Praise

FOUR
WING

A #1 *New York Times* bestseller • Optioned for TV by Amazon Studios • Amazon Best Books of the Year, #4 • Apple Best Books of the Year 2023 • Barnes & Noble Best Fantasy Book of 2023 • NPR "Books We Love" 2023 • Audible Best Books of 2023 • Hudson Book of the Year • Google Play Best Books of 2023 • Indigo Best Books of 2023 • Waterstones Book of the Year finalist • Goodreads Choice Award Winner 2023: Best Romantasy • *Newsweek* Staffers' Favorite Books of 2023 • *Paste* Magazine's Best Books of 2023 • Likewise Choice Award Winner

"I couldn't put it down!"

—Millie Bobby Brown (*Elle*)

"You'll be on the edge of your seat until the very last page."

—USA TODAY

"Completely addicting."

—*Elle* magazine

"An excellent introduction to fantasy…ripe with dragons and magic while also being relatable. It is sure to get your heart pounding while simultaneously making you blush."

—Newsweek

"*Fourth Wing* was everything I hoped it would be."

—Business Insider

★ "Suspenseful, sexy, and with incredibly entertaining storytelling, the first in Yarros' Empyrean series will delight fans of romantic, adventure-led fantasy."

—*Booklist*, starred review

★ "Readers will be spellbound and eager for more."

—*Publishers Weekly*, starred review

More Praise for

Fourth Wing

"A fantasy like you've never read before."

—Jennifer L. Armentrout, #1 *New York Times* bestselling author

"Smart-ass. Bad-ass. Kick-ass. One helluva ride!"

—Tracy Wolff, #1 *New York Times* bestselling author

"An unforgettable adventure from cover to cover. I cheered, laughed, grinned, and refused to put it down."

—Lexi Ryan, #1 *New York Times* bestselling author

"Dragons and war, passion and power...*Fourth Wing* is dazzling. Rebecca Yarros has created a world as compelling as it is deadly, and I can't wait to see where she takes it next."

—Nalini Singh, *New York Times* bestselling author

"Utterly addictive and completely unputdownable... Hands down the best book hangover I've ever experienced. I can't wait for more!"

—Helena Hunting, *New York Times* bestselling author

"KAPOW, what a story!"

—Rachel Howzell Hall, *New York Times* bestselling author

"Phenomenal! Move this one to the top of your TBR."

—Samantha Young, *New York Times* bestselling author

"Buckle up, because with nonstop action, sizzling romance, and the BEST DRAGONS EVER, you will not be able to put down *Fourth Wing* until the last page is turned."

—Mary E. Pearson, *New York Times* bestselling author

FOURTH WING

FOURTH WING

#1 *NEW YORK TIMES* BESTSELLING AUTHOR

REBECCA YARROS

THE CONTINENT
EMERALD SEA
MONTSER
NAVARRE
LUCERAS PROVINCE
IAKOBOS RIVER
MORRAINE PROVINC
ELSUM PROVIN
BASGIATH
CALLDYR CITY
CALLDYR PROVINCE
DEACONSHIRE PROVINCE
SUMERTON
TYRRENDOR PROVINCE
LEWELLEN
ARETIA
CLIFFS OF DRALOR
DRAITHUS
ARCTILE OCEAN

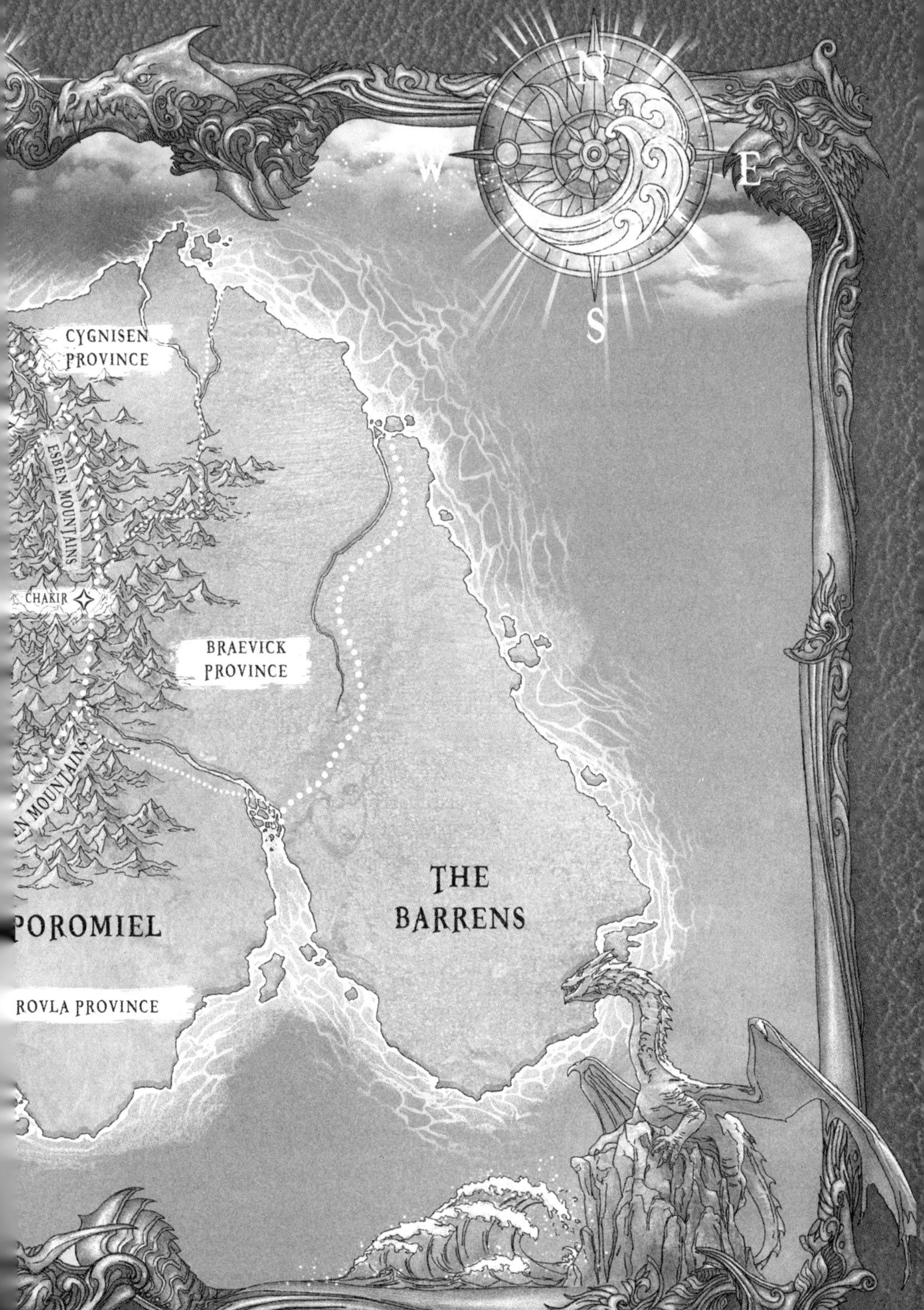
N
W
E
S
CYGNISEN PROVINCE
ESBEN MOUNTAINS
CHAKIR
BRAEVICK PROVINCE
POROMIEL
ROVLA PROVINCE
THE BARRENS

Entangled Publishing, LLC
644 Shrewsbury Commons Ave., STE 181
Shrewsbury, PA 17361
rights@entangledpublishing.com

Red Tower Books is an imprint of Entangled Publishing, LLC.

Visit our website at www.entangledpublishing.com.

Edited by Liz Pelletier
Cover art and design by Bree Archer and Elizabeth Turner Stokes
Stock art by Peratek/Shutterstock
Interior Continent map art by Melanie Korte
Interior Basgiath map art by Amy Acosta and Elizabeth Turner Stokes
Interior design by Toni Kerr and Britt Marczak

Hardcover ISBN 978-1-64937-404-2
Trade Paperback ISBN 978-1-64937-737-1
Ebook ISBN 978-1-64937-408-0

Printed in China at RRD

First Edition September 2024

10 9 8 7 6 5 4 3 2 1

RED TOWER BOOKS™

To Aaron.
My own Captain America.
Through the deployments, the moves,
the sunniest highs, and the darkest lows,
it's always been you and me, kiddo.

Here's to the artists.
You hold the power to shape the world.

Fourth Wing is a nonstop-thrilling adventure fantasy set in the brutal and competitive world of a military college for dragon riders, which includes elements regarding war, battle, hand-to-hand combat, perilous situations, blood, intense violence, brutal injuries, death, poisoning, graphic language, and sexual activities that are shown on the page. Readers who may be sensitive to these elements, please take note, and prepare to enter Basgiath War College...

BWC
BASGIATH WAR COLLEGE
GAUNTLET
FLIGHT FIELD
FIELDS
RIDERS QUADRANT
DRAGON ROTUNDA
ACADEMIC WING
FIRST-YEARS
DORMS
GATHERING HALL
HEALER QUADRANT
BELL TOWER
ADMINISTRATION BUILDING
SCRIBE QUADRANT (UNDERGROUND)
GEN. SORRENGAIL'S OFFICE
INFANTRY QUADRANT

The following text has been faithfully transcribed from Navarrian into the modern language by Jesinia Neilwart, Curator of the Scribe Quadrant at Basgiath War College. All events are true, and names have been preserved to honor the courage of those fallen. May their souls be commended to Malek.

A dragon without its rider is a tragedy.
A rider without their dragon is dead.

—Article One, Section One
The Dragon Rider's Codex

CHAPTER ONE

Conscription Day is always the deadliest. Maybe that's why the sunrise is especially beautiful this morning—because I know it might be my last.

I tighten the straps of my heavy canvas rucksack and trudge up the wide staircase of the stone fortress I call home. My chest heaves with exertion, my lungs burning by the time I reach the stone corridor leading to General Sorrengail's office. This is what six months of intense physical training has given me—the ability to barely climb six flights of stairs with a thirty-pound pack.

I'm so fucked.

The thousands of twenty-year-olds waiting outside the gate to enter their chosen quadrant for service are the smartest and strongest in Navarre. Hundreds of them have been preparing for the Riders Quadrant, the chance to become one of the elite, since birth. I've had exactly six months.

The expressionless guards lining the wide hallway at the top of the landing avoid my eyes as I pass, but that's nothing new. Besides, being ignored is the best possible scenario for me.

Basgiath War College isn't known for being kind to...well, anyone, even those of us whose mothers are in command.

Every Navarrian officer, whether they choose to be schooled as healers, scribes, infantry, or riders, is molded within these cruel walls over three years, honed into weapons to secure our mountainous borders from the violent invasion attempts of the kingdom of Poromiel and their gryphon riders. The weak don't survive here, especially not in the Riders Quadrant. The dragons make sure of that.

"You're sending her to die!" a familiar voice thunders through the general's thick wooden door, and I gasp. There's only one woman on the Continent foolish enough to raise her voice to the general, but she's supposed to be on the border with the Eastern Wing. *Mira.*

There's a muffled response from the office, and I reach for the door handle.

"She doesn't stand a chance," Mira shouts as I force the heavy door open and the weight of my pack shifts forward, nearly taking me down. *Shit.*

The general curses from behind her desk, and I grab onto the back of the crimson-upholstered couch to catch my balance.

"Damn it, Mom, she can't even handle her rucksack," Mira snaps, rushing to my side.

"I'm fine!" My cheeks heat with mortification, and I force myself upright. She's been back for five minutes and is already trying to save me. *Because you need saving, you fool.*

I don't want this. I don't want *any* part of this Riders Quadrant shit. It's not like I have a death wish. I would have been better off failing the admission test to Basgiath and going straight to the army with the majority of conscripts. But I *can* handle my rucksack, and I *will* handle myself.

"Oh, Violet." Worried brown eyes look down at me as strong hands brace my shoulders.

"Hi, Mira." A smile tugs at the corners of my mouth. She might be here to say her goodbyes, but I'm just glad to see my sister for the first time in years.

Her eyes soften, and her fingers flex on my shoulders like she might pull me into a hug, but she steps back and turns to stand at my side, facing our mother. "You can't do this."

"It's already done." Mom shrugs, the lines of her fitted black uniform rising and falling with the motion.

I scoff. So much for the hope of a reprieve. Not that I ever should have expected, or even hoped for, an ounce of mercy from a woman who's been made famous for her lack of it.

"Then *undo* it," Mira seethes. "She's spent her whole life training to become a scribe. She wasn't raised to be a rider."

"Well, she certainly isn't you, is she, Lieutenant Sorrengail?" Mom braces her hands on the immaculate surface of her desk and leans in slightly as she stands, looking us over with narrowed, appraising eyes that mirror the dragons' carved into the furniture's massive legs. I don't need the prohibited power of mind reading to know exactly what she sees.

At twenty-six years old, Mira's a younger version of our mother. She's tall, with strong, powerful muscles toned from years of sparring and hundreds of hours spent on the back of her dragon. Her skin practically glows with health, and her golden-brown hair is sheared short for combat in the same style as Mom's. But more than looks, she carries the same arrogance, the unwavering conviction that she belongs in the sky. She's a rider through and through.

She's everything I'm not, and the disapproving shake of Mom's head says she agrees. I'm too short. Too frail. What curves I do have should be muscle, and my traitorous body makes me embarrassingly vulnerable.

Mom walks toward us, her polished black boots gleaming in the mage lights that flicker from the sconces. She picks up the end of my long braid, scoffs at the section just above my shoulders where the brown strands start to lose their warmth of color and slowly fade to a steely, metallic silver by the ends, and then drops it. "Pale skin, pale eyes, pale hair." Her gaze siphons every ounce of my confidence down to the marrow in my bones. "It's like that fever stole all your coloring along with your strength." Grief flashes through her eyes and her brows furrow. "I told him not to keep you in that library."

It's not the first time I've heard her curse the sickness that nearly killed her while she was pregnant with me or the library Dad made my second home once she'd been stationed here at Basgiath as an instructor and he as a scribe.

"I love that library," I counter. It's been more than a year since his heart finally failed, and the Archives are still the only place that feels like home in this giant fortress, the only place where I still feel my father's presence.

"Spoken like the daughter of a scribe," Mom says quietly, and I see it—the woman she was while Dad was alive. Softer. Kinder...at least for her family.

"I am the daughter of a scribe." My back screams at me, so I let my pack slip from my shoulders, guiding it to the floor, and take my first full breath since leaving my room.

Mom blinks, and that softer woman is gone, leaving only the general. "You're the daughter of a rider, you are twenty years old, and today is

Conscription Day. I let you finish your tutoring, but like I told you last spring, I will not watch one of *my* children enter the Scribe Quadrant, Violet."

"Because scribes are so far beneath riders?" I grumble, knowing perfectly well that riders are the top of the social and military hierarchy. It helps that their bonded dragons roast people for fun.

"Yes!" Her customary composure slips. "And if you dare walk into the tunnel toward the Scribe Quadrant today, I will rip you out by that ridiculous braid and put you on the parapet myself."

My stomach turns over.

"Dad wouldn't want this!" Mira argues, color flushing up her neck.

"I loved your father, but he's dead," Mom says, as if giving the weather report. "I doubt he wants much these days."

I suck in a breath but keep my mouth shut. Arguing will get me nowhere. She's never listened to a damned thing I've had to say before, and today is no different.

"Sending Violet into the Riders Quadrant is tantamount to a death sentence." Guess Mira isn't done arguing. Mira's *never* done arguing with Mom, and the frustrating thing about it is that Mom has always respected her for it. Double standard for the win. "She's not strong enough, Mom! She's already broken her arm this year, she sprains some joint every other week, and she's not tall enough to mount any dragon big enough to keep her alive in a battle."

"Seriously, Mira?" What. The. Hell. My fingernails bite into my palms as I curl my hands into fists. Knowing my chances of survival are minimal is one thing. Having my sister throw my inadequacies in my face is another. "Are you calling me *weak*?"

"No." Mira squeezes my hand. "Just…fragile."

"That's not any better." Dragons don't bond *fragile* women. They incinerate them.

"So she's small." Mom scans me up and down, taking in the generous fit of the cream belted tunic and pants I selected this morning for my potential execution.

I snort. "Are we just listing my faults now?"

"I never said it was a fault." Mom turns to my sister. "Mira, Violet deals with more pain before lunch than you do in an entire week. If any of my children is capable of surviving the Riders Quadrant, it's her."

My eyebrows rise. That sounded an awful lot like a compliment, but with Mom, I'm never quite sure.

"How many rider candidates die on Conscription Day, Mom? Forty? Fifty? Are you that eager to bury another child?" Mira seethes.

I cringe as the temperature in the room plummets, courtesy of Mom's storm-wielding signet power she channels through her dragon, Aimsir.

My chest tightens at the memory of my brother. No one has dared to mention Brennan or his dragon in the five years since they died fighting the Tyrrish rebellion in the south. Mom tolerates me and respects Mira, but she loved Brennan.

Dad did, too. His chest pains started right after Brennan's death.

Mom's jaw tightens and her eyes threaten retribution as she glares at Mira.

My sister swallows but holds her own in the staring competition.

"Mom," I start. "She didn't mean—"

"Get. Out. Lieutenant." Mom's words are soft puffs of steam in the frigid office. "Before I report you absent from your unit without leave."

Mira straightens her posture, nods once, and pivots with military precision, then strides for the door without another word, grabbing a small rucksack on the way out.

It's the first time Mom and I have been alone in months.

Her eyes meet mine, and the temperature rises as she takes a deep breath. "You scored in the top quarter for speed and agility during the entrance exam. You'll do just fine. All Sorrengails do just fine." She skims the backs of her fingers down my cheek, barely grazing my skin. "So much like your father," she whispers before clearing her throat and backing up a few steps.

Guess there are no meritorious service awards for emotional availability.

"I won't be able to acknowledge you for the next three years," she says, sitting back on the edge of her desk. "Since, as commanding general of Basgiath, I'll be your far superior officer."

"I know." It's the least of my concerns, considering she barely acknowledges me now.

"You won't get any special treatment just because you're my daughter, either. If anything, they'll come after you harder to make you prove yourself." She arches an eyebrow.

"Well aware." Good thing I've been training with Major Gillstead for the last several months since Mom made her decree.

She sighs and forces a smile. "Then I guess I'll see you in the valley at

Threshing, candidate. Though you'll be a cadet by sunset, I suppose."

Or dead.

Neither of us says it.

"Good luck, Candidate Sorrengail." She moves back behind her desk, effectively dismissing me.

"Thank you, General." I heft my pack onto my shoulders and walk out of her office. A guard closes the door behind me.

"She's batshit crazy," Mira says from the center of the hallway, right between where two guards are positioned.

"They'll tell her you said that."

"Like they don't already know," she grinds out through clenched teeth. "Let's go. We only have an hour before all candidates have to report, and I saw thousands waiting outside the gates when I flew over." She starts walking, leading me down the stone staircase and through the hallways to my room.

Well…it *was* my room.

In the thirty minutes I've been gone, all my personal items have been packed into crates that now sit stacked in the corner. My stomach sinks to the hardwood floor. She had my entire life boxed.

"She's fucking efficient, I'll give you that," Mira mutters before turning my way, her gaze passing over me in open assessment. "I was hoping I'd be able to talk her out of it. You were never meant for the Riders Quadrant."

"So you've mentioned." I lift an eyebrow at her. "Repeatedly."

"Sorry." She winces, dropping to the ground and emptying her pack.

"What are you doing?"

"What Brennan did for me," she says softly, and grief lodges in my throat. "Can you use a sword?"

I shake my head. "Too heavy. I'm pretty quick with daggers, though." Really damned quick. Lightning quick. What I lack in strength, I make up for in speed.

"I figured. Good. Now, drop your pack and take off those horrible boots." She sorts through the items she's brought, handing me new boots and a black uniform. "Put these on."

"What's wrong with my pack?" I ask but drop my rucksack anyway. She immediately opens it, ripping out everything I'd carefully packed. "Mira! That took me all night!"

"You're carrying way too much, and your boots are a death trap. You'll slip right off the parapet with those smooth soles. I had a set of rubber-bottomed rider boots made for you just in case, and this, my dear Violet, is the worst case." Books start flying, landing in the vicinity of the crate.

"Hey, I can only take what I can carry, and I want those!" I lunge for the next book before she has a chance to toss it, barely managing to save my favorite collection of dark fables.

"Are you willing to die for it?" she asks, her eyes turning hard.

"I can carry it!" This is all wrong. I'm supposed to be dedicating my life to books, not throwing them in the corner to lighten my rucksack.

"No. You can't. You're barely thrice the weight of the pack, the parapet is roughly eighteen inches wide, two hundred feet aboveground, and last time I looked, those were rain clouds moving in. They're not going to give you a rain delay just because the bridge might get a little slick, sis. You'll fall. You'll die. Now, are you going to listen to me? Or are you going to join the other dead candidates at tomorrow morning's roll call?" There's no trace of my older sister in the rider before me. This woman is shrewd, cunning, and a touch cruel. This is the woman who survived all three years with only one scar, the one her own dragon gave her during Threshing. "Because that's all you'll be. Another tombstone. Another name scorched in stone. Ditch the books."

"Dad gave this one to me," I murmur, pressing the book against my chest. Maybe it's childish, just a collection of stories that warn us against the lure of magic, and even demonize dragons, but it's all I have left.

She sighs. "Is it that old book of folklore about dark-wielding vermin and their wyvern? Haven't you read it a thousand times already?"

"Probably more," I admit. "And they're *venin*, not vermin."

"Dad and his allegories," she says. "Just don't try to channel power without being a bonded rider and red-eyed monsters won't hide under your bed, waiting to snatch you away on their two-legged dragons to join their dark army." She retrieves the last book I packed from the rucksack and hands it to me. "Ditch the books. Dad can't save you. He tried. I tried. Decide, Violet. Are you going to die a scribe? Or live as a rider?"

I glance down at the books in my arms and make my choice. "You're a pain in the ass." I put the fables in the corner but keep the other tome in my hands as I face my sister.

"A pain in the ass who is going to keep you alive. What's that one for?" she challenges.

"Killing people." I hand it back to her.

A slow smile spreads across her face. "Good. You can keep that one.

Now, get changed while I sort out the rest of this mess." The bell rings high above us. We have forty-five minutes.

I dress quickly, but everything feels like it belongs to someone else, though it's obviously tailored to my size. My tunic is replaced by a tight-fitting black shirt that covers my arms, and my breezy pants are exchanged for leather ones that hug every curve. Then she laces me into a vest-style corset over the shirt.

"Keeps it from rubbing," she explains.

"Like the gear riders wear into battle." Have to admit, the clothes are pretty badass, even if I feel like an imposter. *Gods, this is really happening*.

"Exactly, because that's what you're doing. Going into battle."

The combination of leather and a fabric I don't recognize covers me from collarbone to just below my waist, wrapping over my breasts and crossing up and over my shoulders. I finger the hidden sheaths sewn diagonally along the rib cage.

"For your daggers."

"I only have four." I grab them from the pile on the floor.

"You'll earn more."

I slide my weapons into the sheaths, as though my ribs themselves have become weapons. The design is ingenious. Between my ribs and the sheaths at my thighs, the blades are easily accessible.

I barely recognize myself in the mirror. I look like a rider. I still feel like a scribe.

Minutes later, half of what I packed is piled onto the crates. She's repacked my rucksack, discarding anything deemed unnecessary and almost everything sentimental while word-vomiting advice about how to survive in the quadrant. Then she surprises me by doing the most sentimental thing ever—telling me to sit between her knees so she can braid my hair into a crown.

It's like I'm a kid again instead of a full-grown woman, but I do it.

"What is this?" I test the material just above my heart, scratching it with my fingernail.

"Something I designed," she explains, tugging my braid painfully tight against my scalp. "I had it specially made for you with Teine's scales sewn in, so be careful with it."

"Dragon scales?" I jerk my head back to look at her. "How? Teine is huge."

"I happen to know a rider whose powers can make big things very small." A devious smile plays across her lips. "And smaller things…much, much bigger."

I roll my eyes. Mira's always been more vocal about her men than I have been…about all two of them. "I mean, how much bigger?"

She laughs, then tugs on my braid. "Head forward. You should have cut your hair." She pulls the strands tight against my head and resumes weaving. "It's a liability in sparring and in battle, not to mention being a giant target. No one else has hair that fades out to silver like this, and they'll already be aiming for you."

"You know very well the natural pigment seems to gradually abandon it no matter the length." My eyes are just as indecisive, a light hazel of varying blues and ambers that never seems to favor either actual color. "Besides, other than everyone else's concern for the shade, my hair is the only thing about me that's perfectly healthy. Cutting it would feel like I'm punishing my body for finally doing something well, and it's not like I feel the need to hide who I am."

"You're not." Mira yanks on my braid, pulling my head back, and our eyes lock. "You're the smartest woman I know. Don't forget that. Your brain is your best weapon. Outsmart them, Violet. Do you hear me?"

I nod, and she loosens her grip, then finishes the braid and pulls me to my feet as she continues to summarize years of knowledge into fifteen harried minutes, barely pausing to breathe.

"Be observant. Quiet is fine, but make sure you notice everything and everyone around you to your advantage. You've read the Codex?"

"A few times." The rule book for the Riders Quadrant is a fraction of the length of the other divisions'. Probably because riders have trouble obeying rules.

"Good. Then you know that the other riders can kill you at any time, and the cutthroat cadets *will* try. Fewer cadets means better odds at Threshing. There are never enough dragons willing to bond, and anyone reckless enough to get themselves killed isn't worthy of a dragon anyway."

"Except when sleeping. It's an executable offense to attack any cadet while sleeping. Article Three—"

"Yes, but that doesn't mean you're safe at night. Sleep in this if you can." She taps the stomach of my corset.

"Rider black is supposed to be earned. You sure I shouldn't wear my tunic today?" I skim my hands over the leather.

"The wind up on the parapet will catch any spare cloth like a sail."

She hands me my now-much-lighter pack. "The tighter your clothes, the better off you are up there, and in the ring once you start sparring. Wear the armor at all times. Keep your daggers on you at *all times*." She points to the sheaths down her thighs.

"Someone's going to say I didn't earn them."

"You're a Sorrengail," she responds, as if that's answer enough. "Fuck what they say."

"And you don't think the dragon scales are cheating?"

"There's no such thing as cheating once you climb the turret. There's only survival and death." The bell chimes—only thirty minutes left. She swallows. "It's almost time. Ready?"

"No."

"Neither was I." A wry smile lifts a corner of her mouth. "And I'd spent my life training for it."

"I'm not going to die today." I sling my pack over my shoulders and breathe a little easier than this morning. It's infinitely more manageable.

The halls of the central, administrative part of the fortress are eerily quiet as we wind our way down through various staircases, but the noise from outside grows louder the lower we descend. Through the windows, I see thousands of candidates hugging their loved ones and saying their goodbyes on the grassy fields just beneath the main gate. From what I've witnessed every year, most families hold on to their candidates right up to the very last bell. The four roads leading to the fortress are clogged with horses and wagons, especially where they converge in front of the college, but it's the empty ones at the edge of the fields that make me nauseous.

They're for the bodies.

Right before we round the last corner that will lead to the courtyard, Mira stops.

"What is— *Oof*." She yanks me against her chest, hugging me tight in the relative privacy of the corridor.

"I love you, Violet. Remember everything I've told you. Don't become another name on the death roll." Her voice shakes, and I wrap my arms around her, squeezing tight.

"I'll be all right," I promise.

She nods, her chin bumping against the top of my head. "I know. Let's go."

That's all she says before pulling away and walking into the crowded courtyard just inside the main gate to the fortress. Instructors, commanders, and even our mother are gathered informally, waiting for the madness outside the walls to become the order within. Out of all the doors in the war college, the main gate is the only one no cadet will enter today, since each quadrant has its own entrance and facilities. Hell, the riders have their own citadel. Pretentious, egotistical fucks.

I follow Mira, catching her with a few quick strides.

"Find Dain Aetos," Mira tells me as we cross through the courtyard, heading for the open gate.

"Dain?" I can't help but smile at the thought of seeing Dain again, and my heart rate jumps. It's been a year, and I've missed his soft brown eyes and the way he laughs, the way every part of his body joins in. I've missed our friendship, and the moments I thought it might turn into more under the right circumstances. I've missed the way he looks at me, like I'm someone worth noticing. I've just missed...him.

"I've only been out of the quadrant for three years, but from what I hear, he's doing well, and he'll keep you safe. Don't smile like that," Mira chides. "He'll be a second-year." She shakes her finger at me. "Don't mess around with second-years. If you want to get laid, and you should"—she lifts her brows—"often, considering you never know what the day brings, then screw around in your own year. Nothing is worse than cadets gossiping that you've slept your way to safety."

"So I'm free to take any of the first-years I want to bed," I say with a little grin. "Just not the second- or third-years."

"Exactly." She winks.

We cross through the gates, leaving the fortress, and join the organized chaos beyond.

Each of Navarre's six provinces has sent this year's share of candidates for military service. Some volunteer. Some are sentenced as punishment. Most are conscripted. The only thing we have in common here at Basgiath is that we passed the entrance exam—both written and an agility test I still cannot believe I passed—which means at least we won't end up as fodder for the infantry on the front line.

The atmosphere is tense with anticipation as Mira leads me along the worn cobblestone path toward the southern turret. The main college is built into the side of Basgiath Mountain, as if it was cleaved from a ridgeline of the peak itself. The sprawling, formidable structure towers over the crowd of anxious, waiting candidates and their tearful families, with its stories-tall stone battlements—built to protect the high rise of the keep within—and defensive turrets at each of its corners, one of which houses the bells.

The majority of the crowd moves to line up at the base of the northern turret—the entrance to the Infantry Quadrant. Some of the mass heads toward the gate behind us—the Healer Quadrant that consumes the southern end of the college. Envy clenches my chest when I spot a few taking the central tunnel into the archives below the fortress to join the Scribe Quadrant.

The entrance to the Riders Quadrant is nothing more than a fortified door at the base of the tower, just like the infantry entrance to the north. But while the infantry candidates can walk straight into their ground-level quadrant, we rider candidates will *climb*.

Mira and I join the riders' line, waiting to sign in, and I make the mistake of glancing up.

High above us, crossing the river-bottomed valley that divides the main college from the even higher, looming citadel of the Riders Quadrant on the southern ridgeline, is the parapet, the stone bridge that's about to separate rider candidates from the cadets over the next few hours.

I can't believe I'm about to cross that thing.

"And to think, I've been preparing for the scribe's written exam all these years." My voice drips with sarcasm. "I should have been playing on a balance beam."

Mira ignores me as the line moves forward and candidates disappear through the door. "Don't let the wind sway your steps."

Two candidates ahead of us, a woman sobs as her partner rips her away from a young man, the couple breaking from the line, retreating in tears down the hillside toward the crowd of loved ones lining the roads. There are no other parents ahead of us, only a few dozen candidates moving toward the roll-keepers.

"Keep your eyes on the stones ahead of you and don't look down," Mira says, the lines of her face tightening. "Arms out for balance. If the pack slips, drop it. Better it falls than you."

I look behind us, where it seems hundreds have filed in within the span of minutes. "Maybe I should let them go first," I whisper as panic fists my heart. What the hell am I doing?

"No," Mira answers. "The longer you wait on those steps"—she motions toward the tower—"the greater your fear has a chance to grow. Cross the parapet before the terror owns you."

The line moves, and the bell chimes again. It's eight o'clock.

Sure enough, the crowd of thousands behind us has separated fully into their chosen quadrants, all lined up to sign the roll and begin their service.

"Focus," Mira snaps, and I whip my head forward. "This might sound harsh, but don't seek friendships in there, Violet. Forge alliances."

There are only two ahead of us now—a woman with a full pack, whose high cheekbones and oval face remind me of renderings of Amari, the queen of the gods. Her dark brown hair is worn in several rows of short braids that just touch the equally dark skin of her neck. The second is the muscular blond man with the woman crying over him. He's carrying an even bigger rucksack.

I look around the pair toward the roll-keeping desk, and my eyes widen. "Is he...?" I whisper.

Mira glances and mutters a curse. "A separatist's kid? Yep. See that shimmering mark that starts on the top of his wrist? It's a relic from the rebellion."

I lift my eyebrows in surprise. The only relics I've ever heard of are when a dragon uses magic to mark the skin of their bonded rider. But those relics are a symbol of honor and power and generally in the shape of the dragon who gifted them. These marks are swirls and slashes that feel more like a warning than a claiming.

"A *dragon* did that?" I whisper.

She nods. "Mom says General Melgren's dragon did it to all of them when he executed their parents, but she wasn't exactly open to further discussion on the topic. Nothing like punishing the kids to deter more parents from committing treason."

It seems...cruel, but the first rule of living at Basgiath is never question a dragon. They tend to cremate anyone they find rude.

"Most of the marked kids who carry rebellion relics are from Tyrrendor, of course, but there are a few whose parents turned traitor from the other provinces—" The blood drains from her face, and she grips the straps of my pack, turning me to face her. "I just remembered." Her voice drops, and I lean in, my heart jumping at the urgency in her tone. "Stay the hell away from Xaden Riorson."

The air rushes from my lungs. That name...

"*That* Xaden Riorson," she confirms, fear lacing her gaze. "He's a third-year, and he *will* kill you the second he finds out who you are."

"His father was the Great Betrayer. He *led* the rebellion," I say quietly. "What is Xaden doing here?"

"All the children of the leaders were conscripted as punishment for their parents' crimes," Mira whispers as we shuffle sideways, moving with the line. "Mom told me they never expected Riorson to make it past the parapet. Then they figured a cadet would kill him, but once his dragon chose him…" She shakes her head. "Well, there's nothing much that can be done then. He's risen to the rank of wingleader."

"That's bullshit," I seethe.

"He's sworn allegiance to Navarre, but I don't think that will stop him where you're concerned. Once you get across the parapet—because you *will* make it across—find Dain. He'll put you in his squad, and we'll just hope it's far from Riorson." She grips my straps tighter. "Stay. Away. From. Him."

"Noted." I nod.

"Next," a voice calls from behind the wooden table that bears the rolls of the Riders Quadrant. The marked rider I don't know is seated next to a scribe I do, and Captain Fitzgibbons's silver eyebrows rise over his weathered face. "Violet Sorrengail?"

I nod, picking up the quill and signing my name on the next empty line on the roll.

"But I thought you were meant for the Scribe Quadrant," Captain Fitzgibbons says softly.

I envy his cream-colored tunic, unable to find the words.

"General Sorrengail chose otherwise," Mira supplies.

Sadness fills the older man's eyes. "Pity. You had so much promise."

"By the gods," the rider next to Captain Fitzgibbons says. "You're Mira Sorrengail?" His jaw drops, and I can smell his hero worship from here.

"I am." She nods. "This is my sister, Violet. She'll be a first-year."

"If she survives the parapet." Someone behind me snickers. "Wind just might blow her right off."

"You fought at Strythmore," the rider behind the desk says with awe. "They gave you the Order of the Talon for taking out that battery behind enemy lines."

The snickering stops.

"As I was saying." Mira puts a hand at the small of my back. "This is my sister, Violet."

"You know the way." The Captain nods and points to the open door into the turret. It looks ominously dark in there, and I fight the urge to run like hell.

"I know the way," she assures him, leading me past the table so the snickering asshole behind me can sign the roll.

We pause at the doorway and turn toward each other.

"Don't die, Violet. I'd hate to be an only child." She grins and walks away, sauntering past the line of gawking candidates as word spreads of exactly who she is and what she's done.

"Tough to live up to that," the woman ahead of me says from just inside the tower.

"It is," I agree, gripping the straps of my rucksack and heading into the darkness. My eyes adjust quickly to the dim light coming in through the equidistant windows along the curved staircase.

"Sorrengail as in…?" the woman asks, looking over her shoulder as we begin to climb the hundreds of stairs that lead to our possible deaths.

"Yep." There's no railing, so I keep my hand on the stone wall as we rise higher and higher.

"The general?" the blond guy ahead of us asks.

"The same one," I answer, offering him a quick smile. Anyone whose mother holds on that tight can't be *that* bad, right?

"Wow. Nice leathers, too." He smiles back.

"Thanks. They're courtesy of my sister."

"I wonder how many candidates have fallen off the edge of the steps and died before they even reach the parapet," the woman says, glancing down the center of the staircase as we climb higher.

"Two last year." I tilt my head when she glances back. "Well, three if you count the girl one of the guys landed on."

The woman's brown eyes flare, but she turns back around and keeps climbing. "How many steps are there?" she asks.

"Two hundred and fifty," I answer, and we climb in silence for another five minutes.

"Not too bad," she says with a bright smile as we near the top and the line comes to a halt. "I'm Rhiannon Matthias, by the way."

"Dylan," the blond guy responds with an enthusiastic wave.

"Violet." I give them a tense smile of my own, blatantly ignoring Mira's earlier suggestion that I avoid friendships and only forge alliances.

"I feel like I've been waiting my entire life for this day." Dylan shifts his pack on his back. "Can you believe we actually get to do this? It's a dream come true."

Right. Naturally, every other candidate but me is excited to be here. This is the only quadrant at Basgiath that doesn't accept conscripts—only volunteers.

"I can't fucking wait." Rhiannon's smile widens. "I mean, who wouldn't want to ride a *dragon*?"

Me. Not that it doesn't sound fun in theory. It does. It's just the abhorrent odds of surviving to graduation that sour my stomach.

"Do your parents approve?" Dylan asks. "Because my mom's been begging me to change my mind for *months*. I keep telling her that I'll have better chances for advancement as a rider, but she wanted me to enter the Healer Quadrant."

"Mine always knew I wanted this, so they've been pretty supportive. Besides, they have my twin to dote on. Raegan's already living her dream, married and expecting a baby." Rhiannon glances back at me. "What about you? Let me guess. With a name like Sorrengail, I bet you were the first to volunteer this year."

"I was more like volun-told." My answer is far less enthusiastic than hers.

"Gotcha."

"And riders do get way better perks than other officers," I say to Dylan as the line moves upward again. The snickering candidate behind me catches up, sweating and red. *Look who isn't snickering now.* "Better pay, more leniency with the uniform policy," I continue. No one gives a shit what riders wear as long as it's black. The only rules that apply to riders are the ones I've memorized from the Codex.

"And the right to call yourself a supreme badass," Rhiannon adds.

"That too," I agree. "Pretty sure they issue you an ego with your flight leathers."

"Plus, I've heard that riders are allowed to marry sooner than the other quadrants," Dylan adds.

"True. Right after graduation." If we survive. "I think it has something to do with wanting to continue bloodlines." Most successful riders are legacies.

"Or because we tend to die sooner than the other quadrants," Rhiannon muses.

"I'm not dying," Dylan says with way more confidence than I feel as he tugs a necklace from under his tunic to reveal a ring dangling from the chain. "She said it would be bad luck to propose before I left, so we're waiting until graduation." He kisses the ring and tucks the chain back under his collar. "The next three years are going to be long ones, but they'll be worth it."

I keep my sigh to myself, though that might be the most romantic thing I've ever heard.

"You might make it across the parapet," the guy behind us sneers. "This one here is a breeze away from the bottom of the ravine."

I roll my eyes.

"Shut up and focus on yourself," Rhiannon snaps, her feet clicking against the stone as we climb.

The top comes into sight, the doorway full of muddled light. Mira was right. Those clouds are going to wreak havoc on us, and we have to be on the other side of the parapet before they do.

Another step, another tap of Rhiannon's feet.

"Let me see your boots," I say quietly so the jerk behind me can't hear.

Her brow puckers, and confusion fills her brown eyes, but she shows me the soles. They're smooth, just like the ones I was wearing earlier. My stomach sinks like a rock.

The line starts moving again, pausing when we're only a few feet from the opening. "What size are your feet?" I ask.

"What?" Rhiannon blinks at me.

"Your feet. What size are they?"

"Eight," she answers, two lines forming between her brows.

"I'm a seven," I say quickly. "It will hurt like hell, but I want you to take my left boot. Trade with me." I have a dagger in the right one.

"I'm sorry?" She looks at me like I've lost my mind, and maybe I have.

"These are rider boots. They'll grip the stone better. Your toes will be scrunched and generally miserable, but at least you'll have a shot at not falling off if that rain hits."

Rhiannon glances toward the open door—and the darkening sky—then back to me. "You're willing to trade a boot?"

"Just until we get on the other side." I look through the open door. Three candidates are already walking across the parapet, their arms stretched out wide. "But we have to be quick. It's almost our turn."

Rhiannon purses her lips in debate for a second, then agrees, and we swap left boots. I barely finish lacing up before the line moves again, and the guy behind me shoves my lower back, sending me staggering onto the platform and into the open air.

"Let's go. Some of us have things to do on the other side." His voice grates on my last freaking nerve.

"You are not worth the effort right now," I mutter, gaining my balance as the wind whips at my skin, the midsummer morning thick with humidity. *Good call on the braid, Mira.*

The top of the turret is bare, the crenelations of stone rising and falling along the circular structure at the height of my chest and doing nothing to obscure the view. The ravine and its river below suddenly feel very, very far. How many wagons do they have waiting down there? Five? Six? I know the stats. The parapet claims roughly fifteen percent of the rider candidates. Every trial in the quadrant—including this one—is designed to test a cadet's ability to ride. If someone can't manage to walk the windy length of the slim stone bridge, then they sure as hell can't keep their balance and fight on the back of a dragon.

And as for the death rate? I guess every other rider thinks the risk is worth the glory—or has the arrogance to think they won't fall.

I'm not in either camp.

Nausea has me holding my stomach, and I breathe in through my nose and out through my mouth as I walk the edge behind Rhiannon and Dylan, my fingers skimming the stonework as we wind our way toward the parapet.

Three riders wait at the entrance, which is nothing more than a gaping hole in the wall of the turret. One with ripped-off sleeves records names as candidates step out onto the treacherous crossing. Another, who's shaved all his hair with the exception of a strip down the top center, instructs Dylan as he moves into position, patting his chest like the ring hidden there will bring him luck. I hope it does.

The third turns in my direction and my heart simply…stops.

He's tall, with windblown black hair and dark brows. The line of his jaw is strong and covered by warm tawny skin and dark stubble, and when he folds his arms across his torso, the muscles in his chest and arms ripple, moving in a way that makes me swallow. And his eyes… His eyes are the shade of gold-flecked onyx. The contrast is startling, jaw-dropping even—everything about him is. His features are so harsh that they look carved, and yet they're astonishingly perfect, like an artist worked a lifetime sculpting him, and at least a year of that was spent on his mouth.

He's the most exquisite man I've ever seen.

And living in the war college means I've seen a *lot* of men.

Even the diagonal scar that bisects his left eyebrow and marks the top corner of his cheek only makes him hotter. Flaming hot. Scorching hot. Gets-you-into-trouble-and-you-like-it level of hot. Suddenly, I can't remember exactly why Mira told me not to fuck around outside my year group.

"See you two on the other side!" Dylan says over his shoulder with an excited grin before stepping onto the parapet, his arms spread wide.

"Ready for the next one, Riorson?" the rider with the ripped sleeves says.

Xaden Riorson?

"You ready for this, Sorrengail?" Rhiannon asks, moving forward.

The black-haired rider snaps his gaze to mine, turning fully toward me, and my heart thunders for all the wrong reasons. A rebellion relic, curving in dips and swirls, starts at his bare left wrist, then disappears under his black uniform to appear again at his collar, where it stretches and swirls up his neck, stopping at his jawline.

"Oh shit," I whisper, and his eyes narrow, as if he can hear me over the howl of wind that rips at my secured braid.

"Sorrengail?" He steps toward me, and I look up…and up.

Good gods, I don't even reach his collarbone. He's massive. He has to be more than four inches over six feet tall.

I feel exactly what Mira called me—*fragile*—but I nod once, and the shining onyx of his eyes transforms to cold, unadulterated hatred. I can almost taste the loathing wafting off him like a bitter cologne.

"Violet?" Rhiannon asks, moving forward.

"You're General Sorrengail's youngest." His voice is deep and accusatory.

"You're Fen Riorson's son," I counter, the certainty of this revelation settling in my bones. I lift my chin and do my best to lock every muscle in my body so I don't start trembling.

He will *kill you the second he finds out who you are.* Mira's words bounce around my skull, and fear knots in my throat. He's going to throw me over the edge. He's going to pick me up and drop me right off this turret. I'm never going to get the chance to even walk the parapet. I'll die being exactly what my mother's always danced around calling me—weak.

Xaden sucks in a deep breath, and the muscle in his jaw flexes once. Twice. "Your mother captured my father and oversaw his execution."

Wait. Like *he* has the only right to hatred here? Rage races through my veins. "Your father killed my older brother. Seems like we're even."

"Hardly." His glaring gaze strokes over me like he's memorizing every detail or looking for any weakness. "Your sister is a rider. Guess that explains the leathers."

"Guess so." I hold his glare, as if winning this staring competition will gain me entrance to the quadrant instead of crossing the parapet behind him. Either way, I'm getting across. Mira isn't going to lose both her siblings.

His hands clench into fists, and he tenses.

I prepare for the strike. He might throw me off this tower, but I won't make it easy for him.

"You all right?" Rhiannon asks, her gaze jumping between Xaden and me.

He glances at her. "You're friends?"

"We met on the stairs," she says, squaring her shoulders.

He looks down, noting our mismatched shoes, and arches a brow. His hands relax. "Interesting."

"Are you going to kill me?" I lift my chin another inch.

His gaze clashes with mine as the sky opens and rain falls in a deluge, soaking my hair, my leathers, and the stones around us in seconds.

A scream rends the air, and Rhiannon and I both jerk our attention to the parapet just in time to see Dylan slip.

I gasp, my heart jolting into my throat.

He catches himself, hooking his arms over the stone bridge as his feet kick beneath him, scrambling for a purchase that isn't there.

"Pull yourself up, Dylan!" Rhiannon shouts.

"Oh gods!" My hand flies to cover my mouth, but he loses his grip on the water-slick stone and falls, disappearing from view. The wind and rain steal any sound his body might make in the valley below. They steal the sound of my muffled cry, too.

Xaden never takes his eyes from me, watching silently with a look I can't interpret as I bring my horrified gaze back to his.

"Why would I waste my energy killing you when the parapet will do it for me?" A wicked smile curves his lips. "Your turn."

There's a misconception that it's kill or be killed in the Riders Quadrant. Riders, as a whole, aren't out to assassinate other cadets...unless there's a shortage of dragons that year or a cadet is a liability to their wing. Then things may get...interesting.

—Major Afendra's Guide to the Riders Quadrant (Unauthorized Edition)

CHAPTER TWO

I will not die today.

The words become my mantra, repeating in my head as Rhiannon gives her name to the rider keeping tally at the opening to the parapet. The hatred in Xaden's stare burns the side of my face like a palpable flame, and even the rain pelting my skin with each gust of wind doesn't ease the heat—or the shiver of dread that jolts down my spine.

Dylan is dead. He's just a name, another soon-to-be stone in the endless graveyards that line the roads to Basgiath, another warning to the ambitious candidates who would rather chance their lives with the riders than choose the security of any other quadrant. I get it now—why Mira warned me not to make friends.

Rhiannon grips both sides of the opening in the turret, then looks over her shoulder at me. "I'll wait for you on the other side," she shouts over the storm. The fear in her eyes mirrors my own.

"I'll see you on the other side." I nod and even manage a grimace of a smile.

She steps out onto the parapet and begins walking, and even though I'm sure his hands are full today, I send up a silent prayer to Zihnal, the god of luck.

"Name?" the rider at the edge asks as his partner holds a cloak over the scroll in a pointless attempt to keep the paper dry.

"Violet Sorrengail," I answer as thunder cracks above me, the sound oddly comforting. I've always loved the nights where storms beat against the fortress window, both illuminating and throwing shadows over the books I curled up with, though this downpour might just cost me my life. With a quick glance, I see Dylan's and Rhiannon's names already blurring at the end where water has met ink. It's the last time Dylan's name will be written anywhere but his stone. There will be another roll at the end of the parapet so the scribes have their beloved statistics for casualties. In another life, it would be me reading and recording the data for historical analysis.

"Sorrengail?" The rider looks up, his eyebrows rising in surprise. "As in General Sorrengail?"

"The same." Damn, that's already getting old, and I know it's only going to get worse. There's no avoiding the comparison to my mother, not when she's the commander here. Even worse, they probably think I'm a naturally gifted rider like Mira or a brilliant strategist like Brennan was. Or they'll take one look at me, realize I'm nothing like the three of them, and declare open season.

I place my hands on either side of the turret and drag my fingertips across the stone. It's still warm from the morning sun but rapidly cooling from the rain, slick but not slippery from moss growth or anything.

Ahead of me, Rhiannon is making her way across, her hands out for balance. She's probably a fourth of the way, her figure becoming blurrier the farther she walks into the rain.

"I thought she only had one daughter?" the other rider asks, angling the cloak as another gust of wind blows into us. If it's this windy here, my bottom half sheltered by the turret, then I'm about to be in for a world of hurt on the parapet.

"I get that a lot." In through my nose, out through my mouth, I force my breathing to calm, my heart rate to slow from its gallop. If I panic, I'll die. If I slip, I'll die. If I… *Oh, fuck it.* There's nothing more I can do to prepare for this.

I take the lone step up onto the parapet and grip the stone wall as another gust hits, knocking me sideways against the opening in the turret.

"And you think you'll be able to ride?" the asshole candidate behind me mocks. "Some Sorrengail, with that kind of balance. I pity whatever wing you end up in."

I regain my balance and yank the straps of my pack tighter.

"Name?" the rider asks again, but I know he's not talking to me.

"Jack Barlowe," the one behind me answers. "Remember the name. I'm going to be a wingleader one day." Even his voice reeks of arrogance.

"You'd better get going, Sorrengail," Xaden's deep voice orders.

I look over my shoulder and see him pinning me with a glare.

"Unless you need a little motivation?" Jack lunges forward, his hands raised. Holy shit, he's going to shove me off.

Fear shoots through my veins, and I move, leaving the safety of the turret as I bolt onto the parapet. There's no going back now.

My heart beats so hard that I hear it in my ears like a drum.

Keep your eyes on the stones ahead of you and don't look down. Mira's advice echoes in my head, but it's hard to heed it when every step could be my last. I throw my arms out for balance, then take the measured mini strides I practiced with Major Gillstead in the courtyard. But with the wind, the rain, and the two-hundred-foot drop, this is nothing like practice. The stones beneath my feet are uneven in places, held together by mortar in the joints that make it easy to trip, and I concentrate on the path ahead of me to keep my eyes off my boots. My muscles are tight as I lock my center of gravity, keeping my posture upright.

My head swims as my pulse skyrockets.

Calm. I have to stay calm.

I can't carry a tune, or even decently hum, so singing for a distraction is out, but I am a scholar. There's nowhere as calming as the archives, so that's what I think of. Facts. Logic. History.

Your mind already knows the answer, so just calm down and let it remember. That's what Dad always told me. I need something to keep the logical side of my brain from turning around and walking straight back to the turret.

"The Continent is home to two kingdoms—and we've been at war for four hundred years," I recite, using the basic, simple data that has been drilled into me for easy recall in preparation for the scribe's test. Step after step, I make my way across the parapet. "Navarre, my home, is the larger kingdom, with six unique provinces. Tyrrendor, our southernmost and largest province, shares its border with the province of Krovla within the Poromiel kingdom." Each word calms my breathing and steadies my heart rate, lessening the dizziness.

"To our east lie the remaining two Poromiel provinces of Braevick and

Cygnisen, with the Esben Mountains providing a natural border." I pass the painted line that marks halfway. I'm over the highest point now, but I can't think about that. *Don't look down.* "Beyond Krovla, beyond our enemy, lie the distant Barrens, a desert—"

Thunder cracks, the wind slams into me, and I flail my arms. "Shit!"

My body sways left with the gale, and I drop to the parapet, holding on to the edges and crouching so I don't lose my footing, making myself as small as possible as the wind howls over and around me. Stomach churning, I feel my lungs threaten to hyperventilate as panic seizes me at knifepoint.

"Within Navarre, Tyrrendor was the last of the bordering provinces to join the alliance and swear fealty to King Reginald," I shout into the howling wind, forcing my mind to keep moving against the very real threat of paralyzing anxiety. "It was also the only province to attempt secession six hundred and twenty-seven years later, which would have eventually left our kingdom defenseless had they been successful."

Rhiannon is still ahead of me, at what I think is the three-quarters point. Good. She deserves to make it.

"The kingdom of Poromiel mainly consists of arable plains and marshlands and is known for exceptional textiles, endless fields of grain, and unique crystalline gems capable of amplifying minor magics." I spare only a quick glance at the dark clouds above me before inching forward, one foot carefully placed in front of the other. "In contrast, Navarre's mountainous regions offer an abundance in ore, hardy timber from our eastern provinces, and limitless deer and elk."

My next step knocks a couple of pieces of mortar loose, and I pause as my arms wobble until I regain my balance. I swallow and test my weight before moving forward again.

"The Trade Agreement of Resson, signed more than two hundred years ago, ensures the exchange of meat and lumber from Navarre for the cloth and agriculture within Poromiel four times a year at the Athebyne outpost on the border of Krovla and Tyrrendor."

I can see the Riders Quadrant from here. The enormous stone footings of the citadel rise up the mountain to the base of the structure, where I know this path ends if I can just get there. Scraping the rain from my face with the leather on my shoulder, I glance back to see where Jack is.

He's stalled at just after the quarter mark, his stocky form standing still…like he's waiting for something. His hands are at his sides. The wind seems to have no effect on his balance, lucky bastard. I swear he's grinning across the distance, but it could just be the rain in my eyes.

I can't stay here. Living to see the sunrise means I have to keep moving. Fear can't rule my body. Squeezing the muscles of my legs together for balance, I slowly let go of the stone beneath me and stand.

Arms out. Walk.

I need to get as far as possible before the next gust of wind.

I look back over my shoulder to see where Jack is, and my blood chills to ice.

He's turned his back on me and is facing the next candidate, who wobbles dangerously as he approaches. Jack grabs the gangly boy by the straps of his overpacked rucksack, and I watch, shock locking my muscles, as Jack throws the scrawny candidate from the parapet like a sack of grain.

A scream reaches my ears for an instant before fading as he falls out of sight.

Holy shit.

"You're next, Sorrengail!" Jack bellows, and I jerk my gaze from the ravine to see him pointing at me, a sinister smile curving his mouth. Then he comes for me, his strides eating up the distance between us with horrifying speed.

Move. Now.

"Tyrrendor encompasses the southwest of the Continent," I recite, my steps even but panicked on the slick, narrow path, my left foot slipping a little at the beginning of each step. "Made up of hostile, mountainous terrain and bordered by the Emerald Sea to the west and the Arctile Ocean to the south, Tyrrendor is nearly impenetrable. Though separated geographically by the Cliffs of Dralor, a natural protective barrier—"

Another gust slams into me, and my foot slips off the parapet. My heart lurches. The parapet rushes up to meet me as I stumble and fall. My knee slams into the stone, and I yelp at the sharp bite of pain. My hands scramble for purchase as my left leg dangles off the edge of this bridge from hell, Jack not far behind now. Then I make the gut-twisting error of looking down.

Water runs off my nose and chin, splattering against the stone before falling to join the river gushing through the valley more than two hundred feet below. I swallow the growing knot in my throat and blink, fighting to steady my heart rate.

I will not die today.

Gripping the sides of the stone, I brace as much of my weight as I can trust on the slick stones to hold and swing my left leg up. The ball of my foot finds the walkway. From here, there aren't enough facts in the world to steady my thoughts. I need to get my right foot under me, the one that has better traction, but one wrong move and I'll find out just how cold that river is beneath me.

You'll be dead on impact.

"I'm coming for you, Sorrengail!" I hear from behind me.

I shove off the stone and pray my boots find the pathway as I burst to my feet. If I fall, fine, that would be my error. But I'm not about to let this asshole murder me. *Best to get to the other side, where the rest of the murderers wait.* Not that everyone in the quadrant is going to try to kill me, just the cadets who think I'll be a liability to the wing. There's a reason strength is revered among riders. A squad, a section, a wing is only as effective as its weakest link, and if that link breaks, it puts everyone in danger.

Jack either thinks I'm that link or he's an unstable asshole who just enjoys killing. Probably both. Either way, I need to move faster.

Throwing my arms out to the side, I focus on the end of the path, the courtyard of the citadel, where Rhiannon steps to safety, and I hustle despite the rain. I keep my body tight, my center locked, and for once am grateful I'm shorter than most.

"Will you scream the whole way down?" Jack mocks, still shouting, but his voice is closer. He's gaining on me.

There's no room for fear, so I block it out, envisioning shoving the emotion behind locked iron bars in my mind. I can see the end of the parapet now, the riders who wait at the entrance to the citadel.

"There's no way someone who can't even carry a full rucksack passed the entrance exam. You're a mistake, Sorrengail," Jack calls out, his voice clearer, but I don't chance losing my speed to check how far he is behind me. "It's really for the best that I take you out now, don't you think? It's so much more merciful than letting the dragons have at you. They'll start to eat you leg by rickety leg while you're still alive. Come on," he cajoles. "It will be my *pleasure* to help you out."

"The fuck you will," I mutter. There are only a dozen feet left to the outside of the citadel's enormous walls. My left foot slips, and I wobble, but I only lose a heartbeat before I'm moving forward again. The fortress looms behind those thick battlements, carved into the mountain in an L-shaped formation of tall stone buildings, built to withstand fire, for obvious reasons. The walls that surround the citadel's courtyard are ten feet thick and eight feet tall, with one opening—and I'm just. About. There.

I bite back a sob of relief as stone rises up on both sides of me.

"You think you'll be safe in there?" Jack's voice is harsh…and close.

Secure on both sides by the walls, I run the last ten feet, my heart pounding as adrenaline pushes my body to its max, and his footsteps charge behind me. He lunges for my pack and misses, his hand hitting my hip as we reach the edge. I hurtle forward, jumping the twelve inches off the elevated parapet down to the courtyard, where two riders wait.

Jack roars in frustration, and the sound grips my heaving chest like a vise.

Spinning, I rip a dagger from its sheath at my ribs just as Jack skids to a halt above me on the parapet, his breath choppy and his face ruddy. Murder is etched in his narrowed, glacial blue eyes as he glares down at me…and where the tip of my dagger now indents the fabric of his breeches—against his balls.

"I think. I'll be safe. For right. Now," I manage between ragged breaths, my muscles trembling but my hand more than steady.

"Will you?" Jack vibrates with rage, his thick blond brows slashing down over arctic blue eyes, every line of his monstrous frame leaning my way. But he doesn't take another step.

"It is unlawful for a rider to cause another harm. While in a quadrant formation or in the supervisory. Presence of a superior-ranking cadet," I recite from the Codex, my heartbeat still in my throat. "As it will diminish the efficacy of the wing. And given the crowd behind us, I think it's clear to argue that it's a formation. Article Three, Section— "

"I don't give a shit!" He moves, but I hold my ground, and my dagger slices through the first layer of his breeches.

"I suggest you reconsider." I adjust my stance just in case he doesn't. "I might slip."

"Name?" the rider next to me drawls, as if we're the least interesting thing she's seen today. I glance in her direction for a millisecond. She pushes the chin-length, fire-red strands of her hair behind her ear with one hand and holds the roll with the other, watching the scene play out. The three silver four-point stars embroidered on the shoulder of her cloak tell me she's a third-year. "You're pretty small for a rider, but it looks like you made it."

"Violet Sorrengail," I answer, but a hundred percent of my focus is on

Jack again. The rain drips off the lowered ridge of his brow. "And before you ask, yes, I'm *that* Sorrengail."

"Not surprised, with that maneuver," the woman says, holding a pen like Mom uses over the roll.

It might be the nicest compliment I've ever been given.

"And what's your name?" she asks again. Pretty sure she's asking Jack, but I'm too busy studying my opponent to glance her way.

"Jack. Barlowe." There's no sinister little smile on his lips or playful taunts about how he'll enjoy killing me now. There's nothing but pure malice in his features, promising retribution.

A chill of apprehension lifts the hairs on my neck.

"Well, Jack," the male rider on my right says slowly, scratching the trim lines of his dark goatee. He's not wearing a cloak, and the rain soaks into the bevy of patches stitched into a worn leather jacket. "Cadet Sorrengail has you by the actual balls here, in more ways than one. She's right. Regs state that there's nothing but respect among riders at formation. You want to kill her, you'll have to do it in the sparring ring or on your own time. That is, if she decides to let you off the parapet. Because technically, you're not on the grounds yet, so *you* are not a cadet. *She* is."

"And if I decide to snap her neck the second I step down?" Jack growls, and the look in his eyes says he'll do it.

"Then you get to meet the dragons early," the redhead answers, her tone bland. "We don't wait for trials around here. We just execute."

"What's it going to be, Sorrengail?" the male rider asks. "You going to have Jack here start as a eunuch?"

Shit. What *is* it going to be? I can't kill him, not at this angle, and slicing off his balls is only going to make him hate me more, if possible.

"Are you going to follow the rules?" I ask Jack. My head is buzzing, and my arm feels so damned heavy, but I keep my knife on target.

"Guess I don't have a choice." A corner of his mouth tilts into a sneer, and his posture relaxes as he raises his hands, palms out.

I lower my dagger but keep it palmed and ready as I move sideways, toward the redhead keeping roll.

Jack steps down into the courtyard, his shoulder knocking mine as he walks by, pausing to lean in close. "You're dead, Sorrengail, and I'm going to be the one to kill you."

Blue dragons descend from the extraordinary Gormfaileas line. Known for their formidable size, they are the most ruthless, especially in the case of the rare Blue Daggertail, whose knifelike spikes at the tip of their tail can disembowel an enemy with one flick.

—Colonel Kaori's Field Guide to Dragonkind

CHAPTER THREE

If Jack wants to kill me, he needs to get in line. Besides, I have a feeling Xaden Riorson is going to beat him to it.

"Not today," I respond to Jack, the hilt of my dagger solid in my hand, and I somehow manage to suppress a shudder as he leans over and breathes in. He's scenting me like a fucking dog. Then he scoffs and walks off into the crowd of celebrating cadets and riders that's gathered in the sizable courtyard of the citadel.

It's still early, probably around nine, but already I see there aren't as many cadets as there were candidates ahead of me in line. Based on the overwhelming presence of leather, both the second- and third-years are here as well, taking stock of the new cadets.

The rain eases into a drizzle, as if it had only come to make the hardest test of my life even harder…but I did it.

I'm alive.

I made it.

My body begins to tremble, and a throbbing pain erupts in my left knee—the one I slammed on the parapet. I take a step, and it threatens to give out on me. I need to bind it before anyone notices.

"I think you made an enemy there," the redhead says, casually shifting the lethal crossbow she wears strapped along her shoulder. She glances at me over the scroll with a shrewd look in her hazel eyes as she looks me up and down. "I'd watch your back with that one if I were you."

I nod. I'm going to have to watch my back and every other part of my body.

The next candidate approaches from the parapet as someone grips my shoulders from behind and spins me.

My dagger is halfway up when I realize it's Rhiannon.

"We made it!" She grins, giving my shoulders a squeeze.

"We made it," I repeat with a forced smile. My thighs are shaking now, but I manage to sheath my dagger at my ribs. Now that we're here, both cadets, can I trust her?

"I can't thank you enough. There were at least three times I would have fallen off if you hadn't helped me. You were right—those soles were slick as shit. Have you seen the people around here? I swear I just saw a second-year with pink streaks in her hair, and one guy has dragon scales tattooed up his entire biceps."

"Conformity is for the infantry," I say as she loops her arm through mine and tugs me along toward the crowd. My knee screams, pain radiating up to my hip and down to my foot, and I limp, my weight falling into Rhiannon's side.

Damn it.

Where did this nausea come from? Why can't I stop shaking? I'm going to fall any second now—there's no way my body can remain upright with this earthquake in my legs or the whirring in my head.

"Speaking of which," she says, glancing down. "We need to trade boots. There's a bench—"

A tall figure in a pristine black uniform steps out of the crowd, charging toward us, and though Rhiannon manages to dodge, I stumble smack into his chest.

"Violet?" Strong hands catch my elbows to steady me, and I look up into a pair of familiar, striking brown eyes, flared wide in obvious shock.

Relief sweeps through me, and I try to smile, but it probably comes out like a distorted grimace. He seems taller than he was last summer, the beard that cuts across his jaw is new, and he's filled out in a way that makes me blink…or maybe that's just my vision going hazy at the edges. The beautiful, easygoing smile that's starred in way too many of my fantasies is far from the scowl that purses his mouth, and everything about him seems a little…harder, but it works for him. The line of his chin, the set of his brow, even the muscles of his biceps are rigid under my fingers as I try to find my balance. Sometime in the last year, Dain Aetos went from attractive and cute to *gorgeous*.

And I'm about to be sick all over his boots.

"What the hell are you doing here?" he barks, the shock in his eyes transforming to something foreign, something deadly. This isn't the same boy I grew up with. He's a second-year rider now.

"Dain. It's good to see you." That's an understatement, but the trembles turn to full-on shakes, and bile creeps up my throat, dizziness only making the nausea worse. My knees give out.

"Damn it, Violet," he mutters, hauling me back to my feet. With one hand on my back and the other under my elbow, he quickly guides me away from the crowd and into an alcove in the wall, close to the first defensive turret of the citadel. It's a shady, hidden spot with a hard wooden bench, which he sits me on, then helps me out of my rucksack.

Spit floods my mouth. "I'm going to be sick."

"Head between your knees," Dain orders in a harsh tone I'm not used to from him, but I do it. He rubs circles on my lower back as I breathe in through my nose and out through my mouth. "It's the adrenaline. Give it a minute and it'll pass." I hear approaching footsteps on the gravel. "Who the hell are you?"

"I'm Rhiannon. I'm Violet's…friend."

I stare at the gravel under my mismatched boots and will the meager contents of my stomach to stay put.

"Listen to me, Rhiannon. Violet is fine," he commands. "And if anyone asks, then you tell them exactly what I said, that it's just the adrenaline working out of her system. Understand?"

"It's no one's business what's going on with Violet," she retorts, her tone just as sharp as his. "So I wouldn't say shit. Especially not when she's the reason I made it across the parapet."

"You'd better mean that," he warns, the bite in his voice at odds with the ceaseless, comforting circles he makes on my back.

"I could ask you just who the hell *you* are," she retorts.

"He's one of my oldest friends." The trembles slowly subside, and the nausea wanes, but I'm not sure if it's from timing or my position, so I keep my head between my knees while I manage to unlace my left boot.

"Oh," Rhiannon answers.

"And a second-year rider, *cadet*," he growls.

Gravel crunches, like Rhiannon has backed up a step.

"No one can see you here, Vi, so take your time," Dain says softly.

"Because puking my guts up after surviving the parapet and the asshole who wanted to throw me off it would be considered weak." I rise slowly, sitting upright.

"Exactly," he answers. "Are you hurt?" His gaze rakes over me with a desperate edge, like he needs to see every inch for himself.

"My knee is sore," I admit in a whisper, because it's Dain. Dain, whom I've known since we were five and six. Dain, whose father is one of my mother's most trusted advisers. Dain, who held me together when Mira left for the Riders Quadrant and again when Brennan died.

He takes my chin between his thumb and forefinger, turning my face left and right for his inspection. "That's all? You're sure?" His hands run down my sides and pause at my ribs. "Are you wearing *daggers*?"

Rhiannon takes my boot off and sighs in relief, wiggling her toes.

I nod. "Three at my ribs and one in my boot." Thank gods, or I'm not sure I'd be sitting here right now.

"Huh." He drops his hands and looks at me like he's never seen me before, like I'm a complete stranger, but then he blinks and it's gone. "Get your boots switched. You two look ridiculous. Vi, do you trust this one?" He nods toward Rhiannon.

She could have waited for me at the security of the citadel walls and thrown me off just like Jack tried to do, but she didn't.

I nod. I trust her as much as anyone can trust another first-year around here.

"All right." He stands and turns toward her. There are sheaths at the sides of his leathers, too, but there are daggers in each of them, where mine are still empty. "I'm Dain Aetos, and I'm the leader for Second Squad, Flame Section, Second Wing."

Squad leader? My brows jump. The highest ranks among the cadets in the quadrant are wingleader and section leader. Both positions are held by elite third-years. Second-years can rise to squad leaders, but only if they're exceptional. Everyone else is simply a cadet before Threshing—when the dragons choose who they will bond—and a rider after. People die too often around here to hand out ranks prematurely.

"Parapet should be over in the next couple of hours, depending on how fast the candidates cross or fall. Go find the redhead with the roll—she's usually carrying a crossbow—and tell her that Dain Aetos put both you and Violet Sorrengail into his squad. If she questions you, tell her she owes me from saving her ass at Threshing last year. I'll bring Violet back to the courtyard shortly."

Rhiannon glances at me, and I nod.

"Go before someone sees us," Dain barks.

"Going," she answers, shoving her foot into her boot and lacing it quickly as I do the same with mine.

"You crossed the parapet with an equestrian boot too big for you?" Dain asks, glaring down at me with incredulity.

"She would have died without trading mine." I stand and wince as my knee objects and tries to buckle.

"And you're going to die if we don't find you a way out of here." He offers his arm. "Take it. We need to get you to my room. You need to wrap that knee." His eyebrows rise. "Unless you found some miracle cure I don't know about in the last year?"

I shake my head and take his arm.

"Damn it, Violet. *Damn it.*" He tucks mine discreetly against his side, grabs my rucksack with his empty hand, then leads me into a tunnel at the end of the alcove in the outer wall I hadn't even seen. Mage lights flicker on in the sconces as we pass and extinguish after we go by. "You're not supposed to be here."

"Well aware." I let myself limp a little, since no one can see us now.

"You're supposed to be in the Scribe Quadrant," he seethes, leading me through the tunnel in the wall. "What the hell happened? Please tell me you did not *volunteer* for the Riders Quadrant."

"What do you think happened?" I challenge as we reach a wrought-iron gate that looks like it was built to keep out a troll…or a dragon.

He curses. "Your mother."

"My mother." I nod. "Every Sorrengail is a rider, don't you know?"

We make it to a set of circular steps, and Dain leads me up past the first and second floor, stopping us on the third and pushing open another gate that creaks with the sound of metal on metal.

"This is the second-year floor," he explains quietly. "Which means—"

"I'm not supposed to be up here, obviously." I tuck in a little closer. "Don't worry—if someone sees us, I'll just say that I was overcome with lust at first sight and couldn't wait another second to get you out of your pants."

"Ever the smart-ass." A wry smile tugs at his lips as we start down the hall.

"I can throw in a few *oh, Dain* cries once we're in your room just for believability," I offer, and actually mean it.

He snorts as he drops my pack in front of a wooden door, then makes a twisting motion with his hand in front of the handle. A lock audibly clicks.

"You have powers," I say.

It's not news, of course. He's a second-year rider, and all riders can perform lesser magics once their dragons choose to channel their power…but it's…Dain.

"Don't look so surprised." He rolls his eyes and opens the door, carrying my pack as he helps me inside.

His room is simple, with a bed, dresser, desk, and wardrobe. There's nothing personal about it other than a few books on his desk. I note with a tiny burst of satisfaction that one is the tome on the Krovlan language that I gave him before he left last summer. He's always had a gift for languages. Even the blanket on his bed is simple, rider black, as if he might forget why he's here while sleeping. The window is arched, and I move toward it. I can see the rest of Basgiath across the ravine through the clear glass.

It's the same war college and yet an entire world away. There are two more candidates on the parapet, but I look away before I can feel invested just to watch them fall. There is only so much death one person can take in a day, and I'm at my fucking maximum.

"Do you have wraps in here?" He hands me the rucksack.

"Got them all from Major Gillstead," I answer with a nod, plopping down on the edge of his expertly made bed and starting to dig through my pack. Luckily for me, Mira is an infinitely better packer than I am, and the wraps are easy to spot.

"Make yourself at home." He grins, leaning back against the closed door and hooking one ankle over the other. "As much as I hate that you're here, I have to say it's more than nice to see your face, Vi."

I look up, and our eyes meet. The tension that's been in my chest for the last week—hell, the last six months—eases, and for a second, it's just us. "I've missed you." Maybe it's exposing a weakness, but I don't care. Dain knows almost everything there is to know about me anyway.

"Yeah. I've missed you, too," he says quietly, his eyes softening.

My chest draws tight, and there's an awareness between us, an almost tangible sense of…anticipation as he looks at me. Maybe after all these years, we're finally on the same page when it comes to wanting each other. Or maybe he's just relieved to see an old friend.

"You'd better get that leg wrapped." He turns around to face the door. "I won't look."

"It's nothing you haven't seen before." I arch my hips and shimmy my leather pants down past my thighs and over my knees. Shit. The one on the left is swollen. If anyone else had taken that stumble, they would have ended up with a bruise, maybe even a scrape. But me? I have to fix it so my kneecap stays where it's supposed to. It's not just my muscles that are weak. My ligaments that hold my joints together don't work for shit, either.

"Yeah, well, we're not sneaking away to swim in the river, are we?" he teases. We grew up together through every post our parents had been stationed at, and no matter where we were, we always managed to find a place to swim and trees to climb.

I fasten the wrap at the top of my knee, then wind and secure the joint in the same way I've done since I was old enough for the healers to teach me. It's a practiced motion that I could do in my sleep, and the familiarity of it is almost soothing, if it didn't mean I was starting in the quadrant wounded.

As soon as I get it fastened with the little metal clasp, I stand and tug my leathers back up over my ass and button them. "All covered."

He turns and glances over me. "You look…different."

"It's the leathers." I shrug. "Why? Is different bad?" It takes a second to close my rucksack and haul it up and over my shoulders. Thank you, gods, the ache in my knee is manageable with it bound like this.

"It's just…" He shakes his head slowly, teasing his lower lip with his teeth. "Different."

"Why, Dain Aetos." I grin and walk toward him, then grasp the door handle at his side. "You've seen me in swimwear, tunics, and even ballgowns. Are you telling me it's the leather that does it for you?"

He scoffs, but there's a slight flush to his cheeks as his hand covers mine to open the door. "Glad to see our year apart hasn't dulled your tongue, Vi."

"Oh," I toss over my shoulder as we walk into the hallway, "I can do quite a few things with my tongue. You'd be impressed." My smile is so wide that it almost hurts, and just for a second, I forget that we're in the Riders Quadrant or that I've just survived the parapet.

His eyes heat. Guess he's forgotten, too. Then again, Mira's always made it clear that riders aren't an inhibited bunch behind these walls. There's not much reason to deny yourself when you might not live through tomorrow.

"We have to get you out of here," he says, shaking his head like he needs to clear it. Then he does the hand thing again, and I hear the lock slide into place. There's no one in the hallway, and we make it to the stairwell quickly.

"Thanks," I say as we start descending. "My knee feels way better now."

"I still can't believe your mother thought putting you into the Riders Quadrant was a good idea." I can practically feel the anger vibrating off him next to me as we walk down the stairs. There's no banister on his side, but he doesn't seem to mind, even though a single misstep would be the end of him.

"Me neither. She announced her decree about which quadrant I'd choose last spring, after I passed the initial entrance exam, and I immediately started working with Major Gillstead." He'll be so proud when he reads the rolls tomorrow and sees that I'm not on them.

"There's a door at the bottom of this stairwell, below the main level, that leads to the passage into the Healers Quadrant farther up the ravine," he says as we approach the first floor. "We'll get you through that and into the Scribe Quadrant."

"What?" I stop as my feet hit the polished stone landing at the main floor, but he continues downward.

He's already three steps beneath me when he realizes I'm not with him. "The Scribe Quadrant," he says slowly, turning to face me.

This angle makes me taller than he is, and I glare down at him. "I can't go to the Scribe Quadrant, Dain."

"I'm sorry?" His eyebrows fly up.

"She won't stand for it." I shake my head.

His mouth opens, then shuts, and his fists clench at his sides. "This place will kill you, Violet. You can't stay here. Everyone will understand. You didn't volunteer—not really."

Anger bristles up my spine, and my gaze narrows on him. Ignoring who did or did not volunteer me, I snap, "One, I'm well aware of what my chances are here, *Dain*, and two, usually fifteen percent of candidates don't make it past the parapet, and I'm still standing, so I guess I'm beating those odds already."

He backs up another step. "I'm not saying you didn't just kick absolute ass by getting here, Vi. But you have to leave. You'll break the first time they put you in the sparring ring, and that's *before* the dragons sense that you're..." He shakes his head and looks away, his jaw clenching.

"I'm *what*?" My hackles rise. "Go ahead and say it. When they sense I'm *less than* the others? Is that what you mean?"

"Damn it." He rakes his hand over his close-cropped light-brown curls. "Stop putting words in my mouth. You know what I mean. Even if you survive to Threshing, there's no guarantee a dragon will bond you. As it was, last year we had thirty-four unbonded cadets who have just been sitting around, waiting to restart the year with this class to get a chance at bonding again, and they're all perfectly healthy—"

"Don't be an asshole." My stomach falls. Just because he might be right doesn't mean I want to hear it...or want to be called *unhealthy*.

"I'm trying to keep you alive!" he shouts, his voice echoing off the stone of the stairwell. "If we get you to the Scribe Quadrant right now, you can still ace their test and have a phenomenal story to tell when you're out drinking. I take you back out there"—he points to the doorway that leads to the courtyard—"it's out of my hands. I can't protect you here. Not fully."

"I'm not asking you to!" Wait...didn't I want him to? Wasn't that what Mira suggested? "Why would you tell Rhiannon to put me in your squad if you just wanted to sneak me out the back door?"

The vise around my chest squeezes tighter. Next to Mira, Dain is the person who knows me best on the entire damned Continent, and even he thinks I can't hack it here.

"To make her leave so I could get you out!" He climbs two steps, shortening the distance between us, but there's no give in the set of his shoulders. If determination had a physical form, it would be Dain Aetos right now. "Do you think I want to watch my best friend die? Do you think it'll be fun to see what they'll do to you, knowing you're General Sorrengail's daughter? Putting on leathers doesn't make you a rider, Vi. They're going to tear you to shreds, and if they don't, the dragons will. In the Riders Quadrant, you either graduate or die, and you know that. Let me save you." His entire posture droops, and the plea in his eyes shreds some of my indignation. "Please let me save you."

"You can't," I whisper. "She said she'd haul me right back. I either leave here as a rider or as a name on a stone."

"She didn't mean it." He shakes his head. "She can't mean that."

"She means it. Even Mira couldn't talk her out of it."

He searches my eyes and tenses, as if he sees the truth of it there. "Shit."

"Yeah. Shit." I shrug, like it's not my life we're talking about here.

"All right." I can see him mentally changing gears, adapting to the information. "We'll find another way. For now, let's go." He takes my hand and leads me to the alcove we disappeared from. "Get out there and meet the other first-years. I'll go back and enter from the turret doorway. They'll figure out we know each other soon enough, but don't give anyone ammunition." He squeezes my hand and lets go, walking away without another word and disappearing into the tunnel.

I grip the straps of my rucksack and walk into the dappled sunlight of the courtyard. The clouds are breaking, and the drizzle is burning off as the gravel crunches beneath my feet on my way toward the riders and cadets.

The massive courtyard, which could easily fit a thousand riders, is just like the map in the archives recorded. Shaped like an angular teardrop, the rounded end is formed by a giant outer wall at least ten feet thick. Along the sides are stone halls. I know the four-story building carved into the mountain with the rounded end is for academics, and the one on the right, towering over the cliff, is the dorms, where Dain took me. The imposing rotunda linking the two buildings also serves as the entrance to the gathering hall, commons, and library behind it. I quit gawking and turn in the courtyard to face the outer wall. There's a stone dais on the right side of the parapet, occupied by two uniformed men I recognize as the commandant and executive commandant, both in full military dress, their medals winking in the sunlight.

It takes me a few minutes to find Rhiannon in the growing crowd, talking to another girl whose jet-black hair is cut just as short as Dain's.

"There you are!" Rhiannon's smile is genuine and full of relief. "I was worried. Is everything..." She lifts her eyebrows.

"I'm good to go." I nod and turn toward the other woman as Rhiannon introduces us. Her name is Tara, and she's from the Morraine province to the north, along the coast of the Emerald Sea. She has that same air of confidence Mira does, and her eyes dance with excitement as she and Rhiannon talk about how they've both obsessed over dragons since childhood. I pay attention but only enough to recall details if we need to form an alliance.

An hour passes, then another, according to the Basgiath bells, which we can hear from here. Then the last of the cadets walks into the courtyard, followed by the three riders from the other turret.

Xaden is among them. It's not just his height that makes him stand out in this crowd but the way the other riders all seem to move around him, like he's a shark and they're all fish giving him a wide berth. For a second, I can't help but wonder what his signet is, the unique power from the bond with his dragon, and if that's why even the third-years seem to scurry out of his way as he strides up to the dais with lethal grace. There are ten of them in total up there now, and from the way Commandant Panchek moves to the front, facing us—

"I think we're about to start," I say to Rhiannon and Tara, and they both turn to face the dais. Everyone does.

"Three hundred and one of you have survived the parapet to become cadets today," Commandant Panchek starts with a politician's smile, gesturing to us. The guy has always talked with his hands. "Good job. Sixty-seven did not."

My chest clenches as my brain spins the calculation quickly. Almost twenty percent. Was it the rain? The wind? That's more than average. *Sixty-seven* people died trying to get here.

"I've heard this position is just a stepping stone for him," Tara whispers. "He wants Sorrengail's job, then General Melgren's."

The commanding general of all Navarre's forces. Melgren's beady eyes have always made me shrivel every time we've met during my mother's career.

"General Melgren's?" Rhiannon whispers from my other side.

"He'll never get it," I say quietly as the commandant welcomes us to the Riders Quadrant. "Melgren's dragon gives him the signet ability to see a battle's outcome before it happens. There's no beating that, and you can't be assassinated if you know it's coming."

"As the Codex says, now you begin the true crucible!" Panchek shouts, his voice carrying over the five hundred of us that I estimate are in this courtyard. "You will be tested by your superiors, hunted by your peers, and guided by your instincts. If you survive to Threshing, and if you are chosen, you will be riders. Then we'll see how many of you make it to graduation."

Statistics say about a quarter of us will live to graduate, give or take a few on any year, and yet the Riders Quadrant is never short volunteers. Every cadet in this courtyard thinks they have what it takes to be one of the elite, the very best Navarre has to offer…a dragon rider. I can't help but wonder for the smallest of seconds if maybe I do, too. Maybe I can do more than just survive.

"Your instructors will teach you," Panchek promises, his hand sweeping to the line of professors standing at the doors to the academic wing. "It's up to you how well you learn." He swings his pointer finger at us. "Discipline falls to your units, and your wingleader is the last word. If I have to get involved..." A slow, sinister smile spreads across his face. "You don't want me involved.

"With that said, I'll leave you to your wingleaders. My best advice? Don't die." He walks off the dais with the executive commandant, leaving only the riders on the stone stage.

A brunette woman with wide shoulders and a scarred sneer stalks forward, the silver spikes on the shoulders of her uniform flashing in the sunlight. "I'm Nyra, the senior wingleader of the quadrant and the head of the First Wing. Section leaders and squad leaders, take your positions now."

My shoulder is jostled as someone walks by, pushing between Rhiannon and me. Others follow suit until there are about fifty people in front of us, spaced out in formation.

"Sections and squads," I whisper to Rhiannon, in case she didn't grow up in a military family. "Three squads in each section and three sections in each of the four wings."

"Thank you," Rhiannon answers.

Dain stands in the section for Second Wing, facing me but averting his eyes.

"First Squad! Claw Section! First Wing!" Nyra calls out.

A man closer to the dais raises his hand.

"Cadets, when your name is called, take up formation behind your squad leader," Nyra instructs.

The redhead with the crossbow and roll steps forward and begins calling names. One by one, cadets move from the crowd to the formation, and I keep count, making snap judgments based off clothing and arrogance. It looks like each squad will have about fifteen or sixteen people in it.

Jack is called into the Flame Section of First Wing.

Tara is called into the Tail Section, and soon they start on Second Wing.

I let loose a thankful sigh when the wingleader steps forward and it isn't Xaden.

Rhiannon and I are both called to Second Squad, Flame Section, Second Wing. We get into formation quickly, lining up in a square. A quick glance tells me that we have a squad leader—Dain, who isn't looking at me—a female executive squad leader, four riders who look like they might be second- or third-years, and nine first-years. One of the riders with two stars on her uniform and half-shaved, half-pink hair has a rebellion relic that winds around her forearm, from her wrist to above her elbow, where it disappears under her uniform, but I look away so she won't catch me staring.

We're silent as the rest of the wings are called. The sun is out in full now, beating into my leathers and scorching my skin. *I told him not to keep you in that library.* Mom's words from this morning haunt me, but it's not like I could have prepared for this. I have exactly two shades when it comes to the sun, pale and burned.

When the order sounds, we all turn to face the dais. I try to keep my gaze on the roll-keeper, but my eyes jerk right like the traitors they are, and my pulse leaps.

Xaden watches me with a cold, calculating look that feels like he's plotting my death from where he stands as the wingleader for Fourth Wing.

I lift my chin.

He cocks his scarred eyebrow. Then he says something to Second Wing's wingleader, and then every wingleader joins in on what's obviously a heated discussion.

"What do you think they're talking about?" Rhiannon whispers.

"Quiet," Dain hisses.

My spine stiffens. I can't expect him to be *my* Dain here, not under these circumstances, but still, the tone is jarring.

Finally, the wingleaders turn around to face us, and the slight tilt to Xaden's lips makes me instantly queasy.

"Dain Aetos, you and your squad will switch with Aura Beinhaven's," Nyra orders.

Wait. What? Who is Aura Beinhaven?

Dain nods, then turns to us. "Follow me." He says it once, then strides through formation, leaving us to scurry after him. We pass another squad on the way from…from…

The very breath freezes in my lungs.

We're moving to Fourth Wing. Xaden's wing.

It takes a minute, maybe two, and we take our place in the new formation. I force myself to breathe. There's a fucking smirk on Xaden's arrogant, handsome face.

I'm now entirely at his mercy, a subordinate in his chain of command. He can punish me however he likes for the slightest infraction, even imaginary ones.

Nyra looks at Xaden as she finishes assignments, and he nods, stepping forward and finally breaking our staring contest. I'm pretty sure he won, considering my heart is galloping like a runaway horse.

"You're all cadets now." Xaden's voice carries out over the courtyard, stronger than the others. "Take a look at your squad. These are the only people guaranteed by Codex not to kill you. But just because they can't end your life doesn't mean others won't. You want a dragon? Earn one."

Most of the others cheer, but I keep my mouth shut.

Sixty-seven people fell or died in some other way today. Sixty-seven just like Dylan, whose parents would either collect their bodies or watch them be buried at the foot of the mountain under a simple stone. I can't force myself to cheer for their loss.

Xaden's eyes find mine, and my stomach clenches before he looks away. "And I bet you feel pretty badass right now, don't you, first-years?"

More cheers.

"You feel invincible after the parapet, don't you?" Xaden shouts. "You think you're untouchable! You're on the way to becoming the elite! The few! The chosen!"

Another round of cheers goes up with each declaration, louder and louder.

No. That's not just cheering, it's the sound of wings beating the air into submission.

"Oh gods, they're beautiful," Rhiannon whispers at my side as they come into view—a riot of dragons.

I've spent my life around dragons, but always from a distance. They don't tolerate humans they haven't chosen. But these eight? They're flying straight for us—at speed.

Just when I think they're about to fly overhead, they pitch vertically, whip the air with their huge semitranslucent wings, and stop, the gusts of wing-made wind so powerful that I nearly stagger backward as they land on the outer semicircular wall. Their chest scales ripple with movement, and their razor-sharp talons dig into the edge of the wall on either side. Now I understand why the walls are ten feet thick. It's not a barrier. The edge of the fortress is a damned *perch.*

My mouth drops open. In my five years of living here, I've never seen this, but then again, I've never been allowed to watch what happens on Conscription Day.

A few cadets scream.

Guess everyone wants to be a dragon rider until they're actually twenty feet away from one.

Steam blasts my face as the navy-blue one directly in front of me exhales through its wide nostrils. Its glistening blue horns rise above its head in an elegant, lethal sweep, and its wings flare momentarily before tucking in, the tip of their top joint crowned by a single fierce talon. Their tails are just as fatal, but I can't see them at this angle or even tell which breed of dragon each is without that clue.

All are deadly.

"We're going to have to bring the masons in again," Dain mutters as chunks of rock crumble under the dragons' grips, crashing to the courtyard in boulders the size of my torso.

There are three dragons in various shades of red, two shades of green—like Teine, Mira's dragon—one brown like Mom's, one orange, and the enormous navy one ahead of me. They're all massive, overshadowing the structure of the citadel as they narrow their golden eyes at us in absolute judgment.

If they didn't need us puny humans to develop signet abilities from bonding and weave the protective wards they power around Navarre, I'm pretty sure they'd eat us all and be done. But they like protecting the Vale—the valley behind Basgiath the dragons call home—from merciless gryphons and we like living, so here we are in the most unlikely of partnerships.

My heart threatens to beat out of my chest, and I absolutely agree with it, because I'd like to run, too. Just thinking that I'm supposed to *ride* one of these is fucking ludicrous.

A cadet bolts out of Third Wing, screaming as he makes a run for the stone keep behind us. We all turn to look as he sprints for the giant arched door at the center. I can almost see the words carved into the arch from here, but I already know them by heart. *A dragon without its rider is a tragedy. A rider without their dragon is dead.*

Once bonded, riders can't live without their dragons, but most dragons can live just fine after us. It's why they choose carefully, so they're not humiliated by picking a coward, not that a dragon would ever admit to making a mistake.

The red dragon on the left opens its vast mouth, revealing teeth as big as I am. That jaw could crush me if it wanted, like a grape. Fire erupts along its tongue, then shoots outward in a macabre blaze toward the fleeing cadet.

He's a pile of ash on the gravel before he can even make it to the shadow of the keep.

Sixty-eight dead.

Heat from the flames blasts the side of my face as I jerk my attention forward. If anyone else runs and is likewise executed, I don't want to see it. More screaming sounds around me. I lock my jaw as hard as I can to keep quiet.

There are two more gusts of heat, one to my left and then another to my right.

Make that seventy.

The navy dragon seems to tilt its head at me, as if its narrowed golden eyes can see straight through me to the fear fisting my stomach and the doubt curled insidiously around my heart. I bet it can even see the wrap binding my knee. It knows I'm at a disadvantage, that I'm too small to climb its foreleg and mount, too frail to ride. Dragons always know.

But I will not run. I wouldn't be standing here if I'd quit every time something seemed impossible to overcome. *I will not die today.* The words repeat in my head just like they had before the parapet and on it.

I force my shoulders back and lift my chin.

The dragon blinks, which might be a sign of approval, or boredom, and looks away.

"Anyone else feel like changing their mind?" Xaden shouts, scanning the remaining rows of cadets with the same shrewd gaze of the navy-blue dragon behind him. "No? Excellent. Roughly half of you will be dead by this time next summer." The formation is silent except for a few untimely sobs from my left. "A third of you again the year after that, and the same your last year. No one cares who your mommy or daddy is here. Even King Tauri's second son died during his Threshing. So tell me again: Do you feel invincible now that you've made it into the Riders Quadrant? Untouchable? Elite?"

No one cheers.

Another blast of heat rushes—this time directly at my face—and every muscle in my body clenches, preparing for incineration. But it's not flames...just steam, and it blows back Rhiannon's braids as the dragons finish their simultaneous exhale. The breeches on the first-year ahead of me darken, the color spreading down his legs.

They want us scared. Mission accomplished.

"Because you're not untouchable or special to them." Xaden points toward the navy dragon and leans forward slightly, like he's letting us in on a secret as we lock eyes. "To them, you're just the prey."

The sparring ring is where riders are made or broken. After all, no respectable dragon would choose a rider who cannot defend themselves, and no respectable cadet would allow such a threat to the wing to continue training.

—Major Afendra's Guide to the Riders Quadrant (Unauthorized Edition)

CHAPTER FOUR

"Elena Sosa, Brayden Blackburn." Captain Fitzgibbons reads from the death roll, flanked by two other scribes on the dais as we stand in silent formation in the courtyard, squinting into the early sun.

This morning, we're all in rider black, and there's a single silver four-pointed star on my collarbone, the mark of a first-year, and a Fourth Wing patch on my shoulder. We were issued standard uniforms yesterday, summer-weight tight-fitted tunics, pants, and accessories after Parapet was over, but not flight leathers. There's no point handing out the thicker, more protective combat uniforms when half of us won't be around come Threshing in October. The armored corset Mira made me isn't regulation, but I fit right in among the hundreds of modified uniforms around me.

After the last twenty-four hours and one night in the first-floor barracks, I'm starting to realize that this quadrant is a strange mix of we-might-die-tomorrow hedonism and brutal efficiency in the name of the same reason.

"Jace Sutherland." Captain Fitzgibbons continues to read, and the scribes next to him shift their weight. "Dougal Luperco."

I think we're somewhere in the fifties, but I lost count when he read Dylan's name a few minutes ago. This is the only memorial the names will get, the only time they'll be spoken of in the citadel, so I try to concentrate, to commit each name to memory, but there's just too many.

My skin is agitated from wearing the armor all night like Mira suggested, and my knee aches, but I resist the urge to bend down and adjust the wrap I managed to put on in the nonexistent privacy of my bunk in the first-year barracks before anyone else woke up.

There are a hundred and fifty-six of us in the first floor of the dormitory building, our beds positioned in four neat rows in the open space. Even though Jack Barlowe was put in the third-floor dorms, I'm not about to let any of them see my weaknesses. Not until I know who I can trust. Private rooms are like flight leathers—you don't get one until you survive Threshing.

"Simone Casteneda." Captain Fitzgibbons closes the scroll. "We commend their souls to Malek." The god of death.

I blink. Guess we were closer to the end than I thought.

There's no formal conclusion to the formation, no last moment of silence. The names on the scroll leave the dais with the scribes, and the quiet is broken as the squad leaders all turn and begin to address their squads.

"Hopefully you all ate breakfast, because you're not going to get another chance before lunch," Dain says, his eyes meeting mine for the span of a heartbeat before he glances away, feigning indifference.

"He's good at pretending he doesn't know you," Rhiannon whispers at my side.

"He is," I reply just as softly. A smile tugs at the corners of my mouth, but I keep my expression as bland as possible as I soak in the sight of him. The sun plays in his sandy-brown hair, and when he turns his head, I see a scar peeking from his beard along his chin I'd somehow missed yesterday.

"Second- and third-years, I'm assuming you know where to go," Dain continues as the scribes wind their way around the edge of the courtyard to my right, headed back to their quadrant. I ignore the tiny voice inside me protesting that it was supposed to be *my* quadrant. Lingering on what could have been isn't going to help me survive to see tomorrow's sunrise.

There's a mutter of agreement from the senior cadets ahead of us. As first-years, we're in the back two rows of the little square that makes up Second Squad.

"First-years, at least one of you should have memorized your academic schedule when it was handed out yesterday." Dain's voice booms over us, and it's hard to reconcile this stern-faced, serious leader with the funny, grinning guy I've always known. "Stick together. I expect you all to be alive when we meet this afternoon in the sparring gym."

Fuck, I'd almost forgotten that we're sparring today. We only have the gym twice a week, so as long as I can get through today's session unscathed, I'm in the clear for another couple of days. At least I have some time to get my feet under me before we'll have to handle the Gauntlet—the terrifying vertical obstacle course they told us we'll have to master when the leaves turn colors in two months.

If we can complete the final Gauntlet, we'll walk through the natural box canyon above it that leads to the flight field for Presentation, where this year's dragons willing to bond will get their first look at the remaining cadets. Two days after that, Threshing will occur in the valley beneath the citadel.

I glance around at my new squadmates and can't help but wonder which of us, if any, will make it to that flight field, let alone that valley.

Don't borrow tomorrow's trouble.

"And if we're not?" the smart-ass first-year behind me asks.

I don't bother looking, but Rhiannon does, rolling her eyes as she turns back forward.

"Then I won't have to be concerned with learning your name, since it will be read off tomorrow morning," Dain answers with a shrug.

A second-year ahead of me snorts a laugh, the movement jangling two small hoop earrings in her left lobe, but the pink-haired one stays silent.

"Sawyer?" Dain looks at the first-year to my left.

"I'll get them there." The tall, wiry cadet whose light complexion is covered with a smattering of freckles answers with a tight nod. His freckled jaw ticks, and my chest pangs with sympathy. He's one of the repeats—a cadet who didn't bond during Threshing and now has to start the entire year over.

"Get going," Dain orders, and our squad breaks apart around the same time the others do, transforming the courtyard from an orderly formation to a crowd of chatting cadets. The second- and third-years walk off in another direction, including Dain.

"We have about twenty minutes to get to class," Sawyer shouts at the eight of us first-years. "Fourth floor, second room on the left in the academic wing. Get your shit and don't be late." He doesn't bother waiting to confirm we've heard him before he heads off toward the dormitory.

"That has to be hard," Rhiannon says as we follow the crowd toward the dorms. "Being set back and having to do this all over again."

"Better than being dead," the smart-ass says as he passes us on the right, his dark-brown hair flopping against the brown skin of his forehead with every step the shorter cadet takes. His name is Ridoc, if I remember correctly from the brief introductions we went through before dinner last night.

"That's true," I reply as we head into the bottleneck that's formed at the door.

"I overheard a third-year say when a first-year survives Threshing unbonded, the quadrant lets them repeat the year and try again if they want," Rhiannon adds, and I can't help but wonder how much determination it would take to survive your first year and then be willing to repeat it just for the chance you might one day become a rider. You could just as easily die the second time around.

A bird whistles to the left, and I look over the crowd, my heart leaping because I immediately recognize the tone. *Dain.*

The call sounds again, and I narrow it down to somewhere near the door to the rotunda. He's standing at the top of the wide staircase, and the second our eyes lock, he motions toward the door with a subtle nod.

"I'll be—" I start saying to Rhiannon, but she's already followed my line of sight.

"I'll grab your stuff and meet you there. It's under your bunk, right?" she asks.

"You don't mind?"

"Your bunk is next to mine, Violet. It's not a hassle. Go!" She gives me a conspiratorial smile and shoulder bumps me.

"Thank you!" I smile quickly, then wade across the crowd until I break free at the edge. Lucky for me, there aren't many cadets headed into commons, which means there aren't any eyes on me once I slip inside one of the four giant doors of the rotunda.

My lungs pull in a sharp breath. It looks like the renderings I've seen in the Archives, but there is no drawing, no artistic medium, that can capture just how overwhelming the space is, how exquisite every detail. The rotunda might be the most beautiful piece of architecture not only in the citadel but in all of Basgiath. The room is three stories tall, from its polished marble floors to the domed glass ceiling that filters in the soft morning light. To the left are two massive arched doors to the academic wing, echoed by the same on the right, leading to the dorms, and up a half dozen steps, there are four doorways in front of me that open into the gathering hall.

Equally spaced around the rotunda, shimmering in their various colors of red, green, brown, orange, blue, and black, stand six daunting marble pillars carved into dragons, as if they'd come crashing down from the ceiling above. There's enough room between the snarling mouths at the base of each to fit at least four squads in the center, but it's empty right now.

I pass by the first dragon, chiseled from dark-red marble, and a hand grips my elbow, pulling me back behind the pillar where there's a gap between the claw and the wall.

"It's just me." Dain's voice is low and quiet as he turns me to face him. Tension radiates from every line of his frame.

"I figured, since you were the one birdcalling me." I grin, shaking my head. He's been using that signal since we were kids living near the Krovlan border while our parents were stationed there with the Southern Wing.

His brow furrows as his gaze scans over me, no doubt looking for new injuries. "We only have a few minutes before this place is packed. How is your knee?"

"It hurts, but I'll live." I've had far worse injuries and we both know it, but there's no use telling him to relax when he's obviously not going to.

"No one tried to screw with you last night?" Concern creases his forehead, and I fold my arms to keep from smoothing the lines with my fingers. His worry sits on my chest like a stone.

"Would it be so bad if they did?" I tease, forcing my smile to widen.

He drops his arms to his sides and sighs so hard, the sound echoes in the rotunda. "You know that's not what I mean, Violet."

"No one tried to kill me last night, Dain, or even hurt me." I lean back against the wall and take some weight off my knee. "Pretty sure we were all too tired and relieved to be alive to start slaughtering one another." The barracks fell quiet pretty quickly after lights out. There was something to be said for the emotional exhaustion of the day.

"And you ate, right? I know they usher you out of the dorms fast when the bells chime for six."

"I ate with the rest of the first-years, and before you even think about lecturing me, I rewrapped my knee under my covers and had my hair braided before the bells sounded. I've been keeping scribe hours for *years*, Dain. They're up an hour earlier. It makes me want to volunteer for breakfast duty, actually."

He glances at the tight, silver-tipped braid I've pinned into a bun against the darker hair near the crown of my head. "You should cut it."

"Don't start with me." I shake my head.

"There's a reason women keep it short here, Vi. The second someone gets ahold of your hair in the sparring ring— "

"My hair is the *least* of my concerns in the sparring ring," I retort.

His eyes widen. "I'm just trying to keep you safe. You're lucky I didn't shove you into Captain Fitzgibbons's hands this morning and beg him to take you out of here."

I ignore the bluster of a threat. We're wasting time, and there's one piece of information I need from Dain. "Why was our squad moved from Second Wing to Fourth yesterday?"

He stiffens and looks away.

"Tell me." I need to know if I'm reading into a situation that doesn't exist.

"Fuck," he mutters, ripping his hand over his hair. "Xaden Riorson wants you dead. It's common knowledge among the leadership cadre after yesterday."

Nope. Not overreacting.

"He moved the squad so he has a direct line to me. So he can do whatever he wants and no one will question a thing. I'm his revenge against my mother." My heart doesn't even jump at the confirmation of what I already knew. "That's what I thought. I just needed to be sure my imagination wasn't running away with me."

"I'm not going to let anything happen to you." Dain steps forward and cups my face, his thumb stroking over my cheekbone in a soothing motion.

"There's not much you can do." I push off the wall, stepping out of his reach. "I have to get to class." Already, there are a few voices echoing in the rotunda as cadets pass through.

His jaw works for a second, and the lines are back between his eyebrows. "Just do your best to keep a low profile, especially when we're in Battle Brief. Not like the colors in your hair don't give you away, but that's the one class the entire quadrant takes. I'll see if one of the second-years can stand guard— "

"No one is going to assassinate me during history." I roll my eyes. "Academics are the one place I don't have to worry. What is Xaden going to do? Pull me out of class and run me through with a sword in the middle of the hallway? Or do you honestly think he'll stab me in the middle of

Battle Brief?"

"I wouldn't put it past him. He's fucking *ruthless*, Violet. Why do you think his dragon chose him?"

"The navy-blue one who landed behind the dais yesterday?" My stomach twists. The way those golden eyes assessed me...

Dain nods. "Sgaeyl is a Blue Daggertail, and she's...vicious." He swallows. "Don't get me wrong. Cath is a nasty piece of work when he gets riled—all Red Swordtails are—but even most dragons steer clear of Sgaeyl."

I stare at Dain, at the scar that defines his jaw and the hard set of his eyes that are familiar and yet not.

"What?" he asks. The voices around us grow louder, and there are more footsteps coming and going.

"You bonded a dragon. You have powers I don't even know about. You open doors with magic. You're a squad leader." I say the sentences slowly, hoping they'll sink in, that I'll truly grasp how much he's changed. "It's just hard to wrap my head around you still being...Dain."

"I'm still me." His posture softens, and he lifts the short sleeve of his tunic, revealing the relic of a red dragon on his shoulder. "I just have this now. And as for the powers, Cath channels a pretty significant amount of magic compared to some of the other dragons, but I'm nowhere near adept at it yet. I haven't changed that much. As for lesser magic powered through the bond of my relic, I can do the typical stuff like open doors, crank up my speed, and power ink pens instead of using those inconvenient quills."

"What's your signet power?" Every rider can do lesser magic once their dragon begins channeling power to them, but the signet is the unique ability that stands out, the strongest skill that results from each unique bond between dragon and rider.

Some riders have the same signets. Fire wielding, ice wielding, and water wielding are just a few of the most common signet powers, all useful in battle.

Then there are the signets that make a rider extraordinary.

My mother can wield the power of storms.

Melgren can see the outcome of battles.

I can't help but wonder again what Xaden's signet is—and if he'll use it to kill me when I least expect it.

"I can read a person's recent memories," Dain admits quietly. "Not like an inntinnsic reads minds or anything—I have to put my hands on the person, so I'm not a security risk. But my signet's not common knowledge. I think they'll use me in intelligence." He points to the compass patch beneath his Fourth Wing one on his shoulder. Wearing that sigil indicates that a signet is too classified. I just didn't notice it yesterday.

"No way." I smile, taking a calming breath as I remember Xaden's uniform didn't have any patches on it.

He nods, an excited smile shaping his mouth. "I'm still learning, and of course I'm better at it the closer I am to Cath, but yeah. I just put my hands on someone's temples, and I can see what they saw. It's…incredible."

That signet will more than set Dain apart. It will make him one of the most valuable interrogation tools we have. "And you say you haven't changed," I half tease.

"This place can warp almost everything about a person, Vi. It cuts away the bullshit and the niceties, revealing whoever you are at your core. They want it that way. They want it to sever your previous bonds so your loyalty is to your wing. It's one of the many reasons that first-years aren't allowed to correspond with their family and friends, otherwise you know I would have written you. But a year doesn't change that I still think of you as my best friend. I'm still Dain, and this time next year, you will still be Violet. We will still be us."

"If I'm still alive," I joke as the bells ring. "I have to get to class."

"Yeah, and I'm going to be late to the flight field." He motions toward the edge of the pillar. "Look, Riorson is still a wingleader. He'll be after you, but he'll find a way to do it within the rules of the Codex, at least when people are watching. I was…" His cheeks flush. "Really good friends with Amber Mavis—the current wingleader for Third Wing—last year, and I'm telling you, the Codex is sacred to them. Now, you go first. I'll see you in the sparring gym." He smiles reassuringly.

"I'll see you." I smile back and turn on my heel, walking around the base of the massive pillar into the semi-crowded rotunda. There're a couple dozen cadets in here, walking from one building to another, and it takes a second to get my bearings.

I spot the academic doors between the orange-and-black pillars and start that way, blending into the crowd.

The hairs on the back of my neck stand up and a chill races down my spine as I cross the center of the rotunda, then my steps halt. Cadets move around me, but my eyes are drawn upward, toward the top of the steps that lead to the gathering hall.

Oh shit.

Xaden Riorson is watching me with narrowed eyes, the sleeves of his uniform rolled up his massive arms that remain folded across his chest, the warning in his relic-covered arm on full display as a third-year next to him says something that he blatantly ignores.

My heart jumps and lodges in my throat. There's maybe twenty feet between us. My fingers twitch, ready to grab one of the blades sheathed at my ribs. Is this where he'll do it? In the middle of the rotunda? The marble floor is gray, so it shouldn't be that hard for the staff to get the blood out.

His head tilts, and he studies me with those impossibly dark eyes, like he's deciding where I'm most vulnerable.

I should run, right? But at least I can see him coming if I hold this position.

His attention shifts, glancing to my right, and he lifts a single brow at me.

My stomach pitches as Dain emerges from behind the pillar.

"What are you—" Dain starts as he reaches me, his brow furrowed in confusion.

"Top of the steps. Fourth door," I hiss, interrupting him.

Dain's gaze snaps up as the crowd thins out around us, and he mutters a curse, not-so-subtly stepping closer to me. Fewer people mean fewer witnesses, but I'm not foolish enough to think Xaden won't kill me in front of the whole quadrant if he wants.

"I already knew your parents are tight," Xaden calls out, a cruel smile tilting his lips. "But do you two have to be so fucking obvious?"

The few cadets who are still in the rotunda turn to look at us.

"Let me guess," Xaden continues, glancing between Dain and me. "Childhood friends? First loves, even?"

"He can't hurt you without cause, right?" I whisper. "Without cause and calling a quorum of wingleaders because you're a squad leader. Article Four, Section Three."

"Correct," Dain answers, not bothering to lower his voice. "But you're not."

"I expected you to do a better job of hiding where your affections lie, Aetos." Xaden moves, walking down the steps.

Shit. Shit. *Shit.*

"Run, Violet," Dain orders me. *"Now."*

I bolt.

Knowing I am in direct disagreement with General Melgren's orders, I am officially objecting to the plan set forth in today's briefing. It is not this general's opinion that the children of the rebellion's leaders should be forced to witness their parents' executions. No child should watch their parent put to death.

—The Tyrrish Rebellion, an official brief for King Tauri by General Lilith Sorrengail

CHAPTER FIVE

"Welcome to your first Battle Brief," Professor Devera says from the recessed floor of the enormous lecture hall later in the morning, a bright purple Flame Section patch on her shoulder matching her short hair perfectly. This is the only class held in the circular, tiered room that curves the entire end of the academic hall and one of only two rooms in the citadel capable of fitting every cadet. Every creaky wooden seat is full, and the senior third-years are standing against the walls behind us, but we all fit.

It's a far cry from history last hour, where there were only three squads of first-years, but at least the first-years in our squad are all seated together. Now if I could only remember all their names.

Ridoc is easy to remember—he cracked wise-ass comments all through history. Hopefully he knows better than to try the same in here, though. Professor Devera isn't the joking kind.

"In the past, riders have seldom been called into service before graduation," Professor Devera continues, her mouth tensing as she paces slowly in front of a twenty-foot-high map of the Continent mounted to the back wall that's intricately labeled with our defensive outposts along our borders. Dozens of mage lights illuminate the space, more than making up for the lack of windows and reflecting off the longsword she keeps strapped to her back.

"And if they were, they were always third-years who'd spent time shadowing forward wings, but we expect you to graduate with the full knowledge of what we're up against. It's not about just knowing where every wing is stationed, either." She takes her time, making eye contact with every first-year she sees. The rank on her shoulder says captain, but I know she'll be a major before she leaves her rotation teaching here, given the medals pinned on her chest. "You need to understand the politics of our enemies, the strategies of defending our outposts from constant attack, and have a thorough knowledge of both recent and current battles. If you cannot grasp these basic topics, then you have no business on the back of a dragon." She arches a black brow a few shades darker than her deep-brown skin.

"No pressure," Rhiannon mutters at my side, furiously taking notes.

"We'll be fine," I promise her in a whisper. "Third-years have only been sent to midland posts as reinforcements, never the front." I'd kept my ears open around my mother enough to know that much.

"This is the only class you will have every day, because it's the only class that will matter if you're called into service early." Professor Devera's gaze sweeps from left to right and pauses on me. Her eyes flare wide for a heartbeat, but she gives an approving smile and nod before moving on. "Because this class is taught every day and relies on the most current information, you will also answer to Professor Markham, who deserves nothing but your utmost respect."

She waves the scribe forward, and he moves to stand next to her, the cream color of his uniform contrasting with her stark black one. He leans in when she whispers something to him, and his thick eyebrows fly high as he whips his head in my direction.

There's no approving smile when the colonel's weary eyes find mine, only a sigh that fills my chest with heavy sorrow when I hear it. I was supposed to be his star pupil in the Scribe Quadrant, his crowning achievement before he retires. How absolutely ironic that I'm now the least likely to succeed in this one.

"It is the duty of the scribes not only to study and master the past but to relay and record the present," he says, rubbing the bridge of his bulbous nose after finally tearing his disappointed gaze from mine. "Without accurate depictions of our front lines, reliable information with which to make strategic decisions, and—most importantly—veracious details to document our history for the good of future generations, we're doomed, not only as a kingdom but as a society."

Which is exactly why I've always wanted to be a scribe. Not that it matters now.

"First topic of the day." Professor Devera moves toward the map and flicks her hand, bringing a mage light directly over the eastern border with the Poromiel province of Braevick. "The Eastern Wing experienced an attack last night near the village of Chakir by a drift of Braevi gryphons and riders."

Oh shit. A murmur rips through the hall, and I dip my quill into the inkpot on the desk in front of me so I can take notes. I can't wait to channel so I can use the type of coveted pens Mom keeps on her desk. A smile curves my lips. There could definitely be perks to being a rider. There *will* be.

"Naturally, some information is redacted for security purposes, but what we can tell you is that the wards faltered along the top of the Esben Mountains." Professor Devera pulls her hands apart and the light expands, illuminating the mountains that form our border with Braevick. "Allowing the drift not only to enter Navarrian territory but for their riders to channel and wield sometime around midnight."

My stomach sinks as a murmur rises from the cadets, especially the first-years. Dragons aren't the only animals capable of channeling powers to their riders. Gryphons from Poromiel also share the ability, but dragons *are* the only ones capable of powering the wards that make all other magic but their own impossible within our borders. They're the reason Navarre's borders are somewhat circular—their power radiates from the Vale and can only extend so far, even with squads stationed at every outpost. Without those wards, we're fucked. It would be open season on Navarrian villages when the raiding parties from Poromiel inevitably descend. Those greedy assholes are never content with the resources they have. They always want ours, too, and until they learn to be content with our trade agreements, we have no chance of ending conscription in Navarre. No chance of experiencing peace.

But if we're not on high alert, then they must have gotten the wards rewoven, or at least stabilized.

"Thirty-seven civilians were killed in the attack in the hour before a squad from the Eastern Wing could arrive, but the riders and dragons managed to repel the drift," Professor Devera finishes, folding her arms over her chest. "Based on that information, what questions would you ask?" She holds up a finger. "I only want answers from first-years to start."

My initial question would be why the hell the wards faltered, but it's not like they're going to answer a question like that in a room full of cadets with zero security clearance.

I study the map. The Esben Mountain Range is the highest along our eastern border with Braevick, making it the least likely place for an attack, especially since gryphons don't tolerate altitude nearly as well as dragons, probably due to the fact that they're half-lion, half-eagle and can't handle the thinner air at higher altitudes.

There's a reason we've been able to fend off every major assault on our territory for the last six hundred years, and we've successfully defended our land in this never-ending four-hundred-year-long war. Our abilities, both lesser and signet, are superior because our dragons can channel more power than gryphons. So why attack in that mountain range? What caused the wards to falter there?

"Come on, first-years, show me you have more than just good balance. Show me you have the critical-thinking skills to be here," Professor Devera demands. "It's more important than ever that you're ready for what's beyond our borders."

"Is this the first time the wards have faltered?" a first-year a couple of rows ahead asks.

Professors Devera and Markham share a look before she turns toward the cadet. "No."

My heart jolts into my throat and the room falls pin-drop quiet.

It's not the first time.

The girl clears her throat. "And how…often are they faltering?"

Professor Markham's shrewd eyes narrow on her. "That's above your pay grade, cadet." He turns his attention to our section. "Next relevant question to the attack we're discussing?"

"How many casualties did the wing suffer?" a first-year down the row to my right asks.

"One injured dragon. One dead rider."

Another murmur rises from the hall. Surviving graduation doesn't mean we'll survive service. Statistically, most riders die before retirement age, especially at the rate riders have been falling over the last two years.

"Why would you ask that particular question?" Professor Devera asks the cadet.

"To know how many reinforcements they'll need," he answers.

Professor Devera nods, turning toward Pryor, the meekest first-year in our squad, who has his hand up, but he lowers it quickly, scrunching his dark eyebrows. "Did you want to ask a question?"

"Yes." He nods, sending a few locks of black hair into his eyes, then shakes his head. "No. Never mind."

"So decisive," Luca—the catty first-year in our squad I'll do just about *anything* to avoid—mocks from next to him, tilting her head as cadets laugh around them. A corner of her mouth tilts up into a smirk, and she flips her long brown hair over her shoulder in a move that's anything but casual. Like me, she's one of the few women in the quadrant who didn't cut her hair. I envy her confidence that it won't be used against her, but not her attitude, and I've known her less than a day.

"He's in our squad," Aurelie—at least I think that's her name—chastises, her no-nonsense black eyes narrowing on Luca. "Show some loyalty."

"Please. No dragon is bonding to a guy who can't even decide if he wants to ask a question. And did you see him at breakfast this morning? He held the entire line up because he couldn't choose between bacon or sausage." Luca rolls her kohl-rimmed eyes.

"If Fourth Wing is done picking at one another?" Professor Devera asks, lifting a brow.

"Ask what altitude the village is at," I whisper to Rhiannon.

"What?" Her brow furrows.

"Just ask," I reply, trying to keep Dain's advice in mind. I swear I can feel him staring at the back of my neck from seven rows behind me, but I'm not going to turn and look, not when I know Xaden's up there somewhere, too.

"What altitude is the village at?" Rhiannon asks.

Professor Devera's eyebrows rise as she turns to Rhiannon. "Markham?"

"A little less than ten thousand feet," he answers. "Why?"

Rhiannon darts a dose of side-eye at me and clears her throat. "Just seems a little high for a planned attack with gryphons."

"Good job," I whisper.

"It *is* a little high for a planned attack," Devera says. "Why don't you tell me why that's bothersome, Cadet Sorrengail? And maybe you'd like to ask your own questions from here on out." She levels a stare on me that has me squirming in my seat.

Every head in the room turns in my direction. If anyone had an inkling of doubt about who I am, it's long gone now. *Awesome.*

"Gryphons aren't as strong at that altitude, and neither is their ability to channel," I say. "It's an illogical place for them to attack unless they *knew* the wards would fail, especially since the village looks to be about what…an hour's flight from the nearest outpost?" I glance at the map to be sure I'm not making a fool of myself. "That is Chakir right there, isn't it?" *Scribe's training for the win.*

"It is." A corner of Professor Devera's mouth lifts into a smirk. "Keep going with that line of thought."

Wait a second. "Didn't you say it took an hour for the *squad* of riders to arrive?" My gaze narrows.

"I did." She looks at me with expectation.

"Then they were already on their way," I blurt, immediately recognizing how silly that sounds. My cheeks heat as a mumble of laughter sounds around me.

"Yeah, because that makes sense." Jack turns around in his seat from the front row and openly laughs at me. "General Melgren knows the outcome of a battle before it happens, but even he doesn't know *when* it will happen, dumbass."

I feel the chuckling of my classmates reverberate in my bones. I want to crawl under this ridiculous desk and disappear.

"Fuck off, Barlowe," Rhiannon snaps.

"I'm not the one who thinks precognition is a thing," he retorts with a sneer. "Gods help us if that one ever gets on the back of a dragon." Another round of laughter has my neck flaming, too.

"Why do you think that, Violet—" Professor Markham winces. "Cadet Sorrengail?"

"Because there's no logical way they get there within an hour of the attack unless they were already on their way," I argue, shooting a glare at Jack. Fuck him and his laughter. I might be weaker than he is, but I'm a hell of a lot smarter. "It would take at least half that long to light the beacons in the range and call for help, and no full squad is sitting around just waiting to be needed. More than half those riders would have been asleep, which means they were already on their way."

"And why would they already be on their way?" Professor Devera prods, and the light in her eyes tells me I'm right, giving me the confidence to take my train of thought a step further.

"Because they somehow knew the wards were breaking." I lift my chin, simultaneously hoping I'm right and praying to Dunne—the goddess of war—that I'm wrong.

"That's the most—" Jack starts.

"She's right," Professor Devera interrupts, and a hush falls over the room. "One of the dragons in the wing sensed the faltering ward, and the wing flew. Had they not, the casualties would have been far higher and the destruction of the village much worse."

A little bubble of confidence rises in my chest, which is promptly popped by Jack's glare, telling me he hasn't forgotten his promise to kill me.

"Second- and third-years, take over," Professor Devera orders. "Let's see if you can be a little more respectful to your fellow cadets." She arches a brow at Jack as questions begin to fire off from the riders behind us.

How many riders were deployed to the site?

What killed the lone fatality?

How long did it take to clear the village of the gryphons?

Were any left alive for questioning?

I write down every question and answer, my mind organizing the facts into what kind of report I would have filed if I'd been in the Scribe Quadrant, which information was important enough to include, and what was extraneous.

"What was the condition of the village?" a deep voice asks from the back of the lecture hall.

The hairs on my neck rise, my body recognizing the imminent threat behind me.

"Riorson?" Markham asks, shielding his eyes from the mage lights as he looks toward the top of the hall.

"The village," Xaden restates. "Professor Devera said the damage would have been worse, but what was the actual condition? Was it burned? Destroyed? They wouldn't demolish it if they were trying to establish a foothold, so the condition of the village matters when trying to determine a motive for the attack."

Professor Devera smiles in approval. "The buildings they'd already gone through were burned, and the rest were being looted when the wing arrived."

"They were looking for something," Xaden says with complete conviction. "And it wasn't riches. That's not a gem mining district. Which begs the question, what do we have that they want so badly?"

"Exactly. That's the question." Professor Devera glances around the room. "And that right there is why Riorson is a wingleader. You need more than strength and courage to be a good rider."

"So what's the answer?" a first-year to the left asks.

"We don't know," Professor Devera answers with a shrug. "It's just another piece in the puzzle of why our constant bids for peace are rejected by the kingdom of Poromiel. What were they looking for? Why *that* village? Were they responsible for the collapse of the ward, or was it already faltering? Tomorrow, next week, next month, there will be another attack, and maybe we'll get another clue. Go to history if you're looking for answers. Those wars have already been dissected and examined. Battle Brief is for fluid situations. In this class, we want you to learn which questions to ask so *all* of you have a chance at coming home alive."

Something in her tone tells me it's not just third-years who might be called into service this year, and a chill settles in my bones.

"You seriously knew every answer in history and apparently every right question to ask in Battle Brief," Rhiannon says, shaking her head as we stand on the sidelines of the sparring mat after lunch, watching Ridoc and Aurelie circle each other in their fighting leathers. They're evenly matched in size. Ridoc is on the smaller side, and Aurelie is built just like Mira, which doesn't surprise me because she's a legacy on her father's side. "You're not even going to have to study for tests, are you?"

The rest of the first-years stand on our side, but the second- and third-years line the others. They're definitely at an advantage here, considering they've already had at least a year of combat training.

"I was trained to be a scribe." I shrug, and the vest Mira made me shimmers slightly with the movement. Other than the times the scales catch the light under the camouflaging mesh, it fits right in with the tops we'd been given from central issue yesterday. All the women are dressed similarly now, though the cuts of their leathers are chosen by preference.

The guys are mostly shirtless because they think shirts give their opponent something to grab onto. Personally, I'm not arguing with their logic, just enjoying the view…respectfully, of course, which means keeping my eyes on my own squad's mat and off the other twenty mats in the massive gym that consumes the first floor of the academic wing. One wall is made entirely of windows and doors, all left open to let in the breeze, but it's still stiflingly hot. Sweat trickles down my spine under my vest.

There are three squads from each wing here this afternoon, and lucky me, First Wing has sent their third squads, which include Jack Barlowe, who's been glaring at me from two mats over since I walked in.

"Guess that means you're not worried about academics," Rhiannon says, her brows rising at me. She's chosen a leather vest, too, but hers cuts in above the collarbone and secures at her neck, leaving her shoulders bare for movement.

"Stop circling each other like you're dance partners and attack!" Professor Emetterio orders from across the mat, where Dain watches Aurelie and Ridoc's match with our squad executive leader, Cianna. Thank God Dain's shirt is on, because I don't need another distraction when it's time for my turn.

"I'm worried about this," I tell Rhiannon, tilting my chin toward the mat.

"Really?" She shoots me a skeptical look. Her braids are twisted into a small bun at the nape of her neck. "I figured as a Sorrengail, you'd be a hand-to-hand threat."

"Not exactly." At my age, Mira had been training in hand-to-hand for twelve years. I have a whopping six months under my belt, which wouldn't matter as much if I wasn't as breakable as a porcelain teacup, but here we are.

Ridoc launches toward Aurelie, but she ducks, sweeping out her leg and tripping him. He staggers but doesn't go down. He pivots quickly, palming a dagger in his hand.

"No blades today!" Professor Emetterio bellows from beside the mat. He's only the fourth professor I've met, but he's definitely the one who intimidates me most. Or maybe it's just the subject he teaches that has me envisioning his compact frame as giant. "We're just assessing!"

Ridoc grumbles and sheathes his knife just in time to deflect a right hook from Aurelie.

"The brunette packs a punch," Rhiannon says with an appreciative smile before glancing my way.

"What about you?" I ask as Ridoc lands a jab to Aurelie's ribs.

"Shit!" He shakes his head and backs up a step. "I don't want to hurt you."

Aurelie holds her ribs but lifts her chin. "Who said you hurt me?"

"Pulling your punches does her a disservice," Dain says, folding his arms. "The Cygnis on the northeast border aren't going to give her any quarter because she's a woman if she falls from her dragon behind enemy lines, Ridoc. They'll kill her just the same."

"Let's go!" Aurelie shouts, beckoning Ridoc by curling her fingers. It's obvious that most cadets have trained their whole lives to enter the quadrant, especially Aurelie, who slips a jab from Ridoc and twists to land a quick tap to his kidneys.

Ouch.

"I mean…damn," Rhiannon mutters, giving Aurelie another look before turning back to me. "I'm pretty good on the mat. My village is on the Cygnisen border, so we all learned to defend ourselves fairly young. Physics and math aren't problems, either. But history?" She shakes her head. "That class might be the death of me."

"They don't kill you for failing history," I say as Ridoc charges Aurelie, taking her to the mat with enough force to make me wince. "I'm probably going to die on these mats."

She hooks her legs around his and somehow leverages him over until she's the one on top, landing punch after punch to the side of his face. Blood spatters the mat.

"I could probably offer some tips to survive combat training," Sawyer says from Rhiannon's other side, running his hand over a day's growth of brown stubble that doesn't quite cover his freckles. "History isn't my strongest subject, though."

A tooth goes flying and bile rises in my throat.

"Enough!" Professor Emetterio shouts.

Aurelie rolls off Ridoc and stands, touching her fingers to her split lip and examining the blood, then offers her hand to help him up.

He takes it.

"Cianna, take Aurelie to the healers. No reason to lose a tooth during assessment," Emetterio orders.

"I'll make you a deal," Rhiannon says, locking her brown eyes with mine. "Let's help each other out. We'll help you with hand-to-hand if you help us with history. Sound like a deal, Sawyer?"

"Absolutely."

"Deal." I swallow as one of the third-years wipes down the mat with a towel. "But I think I'm getting the better end of that."

"You haven't seen me try to memorize dates," Rhiannon jokes.

A couple of mats over, someone shrieks, and we all turn to look. Jack Barlowe has another first-year in a headlock. The other guy is smaller, thinner than Jack, but still has a good fifty pounds on me.

Jack yanks his arms, his hands still secure around the other man's head.

"That guy is such an ass—" Rhiannon starts.

The sickening crack of bones breaking sounds across the gym, and the first-year goes limp in Jack's hold.

"Sweet Malek," I whisper as Jack drops the man to the ground. I'm starting to wonder if the god of death lives here for how often his name must be invoked. My lunch threatens to reappear, but I breathe in through my nose and out through my mouth, since it's not like I can shove my head between my knees here.

"What did I say?" their instructor shouts as he charges onto the mat. "You broke his damned neck!"

"How was I supposed to know his neck was that weak?" Jack argues.

You're dead, Sorrengail, and I'm going to be the one to kill you. His promise from yesterday slithers through my memory.

"Eyes forward," Emetterio orders, but his tone is kinder than it has been as we all look away from the dead first-year. "You don't have to get used to it," he tells us. "But you do have to function through it. You and you." He points to Rhiannon and another first-year in our squad, a man with a stocky build, blue-black hair, and angular features. Shit, I can't remember his name. Trevor? Thomas, maybe? There are too many new people to remember who is who at this point.

I glance at Dain, but he's watching the pair as they take the mat.

Rhiannon makes quick work of the first-year, stunning me every time she dodges a punch and lands one of her own. She's fast, and her hits are powerful, the kind of lethal combination that will set her apart, just like Mira.

"Do you yield?" she asks the first-year guy when she takes him to his back, her hand stopped mid-hit just above his throat.

Tanner? I'm pretty sure it's something that starts with a T.

"No!" he shouts, hooking his legs around Rhiannon's and slamming her to her back. But she rolls and quickly gains her feet before putting him in the same position again, this time with her boot to his neck.

"I don't know, Tynan, you might want to yield," Dain says with a grin. "She's handing you your ass."

Ah, that's right. Tynan.

"Fuck off, Aetos!" Tynan snaps, but Rhiannon presses her boot into his throat, garbling the last word. He turns a mottled shade of red.

Yeah, Tynan has more ego than common sense.

"He yields," Emetterio calls out, and Rhiannon steps back, offering her hand.

Tynan takes it.

"You—" Emetterio points to the pink-haired second-year with the rebellion relic. "And you." His finger swings to me.

She's at least a head taller than me, and if the rest of her body is as toned as her arms, then I'm pretty much fucked.

I can't let her get her hands on me.

My heart threatens to beat out of my chest, but I nod and step onto the mat. "You've got this," Rhiannon says, tapping my shoulder as she passes me.

"Sorrengail." The pink-haired girl looks me over like I'm something she's scraped off the side of her boot, narrowing her pale green eyes. "You really should dye your hair if you don't want everyone to know who your mother is. You're the only silver-haired freak in the quadrant."

"Never said I cared if everyone knows who my mother is." I circle the second-year on the mat. "I am proud of her service to protect our kingdom—from enemies both without *and* within."

As her jaw tightens at the dig, a bubble of hope rises in my chest. Marked ones, as I'd heard some people this morning refer to those carrying rebellion relics on their arms, blame my mother for the execution of their parents. Fine. Hate me. Mom often says the minute you let emotion enter a fight, you've already lost. I've never prayed harder that my ice-in-her-veins mother was right.

"You bitch," she seethes. "Your mother *murdered* my family."

She lunges forward and swings wildly, and I quickly sidestep, spinning away with my hands up. We do that for a few more rounds, and I land a few jabs, start to think that my plan might just work.

She growls low in her throat as she misses me again, and her foot flies at my head. I easily duck, but then she drops to the ground and kicks out with her other foot, which lands square in my chest, sending me backward.

I hit the mat with a *thud*, and she's already above me, so damn *fast.*

"You can't use your powers in here, Imogen!" Dain shouts.

Imogen is trying her best to kill me.

Her eyes are above mine, and I feel the quick slide of something hard against my ribs as she smiles at me. But her smile fades as we both look down, and I can't help but notice a dagger being re-sheathed.

The armor just saved my life. *Thank you, Mira.*

Confusion mars Imogen's face for just a second, long enough for me to send my fist into her cheek and roll out from under her.

My hand screams with pain even though I'm sure I formed the fist right, but I block it out as we both gain our feet.

"What kind of armor is that?" she asks, staring at my ribs as we circle each other.

"Mine." I duck and dodge as she comes at me again, but her movements are a blur.

"Imogen!" Emetterio shouts. "Do it again, and I'll—"

I swerve the wrong way this time and she catches me, taking me to the floor. The mat smacks my face, and her knee digs into my back as she pulls my right arm behind me.

"Yield!" she shouts.

I can't. If I yield on the first day, what will the second bring? "No!" Now I'm the one lacking common sense like Tynan, and I'm far more breakable.

She pulls my arm farther, and pain consumes every thought, blackening the edges of my vision. I cry out as the ligaments stretch, shred, then pop.

"Yield, Violet!" Dain yells.

"Yield!" Imogen demands.

Gasping for breath against the weight of her on my back, I turn my face to the side as she wrenches my shoulder apart, the pain consuming me.

"She yields," Emetterio says. "That's enough."

I hear it again—the macabre sound of snapping bone—but this time it's mine.

It is my opinion that of all the signet powers riders provide, mending is the most precious, but we cannot allow ourselves to become complacent when in the company of such a signet. For menders are rare, and the wounded are not.

—Major Frederick's Modern Guide for Healers

CHAPTER SIX

Flames of agony engulf my upper arm and chest as Dain carries me through the lower, covered passage out of the Riders Quadrant, over the ravine, and into the Healer Quadrant. It's basically a stone bridge, covered and sided with more stone, which pretty much makes it a suspended tunnel with a few windows, but I'm not thinking clearly enough to take it in as we rush through, his strides eating up the distance.

"Almost there," he reassures me, his grip firm but careful on my rib cage and beneath my knees as my useless arm rests on my chest.

"Everyone saw you lose it," I whisper, doing my best to mentally block the pain like I have countless times before. It's usually as easy as building a mental wall around the pulsing torment in my body, then telling myself the pain only exists in that box so I can't feel it, but it isn't working so well this time.

"I didn't lose it." He kicks the door three times when we reach it.

"You shouted and carried me out of there like I mean something to you." I focus on the scar on his jaw, the stubble on his tan skin, anything to keep from feeling the utter destruction in my shoulder.

"You do mean something to me." He kicks again.

And now everyone knows.

The door swings open and Winifred, a healer who has been at my side too many times to mention, stands back so Dain can carry me in. "Another injury? You riders certainly are trying to fill our beds to— Oh no, Violet?" Her eyes fly wide.

"Hi, Winifred," I manage over the pain.

"This way." She leads us into the infirmary, a long hall of beds, half of which are full of people in rider black. Healers do not have magic, relying on traditional tinctures and medical training to heal as best they can, but menders do. Hopefully Nolon's around tonight, since he's been mending me for the last five years.

The signet of mending is exceptionally rare among riders. They have the power to fix, to restore, to return anything to its original state—from ripped cloth to pulverized bridges, including broken human bones. My brother, Brennan, was a mender—and would have become one of the greatest had he lived.

Dain gently lays me onto the bed Winifred brings us to, then she leans into the edge of the mattress, near my hip. Every creased line in her face is a comfort as she strokes a weathered hand across my forehead. "Helen, go get Nolon," Winifred orders a healer in her forties walking by.

"No!" Dain barks, panic lacing his tone.

Excuse me?

The middle-aged healer glances between Dain and Winifred, clearly torn.

"Helen, this is Violet Sorrengail, and if Nolon finds out she was here and you *didn't* call him, well…that's on you," Winifred says in a deceptively calm tenor.

"Sorrengail?" the healer repeats, her voice rising.

I try to focus on Dain through the throbbing in my shoulder, but the room is starting to spin. I want to ask him why wouldn't he want my shoulder mended, but another wave of pain threatens to pull me into unconsciousness and all I can do is moan.

"Get Nolon or he will let his dragon eat you alive, sour face and all, Helen." Winifred arches a silver eyebrow as she ignores Dain insisting again not to call the mender.

The woman blanches and disappears.

Dain pulls a wooden chair closer to my bed, and it scrapes the floor with a god-awful sound. "Violet, I know you're hurting, but maybe…"

"Maybe what, Dain Aetos? You want to see her suffer?" Winifred lectures. "I told her they'd break you," she mutters as she leans over me, her gray eyes full of worry as she assesses me. Winifred is the best healer Basgiath has, and she prepares every tonic she prescribes herself—and has seen me through more scrapes than I care to count over the years. "Would she listen to me? Absolutely not. Your mother is so damned stubborn."

She reaches for my injured arm, and I wince as she raises it a couple of inches, prods my shoulder.

"Well, that's certainly broken." Winifred tsks, raising her brows at the sight of my arm. "And it looks like we need a surgeon for that shoulder. What happened?" she asks Dain.

"Sparring," I explain in one word.

"You hush. Save your energy." Winifred looks back at Dain. "Make yourself useful, boy, and pull the curtain around us. The fewer people who see her injured, the better."

He jumps to his feet and quickly complies, drawing the blue fabric around us to make a small but effective room, separating us from the other riders who have been brought in.

"Drink this." Winifred brings out a vial of amber liquid from her belt. "It will handle the pain while we get you sorted."

"You can't ask him to mend her," Dain protests as she uncorks the glass.

"The pair of us have been mending her for the past five years," she lectures, bringing the vial closer. "Don't start telling me what I can and cannot do."

Dain slides one hand under my back, the other under my head, helping me slightly upright so I can get the liquid down. It's bitter like always as I swallow, but I know it will do the trick. He settles me back on the bed and turns to Winifred. "I don't want her in pain—that's why we're here. But if she's injured this severely, surely we can see if the scribes will take her as a late admission. It's only been a day."

As his reasoning for not wanting a mender sinks in, my anger is able to pierce through the pain long enough for me to bite out, "I'm not going to the scribes."

Then I sigh, closing my eyes as a pleasant hum races through my veins. Soon there's enough distance between me and the pain to think somewhat clearly as I force my eyes open again.

At least, I think it's soon, but there's a conversation going on I clearly haven't been paying attention to, so it's obviously been a few minutes.

The curtain whips back and Nolon walks in, leaning heavily on his cane. He smiles at his wife, his bright white teeth contrasting his brown skin. "You sent for me, my—" His smile falters as he sees me. "Violet?"

"Hi, Nolon." I force my mouth to curve upward. "I'd wave, butone ofmyarms doesn't workand theother feels realllllyheavy." Good gods, am I slurring my words?

"Leigheas serum." Winifred offers her husband a crooked smile.

"She's with you, Dain?" Nolon turns an accusing look on Dain, and I feel all of fifteen years old again, being hauled in because I broke my ankle while we were climbing somewhere we shouldn't have been.

"I'm her squad leader," Dain replies, scooting out of Nolon's way so the mender can get closer. "Putting her under my command was the only thing I could think of to keep her safe."

"Not doing such a good job, are you?" Nolon's eyes narrow.

"It was assessment day for hand-to-hand," Dain explains. "Imogen—she's a second-year—dislocated Violet's shoulder and broke her arm."

"On assessment day?" Nolon growls, cutting away the fabric of my short-sleeve shirt with his dagger. The man is eighty-four if he's a day, and he still dresses in rider black, sheathed with all his weapons.

"Hermotherwasssss. OneofFennnnRiorson's sepppara—sepppara—sssseparatisssts," I explain slowly, trying to enunciate and failing. "And I'mmmmmaSorrengail, so I getit."

"I don't," Nolon grumbles. "I've never agreed with the way they conscripted those kids to the Riders Quadrant as punishment for the sins of their parents. We have never forced conscripts into that quadrant. Ever. And for a very good reason. Most cadets don't survive—which was likely the point, I suspect. Regardless, you certainly shouldn't have to suffer for the honor of your mother. General Sorrengail saved Navarre by capturing the Great Betrayer."

"So you won't mend her, right?" Dain asks softly so he can't be heard outside the curtain. "I'm just asking that the healers do their work and let nature take the time it needs. No magic. She doesn't stand a chance if she goes back in there in a cast or has to defend herself while her shoulder heals from reconstruction surgery. The last one took her four months. This is our chance to get her out of the Riders Quadrant while she's still breathing."

"I'mnotgoingtothesibes." So much for not slurring. "Sibes," I try again. "SIBES." Oh, fuck it. "Mendme."

"I will always mend you," Nolon promises.

"Just. This. Once." I concentrate on every word. "If. The others. See I need. Mending. Allthetime, they'll. Think. I'm weak."

"Which is why we have to use this opportunity to get you out!" Panic rises in Dain's voice, and my heart sinks. He can't protect me from everything, and watching me break, watching me eventually die is going to ruin him. "Walking out of here and going straight to the Scribe Quadrant is your best chance at survival."

I glare at Dain and choose my words carefully. "I'm not. Leavingtheriders. Just so Mom. Canthrowmeback. I'm. Staying." I turn my head and the room spins as I look for Nolon. "Mend me...but justthisonce."

"You know it's going to hurt like hell and will still ache for a couple of weeks, right?" Nolon asks, sitting down in the chair beside my bed and staring at my shoulder.

I nod. This isn't my first mending. When you're as brittle as I was born, the pain of mending is only second to the pain of the original injury. Basically another Tuesday.

"Please, Vi," Dain begs quietly. "Please switch quadrants. If not for you, then for me—because I didn't step in fast enough. I should have stopped her. I can't protect you."

I wish I'd figured out his plan before taking Winifred's potion, so I could have explained better. None of this is his fault, but he's going to shoulder the blame just like he always does. Instead, I take a deep breath and say, "I made mychoice."

"Get back to the quadrant, Dain," Nolon orders without looking up. "If she was any other first-year, you would already be gone."

Dain's anguished gaze holds mine, and I insist, "Go. I'll findyouat formmmmation inthe morning." I don't want him to see this anyway.

He swallows the defeat and nods once, then turns and walks through the separation in the curtains without another word. I sincerely hope my choice today doesn't end up destroying my best friend later.

"Ready?" Nolon asks, his hands hovering above my shoulder.

"Bite down." Winifred holds a strap of leather in front of my mouth, and I take it between my teeth.

"Here we go," Nolon mutters, lifting his hands over my shoulder. His brow furrows in concentration before he makes a twisting motion.

White-hot agony erupts in my shoulder. My teeth slice into the leather as I scream, bearing down for one heartbeat, then two before blacking out.

• • •

The barracks are nearly full by the time I make my way back later that night, my throbbing right arm cradled in a light-blue sling that makes me an even bigger target, if that's possible.

Slings say *weak*. They say *breakable*. They say *liability to the wing.* If I break this easily on the mat, what's going to happen if I get on the back of a dragon?

The sun has long since gone down, but the hall is lit by the soft glow of mage lights as the other first-year women get ready for bed. I offer a smile to a girl who's holding a blood-speckled cloth to her swollen lip, and she returns it with a wince.

I count three empty bunks in our row, but that doesn't mean those cadets are dead, right? They could be in the Healer Quadrant just like I was, or maybe they're in the bathing chambers.

"You're here!" Rhiannon jumps off her bed, already dressed in her sleeping shorts and top, relief in her eyes and smile as she sees me.

"I'm here," I assure her. "I'm already down one shirt, but I'm here."

"You can get another at central issue tomorrow." She looks like she might hug me but glances at my sling and backs up a step, sitting on the edge of her bunk as I do the same with mine, facing her. "How bad is it?"

"It's going to hurt for the next few days, but I'll be fine as long as I keep it immobilized. I'll be all healed up before we start on-mat challenges."

I have two weeks to figure out how to keep this from happening again.

"I'll help you get ready," she promises. "You're the only friend I have in here, so I'd rather you didn't die when it gets real." A corner of her mouth lifts in a wry smile.

"I'll try my best not to." I grin through the throbbing ache in my shoulder and arm. The tonic has long since worn off, and it's starting to hurt like hell. "And I'll help you with history." I brace my weight on my left hand, and it slides just beneath my pillow.

There's something there.

"We'll be unstoppable," Rhiannon declares, her gaze tracking Tara, the dark-haired, curvy girl from Morraine, as she walks past our bunks.

I pull out a small book—no, it's a journal—with a folded note on top that says *Violet* in Mira's handwriting. One-handed, I open the note.

Violet,

I stayed long enough to read the rolls this morning, and you aren't on them, thank gods. I can't stay. I'm needed back with my wing, and even if I could stay, they wouldn't let me see you anyway. I bribed a scribe to sneak this into your bunk. I hope you know how proud I am to be your sister. Brennan wrote this for me the summer before I entered the quadrant. It saved me, and it can save you, too. I added my own bits of hard-earned wisdom here and there, but mostly it's his, and I know he'd want you to have it. He'd want you to live.

Love,

Mira.

I swallow past the knot in my throat and set the note aside.

"What is it?" Rhiannon asks.

"It's my brother's." The words barely make it past my lips as I open the cover. Mother burned everything he owned after he died, as tradition dictates. It's been ages since I've seen the bold strokes of his handwriting, and yet there they are. My chest tightens and a fresh wave of grief sweeps through me. "The book of Brennan," I read along with the first page and then flip to the second.

Mira,

You're a Sorrengail, so you will survive. Perhaps not as spectacularly as I have, but we all can't live up to my standards, can we? All kidding aside, this is everything I've learned. Keep it safe. Keep it hidden. You have to live, because Violet is watching. You can't let her see you fall.

Brennan

Tears prick my eyes, but I blink them back. "It's just his journal," I lie, thumbing through the pages. I can hear his quippy, sarcastic tone as I skim over his words, as though he's standing here, making light of every danger with a wink and a grin. Damn, I miss him. "He died five years ago."

"Oh, that's…" Rhiannon leans in, her eyes heavy with sympathy. "We don't always burn everything, either. Sometimes it's nice to have something, you know?"

"Yeah," I whisper. It's *everything* to have this, and yet I know Mom will toss it in the fire if she ever finds it.

Rhiannon sits back on her bed, opening her history book, and I fall back into Brennan's history, starting on the third page.

You survived Parapet. Good. Be observant the next few days, and don't do anything to draw attention to yourself. I've sketched a map that shows you not only where the classrooms are but where the instructors meet, too. I know you're nervous about challenges, but you shouldn't be, not with that right hook of yours. The matches might seem random, but they're not. What the instructors don't tell you is that they decide challenges the week before, Mira. Any cadet can request a challenge, yes, but instructors will assign your matches based on weeding out the weakest. That means once the real hand-to-hand starts, the instructors already know who you'll be up against that day. Here's the secret—if you know where to look and can get out without being seen, you'll know who you're fighting so you can prepare.

I suck in a breath and devour the rest of the entry, hope blossoming in my chest. If I know who I'm fighting, then I can begin the battle before we even step on the mat. My mind spins, a plan taking shape.

Two weeks, that's how long I have to get everything I'll need before challenges begin, and no one knows the grounds of Basgiath like I do. It's all here.

A slow smile spreads across my face. I know how to survive.

In the best interest of preserving peace within Navarre, no more than three cadets carrying rebellion relics may be assigned to any squad of any quadrant.

—Addendum 5.2, Basgiath War College Code of Conduct

In addition to last year's changes, marked ones assembling in groups of three or more will now be considered an act of seditious conspiracy and is hereby a capital offense.

—Addendum 5.3, Basgiath War College Code of Conduct

CHAPTER SEVEN

"Damn it," I mutter as my toe catches a rock, and I stumble in the waist-high grass that grows alongside the river beneath the citadel. The moon is nice and full, illuminating my way, but it means I'm sweating to death in this cloak to keep hidden, just in case anyone else is out here wandering after curfew.

The Iakobos River rushes with summer runoff from the peaks above, and the currents are fast and deadly this time of year, especially coming out of the steep drop of the ravine. No wonder that first-year died when he fell in yesterday during our downtime. Since Parapet, our squad is the only one in the quadrant not to lose anyone, but I know that's unlikely to last much longer in this ruthless school.

Tightening my heavy satchel over my sling, I move closer to the river, along the ancient line of oaks where I know one vine of fonilee berries will be coming into season soon. Ripe, the purple berries are tart and barely edible but, picked prematurely and left to dry, will make an excellent weapon in the growing arsenal that nine nights of sneaking out has given me. This was exactly the reason I brought the book of poisons with me.

Challenges start next week, and I need every possible advantage.

Spotting the boulder I've used as a landmark for the past five years, I count the trees on the riverbank. "One, two, three," I whisper, spotting the exact oak I'll need. Its branches spread wide and high, some even daring to reach out over the river. Lucky for me, the lowest is easily climbable, even more so with the grass oddly trampled underneath.

A twinge of pain shoots up through my shoulder as I slip my right arm out of the sling and begin to climb by moonlight and memory. The pain quickly fades to an ache, just like it has every evening while Rhiannon has been kicking my ass on the mat. Hopefully tomorrow Nolon will let me out of the annoying sling for good.

The fonilee vine looks deceptively like ivy as it winds up the trunk, but I've scaled this particular tree enough times to know this is the one. I've just never had to climb the damn thing in a cloak before. It's a pain in my ass. The fabric catches on almost every branch as I move upward, slowly and steadily, climbing past the wide branch where I used to spend hours reading.

"Shit!" My foot slips on the bark and my heart stutters for a heartbeat while my feet find better holds. This would be so much easier during the day, but I can't risk being caught.

Bark scrapes my palms as I climb higher. The tips of the vine leaves are white at this height, barely visible in the mottled moonlight through the canopy, but I grin as I find exactly what I've been searching for.

"There you are." The purple berries are a gorgeous, unripe lavender. Perfect. Digging my fingernails into the branch above me, I manage to keep from wobbling long enough to retrieve an empty vial in my satchel and uncork it with my teeth. Then I pluck just enough berries off the vine to fill the glass and shove the stopper back in. Between these, the mushrooms I've already hunted tonight, and the other items I've collected, I should be able to make it through the next month of challenges.

I'm almost down the tree, only a handful of branches to go, when I spot movement beneath me and pause. Hopefully it's just a deer.

But it's not.

Two figures in black cloaks—apparently tonight's disguise of choice—walk under the protection of the tree. The smaller one leans back against the lowest limb, removing her hood to reveal a half-shaved head of pink hair I know all too well.

Imogen, the squadmate who nearly ripped off my arm ten days ago.

My stomach tightens, then knots as the second rider slips off his own hood.

Xaden Riorson.

Oh shit.

There's maybe fifteen feet between us and nothing—and no one—out here to stop him from killing me. Fear clenches my throat and holds tight as I white-knuckle the branches around me, debating the merits of holding my breath so he can't hear me versus falling out of the tree if I faint from lack of oxygen.

They begin speaking, but I can't hear what they're saying, not with the river rushing by. Relief fills my lungs. If I can't hear them, they can't hear me, either, as long as I sit tight. But all it takes is for him to look up, and I'll be toast, literally if he decides to feed me to that Blue Daggertail of his. The moonlight I was thankful for a few minutes ago has now become my biggest liability.

Slowly, carefully, quietly, I move out of the patchy moonlight to the next branch over, cloaking myself in shadow. What is he doing out here with Imogen? Are they lovers? Friends? It's absolutely none of my business, and yet I can't help but wonder if she's the kind of woman he goes for—one whose beauty is only outmatched by her brutality. They fucking deserve each other.

Xaden turns away from the river, as though he's looking for someone, and sure enough, more riders arrive, gathering under the tree. They're all dressed in black cloaks as they shake hands. And they all have rebellion relics.

My eyes widen as I count. There are almost two dozen of them, a few third-years and a couple of seconds, but the rest are all firsts. I know the rules. Marked ones can't gather in groups larger than three. They're committing a capital offense simply by being together. It's obviously a meeting of some sort, and I feel like a cat clinging to the leaf-tipped limbs of this tree while the wolves circle below.

Their gathering could be completely harmless, right? Maybe they're homesick, like when the cadets from the Morraine province all spend a Saturday at the nearby lake just because it reminds them of the ocean they miss so much.

Or maybe marked ones are plotting to burn Basgiath to the ground and finish what their parents started.

I can sit up here and ignore them, but my complacency—my fear—could get people killed if they're down there scheming. Telling Dain is the right thing to do, but I can't even hear what they're saying.

Shit. Shit. Shit. Nausea churns in my stomach. I have to get closer.

Keeping myself on the opposite side of the trunk and sticking to the shadows that wrap around me, I climb down another branch with sloth-like speed, holding my breath as I test each branch with a fraction of my weight before lowering myself. Their voices are still muffled by the river, but I can hear the loudest of them, a tall, dark-haired man with pale skin, whose shoulders take up twice the space of any first-year, standing opposite Xaden's position and wearing the rank of a third-year.

"We've already lost Sutherland and Luperco," he says, but I can't make out the response.

It takes two more rungs of branches before their words are clear. My heart pounds like it's trying to escape my ribs. I'm close enough for any one of them to see if they look hard enough—well, everyone except Xaden, since his back is turned toward me.

"Like it or not, we're going to have to stick together if you want to survive until graduation," Imogen says. One little hop to the right and I could repay that callous shoulder maneuver she pulled on me with a quick kick to her head.

I just happen to value my own life more than I want revenge at the moment, so I keep my feet to myself.

"And if they find out we're meeting?" a first-year girl with an olive complexion asks, her eyes darting around the circle.

"We've done this for two years and they've never found out," Xaden responds, folding his arms and leaning back against the limb below my right. "They're not going to unless one of you tells. And if you tell, I'll know." The threat is obvious in his tone. "Like Garrick said, we've already lost two first-years to their own negligence. There are only forty-one of us in the Riders Quadrant, and we don't want to lose any of you, but we will if you don't help yourselves. The odds are always stacked against us, and trust me, every other Navarrian in the quadrant will look for reasons to call you a traitor or force you to fail."

There's a muttered assent, and my breath hitches at the intensity in his voice. Damn it, I don't want to find a single thing about Xaden Riorson admirable, and yet here he is, being all annoyingly admirable. Asshole.

Have to admit, it would be nice if a high-ranking rider from my province gave a shit if the rest of us from the province lived or died.

"How many of you are getting your asses handed to you in hand-to-hand?" Xaden asks.

Four hands shoot into the air, none of which belong to the spiky-blond-haired first-year standing with his arms crossed, a head taller than most others. Liam Mairi. He's in Second Squad, Tail Section of our wing and already the top cadet in our year. He practically ran across the parapet and destroyed every opponent on assessment day.

"Shit," Xaden swears, and I would give anything to see his expression as he lifts a hand to his face.

The big one—Garrick—sighs. "I'll teach them." I recognize him now. He's the Flame Section leader in Fourth Wing. My direct superior above Dain.

Xaden shakes his head. "You're our best fighter—"

"*You're* our best fighter," a second-year near Xaden counters with a quick grin. He's handsome, with tawny brown skin crowned by a cloud of black curls and a litany of patches on what I can see of his uniform under his cloak. His features are close enough to Xaden's that they might be related. Cousins, maybe? Fen Riorson had a sister, if I remember correctly. Shit, what was the guy's name? It's been years since I read the records, but I think it started with a B.

"Dirtiest fighter, maybe," Imogen snarks.

Most everyone laughs, and even the first-years crack a smile.

"Fucking ruthless is more like it," Garrick adds.

There's a general consensus of nods, including one from Liam Mairi.

"Garrick is our best fighter, but Imogen is right up there with him, and she's a hell of a lot more patient," Xaden notes, which is just ludicrous considering she didn't seem too patient while breaking my arm. "So the four of you split yourselves up between the two of them for training. A group of three won't draw any unwanted attention. What else is giving you trouble?"

"I can't do this," a gangly first-year says, rolling his shoulders inward and lifting his slim fingers to his face.

"What do you mean?" Xaden asks, his voice taking on a hard edge.

"I can't do this!" The smaller one shakes his head. "The death. The fighting. Any of it!" The pitch of his voice rises with every statement. "A guy had his neck snapped right in front of me on assessment day! I want to go home! Can you help me with *that*?"

Every head swings toward Xaden.

"No." Xaden shrugs. "You're not going to make it. Best accept it now and not take up more of my time."

It's all I can do to smother my gasp, and some of the others in the group don't bother trying. What. A. Dick.

The smaller guy looks *stricken*, and I can't help but feel bad for him.

"That was a little harsh, cousin," the second-year who looks a little like Xaden says, lifting his eyebrows.

"What do you want me to say, Bodhi?" Xaden cocks his head to the side, his voice calm and even. "I can't save everyone, especially not someone who isn't willing to work to save themselves."

"Damn, Xaden." Garrick rubs the bridge of his nose. "Way to give a pep talk."

"If they need a fucking pep talk, then we both know they're not flying out of the quadrant on graduation day. Let's get real. I can hold their hands and make them a bunch of bullshit empty promises about everyone making it through if that helps them sleep, but in my experience, the truth is far more valuable." He turns his head, and I can only assume he's looking at the panicked first-year. "In war, people die. It's not glorious like the bards sing about, either. It's snapped necks and two-hundred-foot falls. There's nothing romantic about scorched earth or the scent of sulfur. This"—he gestures back toward the citadel—"isn't some fable where everyone makes it out alive. It's hard, cold, uncaring reality. Not everyone here is going to make it home…to whatever's left of our homes. And make no mistake, we are at war every time we step foot in the quadrant." He leans forward slightly. "So if you won't get your shit together and fight to live, then no. You're not going to make it."

Only crickets dare to break the silence.

"Now, someone give me a problem I can actually solve," Xaden orders.

"Battle Brief," a first-year I recognize says softly. Her bunk is only a row away from Rhiannon's and mine. Shit…what's her name? There are too many women in the hall to know everyone, but I'm certain she's in Third Wing. "It's not that I can't keep up, but the information…" She shrugs.

"That's a tough one," Imogen responds, turning to look at Xaden. Her profile in the moonlight is almost unrecognizable as the same person who shredded my shoulder. That Imogen is cruel, vicious even. But the way she's looking at Xaden softens her eyes, her mouth, her whole posture as she tucks a short strand of pink hair behind her ear.

"You learn what they teach you," Xaden says to the first-year, his voice taking a hard edge. "Keep what you know but recite whatever they tell you to."

My brow furrows. What the hell does he mean by *that*? Battle Brief is one of the classes taught by scribes to keep the quadrant up-to-date on all nonclassified troop movements and battle lines. The only things we're asked to recite are recent events and general knowledge of what's going on near the front lines.

"Anyone else?" Xaden asks. "You'd better ask now. We don't have all night."

It hits me then—other than being gathered in a group of more than three, there's nothing *wrong* with what they're doing here. There's no plot, no coup, no danger. It's just a group of older riders counseling first-years from their province. But if Dain knew, he'd be honor bound to—

"When do we get to kill Violet Sorrengail?" a guy toward the back asks.

My blood turns to ice.

The murmur of assent among the group sends a jolt of terror down my spine.

"Yeah, Xaden," Imogen says sweetly, lifting her pale green eyes to him. "When *do* we get to finally have *our* revenge?"

He turns just enough for me to see his profile and the scar that crosses his face as he narrows his eyes at Imogen. "I told you already, the youngest Sorrengail is *mine*, and I'll handle her when the time is right."

He'll...handle me? My muscles thaw with the heat of indignation. I'm not some inconvenience to be *handled*. My short-lived admiration of Xaden is over.

"Didn't you already learn that lesson, Imogen?" the look-alike Xaden chides from halfway down the circle. "What I hear, Aetos has you scrubbing dinner dishes for the next month for using your powers on the mat."

Imogen's head snaps in his direction. "Her mother is responsible for the execution of my mom and sister. I should have done more than just snap her shoulder."

"Her *mom* is responsible for the capture of nearly *all* our parents," Garrick counters, folding his arms over his wide chest. "Not her daughter. Punishing children for the sins of their parents is the Navarrian way, not the Tyrrish."

"So we get conscripted because of what our parents did *years* ago and shoved into this death sentence of a college— " Imogen starts.

"In case you didn't notice, she's in the same death sentence of a college," Garrick retorts. "Seems like she's already suffering the same fate."

Am I seriously watching them debate over whether I should be punished for being Lilith Sorrengail's daughter?

"Don't forget her brother was Brennan Sorrengail," Xaden adds. "She has just as much reason to hate us as we do her." He pointedly looks at Imogen and the first-year who raised the question. "And I'm not going to tell you again. She's *mine* to handle. Anyone feel like arguing?"

Silence reigns.

"Good. Then get back to bed and go in threes." He motions with his head, and they slowly disperse, walking away in groups of threes just like he ordered. Xaden is the last to leave.

I draw a slow breath. Holy shit, I just might live through this.

But I have to be sure they're gone. I don't move a muscle, even when my thighs cramp and my fingers lock as I count to five hundred in my head, breathing as evenly as possible to soften the beats of my galloping heart.

Only when I'm sure I'm alone, when the squirrels scurry past on the ground, do I finish climbing from the tree, jumping the last four feet to the grassy floor. Zihnal must have a soft spot for me, because I'm the luckiest woman on the Continent—

A shadow lunges behind me and I open my mouth to scream, but my air supply is cut off by an elbow around my neck as I'm yanked against a hard chest.

"Scream and you die," he whispers, and my stomach plummets as the elbow is replaced by the sharp bite of a dagger at my throat.

I freeze. I'd recognize the rough pitch of Xaden's voice anywhere.

"Fucking Sorrengail." His hand yanks back the hood of my cloak.

"How did you know?" My tone is outright indignant, but whatever. If he's going to kill me, I'm not going down as some simpering little beggar. "Let me guess, you could smell my perfume. Isn't that what always gives the heroine away in books?"

He scoffs. "I command shadows, but sure, it was your *perfume* that gave you away." He lowers the knife and steps away.

I gasp. "Your signet is a shadow wielder?" No wonder he's risen so high in rank. Shadow wielders are incredibly rare and highly coveted in battle, able to disorient entire drifts of gryphons, if not take them down, depending upon the signet's strength.

"What, Aetos hasn't warned you not to get caught alone in the dark with me yet?"

His voice is like rough velvet along my skin, and I shiver, then draw my own blade from the sheath at my thigh and raise it as I spin toward him, ready to defend myself to the death. "Is this how you plan to *handle* me?"

"Eavesdropping, were we?" He arches a black brow and sheathes his dagger like I couldn't possibly pose a threat to him, which only serves to piss me off even more. "Now I might actually *have* to kill you." There's an undertone of truth in those mocking eyes.

This is just…bullshit.

"Then go ahead and get it over with." I unsheathe another dagger, this one from beneath my cloak where it was strapped in at my ribs, and back up a couple of feet to give me distance to throw them—if he doesn't rush me.

He pointedly looks at one dagger, then the other, and sighs, folding his arms across his chest. "That stance is really the best defense you can muster? No wonder Imogen nearly ripped your arm off."

"I'm more dangerous than you think," I flat-out bluster.

"So I see. I'm quaking in my boots." The corner of his mouth rises into a mocking smirk.

Fucking. Asshole.

I flip the daggers in my hand, pinching them at the tips, then flick my wrists and fire them past his head, one on each side. They land solidly in the trunk of the tree behind him.

"You missed." He doesn't even flinch.

"Did I?" I reach for my last two blades. "Why don't you back up a couple of steps and test that theory?"

Curiosity flares in his eyes, but it's gone in the next second, masked by cold, mocking indifference.

Every one of my senses is on high alert, but the shadows around me don't slide in as he moves backward, his eyes locked with mine. His back hits the tree, and the hilts of my daggers brush his ears.

"Tell me again that I missed," I threaten, taking the dagger in my right hand by the tip.

"Fascinating. You look all frail and breakable, but you're really a violent little thing, aren't you?" An appreciative smile curves his perfect lips as shadows dance up the trunk of the oak, taking the form of fingers. They pluck the daggers from the tree and bring them to Xaden's waiting hands.

My breath abandons me with a sharp exhale. He has the kind of power that could end me without him having to so much as lift a finger—shadow wielding. The futility of even trying to defend myself against him is laughable.

I hate how beautiful he is, how lethal his abilities make him as he strides toward me, shadows curling around his footsteps. He's like one of those poisonous flowers I've read about from the Cygnis forests to the east. His allure is a warning not to get too close, and I am *definitely* too close.

Switching my grip to the hilts of my daggers, I prepare for the attack.

"You should show that little trick to Jack Barlowe," Xaden says, turning his palms upward and offering me my daggers.

"I'm sorry?" This is a trick. It has to be a trick.

He moves closer, and I lift my blade. My heart stumbles, the beat irregular as fear floods my system.

"The neck-snapping first-year who's very publicly vowed to slaughter you," Xaden clarifies as my blade presses against his cloak at the level of his abdomen. He reaches under my own cloak and slides one blade into the sheath at my thigh, then pulls back the side of my cloak and pauses. His gaze locks onto the length of my braid where it falls over my shoulder, and I could swear he stops breathing for a heartbeat before he slides the remaining dagger into one of the sheaths at my ribs. "He'd probably think twice about plotting your murder if you threw a few daggers at his head."

This is…this is…bizarre. It has to be some kind of game meant to confuse me, right? And if so, he's playing it really fucking well.

"Because the honor of my murder belongs to you?" I challenge. "You wanted me dead long before your little club chose my tree to meet under, so I imagine you've all but buried me in your mind by now."

He glances at the dagger poised at his stomach. "Do you plan on telling anyone about my little *club*?" His eyes meet mine, and there's nothing but cold, calculating death waiting there.

"No," I answer truthfully, suppressing a shiver.

"Why not?" He tilts his head to the side, examining my face like I'm an oddity. "It's illegal for the children of separatist officers to assemble in—"

"Groups larger than three. I'm well aware. I've lived at Basgiath longer than you." I lift my chin.

"And you're not going to run off to Mommy, or your precious little Dain, and tell them we've been *assembling*?" His gaze narrows on mine.

My stomach twists just like it did before I stepped out onto the parapet, like my body knows that whatever action I take next will determine my life-span. "You were helping them. I don't see why that should be punished." It wouldn't be fair to him or the others. Was their little meeting illegal? Absolutely. Should they die for it? Absolutely *not*. And that's exactly what will happen if I tell. Those first-years will be executed for nothing more than asking for tutoring, and the senior cadets will join them just because they helped. "I'm not going to tell."

He looks at me like he's trying to see *through* me, and ice prickles my scalp.

My hand is steady, but my nerves tremble at what the next thirty seconds might bring. He can kill me right here, toss my body into the river, and no one will know I'm gone until they find me downstream.

But I won't let him end me without drawing his blood first, that's for damn sure.

"Interesting," he says softly. "We'll see if you keep your word, and if you do, then unfortunately, it looks like I owe you a favor." Then he steps away, turns, and walks off, heading back toward the staircase in the cliff that leads up to the citadel.

Wait. What?

"You're not going to *handle* me?" I call after him, shock raising my brows.

"Not tonight!" he tosses over his shoulder.

I scoff. "What are you waiting for?"

"It's no fun if you expect it," he answers, striding into the darkness. "Now, get back to bed before your wingleader realizes you're out after curfew."

"What?" I gawk after him. "*You're* my wingleader!"

But he's already disappeared into the shadows, leaving me talking to myself like a fool.

He didn't even ask what was in my satchel.

A slow smile spreads across my face as I tuck my arm back into my sling, sighing with relief as the weight is taken off my shoulder. *A fool with fonilee berries.*

There is an art to poison not often discussed, and that is timing. Only a master can properly dose and administer for effective onset. One must take into account the mass of the individual as well as the method of delivery.

—Effective Uses of Wild and Cultivated Herbs by Captain Lawrence Medina

CHAPTER EIGHT

The women's hall is quiet as I dress for the morning, the sun barely peeking above the horizon in the far windows. I take the dragon-scale vest from where I left it to dry on the hanger at the end of my bed and slip it on over my short-sleeve black shirt. It's a good thing I've gotten pretty adept at tightening the laces behind my back, since Rhiannon isn't in her bed.

At least one of us is getting a few much-needed orgasms. Pretty sure there's a person or two scattered with their partners among the full bunks in here, too. The squad leaders talk a good game about enforcing curfew, but no one really cares. Well, except Dain. He cares about every rule.

Dain. My chest tightens, and I smile as I finish braiding my hair into a crown. Seeing him is the best part of my day, even the moments when he's anything but personable in public. Even in the moments where he's consumed with trying to save me from this place.

I grab my bag on the way out, passing by rows of empty beds that belonged to the dozen women who haven't survived to see August, and shove open the door.

There he is.

Dain's eyes light up as he pushes off the wall of the hallway where he's obviously been waiting for me. "Morning."

I can't help the smile that curves my lips. "You don't have to escort me to duty every morning, you know."

"It's the only time I get to see you when I'm not your squad leader," he counters as we walk down the empty hallway, past the halls that will lead to our rooms if we survive Threshing. "Trust me, it's worth getting up an hour early, though I still can't figure out why you'd choose breakfast duty over every other assignment."

I shrug. "I have my reasons." Really, really, *really* good reasons. Though I do miss the extra hour of sleep I'd had before we chose our assignments last week.

A door on the right flies open, and Dain darts in front of me, dragging me behind him with his arm so I face-plant into his back. He smells like leather and soap and—

"Rhiannon?" he snaps.

"Sorry!" Rhiannon's eyes widen.

I slip out of Dain's hold and move to his side so I can see her. "I wondered where you were this morning." A grin spreads across my face as Tara appears next to her. "Hey, Tara."

"Hey, Violet." She gives me a wave, then heads down the hallway, tucking her shirt into her pants.

"We have curfew for a reason, cadet," Dain lectures, and I fight the urge to roll my eyes. "And you know that no one is supposed to be in the private dorms until after Threshing."

"Maybe we were just up early," Rhiannon counters. "You know, like you are right now." She glances between the two of us with a mischievous smirk.

Dain rubs the bridge of his nose. "Just...get back to the dorms and pretend you slept there, will you?"

"Absolutely!" She squeezes my hand as she passes by.

"Way to go," I whisper quickly. She's had a thing for Tara since we got here.

"I know, right?" She backs away with a smile, then turns to push through the hall doors.

"Monitoring the sex lives of first-years was not what I had in mind when I applied to be a squad leader," Dain mutters, and we continue toward the kitchen.

"Oh, come on. Like you weren't a first-year yourself last year."

He lifts his brows in thought and eventually shrugs. "Fair point. And you're a first-year now..." His eyes slide my way as we near the arched doorways that lead to the rotunda, and his lips part like he's going to continue, but he looks away, pivoting to open the door for me.

"Why, Dain Aetos! Are you asking me about my sex life?" I let my fingers trail along the exposed fangs of the green dragon pillar and bite back a smile as we walk by.

"No!" He shakes his head, then pauses in thought. "I mean…is there a sex life to ask about?"

We climb the steps that lead into commons, and I turn just before the door to face him. He's two steps below me, putting us at eye level. "Since I got here?" I tap my chin with my finger and smile. "That's none of your business. Before I got here? Still none of your business."

"Another fair point." His mouth curves into a grin that makes me wish it was his business, though.

I turn around before I do something utterly foolish like *make* it his business. We continue into commons, walking past the empty study tables and the entrance to the library. It's nothing as awe-inspiring as the scribes' Archives, but it has every tome I'll need for studying here.

"Are you ready for today?" Dain asks as we near the gathering hall. "For the challenges to start this afternoon?"

My stomach knots.

"I'll be all right," I assure him, but he moves in front of me, halting my steps.

"I know you've been practicing with Rhiannon, but…" Worry lines his forehead.

"I've got it," I promise, looking into his eyes so he knows I mean it. "You don't have to worry about me." Last night, Oren Seifert's name was posted next to mine right where Brennan said it would be. He's a tall blond in First Wing with tolerable knife skills but one hell of a punch.

"I always worry about you." Dain's hands curl into fists.

"Don't." I shake my head. "I can handle myself."

"I just don't want to see you get hurt again."

My ribs squeeze my heart like a vise.

"Then don't watch." I take his calloused hand in mine. "You can't save me from this, Dain. I'm going to be challenged once a week just like every other cadet. And it's not going to stop there. You can't protect me from Threshing, or the Gauntlet, or Jack Barlowe—"

"You need to lay low with that one." Dain grimaces. "Avoid that pompous ass whenever you can, Vi. Don't give him an excuse to come after you. He's already responsible for too many names on the death roll."

"Then the dragons are going to love him." They always go for the vicious ones.

Dain squeezes my hand gently. "Just steer clear of him."

I blink. The advice is so different from Xaden's throw-a-few-daggers-at-his-head approach.

Xaden. The knot of guilt that's been lodged in my stomach since last week grows a fraction bigger. By code, I should tell Dain about seeing marked ones under the oak tree, but I won't, not because I told Xaden that I wouldn't but because keeping the secret feels like the right thing to do.

I've never kept a secret from Dain in my life.

"Violet? Did you hear me?" Dain asks, lifting a hand to cradle my face.

Jerking my gaze to his, I nod and repeat, "Steer clear of Barlowe."

He drops his hand and shoves it into a pocket of his pants. "Hopefully he'll forget all about his little vendetta against you."

"Do most men forget when a woman holds a knife to their balls?" I cock an eyebrow at him.

"No." He sighs. "You know, it's not too late to sneak you down to the scribes. Fitzgibbons will take you—"

The bells ring, marking quarter past five and saving me from another session of Dain begging me to run away to the Scribe Quadrant.

"I'll be all right. I'll see you at formation." I give his hand a squeeze, then walk away, leaving him as I make my way to the kitchen. I'm always the first here, and today is no exception.

I pocket the vial of dried, powdered fonilee berries from my satchel and get started as the other workers come in, sleepy-eyed and grumbly. The powder is nearly white, nearly invisible as I take my place in the serving line an hour later, and completely undetectable as I sprinkle it over Oren Seifert's scrambled eggs when he approaches.

• • •

"Keep the temperaments of each specific breed in mind when you decide which dragons to approach and which to run from at Threshing," Professor Kaori says, his serious, dark eyes slashing toward his nose as he studies the new recruits for a beat, then he changes the projection he's conjured from a Green Daggertail to a Red Scorpiontail. He's an illusionist and the only professor in the quadrant with the signet ability to project what he sees in his mind, which makes this class one of my favorites. He's also the reason I knew exactly what Oren Seifert looked like.

Do I feel guilty about blatantly misleading a professor about why I needed to find another cadet? No. Do I think it's cheating? Also no. I was doing exactly what Mira suggested and using my brain.

The Red Scorpiontail in the center of our circled tables is a fraction of its actual size, six feet tall at most, but it's an exact replica of the actual firebreather waiting in the Vale for Threshing.

"Red Scorpiontails, like Ghrian here, are the quickest to temper," Professor Kaori continues, his perfectly trimmed mustache curving as he smiles at the illusion like he's the dragon himself. We all take notes. "So if you offend him, you're— "

"Lunch," Ridoc says from my left, and the class laughs. Even Jack Barlowe, who hasn't quit glaring at me since his squad took over their quarter of the room a half hour ago, snorts.

"Precisely," Professor Kaori responds. "So what's the best way to approach a Red Scorpiontail?" He glances around the room.

I know the answer, but I keep my hand to myself, heeding Dain's advice to lay low.

"You don't," Rhiannon mutters next to me, and I huff a laugh under my breath.

"They prefer that you approach from the left and from the front, if possible," a woman from one of the other squads answers.

"Excellent." Professor Kaori nods. "For this Threshing, there are three Red Scorpiontails willing to bond." The image changes in front of us to a different dragon.

"How many dragons are there in total?" Rhiannon asks.

"A hundred for this year," Professor Kaori answers, changing the image again. "But some might change their minds during Presentation in about two months, depending on what they see."

My stomach hits the floor. "That's thirty-seven fewer than last year." Maybe even fewer if they don't like the look of us after we have to parade by them for their perusal two days before Threshing. Then again, there's usually fewer cadets after that particular event anyway.

Professor Kaori's dark eyebrows rise. "Yes, Cadet Sorrengail, it is, and twenty-six fewer than the year before that."

Fewer dragons are choosing to bond, but the number of riders entering the quadrant has remained steady. My mind whirls. Attacks at the eastern borders are increasing, according to every Battle Brief, and yet there are *fewer* dragons willing to bond in order to defend Navarre.

"Will they tell you why they won't bond?" another first-year asks.

"No, jackass," Jack scoffs, his icy-blue gaze narrowing on the cadet. "Dragons only talk to their bonded riders, just like they only give their full name to their bonded rider. You should know that by now."

Professor Kaori sends Jack a look that shuts the first-year's mouth but doesn't stop him from sneering at the other cadet. "They don't share their reasons," our instructor says. "And anyone who respects their life won't ask a question they're not willing to answer."

"Do the numbers affect the wards?" Aurelie asks from where she sits behind me, tapping her quill against the edge of her desk. She's never happy sitting still.

Professor Kaori's jaw ticks twice. "We're not sure. The number of bonded dragons has never affected the integrity of Navarre's wards before, but I'm not about to lie to you and say that we're not seeing increased breaches when you know from Battle Brief that we are."

The wards are faltering at a rate that makes my stomach tense every time Professor Devera starts our daily Battle Brief. Either we're weakening or our enemies are getting stronger. Both possibilities mean the cadets in this room are needed more than ever.

Even me.

The image changes to Sgaeyl, the navy-blue dragon bonded to Xaden.

My stomach pitches as I remember the way she looked right through me that first day.

"You won't have to worry about how to approach blue dragons, since there are none willing to bond this Threshing, but you should be able to recognize Sgaeyl if you see her," Professor Kaori says.

"So you can fucking run," Ridoc drawls.

I nod along while others laugh.

"She's a Blue Daggertail, the rarest of the blues, and yes, if you see her without her bonded rider, you should…definitely find somewhere else to be. *Ruthless* does not begin to describe her, nor does she abide by what we assume to be what the dragons consider law. She even bonded the relative of one of her previous riders, which you all know is typically forbidden, but Sgaeyl does whatever she wants, whenever she wants. In fact, if you see any of the blues, don't approach them. Just..."

"Run," Ridoc repeats, raking his hand through his floppy brown hair.

"Run," Professor Kaori agrees with a smile, the mustache above his top lip quivering slightly. "There are a handful of other blues in active service, but you'll find them all along the Esben Mountains in the east, where the fighting is most intense. They're all intimidating, but Sgaeyl is the most powerful of them all."

My breath catches. No wonder Xaden can wield shadows—shadows that can yank daggers out of trees, shadows that can probably throw those same daggers. And yet...he let me live. I shove the kernel of warmth that thought gives me far, far away.

Probably just to screw with you, a monster playing with his prey before pouncing.

"What about the black dragon?" the first-year next to Jack asks. "There's one here, right?"

Jack's face lights up. "I want that one."

"Not that it's going to matter." Professor Kaori flicks his wrist and Sgaeyl disappears, and a massive black dragon takes her place. Even the illusion is bigger, making me crane my neck slightly to see its head. "But just to appease your curiosity, since this is the only time you'll ever see him, here is the only other black besides General Melgren's."

"He's huge," Rhiannon says. "And is that a clubtail?"

"No. A morningstartail. He has the same bludgeoning power of a clubtail, but those spikes will eviscerate a person just as well as a daggertail."

"Best of both worlds," Jack calls out. "He looks like a killing machine."

"He is," Professor Kaori answers. "And honestly, I haven't seen him in the last five years, so this image is more than a little outdated. But since we have him up here, what can you tell me about black dragons?"

"They're the smartest and most discerning," Aurelie calls out.

"They're the rarest," I add in. "There hasn't been one born in the last... century."

"Correct." Professor Kaori spins the illusion again, and I'm met with a pair of glaring yellow eyes. "They're also the most cunning. There's no such thing as outsmarting a black dragon. This one is a little over a hundred, which makes him about middle-aged. He's revered as a battle dragon among their kind, and if not for him, we probably would have lost during the Tyrrish rebellion. Add to it that he's a morningstartail, and he's one of the deadliest dragons in Navarre."

"I bet he powers one hell of a signet. How do you approach him?" Jack asks, leaning forward in his seat. There's pure avarice in his eyes, mirrored by his friend next to him.

That's the last thing this kingdom needs, someone as cruel as Jack bonding to a black dragon. No thank you.

"You don't," Professor Kaori answers. "He hasn't agreed to bond since his previous and only rider was killed during the uprising, and the only way you'd ever be near him is if you're in the Vale, which you won't be, because you'd be incinerated before you ever got through the gorge."

The pale redhead across the circle from me shifts in her seat and tugs her sleeve down to cover her rebellion relic.

"Someone should ask him again," Jack urges.

"It doesn't work that way, Barlowe. Now, there is only one other black dragon, which is in service—"

"General Melgren's," Sawyer says. His book is closed in front of him, but I can't blame him. I'd hardly be taking notes, either, if this was the second time I'd gone through this class. "Codagh, right?"

"Yes." Professor Kaori nods. "The eldest of their den and a swordtail."

"But just for curiosity's sake." Jack's glacial-blue gaze doesn't stray from the illusion of the unbonded black dragon still being projected. "What signet ability would this guy gift his rider?"

Professor Kaori closes his fist, and the illusion disappears. "There's no telling. Signets are the result of the unique chemistry between rider and dragon and usually say more about the rider than the dragon. The stronger the bond and the more powerful the dragon, the stronger the signet."

"Fine. What was his previous rider's?" Jack asks.

"Naolin's signet was siphoning." Professor Kaori's shoulders fall. "He could absorb power from various sources, other dragons, other riders, and then use it or redistribute it."

"Badass." Ridoc's tone has more than a little hero worship.

"He was," Professor Kaori agrees.

"What kills someone with that kind of signet?" Jack asks, crossing his arms over his thick chest.

Professor Kaori glances at me for a heartbeat before looking away. "He attempted to use that power to revive a fallen rider—which didn't work, because there's no signet capable of resurrection—and depleted himself in the process. To use a phrase you'll become accustomed to after

Threshing, he burned out and died next to that rider."

Something in my chest shifts, a feeling that I can't explain and yet can't shake.

The bells ring, signaling the hour is up, and we all begin to gather our things. The squads filter out to the hallway, emptying the room, and I rise from behind my desk, shouldering my satchel as Rhiannon waits for me by the door, a puzzled expression on her face. "It was Brennan, wasn't it?" I ask Professor Kaori.

Sadness fills his gaze as he meets mine. "Yes. He died trying to save your brother, but Brennan was too far gone."

"Why would he do that?" I shift the weight of my satchel. "Resurrection isn't possible. Why would he essentially kill himself when Brennan was already gone?" A stampede of grief tramples my heart, stealing my breath. Brennan never would have wanted anyone to die for him. That wasn't in his nature.

Professor Kaori sits back against his desk, pulling at the short, dark hairs of his mustache as he stares at me. "Being a Sorrengail doesn't do you any favors in here, does it?"

I shake my head. "There are more than a few cadets who would like to take me—and my last name—down a peg."

He nods. "It won't be like that once you leave. After graduation, you'll find that being General Sorrengail's daughter means others will do just about anything to keep you alive, even pleased, not because they love your mother but because they either fear her or want her favor."

"Which was Naolin?"

"A little bit of both. And sometimes it's hard for a rider with a signet that powerful to accept his limits. After all, bonding makes you a rider, but resurrecting someone from the dead? Now, that makes you a god. I somehow don't think that Malek takes kindly to a mortal treading on his territory."

"Thank you for answering." I turn and start toward the door.

"Violet," Professor Kaori calls out, and I pivot to look back. "I taught both your siblings. A signet like mine is too useful here in the classroom to let me deploy with a wing for long. Brennan was a spectacular rider and a good man. Mira is shrewd and gifted in the seat when it comes to riding."

I nod.

"But you're smarter than both of them."

I blink. It's not often I get compared to my brother and sister and somehow come out on top.

"From what I've seen of you helping your friend study in commons every night, it seems you might be more compassionate, too. Don't forget that."

"Thank you, but being smart and compassionate isn't going to help me when it comes to Threshing." A self-deprecating laugh escapes. "You know more about dragons than anyone else in the quadrant, probably anyone else on the Continent. They choose strength and shrewdness."

"They choose for reasons they don't see fit to share with us." He pushes off his desk. "And not all strength is physical, Violet."

I nod, because I can't find any appropriate words for his well-intentioned flattery, and head over to meet Rhiannon at the door. The only thing I know for certain right now is that compassion isn't going to help me on the mat after lunch.

I'm so nervous I could puke as I stand at the side of the wide black mat, watching Rhiannon beat the ever-loving shit out of her opponent. It's a guy from Second Wing, and it takes almost no time for her to get him into a headlock, cutting off his air supply. It's a move she's tried her best to drill into me over the last couple of weeks.

"She makes it look so easy," I say to Dain as he stands at my side, his elbow brushing mine.

"He's going to try to kill you."

"What?" I glance up, then follow his line of sight two mats over.

Dain's glaring daggers at Xaden across the mat, a look of sheer boredom on his face as Rhiannon squeezes the neck of the Second Wing first-year fighter.

"Your opponent," Dain says softly. "I overheard him and a few *friends*. They think you're a liability to the wing thanks to that Barlowe kid." His gaze shifts to Oren, who's sizing me up like a damned plaything he's planning on breaking.

But there's a greenish twinge to his complexion that makes me grin.

"I'm going to be fine," I recite, because that's my fucking mantra. I'm stripped down to the dragon-scale vest that's starting to feel like a second skin and my fighting leathers. All four of my daggers are sheathed, and if my plan goes correctly, I'll have one more to add to my collection soon.

The Second Wing first-year passes out, and Rhiannon rises victorious as we clap. Then she leans over her opponent and removes the dagger at his side. "Looks like this is mine now. Enjoy your nap." She pats him on the head, which makes me laugh.

"Not sure why you're laughing, Sorrengail," a sneering voice calls out from behind me.

I turn around and see Jack standing with his feet apart against the wood-planked wall about ten feet away, wearing a smile that can only be described as evil.

"Fuck off, Barlowe." I gift him the middle finger.

"I honestly hope you win today's challenge." His eyes dance with a sadistic glee that makes me queasy. "It would be a shame for someone else to kill you before I get the chance. But I wouldn't be surprised. Violets are such delicate…fragile things, you know."

Delicate, my ass.

He'd probably think twice about plotting your murder if you threw a few daggers at his head.

I unsheathe both daggers from my ribs and flick them in his direction in one smooth movement. They land right where I intended—one nearly nicking his ear and the other an inch beneath his balls.

Fear widens his eyes.

I shamelessly grin and wiggle my fingers in a wave.

"Violet," Dain hisses as Jack maneuvers around my blades, stepping away from the wall.

"You'll pay for that." Jack points at me and stalks off, but the rise and fall of his shoulders is a little choppy.

I watch his back retreat, then retrieve my daggers, sheathing them at my ribs before returning to Dain's side.

"What the hell was that?" he seethes. "I told you to lay low when it comes to him, and you…" He shakes his head at me. "You just piss him off even more?"

"Laying low wasn't getting me anywhere," I say with a shrug as Rhiannon's opponent is carried off the mat. "He needs to realize I'm not a liability." *And I'll be harder to kill than he thinks.*

There's no ignoring the prickle at my scalp, and I let my gaze shift to meet Xaden's.

My heart does that damn stuttering thing again, as if he'd sent shadows straight through my ribs to squeeze the organ. He lifts his scarred brow, and I swear there's a hint of a smile on his lips as he leaves, walking over to observe the Fourth Wing cadets at the next mat.

"Badass," Rhiannon says as she moves to my other side. "I thought Jack was going to shit himself."

I smother a smile.

"Stop encouraging her," Dain chastises.

"Sorrengail." Professor Emetterio glances at his notebook and raises one bushy black brow before continuing. "Seifert."

Swallowing back the panic that threatens to creep up my throat, I step onto the mat opposite Oren, who's definitely looking green now.

Right on time.

I've prepared the best I can, wrapping my ankles and my knees just in case he goes for the legs.

"Don't take this personally," he says as we start to circle, both our hands raised. "But you'll only be a hazard to your wing."

He charges at me, but his footwork is sluggish and I spin away, landing a punch to his kidney before bouncing back on my heels and palming a dagger.

"I'm no more a hazard than you are," I accuse.

His chest heaves once and sweat dots his forehead, but he shakes it off, blinking rapidly as he reaches for his own knife. "My sister is a healer. I've heard your bones snap like twigs."

"Why don't you come find out?" I force a smile and wait for him to charge again, because that's what he does. I've had three sessions to watch him from a few mats over. He's a bull, all power and no grace.

His entire body rolls like he's going to vomit, and he covers his mouth with his empty hand, breathing deeply before standing straight again. I should attack, but instead I wait. And then he charges, his blade held high in a striking position.

My heart pounds as I wait the torturous heartbeats it takes for him to reach me, my brain somehow convincing my body to hold my ground until the last possible second. He swings his knife downward, and I dodge to the left, nicking his side with my blade in the process, then turn and deliver a kick to his back, sending him sprawling.

Now.

He falls to the mat, and I take immediate advantage, digging a knee into his spine just like Imogen had with me and putting my blade to his throat. "Yield." Who needs strength when you have speed and steel?

"No!" he shouts, but his body undulates under mine, and he retches, bringing up everything he's eaten since breakfast and splattering it across the mat to the side of us.

So fucking gross.

"Oh my gods," Rhiannon calls out, disgust dripping from her tone.

"Yield," I demand again, but he's heaving in earnest now and I have to pull my knife away so I don't accidentally slit his throat.

"He yields," Professor Emetterio declares, his face contorted in revulsion.

I sheathe my blade and climb off him, dodging the puddles of sick. Then I take the dagger Oren dropped a few feet back as he continues to vomit. The knife is heavier and longer than my others, but it's mine now, and I earned it. I sheathe it in an empty place at my left thigh.

"You won!" Rhiannon says, clasping me in a hug as I walk off the mat.

"He's sick," I say with a shrug.

"I'll take being lucky over being good any day," Rhiannon counters.

"I have to find someone to get this cleaned up," Dain says, his own complexion turning peaked.

I won.

Timing is the hardest thing about my plan.

I win the next week when a stocky girl from First Wing can't concentrate long enough to throw a decent punch thanks to a few leighorrel mushrooms and their hallucinogenic properties that somehow wind up in her lunch. She gets in a good kick to my knee, but it's nothing a few days in a wrap won't heal.

I win the week after that when a tall guy from Third Wing stumbles because his large feet temporarily lose all feeling, courtesy of the zihna root that grows on one outcropping near the ravine. My timing is off a little, though, and he lands a few good punches to my face, leaving me with a split lip and a bruise that colors my cheek for the next eleven days, but at least he doesn't break my jaw.

I win again the next week when a buxom cadet's vision turns blurry mid-match, on account of the tarsilla leaves that found their way into her tea. She's fast, tossing me to the mat and delivering some overwhelmingly painful kicks to my abdomen that leave colorful contusions and one distinct boot print on my ribs. I almost broke down and went to see Nolon after that one, but I gritted my teeth and wrapped my ribs, determined not to give the others a reason to weed me out like Jack or any marked ones wanted.

I earn my fifth dagger, this one with a pretty ruby in the hilt, the last challenge in August when I take a particularly sweaty guy with a gap between his front teeth to the mat. The bark of the carmine tree that finds its way into his waterskin makes him sluggish and ill. The effects are a little too similar to the fonilee berries, and it's just a shame that the entire Third Squad, Claw Section of Third Wing is suffering the same stomach upset. Must be something viral, at least that's what I say when he finally yields to my headlock after dislocating my thumb and nearly breaking my nose.

Come early September, there's a spring in my step as I walk onto the mat. I've taken down five opponents without killing any of them, something a quarter of our year can't say after almost twenty more names have been added to the death roll the last month for the first-years alone.

I roll my sore shoulders and wait for my opponent.

But Rayma Corrie from Third Wing doesn't step forward this week like she's supposed to.

"Sorry, Violet," Professor Emetterio says, scratching his short black beard. "You were supposed to challenge Rayma, but she's been taken to the healers because she can't seem to walk in a straight line."

Peels of the walwyn fruit will do that when ingested raw…say, like when they're mixed into the icing of your morning pastry.

"That's"—*shit*—"too bad." I wince. *You served it to her too early.* "Should I just…" I start, already backing up to get off the mat.

"I'm happy to step in." That voice. That tone. That prickle of ice along my scalp…

Oh no. Hell no. No. No. *No.*

"You sure?" Professor Emetterio asks, glancing over his shoulder.

"Absolutely."

My stomach hits the floor.

And Xaden walks onto the mat.

I will not die today.

—Violet Sorrengail's personal addendum to the Book of Brennan

CHAPTER NINE

I'm so completely screwed.

Xaden steps forward—all six-foot-everything of him—dressed in midnight fighting leathers and a tight-fitted short-sleeve shirt that only seems to make the shimmering, dark rebellion relics on his skin seem like an even bigger warning, which I know is ridiculous but somehow true.

My heartbeat kicks up to a full gallop, as if my body knows the truth my mind hasn't quite accepted yet. I'm about to have my ass kicked…or worse.

"You are all in for a treat," Professor Emetterio says, clapping his hands. "Xaden's one of the best fighters we have. Watch and learn."

"Of course you are," I mutter, my stomach twisting like I'm the one who's been snacking on walwyn fruit peels.

A corner of Xaden's mouth rises in a smirk, and the gold flecks in his eyes seem to dance. The sadistic ass is enjoying this.

My knees, ankles, and wrist are wrapped, the white cloth protecting my healing thumb a startling contrast against my black leathers.

"A little out of her league, don't you think?" Dain argues from the side of the mat, tension radiating from every word.

"Relax, Aetos." Xaden looks over my shoulder, his gaze hardening toward where I know Dain is standing, where he always stands when I'm on the mat. The look Xaden gives him makes me realize he's been taking it easy on me in the glaring department. "She'll be in one piece when I'm finished *teaching* her."

"I hardly think it's fair—" Dain's voice rises.

"No one asked you to think, *squad leader*," Xaden fires back as he moves to the side, discarding every weapon on his body—and there's a lot of them—and handing them to Imogen.

The bitter, illogical taste of jealousy fills my mouth, but there's no time to examine that particular oddity, not when there're only seconds before he's in front of me again.

"You don't think you'll need those?" I ask, palming my own blades. His chest is massive, with wide shoulders and heavily muscled arms alongside. A target this big should be easy to hit.

"Nope. Not when you brought enough for the both of us." A wicked smile curves his mouth as he stretches out his hand and curls his fingers in a come-hither motion. "Let's go."

My heart beats faster than the wings of a hummingbird as I take a fighting stance and wait for him to strike. This mat is only twenty feet in either direction, and yet my entire world narrows to its confines and the danger within.

He's not in my squad. He can kill me without punishment.

I fling a dagger straight at his ridiculously well-sculpted chest.

He fucking *catches* it and clucks his tongue. "Already seen that move."

Holy shit is he fast.

I have to be faster. It's the single advantage I have—that's my only thought as I move forward in a swipe-and-kick combo Rhiannon's drilled into me over the past six weeks. He artfully dodges my blade and then captures my leg. The earth spins and I slam onto my back, the sudden impact driving the air from my lungs.

But he doesn't go for the kill. Instead, he drops the dagger he's caught and kicks it off the mat, and a second later, when air squeaks into my lungs, I lunge up with the next blade, going for his thigh.

He blocks my strike with his forearm, then grips my wrist with his opposite hand and plucks the knife out of my hand, leaning down so his face is only inches from mine. "Going for blood today, are we, Violence?" he whispers. Metal hits the mat again and he kicks it past my head and out of my reach.

He's not taking my daggers to use against me; he's disarming me just to prove he can. My blood boils.

"My name is *Violet*," I seethe.

"I think my version fits you better." He releases my wrist and stands, offering me a hand. "We're not done yet."

My chest heaves, still recovering from the way he's knocked the wind out of me, and I take the offering. He tugs me to my feet, then twists my arm behind my back and yanks me against his hard chest, pinning our joined hands before I have a chance to get my balance.

"Damn it!" I snap.

There's a tug at my thigh and another of my daggers is pressed to my throat as his chest rests against the back of my head. His forearm is locked across my ribs, and he might as well be a statue for all the give there is in his frame. There's no use slamming my head back—he's so tall that I'd only annoy him.

"Don't trust a single person who faces you on this mat," he warns in a hiss, his breath warm against the shell of my ear, and even though we're surrounded by people, I realize he's quiet for a reason. This lesson is just for me.

"Even someone who owes me a favor?" I counter, my voice just as low. My shoulder starts to protest the unnatural angle, but I don't move. I won't give him the satisfaction.

He drops the third dagger he's taken from me and kicks it forward—to where Dain stands, the other two already in his hand. There's murder in his eyes as he glares at Xaden.

"I'm the one who decides when to grant that favor. Not you." Xaden releases my hand and steps back.

I whirl, punching for his throat, and he knocks my hand aside.

"Good," he says with a smile, deflecting my next blow without so much as a hitch to his breath. "Going for the throat is your best option, as long as it's exposed."

Fury makes me kick out again in the same pattern, muscle memory taking over, and he captures that leg again, this time snatching the dagger sheathed there and dropping it to the mat before he lets me go, cocking a disappointed eyebrow at me. "I expect you to learn from your mistakes." He kicks it away.

I only have five left, all sheathed at my ribs.

Gripping one and putting my hands up defensively, I begin to circle him, and to my absolute annoyance, he doesn't even bother facing me. He just stands there in the center of the mat, his boots planted and his arms loose as I move around him.

"You going to prance or are you going to strike?"

Fuck him.

I punch forward, but he dips and my knife sails over his shoulder, missing him by six inches. My stomach drops as he grips my arm, yanking me forward and flipping me around the side of his body. I'm airborne for a heartbeat before I smack into the mat, my ribs taking the impact.

He cranks my arm into a submission hold and white-hot pain shoots down the limb as I cry out, dropping the dagger, but he's not done. No, his knee is in my ribs and, though he holds my arm captive with one hand, the other plucks a dagger from its sheath and flings it toward Dain's feet before taking another and holding it to the tender area where my jaw meets my neck.

Then he leans closer. "Taking out your enemy before the battle is really smart; I'll give that to you," he whispers, his warm breath brushing the shell of my ear.

Oh gods. He knows what I've been doing. The pain in my arm is nothing compared to the nausea churning in my stomach at the thought of what he might do with that knowledge.

"Problem is, if you aren't testing yourself in here"—he scrapes the dagger down my neck, but there's no warm trickle of blood, so I know he hasn't cut me—"then you're not going to get any better."

"You'd rather I die, no doubt," I fire back, the side of my face pressed into the mat. This isn't just painful, it's humiliating.

"And be denied the pleasure of your company?" he mocks.

"I fucking hate you." The words are past my lips before I can shut my mouth.

"That doesn't make you special."

The pressure releases from my chest and arm as he gets on his feet, kicking both daggers toward Dain.

Two more. I only have two more, and now my indignation and anger far outweigh my fear.

Ignoring Xaden's outstretched hand, I gain my feet and his lips curve into an approving smile. "She can be taught."

"She's a quick learner," I retort.

"That remains to be seen." He backs up two steps, putting a little space between us before crooking his fingers at me again.

"You've made your damn point," I snap loud enough that I hear Imogen gasp.

"Trust me, I've barely gotten started." He folds his arms and leans back on his heels, clearly waiting for me to move.

I don't think. I just act, going low and kicking out the backs of his knees.

He goes down like a tree, the sound more than satisfying, and I pounce, trying for a headlock. Doesn't matter how big someone is—they still need air. Catching his throat in the crook of my elbow, I squeeze.

Instead of going for my arms, he twists, grabbing ahold of the backs of my thighs so I lose my leverage and our bodies careen into a roll. He comes out on top.

Of course he does.

His forearm rests against my throat, not cutting off air but definitely capable of it, and his hips have mine pinned, my legs useless on either side of his as he lies heavily between my thighs. He's unmovable.

Everything around us fades as my world narrows to the arrogant glint in his gaze. He's all I can see, all I can feel.

And I can't let him win.

I slip one of my last daggers free and go for his shoulder.

He seizes my wrist and pins it above my head.

Shit. Shit. SHIT.

Heat rushes up my neck and flames lick my cheeks as he lowers his face so his lips are only inches away from mine. I can make out every speck of gold in his onyx eyes, every bump and ridge of his scar.

Beautiful. Fucking. Asshole.

My breath catches and my body warms, the traitorous bitch. *You are not attracted to toxic men*, I remind myself, and yet, here I am, getting all attracted. I have been since the first second I saw him, if I feel like being honest.

He pushes his fingers into my fist, forcing it open, then sends the blade skittering across the mat before letting go of my wrist.

"Get your dagger," he orders.

"What?" My eyes fly wide. He has me defenseless and in the kill position already.

"Get. Your. Dagger," he repeats, taking my hand in his and retrieving the last blade I have. His fingers curl over mine, clasping the hilt.

Fire races along my skin at the feel of his fingers lacing with mine.

Toxic. Dangerous. Wants to kill you. Nope, doesn't matter. My pulse still skitters like a teenager.

"You're tiny." He says it like an insult.

"Well aware." My eyes narrow.

"So stop going for bigger moves that expose you." He drags the tip of the dagger down his side. "A rib shot would have worked just fine." Then he guides our hands around his back, making himself vulnerable. "Kidneys are a good fit from this angle, too."

I swallow, refusing to think of other things that are a good fit at this angle.

He leads our hands to his waist, his gaze never leaving mine. "Chances are, if your opponent is in armor, it's weak here. Those are three easy places you could have struck before your opponent would have had time to stop you."

They're also fatal wounds, and I've avoided those at all costs.

"Do you hear me?"

I nod.

"Good. Because you can't poison every enemy you come across," he whispers, and I blanche. "You're not going to have time to offer tea to some Braevi gryphon rider when they come at you."

"How did you know?" I finally ask. My muscles lock, including my thighs, which just happen to still be bracketing his hips.

His eyes darken. "Oh, Violence, you're good, but I've known better poison masters. The trick is to not make it quite so obvious."

My lips part, and I bite back a retort that I was careful *not* to be obvious.

"I think she's been taught enough for the day," Dain barks, reminding me that we're far from alone. No, we're a damned spectacle.

"He always that overprotective?" Xaden grumbles, pressing up from the mat a few inches.

"He cares about me." I glare at him.

"He's holding you back. Don't worry. Your little poisoning secret is safe with me." Xaden arches a brow as if to remind me that I'm the keeper of one of *his* secrets, too. Then he guides our hands back to my ribs and slides the ruby-hilted blade back into its sheath.

The move is unnervingly...hot.

"You're not going to disarm me?" I challenge as he releases his grip and pushes up more, removing his weight from my body. My ribs expand as I take my first full breath.

"Nope. Defenseless women have never been my type. We're done for today." He stands, then walks away without another word, taking his weapons from Imogen as I roll to my knees. Every part of my body aches, but I manage to stand.

There's pure relief in Dain's eyes when I reach his side to retrieve the daggers Xaden took from me. "You all right?"

I nod, my fingers trembling as I rearm myself. He's had every chance, and every reason, to kill me, and now he's let me walk away *twice*. What kind of game is he playing?

"Aetos," Xaden calls out from across the mat.

Dain's head snaps up and his jaw locks.

"She could use a little less protection and a little more instruction." Xaden stares Dain down until he nods.

Professor Emetterio calls the next challenge.

"I'm just surprised he let you live," Dain says later that night in his room as his thumbs dig into the muscle between my neck and shoulder.

It hurts so deliciously, it was well worth the pain of sneaking up here.

"I hardly think he'd command respect by snapping my neck on the mat." His blankets are soft against my belly and chest as I lay on his bed, bare from the waist up except for the constricting band around my breasts and ribs. "Besides, that's not his way."

Dain's hands pause on my skin. "Because you know what his way is?"

The guilt of keeping Xaden's secret makes my stomach drop. "He told me he didn't see a reason to kill me himself when the parapet would do it," I answer truthfully. "And let's face it, he's had plenty of chances to take me out if he really wanted."

"Hmm." Dain hums in that thoughtful tone of his, continuing to work out my stiff and aching muscles as he leans over from the side of his bed. Rhiannon drilled me for another two hours after dinner, and I was barely able to move by the end of it.

Guess I wasn't the only one Xaden scared this afternoon.

"Do you think he could be plotting against Navarre and still have bonded Sgaeyl?" I ask, my cheek against his blanket.

"I did at first." His hands move down my spine, pressing into the knots that made lifting my arms almost impossible that last half hour of training tonight. "But then I bonded Cath, and I realized that dragons would do anything to protect the Vale and their sacred hatching grounds. There's no way any dragon would have bonded Riorson or any of the separatists if they weren't honest about protecting Navarre."

"But would a dragon even know if you were lying?" I turn my head so I can see his face.

"Yeah." He grins. "Cath would know because he's in my head. It's impossible to hide something like that from your dragon."

"Is he always in your head?" I know it's against the rules to ask—almost everything about bonds are off-limits for discussion, given how secretive dragons are, but it's Dain.

"Yeah," he answers, his smile softening. "I can block him out if I need to, and they'll teach you that after Threshing—" His expression falls.

"What is it?" I sit up, sliding one of his pillows across my chest and leaning back against the headboard.

"I talked to Colonel Markham this evening." He walks over and pulls his chair out from his desk and takes a seat, then rests his head in his hands.

"Did something happen?" Fear races down my spine. "Is it Mira's wing?"

"No!" Dain's head snaps up, and there's so much misery in his eyes that I swing my feet off the bed. "It's nothing like that. I told him…that I think Riorson wants to kill you."

I blink, sitting fully back onto the bed. "Oh. Well, that's not really news, is it? Everyone who's read a history of the rebellion can put two and two together, Dain."

"Yeah, well, I told him about Barlowe, too, and Seifert." He rubs his hand over his hair. "Don't think I didn't notice the way Seifert shoved you into the wall before formation this morning." He lifts his brows at me.

"He's just pissed that I took his dagger at that first challenge." I squeeze the pillow tighter.

"And Rhiannon told me you found crushed flowers on your bed last week?" He stares me down.

I shrug. "They were just dead flowers."

"They were mutilated *violets*." His mouth tightens and I go to him, resting my hands on his head.

"It's not like they came with a death note or anything," I tease, stroking his soft brown hair.

He looks up at me, the mage lights making his eyes a little brighter above his trim beard. "They're threats."

I shrug. "Every cadet gets threatened."

"Every cadet doesn't have to wrap their knees every day," he fires back.

"The injured ones do." My brow furrows, annoyance taking root in my chest. "Why would you tell Markham about it anyway? He's a scribe, and there's nothing he would do even if he could."

"He said he'd still take you," Dain blurts, his hands flying to my hips, holding me in place when I try to step away. "I asked him if he'd allow you into the Scribe Quadrant for your own safety, and he said yes. They'd put you with the first-years. It's not like you'd have to wait until next Conscription Day or anything."

"You what?" I twist, breaking my hold, and back away from my best friend.

"I saw a way to get you out of danger, and I took it." He stands.

"You went behind my back because you think I'm not cutting it." The truth of the words tightens around my chest like a vise, cutting off my air instead of holding me together, leaving me weak and breathless. Dain knows me better than *anyone*, and if he *still* thinks I can't do this after I've made it this far…

Tears well in my eyes, but I refuse to let them fall. Instead, I tuck my chin and grab my dragon-scale vest, pull it over my head, then wrench the laces together at the small of my back and tie them.

Dain sighs. "I never said I don't think you can cut it, Violet."

"You say it every day!" I snap. "You say it when you walk me from formation to class, which I know makes you late for flight line. You say it when you yell at your wingleader when he takes me to the mat—"

"He had no right to—"

"He's my *wingleader*!" I shrug my tunic over my head. "He has the right to do *whatever* he wants—including execute me."

"And that's why you need to get the hell out of here!" Dain laces his fingers behind his neck and begins to pace. "I've been watching, Vi. He's just toying with you, like a cat plays with a mouse before the kill."

"I've held my own so far." My satchel is heavy with books as I settle it over my shoulder. "I've won every challenge—"

"Except today when he wiped the floor with you time and again." He grasps my shoulders. "Or did you miss the part where he took every weapon so you knew exactly how easy it is to defeat you?"

I raise my chin and glare at him. "I was there, and I've survived almost two months in this place, which is more than I can say for a fourth of my year!"

"Do you know what happens at Threshing?" he asks, his tone dropping.

"Are you calling me ignorant?" Rage bubbles in my veins.

"It's not just about bonding," he continues. "They throw every first-year into the training grounds, the ones you've *never* been to, and then the second- and third-years are supposed to watch as you decide which dragons to approach and which to run from."

"I know how it works." My jaw clenches.

"Yeah, well, while the riders are watching, the first-years are taking out their vendettas and eliminating any…liabilities to the wing."

"I'm not a damned liability." My chest tightens again, because deep down I know, on the physical level, that I am.

"Not to me," he whispers, a hand rising to cradle my cheek. "But they don't know you the way I do, Vi. And while the first-years like Barlowe and Seifert are hunting you, we'll have to *watch*. I'll have to *watch*, Violet." The break in his voice takes the anger right out of me. "We are not *allowed* to help you. To save you."

"Dain—"

"And when they gather the bodies for the roll, no one's going to document *how* that cadet died. You're just as likely to fall under Barlowe's knife as a dragon's talon."

I breathe through the jolt of fear.

"Markham says that he'll put you through the first year without telling your mother. By the time she finds out, you'll already be inducted as a scribe. There's nothing she can do after that." He lifts his other hand so he's holding my face between both palms, tipping it up toward his. "Please. If you won't do it for yourself, then do it for me."

My heart stutters, and I sway, his reasoning tugging me toward exactly what he's suggesting. *But you've made it this far*, a part of me whispers.

"I can't lose you, Violet," he whispers, resting his forehead against mine. "I just…can't."

I squeeze my eyes shut. This is my way out, and yet, I don't want to take it.

"Just promise me you'll think about it," he begs. "We still have four weeks until Threshing. Just…think about it." The hope in his tone and the tender way he holds me cuts through my defenses.

"I'll think about it."

Don't underestimate the challenge of the Gauntlet, Mira. It's designed to test your balance, strength, and agility. The times don't matter for shit, only that you make it to the top. Reach for the ropes when you have to. Coming in last is better than coming in dead.

—Page forty-six, the Book of Brennan

CHAPTER TEN

I look up, and up, and *up*, fear coiling in my stomach like a snake ready to strike.

"Well, that's..." Rhiannon swallows, her head tilted just as far back as mine as we stare at the menacing obstacle course that's carved into the front of a ridgeline so steep, it might as well be a cliff. The zigzagging death trap of a trail rises above us, climbing in five distinct switchbacks of 180-degree turns, each increasing in difficulty on the way to the top of the bluff that divides the citadel from the flight field and the Vale.

"Amazing." Aurelie sighs.

Rhiannon and I turn, both staring at her like she must have hit her head.

"You think that hellscape looks *amazing*?" Rhiannon asks.

"I've been waiting *years* for this!" Aurelie grins, her normally serious black eyes dancing in the morning sun as she rubs her hands together, shifting from one toned leg to the other in glee. "My dad—he was a rider until he retired last year—used to set up obstacle courses like this all the time so we could practice, and Chase, my brother, said it's the best part of being here before Threshing. It's a real adrenaline rush."

"He's with the Southern Wing, right?" I ask, focusing on the obstacle course running up *the side of a fucking cliff*. It looks more like a death trap than an adrenaline rush, but sure, we can go with that. Positive thinking for the win, right?

"Yep. Pretty much desk duty for all the action they see near the Krovlan border." She shrugs and points about two-thirds up the course. "He said to watch out for those giant posts jutting from the side of the cliff. They spin, and you can get crushed between them if you're not fast enough."

"Oh, good, I was wondering when it might get difficult," Rhiannon mutters.

"Thanks, Aurelie." I locate the series of nearly touching, three-foot-wide logs that jut out from the rocky terrain like a set of round steps rising from the ground to the switchback above it and nod. Go fast. Got it. *You could have included that tidbit, Brennan.*

The obstacle course is the embodiment of my worst nightmare. For the first time since Dain begged me to leave last week, I consider Markham's offer. There are no death courses in the Scribe Quadrant, that's for certain.

But you've already made it this far. Ahh, there she is, the little voice that's been riding my shoulder lately, daring to give me hope that I might actually survive Presentation.

"Still not sure why they call it the Gauntlet," Ridoc says from my right, blowing into his cupped hands to ward off the morning chill. The sun hasn't touched this little crevice, but it's shining above the last quarter of the course.

"To ensure dragons keep coming to Threshing by weeding out the weaklings." Tynan sneers from Ridoc's other side, folding his arms over his chest as he casts a pointed look at me.

I shoot him a glare and then shake it off. He's been pissy ever since Rhiannon handed his ass to him on the mat at assessment.

"Knock it the fuck off," Ridoc snaps, earning the entire squad's attention.

My eyebrows lift. I've never seen Ridoc lose his temper or use anything but humor to defuse a situation before.

"What's your problem?" Tynan shoves a strand of thick, dark hair from his eyes and pivots like he's going to stare some intimidation into Ridoc, but it doesn't really work out, seeing as Ridoc is twice as wide and half a foot taller.

"My problem? You think because you made friends with Barlowe and Siefert that you have the right to be a dick to your own squadmate?" Ridoc challenges.

"Exactly. *Squadmate.*" Tynan gestures toward the obstacle course. "Our times aren't just ranked individually, Ridoc. We're scored as a squad, too, which is how the order for Presentation is decided. Do you really think any dragon wants to bond a cadet who walks in after every other squad in the processional?"

Fine, he has a point. It's a shitty one, but it's there.

"They're not timing us for Presentation today, asshole." Ridoc takes a step forward.

"Stop." Sawyer shuffles between the two, shoving Tynan's chest hard enough to make him stagger back into the girl behind him. "Take it from someone who made it through Presentation last year: your time doesn't mean anything. The last cadet to walk in last year bonded just fine, and some of the cadets in the first squad onto the field were passed over."

"Little bitter about that, aren't you?" Tynan smirks.

Sawyer ignores the barb. "Besides, it's not called the Gauntlet because it weeds out cadets."

"It's called the Gauntlet because this is the cliff that guards the Vale," Professor Emetterio says, walking up behind our squad, his shaved head glinting in the growing sunlight. "Plus, actual gauntlets—armored gloves made of metal—are slippery as hell, and the name stuck about twenty years ago." He cocks a brow at Tynan and Sawyer. "Are you two done arguing? Because all nine of you have exactly an hour to get to the top before it's another squad's chance to practice, and from what I've seen of your agility on the mat, you're going to need every second."

There's a grumble of assent in our little group.

"As you know, hand-to-hand challenges are on hold for the next two and a half weeks before Presentation so you can focus here." Professor Emetterio flips a page on the little notebook he carries. "Sawyer, you're going to show them how it's done, since you already have the lay of the land. Then Pryor, Trina, Tynan, Rhiannon, Ridoc, Violet, Aurelie, and Luca." A smile curves the harsh line of his mouth as he finishes calling out every name in our squad, and we file into order. "You're the only squad to remain intact since Parapet. That's incredible. Your squad leader must be very proud. Wait here for a second." He walks past us, waving at someone high up on the cliff.

No doubt that someone has a watch.

"Aetos is especially proud of Sorrengail." Tynan gifts me with a mocking sneer once our instructor is out of hearing range.

I see red. "Look, if you want to talk shit about me, that's one thing, but leave Dain out of it."

"Tynan," Sawyer warns, shaking his head.

"Like it doesn't bother any of you that our squad leader is fucking one of us?" Tynan throws out his hands.

"I'm not—" I start, indignation getting the best of me before I can take a deep breath. "Honestly, it's none of your godsdamned business who I'm sleeping with, Tynan." Though if I'm going to get accused, can't I have some of the perks? If I know Dain, he's hung up on the whole fraternization-is-discouraged-within-the-chain-of-command thing like this asshole. But surely Dain would actually make a move if he really wanted to, right?

"It is if it means you get preferential treatment!" Luca adds in.

"For fuck's sake," Rhiannon mumbles, rubbing the bridge of her nose. "Luca, Tynan, shut up. They're not sleeping together. They've been friends since they were kids, or do you not know enough about our own leadership to know his dad is her mom's aide?"

Tynan's eyes widen, like he's actually surprised. "Really?"

"Really." I shake my head and study the course.

"Shit. I'm...sorry. Barlowe said—"

"And that's your first mistake," Ridoc interjects. "Listening to that sadistic ass is going to get you killed. And you're lucky Aetos isn't here."

True. Dain would more than take exception to Tynan's assumptions and probably assign him cleanup duty for a month. Good thing he's on the flight field this time of day.

Xaden would just beat the shit out of him.

I blink, shoving that comparison and any other thought of Xaden Riorson far out of my head.

"Here we go!" Professor Emetterio walks to the head of our line. "You'll get your time at the top of the course, if you make it, but remember, you'll still have nine practice sessions before we rank you for Presentation in two and a half weeks, which will determine if the dragons find you worthy at Threshing."

"Wouldn't it make more sense to let first-years start practicing this thing right after Parapet?" Rhiannon asks. "You know, to give us a little more time so we don't die?"

"No," Professor Emetterio replies. "The timing is part of the challenge. Any words of wisdom, Sawyer?"

Sawyer blows out a slow breath, his gaze following the treacherous course. "There are ropes every six feet that run from the top of the sheer cliffside to the bottom," he says. "So if you start to fall, reach out and grab a rope. It'll cost you thirty seconds, but death costs you more."

Awesome.

"I mean, there's a perfectly good set of steps over there." Ridoc points to the steep staircase carved into the cliff beside the wide switchbacks of the Gauntlet.

"Stairs are for reaching the flight field on the top of the ridgeline *after* Presentation," Professor Emetterio says, then lifts his hands toward the course and flicks his wrist, pointing at various obstacles.

The fifteen-foot log at the start of the uphill climb begins to spin. The pillars on the third ascent shake. The giant wheel at the first switchback starts its counterclockwise rotation, and those little posts Aurelie mentioned? They all twist in opposite directions.

"Every one of the five ascents on this course is designed to mimic the challenges you'll face in battle." Professor Emetterio turns to look at us, his face just as stern as it is during our usual combat training. "From the balance you must keep on the back of your dragon, to the strength you'll need to hold your seat during maneuvers, to"—he gestures upward, toward the last obstacle that looks like a ninety-degree ramp from this angle—"the stamina you'll need to fight on the ground, then still be able to mount your dragon at a second's notice."

The posts knock a chunk of granite loose, and the rock tumbles down the course, smacking every obstacle in its path until it crashes twenty feet in front of us. If there was ever a metaphor for my life, well…that's it.

"Whoa," Trina whispers, her brown eyes wide as she stares at the pulverized rock. I'm the smallest of our squad, but Trina is the quietest, the most reserved. I can count on both hands the number of times she's spoken to me since Parapet. If she didn't have friends in First Wing, I'd worry, but she doesn't have to open up to us to survive the quadrant.

"You all right?" I ask her in a whisper.

She swallows and nods, one of her auburn ringlet curls bouncing against her forehead.

"What if we can't make it up?" Luca asks from my right, securing her long hair in a loose braid, her usual haughtiness not so in-your-face today. "What's the alternative route?"

"There's no alternative. If you don't make it, you can't get to

Presentation, can you? Take your position, Sawyer," Professor Emetterio orders, and Sawyer moves to the beginning of the course. "After he makes it past the final obstacle, so everyone can learn from this cadet completing the course, the rest of you will start every sixty seconds. And…go!"

Sawyer is off like a shot. He easily runs the fifteen feet across the single log spinning parallel with the cliff face and then the raised pillars, but it takes him three rotations inside the wheel before he jumps through the lone opening, but other than that, I don't see a single misstep in the first ascent. Not. One.

He turns and rushes toward a series of giant hanging balls that makes up the second ascent, jumping and hugging one after another. His feet back on the ground, he turns again and heads up the third ascent, which is divided into two sections. The first part has giant metal rods hanging parallel to the cliff wall, and he easily swings arm over arm, using his body's weight and momentum to swing the bar forward and reach the next bar hanging half a foot higher than the previous as he climbs the side of the cliff. From the last bar, he jumps onto a series of shaking pillars that make up the second half of this ascent before finally leaping back onto the gravel path.

By the time he reaches the fourth ascent, the spinning logs Aurelie's brother warned us about, Sawyer's made it all look like child's play, and I start to feel a bubble of hope that maybe the course isn't as difficult as it looks from the ground.

But then he faces a giant chimney formation rising high above him at a twenty-degree angle and pauses.

"You got this!" Rhiannon yells from my side.

As though he heard, he sprints toward the leaning chimney and flings himself upward, grabbing onto the sides by forming an X with his body, then starts hopping up the conduit until he reaches the end and drops down in front of the final obstacle, a massive ramp that reaches up to the top of the cliff's edge at a nearly vertical climb.

My breath catches in my throat as Sawyer sprints toward the ramp, using his speed and momentum to carry him two-thirds of the way up the ramp. Just before he starts to fall, he reaches up with one arm and grasps the lip of the ramp and hauls himself over the edge.

Rhiannon and I scream and cheer for him. He made it. In an almost flawless approach.

"Perfect technique!" Professor Emetterio calls out. "That's exactly what you should all be doing."

"Perfect, and yet he was still passed over at Threshing," Luca snarks. "Guess the dragons have some sense of taste."

"Give it a rest, Luca," Rhi says.

How could someone as smart and athletic as Sawyer not bond? And if *he* didn't, what the hell kind of hope is there for the rest of us?

"I'm too short for the ramp," I whisper to Rhi.

She glances over at me, and then back to the obstacle. "You're wicked fast. If you get your speed up, I bet the momentum will take you to the top."

Pryor—the shy cadet from the Krovlan border region—struggles on the swinging steel rods in the third ascent due to some rather predictable hesitation on his part, but he makes it just as Trina nearly falls at the shaking pillars, reaching for a rope. I can only make out the flash of red from her hair when she starts the rotating stair steps, but I hear her scream all the way to my toes as that particular rope sways near the ground.

"You can do it!" Sawyer shouts down from the top.

"They go in opposite directions!" Aurelie calls up.

"Tynan, start," Professor Emetterio orders, watching his pocket watch and not the course.

My heart thuds in my ears when Trina makes it past the steps, and the drumming doesn't let up as Rhiannon is called to start. She passes the first ascent with the grace I've come to expect from her before coming to a halt.

Tynan hangs from the second of five buoy balls on the second ascent, right where the ground drops out. If he falls, he's got a minuscule chance of hitting the single spinning log from the first ascent and overwhelming odds of dropping thirty feet to the ground below.

"You have to keep moving, Tynan!" I shout, though it's doubtful he can hear me from here. He might be a gullible ass, but he's still my squadmate.

He shrieks, his arms wrapped around the swinging ball. It's impossible for him to reach his hands completely around—that's the point, and he's slipping.

"He's going to screw her time," Aurelie says, blowing out a bored sigh.

"Good thing this is only practice, then," Ridoc says, then bellows up at Tynan. "What's the matter, Tynan? Scared of heights? Who's the liability now?"

"Stop." I elbow Ridoc in the side. He's not quite as lean now. The last seven weeks have put some muscle on him. "Just because he's a dick doesn't mean you have to be."

"But he's giving me so much material to work with," Ridoc replies, a corner of his mouth lifting into a smirk as he backs away, heading toward the starting position.

"Swing to the next one!" Trina suggests from the top of the course.

"I can't!" Tynan's shriek could break glass as it echoes down the mountain, and it makes my chest tighten.

"Ridoc, start!" Professor Emetterio commands.

Ridoc charges over the log.

"Rhi!" I shout up. "The rope is between the first and second!"

She nods down at me, then jumps for the first buoy ball, clasping it up top, near where the chains hold it to the iron rail above, and swinging her weight around the side.

It's an utterly inspired approach, one that might just work for me.

Gravel crunches beneath my boots as I move to the starting position. Oh, look, it *is* possible for my heart to beat faster. The damned thing practically flutters as I wipe my clammy palms on my leather pants.

Rhiannon gets the rope into Tynan's hand, but instead of using it to swing to the next ball, he climbs…*down*.

My jaw practically unhinges as he descends. Definitely didn't see *that* one coming.

"Violet, begin!" Emetterio orders.

Be with me, Zihnal. I haven't spent nearly enough time at temple for the god of luck to care much about what happens to me right now, but it's worth a shot.

I bolt up the first part of the ascent, coming to the spinning log within seconds. My stomach feels like it's being stirred by this balance beam from hell. "It's just balance. You can balance," I mumble and start across. "Quick feet. Quick feet. Quick feet," I repeat all the way across, jumping off the end to land on the first of four granite columns, each one higher than the last.

There are about three feet between them, but I manage to leap from one pillar to the next without skidding off the ends. *And this is the easy part.* A knot of fear works its way up my throat.

I jump into the rotating wheel and run, leaping over the only opening as it flies by once, then watching it come around a second time. Timing. This one is all about timing.

The opportunity comes and I seize it, racing through the opening and turning back onto the gravel path of the second ascent. The buoy balls are just ahead, but I'm going to fall on my ass if I don't calm down and get my palms to stop sweating.

Feathertail dragons are the breed we know the least about, I recite in my mind, needing every ounce of my lung capacity as I spring from the edge of the path onto the first ball, grasping it up top like Rhiannon did. The immediate strain on my shoulders makes me tense every muscle to keep the joints from dislocating.

Stay calm. Stay calm.

Throwing my weight, I force the ball to rotate, swinging me toward the next one. *This is because feathertails reportedly abhor violence and are not suitable for bonding.*

I repeat motions, grasping from one ball to the next, keeping my eyes on the chains and nothing else.

Though this scholar cannot be certain, as one has never left the Vale within my lifetime. I continue reciting from memory as I reach the fifth and final ball. With one last swing, I throw myself sideways, releasing the ball and landing on the shoulder-wide gravel path without rolling an ankle.

It's all momentum for the next ascent.

"Green dragons," I mutter under my breath, "known for their keen intellect, descend from the honorable Uaineloidsig line, and continue to be the most rational of dragonkind, making them the perfect siege weapons, especially in the case of clubtails." I finish as I line my body up with the first metal rod and get ready to sprint forward.

"Are you...*studying*?" Aurelie calls up from where she leaps onto the first ball below.

"Calms me down," I shoot back in quick explanation. There's no time to be embarrassed here—that can wait for later.

There are three iron rails in front of me, each lined up like a battering ram toward the next. "The Scribe Quadrant is looking pretty good right now," I grumble under my breath, then launch myself toward the first. At least the texture gives me something to keep hold of as I work my way hand over hand. The ache in my shoulders grows into a throbbing pain when I reach the end of the first rail, swinging my feet to work up the momentum for the next.

The first clang of iron as the rails meet makes my fingers slip, and I gasp as terror claws its way out of my stomach. *Orange dragons, coming in various shades of apricot to carrot, are the most*—I throw myself to the next rail—*unpredictable of dragonkind and therefore always a risk.* I move across the rail with the same hand-over-hand motion, ignoring the outright protests of my shoulders. *Descending from the Fhaicorain line—*

My right hand loses purchase and my weight swings me into the face of the steep mountainside, my cheek slamming into the rock. A high-pitched ringing erupts in my ears and my vision darkens at the edges.

"Violet!" Rhiannon shouts from the top.

"Next to you! The rope is next to you!" Aurelie calls up.

Iron scrapes my fingertips as my left hand slips, but I spot the rope and take hold, bracing my feet on the knot beneath me and clinging tight until the ringing fades in my head. I have to swing over or climb down.

I've survived seven weeks in this damned quadrant, and this course isn't going to beat me today.

Pushing off the edge, I swing out for the rail and make it, immediately starting the hand over hand to get me to the next one and then the next, until I finally let go, landing on the first shaking iron pillar. My brain is rattled as the thing shudders violently, and I leap to the next, barely gaining a foothold before jumping to the gravel path at the end of the ascent.

Aurelie is right behind me, landing with a grin. "This is the best!"

"You clearly need to see the healers. You must have hit your head if you think *this* is fun." My breaths are choppy gasps, but I can't help but smile at her obvious joy.

"Just run straight across this one," she says as we reach the twisting staircase posts jutting straight from the side of the cliff face.

Each three-foot-wide timber rotates from its base in one of the steepest sections of the course. I quickly calculate if you fall off one of the posts, you'd probably drop at least thirty or forty feet onto the rocky terrain below. I swallow down the terror trying to crawl up my throat and focus on the possibility my agility and lightness will give me an edge on this particular obstacle.

She continues. "Trust me. If you pause, it'll roll you right off."

I nod and bounce on my feet, dredging up whatever courage I have left. Then I run. My feet are quick, making contact with each post only long enough to push off for the next, and within a few heartbeats, I'm on the other side.

"Yes!" I shout, throwing my fist up in celebration as I get out of the way for Aurelie.

"Go, Violet!" she shouts. "Here I come!" Her footwork is more agile than mine as she springs from spinning post to post.

A roar sounds from overhead, and I jerk my gaze up just in time to see the underbelly of a Green Daggertail as it flies directly over us, headed back to the Vale.

I'm never going to get used to that.

Aurelie cries out and my head snaps toward hers just in time to see her wobble and slip on the fifth post. The air freezes in my lungs as she careens forward, her belly hitting the next-to-last spinning log as if in slow motion.

"Aurelie!" I scream, lunging for her, my fingertips skimming the seventh post.

Our eyes meet, shock and terror filling her wide black eyes as the post rolls her away from me and she falls. Halfway down the cliff.

The sun burns my eyes as we stand in morning formation.

"Calvin Atwater," Captain Fitzgibbons reads, his voice solemn like always.

First Squad, Claw Section, Fourth Wing. He sits two rows behind me in Battle Brief. *He sat.*

There's nothing special about this morning. Our first trial on the Gauntlet has made the roll longer, but it's just another list on just another day...except it's not. The exceptional cruelty of this ritual has never hit me this hard before. It's not like the first day anymore. I know more than half of the names as they're called. My vision blurs. "Newland Jahvon," he continues.

Second Squad, Flame Section, Fourth Wing. He had breakfast duty with me.

We have to be in the twenties by now. How can this be all there is? We say their names once and then go on as if they never existed?

Rhiannon shifts her weight at my side, and she abruptly sniffles, the motion jerking her shoulders once.

"Aurelie Donans."

A single tear escapes and I bat it away, ripping open one of the scabs along my cheek. A trickle of blood follows as the next name is called, but I let that one stain me.

• • •

"You're sure about this?" Dain asks the next night, two worried lines between his brows as he clasps my shoulders.

"If her parents aren't coming to bury her body, then I should be the one to handle her things. I'm the last person she saw," I explain, rolling my shoulders to adjust the weight of Aurelie's pack.

Every Basgiath parent has the same option when their cadet is killed. They can retrieve the body and personal effects for burial or burning or the school will put their body under a stone and burn their effects themselves. Aurelie's parents have chosen door number two.

"And you don't want me to go with you?" he asks, palming my neck.

I shake my head. "I know where the burn pit is."

He mutters a curse. "I should have been there."

"You couldn't have done anything, Dain," I say softly, covering his hand with mine so our fingers lightly lace. "None of us could have. She didn't even have time to reach for the rope," I whisper. I've replayed that moment over and over in my head, coming to the same conclusion each time.

"I never got the chance to ask you if you made it all the way up," he says.

I shake my head. "I got caught at the chimney formation and had to use a rope to get back down. I'm too short to span the distance, but I'm not thinking about that tonight. I'll figure something out before the official timed Gauntlet on Presentation day."

I'll have to. They don't allow cadets to climb back down on the final day. You either complete the Gauntlet—or you fall to your death.

"All right. Let me know if you need me." He lets me go.

I nod and make every excuse to get out of the dormitory hallway. The weight of Aurelie's pack is staggering. She was strong enough to carry so much over the parapet, and yet she fell.

And I'm somehow still standing.

I can't shake the feeling that I'm carrying her with me as I climb the stairs of the academic tower's turret, past the Battle Brief room and up to the stone roof, going by a few other cadets on their way down. The burn pit is nothing more than an extra-wide iron barrel, whose only purpose is to incinerate, and the flames burn bright against the night sky as I stumble out onto the roof, my lungs straining for oxygen.

A couple of months ago, I couldn't have carried a pack this heavy.

There's no one else up here as I slip the bag from my shoulder.

"I'm so sorry," I whisper, my fingers digging into the wide strap of the pack as I fling it up and over the metal edge of the bin.

The flames catch and *whoosh* as it becomes more fuel for the fire, just another tribute to Malek, the god of death.

Instead of walking back down the stairs, I make my way to the edge of the turret. It's a cloudy night, but I can make out the shadows of three dragons as they approach from the west and even see the ridge where the Gauntlet lays, waiting to claim its next victim.

It won't be me.

But why? Because I'll conquer it? Or because I'll give in to Dain's request and hide in the Scribe Quadrant? My entire being rebels against the second option, which makes me question everything as I stand here, letting minutes tick by before the bells sound for curfew. I climb back down the stairs without a solid answer as to why.

I walk through the courtyard, empty but for a couple who can't decide if they'd rather kiss or walk near the dais, and I avert my gaze, heading for the alcove where Dain and I first sat after Parapet.

It's almost been two months, and I'm still here. Still waking every morning to the sunrise. Doesn't that mean something? Isn't there a chance, no matter how small, that I might just be enough to make it through Threshing? That I might just belong here?

The door that leads to the tunnel we took to cross the ridgeline to the Gauntlet this morning opens along the courtyard wall, just left of the academic building, and my brow furrows. Who would be returning this late?

Sitting back against the wall, I let the darkness conceal me as Xaden, Garrick, and Bodhi—Xaden's cousin—pass under a mage light, headed in my direction.

Three dragons. They were out…doing what? There were no training ops that I know of tonight, not that I'm privy to everything third-years do.

"There has to be something more we can do," Bodhi argues, looking to Xaden, his voice low as they pass by me, their boots crunching on the gravel.

"We're doing everything we can," Garrick hisses.

My scalp prickles and Xaden stops mid-step ten feet away, the set of his shoulders rigid.

Shit.

He knows I'm here.

Instead of the usual fear that spikes in his presence, only anger rises in my chest. If he wants to kill me, then fine. I'm over waiting for it to happen.

Over walking through the halls in fear.

"What's wrong?" Garrick asks, immediately looking over his shoulder in the opposite direction, toward the couple who definitely decided making out is more important than getting into the dorms by curfew.

"Go on. I'll meet you inside," Xaden says.

"You sure?" Bodhi's forehead puckers, and his gaze sweeps over the courtyard.

"Go," Xaden orders, standing completely still until the other two walk into the barracks, turning left toward the stairwell that will take them to the second- and third-year floors. Only when they're gone does he turn and face the exact spot where I'm sitting.

"I know you know I'm here." I force myself to stand and move toward him so he doesn't think I'm hiding or worse—scared of him. "And please don't prattle on about commanding the dark. I'm not in the mood tonight."

"No questions about where I've been?" He folds his arms across his chest and studies me in the moonlight. His scar looks even more menacing in this light, but I can't seem to find the energy to be scared.

"I honestly don't care." I shrug, the movement making the throb in my shoulders intensify. *Awesome, just in time to practice on the Gauntlet tomorrow.*

He cocks his head to the side. "You really don't, do you?"

"Nope. It's not like I'm not out after curfew myself." A heavy sigh blows through my lips.

"What *are* you doing out after curfew, first-year?"

"Debating running away," I retort. "How about you? Feel like sharing?" I ask mockingly, knowing he's not about to answer me.

"The same."

Sarcastic ass.

"Look, are you going to kill me or not? The anticipation is starting to annoy the fuck out of me." I lift a hand to my shoulder and roll it, pressing in on the sore muscles, but it doesn't help the ache.

"Haven't decided yet," he answers, like I've just inquired about his dinner preferences, but his gaze narrows on my cheek.

"Well, could you?" I mutter. "It would definitely help me make my plans for the week." Markham or Emetterio. Scribe or rider.

"Am I affecting your schedule, Violence?" There's a definite smirk on those lips.

"I just need to know what my chances are here." My hands curl into fists.

The ass has the nerve to smile. "That's the oddest way I've ever been hit on—"

"Not my chances with *you*, you conceited prick!" Fuck this. Fuck *all* of this. I move past him, but he catches my wrist, his grip light but his hold firm.

His fingertips on my pulse make it skitter.

"Chances at what?" he asks, tugging me just close enough that my shoulder brushes his biceps.

"Nothing." He wouldn't understand. He's a damned *wingleader*, which means he's excelled at everything in the quadrant, even somehow managing to get past his own last name.

"Chances at *what*?" he repeats. "Do not make me ask three times." His ominous tone is at odds with his gentle grasp, and *shit*, does he have to smell so good? Like mint and leather and something I can't quite identify, something that borders between citrus and floral.

"At living through all of this! I can't make it up the damned Gauntlet." I half-heartedly tug at my wrist, but he doesn't let go.

"I see." He's so infuriatingly calm, and I can't even get a grip on *one* of my emotions.

"No, you don't. You're probably celebrating because I'll fall to my death and you won't have to go to the trouble of killing me."

"Killing you wouldn't be any trouble, Violence. It's leaving you alive that seems to cause the majority of my trouble."

My gaze swings up to clash with his, but his face is unreadable, cloaked in shadow, go figure.

"Sorry to be a hassle." Sarcasm drips from my voice. "You know the problem with this place?" I tug my arm back again, but he holds fast. "Besides you touching things that don't belong to you?" My eyes narrow on him.

"I'm sure you're going to tell me." My stomach flutters as his thumb brushes my pulse and he releases my wrist.

I answer before I can think better of it. "Hope."

"Hope?" He tips his head closer to mine, as if he wasn't sure he heard me right.

"Hope." I nod. "Someone like you would never get it, but I knew coming here was a death sentence. It didn't matter that I've been trained my entire life to enter the Scribe Quadrant; when General Sorrengail gives an order, you can't exactly ignore it." Gods, why am I running off at the mouth to this man? *What's the worst he'll do? Kill you?*

"Sure you can." He shrugs. "You just might not like the consequences."

I roll my eyes, and to my utter embarrassment, instead of pulling away now that I'm free, I lean in just a little, like I can siphon off some of his strength. He certainly has enough to spare.

"I knew what the odds were, and I came anyway, concentrating on that tiny percentage of a chance that I would live. And then I make it almost two months and I get…" I shake my head, clenching my jaw. "Hopeful." The word tastes sour.

"Ah. And then you lose a squadmate, and you can't quite get up the chimney, and you give up. I'm starting to see. It's not a flattering picture, but if you want to run off to the Scribe Quadrant—"

I gasp, fear punching a hole in my stomach. "How do you know about that?" If he knows…if he tells, Dain is in danger.

A wicked smile curves Xaden's perfect lips. "I know everything that goes on here." Darkness swirls around us. "Shadows, remember? They hear everything, see everything, *conceal* everything." The rest of the world disappears. He could do anything to me in here and no one would be the wiser.

"My mother would definitely reward you if you told her about Dain's plan," I say softly.

"She'd definitely reward *you* for telling her about my little…what did you call it? *Club*."

"I'm not going to tell her." The words sound defensive.

"I know. It's why you're still alive." He holds my gaze locked with his. "Here's the thing, Sorrengail. Hope is a fickle, dangerous thing. It steals your focus and aims it toward the possibilities instead of keeping it where it belongs—on the probabilities."

"So I'm supposed to what? Not hope that I live? Just plan for death?"

"You're supposed to focus on the things that can kill you so you find ways to *not* die." He shakes his head. "I can barely count the number of people in this quadrant who want you dead, either as revenge against your mother or because you're just really good at pissing people off, but you're still here, defying the odds." Shadows wrap around me, and I swear I feel a caress along the side of my wounded cheek. "It's been rather surprising to watch, actually."

"Happy to be your entertainment. I'm going to bed." Spinning on my heel, I head toward the entrance to the barracks, but he's right behind me, close enough that the door would slam in his face if he wasn't so unnaturally fast at catching it.

"Maybe if you stopped sulking in your self-pity, you'd see that you have *everything* you need to scale the Gauntlet," he calls after me, his voice echoing down the hallway.

"My self-*what*?" I turn around, my jaw dropping.

"People die," he says slowly, his jaw ticking before he drags in a deep breath. "It's going to happen over and over again. It's the nature of what happens here. What makes you a rider is what you do *after* people die. You want to know why you're still alive? Because you're the scale I currently judge myself against every night. Every day I let you live, I get to convince myself that there's still a part of me that's a decent person. So if you want to quit, then please, spare me the temptation and fucking *quit*. But if you want to do something, then do it."

"I'm too short to span the distance!" I hiss, uncaring that anyone could hear us.

"The right way isn't the only way. Figure it out." Then he turns and walks away.

Fuck. Him.

It is a grave offense against Malek to keep the belongings of a dead loved one. They belong in the beyond with the god of death and the departed. In the absence of a proper temple, any fire will do. He who does not burn for Malek will be burned *by* Malek.

—Major Rorilee's Guide to Appeasing the Gods, Second Edition

CHAPTER ELEVEN

The next practice sessions of the Gauntlet are no more successful than my first, but at least we don't lose another squadmate. Tynan has quit running his mouth, since he can't seem to make it up fully, either.

The buoy balls are his downfall.

The chimney is mine.

By the ninth—and next-to-last—session, I'm ready to set the entire obstacle course on fire. The section of the course that's my downfall is meant to simulate the strength and agility it takes to mount a dragon, and it's becoming clear that my size is going to fuck me.

"Maybe you can climb up onto my shoulders and then…" Rhiannon shakes her head as we study the crevice that's become my nemesis.

"Then I'm still stuck halfway up," I answer, wiping the sweat from my forehead.

"Doesn't matter. You can't touch another cadet on the route." Sawyer folds his arms beside me, the tip of his nose now bright red from the high sun.

"Are you here to squash hopes and dreams, or do you have a suggestion?" Rhiannon retorts. "Because Presentation is tomorrow, so if you've got any bright ideas, now is the time."

If I'm going to run to the Scribe Quadrant, then tonight is the night. My heart clenches against the thought. It's the logical choice. The safe choice.

There are only two thoughts stopping me.

One, there's no guarantee my mother won't find out. Just because Markham would keep quiet doesn't mean the instructors there will.

But most importantly, if I go, if I hide…I'll never know if I'm good enough to make it here. And while I might not survive if I stay, I'm not sure I can live with myself if I leave.

"Doria Merrill," Captain Fitzgibbons says from the dais. Every one of his features is crystal clear, not only because the sun is behind the shade of the clouds but because I'm closer. Our formation gets tighter with every cadet who falls.

According to Brennan and statistics, today will be one of the deadliest for first-years.

It's Presentation Day, and in order to get to the flight field, we'll have to climb the Gauntlet first. Everything about the Riders Quadrant is designed to weed out the weak, and today is no exception.

"Kamryn Dyre." Captain Fitzgibbons continues to read from the roll.

I flinch. His seat was across from mine in Dragonkind.

"Arvel Pelipa."

Imogen and Quinn—both second-years—suck in a breath ahead of me. First-years aren't the only ones at risk; we're just the most likely to die.

"Michel Iverem." Captain Fitzgibbons closes the roll. "We commend their souls to Malek." And with that final word, formation breaks.

"Second- and third-years, unless you're on Gauntlet duty, head to class. First-years, it's time to show us what you've got." Dain forces a smile and skips right over me as he looks at our squad.

"Good luck today." Imogen tucks an errant strand of pink hair behind her ear and aims a sickly-sweet smile right at me. "Hopefully you won't fall…short."

"See you later," I reply, lifting my chin.

She stares at me with complete loathing for a second, then walks off with Quinn and Cianna, our executive officer, her shoulder-length blond curls bouncing.

"Best of luck." Heaton—the thickest third-year in our squad, with red flames cut and dyed into their hair—taps their heart, right over two of their patches, and offers us all a genuine but flat-lipped smile before heading to class.

As I stare at their retreating back, I wonder what the circular patch on their upper right arm with water and floating spheres means. I know the triangular patch to the left of that one, with the longsword, means they're not to be messed with on the mat. Since Dain told me about the patch denoting his top secret signet, I've been paying close attention to the patches other cadets have sewn into their uniforms. Most wear them like badges of honor, but I recognize them for what they really are—intelligence that I might one day need to defeat them.

"I didn't realize Heaton actually knew how to speak." Two lines appear between Ridoc's brows.

"Maybe they figure they should at least say hi before we're potentially roasted today," Rhiannon says.

"Back into formation," Dain orders.

"Are you going with us?" I ask.

He nods, still not looking at me.

The eight of us fall into two lines of four, the same as the other squads around us.

"Awkward," Rhiannon whispers from my side. "He seems kind of pissed at you."

I glance up over Trina's slim shoulders as the breeze whips at the braid I've woven like a crown. It's working a few of Trina's ringlet curls loose, too. "He wants something I can't give him."

Her eyebrows rise.

I roll my eyes. "Not like…that."

"I wouldn't care if it *was* like that," she replies under her breath. "He's hot. He has that whole boy-next-door-who-can-still-kick-your-ass vibe going for him."

I fight a smile because she's right. He so does.

"We're the biggest squad," Ridoc notes behind us as the squads farthest left—from First Wing—file out through the western gate in the courtyard.

"What are we down to?" Tynan asks. "Hundred and eighty?"

"Hundred and seventy-one," Dain answers. Squads from Second Wing begin to move, led by their wingleader, which means Xaden is somewhere ahead of us.

My nerves are reserved for the obstacle course, but I can't help but wonder which way his scales will tip today.

"For a hundred dragons? But what will we…" Trina asks, nerves cutting off her words.

"Stop letting fear leach into your voice," Luca snaps from behind Rhiannon. "If the dragons think you're a coward, you'll be nothing but a name tomorrow."

"She says," Ridoc narrates, "inducing more fear."

"Shut up," Luca fires back. "You know it's true."

"Just portray confidence, and I'm sure you'll be fine." I lean forward so our squadmates behind us can't hear me as Third Wing begins to march for the gate.

"Thanks," Trina whispers in reply.

Dain's narrowed gaze finally locks on mine, but at least he doesn't call me a liar. There's enough accusation in his eyes that I might as well be tried and convicted of it, though.

"Nervous, Rhi?" I ask, knowing we're about to be called next.

"For you?" she asks. "Not at all. We've got this."

"Oh, I meant about the history test tomorrow," I tease. "There's nothing going on today to panic about."

"Now that you mention it, the whole Treaty of Arif might just be the death of me." She grins.

"Ahh, the agreement between Navarre and Krovla for mutually shared airspace for both dragons and gryphons over a narrow strip of the Esben Mountains, between Sumerton and Draithus," I recall, nodding.

"Your memory is terrifying." She shoots me a smile.

But my memory isn't going to get me up the Gauntlet.

"Fourth Wing!" Xaden calls out from somewhere in the distance. I don't even need to see to know that it's him who gave the order and not his executive officer. "Move out!"

We file off, Flame Section, then Claw, and finally Tail.

There's a bit of a bottleneck at the gate, but then we're through, walking into the mage-lit dimness of the tunnel that we take every morning to reach the Gauntlet. Shadows blanket the edges of the rocky floor along our path.

What are the limits of Xaden's power anyway? Could he use shadows to choke out every squad in here? Would he need to rest or recharge after? Does such a vast power come with any sort of checks or balances?

Dain falls back so he walks between Rhiannon and me. "Change your mind." It's barely a whisper.

"No." I sound way more confident than I feel.

"Change. Your. Mind." His hand finds mine, concealed by our tight formation as we descend through the passage. "Please."

"I can't." I shake my head. "Any more than you would leave Cath and run to the scribes yourself."

"That's different." His hand squeezes mine, and I can feel the tension in his fingers, his arm. "I'm a rider."

"Well, maybe I am, too," I whisper as light appears ahead. I didn't believe it before, not when I couldn't leave because my mother wouldn't let me, but now I have a choice. And I choose to stay.

"Don't be—" He cuts himself off and drops my hand. "I don't want to bury you, Vi."

"It's inevitable that one of us will have to bury the other." It's not macabre, just fact.

"You know what I mean."

The light grows into an archway that's ten feet high, leading us to the base of the Gauntlet.

"Please don't do this," Dain begs, not bothering to lower his voice this time as we emerge into the mottled sunlight.

The view is spectacular as always. We're still high on the mountain, thousands of feet above the valley, and the greenery seems to stretch endlessly to the south, with random clusters of squat trees among colorful slopes of wildflowers. My gaze turns to the Gauntlet carved into the face of the cliff, and I can't help but follow each obstacle higher and higher until I'm staring at the top of the ridgeline that the maps I've studied show leads into a box canyon—the flight field. I bite my lip as I stare at the break in the tree line.

Normally, only riders are allowed on the flight field—except for Presentation.

"I don't know if I can watch," Dain says, drawing my attention back to his strong face. His perfectly trimmed beard brackets full lips drawn tight into a frown.

"Then close your eyes." I have a plan—a shitty one, but it's worth a try.

"What changed between Parapet and now?" Dain asks again, a wealth of emotions in his eyes that I can't begin to interpret. Well, except the fear. That doesn't need any interpretation.

"Me."

An hour later, my feet fly over the spinning posts of the staircase, and I jump to the safety of the gravel path. Third ascent complete. Two more to go. And I haven't touched a single rope.

I swear I can feel Dain staring from the bottom of the course, where Tynan and Luca have yet to start their climb, but I don't look down. There's no time for what he thinks will be one last look, and I can't afford the delay of comforting him when there are still two obstacles ahead of me.

Which means there's one I haven't even had the chance to practice—the nearly vertical ramp at the end.

"You can do it!" Rhiannon yells from the top as I reach the chimney structure.

"Or you can do us all a favor and fall!" another voice yells. Jack, no doubt. At least it's only been our squad at practice sessions, but every first-year can watch now, either from the base of the course or the edges of the cliff above.

I look up at the hollow column I'm supposed to climb, then dart back a few feet along the path.

"What are you doing?" Rhiannon shouts as I grab one of the ropes and drag it horizontally across the surface of the cliff, sending pebbles into free fall.

It's heavy as hell and protests the stretch, but I manage to get the bottom portion onto the chimney structure. Pulling the rope as tight as it can go, I plant one foot on the side of the shaft and give the rope a tug, then send up a prayer to Zihnal that this is going to work.

"Can she *do* that?" someone snaps.

I'm doing it now.

Then I lift my other foot and begin to climb up the chimney, using only the right side, walking up stone and leveraging my weight with the rope, hand over hand. The line slips about halfway up as the rope scrapes over a large boulder, but I quickly take up the slack and keep climbing. My heart thunders in my ears, but it's my hands that are killing me. It feels like flames are eating my palms, and I grit my teeth so I don't cry out.

There it is. The top.

The rope barely cuts the corner of the structure now, and I use what's left of my upper-body strength to pull myself up, scrambling to my hands and knees on the path.

"Hell yes!" Ridoc yells, hooting from the top. "That's our girl!"

"Get up!" Rhiannon shouts. "One more!"

My chest heaves and my lungs ache, but I make it to my feet. I'm on the last ascent, the final path to the flight field, and standing in front of me is a ramp made of wood that juts out ten feet from the cliff wall, then curves upward like the inside of a bowl, the highest point level with the cliff top ten feet above.

The obstacle is meant to test a cadet's ability to scale a dragon's foreleg and reach its saddle. And I'm too short.

But Xaden's words that the right way wasn't the only way have played over and over in my head all night long. By the time the sun rose and chased away the darkness, I had a plan.

I only hope I can actually pull it off.

I unsheathe my largest dagger from home and wipe away the sweat on my forehead with the back of my dirty palm. Then I forget the agony in my hands, the throbbing of my shoulders, and the twinge in my knee from landing wrong after the pillars. I block out all the pain, lock it behind a wall like I've done my entire life, and focus on the ramp as though my life depends on making it.

There's no rope here. There's only one way I'm getting over this.

Sheer fucking will.

And so I charge, using my speed to my advantage.

There's a drumlike sound as my feet beat against the ramp and the incline sharpens. Just because I haven't personally conquered this obstacle doesn't mean I haven't watched my squadmates take it over and over again. I throw my body forward and momentum carries me upward, running up the side of the ramp.

I wait until I feel the precious shift, the moment gravity reclaims my body almost two feet from the top, and I swing my arm up and slam my dagger into the slick, soft wood of the ramp—and use it to fling myself the last foot upward.

A primal scream rips from my throat as my shoulder cries in protest just as my fingers graze the lip of the edge. I throw my elbow over the top to gain more leverage and pull myself up and over, using the handle of my dagger as a final step before lurching onto the top of the cliff.

Not done yet.

On my stomach, I turn to face the ramp, then reach over the side and yank my dagger free, sheathing it at my ribs before I stagger to my feet. I made it. Relief sucks the adrenaline straight out of my body.

Rhiannon's arms sweep around me, taking my weight as I gasp for air. Ridoc hugs my back, squeezing me like I'm the filling of a sandwich as he hollers in happiness. I'd protest, but right now they're all that's keeping me upright.

"She can't do that!" someone shouts.

"Yeah, well, she just did!" Ridoc tosses over his shoulder, loosening his grip on me.

My knees shake, but they hold as I suck in breath after breath.

"You made it!" Rhiannon takes my face in her hands, tears filling her brown eyes. "You made it!"

"Luck." I draw in another breath and beg my galloping heart to slow. "And. Adrenaline."

"Cheating!"

I turn toward the voice. It's Amber Mavis, the strawberry-blond wingleader from Third Wing who was Dain's *close friend* last year, and there's nothing but fury on her face as she charges toward Xaden, who's only a couple of feet away with the roll, recording times with a stopwatch and looking rather bored with it all.

"Back the hell up, Mavis," Garrick threatens, the sun flashing off the two swords the curly-haired section leader keeps strapped to his back as he puts his body between Amber and Xaden.

"The cheater clearly used foreign materials not once but *twice*," Amber yells. "It's not to be tolerated! We live by the rules or we die by them!"

No wonder she and Dain are so close—they're both in love with the Codex.

"I don't take kindly to calling anyone in my section a cheater," Garrick warns, his massive shoulders blocking her from view as he turns. "And my *wingleader* will handle any rule-breaking in his own wing." He moves to the side, and I'm met with Amber's glaring blue eyes.

"Sorrengail?" Xaden asks, arching an eyebrow in obvious challenge, a pen poised over the book. I notice not for the first time that other than his Fourth Wing and wingleader emblems, he doesn't wear the patches others are so fond of displaying.

"I expect the thirty-second penalty for using the rope," I answer, my breaths steadying.

"And the knife?" Amber's gaze narrows. "She's disqualified." When Xaden doesn't answer, she turns that glare on him. "Surely she's out! You can't tolerate lawlessness within your own wing, Riorson!"

But Xaden's gaze never leaves mine as he silently waits for me to respond.

"A rider may only bring to the quadrant the items they can carry—" I start.

"Are you quoting the Codex to *me*?" Amber shouts.

"—and they shall not be separated from those items no matter what they may be," I continue. "For once carried across the parapet, they are considered part of their person. Article Three, Section Six, Addendum B."

Her blue eyes flare wide as I glance at her. "That addendum was written to make thievery an executional offense."

"Correct." I nod, looking between her and the onyx eyes that see straight through me. "But in doing so, it gave any item carried across the parapet the status of being a part of the rider." I unsheathe the chipped and battered blade with a sharp bite of pain in my palms. "This isn't a challenge blade. It's one I carried across and therefore considered part of myself."

His eyes flare, and I don't miss the hint of a smirk on that infuriatingly decadent mouth of his. It should be against the Codex to look *that* good and be so ruthless.

"The right way isn't the only way." I use his own words against him.

Xaden holds my gaze. "She has you, Amber."

"On a technicality!"

"She still has you." He turns slightly and delivers a look that I never want directed at me.

"You think like a scribe," she barks at me.

It's intended as an insult, but I just nod. "I know."

She marches off, and I sheathe the dagger again, letting my hands fall to my sides and closing my eyes as relief shucks the weight from my shoulders. I did it. I passed another test.

"Sorrengail," Xaden says, and my eyes fly open. "You're leaking." His gaze drops pointedly to my hands.

Where blood is dripping from my fingertips.

Pain erupts, pushing past my mental dam like a raging river at the sight of the mess I've made of my palms. I've shredded them.

"Do something about it," he orders.

I nod and back away, joining my squad. Rhiannon helps me cut off the sleeves of my shirt to bandage my hands, and I cheer our last two squadmates up the cliff.

We all make it.

Presentation Day is unlike any other. The air is ripe with possibilities, and possibly the stench of sulfur from a dragon who has been offended. Never look a red in the eye. Never back down from a green. If you show trepidation to a brown...well, just don't.

—Colonel Kaori's Field Guide to Dragonkind

CHAPTER TWELVE

There are 169 of us by the time the morning is done and, even with my penalty for the rope, we've placed eleventh out of the thirty-six squads for Presentation—the piss-inducing parade of cadets before this year's dragons willing to bond.

Anxiety seizes my legs at the thought of walking so close to dragons determined to weed out the weak before Threshing, and I suddenly wish we'd placed last.

The fastest up the Gauntlet was Liam Mairi, of course, earning him the Gauntlet patch. Pretty sure that guy doesn't know how to take second place, but I wasn't the slowest, and that's good enough for me.

The box canyon that makes up the training field is spectacular in the afternoon sun, with miles of autumn-colored meadows and peaks rising on three sides of us as we wait at the narrowest part, the entrance to the valley. At the end, I can make out the line of the waterfall that might be just a trickle of a creek now but will rush at runoff season.

The leaves of the trees are all turning gold, as though someone has brought in a paintbrush with only one color and streaked it across the landscape.

And then there are the dragons.

Averaging twenty-five feet tall, they're in a formation of their own, lined up several feet back from the path—close enough to pass judgment on us as we walk by.

"Let's go, Second Squad, you're up next," Garrick says, beckoning us with a wave that makes the rebellion relic on his bared forearm gleam.

Dain and the other squad leaders stayed behind. I'm not sure if he'll be thrilled I made it up the Gauntlet or disappointed that I bent the rules. But *I've* never felt more thrilled.

"Into formation," Garrick orders, his tone all business, which doesn't surprise me given that his leadership style is more mission first, niceties last. Go figure he seems to be so close to Xaden. Unlike Xaden, though, the right side of his uniform has a neat line of patches proclaiming him Flame's section leader as well as more than five patches advertising his skill with a multitude of weapons.

We comply, and Rhiannon and I end up near the back this time.

There's a sound like rushing wind in the distance that stops as quickly as it starts, and I know someone else has been found lacking.

Garrick's hazel eyes skim over us. "Hopefully Aetos has done his job, so you know that it's a straight walk down the meadow. I'd recommend staying at least seven feet apart—"

"In case one of us gets torched," Ridoc mutters from ahead.

"Correct, Ridoc. Cluster if you want, just know if a dragon finds disfavor with one of you, it's likely to burn the whole lot to weed one out," Garrick warns, holding our gazes for a beat. "Also, remember you're not here to approach them, and if you do, you won't be making it back to the dormitory tonight."

"Can I ask a question?" Luca says from the front row.

Garrick nods, but the ticking of his jaw says he's annoyed. I can't blame him. Luca annoys the shit out of me, too. It's her constant need to tear everyone down that makes most of us keep our distance.

"Third Squad, Tail Section of Fourth Wing already went through, and I talked to some of the cadets..."

"That's not a question." He lifts his brows.

Yep, he's annoyed.

"Right. It's just that they said there's a feathertail?" Her voice pitches upward.

"A f-feathertail?" Tynan sputters from directly in front of me. "Who the hell would ever want to bond a feathertail?"

I roll my eyes, and Rhiannon shakes her head.

"Professor Kaori never told us there would be a feathertail," Sawyer says. "I know because I memorized every single dragon he showed us. All hundred of them."

"Well, guess there's a hundred and one now," Garrick replies, looking at us as if we're children he'd like to be rid of before glancing back over his shoulder at the entrance to the valley. "Relax. Feathertails don't bond. I can't even remember the last time one has been seen outside the Vale. It's probably just curious. You're up. Stay on the path. You walk up, you wait for the entire squad, you walk back down. It really doesn't get any easier than this from here on out, kids, so if you can't follow those simple instructions, then you deserve whatever happens in there." He turns and heads over to a path before the canyon wall where the dragons are perched.

We follow, breaking away from the crowd of first-years. The breeze bites at my bare shoulders from where we ripped my sleeves for bandages, but we got the blood flow stopped at my hands.

"They're all yours," Garrick says to the quadrant's senior wingleader, a woman I've seen a few times in Battle Brief murmuring to Xaden. Her uniform still has her signature spikes on the shoulders, but this time they're gold and look sharp as hell—like she wanted to throw in a little extra badass today.

She nods and dismisses him. "Single file."

We all shuffle into a line. Rhiannon is at my back and Tynan just ahead of me, which means I'll be treated to his commentary the whole time, no doubt. *Awesome.*

"Talk," the senior wingleader says, folding her arms across her chest.

"Nice day for a Presentation," Ridoc jokes.

"Not to me." The senior wingleader narrows her gaze on Ridoc, then motions to the line of cadets before her. "Talk to your nearby squadmates while you're on the path, as it will help the dragons get a sense of who you are and how well you play with others. There's a correlation between bonded cadets and level of chatter."

And now I want to switch places.

"Feel free to look at the dragons, especially if they're showing off their tails, but I would abstain from eye contact if you value your life. If you come across a scorch mark, just make sure nothing's currently on fire before continuing along." She pauses long enough for that bit of advice to sink in, then adds, "See you after your stroll."

With a sweep of her hand, the senior wingleader steps to the side, revealing the dirt path that leads through the center of the valley, and up ahead, sitting so perfectly still that they might be gargoyles, are the hundred and one dragons who have decided to bond this year.

The line starts, and we give one another the suggested seven feet before following.

I'm hyperaware of every step as I walk down the path. The trail is hard beneath my boots, and there's a definite lingering odor of sulfur.

We pass a trio of red dragons first. Their talons are almost half my size.

"I can't even see their tails!" Tynan shouts from in front of me. "How are we supposed to know what breed they are?"

I keep my eyes locked at the level of their massive, muscled shoulders as we walk by. "We're not supposed to know what breed they are," I respond.

"Fuck that," he says over his shoulder. "I need to figure out which one I'm going to approach during Threshing."

"Pretty sure this little walk is so *they* can decide," I retort.

"Hopefully one of them will decide you don't get to make it to Threshing," Rhiannon says, her voice quiet so it barely reaches me.

I laugh as we approach a set of browns, both slightly smaller than my mother's Aimsir, but not by much.

"They're a little bigger than I thought they would be," Rhiannon says, her voice rising. "Not that I didn't see the ones at Parapet, but..."

I look over my shoulder to see her wide gaze flickering between the path and the dragons. She's nervous.

"So do you know if you're having a niece or nephew?" I ask, continuing to walk forward past a handful of oranges.

"What?" she answers.

"I've heard some of the healers can make pretty good guesses once a woman is further along in her pregnancy."

"Oh. No," she says. "No clue. Though I'm kind of hoping she'll have a girl. I guess I'll find out once we finish the year and can write our families."

"That's a bullshit rule," I say over my shoulder, lowering my gaze immediately when I accidentally make eye contact with one of the oranges. *Breathe normally. Swallow the fear.* Fear and weakness will get me killed, and since I'm already bleeding, the odds aren't exactly in my favor here.

"You don't think it encourages loyalty to the wing?" Rhiannon asks.

"I think I'm just as loyal to my sister whether I've had a letter from her or not," I counter. "There are bonds that can't be broken."

"I'd be loyal to your sister, too," Tynan says, turning around and grinning as he walks backward. "She's one hell of a rider, and that *ass*. I saw her right before Parapet and damn, Violet. She's *hot*."

We pass by another set of reds, then a single brown and a pair of greens.

"Turn around." I make the spinning motion with my finger. "Mira would eat you for breakfast, Tynan."

"I'm just wondering how one of you got all the good traits and the other looks like she got the leftovers." His gaze skims down my body.

Full-body-shudder gross.

"You're an asshole." I flip him the middle finger.

"Just saying, maybe I'll write a letter of my own once we get privileges." He turns and continues walking.

"A nephew would be good," Rhiannon says, like the conversation was never interrupted. "Boys aren't too bad."

"My brother was awesome, but he and Dain are my only experience with growing up around little boys." We pass more dragons, and my breathing starts to settle. The smell of sulfur disappears, or maybe I've just grown accustomed to it. They're close enough to torch us, the half dozen singe marks testify to that, but I can't hear them breathing or feel it, either. "Though I think Dain was probably a little more rule-abiding than most kids. He likes order and pretty much detests anything that doesn't fit neatly into his plan. He's probably going to give me shit about how I got up the Gauntlet, just like Amber Mavis did."

We pass the halfway mark and continue.

Is the way the dragons stare at us scary as hell? Absolutely, but they want to be here the same as we do, so at least I hope they'll be judicious with their firepower.

"Why didn't you tell me about the rope plan? Or the dagger?" Rhiannon asks, hurt pitching her tone. "You can trust me, you know."

"I didn't think of it until yesterday," I answer, taking the time to look over my shoulder so I can see her. "And if it didn't work, I didn't want you to be an accomplice. You have a real future here, and I refuse to bring you down with me if I didn't make it."

"I don't need you to protect me."

"I know. But it's just what friends do, Rhi." I shrug as we walk by a trio of browns, the soft crunch of our boots on the dark gravel path the only sound for a few minutes.

"You keeping any other secrets up there?" Rhiannon eventually asks.

Guilt settles in my stomach when I think of Xaden and his meeting with the other marked ones. "I think it's impossible to know everything there is to know about someone." I feel like shit but keep from lying, at least.

She snorts a laugh. "If that wasn't skirting the question. How about this? Promise me that if you need help, you'll let me give it to you."

A smile spreads across my face despite the terrifying greens we're walking by. "How about this," I toss over my shoulder. "I promise that if I need help you're capable of giving, I'll ask, but only"—I hold up my forefinger—"if you promise the same."

"Deal." She smiles wide.

"You guys done bonding back there?" Tynan sneers. "Because we're almost to the end of the line, if you haven't noticed." He pauses in the middle of the path, his gaze swinging right. "And I still can't figure out which one I'm going to choose."

"With arrogance like that, I'm sure any dragon would feel lucky to share your mind for the rest of your life." I pity whatever dragon—if any—chooses him.

The rest of the squad is gathered ahead of us, facing our direction at the end of the path, but all their attention is focused to the right.

We pass the last brown dragon, and I inhale sharply.

"What the hell?" Tynan stares.

"Keep walking," I order, but my gaze is transfixed.

Standing at the end of the line is a small *golden* dragon. Sunlight reflects off its scales and horns as it stands to its full height, flicking a feathered tail around the side of its body. *The feathertail.*

My jaw drops as I take in the sharp teeth and quick, darting movements of its head as it studies us. At its full height, it's probably only a few feet taller than I am, like a perfect miniature of the brown next to it.

I walk straight into Tynan's back and startle. We've reached the end of the path, where the rest of the squad has been waiting.

"Get off me, Sorrengail," Tynan hisses and shoves me back. "Who the hell would bond that thing?"

My chest tightens. "They can hear you," I remind him.

"It's fucking *yellow*." Luca points right at the dragon, disgust curling her lip. "So not only is it obviously too small to carry a rider in battle, but it's not even powerful enough to be a real color."

"Maybe it's a mistake," Sawyer says quietly. "Maybe it's a baby orange."

"It's full grown," Rhiannon argues. "There's no way the other dragons allow a baby to bond. No human alive has ever *seen* a baby."

"It's a mistake all right." Tynan looks at the golden one and scoffs. "You should totally bond it, Sorrengail. You're both freakishly weak. It's a match made in heaven."

"It looks powerful enough to burn you to death," I counter, heat flushing my cheeks. He called me *weak*, and not just in front of our squad but in front of *them.*

Sawyer lunges between us, grabbing Tynan's collar. "Don't ever say that about a squadmate, especially not in front of unbonded dragons."

"Let him go—he's just saying what we're all thinking," Luca mutters.

I turn slowly to stare at her, my mouth slightly agape. Is this what happens to us the second we're out of hearing range of any superior cadet? We turn on one another.

"What?" She gestures to my hair. "Half your hair is silver and you're… petite," she finishes with a fake smile. "Golden and…small. You match."

Trina puts her hand on Sawyer's arm. "Don't make a mistake in front of them. We don't know what they'll do," she whispers. And now we're grouped up.

I shuffle backward a little as Sawyer drops Tynan's collar.

"Someone should kill it before it bonds," Tynan sputters, and for the first time in my life, I actually want to kick someone while they're down… and keep kicking until they stay down. "It's just going to get its rider killed, and it's not like we get a choice if it wants to bond us."

"You're just picking up on that now, are you?" Ridoc shakes his head.

"We should go back," Pryor says, his gaze darting around the group. "I mean…if you think we should. We don't have to, of course."

"For once in your life," Tynan says, pushing past Pryor to start down the path, "make a damn decision, Pryor."

We take off one by one, leaving the suggested space between us. Rhiannon goes before me this time and Ridoc follows behind, with Luca bringing up the rear.

"They're pretty incredible, aren't they?" Ridoc says, and the wonder in his voice makes me smile.

"They are," I agree.

"They're honestly a little underwhelming after seeing that blue at Parapet." Luca's voice carries all the way to Rhiannon, who turns around with an incredulous look.

"Like this isn't stressful enough without you insulting them?" Rhi asks.

I need to defuse this quickly. "I mean, it could be worse. We could be walking past a line of wyvern, right?"

"Oh please, Violet, do give us one of your nervous-babble story times," Luca says sarcastically. "Let me guess. Wyvern are some elite squad of gryphon riders created because of something we did at a battle only you can manage to remember with your scribe brain."

"You don't know what a wyvern is?" Rhi asks, then begins walking again. "Didn't your parents tell you bedtime stories, Luca?"

"Do enlighten me," Luca drawls.

I roll my eyes, continuing along the path. "They're folklore," I say over my shoulder. "Kind of like dragons but bigger, with two feet instead of four, a mane of razor-sharp feathers streaking down their necks, and a taste for humans. Unlike dragons, who think we're a little gamey."

"My mom used to love telling my sister Raegan and me that we'd be plucked right off the front porch by one if we talked back, and their eerie-eyed venin riders would take us prisoner if we took treats we weren't allowed to have," Rhi says, flashing a grin at me, and I can't help but notice that her step is lighter.

Mine is, too. I notice each dragon as we pass, but my heartbeat steadies. "My dad used to read to me those fables every night," I tell her. "And I seriously asked him one time if Mom was going to turn into a venin because she could channel."

Rhiannon chuckles as we walk by a set of glaring reds. "Did he tell you people supposedly only turn into venin if they channel directly from the source?"

"He did, but it was after my mom had a really long night while we were stationed near the eastern border, and her eyes were bloodshot red, so I freaked out and started shrieking." I can't help but smile at the memory. "She took my book of fables away for a *month* because the outpost guards all came running, and I was hiding behind my brother, who couldn't stop laughing, and, well…it was a mess." I keep my eyes front and center as a large orange sniffs the air when I pass.

Rhiannon's shoulders shake with laughter. "I wish we'd had a book like that. I seriously think Mom just altered the stories to scare us whenever we stepped out of line."

"That sounds like some border-village nonsense." Luca scoffs. "Venin? Wyvern? Anyone with a modicum of education knows that our wards stop all magic that isn't channeled directly from dragons."

"They're *stories*, Luca," Rhi says over her shoulder, and I can't help but notice how much ground we've covered. "Pryor, you can walk a little faster if you want up there."

"Maybe we should slow down and take our time?" Pryor suggests from ahead of Rhiannon, rubbing his palms along the sides of his uniform. "Or I guess we can go faster if we want to get out of here."

A red steps out of line, putting one claw forward toward us, and my stomach drops to the ground from the weight of the dread filling my entire body. "No, no, no," I whisper, freezing in place, but it's too late.

The red opens its mouth, exposing sharp, glistening fangs, and fire erupts along the sides of its tongue, streaming through the air and into the path ahead of Rhiannon.

She yells in shock.

Heat blasts the front of my face.

Then it's over.

The scent of sulfur and burned grass...burned...*something* fills my lungs, and I see a charred patch of ground in front of Rhiannon that hadn't been there before.

"Are you all right, Rhi?" I call forward.

She nods, but the movement is hurried and jerky. "Pryor is... He's..."

Pryor's dead. My mouth waters like I'm going to vomit, but I breathe in through my nose and out through my mouth until the feeling passes.

"Keep walking!" Sawyer shouts from farther down the path.

"It's all right, Rhi. You just have to..." She just has to *what*? Walk over his corpse? Is there a corpse?

"Fire's out," Rhiannon says over her shoulder.

I nod, because there's nothing I can say to reassure her.

Holy shit are we insignificant.

She walks forward and I follow, maneuvering around the pile of ash that used to be Pryor.

"Oh my gods, the *smell*," Luca complains.

"Could you please have some level of decency?" I snap, turning around to level a glare at her, but Ridoc's face makes me pause.

His eyes are as wide as saucers, and his mouth hangs open. "Violet."

It's a whisper, and I wonder briefly if I heard him as much as I saw the word forming on his lips.

"Vi—"

A warm huff of steam blows against the back of my neck. My heart thunders, the beat increasing erratically as I take what might be my last breath and turn toward the line of dragons.

The golden eyes of not one but two greens meet mine, consuming my field of vision.

Oh. Fuck.

To approach a green dragon, lower your eyes in supplication and wait for their approval. That's what I read, right?

I drop my gaze as one chuffs another breath at me. It's hot and appallingly wet, but I'm not dead yet, so that's a plus.

The one on the right chortles deep in its throat. Wait, is that the sound of approval I'm looking for? Shit, I wish I'd asked Mira.

Mira. She's going to be devastated when she reads the rolls.

I lift my head and suck in a sharp breath. They're even closer. The one on the left nudges my hands with its giant nose, but I somehow stand my ground, rocking back on my heels to keep from falling over.

Greens are the most reasonable.

"I cut my hands climbing the obstacle course." I lift my palms, like they can see through the black fabric binding my wounds.

The one on the right sets its nose right at my breasts and chuffs again.

What. The. Hell.

It inhales, making that noise in its throat, and the other shoves its nose into my ribs, making me raise my arms just in case they feel like taking a little nibble.

"Violet!" Rhiannon whisper-shouts.

"I'm all right!" I call back, then wince, hoping I didn't just seal my fate by screaming in their ears.

Another chuff. Another chortle, like they're talking to each other as they sniff me.

The one under my arm moves its nostrils to my back and sniffs again.

Realization hits and I choke out a tight, surreal laugh. "You smell Teine, don't you?" I ask quietly.

They both draw back, just far enough for me to look them in their golden eyes, but they keep their jaws shut, giving me the courage to keep talking.

"I'm Mira's sister, Violet." Slowly lowering my arms, I run my hands over my snot-covered vest and the armor carefully sewn into it. "She collected Teine's scales after he shed them last year and had them shrunk down so she could sew them into the vest to help keep me safe."

The one on the right blinks.

The one on the left sticks its nose in again, sniffing loudly.

"The scales have saved me a few times," I whisper. "But no one else knows they're in there. Just Mira and Teine."

They both blink at me, and I lower my gaze, bowing my head because it feels like the thing to do. Professor Kaori taught us every way to approach a dragon and exactly zero ways to disengage one.

Step by step, they retreat until I see them take up their places in line in my peripherals, and I finally raise my head.

Taking several deep breaths, I try to lock my muscles to keep from trembling.

"Violet." Rhiannon is only a few feet away, a look of terror in her eyes. She must have been right behind their heads.

"I'm fine." I force a smile and nod. "I have dragon-scale armor under the vest," I whisper. "They smell my sister's dragon." If she wants trust, there it is. "Please don't tell anyone."

"I won't," she whispers. "You're all right?"

"Other than having a few years of my life shaved off." I laugh. The sound is shaky, bordering on hysteria.

"Let's get out of here." She swallows, her gaze darting toward the line of dragons.

"Good idea."

She turns and walks back to her place, and once there's fifteen feet between us, I follow.

"I think I just shat myself," Ridoc says, and my laughter only pitches higher as we move through the field.

"Honestly, I thought they were going to eat you," Luca remarks.

"Me too," I admit.

"I wouldn't have blamed them," she continues.

"You're insufferable," Ridoc calls back.

I focus on the path and keep walking.

"What? She's obviously our weakest link after Pryor, and I don't blame them for snuffing him out," she argues. "He could never make a decision, and no one wants someone like that as their rider—"

A blast of heat singes my back and I halt.

Don't be Ridoc. Don't be—

"Guess the dragons think she's insufferable, too," Ridoc mutters.

Our squad is down to six first-years.

There is nothing quite as humbling,
or as awe-inspiring, as witnessing Threshing…
for those who live through it anyway.

—Colonel Kaori's Field Guide to Dragonkind

CHAPTER THIRTEEN

October first is always Threshing.

Monday, Wednesday, or Sunday, it doesn't matter where it falls on any given year. On the first of October, the first-year cadets of the Riders Quadrant enter the bowl-shaped forested valley to the southwest of the citadel and pray they come out alive.

I will not die today.

I didn't bother eating this morning, and I pity Ridoc, who's currently heaving up the contents of his stomach against a tree to my right.

A sword is strapped to Rhiannon's back, the hilt jostling against her spine as she bounces, stretching her arms across her chest one at a time.

"Remember to listen here," Professor Kaori says from in front of the 147 of us here, tapping his chest. "If a dragon has already selected you, they'll be calling." He thumps his chest again. "So pay attention to not just your surroundings but your feelings, and go with them." He grimaces. "And if your feelings are telling you to go in the other direction…listen to that, too."

"Which one are you going for?" Rhiannon asks quietly.

"I don't know." I shake my head but can't ditch the feeling of absolute failure in my chest. At this point, Mira knew she wanted to seek out Teine.

"You memorized the cards, right?" she asks, lifting her brows. "So you know what's out there?"

"Yes. I just don't feel *connected* to any of them." Which is better than feeling connected to a dragon another rider has their eye on. I have no desire to fight to the death today. "Dain tried talking me into a brown."

"Dain lost his vote when he tried talking you into *leaving*," she counters.

There's a lot of truth to that. I've only talked to him once in the past two days since Presentation, and he tried to get me to run within the first five minutes. We've only seen professors this morning, but I know the second- and third-year riders are scattered throughout this valley in order to observe. "What about you?"

She grins. "I'm thinking about that green. The one closest to me when they got all up close and personal with you."

"Well, it didn't eat you, so that's a promising start." I smile despite the fear racing through my veins.

"I think so, too." She links her arm with mine, and I focus back on what Professor Kaori is telling us.

"If you go in groups, you're more likely to be incinerated than bonded," Professor Kaori argues with someone near the center of the valley. "The scribes have run the statistics. You're better off on your own."

"And what if we aren't chosen by dinner?" a man with a short beard to my left asks.

Looking past him, I catch Jack Barlowe running a finger across his neck at me. So original. Then Oren and Tynan flank his sides.

So much for squad loyalty. It's everyone for themselves today.

"If you're not chosen by nightfall, there's a problem," Professor Kaori responds, his thick mustache turned down at the ends. "You'll be brought out by a professor or senior leadership, so don't give up and think we've forgotten about you." He checks his pocket watch. "Remember to spread out and use every foot of this valley to your advantage. It's nine, which means they should be flying in any minute now. The only other words I have for you are 'good luck.'" He nods, sweeping his gaze over the crowd of us with such intensity that I know he'll be able to re-create this moment in a projection.

Then he leaves, marching up the hill to our right and disappearing into the trees.

My mind whirls. It's time. I'll either leave this forest as a rider…or likely never leave.

"Be careful." Rhiannon pulls me into a hug, her braids swinging over my shoulder as she tightens her arms around me.

"You too." I squeeze her back and am immediately swept into another pair of arms.

"Don't die," Ridoc orders.

That's our only goal as what's left of our squad separates, each heading in our own direction like we've been flung apart by centrifugal motion, at the mercy of a spinning wheel.

Guessing by the position of the sun, it's been at least a couple of hours since the dragons flew overhead, landing in the valley in a succession that sounded like thunder and making the earth shake.

I've come across two greens, a brown, four oranges, and—

My heart stumbles and my feet freeze to the forest floor as a red steps into my field of vision, its head just under the canopy of enormous trees.

This is not my dragon. I'm not sure how I know, but I do.

I hold my breath, trying not to make a sound as its head sweeps right, then left, and my gaze plummets to the ground as I bow my head.

For the last hour or so, I've seen dragons launch into the air with a cadet—now a rider—on their back, but I've also seen more than a couple of plumes of smoke, and I have no desire to be one of those.

The dragon huffs a breath, then continues along its path, its clubtail flicking upward and catching one of the lower-hanging branches. The limb falls to the ground with a monstrous crash, and only after the footsteps recede do I finally raise my head.

I've now come across every color of dragon, and none of them has spoken to me or given me the sense of connection we're reportedly supposed to feel.

My stomach sinks. What if I'm one of the cadets who's destined to never become a rider? One who's thrown back time and again to restart first year until eventually something puts me on the death roll? Has this all been for nothing?

The thought is too heavy to carry.

Maybe if I could just see the valley, then I'd get a feeling like Professor Kaori was talking about.

I spot the nearest climbable tree and get to work, scaling branch after branch. Pain radiates from my hands, but I don't let it distract me. The bark catching the wraps that still cover my palms… Now that's an annoyance that makes me pause every few feet and pull the cloth free of the bark.

Pretty sure the higher branches aren't going to support my weight, so I stop about three-quarters to the top and survey the immediate area.

There are a few greens in plain sight to my left, standing out against the fall foliage. Oddly enough, this is the one time of year when oranges, browns, and reds have the highest chance of blending in. I watch the trees for movement and spot a couple more directly south, but there's no pull, no aching need to head in that direction, which probably means those aren't mine, either.

Relief hits me embarrassingly hard when I count at least half a dozen first-years wandering aimlessly. I shouldn't be so happy that they haven't found their dragons, either, but at least I'm not the only one, which gives me hope.

There's a clearing to the north, and my eyes narrow as a flash, like a mirror, catches the sun.

Or like a golden dragon.

Guess the little feathertail is still out here appeasing its curiosity. But I'm apparently not going to find my dragon up a tree, so I climb down carefully and as quietly as possible. My feet hit the ground just before voices approach, and I tuck myself against the trunk to hide from being seen.

We're not supposed to be in groups.

"I'm telling you, I think I saw it headed this way." It's a cocky voice I immediately recognize as Tynan.

"You'd better be right, because if we just hiked all the way the fuck over here just to find nothing, I'm going to run you through." My stomach twists. It's Jack. No one else's voice has that physical effect on me, not even Xaden's.

"You sure we shouldn't be spending our time looking for our own dragons instead of hunting the freak down?" Recognition tickles the edges of my mind, but I lean out from my hiding place just to be sure. Yep, it's Oren.

I dart back behind the cover of the tree as the trio passes, each strapped with a deadly sword. There are nine daggers tucked against my body in various places, so it's not like I'm unarmed, but I feel tragically disadvantaged by my inability to wield a sword effectively. They're just too damned heavy.

Wait…what did they say they were doing? Hunting?

"It's not like our dragons are going to bond other riders," Jack snaps.

"They'll wait for us. This has to be done. That scrawny one is going to get someone killed. We have to take it out."

Nausea swirls in my stomach, and my fingernails bite into my palms. They're going to try and kill the little golden one.

"If we get caught, we're fucked," Oren comments.

That's an understatement. I can't imagine dragons would take kindly to killing one of their own, but they seem to be focused on culling the weak from the herd in our species, so it's not a stretch to imagine they do the same with their own.

"Then you'd better shut your mouth so no one hears us," Tynan counters, his voice rising in that mocking tone that makes me want to punch him in the face.

"It's for the best," Jack argues, his tone dropping. "It's unrideable, a certified freak, and you know feathertails are useless in combat. They refuse to fight." His voice fades as they walk farther away, headed north.

Toward the clearing.

"Shit," I mutter under my breath even though the assholes are out of hearing range by now. No one knows anything about feathertails, so I don't know where Jack is getting his information, but I don't have time to focus on his assumptions right now.

I have no way of contacting Professor Kaori, and there hasn't even been a hint that the senior riders are watching us, so I can't count on them to stop this madness, either. The golden dragon should be able to breathe fire, but what if it can't?

There's a chance they won't find it, but… Shit, I can't even convince myself of that one. They're headed the right way and that dragon is pretty much a shiny beacon. They'll find it.

My shoulders sag and I sigh at the sky, blowing out a frustrated breath.

I can't just stand here and do nothing.

You can get there first and warn it.

Solid plan, and way better than option two, where I'd be forced to take on three armed men with at least a combined two hundred pounds on me.

I keep my footsteps silent and race across the forest floor at a slightly different angle than Jack's little posse, thankful I grew up playing hide-and-seek with Dain in the woods. This is one area of expertise I can confidently claim.

They've got a head start on me, and the clearing is closer than I realized, so I kick up my speed, my gaze darting between the leaf-covered path I've chosen and where I think—scratch that, where I know they are toward the left. I can make out their lumbering shapes in the distance.

I hear a *pop*, and the ground falls out from under me, then rushes for my face. My hands fly out to brace myself a second before I slam into the forest floor. I bite into my lower lip to keep from crying out as my ankle screams. Popping isn't good. It's never good.

Glancing back, I curse at the fallen branch, hidden by fall foliage, that's just wrecked my ankle. Shit.

Block the pain. Block it. But there's no mental trick to keep the shooting agony from turning my stomach as I drag myself to my knees and rise carefully, keeping my weight on my left ankle.

There's nothing to do but limp the final dozen feet to the clearing, gritting my teeth the whole way. The tinge of satisfaction that I beat Jack here is almost enough to make me smile.

The meadow is big enough for ten dragons, ringed by several large trees, but the golden one stands alone in the center, like it's trying to get a suntan. It's just as beautiful as I remember, but unless it can breathe fire, it's a sitting duck.

"You have to get out of here!" I hiss from the cover of the trees, knowing it should be able to hear me. "They're going to kill you if you don't leave!"

Its head pivots toward me, then tilts at an angle that makes my own neck hurt.

"Yes!" I whisper loudly. "You! Goldie!"

It blinks its golden eyes and swishes its tail.

You have to be fucking kidding me.

"Go! Run! Fly!" I shoo at it, then remember it's a godsdamned dragon, capable of shredding me with its claws alone, and drop my hands. This is not going well. It's going the *opposite* of well.

The trees rustle from the south, and Jack steps into the clearing, his sword swaying in his right hand. A step later, he's flanked by Oren and Tynan, both their weapons drawn.

"Shit," I mutter, my chest tightening. This is now officially going *horribly.*

The golden dragon's head snaps in their direction, a low growl rumbling in its chest.

"We'll make it painless," Jack promises, like that makes the murder acceptable.

"Scorch them," I whisper-shout, my heart pounding as they draw closer. But the dragon doesn't, and somehow, I'm certain in the marrow of my bones that it can't. Other than its teeth, it's defenseless against three trained warriors.

It's going to die just because it's smaller, weaker than the other dragons…just like me. My throat closes.

The dragon backs up, its growl growing louder as it bares its teeth.

Stomach pitching, I have that Parapet feeling again—whatever I do next has overwhelming odds of ending my life.

And yet, I'm still going to do it because this is *wrong.*

"You can't do this!" I take the first step into the shin-high grass and Jack's attention swings my way. My ankle has a heartbeat of its own, and agony streaks up my spine, chattering my teeth as I force my weight onto my ruined joint so they won't see me limping. They can't know I'm hurt, or they'll just attack faster.

One at a time, I stand a chance of holding them off long enough for the dragon to escape, but together…

Don't think about it.

"Oh, look!" Jack grins, pointing his sword my way. "We can take out both the weakest links at the same time!" He looks at his friends and laughs, pausing their advance.

Each step hurts worse than the last, but I make it to the center of the clearing, putting myself between Jack's group and the golden dragon.

"Been waiting a long time for this, Sorrengail." He walks forward slowly.

"If you can fly, now would be a good time," I shout over my shoulder at the small dragon, drawing two daggers from the sheaths at my ribs.

The dragon chuffs. So helpful.

"You can't kill a dragon," I try reasoning, shaking my head at the trio, fear lacing my veins with adrenaline.

"Sure we can." Jack shrugs, but Oren looks a little uncertain, so I pin my gaze on him as they spread out slightly about a dozen feet away, setting up the perfect formation for an attack.

"You can't," I say directly to Oren. "It goes against everything we believe in!"

He flinches. Jack doesn't.

"Letting something so *weak*, so incapable of fighting, live is against our beliefs!" Jack shouts, and I know he's not just talking about the dragon.

"You're going to have to get through me, then." My heart thunders against my ribs as I raise my daggers, flipping one to pinch the tip so I'm ready to throw and measuring the twenty or so feet separating me from my attackers.

"I don't really consider that a problem," Jack snarls.

They all lift their swords, and I draw a deep breath, readying myself to fight. This isn't the mat. There are no instructors. No yielding. Nothing to stop them slaughtering me…slaughtering *us*.

"I would strongly recommend you rethink your actions," a voice—*his* voice—demands from across the field to my right.

My scalp prickles as each of our heads swivel in his direction.

Xaden is leaning against the tree, his arms folded across his chest, and behind him, watching with narrowed golden eyes, her fangs exposed, is Sgaeyl, his terrifying navy-blue daggertail.

In the six centuries of recorded history of dragon and rider, there have been hundreds of known cases where a dragon simply cannot emotionally recover from the loss of their bonded rider. This happens when the bond is particularly strong and, in three documented cases, has even caused the untimely death of the dragon.

—Navarre, an Unedited History by Colonel Lewis Markham

CHAPTER FOURTEEN

Xaden. For the first time, the sight of him fills my chest with hope. He won't let this happen. He might hate me, but he's a wingleader. He can't just watch them kill a dragon.

But I know the rules probably better than anyone else in this quadrant.

He has to. Bile rises in my throat, and I tilt my chin to quell the burning. What Xaden wants, which is always debatable, doesn't matter here. He can only observe, not interfere.

I'm going to have an audience for my death. Fantastic.

So much for hope.

"And if we don't want to *rethink our actions*?" Jack shouts.

Xaden looks toward me, and I swear I can see his jaw clench, even from this far away.

Hope is a fickle, dangerous thing. It steals your focus and aims it toward the possibilities instead of keeping it where it belongs—on the probabilities. Xaden's words come back to me with alarming clarity, and I rip my gaze from his and concentrate on the three *probabilities* in front of me.

"There's nothing you can do, right? *Wingleader?*" Jack bellows.

Guess he knows the rules, too.

"It's not me you should worry about today," Xaden responds and Sgaeyl tilts her head, nothing but menace in her eyes when I glance over.

"You really going to do this?" I ask Tynan. "Attack a squadmate?"

"Squads don't mean shit today," he seethes, menace curling his lips into a sinister smile.

"So I guess that's a no on the flying?" I toss over my shoulder again, and the golden dragon chuffs low in its throat in response. "Great. Well, if you can back me up with those claws, I'd really appreciate it."

It chuffs twice, and I spare a glance down at its claws.

Or should I say…paws.

"Oh, fucking *hell.* You don't have any claws?"

I turn back to the three men just as Jack roars a battle cry and sprints toward me. I don't hesitate. I whip my blade across the rapidly closing space between us, and the dagger finds its mark in the shoulder of his sword arm. His sword falls as he hits his knees, crying out this time in pain.

Good.

But Oren and Tynan have charged at the same time, and they're almost on me. I fling my second dagger at Tynan and catch him in the thigh, slowing but not stopping him.

Oren swings for my neck and I duck, unsheathing another blade and slicing him along the ribs just like I did during our challenge. My ankle isn't going to let me kick, or even land a decent punch, so it's up to my blades.

He recovers quickly and pivots with the sword, catching me at my stomach in a clean slice that would eviscerate me if not for Mira's armor. Instead, the blade skims the scales, sliding right off me.

"What the hell?" Oren's eyes fly wide.

"She's destroyed my shoulder!" Jack cries, stumbling to his feet and distracting the others. "I can't move it!" He clutches the joint, and I grin.

"That's the thing about having weak joints," I say, palming another blade. "You know *exactly* where to strike."

"Kill her!" Jack orders, still clutching his shoulder as he backs away a few steps, then turns and runs in the opposite direction, disappearing into the tree line in no time.

Fucking coward.

Tynan jabs with his sword and I spin away, white-hot pain stealing my sight for a heartbeat before I swipe backward, plunging my dagger into his side, then pivoting, shoving my elbow up into Oren's chin as he attacks, rattling his head.

"You fucking *bitch*!" Tynan screams, pressing his palm against his oozing side.

"Such an original"—I take advantage of Oren's dazed expression and slice open his hip—"insult!"

The move costs me, and a scream rips from my throat as Tynan's sword cuts into my upper right arm, along the direction of the bone.

The armor keeps it from penetrating my ribs, but I know I'll have a hell of a bruise tomorrow as I wrench myself away, blood flowing freely as I peel myself off the sword.

"Behind you!" Xaden shouts.

I pivot to see Oren's sword held high, ready to separate my head from my shoulders, but the golden dragon snaps its jaw and Oren stumbles to the side with terror-filled eyes, as if he's just now realized that it has teeth.

I sidestep and knock the handle of my blade against the base of his skull.

He crumples, unconscious, and I don't wait to see him fall before turning back toward Tynan, who has his bloodied sword ready.

"You can't interfere!" Tynan shouts at Xaden, but I don't dare look away from my opponent long enough to see how the wingleader reacts.

"No, but I can narrate," Xaden retorts.

He's obviously on my side here, which confuses the hell out of me, since more than anything, I'm certain he wants me dead. But maybe it's not my life he's protecting but the golden dragon's.

I chance a quick glance. Yeah, Sgaeyl looks pissed. Her head undulates in a serpentine motion—a clear sign of agitation—and those narrowed golden eyes of hers are focused on Tynan, who is now trying to circle me like we're on the mat, but I won't let him get between me and the little golden dragon.

"Your arm is shot, Sorrengail," Tynan hisses, his face pale and sweaty.

"I'm used to functioning in pain, asshole. Are you?" I raise the dagger in my right hand just to prove that I can despite the blood that runs down my arm and drips from the tip of my blade, saturating the wrap across my palm. My gaze drops meaningfully to his side. "I know exactly where I sliced into you. If you don't get to a healer soon, you'll bleed out internally."

Rage contorts his features, and he moves to strike.

I try to flick my knife at him, but it slips from my blood-soaked hand and lands with a thud in the grass several feet away.

And I know my bravado won't be enough to save me now.

My arm is shot. My leg is shot. But at least I made Jack Barlowe run away before I died.

As a last thought, that's not a bad one.

Just as Tynan reaches up to two-hand his sword, preparing for a killing blow, I catch a glimpse of movement to my right. It's Xaden. And rules be damned, he steps forward as though he intends to stop Tynan from killing me.

I barely have a moment to register surprise that Xaden would ever save me, for *any* reason, when a gust of wind slams into my back, and I stumble forward onto my destroyed ankle, flinging my arms out to keep my balance and grimacing at the shooting pain.

Tynan's mouth hangs open and he staggers backward, his head tilting so far back it's nearly perpendicular to his torso. Shade envelops us both as he continues to back away.

Chest heaving, my lungs desperate for air, I chance a look over my shoulder to see why Tynan's retreating.

And my heart lurches into my throat.

Standing with the golden one tucked under an enormous, scarred black wing is the biggest dragon I've ever seen in my life—the unbonded black dragon Professor Kaori showed us in class. I don't even come close to reaching its *ankle*.

A growl resonates through its chest, vibrating the ground around me as it lowers its gigantic head, baring dripping teeth.

Fear ripples through every cell in my body as its hot breath blows over me.

"Step aside, Silver One," a deep, gruff, definitely male voice orders.

I blink. Wait. *What?* Did he just speak to me?

"Yes. You. Move." There's zero room for argument in his tone, and I limp to the side, nearly stumbling over Oren's unconscious body as Tynan breaks into a screaming run, fleeing for the trees.

The black dragon's eyes narrow to glare at Tynan and he opens his mouth wide a second before fire shoots across the field, blasting heat against the side of my face and incinerating everything in its path... including Tynan.

Flames crackle at the edges of the blackened path, and I turn slowly to face the dragon, wondering if I'm about to be next.

His giant golden eyes study me, but I hold my ground, tilting my chin upward.

"You should end the enemy at your feet."

My eyebrows jerk upward. His mouth didn't move. He spoke to me, but…his mouth didn't move. Oh shit. Because he's in my head. "I can't kill an unconscious man." I shake my head, though whether it's in protest at his suggestion or a result of my confusion is up for debate.

"He would kill you if given the same chance."

I glance down at Oren, still unconscious in the grass beside my feet. It's not like I can argue that astute assessment. "Well, that's a statement on his character. Not mine."

The dragon only blinks in response, and I can't quite tell if that's a good thing or not.

There's a flash of blue out of the corner of my eye, then a whoosh of air as Xaden and Sgaeyl take off, leaving me here with the giant black dragon and the little golden one. Guess Xaden's momentary concern for my life is over.

The dragon's giant nostrils flare. *"You're bleeding. Stop it."*

My arm.

"It's not that simple when you've been run through with a—" I shake my head again. Am I seriously arguing with a dragon? This is so fucking surreal. "You know what? That's a great idea." I manage to cut off what remains of my right shirtsleeve and wrap it around the wound, holding one end of the fabric with my teeth as I tie it tight to apply pressure and slow the bleeding. "There. Better?"

"It will do." He tilts his head at me. *"Your hands are bound, too. Do you bleed often?"*

"I try not to."

He scoffs. *"Let's go, Violet Sorrengail."* He lifts his head, and the golden dragon peeks out from under his wing.

"How do you know my name?" I gawk up at him.

"And to think, I'd almost forgotten just how loquacious humans are." He sighs, the gust of his breath rattling the trees. *"Get on my back."*

Oh. Shit. He's choosing…*me.*

"Get on your back?" I repeat like a fucking parrot. "Have you seen you? Do you have any idea how huge you are?" I'd need a damned ladder to get up there.

The look he gives me can only be described as annoyance. *"One does not live a century without being well aware of the space one takes up. Now get on."*

The golden one moves out from under the shelter of the big one's wing. It's tiny compared to the monstrosity before me, and apparently completely defenseless with the exception of those teeth, like a playful puppy. "I can't just leave it," I say. "What if Oren wakes up or Jack comes back?"

The black dragon chuffs.

The golden one bends down, flexing its legs, and then launches into the sky, its golden wings catching the sun as it flies off, skimming the tops of the trees.

So it *can* fly. That would have been nice to know twenty minutes ago.

"Get. On," the black dragon growls, shaking the ground and trees at the edge of the field.

"You don't want me," I argue. "I'm—"

"I'm not going to tell you again."

Point taken.

Fear grasps my throat like a fist, and I hobble over to his leg. This isn't like climbing a tree. There are no handholds, no easy path, just a series of hard-as-stone scales that don't exactly give me a foothold. My ankle and arm aren't doing me any favors, either. How the hell am I going to get up there? I raise my left arm and suck in a breath before placing my hand on his front leg.

The scales are larger and thicker than my hand and surprisingly warm to the touch. They layer into the next above them in an intricate pattern that leaves no space to grab hold.

"You are a rider, are you not?"

"That seems up for debate at the moment." My heart thunders. Is he going to cook me alive for being too slow?

A low, frustrated grumble sounds in his chest, and then he shocks me to the core as he stretches forward, his front leg becoming a ramp. Dragons never supplicate for *anyone*, and yet here he is, bowing to make it easier for me to climb on. It's steep but manageable.

I don't hesitate, crawling up his front leg on my hands and knees to balance my weight and spare my ankle, but the strain on my arm has me gasping by the time I climb over his shoulder and reach his back, dodging the pointed spikes that ripple down most of his neck like a mane.

Holy shit. I'm on the back of a dragon.

"Sit."

I see the seat—the smooth, scaly divot, just in front of his wings—and sit, bending my knees like Professor Kaori taught us. Then I grab ahold of the thick ridges of scales we call the pommel, where his neck meets his shoulders. Everything about him is bigger than any model we practiced on. My body isn't built to stay on *any* dragon, let alone one of his size. There's no way I'll be able to stay seated. This is about to be the first and last ride of my life.

"My name is Tairneanach, son of Murtcuideam and Fiaclanfuil, descended from the cunning Dubhmadinn line." He stands to his full height, bringing me eye level with the canopy of trees around the clearing, and I squeeze a little tighter with my thighs. *"But I'm not going to assume that you'll be able to remember that once we reach the field, so Tairn will do until I inevitably have to remind you."*

I inhale swiftly, but there's no time to process his name—his history—before he bends slightly and launches us into the sky.

It feels like I imagine a stone does after being flung from a catapult, except it takes every ounce of strength I have to stay on this particular stone.

"Holy shit!" The ground falls away as we soar, Tairn's enormous wings beating the air into submission and pitching upward.

My body lifts off his back, and I dig in with my hands, trying to keep anchored, but the wind, the angle, it's all too much, and my grip falters.

My hands slip.

"Fuck!" Scrambling for purchase, my hands rake down Tairn's back as I skid past his wings, rapidly approaching the sharp scales of his morningstar tail. "No, no, NO!"

He banks left and whatever hope I had of getting a handhold tumbles right off with me.

I'm in free fall.

Just because you survive Threshing doesn't mean you'll survive the ride to the flight field. Being chosen isn't the only test, and if you can't hold your seat, then you'll fly straight into the ground.

—Page fifty, the Book of Brennan

CHAPTER FIFTEEN

Terror clogs my throat and stutters my heart. Air rushes past me as I plummet toward the mountainous terrain beneath, and the sun catches the scales of the golden one far beneath me.

I'm going to die. That's the only possible outcome.

Vises clamp around my ribs and over my shoulders, stopping my descent, and my body jerks with whiplash as I'm yanked upward again.

"You're making us look bad. Stop it."

I'm clasped in Tairn's claws. He's actually…caught me instead of finding me unworthy and letting me fall to my death. "It's not like it's easy to stay on your back when you're doing acrobatics!" I shout up.

He glances down at me, and I swear the ridge above his eye arches. *"Simple flight is hardly acrobatics."*

"There is absolutely *nothing* simple about you!" I wrap my arms around the knuckles of his claws, noting that his sharp talons are draped harmlessly around the sides of my body. He's huge, but he's also careful as he flies us along the mountain.

He's one of the deadliest dragons in Navarre. Professor Kaori's lesson. What else had he said? The only unbonded black dragon hadn't agreed to bond this year. He hadn't even been seen in the last five years. His rider died in the Tyrrish rebellion.

Tairn swings me upward and then releases me, sending me flying high above him, and I flail. My stomach drops at the height of his toss, and then I fall for two heartbeats before Tairn rushes up, catching me on his back between his wings.

"Now get in the seat and actually hold on this time, or no one is going to believe that I've actually chosen you," he growls.

"*I* still can't believe you've chosen me!" I have half a mind to tell him that getting back to the seat isn't as easy as he's implying, but he levels out and his wings catch the air in a gentle glide, cutting the wind resistance. Inch by inch, I crawl up his back until I reach the seat and settle in again. I hold on to his ridges so hard, my hands cramp.

"You're going to have to strengthen your legs. Didn't you practice?"

Indignation ripples up my spine. "Of course I practiced!"

"There's no need to shout. I can hear you just fine. The entire mountain can probably hear you."

Was everyone's dragon a curmudgeon? Or just mine?

My eyes widen. I have…a dragon. And not just any dragon. I have Tairneanach.

"Grip harder with your knees. I can barely feel you back there."

"I'm trying." I push my knees in and the muscles of my thighs tremble as he banks left, softer this time than last, his angle not quite as steep as he changes course in a wide arc, taking us back toward Basgiath. "I'm just… not as strong as other riders."

"I know exactly who and what you are, Violet Sorrengail."

My legs shake until they lock, the muscles freezing in place as though bands have been wrapped around them, but there's no pain. I glance over my shoulder and see his morningstar tail, what feels like miles behind us.

He's doing this. He's holding me in place.

Guilt settles in my stomach. I should have focused more on strength training for my legs. I should have spent more time preparing myself for this. He shouldn't have to spend his energy on keeping his rider seated. "I'm sorry. I just didn't think I'd make it this far."

A loud sigh resonates through my mind. *"I didn't think I would, either, so we have that in common."*

I sit higher in the seat and look out over the landscape, wind ripping tears from the corners of my eyes. No wonder most riders choose to wear goggles. There are at least a dozen dragons in the air, each putting their rider through a trial of dips and turns. Reds, oranges, greens, browns, the sky is speckled with color.

My heart lurches as I see a rider fall from the back of a Red Swordtail and, unlike Tairn, the dragon doesn't dip to catch the first-year. I look away before the body hits the ground.

It's not anyone you know. That's what I tell myself. Rhiannon, Ridoc, Trina, Sawyer… They're all probably safely bonded and already waiting at the field.

"We're going to have to put on a show."

"Awesome." The idea is anything but.

"You will not fall. I will not allow it." The bands around my legs extend to my hands, and I feel the pulse of invisible energy. *"You will trust me."*

Not a question. An order.

"Let's get it over with." I can't move my legs, my fingers, my hands, so there's nothing I can do but sit back and hope I enjoy whatever hell he's about to put me through.

His wings give a mighty beat, and we lurch upward in what feels like a ninety-degree climb, leaving my stomach back at the lower altitude. He crests the top of the snow-dusted peaks, and we hang there for a breath of a second before he twists, diving back down at the same terrifying angle.

It's the most horrifying and yet exhilarating moment of my life.

Until he twists again, sending us into a spiral.

My body is wrenched this way and that as he completes turn after turn, pulling us out of the dive only to bank so hard, I swear the land becomes the sky, then repeats it all until my face splits into a grin.

There is *nothing* like this.

"I think we made our point." He pulls us level, then banks right, starting up the valley that leads to the box canyon of the training fields. The sun is close to setting behind the peaks, but there's plenty of light to see the golden dragon up ahead, hovering as though it's waiting. Maybe it didn't choose a rider, but it will live to decide again next year, and that's all that matters.

Or maybe it will see that we humans aren't so great after all.

"Why did you choose me?" I have to know, because as soon as we land, there are going to be questions.

"Because you saved her." Tairn's head inclines toward the golden as we approach, and she follows after us. Our speed slows.

"But…" I shake my head. "Dragons value strength and cunning and… ferocity in their riders." None of which defines me.

"Please, do tell me more about what I should value." Sarcasm drips

from his tone as we pass over the Gauntlet and crest the narrow entrance to the training fields.

I suck in a sharp breath at the sight of so many dragons. There are hundreds gathered along the rocky edges of the mountain slopes behind the bleachers that were erected overnight. Spectators. And at the bottom of the valley, in the same field I'd walked only a couple of days before, are two lines of dragons facing each other.

"They are divided between those still in the quadrant who chose in years past and those who chose today," Tairn tells me. *"We are the seventy-first bond to enter the fields."*

Mom will be here, on the dais in front of the bleachers, and maybe I'll get more than a cursory glance, but her attention will mostly be on the seventy or so newly bonded pairs.

A ferocious roar of celebration goes up among the dragons as we fly in, every head swinging our way, and I know it's in deference to Tairn. So is the parting of the dragons at the very center of the field, making room for Tairn to land. He releases the bands holding me in my seat, then hovers over the grass for a few wing beats, and I see the golden dragon flying furiously to catch up.

How ironic. Tairn is the most celebrated dragon in the Vale, and I'm the most unlikely rider in the quadrant.

"You are the smartest of your year. The most cunning."

I gulp at the compliment, brushing it off. I was trained as a scribe, not a rider.

"You defended the smallest with ferocity. And strength of courage is more important than physical strength. Since you apparently need to know before we land."

My throat tightens from his words, emotion forming a knot I have to swallow past.

Oh. Shit. I hadn't spoken those words. I'd thought them.

He can read my thoughts.

"See? Smartest of your year."

So much for privacy.

"You'll never be alone again."

"That sounds more like a threat than a comfort," I think. Of course I knew that dragons maintain a mental bond with their riders, but the extent of it is more than a little daunting.

Tairn scoffs in reply.

The golden dragon reaches us, her wings beating twice as fast as Tairn's, and we land in the dead center of the field. The impact jars me slightly, but I sit up tall in the seat and even let go of the pommel ridges.

"See, I can hang on just fine when you're not moving."

Tairn tucks his wings up and looks over his shoulder at me with an expression that's the closest thing to a dragon rolling his eyes that I've ever seen. *"You need to dismount before I rethink my selection, then tell the roll-keeper—"*

"I know what to do." I pull in a shaky breath. "I just didn't think I'd be alive to do it." Surveying both options for dismount, I move right to shelter my ankle as long as possible. There are no healers allowed in the flight field, only riders, but hopefully someone thought to pack a medical kit, because I'm going to need stitches and a splint.

I scoot over the scales of Tairn's shoulder and, before I can lament the distance I'm about to have to jump on the wreckage of my ankle, Tairn shifts slightly, angling his front leg.

There's a sound from the slopes that reminds me of muttering…if dragons mutter.

"They do and they are. Ignore it." Again, there's no room for argument in his tone.

"Thanks," I whisper, then slide down on my butt like he's a bumpy piece of lethal playground equipment, taking the brunt of the impact with my left leg when I hit the ground.

"That's one way to do it."

I can't stop the smile on my face or the joy that stings my eyes at the sight of other first-years standing in front of their dragons. I'm alive, and I'm no longer a cadet. *I'm a rider.*

The first step hurts like hell, but I pivot toward the golden one, who is tucked in tight next to Tairn, surveying me with bright eyes as she flicks her feathertail.

"I'm glad you made it." "Glad" isn't even the right word. Thrilled, relieved, grateful. "But maybe you should fly off the next time someone suggests you save yourself, eh?"

She blinks. *"Maybe I was saving you."* Her voice is higher, sweeter in my mind.

My lips part, and the muscles in my face go slack with shock. "Didn't anyone tell you that you're not supposed to speak to humans who aren't your rider? Don't go getting yourself in trouble, Goldie," I whisper. "From what I hear, dragons are pretty strict about breaking that rule."

She simply sits, tucking her wings in, and tilts her head at me in that should-be-impossible angle that almost makes me laugh.

"Holy hell!" the rider of the red dragon to my right exclaims, and I turn toward him. He's a first-year from Claw Section, Fourth Wing, but I don't remember his name. "Is that…" He openly stares with fear-wide eyes at Tairn.

"Yeah," I say, smiling wider. "He is."

My ankle throbs, aches, and generally feels like it's going to come apart at any second as I limp across the wide field, heading for the small formation directly ahead of me. Behind me, wind sporadically gusts as more dragons land and their riders dismount to have their names recorded, but it's softer and softer as the line spreads farther down the field.

Dusk falls, and a series of mage lights illuminates the crowd in the bleachers and on the dais. In the very center, right above where the redhead from Parapet is recording roll, sits my mother, dressed in all her military finery, medals and all, lest anyone forget exactly who she is. Though there is an assortment of generals on the dais, each representing their wing, there's only one more highly decorated than Lilith Sorrengail.

And Melgren, the commanding general of all Navarrian forces, has his beady eyes on Tairn in open assessment. His focus flicks toward me, and I suppress a shudder. There's nothing but cold calculation in those eyes.

Mom rises as I approach the roll-keeper at the base of the dais, who's recording bonded pairs before motioning the next rider forward to maintain secrecy of a dragon's full name.

Professor Kaori jumps off the six-foot platform to my left and stares open-mouthed at Tairn, his gaze sweeping over the massive black dragon, memorizing every single detail.

"Is that really—" Commandant Panchek starts, hovering at the edge of the dais with more than a dozen other uniformed, high-ranking officers, all gaping.

"Don't say it," Mom hisses, her eyes on Tairn, not me. "Not until she does."

Because only a rider and the roll-keeper know a dragon's full name and she's not certain I'm really his. That's *exactly* what she's implying. *Like I'd be able to hijack Tairn.* Anger simmers in my veins, overtaking the pain coursing through my body as I move forward in the line so there's only one other rider ahead of me.

Mom forced me into the Riders Quadrant. She didn't care if I lived or died as I crossed the parapet. The only thing she cares about now is how my flaws might mar her sterling reputation or how my bonding might further her own agenda.

And now she's staring at my dragon without even bothering to look down and see if I'm all right.

Fuck. Her.

It's everything I expected and yet still so disappointing.

The rider ahead finishes, moving out of the way, and the roll-keeper looks up, glancing wide-eyed at Tairn before lowering her shocked gaze to mine and beckoning me forward.

"Violet Sorrengail," she says as she writes in the Book of Riders. "Nice to see that you made it." She offers me a quick, shaky smile. "For the record, please tell me the name of the dragon who chose you."

I lift my chin. "Tairneanach."

"Pronunciation could use some work." Tairn's voice rumbles through my head.

"Hey, at least I remembered," I think back in his general direction, wondering if he'll hear me across the field.

"At least I didn't let you fall to your death." He sounds utterly bored, but he definitely heard me.

The woman grins, shaking her head as she writes down his name. "I can't believe he bonded. Violet, he's a legend."

I open my mouth to agree—

"Andarnaurram." The sweet, high voice of the golden fills my mind. *"Andarna for short."*

I feel the blood rush from my face, and the edges of my vision sway as I pivot on my good ankle, staring back across the field at where the golden dragon—Andarna—now stands between Tairn's front legs. "Excuse me?"

"Violet, are you all right?" the redhead asks, and everyone around me, above me, leans in.

"Tell her," the golden insists.

"Tairn. What am I supposed to—" I think at him.

"Tell the roll-keeper her name," Tairn echoes.

"Violet?" the roll-keeper repeats. "Do you need a mender?"

I turn back to the woman and clear my throat. "And Andarnaurram," I whisper.

Her eyes fly wide. "*Both* dragons?" she squawks.

I nod.

And all hell breaks loose.

Though this officer considers himself to be an expert on all matters dragonkind, there is a great deal we don't know about the way dragons govern themselves. There is a clear hierarchy among the most powerful, and deference is paid to elders, but I have not been able to discern how it is they make laws for themselves or at what point a dragon decided to bond only one rider, rather than go for better odds with two.

—Colonel Kaori's Field Guide to Dragonkind

CHAPTER SIXTEEN

"Absolutely not!" one general shouts loud enough that I can hear her all the way from the little medical station that's been set up at the end of the bleachers for riders. It's nothing but a row of a dozen tables and some flown-in supplies to tide us over until we can get to the Healer Quadrant, but at least the pain medication is taking effect.

Two dragons. I have...*two* dragons.

The generals have been screaming at each other for the last half hour, long enough for a chill to settle in the night air and for an instructor I've never met to sew up both sides of my arm.

Lucky for me, Tynan mostly sliced through muscle but didn't sever it.

Unlucky for me, Jack is getting his shoulder examined about a dozen feet away. He strutted over from the back of an Orange Scorpiontail to record his bond with the roll-keeper, who'd kept doing her job regardless of the generals arguing on the dais behind her.

Jack hasn't quit staring at Tairn across the field.

"How is that?" Professor Kaori asks quietly, tightening the straps around my splinted ankle. There are about a million other questions in his slashing, dark eyes, but he keeps them to himself.

"Hurts like hell." The swelling made it nearly impossible to get my boot back on without loosening every single lace to its widest position, but at least I didn't have to crawl across the field like a girl from Second Wing who had broken her leg during dismount. She's seven tables back, crying softly as the rider field medics try to set her leg.

"You'll be focused on strengthening your bonds and riding in the next couple of months, so as long as you don't have trouble mounting or dismounting"—his head tilts as he ties off the straps of my splint—"which, after what I saw, I don't think you will—this sprain should heal before your next round of challenges." Two lines deepen between his brow. "Or I can call Nolon—"

"No." I shake my head. "I'll heal."

"If you're sure?" He obviously isn't.

"Every eye in this valley is on me and my dragon—*dragons*," I correct myself. "I can't afford to appear weak."

He frowns but nods.

"Do you know who made it out of my squad?" I ask, fear knotting my throat. *Please let Rhiannon be alive. And Trina. And Ridoc. And Sawyer. All of them.*

"I haven't seen Trina or Tynan," Professor Kaori answers slowly, like he's trying to soften a blow. It doesn't.

"Tynan won't be coming," I whisper, guilt gnawing at my stomach.

"That is not your kill to take credit for," Tairn mentally growls.

"I see," Professor Kaori murmurs.

"What the hell do you mean you think it needs surgery?" Jack bellows from my left.

"I mean, it looks like the weapon severed a couple of ligaments, but we'll have to get you to the healers to be sure," the other instructor says, his voice infinitely patient as he secures Jack's sling.

I look Jack straight in those evil eyes and smile. I'm done being scared of him. He *ran* back in that meadow.

Rage mottles his cheeks in the mage light, and he swings his feet over the end of his table and charges toward me. "You!"

"I what?" I slip off the end of my table and leave my hands loose by the sheaths at my thighs.

Professor Kaori's eyebrows jump as he glances between us. "You?" he murmurs.

"Me," I answer, keeping my focus on Jack.

But Professor Kaori moves between us, throwing his palm out at Jack. "I wouldn't get any closer to her."

"Hiding behind our instructors now, Sorrengail?" Jack's uninjured fist curls.

"I didn't hide out there, and I'm not hiding here." I raise my chin. "I'm not the one who ran."

"She doesn't need to hide behind me when she's bonded to the most powerful dragon of your year," Professor Kaori warns Jack, whose eyes narrow on me. "Your orange is a good choice, Barlowe. Baide, right? He's had four other riders before you."

Jack nods.

Professor Kaori looks back over his shoulder at the line of dragons. "As aggressive as Baide might be, from the way Tairn's looking at you, he'll have no problem scorching your bones into the earth if you take another step toward his rider."

Jack stares at me in disbelief. "You?"

"Me." The throbbing in my ankle is down to a manageable, dull ache, even standing on it.

He shakes his head, and the look in his eyes transforms from shock, to envy, to fear as he pivots toward the professor. "I don't know what she told you about what happened out there—"

"Nothing." The instructor folds his arms across his chest. "Is there something I need to know?"

Jack pales, going white as a sheet in the mage light as another injured first-year hobbles over, blood streaming from his thigh and torso.

"Everyone who needs to know already knows." I lock eyes with Jack.

"Guess we're done for the night," Kaori says as a line of dragons flies in, only visible by their silhouettes in the darkness. "The senior riders are back. You two should return to your dragons."

Jack huffs and marches off across the field.

I glance at the generals still gathered in heated discussion on the dais. "Professor Kaori, has anyone ever bonded two dragons?" If anyone knows, it's the professor of Dragonkind.

He turns with me to face the arguing leadership. "You would be the first. Not sure why they're fighting about it, though. The decision won't be up to them."

"It won't?" Wind gusts as dozens of dragons land on the opposite side of the first-years, rows of mage lights hanging between them.

"Nothing about who dragons choose is up to humans," Kaori assures me. "We only like to maintain the illusion that we're in control. Something tells me they've just been waiting for the others to make it back before they meet."

"The leadership?" My brow furrows.

Kaori shakes his head. "The dragons."

The dragons are going to meet? "Thank you for tending to my ankle. I'd better get back over there." I offer him a tentative smile and head across the dimly lit field to Tairn and Andarna, feeling the weight of every stare in the valley as I stop and stand between the two dragons.

"You two are causing a ruckus, you know." I look at Andarna, then glance up at Tairn before turning around to face the field like the other first-years. "They're not going to let us do this." Oh shit, what if they make me choose?

My stomach plummets.

"It's up to the Empyrean to decide," Tairn says, but there's an edge of tension in his tone. *"Don't leave the field. This might take a while."*

"What might—" My question dies on my tongue as the biggest dragon I've ever seen, even larger than Tairn, stalks toward us from the opening to the valley. Each dragon it passes walks into the center of the field and follows after, gathering dozens as it walks. "Is that…"

"Codagh," Tairn answers.

General Melgren's dragon.

I make out the patchy holes in his battle-scarred wings as he comes closer, his golden gaze focused on Tairn in a way that makes me nauseous. He growls, low in his throat, turning those sinister eyes on me.

Tairn rumbles his own growl, stepping forward so I'm between his massive claws.

There's zero doubt I'm the subject of both disgruntled snarls.

"Yep! We're talking about you!" Andarna says as the line passes by, and she joins.

"Stay close to the wingleader until we return," Tairn orders.

Surely he meant to say *squad leader*.

"You heard what I said."

Or not.

I glance around and spot Xaden standing across the field, his arms crossed and legs spread as he stares at Tairn.

The riders are eerily silent as the dragons empty the meadow, taking flight in a steady stream near the end and landing halfway up the southernmost peak in a shadowy grouping I can barely define in the moonlight.

The second the last of the dragons flies off, chaos erupts. First-years swarm the center of the field, where I happen to be standing, shouting in exuberance and searching for their friends. My eyes scan the crowd, hoping for some glimpse of—

"Rhi!" I shout, spotting Rhiannon in the mob and limping her way.

"Violet!" She crushes me into a hug, pulling away when I wince at the fresh pain in my arm. "What happened?"

"Tynan's sword." I barely get the answer out of my mouth before I'm snatched off my feet by Ridoc, who spins me around, my feet flying out in front of me.

"Look who rode in on the baddest motherfucker around!"

"Put her down!" Rhiannon chides. "She's bleeding!"

"Oh shit, sorry," Ridoc says, and my feet find the ground.

"It's fine." There's fresh blood on the bandage, but I don't think I've torn my stitches. And painkillers are awesome. "Are you all right? Who did you guys bond?"

"The Green Daggertail!" Rhiannon grins. "Feirge. And it was just… easy." She sighs. "I saw her and just knew."

"Aotrom," Ridoc says with pride. "Brown Swordtail."

"Sliseag!" Sawyer throws his arms around Rhiannon's and Ridoc's shoulders. "Red Swordtail!" We all cheer, and I'm swept into his hug next. Out of all of us, I'm happiest for him, for all he's had to endure to get here.

"Trina?" I ask as he lets me go.

One by one, they shake their heads, looking to the others for answers. An impossible heaviness settles in my heart, and I search for any other reason. "I mean…there's a possibility she's just unbonded, right?"

Sawyer shakes his head, sorrow slackening his shoulders. "I saw her fall from the back of an Orange Clubtail."

My heart sinks.

"Tynan?" Ridoc asks, his gaze jumping between us.

"Tairn killed him," I say softly. "In his defense, Tynan had already run me through once." I gesture to the wound on my arm. "And he was trying to—"

"He tried *what*?"

I'm spun around by the shoulders and yanked against a chest. *Dain.*

My arms wind around his back and hold fast as I breathe deeply.

"Damn it. Violet. Just…damn." He squeezes me tight, then pushes me to arm's length. "You're hurt."

"I'm fine," I assure him, but that doesn't quell the worry in his eyes. I'm not sure anything ever will. "But we're all that's left of our squad's first-years."

Dain's gaze rises to look at the others, and he nods. "Four out of nine. That's"—his jaw ticks once—"to be expected. The dragons are currently holding a meeting of the Empyrean—their leadership. Stay here until they return," he says to the others before looking down at me. "You come with me."

It's probably my mother, beckoning me through him. Surely she'll want to see me with everything that's going on. I glance across the field, but it's not Mom I find watching me but Xaden, his expression unreadable.

When Dain takes my hand and tugs, I turn away from Xaden, following Dain to the opposite edge of the field, where we're hidden in shadow. *Guess it's not about Mom.*

"What the actual fuck happened out there? Because I've got Cath telling me that not only did Tairn choose you but so did the small one—Adarn?" His fingers lace with mine, panic swirling in his brown eyes.

"Andarna," I correct him, a smile playing on my lips at the thought of the small golden dragon.

"They're going to make you choose." His expression hardens, and the certainty there makes me recoil.

"I'm not choosing." I shake my head, disengaging our hands. "No human has ever *chosen*, and I'm not about to be the first." And who the hell is Dain to tell me that?

"You are." He rips his hand over his hair, and his composure slips. "You have to trust me. You do trust me, right?"

"Of course I do—"

"Then you have to choose Andarna." He nods as if his decree equals a decision made. "The gold one is the safest choice of the two."

Why, because Tairn is…Tairn? Does Dain think I'm too weak for a dragon as strong as Tairn?

My mouth opens, then shuts like a fish out of water as I search for any reply that isn't *fuck off.* There's no way in hell I'm rejecting Tairn. But my heart won't let me reject Andarna, either.

"Are they going to make me choose?" I think in their direction.

There's no response, and where I've felt an…extension in my mind, of who I am, stretching my mental boundaries since Tairn first spoke to me in that field, there's nothing now.

I'm cut off. *Don't panic.*

"I'm not choosing," I repeat, softer this time. What if I can't have either of them? What if they've broken some sacred rule and now we'll all be punished?

"You are. And it has to be Andarna." He grips my shoulders and leans in, an edge of urgency in his tone. "I know she's too small to bear a rider—"

"That hasn't been tested," I say defensively even though I know it's true. The physics just don't match up.

"And it doesn't matter. It will mean that you won't be able to ride with a wing, but they'll probably make you a permanent instructor here like Kaori."

"That's because his signet power makes him indispensable as a teacher, not because his dragon can't fly," I argue. "And even he had the requisite four years with a combat wing before he was put behind a desk."

Dain looks away, and I can almost see the gears in his mind turning as he calculates…what? My risk? My choice? My freedom? "Even if you take Andarna into combat, there's only a *chance* you'll be killed. You take Tairn, and Xaden will *get* you killed. You think Melgren is terrifying? I've been here for a year longer than you have, Vi. At least you know what you're getting when it comes to Melgren. Xaden isn't only twice as ruthless, but he's dangerously unpredictable."

I blink. "Wait. What are you saying?"

"They're a mated pair, Tairn and Sgaeyl. The strongest bonded pair in centuries."

My mind whirs. Mated pairs can't be separated for long or their health diminishes, so they're always stationed together. *Always*. Which means—oh gods.

"Just…tell me how it happened." He must see me fumbling because his voice softens.

So I do. I tell him about Jack and his band of murderous friends hunting Andarna. I tell him about falling, and the field, and Xaden watching, Xaden…shockingly protecting me with his warning when Oren was at my back. He had the perfect opportunity to end me without it tipping his scales, and he chose to help. What the hell am I supposed to do with that?

"Xaden was there," Dain says quietly, but the gentleness leaches from his voice.

"Yes." I nod. "But he left after Tairn showed up."

"Xaden was there when you defended Andarna, and then Tairn just… showed up?" he asks slowly.

"Yes. That's what I just said." Was the timeline confusing him? "What are you getting at?"

"Don't you see what happened? What Xaden's done?" His grip tightens. Thank gods for the dragon-scale armor, or I might have bruises tomorrow.

"Please, do tell me what it is you think I've done." A shape emerges from the shadows, and my pulse quickens as Xaden steps into the moonlight, darkness falling off him like a discarded veil.

Heat rushes through every vein, wakes every nerve ending. I hate the reaction of my body to the sight of him, but I can't deny it. His appeal is so fucking inconvenient.

"You manipulated Threshing." Dain's hands drop from my shoulders, and he turns to face our wingleader, the set of his shoulders rigid as he puts himself between us.

Oh shit, that's a huge allegation to hurl.

"Dain, that's…" *Paranoid.* I sidestep Dain's back. If Xaden was going to kill me, he wouldn't have waited this long to do it. He's had every possible opportunity, and yet I'm still standing here. Bonded. To *his* dragon's mate.

Xaden's not going to kill me. The realization makes my chest tighten, makes me reexamine everything that happened in that field, makes my sense of gravity shift beneath my feet.

"Is that an official accusation?" Xaden looks at Dain like a hindrance, an annoyance.

"Did you step in?" Dain demands.

"Did I what?" Xaden arches a dark brow and levels a look on Dain that would make a lesser person wither. "Did I see her outnumbered and already wounded? Did I think her bravery was as admirable as it was fucking *reckless*?" He turns that stare on me, and I feel the impact all the way to my toes.

"And I would do it again." I raise my chin.

"Well-the-fuck-aware," Xaden roars, losing his temper for the first time since I met him on Parapet.

I pull in a quick breath, and Xaden does the same, as if he's just as shocked by his outburst as I am.

"Did I see her fight off *three* bigger cadets?" His glare pivots to Dain. "Because the answer to all of those is yes. But you're asking the wrong question, Aetos. What you should be asking is if *Sgaeyl* saw it, too."

Dain swallows and looks away, obviously rethinking his position.

"His mate told him," I whisper. Sgaeyl called for Tairn.

"She's never been a fan of bullies," Xaden says to me. "But don't mistake it as an act of kindness toward you. She's fond of the little dragon. Unfortunately, Tairn chose you all on his own."

"Fuck," Dain mutters.

"My thought exactly." Xaden shakes his head at Dain. "Sorrengail is the last person on the Continent I'd ever want to be chained to me. I didn't do this."

Ouch. It takes all the willpower in my body not to reach for my chest and make sure he didn't just rip my heart out from behind my ribs, which makes absolutely zero sense, since I feel the same way about him. He's the son of the Great Betrayer. His father was directly responsible for Brennan's death.

"And even if I had." Xaden moves toward Dain, towering over him. "Would you really level that accusation knowing it would have been what saved the woman you call your best friend?"

My gaze flies to Dain, and a silent, damning moment passes. It's a simple question, and yet I find myself holding my breath for his answer. What do I really mean to him?

"There are…rules." Dain tilts his chin to look Xaden in the eyes.

"And out of curiosity, would you have, let's say, *bent* those rules to save your precious little Violet in that field?" His voice ices over as he studies Dain's expression with rapt fascination.

Xaden had taken a step. Right before Tairn landed, he'd moved… toward *me*.

Dain's jaw flexes, and I see the war in his eyes.

"That's unfair to ask him." I move to Dain's side as the sound of whipping wings interrupts the night. The dragons are flying back. They've made their decision.

"I'm ordering you to answer, *squad leader.*" Xaden doesn't even spare me a glance.

Dain swallows, his eyes slamming shut. "No. I wouldn't have."

My heart hits the ground. I've always known deep down that Dain valued rule and order more than relationships, more than me, but to have it so cruelly displayed cuts deeper than Tynan's sword.

Xaden scoffs.

Dain immediately jerks his head toward mine. "It would have killed me to watch something happen to you, Vi, but the rules—"

"It's all right," I force out, touching his shoulder, but it isn't.

"The dragons are returning," Xaden says as the first of them lands on the illuminated field. "Get back to formation, squad leader."

Dain rips his gaze from mine and walks away, blending into the crowd of hurried riders and their dragons.

"Why would you do that to him?" I hurl at Xaden, then shake my head. I don't care why. "Forget it," I mutter, then march off, heading back toward the spot where Tairn told me to wait.

"Because you put too much faith in him," Xaden answers anyway, catching up to me without even lengthening his stride. "And knowing who to trust is the only thing that will keep you alive—keep *us* alive—not only in the quadrant but after graduation."

"There is no *us*," I say, dodging a rider as she races past. Dragons land left and right, the ground trembling with the force of the riot's movement. I've never seen so many dragons at flight in the same moment.

"Oh, I think you'll find that's no longer the case," Xaden murmurs next to me, gripping my elbow and yanking me out of the path of another rider running from the other direction.

Yesterday, he would have let me run headfirst into him.

Hell, he might have even pushed me.

"Tairn's bonds are so powerful, both to mate and rider, because *he's* so powerful. Losing his last rider nearly killed him, which, in turn, nearly killed Sgaeyl. Mated pairs' lives are—"

"Interdependent, I know that." We move forward until we're dead center in the line of riders. If I wasn't so aggravated by Xaden's callous attitude toward Dain, I would take the time to admire just how spectacular it is to see hundreds of dragons land all around us. Or maybe I'd question how the man next to me manages to consume all the air in the massive field.

"Each time a dragon chooses a rider, that bond is stronger than the last, which means that if you die, Violence, it sets off a chain of events that potentially ends with *me* dying, too." His expression is immovable marble, but the anger in his eyes leaves me breathless. It's pure…rage. "So yeah, unfortunately for everyone involved, there's now an *us* if the Empyrean lets Tairn's choice stand."

Oh. Gods.

I'm tethered to Xaden Riorson.

"And now that Tairn is in play, that other cadets know he's willing to bond..." He sighs, annoyance rippling over his features, his strong jaw working as he looks away.

"That's why Tairn told me to stay with you," I whisper as the consequences of today's actions settle in my churning stomach. "Because of the unbonded." There are at least three dozen of them standing on the opposite side of the field, watching us with avarice in their eyes—including Oren Seifert.

"The unbonded are going to try to kill you in hopes they'll get Tairn to bond *them*." Xaden shakes his head at Garrick as he approaches, and the section leader glances between us, his mouth set in a firm line before retreating across the field. "Tairn is one of the strongest dragons on the Continent, and the vast power he channels is about to be yours. The next few months, the unbonded will try to kill a newly paired rider while the bond is weak, while they still have a chance of that dragon changing its mind and picking them so they're not set back a full year. And for Tairn? They'll do just about anything." He sighs again like it's his new full-time job. "There are forty-one unbonded riders for which you are now target number one." He holds up a single finger.

"And Tairn thinks you'll play bodyguard." I snort. "Little does he know just how much you dislike me."

"He knows exactly how much I value my *own* life," Xaden retorts, glancing down my body. "You're freakishly calm for someone who just heard she's about to be hunted."

"It's a typical Wednesday for me." I shrug, ignoring the way his gaze heats my skin. "And honestly, being hunted by forty-one people is a lot less intimidating than constantly watching dark corners for *you*."

A breeze hits my back as Andarna lands behind me, followed by a gust of wind and shuddering ground when it's Tairn.

Without another word, Xaden rips his gaze from mine and walks away, cutting a slightly diagonal path across the field to where Sgaeyl overshadows the other wingleaders' dragons.

"Tell me it's going to be all right," I murmur toward Andarna and Tairn.

"It is how it should be," Tairn answers, his voice gruff and bored at the same time.

"You didn't answer before." Fine, it sounds a little accusatory.

"Humans can't know what's said within the Empyrean," Andarna answers. *"It's a rule."*

So every rider was blocked, not just me. The thought is oddly comforting. Also, the whole *Empyrean* is a new term for me today. Kaori must be in heaven tonight with all the dragon politics coming to light. What did they decide?

I glance at my mother, but she's looking everywhere *but* my direction.

General Melgren moves toward the front of the dais, his uniform dripping in medals. Dain's right in one way—the top general in our kingdom is *terrifying*. He's never had an issue using infantry for fodder, and his cruelty when it comes to overseeing the interrogation—and execution—of prisoners is well-known, at least at my family's dining room table. His enormous nightmare of a dragon takes up the entire space beside the dais, and a hush falls over the crowd as Melgren angles his hands in front of his face.

"Codagh has relayed that the dragons have spoken regarding the Sorrengail girl." Lesser magic allows his voice to magically amplify over the field for all to hear.

Woman, I mentally correct him, my stomach knotting.

"While tradition has shown us that there is one rider for every dragon, there has never been a case of two dragons selecting the same rider, and therefore there is no dragon law against it," he declares. "While we riders may not feel as though this is...equitable"—his tone implies that he's one of them—"dragons make their own laws. Both Tairn and..." He looks over his shoulder and his aide rushes forward to whisper in his ear. "Andarna have chosen Violet Sorrengail, and so their choice stands."

The crowd murmurs, but my shoulders sag in acute relief. I don't have to make an impossible choice.

"As it should be," Tairn grumbles. *"Humans have no say in the laws of dragons."*

Mom steps forward and makes the same gesture with her hands to project her voice, but I can't concentrate on what she's saying as she closes out the formal portion of the Threshing ceremony, promising the unbonded riders another chance next year. *If they don't manage to kill one of us while our bonds are weak in the next few months and try to bond our dragons themselves.*

I belong to Tairn and Andarna...and, in some really fucked-up way... Xaden.

My scalp prickles, and I glance across the field at him.

As if sensing my gaze, he looks over and holds up a single finger. *Target number one.*

"Welcome to a family that knows no boundaries, no limits, and no end," my mother finishes, and a cheer resounds around the field. "Riders, step forward."

I look left and right in confusion, but so does every other rider.

"Five steps or so," Tairn says.

I take them.

"Dragons, it is our honor as always," Mom calls out. "Now we celebrate!"

Heat blasts my back, and I hiss in pain as riders on both sides of me cry out. My back feels like it's on fucking *fire*, and yet everyone across the field is cheering raucously, some of them racing our way.

Other riders are caught up in embraces.

"You'll like it," Tairn promises. *"It's unique."*

The pain fades to a dull ache, and I glance over my shoulder. There's a solid black…*something* peeking out from the vest. *"I'll like what?"*

"Violet!" Dain reaches me, his smile wide as he cups my face. "You kept *both* of them!"

"I guess I did." My lips curve. It's all…surreal, all too much for one day.

"Where's your…" He lets go and circles me. "Can I unlace this? Just the top?" he asks, tugging at the raised neck of the back of my vest.

I nod. A few pushes and pulls later, the crisp October air nips at the base of my neck.

"Holy shit. You have to see this."

"Tell the boy to move," Tairn orders.

"Tairn says you should move."

Dain steps out of the way.

Suddenly, my vision isn't mine. I'm looking at my own back through… Andarna's eyes. A back that has a glistening black relic of a dragon mid-flight stretching from shoulder to shoulder and, in the center, the silhouette of a shimmering golden one.

"It's beautiful," I whisper. I'm marked by their magic as a rider now, as *their* rider.

"We know," Andarna answers.

I blink, and my vision is mine again, and Dain's hands lace up my corset quickly, then are on my face, tipping it up toward his.

"You have to know that I would do anything to save you, Violet, to keep you safe," he blurts, panic in his eyes. "What Riorson said…" He shakes his head.

"I know," I say reassuringly, nodding even as something cracks in my heart. "You always want me safe." He'd do anything. *Except break the rules.*

"You have to know how I feel about you." His thumb strokes over my cheek, his eyes searching for something, and then his mouth is on mine.

His lips are soft, but the kiss is firm, and delight races up my spine. After years, Dain is *finally* kissing me.

The thrill is gone in less than a heartbeat. There's no heat. No energy. No sharp slice of lust. Disappointment sours the moment, but not for Dain. He's all smiles as he pulls away.

It was over in an instant.

It was everything I've ever wanted…except…

Shit. I don't want it anymore.

It is therefore only natural that the more powerful the dragon, the more powerful the signet its rider manifests. One should beware of a strong rider who bonds a smaller dragon, but even warier of the unbonded cadet, who will stop at nothing to seize a chance to bond.

—Major Afendra's Guide to the Riders Quadrant (Unauthorized Edition)

CHAPTER SEVENTEEN

After sleeping in the crowded barracks for the last two months, it's weird, and oddly decadent, to have my own room. I'll never take the luxury of privacy for granted again.

I close my door behind me as I limp into the hallway.

Rhiannon's door, across the small hall from mine, opens and I see Sawyer's tall, lean frame come out. He runs his fingers through his hair, and when he sees me, his eyebrows rise and he freezes—his cheeks almost as red as his freckles.

"Good morning." I grin.

"Violet." He forces an awkward smile and walks off, headed toward the main hallway of the first-year dormitory.

A couple from Second Wing holds hands as they come out of the room next to Rhiannon's, and I offer them a smile as I lean back against my door and wait, testing my ankle by rolling it. It's sore, just like every time I sprain it, but the brace and my boot hold it in place well enough to keep my weight on it. If I were anywhere else, I would call for crutches, but that would just put another target on my back, and according to Xaden, I already have a big enough one as it is.

Rhiannon walks out of her room and smiles as soon as she sees me.

"No more breakfast duty?"

"I was told last night that all the *less desirable* duties were being handed off to the unbonded so our energy can be redirected for flight lessons." Which means I'll have to find another way to weaken my opponents before challenges. Xaden's right. I can't always count on taking every enemy down with poison, but I'm not going to ignore the only advantage I have here, either.

"One more reason for the unbonded to hate us," Rhiannon mutters.

"So, Sawyer, huh, Rhi?" We start down our hallway, passing a few other rooms before meeting up with the main corridor that leads to the rotunda. Have to say, the first-year rooms aren't as spacious as the second-years', but at least we both got ones with windows.

A grin curves her lips. "I felt like celebrating." She darts a quick side-eye at me. "And why have I not heard of *you* celebrating?"

We melt into the crowd moving toward the gathering hall. "Haven't found anyone I want to celebrate with."

"Really? Because I heard that you and a certain squad leader had a moment last night."

My gaze whips toward hers, and I nearly stumble over my feet.

"Come on, Vi. The entire quadrant was out there, and you don't think someone saw you?" She rolls her eyes. "You're not going to get a lecture from me. Who gives a shit if it's frowned upon to be in a relationship with a superior officer? There's no regulation, and it's not like any of us is guaranteed to live through the day."

"Solid points," I admit. "But it's..." I shake my head, searching for the right words. "It's not like that with us. I'd always hoped it would be, but when he kissed me—there was nothing there. Like. *Nothing*." It's impossible to keep the disappointment out of my voice.

"Well, that's shitty to hear." She hooks her arm through mine. "I'm sorry."

"Me too." I sigh.

A door opens farther down the hall, and Liam Mairi walks out with his arm wrapped around the waist of another first-year who bonded a Brown Clubtail. Looks like everyone was *celebrating* last night except me.

"Good morning, ladies." Ridoc forces his way through the crowd and slings an arm around each of our shoulders as we enter the rotunda. "Or should I say, *riders*?"

"I like the sound of *riders*," Rhiannon replies, shooting a smile in his direction.

"It has a certain ring to it," Ridoc agrees.

"It's definitely better than *dead*. Where's your relic?" I ask Ridoc as we pass through the columns of carved dragons and take the steps into commons.

"Right here." His arm falls off my shoulders, and he shoves the sleeve of his tunic up to reveal the brown mark of a dragon silhouette on his upper arm. "You?"

"Can't see it. It's on my back."

"That will keep you safer if you're ever separated from that massive dragon of yours." His eyes dance. "I swear, I thought I was going to shit myself when I saw him on the field. What about yours, Rhi?"

"Somewhere you'll never see," she responds.

"You wound me." He slaps his hand over his heart.

"I highly doubt that," she retorts, but there's a smile on her face. We move through commons and into the gathering hall, then make our way through the line for breakfast.

It's odd to be on this side of it, and I startle at the sight of the guy behind the counter.

It's Oren.

He glares at me with a hatred that trickles like ice down my spine. I skip his station, opting for fresh fruit that I know can't be tampered with, just in case he decides to take my approach to conflict and poison me.

"Asshole," Ridoc mutters behind me. "I still can't believe they tried to kill you."

"I can." I shrug, taking my chances with a mug of apple juice. "I'm the weakest link, right? Unfortunately for me, that means people are bound to try and take me out for the good of the wing." We head toward the Fourth Wing section and find a table with three extra seats.

"Mind if we—" Ridoc starts.

"Absolutely! It's yours!" A couple of guys from Tail Section scurry off the bench.

"Sorry, Sorrengail!" the other says over his shoulder as they find another table, leaving this one empty.

What the hell?

"Well, that was really fucking weird." Rhiannon rounds the other side of the table, and I follow, putting our backs to the wall as we step over the bench and sit, setting our trays in front of us.

I'm half tempted to give my underarms a whiff to see if I smell.

"Even weirder?" Ridoc remarks, gesturing across the hall toward First Wing.

Following his line of sight, my eyebrows lift. Jack Barlowe is being squeezed out of his table. He's forced to stand as others take his seat.

"What the hell is going on?" Rhiannon bites into a pear and chews.

Jack moves to another table—whose occupants won't make room for him—and then finds a place two tables down.

"How the mighty have fallen," Ridoc notes, watching the same show I am, but there's no satisfaction in watching Jack struggle. Feral dogs bite harder when they're cornered.

"Hey, Sorrengail," the stocky girl from First Wing I beat in my second challenge says with a tight smile as she walks past our table.

"Hi." I wave awkwardly as she walks away, then turn to whisper to Ridoc and Rhiannon. "She hasn't spoken to me since I took one of her daggers in that challenge."

"It's because you bonded Tairn." Imogen blows her pink hair out of her face and throws her leg over the bench across from us to sit, pushing up the sleeves of her tunic and revealing her rebellion relic. "The morning after Threshing is always a clusterfuck. Power balance shifts, and you, little Sorrengail, are now about to be the most powerful rider in the quadrant. Anyone with common sense is going to be scared of you."

I blink, my pulse elevating. Is that what's going on? I look around the hall and take note. Social groups have split up, and some of the cadets I would have considered threats are no longer sitting where they usually do.

"Which is why *you're* now sitting with us?" Rhiannon arches a brow at the second-year. "Because I can count on one hand the number of nice words you've said to any of us." She holds up a fist with zero fingers raised.

Quinn—the tall second-year in our squad who hasn't bothered to so much as look our way since Parapet—takes a seat next to Imogen, and Sawyer arrives, sitting on Rhiannon's other side. Quinn tucks her blond curls behind her ears and brushes her bangs out of her eyes, her round cheeks rising as she smiles at something Imogen says. Have to admit, the hooped piercings that line the shells of both her ears are pretty awesome, and among her half dozen patches, it's the dark-green one—the same color as her eyes—with two silhouettes that's most intriguing. I should have studied up on what all the patches mean, but according to what I've heard, they change every year.

I'm personally a fan of the first ones we've been given. I had to sew the flame-shaped patch with the emblem for Fourth Wing and the centered, reddish number two with great care, being sure to only stitch the fabric of my corseted armor, since it's not like any needle is going to penetrate the scales.

My favorite patch, though, is the one beside the Flame Section one. We're the squad to have the most surviving members since Parapet, this year's Iron Squad.

"You weren't interesting enough to sit with before," Imogen responds, then bites into a muffin.

"I usually sit with my girlfriend in Claw Section. Besides, no use getting to know you when most of you die," Quinn adds, tucking her curls away again, just to have them spring forward. "No offense."

"None taken?" I start on my apple.

I nearly spit it out when Heaton and Emery, the only third-years in our squad, flank Imogen and Quinn on the bench across from us.

The only people we're missing are Dain and Cianna, who are eating with leadership as usual.

"I thought Seifert would bond," Heaton says to Emery across the table, as though we've caught them mid-discussion. The normally red flames in their hair are green today. "Other than losing to Sorrengail, he nailed every challenge."

"He tried to kill Andarna." *Shit. Maybe I should have kept that to myself.*

Every head at the table turns toward me.

"My guess would be that Tairn told the others." I shrug.

"But Barlowe bonded?" Ridoc questions. "Though from what I've heard, his Orange Scorpiontail is on the smaller side."

"She is," Quinn confirms. "Which is why he's struggling this morning."

"Don't worry—I'm sure he'll make up for his lack of social standing in other ways," Rhiannon mutters, her gaze narrowing on my tray. "You have to have some protein, Vi. You can't just survive on fruit."

"It's the only food I can be sure isn't tampered with, especially with Oren behind the counter." I busy myself with peeling an orange.

"Oh, for fuck's sake." Imogen scrapes three pieces of sausage onto my plate. "She's right. You're going to need all your strength to ride, especially with a dragon as big as Tairn."

I stare at the sausage. Imogen hates me just as much as Oren does. Hell, she's the one who broke my arm and ripped out my shoulder on assessment day.

"You can trust her," Tairn says, and I startle, dropping the orange.

"She hates me."

"Stop arguing with me and eat something." There's zero room for debate in his tone.

My gaze rises to meet Imogen's, and she tilts her head, staring back in challenge.

I use my fork to cut the link, then pop it into my mouth and chew, focusing on the conversation at the table again.

"What's your signet?" Rhiannon asks Emery.

Air rushes down the table, rattling the glasses. Air manipulation. Got it.

"That's epic." Ridoc's eyes widen. "How much air can you move?"

"None of your business." He barely spares him a glance.

"Sorrengail, after class is out today, you're mine," Imogen says.

I swallow my current bite. "I'm sorry?"

Her pale green eyes lock on mine. "Meet me in the sparring gym."

"I'm already working with her on sparring—" Rhiannon starts.

"Good. We can't afford her to lose any challenges," Imogen retorts. "But I'm going to help you with weights. We need to strengthen the muscles around your joints before challenges resume. That's the only way you'll survive."

The hairs rise on the back of my neck. "And since when do you care about my survival?" This isn't a squad thing. It can't be. Not when she didn't give a shit before.

"Since now," she says, gripping her fork in her fist, but it's the lightning-fast glance toward the dais at the end of the hall that gives her away. Her concern isn't coming from the goodness of her heart. Something tells me it's an order. "Squads are about to be condensed at morning formation. We'll be down to two in every section," she continues. "Aetos kept the highest number of his first-years alive—hence the patch—so he'll be allowed to retain his squad, but we'll probably gain a few when they strip the squads from those who weren't as successful."

As discreetly as I can, I look to my right, past the other Fourth Wing tables and to the dais where Xaden sits with his executive officer and the section leaders, including Garrick, whose shoulders look like they should take up at least two seats. It's Garrick who looks my way first, his forehead lining with… What is that? Worry? Then he looks away.

The only reason he'd be remotely worried—*he knows.* He knows my fate is tethered to Xaden's.

My gaze snaps to Xaden, and my chest tightens. So. Freaking. Beautiful. Apparently my body doesn't care that he's as dangerous as they come in the quadrant, because heat rushes through my veins, flushing my skin.

He's using a dagger to peel an apple, removing the rind in one long curl, and the blade continues its path as his eyes lift, locking with mine.

My whole head tingles.

Gods, is there any part of my body that doesn't physically react to the sight of him?

He glances toward Imogen and back to me, and that's all it takes for me to know for certain. He's ordered her to help train me. Xaden Riorson is now in the business of keeping his mortal enemy alive.

A few hours later, after the squads are rearranged and the death roll is read, all the first-year riders in Fourth Wing stand in our newly issued flight leathers, waiting in front of our dragons on the flight field. The uniform is thicker than our usual one, with a full jacket I've buttoned over my dragon-scale armor.

And unlike our regular uniforms, whatever we choose them to be, flight leathers bear no insignia besides our rank at our shoulder and any leadership designation. No names. No patches. Nothing that could give us away if we're separated from our dragons behind enemy lines. Just a lot of sheaths for weapons.

I try not to think about possibly fighting in the war effort one day and focus on the organized chaos evolving on the flight field this morning. I can't miss the way the other cadets look at Tairn or the wide berth the other dragons give him. Honestly, if I had those teeth bared at me, I'd back away, too.

"No you wouldn't, because you didn't. You stayed and defended Andarna." His voice fills my head, and I can tell from his tone there are

places he'd rather be.

"Only because there was a lot going on at the moment," I respond. *"Andarna isn't coming this morning?"*

"She has no need for flight lessons when she can't bear you."

"Good point." Though it would have been nice to see her. She's quieter in my head, too, not as meddlesome as Tairn.

"I heard that. Now pay attention."

I roll my eyes but focus on what Kaori is saying from the center of the field. His hand is up, using common lesser magic to project his voice so we can all hear.

God help us when Ridoc figures out how to do that. I bite back a smile, knowing he'll find some way to annoy the shit out of every rider in the quadrant, not just his squad.

"...and at only ninety-two riders, you are our smallest class to date."

My shoulders dip. *"I thought a hundred and one were willing to bond, plus you?"*

"Willing doesn't mean they found worthy riders," Tairn answers.

"And yet two of you chose me?" With forty-one unbonded? That's quite the insult.

"You're worthy. At least I think you are, but you apparently don't pay attention in class." He chuffs and a warm puff of steam blasts the back of my neck.

"There are forty-one unbonded riders who would kill to be standing where you are," Kaori continues. "And your dragons know that your bond is at its weakest point right now, so if you fall, if you fail, there's a good chance your dragon might let you if it thinks the unbonded will be a better choice."

"Comforting," I mutter.

Tairn makes a noise that reminds me of a scoff.

"Now, we're going to mount, then follow a series of specific maneuvers your dragons already know. Your orders are simple today. Stay in your seat," Kaori finishes. Then he turns and breaks into a sprint, racing the dozen feet toward his dragon's foreleg and making the vertical climb to mount.

Just like the last obstacle on the Gauntlet.

I swallow, wishing I hadn't eaten so much for breakfast, and turn to face Tairn. To my left and right, other riders are doing the same mounting maneuver. There's no way I can pull that off normally, let alone with my ankle still healing.

Tairn dips his shoulder and makes his leg into a ramp for me.

Defeat just about swallows me whole. I've bonded the biggest—and certainly grumpiest—dragon in the quadrant, and yet he has to make accommodations for me.

"They're accommodations for me. I've seen your memories. I'm not about to have you sticking daggers into my leg to climb up. Now let's go."

I snort but make the ascent, shaking my head as I navigate his spikes to find the seat. My thighs ache from yesterday, and I wince as I get into position, gripping the pommel of scales.

Kaori's dragon launches into the sky.

"Hold tight."

I feel the same bands of energy clamp around my legs, and Tairn crouches a millisecond before he hurls us skyward.

The wind tears at my eyes as my stomach falls away, and I risk holding on with one hand to lower my flight goggles. Immediate relief.

"We had to go second?" I ask Tairn as we fly out of the canyon and higher into the mountain range. I get it now, why I didn't see the dragons training often even though I've basically grown up at Basgiath. The only people around us are other riders. *"Everyone is going to see when I slide right off."*

"I only agreed to follow Smachd because his rider is your instructor."

"So you're an in-front kind of guy. Good to know. Remind me to spend some time at temple so I can make multiple appeals to Dunne." I keep my focus on Kaori, watching for when the maneuvers will start.

"The goddess of strength and war?" Tairn clearly scoffs this time.

"What, dragons don't think we need the gods on our side?" Shit, it's cold up here. My gloved hands tighten on the pommel.

"Dragons pay no heed to your puny gods."

Kaori banks right, and Tairn follows suit, leading us into a steep dive down the face of one of the peaks. I clench with my legs, but I know it's Tairn keeping me in the seat.

He holds me there through another climb and even a near-spiral of a turn, and I can't help but notice that he's taking everything Kaori is doing and making it harder.

"You can't hold me here the entire time, you know."

"Watch me. Unless you'd rather be scraped off the glacier below like Gleann's rider back there?"

I whip my head around to look, but all I see is Tairn's tail swinging, his massive spikes blocking the view.

"Don't look."

"We already lost a rider?" My throat knots.

"Gleann chose poorly. He never bonds strongly anyway."

Oh. My. God.

"If you keep holding me like this, your energy will go into keeping me on instead of channeling when we need power for battle," I argue.

"It's a minuscule amount of my power."

How the hell am I supposed to be a rider if I can't stay on my damn dragon by myself?

"Have it your way."

The bands fall away.

"Thank yoooooh shit!" He banks left and my thighs slip. My hands slide. I skid right off his side, my fingers fumbling for purchase and finding none.

Rushing air fills my ears as I plummet toward the glacier, raw fear gripping my heart and squeezing like a vise. The shape of a body below grows bigger and bigger.

I'm yanked upward as Tairn's claws catch me, harnessing me just like he did during Threshing. He climbs high, then tosses me again, but at least I'm prepared for impact this time as his back rises to meet my falling bottom.

There's a disgusted roar of something I don't understand in my head.

"What the hell does that mean?" I scramble for the seat and get myself into position as he flies level.

"The closest translation for humans is probably 'for fuck's sake.' Now. Are you going to stay in your seat this time?" He dips back into formation, and I manage to stay on.

"I have to be able to do this by myself. We both need me to do this," I argue.

"Stubborn silver human," Tairn mutters, following Kaori into a dive.

I fall again.

And again.

And again.

Later that evening, after dinner, I make my way to the sparring gym. Everything hurts from how many times I slid off Tairn's back, and I'm pretty sure there are bruises under my arms from him catching me.

I'm through the rotunda and crossing into the academic wing when I hear Dain calling my name, jogging to catch up with me.

I wait for that familiar swell of happiness that we might have a minute alone, but it doesn't come. Instead, there's a sea of awkwardness that I don't know how to navigate.

What the hell is wrong with me? Dain is gorgeous and kind and a really, *really* good man. He's honorable and my very best friend. So why don't we have any chemistry?

"Rhiannon said you were headed this way," he says once he reaches my side, concern knitting his brow.

"I'm going to work out." I force a smile as we turn the corner where the gym is just ahead of us, the large arched doors open.

"You didn't get enough during flight today?" He touches my shoulder and stops, so I do, too, pivoting to face him in the empty hallway.

"I definitely fell enough today." I check the bandage on my arm. At least I didn't tear open my stitches.

His jaw works. "I honestly thought you'd be all right once Tairn chose you."

"And I will be," I assure him, my voice rising. "I just need to strengthen my muscles to stay seated through maneuvers, and Tairn insists on making everything harder than what Kaori is doing."

"For your own good."

"Are you always around?" I snap back mentally.

"Yes. Get used to it."

I fight the urge to growl at the intrusive, overbearing—

"Still here."

"Violet?" Dain asks.

"Sorry, I'm not used to Tairn butting into my thoughts."

"It's a good sign. Means your bond is strengthening. And honestly, I'm not sure why he's giving you a hard time with maneuvers. It's not like there's any aerial threat out there besides gryphons, and we all know one breath of fire means those birds are goners. Tell him to ease up on you."

"Tell him to mind his own business."

"I'll…uh…do that." I bite back a laugh. *"Take it easy on him. He's my best friend."*

Tairn snorts.

A sigh rips from Dain's lips, and he palms my face gently, his gaze dropping to my lips for a heartbeat before he steps back. "Look. About last night…"

"The part where you told me Xaden would get me killed if I bonded Tairn? Or the part where you kissed me?" I fold my arms across my chest, careful with my right.

"The kiss," he admits, his voice lowering. "It…it never should have happened."

Relief courses through me. "Right?" I crack a smile. Thank gods he feels the same way. "And it doesn't mean we're not friends."

"The best of friends," he agrees, but his eyes are heavy with a sadness I don't understand. "And it's not that I don't want you—"

"What?" My eyebrows rise. "What are you saying?" Are our wires somehow crossed?

"I'm saying the same thing you are." Two lines appear between his brows. "It's incredibly frowned upon to have a physical relationship with anyone in our chain of command."

"Oh." Yeah, that definitely *isn't* what I'm saying.

"And you know how hard I've worked to be a squad leader. I'm determined to be a wingleader next year, and as much as you mean to me…" He shakes his head.

Oh. This is all about politics for him. "Right." I nod slowly. "I get it." It shouldn't matter that the only reason he isn't pursuing me is rank, and it honestly doesn't. But it definitely makes me lose a little respect for him, which is something I never expected.

"And maybe next year, if you're in a different wing, or even after graduation," he starts, hope lighting up his eyes.

"Sorrengail, let's go. I am not sitting around all night," Imogen calls from the doorway, her arms folded across her chest. "If our *squad leader* is done with you, that is."

Dain rears back, glancing between Imogen and me. "She's training you?"

"She offered." I shrug.

"Squad loyalty and all that. Blah, blah." Imogen offers a smile that doesn't reach her eyes. "Don't worry. I'll take good care of her. Bye, Aetos."

I toss Dain a quick smile and walk away, refusing to look over my shoulder to see if he's still there. She quickly follows after me, then leads me toward the corner on the left where glass meets stone and pushes open a door I've never taken the time to notice before.

The room is lit with mage lights and full of a variety of wooden machinery with racks and ropes and pulleys, benches with levers, and bars attached to the wall.

And on the other side, doing push-ups on a mat, is one of the first-year Tyrs I saw in the woods that night, Garrick crouched down next to her, urging her on.

"Don't worry, Sorrengail," Imogen coos in a saccharine-sweet tone. "There's only three of us in here. You're perfectly safe."

Garrick turns, his gaze meeting mine even as he continues calling off reps for the other first-year. He nods once, then goes back to his task.

"You're the only one I worry about," I say as she leads me to a machine with a polished wooden seat and two cushioned squares that meet in front of it at knee height.

She laughs, and I think it's the first genuine sound I've heard her make. "Fair point. Since we can't work that ankle of yours or your arms until they heal, we're going to start with the most important muscles you have for staying on a dragon." She glances down my body and sighs with obvious distaste. "Those weak-ass inner thighs."

"You're only doing this because Xaden is making you, right?" I ask, parking my ass in the seat of the machine with the cushioned wood between my knees as she makes adjustments.

Her eyes meet mine and narrow. "Rule number one. He's Riorson to you, *first-year*, and you never get to question me about him. Ever."

"That's two rules." I'm starting to think my first guess about them is right. With that kind of fierce loyalty, they have to be lovers.

I am not jealous. Nope. That pit of ugliness spreading inside my chest isn't jealousy. It can't be.

She scoffs and pulls a lever that puts immediate tension on the wood, and they rush outward, separating my thighs. "Now get to work. Push them back together. Thirty reps."

There is nothing more sacred than the Archives. Even temples can be rebuilt, but books cannot be rewritten.

—Colonel Daxton's Guide to Excelling in the Scribe Quadrant

CHAPTER EIGHTEEN

The wooden library cart squeaks as I push it over the bridge that connects the Riders Quadrant to the Healer, and then past the clinic doors into the heart of Basgiath.

Mage lights illuminate my way down the tunnels as I take a path so familiar that I could walk it with my eyes shut. The scent of earth and stone fills my lungs the deeper I descend, and the stab of longing that's hit me nearly every day for the past month since I was assigned to Archives duty isn't quite as sharp as it was yesterday, and that wasn't as sharp as the day before.

I nod to the first-year scribe at the entrance to the Archives and he jumps out of his seat, hurrying to open the vault-like door.

"Good morning, Cadet Sorrengail," he says, holding the entrance open so I can pass. "I missed you yesterday."

"Good morning, Cadet Pierson." I offer him a smile as I push the cart through. As quadrant chores go, I've scored my favorite. "I wasn't feeling well." I'd had dizzy spells all day, no doubt from not drinking enough water, but at least I'd been able to rest.

The Archives smell like parchment, book-binding glue, and ink. They smell like home.

Rows of twenty-foot-high shelves run the length of the cavernous structure, and I soak in the sight as I wait by the table nearest the entrance, the place where I spent the majority of my hours these past five years. Only scribes may pass any farther, and I am a rider.

The thought brings a smile to my lips as a woman approaches in a cream tunic and hood, a single rectangle of gold woven onto her shoulder. A first-year. When she pulls the fabric from her head, baring long brown hair, and brings her gaze to meet mine, I full-on grin. I sign, "Jesinia!"

"Cadet Sorrengail," she signs back. Her bright eyes sparkle, but she smothers her smile.

For just this second, I abhor the rituals and customs of the scribes. There would be nothing wrong with pulling my friend into a hug, but she'd be chastised for a loss of composure. After all, how could we know how earnest the scribes are about their work, how dedicated they remain, if they were to crack a smile?

"It's really good to see you," I sign and can't quit grinning. "I knew you'd pass the test."

"Only because I studied with you for the past year," she signs back, pressing her lips together so they don't curve upward. Then her face falls. "I was horrified to hear about you being forced into the Riders Quadrant. Are you all right?"

"I'm fine," I assure her, then pause to search my memory for the correct sign for a dragon bond. "I'm bonded and..." My feelings are complicated, but I think about the way it felt to soar on Tairn's back, the gentle nudges from Andarna to keep going when I thought my muscles might give out during Imogen's training sessions, and my relationships with my friends, and I can't deny the truth. "I'm happy."

Her eyes widen. "Aren't you constantly worried you're going to—" She glances left and right, but there's no one near enough to see us. "You know...die?"

"Sure." I nod. "But oddly enough, you kind of get used to that."

"If you say so." She looks skeptical. "Let's get you taken care of. Are these all returns?"

I nod and reach into the pocket of my pants for a small scroll of parchment and hand it to her before signing, "And a few requests from Professor Devera." The rider in charge of our small library sends a list of requests and the returns every night, and I fetch them before breakfast, which is probably why my stomach is growling.

Burning all the extra calories from a combination of flight, Rhiannon's sparring lessons, and Imogen's torture sessions means I have an all-new capacity for food.

"Anything else?" she asks after putting the scroll in a hidden pocket in her robes.

Maybe it's being in the Archives, but a stab of homesickness nearly bowls me over. "Any chance you guys have a copy of *The Fables of the Barren*?" Mira was right, I had no business bringing the book of fables with me, but it would be nice to spend an evening curled up with a familiar story.

Jesinia's brow furrows. "I'm not familiar with that text."

I blink. "It's not for academics or anything, just a collection of folklore my dad shared with me. A little on the dark side, honestly, but I love it." I think for a moment. There's no sign for wyvern or venin, so I spell them out. "Wyvern, venin, magic, the battles of good and evil—you know, the good stuff." I grin. If anyone understands my love of books, it's Jesinia.

"I've never heard of that one, but I'll look for it while I pull these."

"Thank you. I'd really appreciate it." Now that I'm going to be the one wielding magic, I could use a few good folktales of what happens when humans defile the power channeled to them. No doubt they were written as a parable to warn us of the dangers of bonding dragons, but in Navarre's six-hundred-year history of unification, I've never read of a single rider losing their soul to their powers. The dragons keep us from that.

Jesinia nods and pushes the cart, disappearing into the shelves.

It usually takes about fifteen minutes to gather the requests that come in from both professors and cadets in my quadrant, but I'm more than content to wait. Scribes come and go, some in groups as they train to become our kingdom's historians, and I find myself staring at every hooded figure, searching for a face I know I can't find—searching for my father.

"Violet?"

I turn to the left and see Professor Markham leading a squad of first-year scribes. "Hello, Professor." Keeping my face emotionless around him is easier because I know he'll expect it.

"I didn't realize you had library chore duty." He glances toward the spot in the shelves where Jesinia disappeared. "Are you being helped?"

"Jesinia—" I cringe. "I mean, Cadet Neilwart is most helpful."

"You know," he says to the squad of five as they arc around me, "Cadet Sorrengail here was my prized student until the Riders Quadrant stole her away." His gaze meets mine under his hood. "I had hopes she would return, but alas, she has bonded to not one but two dragons."

A girl to his right gasps, then covers her mouth and mutters an apology.

"Don't worry, I felt the same way," I tell her.

"Perhaps you can explain something to Cadet Nasya over here, who was just griping that there's not nearly enough fresh air in here." Professor Markham turns his focus to a boy on his left. "This group is just starting their rotation in the Archives."

Nasya turns beet red under his cream hood.

"It's part of the fire mitigation system," I tell him. "Less air, less risk of our history burning to the ground."

"And the stuffy hoods?" Nasya lifts a brow at me.

"Makes it harder for you to stand out against the tomes," I explain. "A symbol that no one and nothing is more important than the documents and books in this very room." My gaze darts around the chamber, and a new pang of homesickness hits me.

"Exactly." Professor Markham levels a glare at Nasya. "Now, if you'll excuse us, Cadet Sorrengail, we have work to attend. I'll see you tomorrow in Battle Brief."

"Yes, sir." I step back, giving the squad room to pass.

"You are sad?" Andarna asks, her voice soft.

"Just visiting the Archives. No need to worry," I tell her.

"It's hard to love a second home as much as the first."

I swallow. *"It's easy when the second home is the right one."* And that is what the Riders Quadrant has become to me—the right home. The longing for the kind of peace and solitude I found only here can't match the adrenaline rush of flight.

Jesinia reappears with the cart, laden down with the requested books and bits of mail for the professors of my quadrant. She signs, "I'm so sorry, but I couldn't find that book. I even searched the catalog for wyvern—I think that's what you said—but there's nothing."

I stare for a second. Our Archives have either a copy or the original of almost every book in Navarre. Only ultrarare or forbidden tomes are excluded. When did folklore become either of those? Though, come to think of it, I never came across anything like *The Fables of the Barren* on the shelves while I was studying to become a scribe. Chimera? Yes. Kraken? Sure. But wyvern or the venin that create them? None. Bizarre.

"That's all right. Thank you for looking," I sign back.

"You look different," she signs, then hands the cart over.

My eyes widen.

"Not bad different, just...different. Your face is leaner, and even your posture..." She shakes her head.

"I've been training." I pause, my hands hanging by my sides while I consider my answer. "It's hard, but great, too. I'm getting quicker on the mat."

"The mat?" Her brow furrows.

"For sparring."

"Right. I forget that you guys fight each other, too." Sympathy fills her eyes.

"I'm really all right," I promise her, leaving out the times I've caught Oren gripping a dagger in my presence or the way Jack seethes in my direction. "How about you? Is it everything you wanted?"

"It's everything and more. So much more. The responsibility we have not only to record history but to speed information from the front lines is more than I ever could have imagined, and it's so fulfilling." She presses her lips together again.

"Good. I'm happy for you." And I mean it.

"But I worry for you." She sucks in a breath. "The uptick in attacks along the border..." Concern etches lines into her forehead.

"I know. We hear about them in Battle Brief." It's always the same, striking at faltering wards, ransacking villages high in the mountains, and more dead riders. My heart breaks every time we get a report, and a part of me shuts down with each attack that I have to analyze.

"And Dain?" she asks as we head for the door. "Have you seen him?"

My smile falters. "That's a story for another day."

She sighs. "I'll try and be here around this time so I can see you."

"Sounds wonderful." I refrain from pulling her into a hug and walk through the door she opens.

By the time I return the cart to the library and make it through the lunch line, our time is almost up, which means I'm busy shoveling food in my mouth as fast as I can while the members of our original squad chat around me. The newbies, two first-years and two second-years we took on when the third squad was dissolved, are a table away. They've refused to sit with anyone with a rebellion relic.

So, fuck them.

"It was the coolest thing *ever*," Ridoc continues. "One second he was sparring against that third-year with the wicked broadsword skills, and then Sawyer—"

"You could let *him* tell the story," Rhiannon chides, rolling her eyes.

"No thank you," Sawyer counters, shaking his head, staring at his fork with a hefty dose of fear.

Ridoc grins, in all his glory telling the story. "And then the sword just twists in Sawyer's hand, curving toward the third-year even though Sawyer was *way* off the mark." He grimaces in Sawyer's direction. "Sorry, man, but you were. If your sword hadn't decided to warp and go straight for that guy's arm—"

"You're a metallurgist?" Quinn's eyebrows rise. "Really?"

Holy crap, Sawyer can manipulate metals. I force down a little more turkey and openly stare at him. As far as I know, he's the first of us to display any form of power, let alone a signet.

Sawyer nods. "That's what Carr says. Aetos dragged me straight to the professor when he saw it happen."

"I'm so jealous!" Ridoc grabs his chest. "I want my signet power to manifest!"

"You wouldn't be so excited if it meant you weren't sure if your fork would stab into the roof of your mouth because you can't control it yet." Sawyer shoves his tray away.

"Good point." Ridoc looks at his own tray.

"You'll manifest when your dragon is ready to trust you with all that power," Quinn says, then finishes off her water. "Just hope your dragons trust you before about six months and—" She makes a sound like an explosion and mimics it with her hands.

"Stop scaring the children," Imogen says. "That hasn't happened in"—she pauses to think—"decades." When we all stare at her, she rolls her eyes. "Look, the relic your dragons transferred onto you at Threshing is the conduit to let all that magic into your body. If you don't manifest a signet and let it out, then after a bunch of months, bad things happen."

We all gawk.

"The magic consumes you," Quinn adds, making the explosion sound again.

"Relax, it's not like a hard deadline or something. It's just an average." Imogen shrugs.

"Fuck me, it's always *something* around here," Ridoc mutters.

"Feeling a little luckier now," Sawyer says, staring at his fork.

"We'll get you some wooden utensils," I tell Sawyer. "And you should probably avoid the armory or sparring with…anything."

Sawyer scoffs. "That's the truth. At least I'll be safe during flight this afternoon."

Adding flight classes to our schedule has been essential since Threshing.

The wings rotate for access to the flight field, and today is one of our lucky days of the week.

I feel a tingle in my scalp and know if I turn, I'll find Xaden watching us. Watching me. But I don't give him the satisfaction of looking. He hasn't said so much as a word to me since Threshing. That doesn't mean I'm alone—oh, I'm never alone. There's always an upperclassman somewhere near when I'm walking the halls or headed to the gym at night.

And they all have rebellion relics.

"I like it better when we have it in the morning," Rhiannon says, her face souring. "It's way worse after we've eaten breakfast *and* lunch."

"Agreed," I manage between mouthfuls.

"Finish the turkey," Imogen orders. "I'll see you tonight." She and Quinn clear their trays, taking them back to the window for scullery.

"Is she *any* nicer when she's training you?" Rhiannon asks.

"No. But she's efficient." I finish the turkey as the room begins to clear, and we all make our way toward the scullery window. "What's Professor Carr like?" I ask Sawyer, then tuck my tray onto the stack. The wielding professor is one of the only ones I haven't met, since I haven't manifested a signet.

"Fucking terrifying," Sawyer answers. "I can't wait for the entire year to start wielding lessons so everyone can enjoy his particular brand of instruction."

We head out through commons and the rotunda and into the courtyard, all buttoning up our coats. November has hit hard with gusty winds and frosted grass in the morning, and the first snow isn't far behind.

"I knew it would work!" Jack Barlowe says ahead of us, dragging someone under his arm and thumping her head affectionately.

"Isn't that Caroline Ashton?" Rhiannon asks, her mouth hanging open as Caroline heads toward the academic wing with Jack.

"Yeah." Ridoc tenses. "She bonded Gleann this morning."

"Wasn't he already bonded?" Rhiannon watches them until they disappear into the wing.

"His rider died on our first flight lesson." I focus on the gate ahead that leads to the flight field.

"So I guess the unbonded still have that shot they're looking for," Rhiannon mutters.

"Yeah." Sawyer nods, his features tense. "They do."

• • •

"You only fell about a dozen times that trip," Tairn remarks as we land on the flight field.

"I can't tell if that's a compliment or not." I take deep breaths and try to calm my racing heart.

"Take it as you wish."

I mentally roll my eyes and scoot out of the seat as he dips his shoulder so I can slide down his foreleg. The move has become so practiced that I barely even notice that other riders are capable of leaping to the ground or descending the *proper* way. *"Besides, you could make it easier, you know."*

"Oh, I know."

"I'm not the one putting us into spirals with steep banks while Kaori is teaching plain dives." My feet hit the ground of the field, and I arch an eyebrow at Tairn.

"I'm training you for battle. He's teaching you parlor tricks." He blinks a golden eye at me and looks away.

"Do you think we can get Andarna to join us next week? Even if it's just to fly along?" I do all the checks Kaori has taught us, looking for any debris that could have lodged between the long, taloned toes of Tairn's claws or between the rock-hard scales of his underbelly.

"I'm not foolish enough to not know that I have something stuck in my flesh. And I wouldn't ask Andarna to join us unless she requested it. She can't keep up the speed, and it would only draw unwanted attention."

"I never get to see her," I blatantly whine. *"I'm always stuck with your grumpy ass."*

"I'm always here," Andarna answers, but there's no flicker of gold. She's most likely in the Vale as usual, but at least she's protected there.

"This grumpy ass just caught you a dozen times, Silver One."

"Eventually you could call me Violet, you know." I take the time to examine every row of his scales. One of the biggest dangers to dragons are the smallest things they can't remove that penetrate between the scales, causing infection.

"I know," he repeats. *"And I could call you Violence like the wingleader."*

"You wouldn't dare." I narrow my eyes as I move forward, checking where his chest begins to rise. *"And you know how much that ass annoys me."*

"Annoys you?" Tairn chuckles above me, the sound like a chuffing cat.

"Is that what you call it when your heart rate—"

"Don't even start with me."

A growl rumbles through Tairn's chest above me and vibrates my very bones. I pivot, my hands hovering along my sheathed daggers as Dain approaches.

"It's just Dain." I walk out from between Tairn's forelegs when Dain pauses a dozen feet away.

"Anger does not suit him." He growls again, and a puff of steam hits the back of my neck.

"Relax," I say and glance back over my shoulder at him. My eyebrows shoot up.

Tairn's golden eyes are narrowed in a glare on Dain, and his teeth are bared, dripping saliva as another growl rumbles.

"You're a menace. Stop it," I say.

"Tell him if he harms you, I'll scorch the ground where he stands."

"Oh, for fuck's sake, Tairn." I roll my eyes and walk to Dain, whose jaw is locked, but his eyes are wide with apprehension.

"Tell him, or I'll take it up with Cath."

"Tairn says if you harm me, he'll burn you," I say as dragons to the left and right launch skyward without their riders, headed back to the Vale. But not Tairn. Nope, he's still standing behind me like an overprotective dad.

"I'm not going to harm you!" Dain snaps.

"Word for word, Silver One."

I blow a breath out slowly. "Sorry, he actually said, if you harm me, he'll scorch the ground where you stand." I turn and look over my shoulder. "Better?"

Tairn blinks.

Dain keeps his eyes on me, but I see it there, the swirling anger Tairn warned me about. "I would rather die than harm you, and you know it."

"Happy now?" I ask Tairn.

"I'm hungry. I think I'll partake in a flock of sheep." He launches with great beats of his wings.

"I need to talk to you." Dain's voice drops, and he narrows his eyes.

"Fine. Walk me back." I motion at Rhiannon to go on without me, and she walks ahead with the others, leaving Dain and me to bring up the rear.

We fall back at the edge of the field.

"Why didn't you tell me you can't keep your fucking seat?" he shouts at me, grabbing my elbow.

"I'm sorry?" I yank my arm out of his hold.

Tairn growls in my mind.

"I've got this," I shout back at him.

"All this time, I've been letting Kaori teach you, thinking he must have everything under control. After all, if the rider of the strongest dragon in the quadrant couldn't keep her seat, then surely we'd all know." He rips his hand over his hair. "Surely *I* would know if my best friend fell every fucking day that she flew!"

"It's not a secret!" Anger bubbles in my veins. "Everyone in our wing knows! I'm sorry if you haven't been keeping tabs on your squad, but trust me, Dain. Everyone knows. And I'm not going to stand here while you lecture me like I'm a child." I stalk off, my strides eating up the ground as I follow my wing.

"*You* didn't tell me," he says, anger in his voice giving way to hurt as he catches up, more than matching my pace.

"There's not a problem." I shake my head. "Tairn can keep me buckled in magically if he needs to. I'm the one asking him to loosen the restraints. And I'd think twice before you question him. He's more of the char-first-ask-questions-later type."

"It's a huge problem, because he can't channel—"

"His full powers?" I ask as we make it out of the field, heading toward the steps that descend next to the Gauntlet. "I know that. Why do you think I'm up there asking him to loosen up?" Frustration is a living, breathing thing inside me, eating up all rational thought.

"You've been flying for a month, and you're still falling." His voice follows me down the staircase.

"So is half the wing, Dain!"

"Not a dozen times, they aren't," he shoots back. He's on my heels as I pick up my pace toward the path that will lead back to the citadel, the gravel crunching beneath my boots. "I just want to help you, Vi. How can I help?"

I sigh at the plaintive tone in his voice. I keep forgetting this is my best friend, and he's having to watch me risk my life every day. I don't know how I'd feel if our roles were reversed. Probably just as concerned. So I try to lighten the mood and say, "You should have seen me a month ago when it was three dozen times."

"Three *dozen*?" His voice rises on the last word.

I halt at the mouth of the tunnel and offer a smile. "It sounds worse than it is, Dain. I promise."

"Will you at least tell me what part of flight you have trouble with? At least let me help you."

"You want a list of my flaws?" I roll my eyes. "My thighs are too weak, but I'm building muscle. My hands can't grip the pommel, but they're getting stronger. It took weeks for my biceps to heal, so I'm training that one, too. But you don't have to worry about me, Dain—Imogen is training me."

"Because Riorson asked her to," he guesses, folding his arms across his chest.

"Probably. Why does it matter?"

"Because he doesn't have your best interest at heart." He shakes his head, looking more like a stranger than I've ever seen him before. "First, it was bending the rules to make it up the Gauntlet, and yes, Amber lit into me for an *hour* about how you acted dishonorably."

Dishonorably? Fuck this.

"And you just took her word for it? Without asking me what happened?"

"She's a wingleader, Vi. I'm not about to question her integrity!"

"I proved myself with the Codex, and Riorson accepted it. He's a wingleader, too."

"Fine. You made it up. Don't get me wrong, I couldn't stand myself if something happened to you, whether you were handling the trial the right or wrong way. And then I thought you'd be fine if you survived Threshing, but even bonded to the strongest of them…" He shakes his head.

"Go ahead. Say it." My hands curl into fists, my nails biting into my palms.

"I'm terrified you're not going to make it to graduation, Vi." His shoulders slump. "You know exactly how I feel about you, whether or not I can do anything about it, and I'm *terrified*."

It's that last line that does me in. Laughter bubbles up through my throat and escapes.

His eyes widen.

"This place cuts away the bullshit and the niceties, revealing whoever you are at your core." I repeat his words from this summer. "Isn't that what you said to me? Is this who you really are at your core? Someone so enamored with rules that he doesn't know when to bend or break them for someone he cares about? Someone so focused on the least I'm capable of doing, he can't believe I can do so much more?"

The warmth drains from his brown eyes.

"Let's get one thing straight, Dain." I take a step closer, but the distance between us only widens. "The reason we'll *never* be anything more than friends isn't because of your rules. It's because you have no faith in me. Even now, when I've survived against all odds and bonded not just one dragon but *two*, you still think I won't make it. So forgive me, but you're about to be some of the bullshit that this place cuts away from *me*." I move to the side and march past him through the tunnel, forcing air through my lungs.

Other than the last year, when he entered the Riders Quadrant, I can't remember a time without Dain in my life.

But I can't take his constant pessimism about my future anymore.

Sunlight overpowers me for a second as I walk into the courtyard. Classes are out for the afternoon, and I see Xaden and Garrick leaned up against the wall of the academic building like gods surveying their domain.

Xaden arches a dark eyebrow as I pass by.

I flip him the middle finger.

I'm not taking his shit today, either.

"Everything all right?" Rhiannon asks as I catch up to her and the guys.

"Dain is an ass—"

"Make it stop!" someone screams, rushing down the steps of the rotunda and holding his head. It's a first-year in Third Wing who sits two rows beneath me in Battle Brief and perpetually drops his quill. "For gods' sake, make it stop!" he shrieks, stumbling into the courtyard.

My hands hover over my blades.

A shadow moves to my left, and a glance tells me Xaden has moved, casually putting himself just ahead of me.

The crowd hollows, forming a circle around the first-year as he screams, clutching his head.

"Jeremiah!" someone shouts, coming forward.

"You!" Jeremiah spins, pointing his finger at the third-year. "You think I've lost it!" His head tilts, and his eyes flare. "How does he know? He shouldn't know!" His tone shifts, like the words aren't his own.

Chills race down my spine, dragging my stomach to the ground.

"And you!" He spins again, pointing at a second-year in First Wing. "What the hell is wrong with him? Why is he screaming?" He turns again, focused on Dain. "Is Violet going to hate me forever? Why can't she see that I just want to keep her alive? How is he…? He's reading my thoughts!" The impression is uncanny, embarrassing, and terrifying.

"Oh gods," I whisper, my heart thundering so loud, I can hear the pounding blood in my ears. Forget the embarrassment. Who cares if people know Dain is thinking about me? Jeremiah's *signet power* is manifesting. He can read minds—an inntinnsic. His power is a death sentence.

Ridoc stumbles backward on my left—shoved aside—and I don't need to look to know whose muscled arm now brushes my shoulder. The scent of mint somehow steadies my heartbeat.

Jeremiah unsheathes his shortsword. "Make it stop! Can't any of you see? The thoughts won't stop!" His panic is palpable, clogging my own throat.

"Do something," I beg Xaden, glancing up at him.

His unwavering, lethal focus is on Jeremiah, but his body tenses at my plea, poised, ready to strike. "Start mentally reciting whatever bookish shit you've learned."

"I'm sorry?" I hiss up at him.

"If you value your secrets, clear your thoughts. *Now*," Xaden orders.

Oh. Shit.

Nothing comes to mind, and we're clearly in imminent danger. Um... *Many Navarrian defense posts exist beyond the safety of our wards. Such posts are considered to be in a zone of imminent danger and should only be staffed by military personnel and never the civilians who usually accompany them.*

"And you!" Jeremiah turns, his gaze locking on Garrick. "Damn it all to hell. He'll know about—" The shadows around Jeremiah's feet snake up his legs in a heartbeat, winding around his chest until they cover his mouth in bands of black.

I swallow the boulder in my throat.

A professor pushes through the crowd, his shock of white hair bouncing with every step of his large frame.

"He's an inntinnsic!" someone shouts, and that seems to be all that's necessary.

The professor grips Jeremiah's head with both hands, and a *crack* echoes off the walls of the silent courtyard. Xaden's shadows melt away and Jeremiah falls to the ground, his head at an unnatural, macabre angle. His neck is broken.

The professor bends down and lifts Jeremiah's body with surprising strength, carrying him into the rotunda.

Xaden inhales sharply beside me, then walks away with Garrick, headed toward the academic wing. *Nice to see you, too.*

"Maybe I don't want a signet power after all," Ridoc murmurs.

"That death is merciful compared to what will happen if you don't manifest one," Dain says, and I swear I start to feel my relics burn across my back even though my dragons haven't started channeling.

"And that," Sawyer says from Rhiannon's side, "was Professor Carr."

"You always have to check your sources," Dad tells me, ruffling my hair as he stands beside me at the table in the Archives. "Remember that firsthand accounts are always more accurate, but you have to look deeper, Violet. You have to see *who* is telling the story."

"But what if I want to be a rider?" I ask with the voice of a much-younger version of me. "Like Brennan and Mom?"

"WAKE." A familiar, consuming voice rumbles through the Archives. A voice that doesn't belong here.

"You're not like them, Violet. That's not your path." Dad offers me an apologetic smile, the usual kind that says he sympathizes but there's nothing he can do, the kind he gives me when Mom makes a choice he doesn't agree with. "And it's for the best. Your mother has never understood that while riders may be the weapons of our kingdom, it's the scribes who have all the real power in this world."

"Wake before you die!" The bookshelves in the Archives tremble, and my heart jolts. *"Now!"*

My eyes fly open, and I gasp as the dream disintegrates. I'm not in the Archives. I'm in my room in the Riders—

"Move!" Tairn bellows.

"Fuck! She's awake!" Moonlight reflects off a sword slicing through the air above me.

Oh. Shit. I roll toward the opposite side of my bed, but not fast enough, and the blade slams into the side of my back with a force even my thick winter blankets can't diffuse.

Adrenaline camouflages the pain as the sword rebounds, unable to split the dragon scales.

My knees slam into the hardwood floor, and I thrust my hands beneath my pillow, drawing back two daggers as I untangle from the covers and gain my feet. How the hell did they get my door unlocked?

Blowing my unbound hair out of my face, I meet the wide, shocked eyes of an unbonded first-year, and he's not the only one. There are seven cadets in my room. Four are unbonded men. Three are unbonded women—I gasp with recognition—make that two as *she* runs for the door and slams it on the way out.

She opened the door. There's no other explanation.

The rest are all armed. All determined to kill me. All standing between my unlocked door and me. My hands curl around the hilts of my daggers and my heart rate skyrockets. "Guess it won't do me much good to ask you to leave nicely?"

I'm going to have to fight my way out of here.

"Get away from the wall! Don't let them trap you!"

Good point. But there's not exactly a lot of places to go in this tiny room.

"Damn it! I told you her armor is impenetrable!" Oren hisses from the other side of the room, blocking my exit. Fucking asshole.

"I should have killed you during Threshing," I admit. My door is closed, but surely someone will hear if I sc—

A woman lunges for me, scrambling across my bed, and I dodge, sliding along the icy pane of the window. *The window!*

"It's too high. You'll fall to the ravine, and I can't get there fast enough!"

No window. Got it. Another woman throws her knife, rending the fabric of my nightgown's sleeve as it lodges in the armoire, but she missed any flesh. I spin, leaving the sleeve behind as it rips away, and flick my dagger as I round the end of my bed. It lands in her shoulder, my favorite target, and she goes down with a cry, clutching her wound.

The rest of my weapons are stored near the door. Shit. Shit. *Shit.*

"No more throwing things. Keep ahold of that weapon!"

For someone who can't help, Tairn has no problem dishing out opinions.

"You have to go for her throat!" Oren shouts. "I'll do it myself!"

I move my blade to my right hand and fend off one attack from the left, slicing her down her forearm, and then another to the right, stabbing into a man's thigh. I kick out with my heel and catch another in the gut as he attacks, sending him careening back onto my bed, his sword tumbling after him.

But now I'm cornered between my desk and the armoire.

There are too many of them.

And they all rush at the same damn time.

My dagger is kicked out of my hand with appalling ease, and my heart seizes as Oren grips my throat, yanking me toward him. I sweep out for his knees, but my bare feet make no impact as he lifts me off the ground, cutting off my air supply as I kick for purchase.

No. No. No.

I dig my hands into his arm, my fingernails puncturing his skin as I claw, drawing blood. He might bear my scars after this, but his grip doesn't ease as he crushes my throat.

Air. There's no air.

"He's almost there!" Tairn promises, panic lacing his tone.

He *who*? I can't breathe. Can't think.

"Finish her!" one of the men yells. "He'll only respect us if we finish her!"

They're after Tairn.

Tairn's roar of rage fills my head as Oren lowers my body, flipping me around as he curls his arm so my back is against his chest. At least my feet are on the ground, but the edge of my vision goes dark, my lungs fighting for oxygen that isn't there.

The greedy eyes of a bleeding first-year stare back into mine. "Do it!" she demands.

"Your dragon is mine," Oren hisses in my ear, and his hand falls away, replaced by a blade.

Air rushes into my lungs as cold metal caresses my throat, the oxygen flooding my blood and clearing my head enough to realize this is it. I am going to die. From one heartbeat to what will probably be my last, an overwhelming sorrow seizes my chest, and I can't help but wonder if I would have made it. Would I have been strong enough to graduate? Would I have become worthy of Tairn and Andarna? Would I have finally made my mother proud?

The knife tip touches my skin.

My bedroom door flies open, the wood splintering as it slams against the stone wall, but I don't have a chance to turn to see who is standing there before a shriek pierces my vision.

"Mine!" Andarna screams. Skin-prickling energy zings down my spine, then rushes to my fingertips and toes, and the next breath I take is in total, complete silence.

"Go!" Andarna demands.

I blink and realize the first-year in front of me doesn't. She isn't breathing. Isn't moving.

No one is.

Everyone in this room is frozen in place…except me.

In response to the Great War, dragons claimed the western lands and gryphons the central ones, abandoning the Barrens and the memory of General Daramor, who nearly destroyed the Continent with his army. Our allies sailed home and we began a period of peace and prosperity as the provinces of Navarre united for the first time behind the safety of our wards, under the protection of the first bonded riders.

—Navarre, an Unedited History
by Colonel Lewis Markham

CHAPTER NINETEEN

What. The. Hell.

It's as if everyone in my room has turned to stone, but I know that can't be true. Oren's body is warm behind me, his skin malleable under my fingers as I shift my grip and shove his bloody forearm, forcing the blade away from my neck.

A single drop of blood drips from the sharp tip, splattering on the hardwood, and there's a trickle of wetness down my throat.

"Quick! I can't hold it!" Andarna urges, her voice thready.

She's doing this? I gulp heaving breaths through my battered windpipe and duck under Oren's forearm, freeing myself, then sidestep quickly in the silence.

Complete, unearthly silence.

The clock on my desk isn't ticking as I squeeze between Oren's elbow and a giant guy who used to be from Second Wing. No one breathes. Their gazes are frozen. To the left, the woman I sliced open is hunched over, clutching her forearm, and the man I stabbed is leaned against the wall on the right, staring in horror at his thigh.

I mark time in thunderous heartbeats as I stumble into the only open space in my room, but my path to the now-open door isn't clear.

Xaden fills the doorway like some kind of dark, avenging angel, the messenger of the queen of the gods. He's fully dressed, his face a mask of veritable rage as shadows curl from the walls on either side of him, hanging in midair.

For the first time since crossing the parapet, I'm so fucking relieved to see him that I could cry.

Andarna gasps in my mind—and chaos resumes.

Nausea clenches my stomach.

"It's about damned time," Tairn rumbles.

Xaden's gaze snaps to mine, his onyx eyes flaring in shock for no longer than a millisecond before he strides forward, his shadows streaming before him as he stands at my side. He snaps his fingers and the room illuminates, mage lights hovering above us.

"You're all fucking *dead*." His voice is eerily calm and all the scarier for it.

Every head in the room turns.

"Riorson!" Oren's dagger clatters to the floor.

"You think surrendering will save you?" Xaden's lethally soft tone sends goose bumps up my arms. "It is against our code to attack another rider in their sleep."

"But you know he never should have bonded her!" Oren puts his hands up, his palms facing us. "You of all people have reason enough to want the weakling dead. We're just correcting a mistake."

"Dragons don't make mistakes." Xaden's shadows grab every assailant but Oren by the throat, then constrict. They struggle, but it doesn't matter. Their faces turn purple, the shadows holding tight as they sag to their knees, falling in an arc in front of me like lifeless puppets.

I can't find it in my heart to pity them.

Xaden prowls forward as though he has all the time in the world and holds out his palm as yet another tendril of darkness lifts my discarded dagger from the floor.

"Let me explain." Oren eyes the dagger, and his hands tremble.

"I've heard everything I need to hear." Xaden's fingers curl around the hilt. "She should have killed you in the field, but she's merciful. That's not a flaw I possess." He slashes forward so quickly that I barely catch the move, and Oren's throat opens in a horizontal line, blood streaming down his neck and chest in a torrent.

He grabs for his throat, but it's useless. He bleeds out in seconds, crumpling to the floor. A crimson puddle grows around him.

"Damn, Xaden." Garrick walks in, sheathing his sword as his gaze rakes over the room. "No time for questioning?" His glance sweeps to me as if cataloging injuries, catching on my throat.

"No need for it," Xaden counters as Bodhi enters, doing the same quick assessment Garrick had. The similarity between the cousins still gives me pause. Bodhi has the same bronzed skin and strong brow line, but his features aren't as angular as Xaden's, and his eyes are a lighter shade of brown. He looks like a softer, more approachable version of his older cousin, but my body doesn't heat at the sight of him the way it does around Xaden. Or maybe Oren just strangled the common sense out of me.

An illogical laugh bubbles up through my lips, and all three men look at me like I've hit my head.

"Let me guess," Bodhi says, rubbing the back of his neck. "We're on cleanup?"

"Call in help if you need it," Xaden answers with a nod.

Bodies.

I'm alive. I'm alive. I'm alive. I repeat the mantra in my head as Xaden wipes the blood from my dagger on the back of Oren's tunic.

"Yes. You're alive." Xaden steps over Oren's body and two others, retrieving my dagger from the fallen woman's shoulder before reaching my armoire. I don't even recognize her, and yet she tried to kill me.

Garrick and Bodhi haul out the first bodies.

"I didn't realize I'd said that out loud." The trembling starts in my knees, and then nausea overpowers me. Fuck, I thought I'd worked past this kind of reaction to adrenaline, but here I am, shaking like a leaf as Xaden sorts through my armoire like he hasn't just taken out half a dozen people.

As if this kind of slaughter is commonplace.

"It's the shock," he says, whipping my cloak from its hook and retrieving a pair of boots. "Are you hurt?" His words are clipped and break whatever temporary block I had on the pain. It comes flooding back in a throbbing wave that centers in my back. So much for the adrenaline rush.

Every breath feels like I'm shoving my lungs against broken glass, so I keep them short and shallow. But I manage to stay on my feet, retreating until I feel the stone wall against my uninjured side, letting it take my weight.

"Come on, Violence." His cajoling words are at odds with his terse tone as he folds my cloak over his arm and brings my boots through the remaining bodies he's left on my floor. "Pull your shit together and tell me where you're hurt." He's killed six people without so much as a spot of blood on his midnight-black leathers. My boots hit the ground next to my feet and my cloak lands on the little armchair in the corner.

I can barely breathe, but can I risk admitting my current weakness to him?

His fingers are warm under my chin as he tilts my head up so our gazes collide. Wait…is that a hint of panic swirling in his? "You're breathing like crap, so I'm guessing it has to do with—"

"My ribs," I finish before he can guess. Trying to mask the pain isn't going to work with him. "The one by the bed hit the side of my ribs with the sword, but I think they're just bruised." There hadn't been that telltale snap that comes with broken bones.

"Must have been a dull sword." He cocks a dark eyebrow. "Unless it has something to do with why you sleep in your leather vest."

"Trust him," Tairn demands.

"It's not that easy."

"It has to be for now."

"It's dragon-scale." I lift my right arm and pivot slightly so he can see the gaping hole in my nightdress. "Mira made it for me. It's why I've lived this long."

He glances between our bodies, his mouth tensing before he nods once. "Ingenious, though I'd say there are multiple reasons for why you've made it this far." Before I can argue that point, his gaze shifts to my throat and narrows at what I imagine has to be the purple imprint of a hand. "I should have killed him slower."

"I'm fine." I'm not.

His focus snaps back to my eyes. "Never lie to me." He says it with such ferocity, bit out through gritted teeth, that I can't help but nod in promise.

"It hurts," I admit.

"Let me see."

I open and shut my mouth twice. "Is that a request or a demand?"

"Your pick as long as I get to see if that fucker broke your ribs." His hands curl into fists.

Two other men walk in through the open door, Garrick and Bodhi following closely after. They're all…dressed. Fully clothed at—I glance at the clock—two a.m.

"Take those two, and we'll get the last ones," Garrick orders, and the others get to work, carrying the last of the bodies out through the door. I can't help but notice they all have rebellion relics shimmering up their arms, but I keep the observation to myself.

"Thank you," Xaden says, then flicks his hand and my door shuts with a soft *click*. "Now, let me see your ribs. We're wasting time."

I swallow, then nod. Better to know now if they're broken anyway. I turn my back on him, but I can see his face in the full-length mirror as I shrug out of the billowing sleeves of my nightdress, holding the material above my breasts as it dips in the back to my waist. "You'll have to—"

"I know how to handle a corset." His jaw flexes once, and something that reminds me of raw hunger flitters across his expression before he locks it down, drawing my hair over my shoulder with surprising gentleness.

His fingers skim my bare skin and I suppress a shiver, locking my muscles so I don't arch into his touch.

What the hell is wrong with me? There's still blood on my floor and yet my breaths are tight for the entirely *wrong* reason as he makes quick work of the laces, starting at the bottom. He wasn't lying. He absolutely knows his way around a corset.

"How the hell do you get yourself into this thing every morning?" he asks, clearing his throat as inch after inch of my back is exposed.

"I'm freakishly flexible. It's part of the whole bones-snapping, joints-tearing thing," I answer over my shoulder.

Our eyes meet, and warmth flutters through my stomach. The moment is gone as quickly as it came, and he pulls my armor apart, inspecting my right side. Gentle fingers stroke over the abused ribs, then prod carefully.

"You have one hell of a bruise, but I don't think they're broken."

"That's what I thought. Thank you for checking." It should be awkward, but somehow it isn't, even as he laces me back up, securing the ends.

"You'll live. Turn around."

I do, tugging my nightdress back over my shoulders, and he drops to his knees on the floor before me.

My eyes widen. Xaden Riorson is kneeling before me, his black hair at the perfect level for me to run my fingers through the thickness. It's probably the only thing that's soft about him. How many women have felt those strands between their fingers?

Why the hell do I care?

"You're going to have to walk through the pain, and we have to do it fast." He grabs a boot, then taps my foot. "Can you lift it up?"

I nod, lifting my foot. Then he robs me of every logical thought by putting on my boots and lacing them one at a time.

This is the same man who had no problems with my death just a few months ago, and my brain can't seem to wrap itself around the different sides of him.

"Let's go." He wraps my cloak around my shoulders and buttons it at my collar like I'm something precious. Now I know I'm in shock because I'm anything but precious to Xaden Riorson. His gaze drifts over my hair and he blinks once before tugging my hood up over the fading dark-to-light mass. Then he grasps my hand and tugs me into the hallway. His fingers are strong as they curl around mine, his grip firm but not too tight.

Every other door is shut. The attack wasn't even loud enough to rouse my neighbors. I'd be dead by now if Xaden hadn't shown up, even if I had managed to get out of Oren's hold. But *how* did that happen?

"Where are we going?" The hallways are dimly lit by blue mage lights, the kind that signal it's still night for those without windows.

"Keep talking loud enough for others to hear, and someone will stop us before we get anywhere."

"Can't you just hide us in shadows or something?"

"Sure, because a giant black cloud moving down the hallway isn't going to look more suspicious than a couple sneaking around." He shoots me a look that keeps me from countering.

Point taken.

Not that we're a couple.

Not that I wouldn't climb the man like a tree if presented with the right set of circumstances. I cringe as we make it to the main hallway of the dormitory. There will never, *ever* be a right set of circumstances when it comes to him, let alone right after he's executed half a dozen people.

But in my defense, and in a sick, twisted way, his rescue was pretty damned hot, even if he is hauling me down the hallway at an untenable speed. Even if he only did it because my life is tied to his. My chest screams for a break, but there's none to be found as he leads me past the spiral staircase that leads up to the second- and third-year dorms and into the rotunda.

It's going to take weeks for my ribs to fully heal.

Our boots against the marble floor are the only sounds as we pass into the academic wing. Instead of turning left, toward the sparring gym, he takes us right, down a set of stairs that I know leads to storage.

Halfway down the steps, he pauses, and I nearly run into the sword strapped to his back. Then he gestures with his right hand, keeping mine in his left.

Click. Xaden pushes on the stones and a hidden door swings open.

"Holy shit," I whisper at the expansive tunnel revealed before us.

"Hope you're not afraid of the dark." He pulls me inside, and suffocating darkness envelops us as the door closes.

This is fine. This is absolutely fine.

"But just in case you are," Xaden says, his voice at full volume as he snaps. A mage light hovers above our head, illuminating our surroundings.

"Thanks." The tunnel is supported by arches of stone and the floor is smooth, as though it's been traveled more than its entrance lets on. It smells like earth but isn't dank, and it goes on for what seems like an eternity.

He drops my hand and starts walking. "Keep up."

"You could—" I wince. Fuck, my chest hurts. "Be a little more considerate." I trudge after him, dropping my hood.

"I'm not going to baby you like Aetos does," he says without turning around. "That's only going to get you killed once we get out of Basgiath."

"He doesn't baby me."

"He does and you know it. You hate it, too, if the vibe I'm picking up on is any indication." He falls back to walk at my side. "Or did I read that wrong?"

"He thinks this place is too dangerous for someone…like me, and after what just happened, I'm not sure I can really argue with him." I was *asleep*. That's the only time we're supposed to be guaranteed safety around here. "I don't think I'll bother sleeping again." I shoot a look sideways at his irritatingly gorgeous profile. "And if you even *think* about suggesting that you sleep with me for safety from now on—"

He scoffs. "Hardly. I don't fuck first-years—even when I *was* one—let alone…you."

"Who said anything about fucking?" I fire back, cursing myself as the ache in my ribs only intensifies. "I'd have to be a masochist to sleep with you, and I can assure you, I'm not." Fantasizing about it doesn't count.

"Masochist, huh?" A corner of his mouth quirks into a smirk.

"You hardly give off snuggly morning-after vibes." A smile of my own curves my lips. "Unless you're worried about *me* killing *you* while we sleep."

We round a corner, and the tunnel continues.

"I have zero concern about *that.* As violent as you are, and skilled with those daggers, I'm not even sure you could kill a fly. Don't think I didn't notice that you managed to wound three of them and never went for a kill shot." He shoots a disapproving look my way.

"I've never killed anyone," I whisper like it's a secret.

"You're going to have to get over that. All we are after graduation are weapons, and it's best if we're honed before leaving the gates."

"Is that where we're going? Are we leaving the gates?" I've lost all sense of direction in here.

"We're going to ask Tairn what the hell just happened." Xaden's jaw flexes. "And I'm not talking about the attack. How the hell did they get past your locks?"

I shrug but don't bother to explain. There's no way he'll believe me. I barely believe it myself.

"We'd better figure it out so it doesn't happen again. I refuse to sleep on your fucking floor like some kind of guard dog."

"Wait. This is another way to the flight field?" I do my best to mentally wall off the pain in my throat and ribs. *"He's bringing me to you,"* I tell Tairn.

"I know."

"Are you going to tell me what that was in there?"

"I would if I knew."

"Yes," Xaden says, and the path curves again. "It's not exactly common knowledge. And I'm going to ask you to tuck this little tunnel into the file of secrets you keep on my behalf."

"Let me guess, and you'll know if I tell?"

"Yes." Another smirk appears, and I look away before he can catch me staring.

"Are you going to promise me another favor?" The path begins to climb, and the ascent is anything but gentle. Every breath reminds me of what happened less than an hour ago.

"Having one of my favors is more than enough, and we've already reached mutually assured destruction status, Sorrengail. Now, can you push through it, or do you need me to carry you?"

"That sounds like an insult, not an offer."

"You're catching on." But his pace slows to match mine.

The ground shifts beneath my feet as though it's rocking, but I know better. It's my head, the result of the pain and stress. My steps wobble.

Xaden's arm wraps around my waist, steadying me. I hate how his touch elevates my heart rate as we continue the climb, but I don't protest. I don't want to be grateful for anything when it comes to him, but man if that minty scent of his isn't delicious. "What were you doing tonight anyway?"

"What makes you ask?" His tone clearly insinuates that I shouldn't.

Too bad.

"You made it to my room within minutes, and you're not exactly dressed for sleeping." He's strapped with a sword for crying out loud.

"Maybe I sleep in my armor, too."

"Then you should pick more trustworthy bedmates."

He snorts, a flash of a smile appearing for a heartbeat. A real one. Not the fake, forced sneer I'm used to seeing or the cocky little smirk. An honest, heart-stopping smile that I'm anything but immune to. It's gone as fast as it appears, though.

"So you're not going to tell me?" I ask. I'd be frustrated if I didn't hurt so damned much. And I'm not even going to touch why he needed to haul us all the way to Tairn when I can chat with him anytime I want.

Unless *he* wants to talk to Tairn, which is…ballsy.

"Nope. Third-year business." He lets go when we reach the stonewalled end of the tunnel. A few hand gestures and another *click* sounds before he pushes open the door.

We step out into crisp, freezingly cold November air.

"What the hell," I whisper. The door is built into a stack of boulders on the eastern side of the field.

"It's camouflaged." Xaden waves a hand and the door closes, blending into the rock as if it's a part of it.

There's a sound I now recognize as the steady beat of wings, and I look up to see the three dragons block out the stars as they descend. The earth shudders as they land in front of us.

"I'm guessing the wingleader wants a word?" Tairn steps forward and Sgaeyl follows, her wings tucked in tight, her golden eyes narrowing on me.

Andarna scurries between Sgaeyl's claws, galloping toward us. She skids the last dozen feet, paws digging into the ground to stop just in front of me, bringing her nose to my ribs as an urgent sense of anxiety fills my head, swamping me with feelings I know aren't mine.

"No broken bones," I promise, stroking my hand over the bumpy ridges of her head. "They're just bruised."

"You're sure?" she asks, worry widening her eyes.

"As sure as I can be." I force a smile. Trudging out here in the middle of the night is worth it to alleviate her anxiety.

"Yes, I want a word. What the hell kind of powers are you channeling to her?" Xaden demands, staring up at Tairn like he isn't…Tairn.

Yep. Ballsy. Every muscle in my body locks, sure that Tairn is about to torch Xaden for impudence.

"None of your business what I choose or do not choose to channel toward my rider," Tairn answers with a growl.

This is going well.

"He says—" I start.

"I heard him," Xaden counters, not sparing me a glance.

"You what?" My eyebrows hit my hairline, and Andarna retreats to stand with the others. Dragons only talk to their riders. That's what I've always been taught.

"It's absolutely my business when you expect me to protect her," Xaden retorts, his voice rising.

"I got the message to you just fine, human." Tairn's head swivels in that snakelike motion that puts me on alert. He's more than agitated.

"And I *barely* made it." The words come out clipped through clenched teeth. "She would have been dead if I'd been thirty seconds later."

"Seems like you had thirty seconds gifted to you." Tairn's chest rumbles with a growl.

"And I'd like to know what the fuck happened in there!"

I inhale sharply.

"Don't hurt him," I beg Tairn. *"He saved me."* I've never seen someone so much as dare to *speak* to another rider's dragon, yet alone yell at one, especially not one as powerful as Tairn.

He grumbles in response.

"We need to know what happened in that room." Xaden's dark gaze cuts through me like a knife for a millisecond before he glares back at Tairn.

"Do not dare to try and read me, human, or you'll regret it." Tairn's mouth opens, his tongue curling in a motion I know all too well.

I move between the two and tilt my chin at Tairn. "He's just a little freaked out. Don't scorch him."

"At least we agree on something." A feminine voice sounds through my head.

Sgaeyl.

In awe, I blink up at the navy-blue daggertail as Xaden moves to my side. "She talked to me."

"I know. I heard." He folds his arms across his chest. "It's because they're mates. It's the same reason I'm chained to you."

"You make it sound so pleasant."

"It's not." He turns to face me. "But you and I are exactly that, Violence. We're chained. Tethered. You die, I die, so I damn well deserve to know how the hell you were under Seifert's knife one second and across the room in another. Is that the signet power you've manifested with Tairn? Come clean. Now." His eyes bore into me.

"I don't know what happened," I answer honestly.

"Nature likes all things in balance," Andarna says like she's reciting facts, just like I do when I'm nervous. *"That's the first thing we're taught."*

I pivot to face the golden dragon, repeating what she said to Xaden.

"What is that supposed to mean?" he asks me, not her.

Guess that means he can hear Tairn, but not Andarna.

"Well, not the first thing." Andarna sits, flicking her feathertail along the frost-laden grass. *"The first thing is we shouldn't bond until we're full-grown."* She cocks her head to the side. *"Or maybe the first is where the sheep are? I like goats better, though."*

"This is why feathertails don't bond." Tairn sighs with a hefty dose of exasperation.

"Let her explain," Sgaeyl urges, clicking her talons like nails on the ground.

"Feathertails shouldn't bond because they can accidentally gift their powers to humans," Andarna continues. *"Dragons can't channel—not really—until we're big, but we're all born with something special."*

I relay the message. "Like a signet?" I ask out loud so Xaden can hear.

"No," Sgaeyl answers. *"A signet is a combination of our power with your own ability to channel. It reflects who you are at the core of your being."*

Andarna sits up and tilts her head proudly. *"But I gave my gift directly to you. Because I'm still a feathertail."*

I repeat again, staring at the smaller dragon. Almost nothing is known about feathertails because they're never seen outside the Vale. They're guarded. They're… I swallow. *Wait.* What did she say? "You're *still* a feathertail?"

"Yep! For another couple of years, probably." She blinks slowly and

then cracks a yawn, her forked tail curling.

Oh. Gods. "You're…you're a hatchling," I whisper.

"I am not!" Andarna puffs steam into the air. *"I'm two! The hatchlings can't even fly!"*

"She's a what?" Xaden's gaze swings between Andarna and me.

I glare up at Tairn. "You let a *juvenile* bond? A *juvenile* train for war?"

"We mature at a much faster rate than humans," he argues, having the nerve to look affronted. *"And I'm not sure anyone* lets *Andarna do anything."*

"How much faster?" I gasp. "She's two years old!"

"She'll be full-grown in a year or two, but some are slower than others," Sgaeyl answers. *"And if I thought she'd actually bond, I would have objected harder to her Right of Benefaction."* She chuffs at Andarna in obvious disapproval.

"Hold on. Is Andarna *yours*?" Xaden walks a step toward Sgaeyl, and the tone in his voice is one I've never heard. He's…hurt. "Have you hidden a hatchling away from me these last two years?"

"Don't be ridiculous." Sgaeyl blows out a blast of air that ruffles Xaden's hair. *"Do you think I'd let my offspring bond while still feathered?"*

"Her parents passed before hatching," Tairn answers.

My heart sinks. "Oh, I'm sorry, Andarna."

"I have lots of elders," she responds, as though that makes up for it, but having lost my dad…I know it doesn't.

"Not enough to keep you off the Threshing field," Tairn grumbles. *"Feathertails don't bond because their power is too unpredictable. Unstable."*

"Unpredictable?" Xaden questions.

"The same way you wouldn't hand a toddler your signet, would you, wingleader?" Tairn grunts when Andarna sags against his foreleg.

"Gods, no. I could barely control it as a first-year." Xaden shakes his head.

It's odd to imagine Xaden ever *not* being in control. Hell, I'd pay good money to see him lose it. To be the one he lost it with. *Nope.* I shut that thought down immediately.

"Exactly. Bonding too young allows them to give their gift directly, and a rider could easily drain them and burn out."

"I would never!" I shake my head.

"That's why I chose you." Andarna's head flops against Tairn's leg. How could I not see it before now? Her rounded eyes, her paws…

"Of course, you wouldn't know. Feathertails aren't supposed to be seen," Tairn says, glancing sideways at his mate.

She doesn't even roll her eyes.

"If leadership knew riders could take her gifts for themselves, rather than depending on their own signets…" Xaden says, staring at Andarna as she blinks slower and slower.

"She'd be hunted," I finish quietly.

"Which is why you can't tell anyone what she is," Sgaeyl says. *"Hopefully she'll mature once you're out of the quadrant, and the elders are already placing more…stringent protections on the feathertails."*

"I won't," I promise. "Andarna, thank you. Whatever you did saved my life."

"I made time stop." Her mouth drops open into another jaw-cracking yawn. *"But only for a little bit."*

Wait. What? My stomach hits the ground as I stare into Andarna's golden eyes and forget the pain, the solid earth beneath my feet, even the need to breathe as shock rolls through me, robbing me of logic.

No one can stop time. *Nothing* can stop it. It's…unheard of.

"What did she say?" Xaden asks, gripping my shoulders to steady me.

Tairn growls and a puff of steam blasts us both.

"I'd take your hands off the rider," Sgaeyl warns.

Xaden loosens his grip but continues to cradle my shoulders. "Tell me what she said. Please." His mouth tightens and I know that last bit cost him.

"She can pause time," I force out, stumbling over my words. "Briefly."

Xaden's features slacken, and for the first time, he doesn't look like the stalwart, lethal wingleader I met on the parapet. He's flat-out shocked as his gaze swings to Andarna. "You can stop time?"

"And now we *can stop it."* She blinks slowly, and I can feel exhaustion wafting off her. Channeling that gift to me tonight cost her. She can barely keep her eyes open.

"In small increments," I whisper.

"In small increments," Xaden echoes slowly, like he's absorbing the information.

"And if I use it too much, I can kill you," I say softly to Andarna.

"Kill us.*"* She stands on all four paws. *"But I know you won't."*

"I'll do my best to be worthy." The ramifications of this gift, this exceptional power, hit me like a death blow, and my stomach bottoms out.

"Is Professor Carr going to kill me, too?"

Every gaze whips toward me, and Xaden's grip tightens on my shoulders, his thumbs stroking in a soothing motion. "Why would you think that?"

"He killed Jeremiah." I push the panic away and focus on the tiny golden flecks in Xaden's onyx eyes. "You saw him snap his neck like a twig right in front of the whole quadrant."

"Jeremiah was an inntinnsic." Xaden's voice lowers. "A mind reader is a capital offense. You know that."

"And what are they going to do if they find out I can stop time?" Terror freezes the blood in my veins.

"They're not going to find out," Xaden promises. "No one is going to tell them. Not you. Not me. Not them." He motions with one hand toward our trio of dragons. "Understand?"

"He's right," Tairn says. *"They can't find out. And there's no saying how long you'll have the ability. Most feathertail gifts disappear with maturity when they begin to channel."*

Andarna cracks another yawn, looking nearly dead on her feet.

"Get some sleep," I tell her. *"Thank you for helping me tonight."*

"Let's go, Golden One," Tairn says, and they all bend slightly, then launch, wind gusting against my face. Andarna struggles, her wings beating twice as hard, and Tairn flies up underneath her, taking her weight and continuing on to the Vale.

"Promise me you won't tell anyone about the time-stopping," Xaden asks as we head back into the tunnel, but it feels an awful lot like a command. "It's not just for your safety. Rare abilities, when kept secret, are the most valuable form of currency we possess."

My brow furrows as I study the stark lines of the rebellion relic that winds up his neck, marking him as a traitor's son, warning everyone that he's not to be trusted. Maybe he's telling me to keep quiet for his own gain, so he can use me later down the road.

At least that means he intends for me to be alive at a later date.

"We need to figure out how unbonded cadets got in your room," he says.

"There was a rider there," I tell him. "Someone who ran away before you arrived. She must have unlocked it from the outside."

"Who?" He halts, taking my elbow gently and turning me toward him.

I shake my head. There's no way he'll believe me. I barely believe it myself.

"At some point, you and I are going to have to start trusting each other, Sorrengail. The rest of our lives depend on it." Fury swims in Xaden's eyes. "Now tell me *who*."

Accusing a wingleader of wrongdoing is the most dangerous of all accusations. If you're right, then we've failed as a quadrant to select the best wingleaders. If you're wrong, you're dead.

—My Time as a Cadet: A Memoir
by General Augustine Melgren

CHAPTER TWENTY

"Oren Seifert." Captain Fitzgibbons finishes reading the death roll and closes the scroll as we stand in formation the next morning, our breath creating clouds in the chilled air. "We commend their souls to Malek."

There's no room for sorrow in my heart for six of the eight names, not when I'm shifting my weight to soothe the ache of black-and-blue along my ribs and ignoring the way other riders stare at the ring of bruises I wear around my throat.

The two others on today's list are third-years from Second Wing, killed on a training operation near the Braevick border, according to breakfast gossip, and I can't help but wonder if that's where Xaden had been before coming to my rescue last night.

"I can't believe they tried to kill you while you were sleeping." Rhiannon's still seething at breakfast after I told our table what happened.

Maybe Xaden is fighting to keep last night's events a secret, to hide what a liability I really am to him, because no one else in leadership knows. He didn't say a single word after I told him who unlocked the door, so I have no clue if he believes me or not.

"Even worse, I think I'm getting used to it." Either I have kick-ass compartmentalization skills or I really am acclimating to always being a target.

Captain Fitzgibbons makes some minor announcements, and I tune him out as someone strides our way, cutting through the space between the Flame and Tail Sections of our wing.

Just like it always does, my stupid, hormone-driven heart stutters at the first sight of Xaden. Even the most effective poisons come in pretty packages, and Xaden's exactly that—as beautiful as he is lethal. He looks deceptively calm as he approaches, but I can feel his tension as if it's my own, like a panther prowling toward his prey. The wind ruffles his hair, and I sigh at the completely unfair advantage he has over every man in this courtyard. He doesn't even have to try to *look* sexy...he just *is*.

Oh shit. This feeling right here—the way my breath catches and my entire body draws tight when he's near—is why I haven't taken anyone to bed or *celebrated* like the rest of my perfectly normal friends. This feeling is why I haven't wanted anyone...else.

Because I want *him*.

There aren't enough curse words in the world for this.

His gaze locks with mine just long enough to quicken my pulse before he addresses Dain, ignoring Fitzgibbons's announcements behind him. "There's a change to your squad roll."

"Wingleader?" Dain questions, his spine straightening. "We just absorbed four from the dissolution of the third squad."

"Yes." Xaden looks to the right, where Second Squad, Tail Section stands at attention. "Belden, we're making a roll change."

"Yes, sir." The squad leader nods once.

"Aetos, Vaughn Penley will be leaving your command, and you'll be gaining Liam Mairi from Tail Section."

Dain's mouth snaps shut, and he nods.

We all watch as the two first-year riders exchange places. Penley's only been with us since Threshing, so there's no heartfelt goodbye from our original squad, but the other three grumble.

Liam nods at Xaden, and my stomach twists. I know exactly why he's being put under Dain's command. The guy is massive, as tall as Sawyer and as built as Dain, with light-blond hair, prominent nose, blue eyes, and the sprawling rebellion relic that begins at his wrist and disappears under the sleeve of his tunic gives his mission away.

"I do *not* need a bodyguard," I snap at Xaden. Am I out of line speaking to a wingleader that way? Absolutely. Do I care? Not one bit.

He ignores me, facing Dain. "Liam is statistically the strongest first-year in the quadrant. He has the fastest time up the Gauntlet, hasn't lost a single challenge, and is bonded to an exceptionally strong Red Daggertail. Any squad would be lucky to have him, and he's all yours, Aetos. You can thank me when you win the Squad Battle in the spring."

Liam steps into formation behind me, taking Penley's place.

"I. Do. Not. Need. A. Bodyguard," I repeat, a little louder this time. I could give two fucks who hears me.

One of the first-years behind me gasps, mortified by my audacity, no doubt.

Imogen snorts. "Good luck with that approach."

Xaden walks past Dain and stands directly in front of me, leaning into my space. "You do, though, as we both learned last night. And I can't be everywhere you are. But Liam here"—he points back to the blond Tyr—"he's a first-year, so he can be in *every* class, at *every* challenge, and I even had him assigned to library duty, so I hope you get used to him, Sorrengail."

"You're overstepping." My nails bite into my palms.

"You haven't *begun* to see overstepping," he warns, his voice dropping low, sending a shiver down my spine. "Any threat against you is a threat against me, and as we've already established, I have more important things to do than sleep on your floor."

Heat flushes up my neck and stains my cheeks. "He is *not* sleeping in my room."

"Of course not." He freaking *smirks*, and my traitorous stomach dips. "I had him moved into the one next to yours. Wouldn't want to *overstep*." He turns on his heel and walks away, headed back to his place at the front of our formation.

"Fucking mated dragons," Dain seethes, keeping his eyes forward.

Fitzgibbons finishes his announcements and steps to the back of the dais, which would usually signal the end of formation, but Commandant Panchek takes the podium. He makes it a habit to avoid morning formation, which means something is up.

"What's going on with Panchek?" Rhiannon asks at my side.

"Not sure." I take a deep breath, wincing at the pain in my ribs.

"It has to be something big if he's fumbling with a Codex up there," Rhiannon says.

"Quiet," Dain orders, glancing back over his shoulder at us for the first time this morning. He does a double-take, his eyes flaring wide as he catches sight of my neck. "Vi?"

He hasn't spoken to me since our fight yesterday. Gods, how has it been less than twenty-four hours when I feel like a completely different person?

"I'm fine," I assure him, but he's still staring at my throat, locked in shock. "Squad Leader Aetos, people are staring." We hold way more than our share of the attention as Commandant Panchek begins to speak at the podium, telling us that there's another matter to handle this morning, but Dain won't look away. "Dain!"

He blinks, jerking his gaze to mine, and the apology in those soft brown eyes clogs my throat. "Is that what Riorson meant by *last night*?"

I nod.

"I didn't know. Why didn't you tell me?"

Because you wouldn't believe me, even if I did.

"I'm fine," I repeat, nodding toward the dais. "Later."

He turns, but the motion is reluctant.

"It has been brought to my attention as your commandant that a breach of the Codex has occurred," Panchek calls out over the courtyard.

"As you know, breaches of our most sacred laws are not to be tolerated," Panchek continues. "This matter will be addressed here and now. Will the accuser please step forward."

"Someone's in trouble," Rhiannon whispers. "Think Ridoc finally got caught in Tyvon Varen's bed?"

"That's hardly against the Codex," Ridoc murmurs from behind us.

"He's the executive officer for Second Wing." I send a pointed look over my shoulder.

"And?" Ridoc shrugs, grinning without a touch of remorse. "Fraternizing with command is frowned upon, not unlawful."

I sigh, facing forward. "I miss sex." I really do, and it's not just the physical gratification, either. There's a sense of connection in those moments that I crave, a momentary banishment of loneliness.

The first is something I'm sure Xaden would be more than capable of providing, *if* he ever thought of me that way, but the second? He's the last person I should be craving, but lust and logic never seem to go hand in hand.

"If you're looking for a little fun, I'm happy to oblige—" Ridoc starts, shoving his floppy brown hair off his forehead with a wink.

"I miss *good* sex," I counter, smothering a smile as someone walks from the front of formation toward the dais, indistinguishable through the rows of the squads ahead of us. "Besides, apparently you're spoken for." Have to admit, it feels good to tease a friend about something so trivial. It's a tiny slice of normalcy in an otherwise macabre environment.

"We're not exclusive," Ridoc counters. "It's like Rhiannon and what's-her-name…"

"Tara," Rhiannon offers.

"Will you all shut the hell up?" Dain barks in his superior-officer voice.

Our mouths snap shut.

Mine drops open again when I realize it's Xaden climbing the steps to the dais. My stomach lurches as I suck in a tight breath. "This is about me," I whisper.

Dain glances back at me, confusion furrowing his brow before whipping his attention toward the dais, where Xaden now stands at the podium, somehow managing to fill the entire stage with his presence.

From what I remember reading, his father had that same magnetism, the ability to hold and capture a crowd with nothing but his words…words that led to Brennan's death.

"Early this morning," he begins, his deep voice carrying over the formation, "a rider in my wing was brutally, illegally attacked in her sleep with the intent of murder by a group primarily composed of unbondeds."

A collection of murmurs and gasps fills the air, and Dain's shoulders stiffen.

"As we all know, this is a violation of Article Three, Section Two of the Dragon Rider's Codex and, in addition to being dishonorable, is a capital offense."

I feel the weight of a dozen glances, but it's Xaden's I feel most of all.

His hands clench the sides of the podium. "Having been alerted by my dragon, I interrupted the attack along with two other Fourth Wing riders." He dips his chin toward our wing, and two riders—Garrick and Bodhi—break formation, then climb the steps to stand behind Xaden, their hands at their sides. "As it was a matter of life and death, I personally executed six of the would-be murderers, as witnessed by Flame Section Leader Garrick Tavis and Tail Section Executive Officer Bodhi Durran."

"Both Tyrs. How convenient," Nadine, one of our new additions to the squad, says from the row behind Ridoc and Liam.

I look back over my shoulder and pin her with a glare.

Liam keeps his eyes forward.

"But the attack was orchestrated by a rider who fled before I arrived," Xaden continues, his voice rising. "A rider who had access to the map of where all first-years are assigned to sleep, and that rider must be brought to swift justice."

Shit. This is about to get ugly.

"I call you to answer for your crime against Cadet Sorrengail." Xaden's focus shifts to the center of the formation. "Wingleader Amber Mavis."

The quadrant draws a collective breath before an uproar rips through the crowd.

"What the hell?" Dain bites out.

My chest tightens. Gods, I hate it when Dain proves me right.

Rhiannon reaches for my hand, squeezing tight in support as every rider in the courtyard's attention pivots between Xaden, Amber…and me.

"She's a Tyr, too, Nadine," Ridoc says over his shoulder. "Or are you only biased against marked ones?"

Amber's family stayed loyal to Navarre, so she wasn't forced to watch her parents executed and wasn't marked by a rebellion relic.

"Amber would never." Dain shakes his head. "A wingleader would *never*." He turns completely to face me. "Get up there and tell everyone that he's lying, Vi."

"But he's not," I say as gently as I can.

"It's impossible." His cheeks flush a mottled shade of red.

"I was there, Dain." The reality of his disbelief hurts so much more than I expected, like a blow to my already battered ribs.

"Wingleaders are beyond reproach—"

"Then why are you so quick to call our own wingleader a liar?" My brows rise in challenge, daring him to say what he's so careful to keep quiet.

Behind him, Amber steps forward, separating herself from the formation. "I have committed no such crime!"

"See?" Dain swings his arm, pointing toward the redhead. "Put a stop to this *right now*, Violet."

"She was with them in my room," I say simply. Shouting won't convince him. Nothing will.

"That's impossible." He lifts his hands, as though ready to cup my face. "Let me see."

The shock of what he intends to do has me stumbling backward. How have I forgotten that his signet allows him to see others' memories?

But if I let him see my memory of Amber's participation, it will also show him that I stopped time, and I can't let that happen. I shake my head and take another step back.

"Give me the memory," he orders.

Indignation lifts my chin. "Touch me without permission, and you'll spend the rest of your life regretting it."

Surprise ripples over his features.

"Wingleaders." Xaden projects his voice over the chaos. "We need a quorum."

Both Nyra and Septon Izar—the wingleaders for First and Second Wing—climb the stairs to the dais, passing by Amber as she stands utterly exposed in the courtyard.

A familiar chaos fills the air, and we all look toward the ridgeline as six dragons curve along the mountain, flying straight for us. The biggest among them is Tairn.

In a matter of seconds, they reach the citadel and hover over the courtyard walls. Wind from the strong beats of their wings blasts through the courtyard. Then, one by one, they land on their perch, Tairn at the center of the grouping.

Every line of his frame exudes menace as his talons crush the masonry under his grip, and his narrowed, angry eyes focus on Amber.

Sgaeyl is perched to the right, taking her position behind Xaden. She's just as terrifying as she was that first day, but back then I'd never imagined I'd bond a dragon even more frightening…to everyone but me. Nyra's Red Scorpiontail looms behind her as well, and Septon's Brown Daggertail mirrors the stance to the left. On the ends, puffing blasts of steam, are Commandant Panchek's Green Clubtail and Amber's Orange Daggertail.

"Shit's about to get real," Sawyer says, breaking formation to stand at my side, and I feel Ridoc at my back.

"You can stop this all right now, Violet. You have to," Dain implores. "I don't know what you saw last night, but it wasn't Amber. She cares too much about the rules to break them."

And she thinks I broke them by using my dagger on the last ascent of the Gauntlet.

"You're using this to get your revenge on my family!" Amber shouts at Xaden. "For not supporting your father's rebellion!"

That's a low fucking blow.

Xaden doesn't even acknowledge it as he turns to the other wingleaders.

He isn't demanding proof like Dain. He believes me, and he's ready to execute a wingleader on nothing more than my word. As surely as if they're a physical structure, I feel my defenses crack on Xaden's behalf.

"Can you see my memories?" I ask Tairn. *"Share them?"*

"Yes." His head snakes left and right ever so slightly. *"A memory has never been shared outside of a mating bond. It's considered a violation."*

"Xaden's up there fighting because I told him it was her. Help him." And gods, I admire him for it. I take a deep breath. *"Only what they need to see."*

Wanting *and* admiring? I'm so screwed.

Tairn chuffs and every dragon besides Sgaeyl stiffens on the wall, even Amber's. The riders are quick to follow, silence filling the courtyard, and I know they know.

"That spineless wretch," Rhiannon seethes, her hand squeezing mine even tighter.

Dain pales.

"Believe me *now*?" I hurl it like the accusation it is. "You're supposed to be my oldest friend, Dain. My *best* friend. There's a reason I didn't tell you."

He staggers backward.

"The wingleaders have formed a quorum and are in unanimous agreement," Xaden announces, flanked by Nyra and Septon while the commandant hangs back. "We find you guilty, Amber Mavis."

"No!" she shouts. "It is no crime to rid the quadrant of the weakest rider! I did it to protect the integrity of the wings!" She paces in panic, looking to everyone—anyone for help.

As a whole, the formation moves backward.

"And as is our law, your sentence will be carried out by fire," Nyra states.

"No!" Amber looks to her dragon. "Claidh!"

Amber's Orange Daggertail snarls at the other dragons and lifts a claw.

Tairn swivels his massive head toward Claidh, his roar shaking the ground beneath my feet. Then he snaps his teeth at the smaller orange, and she retreats, her head hanging as she grips the wall again.

The sight breaks my heart, not for Amber but for Claidh.

"Do you have to?" I ask Tairn.

"This is our way."

"Please don't," I beg, forgetting to think the words. It's one thing to punish Amber, but Claidh will suffer as well.

Maybe I could talk to Amber. Maybe we can still work through our issues. Maybe we can find common ground, turn our anger to friendship or at least casual indifference. I shake my head, my heart pounding in my throat. I did this. I was so focused on whether anyone would believe me, I didn't stop to think what might happen if they *did*.

I turn to Xaden and beg again, my voice breaking by the end. "Please give her a chance."

He holds my gaze but doesn't so much as show a flicker of emotion.

"I let someone live once, and he almost killed you last night, Silver One," Tairn says. Then, as if this is all that really matters in the end, *"Justice is not always merciful."*

"Claidh," Amber whimpers, the courtyard so unbelievably silent that the sound carries.

The formation splits at the center.

Tairn leans low, extending his head and neck past the dais toward where Amber stands. Then his teeth part, he curls his tongue, and he incinerates her with a blast of fire so hot, I can feel it from here. It's over in a heartbeat.

A gruesome scream rends the air, shattering a window in the academic wing, and every rider slams their hands over their ears as Claidh mourns.

Don't freak out if you can't immediately
channel your dragon's powers, Mira.
Yeah, I know you have to be the best at everything,
but this isn't something you can control.
They'll channel when they feel you're ready.
And once they do, you'd better be ready to manifest a signet.
Until then, you're not ready. Don't push it.

—PAGE SIXTY-ONE, THE BOOK OF BRENNAN

CHAPTER TWENTY-ONE

"This really isn't necessary." I glance sideways at Liam as we make our way toward the door of the Archives. The cart doesn't even squeak anymore. He fixed that the very first day.

"So you've told me for the last week." He shoots me a grin, revealing a dimple.

"And yet you're still here. Every day. All day." It's not that I don't like him. To my absolute annoyance, he's actually…nice. Courteous, funny, and ridiculously helpful. He makes it difficult to loathe his constant presence, even though he leaves wood shavings in little piles everywhere he goes—which is everywhere *I* go now. The guy is constantly whittling with that smaller knife of his. Yesterday he finished the figurine of a bear.

"Until otherwise ordered," he says.

I shake my head at him as Pierson jolts upright at the Archives doors, straightening his cream tunic. "Good morning, Cadet Pierson."

"You as well, Cadet Sorrengail." He offers me a polite smile, which dies as he glances at Liam. "Cadet Mairi."

"Cadet Pierson," Liam responds, as if the scribe's tone hadn't completely changed.

My shoulders tense as Pierson hurries to open the door. Maybe it's just that I haven't been around marked ones before Basgiath, but the outright hostility toward them is becoming glaringly, uncomfortably obvious to me.

We walk into the Archives and wait by the table just like every other morning.

"How do you do that?" I ask Liam in a hushed whisper. "Handle when people are that rude without reacting?"

"You're rude to me all the time," he teases, drumming his fingers on the handle of the cart.

"Because you're my babysitter, not because…" I can't even say it.

"Because I'm the son of the disgraced Colonel Mairi?" His jaw ticks, his brow furrowing for a heartbeat as he looks away.

I nod, my stomach sinking as I think back over the last few months. "I guess I'm really no better, though. I hated Xaden on sight, and I didn't know a single thing about him." Not that I do now, either. He's infuriatingly good at being completely inaccessible.

Liam scoffs, earning us a glare from a scribe near the back corner. "He has that effect on people, especially women. They either despise him for what his father did or want to fuck him for the same reason, just depends on where we are."

"You actually *know* him, don't you?" I crane my neck to look up at him. "He didn't just pick you to shadow me because you're the best in our year."

"Just now catching on, huh?" A grin flashes across his face. "I would have told you that on the first day if you hadn't been so busy huffing and puffing about the pleasure of my company."

I roll my eyes as Jesinia approaches, her hood up over her hair. "Hey, Jesinia," I sign.

"Good morning," she signs back, her mouth curving in a shy smile as her gaze darts up to Liam.

"Good morning." He signs with a wink, clearly flirting.

It shocked me to my toes that first day that he knew how to sign, but honestly, I'd been a little judgy just because I didn't want a shadow.

"Just these today?" Jesinia asks, inspecting the cart.

"And these." I reach for the list of requests amid their obvious glances and hand it to her.

"Perfect." Her cheeks flush and she studies the list before putting it in her pocket. "Oh, and Professor Markham left before his daily report arrived to teach your briefing. Would you mind taking it over?"

"Happy to." I wait until she's pushing the cart away from us, then smack Liam's chest. "Stop it," I whisper out loud.

"Stop what?" He watches her until she turns the corner at the first set of shelves.

"Flirting with Jesinia. She's a long-term-relationship woman, so unless that's what you're looking for...just...don't."

His eyebrows hit his hairline. "How does *anyone* think long-term around here?"

"Not everyone is in a quadrant where death is less of a chance and more of a foregone conclusion." I breathe in the scent of the Archives and try to absorb a little of the peace it brings.

"So you're saying that some people still try to make cute little things like plans."

"Exactly, and those *some people* is Jesinia. Trust me, I've known her for years."

"Right. Because you wanted to be a scribe when you grew up." He scans the Archives with an intensity that almost makes me laugh. As if there's any chance someone is going to lunge out of the shelves and come after me.

"How did you know that?" I lower my voice as a group of second-years passes, their expressions somber as they debate the merits of two different historians.

"I did my research on you after I was...you know...assigned." He shakes his head. "I've seen you practicing this week with those blades of yours, Sorrengail. Riorson was right. You would have been wasted as a scribe."

My chest swells with more than a little pride. "That remains to be seen." At least challenges haven't resumed. Guess enough of us are dying during flight lessons to hold off on killing more through hand-to-hand. "What did you want to be when you grew up?" I ask, just to keep the conversation going.

"Alive." He shrugs.

Well, that's...something.

"How do you know Xaden anyway?" I'm not foolish enough to think that everyone in the province of Tyrrendor knows one another.

"Riorson and I were fostered at the same estate after the apostasy," he says, using the Tyrrish term for the rebellion, which I haven't heard in *ages*.

"You were fostered?" My mouth drops open. Fostering the children of aristocrats was a custom that died out after the unification of Navarre more than six hundred years ago.

"Well, yeah." He shrugs again. "Where did you think the kids of the traitors"—he flinches at the word—"went after they executed our parents?"

I look out over the sprawling shelves of texts, wondering if one of them holds the answer. "I didn't think." My throat catches on that last word.

"Most of our great houses were given to nobles who had remained loyal." He clears his throat. "As it should be."

I don't bother agreeing with what's obviously a conditioned reply. King Tauri's response after the rebellion was swift, even cruel, but I was a fifteen-year-old girl too lost in her own grief to think mercifully on the people who'd caused my brother's death. The burning of Aretia, which had been Tyrrendor's capital, to the ground had never sat well with me, though. Liam was the same age. It wasn't his fault his mother had broken faith with Navarre. "But you didn't go with your father to his new home?"

His gaze swings toward mine, and his brow furrows. "It's hard to live with a man who was executed on the same day as my mother."

My stomach sinks. "No. No, that's not right. Your father was Isaac Mairi, right? I've studied all the noble houses in every province, including Tyrrendor." Had I gotten something wrong?

"Yes. Isaac was my father." He tilts his head, looking toward the area where Jesinia disappeared, and I get the distinct feeling he is over this conversation.

"But he wasn't a part of the rebellion." I shake my head, trying to make sense of it. "He isn't on the death roll of the executions from Calldyr."

"You read the death roll from the Calldyr executions?" His eyes flare.

It takes all my courage, but I hold his stare. "I needed to see that someone was on it."

He draws back slightly. "Fen Riorson."

I nod. "He killed my brother at the Battle of Aretia." My mind scrambles, trying to harmonize what I've read and what he's saying. "But your father wasn't on that roll." But Liam was—as a witness. Mortification sweeps over me. What the hell am I doing? "I'm so sorry. I shouldn't have asked."

"He was executed at our family's house." His features tighten. "Before it was given to another noble, of course. And yes, I watched as they did it that time, too. I already had the rebellion relic by then, but the pain was the same." He looks away, his throat working. "Then I was sent to Tirvainne to be fostered by Duke Lindell, the same as Riorson. My little sister was sent elsewhere."

"They separated you?" My jaw practically unhinges. Neither fostering nor separating siblings is mentioned in any text I've read about the rebellion, and I've read a ton.

He nods. "She's only a year younger than me, though, so I'll get to see her when she enters the quadrant next year. She's strong, quick, and has good balance. She'll make it." The edge of panic in his tone reminds me of Mira.

"She could always choose another quadrant," I say softly, hoping it will soothe him.

He blinks at me. "We're all riders."

"What?"

"We're all riders. It was part of the deal. We're allowed to live, allowed a chance to prove our loyalty, but only if we make it through the Riders Quadrant." He stares at me in bewilderment. "You don't know?"

"I mean…" I shake my head. "I know that the children of the leaders, the officers, were all forced into conscription, but that's all. A lot of those treaty addenda are classified."

"I personally think the quadrant was chosen to give us the best chance of rising in rank, but others…" He grimaces. "Others think it's because the death rate is so much higher for riders, so they were hoping to kill us all off without having to do it themselves. I've heard Imogen say they originally figured the dragons have unimpeachable honor, so they'd never bond a marked one in the first place, and now they don't quite know what to do with us."

"How many of you are there?" I think of my mother and can't help but wonder how much of it she knows, how much of it she agreed to when she became the commanding general of Basgiath after Brennan's death.

"Xaden's never?" He pauses. "Sixty-eight of the officers had kids under the age of twenty. There are one hundred and seven of us, all who carry rebellion relics."

"The oldest is Xaden," I murmur.

He nods. "And the youngest is almost six now. Her name is Julianne."

I think I'm going to be sick. "Is she marked?"

"She was born with it."

I understand it was done by dragon, but what the fucking hell?

"And it's all right that you ask. Someone should know. Someone should remember." His shoulders rise and fall as he breathes deeply. "Anyway, is it hard for you to be in here? Or is it more of a comfort thing?"

Subject change noted.

I take in the rows of tables, slowly filling with scribes readying themselves for work, and imagine my father among them. "It's like coming home, but not. And it's not that it's changed—this place never changes. Hell, I think change is the mortal enemy of a scribe. But I'm starting to realize that *I've* changed. I don't quite fit here. Not anymore."

"Yeah. I get that." Something in his voice tells me he really does.

It's on the tip of my tongue to ask what the last five years were like for him, but Jesinia reappears, the cart laden with the requested tomes.

"I have everything here for you," she signs, then gestures to the scroll on top. "And that is for Professor Markham."

"We'll make sure he gets it," I promise, leaning forward to take the cart. My high collar shifts, and Jesinia gasps, her hand flying to cover her mouth.

"Oh gods, Violet. Your neck!" Her hand movements are sharp, and the sympathy in her eyes makes my chest tighten. "Sympathy" isn't a word found in our quadrant. There's rage, wrath, and indignation...but no sympathy.

"It's nothing." I put my collar back in place, covering the ring of yellowing bruises, and Liam reaches across me, taking the cart. "We'll see you tomorrow."

She bobs her head and wrings her hands as we turn for the door. Pierson closes it after we pass into the hallway.

"Riorson taught me to fight during the years he was at Tirvainne." Liam's change of subject is appreciated and no doubt intentional once again. "I've never seen anyone move the way he does. He's the only reason I made it through the first round of challenges. He might not show it, but he takes care of his own."

"Are you trying to sell me on his finer points?" We make the ascent, and I note with some satisfaction that my legs feel strong today. I love the days when my body cooperates.

"You are slightly stuck with him for..." He makes a face. "Well, forever."

"Or until one of us dies," I joke, but it falls flat as we round the corner and take the path past the Healer Quadrant. "How can you do this anyway? Guard someone whose own mother oversaw the wing that captured yours?" I've wanted to ask the question all week.

"Wondering if you can trust me?" He flashes another easy grin.

"Yes." The answer is simple.

He laughs, the sound echoing off the tunnel walls and glass windows of the clinic. "Good answer. All I can say is that your survival is essential to Riorson's, and I owe him everything. *Everything*." He looks me straight in the eye for that last word, even as the cart hits a raised stone in the paved corridor.

The scroll on top tumbles to the floor, and I wince at the dull ache in my ribs as I hurry to retrieve it and it unrolls along the slight slope of the passage.

"Got it." The thick parchment isn't eager to roll back into place, and I catch a sentence that makes me pause.

The conditions at Sumerton are of particular concern. A village was ransacked and a supply convoy looted last night—

"What does it say?" Liam asks.

"Sumerton was attacked." I flip the scroll to see if it's marked as classified, but it isn't.

"On the southern border?" He looks as confused as I feel.

"Yeah." I nod. "It's another high-altitude attack, too, if I remember my geography correctly. It says a supply convoy was looted." I read a little further. "And the community storage in nearby caves was ransacked. But that doesn't make sense. We have a trade agreement with Poromiel."

"A raiding party, then."

I shrug. "No clue. Guess we'll hear about it in Battle Brief today." Attacks along our southern borders are rising, all with the same description. Mountain villages are being torn apart wherever the wards weaken.

Immense, incredible hunger strikes, my stomach gnawing on emptiness that demands to be appeased with the blood of—

"Sorrengail?" Liam looks over at me, concern etched between his brows.

"Tairn's awake," I manage to say, clutching my stomach like I'm the one who craves a flock of sheep. Or goats. Or whatever he decides for the morning. *"Good gods, please go eat something."*

"The same could be suggested to you," he snarls.

"Such a morning person, aren't you?" The hunger dissipates, and I know it's because he's dampening the bond in that moment because I can't. His emotions only flow into me when they override his control. *"Thank you. Andarna?"*

"Still sleeping. She'll be out another few days after using that much power."

"Does it ever get any easier?" I ask Liam. "Being tackled by what they're feeling?"

He winces. "Good question. Deigh keeps pretty good control of himself, but when he's angry?" Liam shakes his head. "It's supposed to help once they start channeling and we have the power to shield them out, but you know Carr isn't going to bother with us until that happens."

I'd already assumed Liam didn't have his abilities yet, considering he's with me in every single class, but it's comforting to know he's still in the waning population of powerless riders with me. While Andarna has given me her gift for stopping time, I'm pretty sure using it isn't going to be a regular occurrence, especially if it takes her days to recover.

"So Tairn hasn't channeled to you, either, right?" Liam asks, a look of uncertainty, vulnerability on his face.

I shake my head. "I think he has commitment issues," I whisper.

"I heard that."

"Then stay out of my head."

Another wave of paralyzing hunger assaults me, and I nearly crush Markham's scroll in my hand. *"Don't be an ass."*

I swear I hear him chuff a chuckle in response.

"We'd better hurry or we'll miss breakfast."

"Right." I finish rolling the scroll and put it back on the cart.

"I want to be like the cool kids," Rhiannon grumbles as first-years from Second and Third Wings pour out of the stairwell of the turret that leads up to Professor Carr's classroom that afternoon, further clogging the hallway on our way to Battle Brief.

"We will," I promise, linking my arm through hers. Have to admit, there's more than a little twinge of jealousy in my chest.

"You may be cool, but you will never be as cool as I am!" Ridoc pushes past Liam and throws his arm over my shoulder.

"She's talking about everyone who's already channeling," I explain, juggling my books so I don't drop them. "Though at least if we're not channeling, we're not stressed about manifesting a signet before the magic kills us." The relic in the center of my back tingles, and I can't help but wonder if Andarna's gift has triggered that clock for me.

"Oh, I thought we were discussing how I just *owned* that physics test." He grins. "Definitely the highest score in the class."

Rhiannon rolls her eyes. "Please. I scored five points higher than you."

"We stopped counting *your* grades months ago." He leans forward slightly. "Your grades in that class make it unfair for the rest of us." He looks between our shoulders. "Wait. What did you get, Mairi?"

"Not getting into the middle of this," Liam responds.

I laugh as we break apart, entering the bottleneck of cadets to get into the briefing room.

"Sorry, Sorrengail," someone says, stepping out of the way and tugging their friend with them as we enter the tiered classroom.

"Nothing to be sorry about!" I call out, but they're already headed up a few rows. "I'm never going to get used to that."

"It definitely makes getting places easier," Rhiannon teases as we descend the steps that curve along the massive turret.

"They show the appropriate level of deference," Tairn grumbles.

"To what they think I'll be, not who I am." We find our row and walk to our seats, sitting as a squad among the first-years.

"That shows excellent forethought."

The room buzzes with energy as riders file in, and I can't help but notice that no one has to stand anymore. Our numbers have decreased exponentially in the last four months. The number of empty chairs is sobering. We lost another first-year yesterday when he got too close to another rider's Red Scorpiontail on the flight field. One second he was standing there, and the next he was a scorched patch of earth. I kept as close to Tairn as possible the rest of the session.

My scalp prickles, but I fight the urge to turn around.

"Riorson just got here," Liam says from the seat to my right, breaking from the little dragon figurine he's carving and looking up the rows toward the third-years.

"Figured." I hold up my middle finger and keep my eyes forward. Not that I don't like Liam, but I'm still pissed at Xaden for assigning him.

Liam snorts and grins, flashing his dimple. "And now he's glaring. Tell me, is it fun pissing off the most powerful rider in the quadrant?"

"You could try it yourself and find out," I suggest, opening my notebook to the next empty page. I can't turn around. I won't. Wanting Xaden is fine.

It has to be. Indulging the impulses it gives me? That's asinine.

"That's going to be a no from me."

I lose the battle with my self-control and look over my shoulder. Sure enough, Xaden is seated in the top row next to Garrick, mastering the art of looking bored. He gives Liam a nod, which Liam returns.

I roll my eyes and face forward again.

Liam concentrates on his carving, which looks a lot like his Red Daggertail, Deigh.

"I swear, you'd think there were assassination attempts on me during every class with the way he makes you shadow me." I shake my head.

"In his defense, people are fond of trying to kill you." Rhiannon sets out her supplies.

"One time! It's happened one time, Rhi!" I adjust my posture to keep my weight off my bruised ribs. They're wrapped tight, but leaning against the back of my seat isn't an option.

"Right. And what would you call that whole thing with Tynan?" Rhiannon asks.

"Threshing." I shrug.

"And Barlowe's constant threats?" She arches a brow at me.

"She has a point there," Sawyer chimes in, leaning forward from the seat next to Rhiannon's.

"They're just threats. The only time I've actually been targeted was at night, and it's not like Liam here is sleeping in my bedroom."

"I mean, I'm not opposed—" he begins, his knife hovering over the piece of wood.

"Don't even start." I whip my head to face him and can't help but laugh. "You are a *shameless* flirt."

"Thank you." He grins and goes back to carving.

"It wasn't a compliment."

"Don't mind her, she's just sexually frustrated. Makes a girl crabby." Rhiannon writes the date down on her empty page and I follow suit, dipping my quill into my portable inkpot. Those easy, mess-less pens some of the others can already use is just another reason I can't wait to channel. No more quills. No more inkpots.

"That has *nothing* to do with it." Gods, could she have said that a little louder?

"And yet I don't hear you denying it." She smiles sweetly at me.

"I'm sorry I don't make the cut," Liam teases. "But I'm sure Riorson would be fine with my reviewing a couple candidates, especially if it means you'll stop flipping him off in front of his entire wing."

"And how exactly would you be *reviewing* candidates? What will you be scoring?" Rhiannon asks, one eyebrow raised above her wide grin. "This I have to hear."

I manage a straight face for all of two seconds before laughing at how horrified he suddenly looks. "Thanks for the offer, though. I'll make sure to run any potential liaisons by you."

"I mean, you could watch," Rhiannon continues, blinking innocently at him. "Just to be sure she's fully covered. You know, so no one…sticks it to her."

"Oh, are we telling dick jokes now?" Ridoc asks from Liam's side. "Because my entire life has led up to this very moment."

Even Sawyer laughs.

"Fuck me," Liam mutters under his breath. "I'm just saying that since you're protected at night now—" We laugh harder, and he blows out a deep breath.

"Wait." I stop laughing. "What do you mean I'm protected at night? Because you're next door?" My smile vanishes. "Please tell me he's not making you sleep in the hallway or something obnoxious."

"No. Of course not. He warded your door the morning after the attack." His expression clearly says I should know this. "I'm guessing he didn't tell you?"

"He *what*?"

"He warded your door," Liam says, quieter this time. "So only you can open it."

Shit. I don't know how to feel about that. It's more than slightly controlling, and way out of line, but also…sweet. "But if he's the one who warded it, then he can get in, too, right?"

"Well, yeah." Liam shrugs as Professors Markham and Devera walk down the stairs, heading for the front of the room. "But it's not like Riorson is going to kill you."

"Right. You see, I'm still adjusting to that little change of heart." I fumble my quill and it falls to the ground, but before I can lean over, the shadows beneath the arm of my desk lift the instrument like an offering. I pluck it out of the shadows and look back at Xaden.

He's locked in conversation with Garrick, not paying me a speck of attention.

Except, apparently, he is.

"If we can get started?" Markham calls over the room, and we fall silent as he places the scroll Liam and I had delivered to him before breakfast on the podium. "Excellent."

I write *Sumerton* down at the top of the page and Liam trades his knife for a quill.

"First announcement," Devera says, stepping forward. "We've decided that not only will the winners of this year's Squad Battle receive bragging rights—" She grins like we're in for a treat. "But they'll also be given a trip to the front lines to shadow an active wing."

Cheers break out all around us.

"So if we win, we get a chance to die sooner?" Rhiannon whispers.

"Maybe they're trying a reverse psychology thing." I glance at the others around us who are clearly overjoyed and worry about their sanity. Then again, most everyone in this room can stay on their dragon.

"So can you."

"Don't you have better things to do with your day than listen in on my self-loathing?"

"Not particularly. Now pay attention."

"Stop butting in and maybe I can," I counter.

Tairn chuffs. One day I might be able to translate that sound, but it's not today.

"I know the Squad Battle doesn't commence until spring," Devera continues, "but I figured that news would give you all the proper motivation to apply yourselves in every area leading up to the challenges."

Another cheer resounds.

"And now that we have your attention." Markham lifts his hand and the room quiets. "The front lines are relatively quiet today, so we're going to take this opportunity to dissect the Battle of Gianfar."

My quill hovers above my notebook. Surely he didn't say that.

The mage lights rise to the Cliffs of Dralor that separate Tyrrendor, lifting the entire province thousands of feet above the rest of the Continent, before shining brightest on the ancient stronghold along the southern border. "This battle was pivotal to the unification of Navarre, and though it happened more than six centuries ago, there are important lessons that still impact our flight formations to this day."

"Is he serious?" I whisper to Liam.

"Yeah." Liam's grip bends his quill. "I think he is."

"What made this battle unique?" Devera asks, her eyebrows raised. "Bryant?"

"The stronghold was not only set for a siege," the second-year says from high above us, "but was equipped with the first cross-bolt, which proved lethal against dragonkind."

"Yes. And?" Devera prompts.

"It was one of the final battles where gryphons and dragons actually worked alongside each other to annihilate the army of the Barrens," the second-year continues.

I glance left and right, watching the other riders begin to take notes. Surreal. This is just...surreal. Even Rhiannon is writing intensely.

None of them knows what we do, that an entire village of Navarrians was ransacked last night along the border and supplies looted. And yet, we're discussing a battle that happened before the convenience of indoor plumbing was invented.

"Now, pay close attention," Markham lectures. "Because you'll be turning in a detailed report in three days and drawing comparisons to battles from the last twenty years."

"Was that scroll marked classified?" Liam asks under his breath.

"No," I respond just as quietly. "But maybe I missed it?" The battle map doesn't even show activity near that mountain range.

"Yeah." He nods, scratching his quill against the parchment as he begins to take notes. "That has to be it. You missed it."

I blink, forcing my hand through the motions of writing about a battle I've analyzed dozens of times with my father. Liam's right. That's the only possible explanation. Our clearance isn't high enough, or maybe they haven't finished gathering all the information needed to form an accurate report.

Or it had to have been marked classified. I just missed it.

**The first rush of power is unmistakable.
The first time it forms to you, surrounds you with a seemingly endless supply of energy, you'll be addicted to the high, to the possibilities of all you can do with it, to the control you hold in the palm of your hand.But here's the thing, that power can quickly turn and control *you*.**

—Page sixty-four, the Book of Brennan

CHAPTER TWENTY-TWO

The rest of November passes without mention of what happened at Sumerton, and by the time the howling winds bring snow in December, I've given up hoping command will release the information. It's not like Liam or I can directly ask the professors without incriminating ourselves for reading what was obviously a classified report—even if it wasn't marked.

It makes me wonder what else doesn't make it to Battle Brief, but I keep that to myself. Between that and my growing frustration over my inability to channel—unlike three-quarters of my year—I'm keeping a lot to myself these days.

"Not entirely," Tairn grunts.

"No comments from you, not after you almost let me hit the side of a mountain today." My stomach churns just thinking about how far he let me fall.

The first-year from Third Wing wasn't as lucky. She lost her seat during a new maneuver and ended up on the death roll this morning.

Rhiannon swings her bow staff, and I throw my weight into a backbend, narrowly escaping the strike. To my absolute surprise, I keep my balance on the training mat.

"Then stay on next time."

"Start channeling and maybe I'll be able to," I counter.

"You're distracted tonight." Rhiannon backs off as I regain my balance, showing me mercy no opponent would during a challenge. Her gaze flicks across the mat to where Liam sits on a bench, carving yet another dragon, and returns to mine, giving me a look that says she'll follow up later once I've been released from my constant shadow for the night. "But you're faster than you used to be. Whatever Imogen has you doing is working."

"You're not ready to channel yet, Silver One."

"As if there was ever any doubt," Imogen calls from the next mat over, where she casually holds Ridoc in a headlock, waiting for him to tap out.

To my left, Sawyer and Quinn circle each other, preparing for yet another round, and behind Rhiannon, Emery and Heaton are doing their best to coach the other first-years we gained after Threshing while Dain looks on, studiously avoiding anything that has to do with me.

Per his recent orders, Tuesday nights are for squad hand-to-hand practice, because the full academic load we're carrying, coupled with flight lessons and now wielding instruction for some of us isn't leaving much time for the mat. A few of the farther mats are taken up by other riders with the same idea, one of which includes Jack Barlowe.

Hence why Liam refused when Ridoc asked to spar with him.

"You're taking it easy on me," I tell Rhiannon. Sweat drips down my back, dampening the tight-fitted tunic I chose while my dragon-scale vest dries on the bench next to Liam.

It's not like he needs extra practice. He's already taken everyone but Dain down to the mat, and part of me thinks that's only because Dain refuses to be bested by a younger rider.

"We've been at this for an hour." Rhiannon swishes her staff through the air. "You're tired, and the last thing I want is to hurt you."

"Challenges resume after solstice," I remind her. "You're not doing me any favors by holding back."

"She's not wrong," a deep voice says from behind me.

In my peripherals, I see Liam stand, and I mutter a curse under my breath.

"Well aware," I say over my shoulder as Xaden passes by our mat, accompanied by Garrick as usual. It's impossible to rip my eyes away until he passes, though. Gods, I have it bad. "Go away unless you have something useful to say."

"Move faster. You'll be less likely to die. How's that for useful?" he calls back, taking up a position on a mat closer to the center of the sparring gym.

Rhiannon's eyes flare, and Liam shakes his head.

"What?"

"The way you talk to him," Rhiannon murmurs.

"What's he going to do? Kill me?" I charge forward, swinging my staff at her legs.

She jumps over the attack and spins, bringing the staff against mine with a *crack*.

"You're likely to kill each other," Liam chimes in, taking his seat again. "Can't wait to see how you two function after graduation."

After graduation.

"Haven't let myself think past this week, let alone all the way to graduation." Not when there are some very difficult questions I'm not ready to ask.

"Look, I know you're...aggravated by how long it's taking Tairn to channel," Rhiannon says, circling me on the mat again. "I'm just saying on this mat with me is a way safer place for you to take out that anger than the giant, shadow-wielding wingleader."

"I don't want to take any of my anger out on you. You're my friend." I gesture loosely toward Xaden. "He's the one who stuck me with a shadow I can't shake because he thinks I'm his *weakness*. But does he help me?" I lash out with the staff, and she counters. "No. Does he train me?" Another lunge, another clash of our staffs. "No. He's remarkably good at showing up when I'm about to die and eliminating threats, but that's it." He sure as hell doesn't have a problem keeping his eyes off me the way I do him.

"So there's definitely some anger there," Rhiannon drawls as she spins away easily.

"You would be furious if someone took your freedom away. If you had Liam at your door every morning until every night, even as seemingly great as he is." I dodge one of her attacks.

"I appreciate that," Liam butts in, proving my point.

"Yeah," she agrees. "I would. And I'm pissed on your behalf. Now, let's put that anger to use." Rhiannon rains another series of moves down on me and I keep up, but only because she's doing exactly what I accused her of and taking it easy on me.

Then I make the mistake of glancing over her shoulder, toward the center of the gym.

Holy. Fucking. Hot.

Xaden and Garrick have stripped off their shirts and are sparring like their lives depend on it, a blur of kicks, punches, and rippling muscle. I've never seen two people move that fast. It's a beautiful, hypnotizing dance with lethal choreography that makes me hold my breath whenever Garrick goes in for the kill and Xaden deflects.

I've seen countless riders spar without their shirts these past months. This is nothing new. I should be absolutely immune to the male form, but I've never seen *him* shirtless.

Every edge of Xaden's body is honed like a weapon, all sharp lines and barely leashed power. His rebellion relic twists around his upper body and stands out against the deep bronze of his skin, accentuating every punch he throws, and his stomach… I mean, how many muscles *are* there in the abdominals? His are so rigidly defined that I could probably count every single one if the rest of him wasn't so damned distracting. And he has the largest dragon relic I've ever seen. Mine consumes the skin between shoulder blades, but Sgaeyl's mark takes up his entire back.

And I know exactly how that body feels on top of mine, just how much power—

My hip stings, knocking me out of my trance, and I startle.

"Serves you right," Tairn lectures.

"Pay attention!" Rhiannon yells, drawing back her staff. "I could have… Oh." Clearly, she sees what I do, what nearly every other woman—and several of the men—are happily watching.

How can we not when the two of them are mesmerizing?

Garrick's wider, more densely packed with muscle than Xaden, his rebellion relic only extending to his shoulder, the second largest I've seen. Only Xaden's reaches his carved jawline.

"That is…" Rhiannon murmurs beside me.

"It sure is," I agree.

"Stop objectifying our wingleader," Liam teases.

"Is that what we're doing?" Rhiannon asks, not bothering to look away.

My mouth waters at the muscled expanse of his back and that sculpted ass. "Yeah, I think that's what we're doing."

Liam snorts.

"We could just be watching for technique."

"Yeah. We absolutely could be." But I'm not. I'm shamelessly wondering how his skin would feel under my fingertips, how my body would react to having every ounce of that intense focus on *me.* Heat races through my veins and stings my cheeks.

A repetitive smacking sound draws my attention to the right, where Ridoc is tapping out with zeal. Imogen drops him, leaving him gasping for breath on the mat, and an unwanted and absolutely illogical flash of ugly, twisted jealousy stabs me straight in the chest at the pure yearning she can't hide in her expression as she watches Xaden and Garrick.

"If you guys are this easily distracted, we're fucked for the Squad Battle," Dain barks. "You can kiss any thought of visiting the front lines goodbye."

We all snap out of it, and I shake my head like that might clear the dizzying need that demands I do more than look at Xaden, which is just… ridiculous. He only tolerates my existence because our dragons are mated, and here I am salivating over his half-naked body.

It's a *really* nice half-naked body, though.

"Get back to work. We have another half hour," Dain orders, and I feel like he's talking directly to me, which would be the first thing he's said since my memory got Amber killed.

"She got herself killed by breaking the Codex," Tairn growls.

Sure enough, when I glance his way, Dain's eyes are narrowed on me, but I must be reading his face wrong. Surely that's not betrayal pursing his lips.

"Should we?" Rhiannon asks, lifting her staff.

"Yep, we definitely should." I roll my shoulders, and we start again. I match her move for move, using the patterns she taught me, but she switches up the next attack.

"Stop defending and go on offense!" Tairn demands, his anger flooding my system and throwing off my footwork.

Rhiannon sweeps low and flips me onto my back, knocking the wind out of me as I collide with the mat.

I fight for air that isn't there.

"Shit, I'm sorry, Vi." Rhiannon drops down to a knee beside me. "Just relax and give it a second."

"And yet *that* is the rider Tairn chose," Jack mocks, talking to someone in his squad as he grins maliciously at the edge of the mat. "I'm starting to think he chose wrong, but considering I haven't seen you wield any powers, I bet you're thinking the same thing, too, aren't you, Sorrengail? Shouldn't you have twice the ability to channel with two dragons?"

It doesn't work like that with Andarna, but none of them know that.

Liam stands, putting himself between Jack and me as the first trickle of air dances into my lungs.

"Simmer down, Mairi. I'm not going to attack your little charge. Not when I can just challenge her in a couple of weeks and accidentally snap her scrawny neck in front of an audience." Jack folds his arms across his chest and watches me struggle with pure pleasure. "Tell me, though, you are getting tired of playing the nursemaid, aren't you?" His friend from First Wing offers him something—a slice of the orange he's eating—and Jack shoves his hand away at the wrist. "Get that noxious shit away from me. Do you want me to end up in the infirmary?"

"Walk the fuck away, Barlowe," Liam warns, dagger in hand.

I manage one breath, then two as Jack's gaze rises from me to someone standing behind me. That look on his face, half envy, half shitting himself, means it has to be Xaden.

"She's only alive because of you," Jack spits, but the blood drains from his face.

"Right, because I'm the one who buried a dagger in your shoulder at Threshing."

Finally breathing somewhat normally, I scramble for my feet, clutching the staff with both hands.

"We could just settle this now," Jack says, sidestepping Liam to look me in the eyes. "If you're done hiding behind the big, strong men."

My stomach hollows out because he's right. The only reason I don't accept his challenge is because I'm not sure I'll win, and the only reason he isn't attacking me is because of Liam and Xaden. If I attack Jack now, they'll kill him. Garrick's hulking frame appears to the left, and I begrudgingly add him to my list of protectors. Hell, even Imogen has inched closer, but not on my behalf.

It's only on *his*.

"That's what I thought," Jack says, blowing me a kiss.

"You ran," I snarl, wishing I could lunge forward and beat the shit out of him, but forcing my feet to stay planted where they are. "That day in the field, you *fucking ran* when it was three on one, and we both know when it comes down to it, you'll run again. That's what cowards do."

Jack flushes, his eyes nearly bugging out of his face.

"Oh, for fuck's sake, Violet," Dain mutters.

"She's not wrong," Xaden drawls.

Garrick laughs, and Liam muscles Jack off the mat when he leaps at me. Jack's boots squeak against the hardwood floor as he unsuccessfully fights to hold his ground, and Liam forces him from the gym.

With a flick of his hand, Xaden shuts the huge doors with his power, locking Jack out.

"What the hell were you thinking, egging him on like that?" Dain marches toward me, disbelief raising his brows.

"Oh, *now* you feel like talking to me?" I lift my chin, but it's Xaden who fills my vision as he steps between us. The fury in his eyes is palpable, but I don't retreat.

"Give us a second." His gaze is locked on mine, but we both know he's not talking to me.

My pulse skitters.

Rhiannon steps back.

"You want to tell me why the fuck you're not wearing that?" His tone is soft but deadly as he points toward the bench where my armor lies.

"I have to wash it at some point."

"And you thought that would be a good idea during *sparring*?" His chest heaves, like he's battling to keep control of himself.

I'm just trying *not* to notice his chest or the heat he's throwing off like a damned furnace. "I washed it *before* sparring, knowing it could dry while your guard dog keeps watch, as opposed to sleeping without it because we both know what happens behind locked doors around here."

"Not behind yours anymore." His jaw ticks. "I made sure of it."

"Because I'm supposed to trust *you*?"

"Yes." A vein in his neck bulges.

"And you make it *so* easy." Sarcasm drips from my voice.

"You know I can't kill you. Fuck, Sorrengail, the entire *quadrant* knows I can't kill you." He leans into my space, eclipsing the rest of the room.

"That doesn't mean you can't hurt me."

He blinks and shifts backward, composing himself in less than a heartbeat while mine still races. "Stop training with a bow staff. It's too easy to knock out of your hands. Stick to the daggers."

To my surprise, he doesn't snatch it away just to prove he can.

"I was doing just fine until Tairn barged into my head with all his anger and distracted me," I argue, my defenses rising like the hackles of a dog.

"Then learn how to block him out." He says it like it's just that simple.

"What, with all this power I'm wielding?" My brows rise. "Or were you unaware that I'm still not channeling?" I want to throttle him, to shake some ever-loving sense into that beautiful head of his.

He leans in so we're almost nose to nose. "I am annoyingly aware of *everything* you do."

Thanks to Liam.

Every inch of my body vibrates with anger, with irritation, with... whatever this electric tension is between us as we stand there, our eyes locked in combat.

"Wingleader Riorson," Dain starts. "She's just not used to the bond yet. She'll learn how to block it out."

Dain's words sting like a blow. I inhale sharply and step back from Xaden. Good gods, we've been putting on a fucking *show*. What is it about Xaden that makes me tune out the rest of the world?

"You choose the oddest times to defend her, Aetos." Xaden all but rolls his eyes as he looks at Dain. "And the most convenient times *not* to."

Dain's jaw clenches and his hands curl into fists at his sides.

He's talking about Amber. I know it. Dain knows it. Everyone in this whole, awkward room knows it. Our entire squad was there when Dain demanded I call Xaden a liar.

Xaden turns those unfathomable eyes back on me. "Do us both a favor and put the fucking armor back on," he finishes.

Before I can counter, he turns and walks off the mat, meeting Garrick at the edge.

His back.

My quiet gasp is uncontrollable, and Xaden tenses for a second before taking his shirt from Garrick's outstretched hand and tugging it over his head, covering the navy-blue relic of a dragon that sweeps from his waist to over both shoulders—textured intricately with raised silver lines I couldn't see from across the gym.

Silver lines I instantly recognize as scars.

"You held your own and controlled your temper," Tairn says, an immense swell of pride flooding my chest.

"She's ready," Andarna adds with a giddy jolt of joy that makes me instantly light-headed.

"She's ready," he agrees.

• • •

A couple of hours later, I rip my brush through my hair in the privacy of my room, still fully dressed down to my boots *and* armor. I still can't believe I made an ass of myself in front of my entire squad simply because Xaden decided to train shirtless.

I really need to get laid.

I pause mid-brushstroke when a rush of energy races down my spine, dissipating in a heartbeat.

Well, that's...weird.

Maybe it's... *No*. It can't be. It felt completely different when Andarna stopped time through me. That was a full-body flood that expanded through my fingers and toes, then...left afterward.

Another wave ripples through me, stronger this time, and I drop the brush, clutching the edge of the dresser so I don't fall as my knees threaten to buckle. The energy doesn't dissipate this time; it sticks around, humming under my skin, ringing in my ears, overwhelming every sense.

Something within me expands, somehow too big for my own body, too vast to be contained, and pain sears every nerve as I crack open, the sound reverberating through my skull like bones shattering. It's as though I've been split at the very seams of the fabric of my being.

My knees hit the floor, and I throw my hands over my temples, trying to shove everything I am back into my skull, forcing myself to shrink.

Energy pours in—a deluge of raw, endless power—eroding everything I was and forging something completely new as it fills every pore, every organ, every bone. My head screams, and it feels like Tairn has flown too high too fast and I can't pop my ears. All I can do is lie there on the floor and pray the pressure equalizes.

I stare at my brush, the hardwood floor biting into my cheek, and breathe.

In and then out.

In...and then out...surrendering to the onslaught.

Finally, the pain ebbs, but the energy—the power—doesn't. It's simply... there, prowling through my veins, saturating every cell in my body. It is everything I am and everything I can be all at once.

I sit up slowly and flip my hands to examine my tingling palms. It feels like they should look different, changed, but they're not. They're still my fingers, my slender wrists, and yet they're so much more now. They're strong enough to shape the torrent inside me, to mold it into whatever I desire.

"This is your power, isn't it?" I ask Tairn, but he doesn't answer. *"Andarna?"*

There's only silence.

Go figure, they're always around, pushing into my head when I could use a little space, then nowhere to be found when it's the other way around. I'd heard them say I was ready earlier, but I figured it would take a day or two for my mind to fully open that pathway once Tairn started channeling. Guess not.

Rhiannon. I have to tell Rhiannon. She's going to flip that I can finally go to Professor Carr's class with her. And Liam? He can stop pretending that he can't channel just so he isn't forced to leave me for an hour a day.

Heat washes over me, prickling my skin and centering low in my stomach.

Odd, but whatever. It's probably just a side effect of the power. I throw open the lock on my door and yank it open.

My vision blurs and need slams into me, robbing me of every logical thought besides satiating the overwhelming—

"Violet?" The fuzzy shape of a man stands in the hallway, and I blink Liam into focus. "You all right?"

"Are you sleeping in the hallway?" I grip the doorframe as an image of falling fills my mind, and I feel the sizzle of flakes as they make contact with my heated skin. It's gone as quickly as it appeared, but the driving, thundering desire remains.

Oh shit. This is…lust.

"No." Liam shakes his head. "Just hanging out here before turning in."

I look at him then. Really, honestly *look* at him. He's more than handsome, with strong features and sky-blue eyes that are startlingly beautiful.

"Why are you looking at me like that?" He sets his knife and semi-carved dragon down.

"Like what?" My teeth sink into my bottom lip and I debate rubbing against him like a cat in heat while demanding he appease this unimaginable ache.

But he's not who you really want.

He's not Xaden.

"Like…" He cocks his head to the side. "Like something's going on. You don't look like you feel—you know—like yourself."

Oh shit.

It's because I'm not myself. All of this, the need, the lust, the craving for the one person who I'm meant to be with…it's Tairn.

Tairn's emotions aren't just overwhelming me; they're controlling me.

"I'm good! Go to bed!" I step back into my room and slam the door while I still have the mental capacity to do so.

Then I start pacing, but that doesn't stop the next blast of heat or the compulsion to—

I have to get out of here before I make an epic mistake and take Tairn's feelings out on Liam.

Grabbing my fur-lined cloak in one hand and pulling my hair up with the other, I swirl the fabric over my shoulders and fasten the clip beneath my throat. A second later, I peek out the door, and when I'm sure the coast is clear, I fucking *flee*.

I make it to the entrance of the spiral steps—the ones that lead to the river—before I have to lean back against the stone wall and breathe through the fog of Tairn's emotions.

Once the wave passes, I race down the steps, keeping one hand on the wall in case I'm pulled under again.

The mage lights flicker on as I approach and fizzle out as I race by, as though this newfound power is already at work, stretching into the world.

Away. I have to get away from everyone until Tairn finishes…whatever he and Sgaeyl are doing.

I stumble out of the stairwell and emerge at the foundation walls of the citadel. Snow fills the sky, and I tip my head back, savoring the brief kiss of snowflakes on skin that's heated for all the wrong reasons.

The air is crisp and chilled, and—

My eyes pop open at the scent in the air and I whirl, my cloak whipping out behind me as I find the source of the sweet, easily identifiable smoke.

Xaden is leaning back against the wall, one foot braced on the stone, smoking and watching me like he doesn't have a care in the world.

"Is that…churam?"

He blows out a puff of smoke. "Want some? Unless you're here to continue our earlier argument, in which case, none for you."

My jaw practically unhinges. "No! We're not allowed to smoke that!"

"Yeah, well, the people who made that rule obviously weren't bonded to Sgaeyl and Tairn, now were they?" A smirk lifts a corner of his mouth.

Gods, I could stare at his lips forever. They are perfectly shaped and yet entirely too decadent for the slashing line of his jaw.

"It helps with...distancing yourself." He offers me the rolled churam and cocks an eyebrow at me—the one with the scar. "Beyond what shielding does, of course."

I shake my head and cross through the newly fallen snow to brace my weight on the wall beside him, letting my head fall back against the stone.

"Suit yourself." He inhales deeply on the churam and then puts it out against the wall.

"I feel like I'm on fucking *fire*." That's putting it mildly.

"Yeah. That happens." His laugh holds a wicked edge, and I make the utterly unforgivable mistake of turning to see his smile.

Xaden, while brooding and bossy, dangerous and lethal, is a toe-curling sight that makes my pulse quicken. But Xaden laughing, his head thrown back with a smile curving his mouth, is drop-dead beautiful. My stupid, foolish heart feels like there's a fist around it, squeezing tight.

There is nothing I wouldn't sacrifice, nothing I wouldn't give to have one unguarded moment with this man I'm going to be tethered to for the rest of our lives.

This has to be Tairn. It just...has to.

And yet, I know it isn't. While I'd admired Liam upstairs, I am completely, utterly *obsessed* with Xaden.

His eyes meet mine in the moonlight. "Oh, Violence, you're going to have to learn to shield against Tairn or his escapades with Sgaeyl will drive you mad—or into someone's bed."

I squeeze my eyes shut just so I can escape his gorgeous face as a jolt of heat flashes through me, making every inch of my skin tingle and burn. I reach a hand out to steady myself against the wall again. "Oh, I know. I am horrified to see Liam again."

"Liam? Why?" He pivots to face me, leaning against his shoulder. "Where the hell *is* your bodyguard?"

"I'm my own bodyguard," I counter, resting my cheek on the icy stone. "And he's in bed."

"*Your* bed?" His voice is like a crack of lightning.

I pry my eyes open to meet his gaze. The snow makes everything so much brighter, highlighting the furrowed line of his brow, the firm set of his mouth. "No. Not that it should matter to you."

Is he jealous? That's...oddly comforting.

He looses a breath, his shoulders dipping. "It *doesn't* matter to me as long as you're both consenting, and trust me, you're in no condition to consent."

"You have no clue what I'm capable of consenting—" Undeniable, unquenchable need nearly takes me out at the knees.

Xaden's arm wraps around my waist, steadying me. "Why the hell aren't you shielding?"

"Not all of us have been given lessons! He just started channeling before all…this, and in case you forgot, you're only allowed to attend Professor Carr's class if you can wield."

"Always thought that was a ridiculous rule." He sighs. "All right. Crash course. Only because I've been where you are and woken up with more than a few regrets."

"You're actually going to help me?"

"I've been helping you for *months*." His hand flexes at my waist, and I swear I can feel the warmth of his touch through my cloak and leathers.

"No, you sent Liam to help. *He's* been helping me for months." My forehead puckers. "Weeks. Almost months. Whatever."

He has the nerve to look offended. "I'm the one who burst through your door and killed everyone who attacked you, and *then* I removed the other threat to your life with a very public, very polarizing display of vengeance. Liam didn't do that. I did."

"The crowd wasn't polarized. They were all for it. I was there."

"*You* were torn. In fact, you begged Tairn not to kill her, damn well knowing she'd just come after you again."

That point was still debatable.

"Fine. But let's not pretend that you didn't do most of that for yourself. It would be inconvenient for you if I died." I shrug, blatantly poking at him to help ignore the rising tide of lust thundering through me.

He stares at me with disbelief. "You know what? We're not fighting tonight. Not if you want to learn how to shield."

"Fine. We're not fighting. Teach me." I tilt my chin. Gods, I barely reach his collarbone.

"Ask me nicely." He leans closer.

"Have you *always* been this tall?" I blurt the first thing that comes to mind.

"No. I was a child at some point."

I roll my eyes.

"Ask me nicely, Violence," he whispers. "Or I'm gone."

I can feel Tairn at the edge of my mind, his emotions ebbing and flowing, and know the next wave is going to hit hard. How freaking long can those two possibly take? "How often is it like this with them?"

"Often enough that you're going to need proper shields. You won't ever be able to block them out completely, and sometimes *they* forget to block *us*, like tonight. That's why the churam helps, but at least it's like walking by a brothel instead of actively participating in one."

Well…shit. "Right then. All right. Will you teach me to shield?"

A smile curves his mouth, and my gaze drops to his lips. "Say please."

"Are you always this difficult?"

"Only when I know I have something you need. What can I say, I like making you squirm. It's like a sweet little slice of payback for what you've put me through these last couple of months." He brushes the snow off my hair.

"What *I've* put *you* through?" Unbelievable.

"You've scared me nearly to death once or twice, so I think saying *please* is a fair request."

Like he's ever played fair a day in his life. I take a deep breath and swat at a snowflake that lands on my nose. "As you prefer. Xaden?" I smile sweetly up at him and inch a little closer. "Would you pretty, pretty please teach me how to shield before I accidentally climb you like a tree and we *both* wake up with regrets?"

"Oh, I'm firmly in control of my faculties." He smiles again, and I feel it like a caress.

Dangerous. This is so damned dangerous. Heat flushes my skin, so hot that I debate tossing my cloak to the ground just to get a little relief. Notably, Xaden isn't wearing one.

"And since you asked so nicely." He adjusts his stance and brings both his hands up to my cheeks, cradling my face before sliding them back to hold my head. "Close your eyes."

"It requires touching me?" My eyes flutter shut at the sensation of his skin against mine.

"Not at all. Just one of the perks of not thinking too clearly. You have incredibly touchable skin."

The compliment makes me suck in a breath. So much for controlling his faculties.

"You need to envision somewhere. Anywhere. I prefer the top of my favorite hillside near what's left of Aretia. Wherever it is, it needs to feel like home."

The only place I can think of is the Archives.

"Feel your feet hit the ground and dig in some."

I imagine my boots on the polished marble floor of the Archives and wiggle them a little. "Got it."

"That's called grounding, keeping your mental self somewhere so you aren't swept away by the power. Now call to your power. Open your senses."

My palms begin to tingle, and a flood of energy surrounds me, just as saturating as it was in my bedroom but without the pain. It's *everywhere*, filling the Archives and pushing at the walls, making them bow and bend, threatening to break them. "Too much."

"Focus on your feet. Stay grounded. Can you see where the power flows from? If not, just pick a place."

I turn in my mind. The barrage of molten power is flowing through the door. "I see it."

"Perfect. You're a natural. It takes most people a week just to learn how to ground. Now, do whatever you need to mentally do to wall yourself off from that current. Tairn is the source. You block that power, and you'll have some control back."

The door. I just need to close the door and twist the enormous, circular handle that seals the Archives off for fire control.

Desire makes my heart pound, and I grab on to Xaden's arms, anchoring myself in reality.

"You've got this." His voice sounds strained. "Whatever you create in your mind is real to you. Shut off the valve. Build a wall. Whatever makes sense."

"It's a door." My fingers dig into the soft material of his tunic, and I mentally heave myself against the door, forcing it shut one inch at a time.

"There you go. Keep going."

My physical body trembles at the effort it takes to mentally shove the door closed, but I get it there. "I've got the door shut."

"Great. Lock it."

I imagine spinning the giant handle and hearing the locks click into place. The relief is immediate, a cool blast of snow against my feverish skin. Power pulses, turning the door clear. "It changed. I can see through the door."

"Yeah. You'll never be able to fully block him. Got it locked?"

I nod.

"Open your eyes, but do your best to keep that door locked. It means keeping one foot grounded. Don't be surprised if it slips. We'll just start again."

I open my eyes, keeping that mental picture of the shut Archives door, and while my body is still heated and flushed with warmth, that inescapable, driving need is blessedly...somewhat muted. "He's..." I can't find the right words.

Xaden studies me with an intensity that makes me sway toward him. "You are astonishing." He shakes his head. "I couldn't do that for *weeks*."

"Guess I have a superior teacher." The emotion swelling through me is more than joy. It's euphoria that has me grinning like a fool. I'm finally not only good at something, but *astonishing*.

His thumbs stroke over the soft skin under my ears, and his gaze drops to my mouth and heats. Hands flexing, he draws me forward a few inches before he suddenly lets go and retreats a full step. "Damn it. Touching you was a bad idea."

"The worst," I agree, but my tongue skims my lower lip.

He *groans* and my core melts at the sound. "Kissing you would be a cataclysmic mistake."

"Calamitous." What would it take to hear that groan again?

The inches between us feel like kindling, ready to burn at the first suggestion of heat, and I'm a living, breathing flame. This is everything I should run from, and yet denying the primal attraction I feel is completely, utterly impossible.

"We'll both regret it." He shakes his head, but there's more than hunger in his eyes as he stares at my lips.

"Naturally," I whisper. But knowing I'll regret it doesn't stop me from wanting it—wanting him. Regretting is a problem for future Violet.

"Fuck it."

One second he's out of reach and the next his mouth is on mine, hot and insistent.

Gods, *yes*. This is exactly what I need.

I'm trapped between the immovable stone of the wall and the hard lines of Xaden's body, and there's nowhere else I'd rather be. The thought should sober me, but all I do is lean in for more.

He tunnels a hand through my hair, cradling the back of my head, angling me for a deeper kiss, and my lips part eagerly. He takes the invitation, sliding his tongue along mine with expert, teasing strokes that have me clutching at his chest, fisting the material of his shirt to pull him closer as desire dances up and down my spine.

He tastes like churam and mint, like everything I'm not supposed to want and yet can't help needing, and I kiss him back with everything I have, sucking on his lower lip and scraping my teeth over him.

"Violence," he moans, and the sound of the nickname on his lips makes me ravenous.

Closer. I need him *closer.*

As though he can hear my thoughts, he kisses me harder, claiming every line and curve of my mouth with a reckless edge that makes my body sing. He's just as needy as I am, and when he shifts his grip to my ass and picks me up, I wrap my legs around his waist and hold on like my life depends on this kiss never ending.

The wall digs into my back, but I don't care. My hands are finally in his hair and it's just as soft as I imagined. He kisses me until I feel thoroughly devoured and explored, and then he sucks my tongue into his mouth so I can do the same.

This is complete and utter madness, and yet I can't stop. Can't get enough. I could live forever in this tiny slice of insanity if it means keeping his mouth on mine, leaving my world narrowed to the heat of his body and the skilled stroke of his tongue.

His hips rock into mine, and I gasp at the delicious friction. He breaks the kiss, sliding his mouth across my jaw, my neck, and I know I'll do anything to keep him here with me. I want to feel his mouth *everywhere.*

We're a tangle of tongues and teeth, questing lips and hands as the snow falls around us, and the kiss consumes me the same way the power had before, so thoroughly I can feel it in every cell in my body. Need pulses between my thighs, and I jolt at the simple knowledge that there's nothing he could do that I wouldn't welcome. I want him.

Only him. Here. Now. Anywhere. Whenever.

I've never been this out of control over a single kiss. Never wanted someone the way I do him. It's exhilarating and terrifying at the same time because I know that in this moment, he has the power to break me.

And I'd let him.

I surrender completely, melting into him, my body going pliant against his and losing that mental foothold he calls grounding. A flash of light burns behind my closed eyes, followed by the boom of thunder. Thundersnow isn't uncommon around here, but damn does it summarize how this feels, wild and out of control.

But then he breaks the kiss with a sharp gasp, his brow furrowing with something akin to panic before he slams his eyes shut.

I'm still struggling to draw a full breath when he abruptly steps away from the wall and palms the backs of my thighs, setting me on my feet again. He makes sure I'm steady and then retreats a few feet, like the distance will save his life.

"You have to go." His words are clipped and at odds with the heat in his eyes, his ragged breaths.

"Why?" The cold is a shock to my system without his body heat.

"Because I can't." He rakes both hands through his hair and leaves them on the top of his head. "And I refuse to act on desire that isn't yours. So you have to walk back up those steps. Now."

I shake my head. "But I want—" Everything.

"This isn't *your* want." He tilts his head up at the sky. "That's the fucking problem. And I can't leave you out here on your own, so have just a little mercy on me and *go*."

Silence ices over between us as I get ahold of myself. He's saying *no.*

And the shitty part about it isn't the chill of chivalrous rejection. It's that he's *right.* This started because I couldn't tell Tairn's emotions from my own. But those emotions are gone, aren't they? My door is wide open, and I don't feel anything coming from Tairn's direction.

I manage a nod, and then I flee for the second time tonight, climbing the steps as quickly as possible to get back to the citadel. My shields are open, but I don't bother stopping to shut that mental door, since Tairn isn't barging through.

Common sense prevails by the time I reach the top, my thighs burning from the workout. Xaden stopped us from making a huge mistake.

But I didn't.

What the hell is wrong with me? And how could I have been a heartbeat away from ripping off my clothes to get closer to someone I don't like and even worse—can't fully trust?

It's harder than it should be to keep moving in the direction of my dorm room when all I want is to go right back down those stupid freaking steps.

Tomorrow is going to suck.

The most worrisome sight for any instructor is most definitely when powers backfire. We lost nine cadets my first year to signets that could not be controlled from their first manifestation.

Pity.

—Major Afendra's Guide to the Riders Quadrant (Unauthorized Edition)

CHAPTER TWENTY-THREE

"I don't even *know* what I was thinking," I say to Rhiannon as I sit cross-legged on her bed, watching her pack her satchel with books for the afternoon. The relic on my back burns today, as if it needs to remind me that I can channel now, and I roll my shoulders to try and relieve the sensation, but it's impossible. My clock has started.

"I can't believe you managed to wait this long to tell me." She lifts the canvas strap over her head and turns, leaning back against her desk. "And that's not judgment. Far from it. I'm all for you exploring…whatever it is you want to explore."

"I've been with Liam from the second I walked out the door this morning, and last night I was a little too discombobulated to put it into words." The knot between my shoulders has me rolling my neck, looking for some relief. With flight lessons and Imogen using weight training to strengthen the muscles around my joints in hopes they won't subluxate as often—which is hit or miss right now—I'm a mass of aches and tightness. "Between Tairn finally channeling and then everything else, it was just a night."

"Good point." A grin shapes her mouth and her brown eyes sparkle. "Was it good? Tell me it was good. That man looks like he knows exactly what he's doing."

"It was just a kiss." Heat sings in my cheeks at the blatant lie. "But yeah. He knows *exactly* what he's doing." My brow furrows, my imagination running through the thousand different consequences of what I did last night just like it has been all morning.

"Second thoughts?" She tilts her head, studying me. "You look like maybe there are third thoughts, even."

"No." I shake my head. "Well, maybe? But only if it makes stuff between us weird."

"Right. Because you're stuck with him for the rest of your careers. Lives, too. Have you guys talked about what happens after he graduates?" Her eyebrows rise. "Oh, I bet you get the choice of duty stations. Wingleaders always get to pick."

"He'll get to pick," I grumble, toying with an errant string on my satchel. "I will have to follow. Tairn and Sgaeyl haven't been separated for *years*. Her last rider died almost fifty years ago, and as far as I know, she flew wherever and whenever she wanted to be near Tairn before Naolin—his last rider—died in Tyrrendor. It's a two-day flight to that part of our border, depending on where he's stationed, so what are we going to do next year and the year after?"

Her lips purse. "Not sure. Feirge said we won't be able to be apart more than a couple of days, so does that mean one of you has to always follow the other?"

"No clue. I think that's why most mated pairs bond within the same year, so they don't have these issues. How am I supposed to remain competitive next year if I'm constantly flying off to the front line with Tairn? How is Xaden supposed to be effective if he has to fly back here all the time?" My face scrunches. "He's the most powerful rider of our generation. He's going to be needed on the front, not here."

"For now." Rhiannon stares at me with intention, lifting her brows. "He's the most powerful rider in our generation *for now*."

"What—"

Three knocks have both of us looking toward her door.

"Rhi?" Liam asks, panic evident in his voice. "Is Sorrengail in there with you? Because—"

Rhiannon opens the door, and Liam stumbles inside, catching his balance before his gaze sweeps the room, finding mine.

"There you are! I went to the bathroom, and you disappeared!"

"No one's trying to assassinate her in my room, Mairi." Rhiannon rolls her eyes. "You don't have to be with her every second of every fucking day. Now give us five minutes and then we'll start walking to class." She pushes at his chest and he retreats, his mouth opening and shutting like he's trying to think of an argument but can't as she forces him out the door and shuts it in his face.

"He's..." I sigh. "Dedicated."

"That's one word for it," she mutters. "You'd think that guy owes Riorson his life or something, the way he sticks to you like glue."

He's pretty much told me that he does, but I keep that confidence to myself. Between Xaden's meetings, stopping time, and Andarna's age, I'm starting to keep too many secrets.

"Oh!" Her eyes light up, and she sits on the edge of the bed next to me. "Something happened with me last night, too."

"Yeah?" I pivot to face her. "Do go on."

"All right." She takes a deep breath. "I've only done it three times. Twice last night and once this morning, so be patient for a second."

"Of course." I nod.

"Watch the book on my desk."

"Got it." My gaze locks on the history textbook on the left-hand side of the desk. A minute passes, but I don't look away.

Then the thing *vanishes.*

"What the hell, Rhi?" I fly to my feet and whip my head toward her. "What just—" My mouth drops.

She's holding the book, looking up at me with a wide grin.

"Is that the same book?" I lean in just to see. Yep, it's the same.

"I guess I can summon." Her grin grows even wider.

"Holy shit!" I grasp her shoulders in excitement. "That's amazing! That's...incredible! I don't even have words for what that is!" Moving objects and locking doors are the small magics, the baseline of wielding that comes from our constant connection to our dragons through our relics once they begin channeling. But making something disappear and bringing it to you? I haven't read about a signet power like that in a century. It's a hell of a signet.

"Right?" She clutches the book to her chest. "I can only do it from a few feet away, and I can't go through walls or anything."

"Yet," I correct her, joy bubbling through me. "You can't go through walls *yet*. Rhi. That's the kind of rare signet that's going to make your entire career!"

"I hope so." She stands, putting the book back on her desk. "I just have to develop it."

"You will." I say it with the same assurance I feel.

The three of us walk toward the academic wing minutes later, joined by Sawyer and Ridoc as they come out of commons, fresh from the library.

"I finished this for you," Liam says, handing me a figurine as we climb the wide spiral staircase to the third floor.

It's Tairn. He's even mastered his snarl. "This is…incredible. Thank you."

"Thanks." Liam gives me a grin, flashing his dimple. "I wanted to carve Andarna first, but I'm not around her as much, you know?"

"She's pretty private." We break off from the crowd headed to the fourth floor, and I stash the dragon in my bag, then reach out and give him a hug. "Really, I love it. Thank you." The hallway is crowded but clears as we walk farther down, nearing Professor Carr's room.

"You're welcome." He turns to Rhiannon. "I'm starting Feirge next."

Rhiannon jokes with Liam that she hopes he captures her full badassery, but I lose the rest of the conversation as I glance toward the floor-to-ceiling window before the entrance to the Battle Brief tower and my breath catches.

Xaden is standing with the other wingleaders, locked in what looks to be a tense discussion, his arms folded across his chest. It took the commandant all of five minutes to appoint Lamani Zohar as wingleader for Third Wing after Amber was executed, but since she was already executive officer, it made the most sense.

I'll never get over how quickly people move on around here, how callously death is swept under a rug and trampled on minutes later.

Gods, Xaden looks good today, his brow slightly furrowed as he listens intently to something Lamani says, then nods. Hard to believe I had that mouth on mine last night, those arms wrapped around me. Forget second thoughts. I just want more.

As if he feels me staring, Xaden lifts his head, his gaze colliding with mine across the space with the same effect as a touch. My pulse skitters and my lips part.

"We're going to be late," Rhi reminds me, glancing back over her shoulder.

Xaden looks behind me, and his mouth tenses.

"Vi, can we talk?" Dain asks, a little out of breath, like he's run to catch up to me.

"Now?" I rip my gaze from Xaden's and turn to face the person I *thought* was my best friend.

Dain grimaces, rubbing a hand behind his neck, and nods. "I tried to catch you after formation, but you disappeared pretty quickly, and after what happened last night, I figure now is better than later."

"It might be convenient for you to want to talk after weeks of ignoring me, but I have class right now." I grip the strap of my satchel.

"We have a couple of minutes." The plea in his eyes is so heavy that I feel the weight of it on my chest. "Please."

I glance at Rhiannon, who is glaring at Dain with her true feelings for once, instead of the deference owed him as our squad leader. "I'll be right in."

She glances at me and then nods, heading into Carr's room with the rest of our squad.

I follow Dain out of the doorway, to a place along the wall where we won't obstruct traffic.

"You let Tairn share your memory with *everyone* instead of just showing me yourself," he blurts, his hands falling to his sides.

"I'm sorry?" What the hell is he talking about?

"When all that shit went down with Amber, I asked you to show me what happened, and you refused." He shifts his weight, just one of his nervous tells, and the motion strips away some of my anger.

When push comes to shove, he's my oldest friend, even if he's being an ass.

"I didn't believe you, and that part is on me." He raises his hand over his heart. "I should have believed you, but I couldn't reconcile the woman I knew with what you were saying, and you didn't come find me after the attack, either." Hurt laces his tone. "I had to hear about it in formation, Vi. Regardless of the fight we had on the flight field, you're still…*you* to me. And my best friend had been viciously attacked, nearly killed, and you didn't say a single word about it."

"You didn't ask," I say softly. "You reached for my head like you were entitled to my memory after blatantly telling me you didn't believe me, and you demanded I show you." It's everything I can do to keep my voice even.

Two lines appear between his eyebrows. "I didn't ask?"

"You didn't ask." I shake my head. "And after being told countless times that I'm not tough enough for this place, not strong enough…well, what happened on the flight field was a long time coming between you and me. The worst part is that I knew you wouldn't believe me. It's why I almost didn't tell Xaden who it was, because I was sure he wouldn't believe me, either."

"But he did." Dain's voice drops, and his jaw ticks. "And he was the one who killed them in your bedroom."

"Because Tairn told Sgaeyl." I fold my arms across my chest. "Not because he was already there or anything. And I know you hate him—"

"You have *every* reason to hate him, too," he reminds me, reaching for me before thinking better of it and drawing his hand back.

"I *know* that," I counter. "His father put an arrow in Brennan's chest, according to battlefield reports. I live with that knowledge every day. But don't you think he sees me and remembers that my mother put his father to death? It's…" The right words are hard to find. "It's complicated between us." Images of last night flood my mind, from Xaden's first smile to the last brush of his lips, and I shove them away.

Dain flinches. "You trust him more than you trust me." It's not an accusation, but it stings all the same.

"That's not it." My stomach twists. Wait. Is it true? "I just…I have to trust him, Dain. Not with everything, of course." Shit, I'm tying myself into knots here. "Neither of us can do anything about Sgaeyl and Tairn being mated, and trust me, neither of us likes the situation, but we have to figure out a way through it. We don't have a choice."

Dain mutters a curse, but he doesn't disagree.

"I know you just want to keep me safe, Dain," I whisper. "But keeping me safe is keeping me from growing, too." He blinks at me, and something shifts between us. Like maybe, just maybe, he's finally ready to hear me. "When you told me that this place strips everything away from you to reveal what's underneath, I was afraid. What if underneath the brittle bones and frail ligaments, there was just more weakness? Only this time, I wouldn't be able to blame my body."

"You've never been weak to me, Vi—" Dain starts, but I shake my head.

"Don't you get it?" I interrupt. "It doesn't matter what you think—it only matters what *I* think. And you were right. But the Riders Quadrant stripped away the fear and even the anger about being thrown into this quadrant, and it revealed who I really am. At my core, Dain, I'm a rider. Tairn knew it. Andarna knew it. It's why they chose me. And until you can stop looking for ways to keep me in a glass cage, we aren't going to get past this, no matter how many years of friendship we have between us."

He glances over my shoulder. "And what? Riorson gets a free pass for his control issues? Because last time I checked, Liam was moved into our squad specifically to shadow you."

It's an excellent point. "Liam is around because even the *strongest* rider can't watch their back from more than thirty unbonded cadets gunning for them. And if I die, Xaden dies. What's your excuse?"

Dain tenses like a statue, only the muscle in his jaw ticking before he eventually leans forward and whispers, "Look, you don't know everything there is to know about Xaden, Vi. I have a higher security clearance due to my signet, and you need to be careful. Xaden has secrets, reasons to never forgive your mother, and I don't want him to use you to get his revenge."

My hackles rise. There's a sliver of truth in what he's saying, but I don't have time to focus on the confusion that is Xaden right now. One screwed-up relationship at a time.

I narrow my gaze as Dain shuffles his feet again, a kernel of a suspicion growing in my chest. "Wait, did you keep begging me to leave Basgiath because you didn't think I could survive here—or because you were trying to get me away from Xaden?"

I shake my head before he can answer. "You know what? It's irrelevant." And I mean it. "You only want to keep me safe. I appreciate that. But it stops now, Dain. Xaden is tied to me because of Sgaeyl. Nothing more. I do not need protection, and if I do—I've got *two* badass dragons who have my back. Can you respect that?"

He reaches up to cup my cheek, and I hold his gaze, determined for him to understand he either starts valuing my choices or we are never going to fix our friendship. "All right, Vi." His eyes crinkle at the sides as his mouth turns up into a half smile. "How can I argue with someone who has *two badass dragons*?"

A weight shifts in my chest, and suddenly I can breathe again. I toss him a cheeky grin. "Exactly."

"I'm sorry for not asking for the memory." He drops his hand to my shoulder. "You'd better get to class." And then he squeezes my shoulder gently before walking away.

I let out a shaky breath and turn back to the door for Carr's class. The hallway is empty.

I head into Carr's room, a massively long chamber with padded walls and no windows. The entire length is lit by chandeliers of mage lights bright enough to emulate daylight over three dozen students from Third and Fourth Wing, who are seated in rows on the floor, evenly spaced to give one another the most room.

Rhiannon and Liam meet me at the door and Professor Carr raises his bushy white brows at me when we approach where he's positioned at the front of the room, dominating the space by doing nothing more than standing there. The man isn't just imposing, he's intimidating as fuck.

I swallow, remembering how he snapped Jeremiah's neck.

"Finally ready to join us, Cadet Sorrengail?" There's no kindness in his eyes, merely shrewd, clinical observation.

"Yes, sir." I nod.

He studies me like I'm a bug pinned to the wall in the biology room. "Signet power?"

"Not yet." I shake my head, keeping the whole time-stopping thing to myself like Xaden suggested. *You trust him more than you trust me.* In this regard, Dain is right, and guilt drops my stomach.

"I see." He clucks his tongue, glancing over at me. "You know your siblings were both gifted by extraordinary signet powers. Mira's ability to manifest a ward around her and her squad has been an absolute asset to her wing, and she's been highly decorated for her valor behind enemy lines."

"Yes. Mira is an inspiration." I force a smile, more than aware of my sister's prowess on the battlefield.

"And Brennan…" He looks away. "Menders are so very rare, and to lose one so young was tragic."

"I think losing Brennan is the tragedy." I heft my satchel up higher on my shoulder. "But the loss of his signet was a definite blow to the wings."

"Hmm." He blinks twice and turns his chilling gaze back on me. "Well, it seems the Sorrengail line is blessed, even in a rider as…well, delicate as you are. With Tairn having chosen you, we'll expect nothing but an earth-shattering signet from you. Take a seat. You can at least start with the lesser magics through your relic." He waves me off.

"No pressure," I mutter as we walk to obviously empty places in the line with the rest of our squad.

"Don't stress," Rhiannon says as we take our seats on the padded floor. "That's what I was trying to remind you of earlier. You are Tairn's rider."

"What do you mean?" I set my satchel down next to me.

"You're all worried about the integrity of the wing because Riorson might have to visit to keep his dragon happy but, Violet, he's not the most powerful rider of our generation. *You* are." She holds my gaze just long enough to let me know she means it.

My heart lurches into my throat.

"Now let's begin!" Carr calls out.

December turns to January.

Ground. Shield. Imagine closing your door. Build your wall. Sense who and what has access around you. Trace the bond to your dragon. *Dragons* in my case. Build a second entrance—a window—into the archive of my power for Andarna's golden energy. Block those bonds as far as you can.

Visualize.

Imagine a knot of power—not too intricate; no one's ready for that yet—in front of you, then untangle it. Unlock the door.

Visualize.

Keep one foot firmly grounded at all times. You're useless unless you're connected to your power, and you're dangerous if you can't contain it. There is only the in-between that makes you a great rider.

Envision your power like a hand, gripping that pencil and bringing it toward you. Pick it up. No. Not like that. Try again. No, again.

VISUALIZE.

I study for tests. I prep for flights. I lift weights with Imogen. I wonder how long Xaden is going to make me put in hours on the mat with Rhiannon. I win my first challenge, earning a dagger from a girl in Second Wing. But the most exhausting assignment is spending endless hours in the archive of my mind, learning which door is Tairn's and which belongs to Andarna, then working diligently to separate the two.

It turns out that while my power might flow from my dragons, the ability to control it comes from my own exertion, and there are nights I fall into bed, plunging into sleep before I even remove my boots.

By the end of the second week in January, I'm not only pissed that Xaden hasn't bothered to talk to me about that kiss but *exhausted*, and that's without a signet power manifesting, draining my energy to control it.

Ridoc can wield ice, which might be a more common signet, but it's impressive to see.

Sawyer's metallurgy powers grow every day.

Liam can see a single tree *miles* away.

I guess I can stop time, but I'm not willing to drain Andarna just for the sake of trying again, not when it took her more than a week of straight sleeping to recover. Without a signet, all I can wield are the lesser magics. I finally use an ink pen, lock a door, and open it. I'm a party trick.

By the third week in January, I earn yet another dagger in a challenge against a guy in Third Wing, my second without weakening my opponent with poisons. It leaves me with a sore wrist, but my joints are intact.

And in the fourth week, during the coldest weather I've ever experienced at Basgiath, I sneak out in the middle of the night to see the challenge board.

Jack has finally been given the chance to end me on the mat tomorrow.

"He's going to kill me." That's all I can think as I dress for the morning, sheathing all of my daggers in the most advantageous places.

"He's going to try." Tairn is up early.

"Any advice?" I know Liam is waiting for us to make the library run before breakfast.

"Don't let him."

I scoff. He makes it sound so damned simple.

We're already on our way back from the library when I finally work up the nerve to talk to Liam about it. "If I tell you something, will you report it to Xaden?"

His head whips in my direction as he pushes the cart over the bridge between the quadrants. "Why would you think—"

"Oh, come on." I roll my eyes. "We both know you report just about everything I do. I'm not ignorant." Snow pelts the windows, making a dull, chiming sound.

"He worries. I alleviate worries." He glances at me again before looking forward. "I know it's not fair. I know it's a breach of your privacy. But it's nothing compared to what I owe him."

"Yeah. I got that part." I hurry ahead and open the thick, heavy door into the citadel so he can pass through. "Maybe I should rephrase my question. If I were to tell you something and *ask* you specifically to keep this one thing between the two of us, would you agree? Are we friends, or am I just your assignment?"

He pauses while I shut the door, and I can tell he's thinking by the way he drums his fingers on the handle of the cart. "Would me keeping it to myself alter your safety in any way?"

"No." I catch up to him and we start along the incline that will eventually split into two tunnels—one toward the dormitory and the other toward commons. "There's nothing you can do, and that's the point."

"We're friends. Tell me." He grimaces. "I'll keep it to myself."

"Jack Barlowe is going to be allowed to challenge me today."

He stops walking, so I do, too. "How do you know that?"

"And *that* is why I'm asking you to keep it to yourself." I cringe. "Just…try to trust that I know."

"The instructors can't let that happen." He shakes his head, panic creeping into his eyes.

"They're going to." I shrug, forcing a tight smile. "He's been asking since the first day, so it's not like we didn't see this coming. Point is, Jack is going to challenge me today, and when he does, you can't step in, no matter what."

His blue eyes widen. "Vi, if we tell Riorson, he can put a stop to it."

"No." I reach for his hand and lay mine on top of it. "He can't." My stomach twists, but at least I'm not puking like I did when I found out. "There's only so much Xaden can do to protect me both here and once we're on the front lines. You and I both know that if he stops this, there will be an uproar in the quadrant after what happened to Amber."

"And you expect me to stand there and watch whatever happens…happen?" he asks, incredulous.

"Just like you have the last two challenges." I force another smile. "Don't worry. I'm going to use everything I have to my advantage." And everything I have is currently in a vial tucked into the tiny pocket at my waist.

"I don't like this." He shakes his head.

"Yeah, well, that makes two of us."

There's no flight field today—the dragons have deemed it too cold to fly over the last week, which means we're all headed to the sparring gym after formation. I don't bother with breakfast, but I pay close attention to every single thing on Jack's tray as I walk by, noting what's there…and what isn't.

My heart pounds a chaotic, nauseating rhythm by the time all eighty-one of the surviving first-years gather in the gym.

Professor Emetterio calls out the challenges one by one, assigning them to a mat. At least we'll all fight at once, which means not every rider will be watching.

At least Xaden isn't here, which means Liam kept his word.

"Mat seventeen, Jack Barlowe from First Wing versus…" His eyebrows rise, and he takes a deep breath. "Violet Sorrengail."

Thank gods Rhiannon's already across the floor, ready to challenge a woman from Third Wing, so she doesn't have to see how the blood drains from Liam's face. She shouldn't have to see any of this. Sawyer's gone, too, over at mat nine.

"No fucking way," Ridoc mutters, shaking his head.

"Finally!" Jack throws his hands in the air like he's already won.

"Let's do this." I roll my shoulders and head for the mat. Neither Liam nor Ridoc is called to the mat today, so they walk at my sides.

"Tell me I can break the promise," Liam begs, and the pleading look in his eyes tells me exactly what a shitty position I've put him in.

"The third-years are off doing third-year things," I tell him as my toes touch the mat. "You can't get him here in time, but I know what it means to you to keep your word. Especially with him. Go ahead."

He looks from me to Ridoc. "Guard her like you're me."

"You mean like I'm six inches taller and built like a bull?" Ridoc gives him a thumbs-up. "Sure. I'll do my best. In the meantime, you'd better *run*."

Liam's gaze finds mine. "Stay alive."

"Working on it, and not just for my sake." I give him a smile. "Thanks for being a great shadow."

His eyes widen a split second before he sprints out of the gym.

"Barlowe and Sorrengail," Emetterio calls from the opposite side of the mat. "Weapons?"

Jack bounces like a kid who's just been given a gift. "Anything she can hold in those puny hands of hers." The look in his eyes sends a shiver of apprehension down my spine.

I step onto the mat, and Jack does the same, walking forward until we're at the center, facing each other.

"No wielding," Emetterio reminds us. "Tap out or knockout earns you a victory."

Pretty sure everyone gathered around this mat knows that Jack isn't going for either of those options. If he gets his hands around my neck, I'm dead.

"That whole I-die-Xaden-dies thing is really just a hypothesis, right?" I ask, unsheathing the daggers that are hardest to reach during a fight, the

ones in my boots.

"One I'd rather not put to the test," Tairn growls.

I stand, gripping the handles of my daggers, as Jack faces me with a single knife. "You're kidding, right? Only one?"

"I only need one." He grins with sickening excitement.

"Go for the gullet," Tairn suggests.

"I don't have the energy to block you out right now, so I'm going to need you to be quiet for a few minutes here."

An answering growl is the only response I get.

"Keep it clean," Emetterio warns. "Go."

My heart drums so loudly, I can hear it in my ears as we begin to circle each other.

"Offense. Now. Strike first," Tairn snaps.

"Not helping!"

Jack lunges, striking out with his knife, and I slice my dagger across the back of his hand, drawing first blood.

"Shit!" He jumps back, his cheeks blotching.

That's what I want, what I need to win this match, for him to get so angry that he acts without thinking and makes a mistake.

He dances forward and then kicks out, aiming for my midsection, and I stumble back, narrowly avoiding the blow. "Bet you wish you could throw that blade, don't you?" he taunts, knowing I won't break a rule when it can hurt someone in the matches going on around us.

"Bet you wish you didn't know what it feels like to dig out one of my knives, don't you?" I retort.

His lips press into a thin line before he comes at me in a series of punches and swipes with his dagger. I can't deflect—he's too strong for me, as evidenced by the dagger he easily kicks out of my hand—so I use my speed, ducking and diving while getting in another cut, this one along his forearm.

"Damn it!" he rages, twisting to follow as I come around his back. He catches me off guard, locking onto my arm and flipping me over his back to the mat.

I take the blow on my shoulder and wince, but there's no sound of tearing or snapping. Thanking Imogen will be my first order of business if I make it out of this.

Keeping my arm locked, Jack thrusts his knife straight at my chest, but it's deflected by my vest, skimming along my ribs to lodge in the mat.

"He's using death blows!" Ridoc shouts. "That's not allowed!"

"Pull it back, Barlowe!" Emetterio bellows.

"What do you think, Sorrengail?" Jack whispers in my ear, holding me immobile with my arm behind my back. "Admit it. You and I both knew it would be like this between us. Quick. Embarrassingly easy. Fatal. Your precious wingleader isn't here to save you."

No, but Xaden will suffer…if not worse if Jack achieves his goal. The thought spurs me to action. Ignoring the pain, I throw my weight into a roll, subluxating my shoulder but freeing myself from his grip when he gets tangled in my legs.

Then I kick him straight in the balls.

He hits his knees as I gain my feet, clutching himself as his mouth opens in a silent scream.

"Tap out," I order, picking up the dagger I dropped. "I can cut you open at any second. Both you and I know if this were real life, you'd be done."

"If this were real life, I would have killed you the second you stepped onto the mat," he seethes through gritted teeth.

"Tap. Out."

"Fuck off!" He throws his dagger.

I throw up my hands to block, but it lodges in my left fucking forearm. Blood streams and pain sears the nerves along my arm, erupting with alarming poignancy, but I know better than to remove it. Right now, it's holding that wound as shut as it can.

"No throwing!" Emetterio shouts from the sidelines, but Jack is already moving, barreling toward me with a series of kicks and punches that I'm not ready for. His fist slams into my cheek, and I feel the skin split.

His knee forces the air from my body when he rams it into my stomach.

But I stay on my feet until his hands clasp my face. Agony fills every cell in my body as violent, vibrating energy rips through me with an intensity that makes it feel like he's cleaving ligament from bone, muscle from tendon.

I scream as I'm shaken by an internal force I don't understand, as though he's forcing his own power into my body, shocking me with a thousand stings of vibrating energy.

Now. If I don't do it now, he'll kill me. My vision is already darkening at the edges.

I reach a trembling hand into the pocket of my leathers and thumb open the stopper on the vial.

His sadistic grin and a red rim around his eyes are all I can see as he forces more and more power into my body, but his hands are occupied and he's too obsessed with his victory to hear that I've stopped screaming, to see that I'm moving.

"He's using his powers!" Ridoc roars, and from the corner of my decreasing vision, I see movement on both sides.

I shove the vial against Jack's smile so hard, I feel one of his teeth break.

Hands reach for us both, and I hear Ridoc and Emetterio cry out, jerking their hands away after contact. Whatever Jack is doing is transferring from me to them by touch.

My teeth rattle as the pain consumes me, my body fighting to pass out, to escape the unbearable torture, but I refuse to succumb to the darkness until Jack wheezes.

His eyes fly impossibly wide, and he drops his hands, clutching his own neck as his airway closes.

My knees give way, my body still shuddering as I hit the mat, but so does Jack, heaving and clawing at his neck as his face turns purple.

Ridoc's face is in mine within seconds. "Breathe, Sorrengail. Just breathe."

"What the hell is wrong with him?" someone asks as Jack writhes.

"Oranges," I whisper to Ridoc as my body finally gives out. "He's allergic to oranges." I fall into nothingness.

When I wake, I'm not on the mat, and I can tell by the windows of the Healer Quadrant infirmary that night has fallen. I've been out for hours.

And that's not Ridoc lounged in the chair next to my bed, glaring at me like he'd like to kill me himself.

It's Xaden. His hair is tousled, like he's been tugging at it, and he's flipping a dagger end over end, catching it by the tip without so much as looking at it before sheathing it at his side. "Oranges?"

I know you don't want to hear this, but sometimes you have to know when to take the death blow, Mira. It's why you have to be sure that Violet enters the Scribe Quadrant. She'll never be able to take a life.

—Page seventy, the Book of Brennan

CHAPTER TWENTY-FOUR

I move to scoot up the bed so I can sit, but the pain in my arm reminds me that there was a dagger in it a couple of hours ago. Now it's bandaged. "How many stitches?"

"Eleven on one side and nineteen on the other." He arches a dark brow and leans forward, bracing his elbows on his knees. "You turned *oranges* into a weapon, Violence?"

I wiggle to a sitting position and shrug. "I worked with what I had."

"Seeing as it kept you alive—kept *us* alive—I can't really argue, and I'm not going to ask how it is you always know who you'll end up challenging." There's definite anger in that gaze but a touch of relief, too. "Telling Ridoc allowed Emetterio to get him here in time. Unfortunately, he's five beds down from you, and he'll live, unlike the second-year a row over. You could have killed him and saved us all a lot of drama."

"I didn't want to kill him." I roll my shoulder, testing it. Sore, but not dislocated. My face is tender, too. "I just wanted him to stop killing *me*."

"You should have told me." The accusation rips from his lips in a snarl.

"And you could have done *nothing* about it besides make me look weak." I narrow my eyes at him. "And you haven't exactly been around to talk about *anything* in weeks. If I didn't know better, I'd think that kiss scared you." *Shit.* I didn't mean to say that.

"That's not up for discussion." Something flashes in his eyes and is quickly replaced by a cool mask of indifference.

"Seriously?" I should know better, considering he's avoided it this long.

"It was a mistake. You and I are going to be stationed together for the rest of our lives, never able to escape the other. Getting involved—even on a physical level—is a colossal blunder. No point talking about it."

I barely keep from clutching at my chest to see if all my organs are where they're supposed to be, since it feels like he just eviscerated me with four sentences. But he had been just as into it as I was. I was there, and there was no mistaking that kind of…enthusiasm. *But maybe it was the churam.* "What if I want to talk about it?"

"Then feel free, but it doesn't mean I have to be a part of the conversation. We're both allowed our boundaries, and this is one of mine." The finality in his tone makes my stomach curdle. "I'll agree that keeping my distance didn't work out so well, and if today's little stunt was about getting my attention, then congratulations. It's yours."

"I don't know what you're talking about." I swing my feet to the side of the bed. I need my boots and to get the hell out of here before I make an even bigger fool of myself.

"Apparently I can't trust Liam to report deadly situations or Rhiannon to train you on the mat, seeing how easily Barlowe had you pinned, so as of this moment, I'm taking over."

"Taking over what?" My eyes narrow.

"Everything when it comes to you."

The next day, during what should be our flight hours if not for the howling, subzero winds outside, Xaden has me on the mat. Fortunately, he has his shirt on, so I'm not distracted by what I know is under it. No, he's not only wearing fighting leathers and boots, he's strapped to the nines with what looks to be a dozen different daggers in a dozen different sheaths.

Is it absolutely toxic that I'm attracted to this look on him? Probably. But one look, and my temperature rises.

"Leave your blades off the mat," he instructs, and nearly a dozen riders glance our way from other mats.

At least Liam has been given the time to go train himself a couple of mats over against Dain—a first. Most of the squads are in here, making use of the unexpected free time, so thankfully everyone is busy training instead of watching us.

"But you're armed." I glance pointedly to his sheaths.

"You either trust me or you don't." He tilts his head to the side slightly, exposing more of the rebellion relic curving up around his neck. The same relic I caressed with my hand while he had me against the foundation wall more than a month ago.

Nope. Not thinking about that.

But my body has no problem remembering.

I blow out my breath in a long sigh and step to the edge of the mat, unsheathing every dagger I own and the ones I've won, then laying them on the floor.

"I'm unarmed. Happy now?" I turn to face him, putting my arms out. My long sleeve covers the bandage on my arm, but the throb is insistent. "Though we probably could have waited a couple of days for my arm to heal up before doing this." The stitches pull, but I've had worse.

"No." He shakes his head, unsheathing one of his daggers and walking forward. "The enemy doesn't give a shit if you're wounded. They'll use it to their advantage. If you don't know how to fight in pain, then you'll get us both killed."

"Fine." I shift my body weight in annoyance. Little does he know, I'm almost *always* in pain. It's pretty much my comfort zone. "That's actually a good point, so I'll let you have it."

"Thank you for being so gracious." He smirks, and I ignore the immediate surge of warmth low in my belly. He flips his palm upward, showing me the dagger with an oddly short blade. "The problem isn't necessarily your fighting style. You're fast, and you've become pretty damned formidable since August. The problem is you're using daggers that are too easy to pluck out of your hands. You need weaponry designed for your body type."

At least he didn't say *weaknesses.*

I study the blade in his hand. It's beautiful, with a solid black hilt engraved with Tyrrish knots, old, mythical runes of intricate swirls and ties. The blade itself is clearly honed to lethal perfection. "It's spectacular."

"It's yours."

My head snaps up, but there's no lie in his onyx eyes.

"I had it made for you." His lips curve slightly.

"What?" My mouth opens, and my chest tightens. He took the time to have it made? Shit. That gives me feelings I really don't want to have. Soft, confusing feelings.

"You heard me. Take it."

Swallowing the illogical lump in my throat, I take the blade from him. It feels solid in my palm but is infinitely lighter than my other daggers. There's no strain on my wrist, and my fingers comfortably wrap around the hilt, making it much more secure than the knives I've left on the floor. "Who made it?"

"I know someone."

"In the quadrant?" My eyebrows shoot up.

"You'd be surprised how resourceful you get after three years here." A smirk tugs at the corner of his mouth, and I openly stare before remembering where we are.

"It's incredible." I shake my head and hand it back to him. "But you know I can't take it. The only weapons we're allowed to have are the ones we earn." Only challenges or weapons qualifications are acceptable. There's a crossbow I have my eye on that I'm not quite expert at yet.

"Exactly." He smiles for a flash of a second before moving with a speed I've never dreamed possible. He's even faster than Imogen as he sweeps my feet from under me with one strike, taking me to the mat in a single move.

The ease with which he has me on my back is simultaneously appalling and…ridiculously hot, especially with the weight of his hips settled between my thighs. It takes all my willpower not to reach up and brush the stray lock of hair from his forehead. *It was a mistake.*

Well, if that memory doesn't cool me right off.

"And what point are you making with this little move?" I ask, well aware that he's done it all without knocking the wind out of me.

"There are a dozen of these daggers strapped to my body, so start disarming me." He lifts a sardonic brow. "Unless you don't know how to handle an opponent on top of you, and if so, that's a whole other issue."

"I know how to handle *you* on top of me," I challenge quietly.

He lowers his mouth to my ear. "You won't like what happens if you push me."

"Or maybe I will." I turn just enough that my lips brush the shell of his ear.

He jerks up, and the heat in his gaze makes me all too aware of everywhere our bodies connect. "Disarm me before I test that theory in front of everyone in this gym."

"Interesting. I didn't take you for an exhibitionist."

"Keep pushing, and I guess you'll find out." His gaze drops to my mouth.

"I thought you said kissing me was a mistake." I don't care if the entire quadrant is watching if that means he'll kiss me again.

"It was." He smirks. "I'm just teaching you that blades aren't the only way to disarm an opponent. Tell me, Violence, are you disarmed?"

Arrogant ass.

I scoff and start plucking knives from their sheaths, flinging them across the mat while he watches with impatient amusement. Then I lock my legs around his hips and force a roll to the left, putting Xaden on his back. Willingly, of course—there's no way I'm kneeling on top of him if he doesn't want it that way—but I throw a forearm against his collarbone with the pretense of pinning him anyway and proceed to steal the other daggers he has sheathed along his side.

"And lastly," I say with a smile, leaning forward, our heated bodies nearly flush as I snatch the dagger right out of his hand. "Thank you."

The final blade secure, Xaden throws his palms to the mat and shoves with unnatural strength, arching us straight back until my spine kisses the mat again.

"That's." I suck in a breath, the move shocking me to my toes and lodging him firmly between my thighs. It takes everything I have not to arch up against him and see if he really thinks that kiss was a mistake. "Not fair to use your powers on the mat." Magical. Sexual. Whatever. It's all unfair.

"That's the other thing." He jumps to his feet and offers his hand. I take it, my head rushing as I stand. *Not now. Do not get dizzy now*. "Emetterio doesn't allow powers in order to level the playing field when it comes to challenges. But out there? The field is anything but level, and you need to learn to use whatever you've got."

"I can't do much beside ground, shield, and move a piece of parchment." I sheathe the new dagger, then collect the others and do the same. They really are lovely, all marked with different runes. It's a shame there are so many parts of Tyrrish culture that were lost centuries ago during the unification, including most runes. I don't even know what they all mean.

"Well, looks like we're going to have to work on that, too." He sighs and takes up a fighting stance. "Now, earn your nickname and try your best to kill me."

• • •

February flies by in a blur of exhaustion. Xaden takes every unscheduled moment of my day, and Dain's gritted his teeth more than once when the wingleader has pulled me out of squad training because he has something infinitely more important for me to do.

Which usually ends with me getting my ass handed to me repeatedly on the mat.

But I have to say, he doesn't baby me like Dain, and he doesn't take it easy on me like Rhiannon does. He pushes me to my physical limit every session but never further, usually leaving me a boneless, sweaty heap on the sparring gym floor, gasping for breath.

That's usually when Imogen reminds me that I'm needed in the weight room.

I hate them both.

Kind of.

It's hard to argue with the results when I'm learning to take down the strongest fighter in the quadrant. I have yet to beat him, but I'm all right with that. It means he doesn't let me win.

He also doesn't kiss me again, even when I *push*.

March arrives with uncountable feet of snow that have to be shoveled before morning formation every day. And the moments the relic burns in my back and I feel like I might crawl out of my own skin if the power building within me doesn't release reminds me that I still don't have a signet. It's already almost been three months.

Every morning I wake up wondering if today is the day I'll spontaneously combust.

"Sharla Gunter," Captain Fitzgibbons reads from the death roll, his gloved hands slipping on the frozen parchment. It's warmer this week, but not by much. "And Mushin Vedie. We commend their souls to Malek."

"Vedie?" I ask Rhiannon, my eyebrows shooting up as formation ends. I didn't know him well, since he was in Second Wing, but the name is still a shock, considering he was rumored to be one of the best among us.

"You didn't hear?" She pulls her fur-lined cloak closer around her neck. "His signet manifested in the middle of Carr's class yesterday, and he burst into flames."

"He…burned himself to death?"

She nods. "Tara said Carr thinks he was supposed to be able to wield fire, but it just overwhelmed him in that first rush and…"

"He went up like a torch," Ridoc adds. "Kind of makes you glad your signet's still hiding, huh?"

"*Hiding* is one way to put it." Other than the ability I'm not supposed to even whisper about, I'm proving to be the one thing my mother hates—average. And it's not as though I can go to Tairn or Andarna for help. The signet is all about *me*, and I'm apparently not delivering, as the stinging relic on my back constantly reminds me. There's a tiny, secret part of me that hopes my signet hasn't manifested yet because it's different than the others, not only useful but…meaningful, like Brennan's was.

"Definitely makes me want to skip class today," Rhiannon mutters, blowing on her hands to keep them warm.

"No skipping class," Dain admonishes, pinning us with a stare. "We're weeks away from the Squad Battle and we need every single one of you at your best to win."

Imogen snorts. "Come on, Aetos, I think we all know Second Wing has that squad in Tail Section that's going to smoke the rest of us. Have you ever seen them sprint up the Gauntlet? Pretty sure they've been out there even though it's still covered in ice."

"We're going to win," Cianna, our executive officer, proclaims with a decisive nod. "Sorrengail here might slow us down on the Gauntlet"—she wrinkles her hawkish nose—"and probably in the wielding department, too, at the rate she's advancing—"

"Gee, thanks." I fold my arms across my chest. Bet I can shield better than all of them combined.

"But Rhiannon's skills more than make up for that," Cianna continues. "And we all know Liam and Heaton are both going to decimate on the mat for the challenge competition. That only leaves flight maneuvers and whatever task the wingleaders come up with to judge this year."

"Oh, is that all? Man, I thought it was going to be hard." The sarcasm rolling off Ridoc is thick enough to earn him a glare from Dain.

"We're down to ten of you," Dain says, glancing over our group. "Twelve of us in total, which puts us at a slight disadvantage against a couple other squads, but I think we'll manage."

We lost two of the new additions last week when the smaller one's signet manifested in Battle Brief and they both froze to death in seconds, nearly taking out Ridoc with the exposure, too. He was treated for frostbite but didn't have any permanent damage. Now Nadine and Liam are the only ones left from the batch we acquired after Threshing.

"But in order to manage, I need you guys to get to class." He lifts his brows at me. "Especially you. A signet would be *great*, you know. If you can maybe make that happen." It's as if he can't decide how to treat me lately, as the first-year who's struggling but still here or the girl he grew up with.

I hate how unsettled everything feels between us, all wrongly sticky, like putting on clothes before you can dry after a bath, but it's still Dain. At least he's finally being supportive.

"She's going to miss Carr's class today," Xaden interrupts, appearing behind Sawyer, who hurries to clear a path.

"No I'm not." I shake my head and ignore the quick jump of my pulse at the sight of him.

"She needs to go," Dain argues, then grits his teeth. "I mean, unless the wing has more pressing matters for Cadet Sorrengail, her time is best spent developing her wielding skills."

"I think we both know she's not going to manifest a signet in that room. She would have already if that was the key." I wouldn't wish the look Xaden levels Dain with on my worst enemy. It's not anger or even indignation. No, he looks...annoyed, as if Dain's complaints are entirely beneath him, which, according to our chain of command, they are. "And yes, the wing has more pressing matters for her."

"Sir, I'm just not comfortable with her going a day without at least practicing her wielding, and as her squad leader—"

He doesn't know that Xaden's been giving me extra wielding sessions while we spar.

"For Dunne's sake." Xaden sighs, invoking the goddess of war. He reaches into the pocket of his cloak and takes out a pocket watch, holding it in his outstretched palm. "Pick it up, Sorrengail."

I glance at the two men and wish they'd just sort their shit out between themselves, but there's about a zero percent chance of that happening. For the sake of expediency, I throw my mental feet into the floor of the Archives. White-hot power flows around me, raising goose bumps on my arms and lifting the hair at the back of my neck.

Raising my right hand, I envision that power twining between my fingers, and little shocks blossom along my skin as I give form to the energy, making it a hand of its own as I ask it to stretch the few feet that separate me from Xaden.

There's an abrupt halt, as though my tendrils of raw magic hit a wall, but then it gives, and I push forward, keeping tight control of the blazing hand. There's a crackle in my head, like the dying embers of a fire, as my power brushes Xaden's hand, but I close my mental fist around the pocket watch and then pull.

It's fucking *heavy*.

"You got this," Rhiannon urges.

"Let her concentrate," Sawyer chides.

The watch plummets for the ground, but I snap my hand back, yanking on my power as though it's a rope, and the watch flies toward me. I catch it with my left hand before it can smack me in the face.

Rhiannon and Ridoc clap.

Xaden walks forward and plucks the watch from my fingers, dropping it into his cloak. "See? She's practiced. Now, we have things to do." He puts his hand on the small of my back and leads me out of the crowd.

"Where are we going?" I loathe the way my body demands I lean back into his touch, but I miss it the second it's gone.

"I'm assuming you're not wearing flight leathers under that cloak." He opens the door to the dormitory for me, and I walk inside. The motion is so easy that I know it's not only practiced but second nature, which is at complete odds with, well…everything I've come to know about him.

I pause, looking at him like we're meeting for the first time.

"What?" he asks, closing the door behind us and shutting out the blustering cold.

"You opened the door for me."

"Old habits die hard." He shrugs. "My father taught me that—" His voice dies abruptly, and his gaze falls away, every muscle in his body locking as though he's preparing for an attack.

My heart aches at the look that crosses his face, recognizing it well. Grief.

"Don't you think it's a little cold for flying?" I ask, changing the subject in an attempt to help. The pain in his eyes is the kind that never dies, the kind that rises like an unpredictable tide and floods the shoreline without mercy.

He blinks, and it's gone. "I'll wait here."

I nod and hurry to change into the fur-lined leathers we're issued for winter flight. He has that unreadable mask on when I return, and I know there won't be any more doors held on my account today.

We walk out across the emptying courtyard as cadets scurry off to classes. "You didn't answer me."

"About what?" He keeps his eyes on the gate to the flight field path and I have to damn near scurry to keep up with his strides.

"About it being cold for flight."

"Third-years have flight field this afternoon. Kaori and the other professors are just taking it easy on you guys, since the Squad Battle is coming up and they know you need the practice in wielding." He pushes open the gate, and I hurry after him.

"But I don't need the practice?" My voice echoes in the tunnel.

"Winning the Squad Battle is nothing in the scheme of keeping you alive. You'll be on the front lines before the rest of them come next year." The mage lights play off the harsh angles of his face, casting sinister shadows as we pass each one.

"Is that what's going to happen next year?" I ask as we come out the other side, the snow whiting out my vision momentarily. It's piled high on each side of the path, the result of this heavy winter. "I'm going to the front lines?"

"Inevitably. There's no telling how long Sgaeyl and Tairn will tolerate being separated. My best guess is that we'll both have to sacrifice to keep them happy." He's clearly not so happy about it himself, but I can't blame him. After three years in the quadrant, I'd want to get the hell out, too. My stomach sinks as I realize I'll be in his shoes when I graduate as well, with no real control on how our dragons' bond dictates my future posts.

I nod, not knowing what else to say, and we walk to the Gauntlet in companionable silence.

"Second Wing," I note, watching the squad from Tail Section slip and slide their way across the Gauntlet. "You sure you don't want your own squads out here practicing?"

A corner of his mouth lifts, and that inhuman facade of his cracks. "When I was a first-year, I thought winning was the pinnacle, too. But once you're in your third year, and you see the things that we do..." His jaw flexes. "Let's just say that the games are a lot more lethal."

We head toward the staircase that leads to the flight field, but there's already a group coming down, so I move back to let them descend first.

My heart launches into my throat as they come closer, and I snap my frame to an attention stance, my spine stiffening. It's Commandant Panchek and Colonel Aetos.

Reaching the ground first, Dain's dad offers me a smile. "At ease.

You're looking well, Violet. Nice flight lines," he says, gesturing to the ones on his own cheekbones that come from flight goggles. "You must be getting a lot of airtime."

"Thank you, sir, I am." I relax my posture and can't help but return the favor, but my lips are tight. "Dain is doing well, too. He's my squad leader this year."

"He's told me." He grins, his brown eyes just as warm as Dain's. "Mira asked about you while we were touring the Southern Wing last month. Don't worry, you'll get your letter privileges in second year, and then you can keep in touch more often. I'm sure you miss her."

"Every day." I nod, pushing past the swell of emotion the admission brings. It's so much easier to pretend there's nothing outside the walls than to wallow in how much I miss my sister.

Xaden stiffens at my side as Mom steps out of the stairwell. *Oh shit.*

"Mom," I blurt, and her head turns, her eyes meeting mine. It's been more than five months since I've seen her, and even though I want to be as composed as she is, as compartmentalized, I just can't. I'm not built like she is, like Mira is. I'm my father's daughter.

Her assessing gaze sweeps over me with all the familiarity of a commanding general and a Basgiath cadet, and there's no warmth in her expression as she finishes her perusal. "I hear you're having trouble wielding."

I blink and step backward, as though physical distance is going to shelter me from the icy rebuke. "I have the best shields in my year." For the first time, I'm actually glad I haven't manifested a signet, haven't given her something to brag about.

"With a dragon like Tairn, I would certainly hope so." She cocks an eyebrow. "If not, all of that incredible, enviable power will have been…" Her sigh is a puff of steam in the air. "Squandered."

I try my best to swallow the growing knot in my throat. "Yes, General."

"You have been the topic of some conversation, though." Her gaze skims the top of my head, and I know she's looking at the silver-tipped braid she thinks marks me as cursed, the hair she told me I was better off cutting.

"Oh?" She actually talks about me?

"We're all wondering what powers—if any—you're wielding from the golden dragon?" Her lips form a smile I'm sure she thinks is soft, but I know her too well to fall for it.

"No." The single word from Tairn rumbles through my entire body. *"Do not speak of it."*

"Nothing yet." I drag my tongue over my chapped lower lip. Winter is hell on the skin during flight. "Andarna told me that feathertails are known for being unable to channel power to their rider." Only their direct gifts, but I'm not about to say that. "It's why they don't bond often."

"Or ever," Dain's dad chimes in. "We were actually hoping that you might ask your dragon to allow us to study her. For purely academic purposes, of course."

My stomach sours. The group of them would poke and prod Andarna for gods know how long to appease their academic curiosity, and they might stumble onto the untapped power of young dragons. No thank you. "Unfortunately, I don't see her being comfortable with that. She's pretty private, even with me."

"Pity," Colonel Aetos says. "We've had the scribes on it since Threshing, and the only reference they can find in the Archives about the power of feathertails is hundreds of years old, which is funny because I remember your father doing a bit of research about the second Krovlan uprising, and he mentioned something about feathertails, but we can't seem to find that tome." He scratches his forehead.

Mom looks at me with expectation, as though to ask me without actually asking.

"I don't believe he finished his research on that particular historical event before he died, Colonel Aetos. I couldn't even tell you where his notes are." The words are as true as I can make them. I know exactly where his notes are—in the one location he spent the majority of his after-hours time. But there's something about Tairn's warning that makes me simply unable to tell them.

"Too bad." Mom forces another smile. "Glad to see you're alive, Cadet Sorrengail." Her gaze flashes sideways and instantly hardens to steel. "Even if the company you're forced to keep is more than questionable."

Shit. Shit. Shit.

I can't step in front of Xaden and make him look weak. I can't even glance his way without telling my mother where my allegiance lies… without telling *myself.*

"I always felt that we resolved any of those *questions* years ago," Xaden says, his voice low, but he's gone taut as a bowstring next to me.

"Hmm." Mom turns toward the citadel in clear dismissal. "Do see if you can master some kind of signet, Cadet Sorrengail. You have a legacy to live up to."

"Yes, General." The informal words cost more than I'm prepared to admit, ripping into the confidence it's taken me nearly eight months to build with talon-sharp precision.

"Good to see you, Violet." Dain's dad offers me a sympathetic smile, and Panchek outright ignores us, running to catch up with Mom.

I don't say a word to Xaden before I climb the stairs, each step making me only angrier until I'm a ball of rage by the time I reach the top of the cliffside.

"You didn't tell her about how you got out of the attack in your bedroom," he says. It's a statement, not a question. "And I'm not talking about me showing up."

I know exactly what he's talking about.

"I don't ever see her. And you told me not to tell anyone."

"Didn't realize it was quite like that between you," Xaden says, his tone surprisingly soft as we start down the box canyon toward the flight field.

"Oh, that's nothing," I toss out, intentionally making my tone as flippant as possible. "She spent almost an entire year ignoring me when Dad died." A self-deprecating laugh slips past my lips. "Which was almost as wholesome as the years she spent barely tolerating my existence because I wasn't perfect like Brennan or a warrior like Mira." I shouldn't be saying these things. These are the thoughts families keep behind their doors so they can wear their polished, perfect reputations like armor when in public.

"She doesn't know you very well, then," Xaden remarks, keeping pace with my furious strides.

I scoff. "Or she sees right through me. Problem is, I'm never quite sure which it is. I'm too busy trying to live up to whatever impossible standard she sets to ask myself if they're even standards I give a shit about." My narrowed gaze swings to him. "And what was that about anyway? Saying that you resolved questions years ago?"

"Just reminding her that I paid the price for my loyalty." His brow furrows, but he stares ahead of us.

"Paid what price?" The question slips out before I can stop my foolish tongue. I can't help but remember what Dain said, that Xaden has reasons to never forgive my mother.

"Boundaries, Violence." His head lowers for the span of a heartbeat, and when it rises, he's wearing that polished give-no-fucks mask he's so good at donning.

Lucky for us, the strain of the moment is broken as Tairn and Sgaeyl land across the field ahead, accompanied by a shiny smaller dragon who makes me instantly smile.

"We're all flying today?" I ask, following as he walks toward the trio.

"We're all learning today. You need to learn how to stay on, and I need to learn why the hell it's so hard for you," he answers. "Andarna needs to learn how to keep up. Tairn needs to learn how to share his space in a tighter flight formation, and every other dragon but Sgaeyl is too scared to fly closer."

Tairn chuffs in agreement as we approach.

"And what is Sgaeyl learning?" I ask, eyeing the giant blue dragon.

Xaden grins. "She's been leading for almost three years now. She's going to have to learn how to follow. Or at least practice."

Tairn's chuff sounds suspiciously like a laugh, and she snaps at him, baring her teeth and coming within inches of his neck.

"Dragon relationships are absolutely incomprehensible," I murmur.

"Yeah? You should try a human one sometime. Just as vicious, but less fire." He mounts with an ease I envy. "Now let's go."

The Squad Battle is more important than the wingleaders will let on. They like to joke that it's a game, that it's just bragging rights for the squad leaders and the winning squad, but it's not. They're all watching. The commandant, the professors, the commanding officers—they're watching to see who will rise to the top. They're salivating to see who will fall.

—Page seventy-seven, the Book of Brennan

CHAPTER TWENTY-FIVE

"Tap out!" Rhiannon screams as a rider out of Second Wing fights to drag himself forward on the mat, his hands splayed wide, his fingernails digging in as Liam holds him in a leg lock, forcing his back into what should be an impossible arch.

My heart pounds as the excitement of today's matches reaches a fever pitch.

It's the last challenge of this portion of the Squad Battle, and the crowd pushes at our backs, forcing me to continuously struggle not to fall over onto the mat. After two events, we're in seventh out of twenty-four on the leaderboard, but if Liam wins, we'll jump to third.

My flight time in the gauntlet sky race was the slowest in squad, but that's because I kept forcing Tairn to release his magical hold on me—and then we'd lose precious seconds while he had to dip to catch me and toss me back in the saddle. Over and over and over again. I swear, the bruises on my ass from landing in the hard divot hurt less than Tairn's scoff that I'd humiliated his entire family line as we crossed the finish line last.

Mikael cries out in pain, the sound sharp, near earsplitting, and pulling my attention back to the action in front of me. Liam holds fast and presses his advantage.

"Fuck me, that looks like it hurts," I mutter over the cheering first-years.

"Yeah, he's not walking for a while," Ridoc agrees, cringing as the arc of Mikael's back looks like a broken spine waiting to happen.

With another cry, Mikael slams his palm into the mat three times, and the crowd roars.

"Yes! Go, Liam!" Sawyer screams from behind me, and Liam drops Mikael to the mat, where he sprawls out, exhausted.

"We won!" Liam rushes for us, and I'm swept up into a tangle of arms and shouting and joyous squadmates.

I'm pretty sure I even see Imogen in this little melee.

But I don't see Dain. Where the hell is Dain? He would never miss this.

"Your winner!" Professor Emetterio shouts, his voice ringing through the gym and quieting the zealous energy as Liam steps out of our crushing hug. "Liam Mairi from Second Squad, Flame Section, Fourth Wing!"

Liam puts up both hands in victory and turns in a small circle, and the sound of cheering makes my ears ring in the best way.

Commandant Panchek steps onto the mat, and Liam joins the rest of our squad, sweat pouring off his skin. "I know you were all expecting the last portion of the Squad Battle to happen tomorrow, but the cadre and I have a surprise."

He has every single rider's attention now.

"Instead of telling you what the final, unknown task will be and giving you tonight to plan for it, your final task will begin this hour!" He grins, throwing out his hands and turning just like Liam had.

"Tonight?" Ridoc whispers.

My stomach hits the ground. "Dain isn't here. Neither is Cianna."

"Oh shit," Imogen whispers, looking over the crowd herself.

"As you may have noticed, your squad leaders and their executive officers have been…shall we say, sequestered with your section leaders and wingleaders, and no, before someone asks, your task is not to find them." He continues to walk in a small circle, addressing each side of the mat. "You are to break into your squads and accomplish a unique mission this evening without the leadership and instruction of your squad leaders."

"Doesn't that defeat the purpose of having squad leaders?" someone asks across the mat.

"The purpose of a squad leader is to form a tightly knit unit that can carry on with a mission after their demise. Consider your leaders…

demised." Panchek shrugs with a gleeful smile. "You're on your own, riders. Your mission is simple: find and acquire, by any means necessary, the one thing that would be most advantageous to our enemies regarding the war effort. Leadership will serve as unbiased judges, and the winning squad will be awarded sixty points."

"That's enough to put us into first!" Rhiannon whispers, linking her arm with mine. "We could win the glory of going to the front!"

"What are the boundaries?" someone to the right asks.

"Anything within the walls of Basgiath," Panchek answers. "And don't you dare let me see you trying to haul a dragon back here. They'll incinerate you out of sheer annoyance."

The squad to our left mutters their disappointment.

"You have"—Panchek pulls out his pocket watch—"three hours, at which time we'll expect you to present your stolen treasures in the Battle Brief room."

We all stare at him in silence. Out of everything I imagined the third and final task to be…well, this wasn't anywhere near that list.

"What are you waiting for?" Panchek shoos his hands at us. "Go!"

Pandemonium ensues.

This is what happens when you remove our leadership. We're…a hot freaking mess.

"Second Squad!" Imogen yells, putting her hands up. "Follow me!"

Sawyer and Heaton make sure we're all ducklings, following in Imogen's wake as she leads us across the gym to the weight room.

"You did great," I tell Liam as he walks at my side, still struggling to catch his breath.

"It was epic." Ridoc hands Liam a waterskin, which Liam promptly drains.

"Let's go, let's go," Imogen says, ushering us through the open door. She does a quick head count and then closes the door, wielding to lock it.

I find a seat on one of the benches, flanked by Rhiannon and Liam.

"First thing. Who wants to be in command?" Imogen asks, looking at the ten of us.

Ridoc throws his hand in the air.

Rhiannon turns and forces it back down. "No." She shakes her head. "You'll turn this into some kind of prank."

"Fair point." He shrugs.

"Liam?" Quinn asks, lifting her eyebrows.

"No." He shakes his head, but his gaze darts in my direction, giving his reasoning away.

"No one is going to try and off me while we're out tonight," I argue.

He turns back toward Imogen and shakes his head one more time.

Of course she nods. They're both on Team Xaden.

"You keep command," Rhiannon suggests, looking at Imogen. "You've gotten us this far."

A murmur of agreement goes around the room.

"Emery? Heaton?" Imogen asks. "As third-years, it's your right."

"No thanks." Heaton leans back against the wall.

"Nope. There's a reason neither of us wanted to be in leadership," Emery adds, sitting next to Nadine. "Any reason you wouldn't be all right following Imogen's command for a few hours, Nadine?"

Every one of us turns to face the first-year who hasn't been remotely subtle about her hatred of marked ones. Knowing now that she's from a northern village on the border of the provinces of Deaconshire and Tyrrendor, I can see her reasoning. I just don't agree with it, hence why I'm not exactly friendly with her.

She visibly swallows, her nervous gaze skittering over all of us. "I'm fine with it."

"Good." Imogen folds her arms across her chest, the wrist with her rebellion relic peeking out from under her tunic. "We have a little less than three hours. What are your ideas?"

"What about a piece of weaponry?" Ridoc suggests. "A cross-bolt would be deadly to any of our dragons in the hands of our enemies."

"Too big," Quinn says decisively. "There's only one in the museum, and honestly, it's not even the bolt that's deadly, it's the launching system."

"Next?" Imogen glances at each of us.

"We could steal Panchek's underw—" Ridoc starts before Rhiannon slams her hand over his mouth.

"And that's why we don't let you lead." She arches a brow at him.

"Come on, guys! Think! What's the most useful thing to our enemy?" Imogen's brow puckers over her pale green eyes.

"Information," Liam answers. He swings his gaze toward me. "Violet, what about stealing the news missives from the Archives? The ones that come in from the front?"

I shake my head. "It's after seven. The Archives are locked, and it's the kind of vault that even wielding isn't going to touch. The whole room is sealed up airtight in case of fire."

"Damn." Imogen sighs. "That was a good one."

The entire room breaks into conversation, each voice louder than the next as suggestions are hurled into the open.

Information. My stomach twists as an idea takes form. It would be a showstopper, something no one else could compare to. But… I shake my head. It's too risky.

"What are you thinking, Sorrengail?" Imogen asks and the room falls silent. "I can see the little gears turning in your mind."

"It's probably nothing." I glance at the members of our squad. But is it nothing?

"Get up here and work it out in your head," Imogen orders.

"Seriously, it's mad. Like, undoable. We'd get thrown in the brig if we're caught." I snap my mouth shut before I say anything more.

But it's too late—Imogen's eyes are sparkling with interest.

"Get. Up. Here. And. Work. It. Out," she orders, making sure I know it's not a suggestion.

"We can wield, right?" I stand, brushing my hands down my sides and the hilts of the six daggers sheathed there.

"By all means necessary," Heaton repeats, nodding.

"All right." I rock back on my heels, letting my mind whirl through a plan. "I know Ridoc can wield ice, Rhiannon can retrieve, Sawyer can manipulate metal, Imogen can mind-wipe recent memories—"

"And I'm fast," she adds.

Something she has in common with Xaden.

"Heaton, what about you?" I ask.

"I can breathe underwater," they answer.

I blink. "Awesome, but I don't think that's going to come in handy if we do this. Emery?"

"I can control wind." He grins. "A lot of wind."

All right, that one could be defensively useful, but not quite what I'm looking for.

My boots squeak on the floor as I turn to face her. "Quinn?"

"I can astral project. Keep my body in one place and then walk around somewhere else."

My mouth hangs open, matching about half the squad.

"I know, it's pretty awesome." She winks, pulling her curls up into a bun.

"Yes. *That* we can use." My head bobs as I parcel through the easiest way to do this.

"What are you thinking, Sorrengail?" Imogen prompts, tucking the short hair on one side of her shaved head behind her ear.

"You're going to tell me I've lost my mind, but if we pull it off, we'll win for sure." I might not be enough like my mother to win her approval, but I know where she keeps the most valuable information.

"And?"

"We're going to break into my mother's office."

"You are so fucking creepy." Ridoc squirms two hours later, leaning away from Quinn, well, from Quinn's astral form. Her body is currently with Heaton, guarded in the weight room.

The rest of us are sneaking through the hallways past the Healer Quadrant. We've already run into a squad from Second and another from Third, but none of us had time to question or deter the others.

We'll rise or fall on our own merit with this timeline, and we've wasted the last two hours waiting for night to fall so it would even be possible.

"I've never been farther than this," Emery says as we pass the last door to the clinic.

"You've never even been to the Archives?" Imogen asks.

"I avoid that duty like the plague," Emery answers. "Scribes freak me out. Quiet little know-it-alls, acting like they can make or break someone by writing something down."

I grin. There's more truth to that statement than most people realize.

"Infantry is still out camping." Rhiannon points out the windows to the dozens of campfires illuminating the field below.

"Must be nice to get a break," Nadine remarks, but there's no snotty tone I've come to expect, just the same exhaustion I think we all feel. "Scribes will all go home for the summer. Healers get to spend their weekends on those mind-body-health retreats, and the infantry might have to practice making and breaking camp in the snow through winter, but at least they spend those months around a campfire."

"We'll get to go home," Imogen argues.

"After graduation," Rhiannon retorts. "For what? A couple of days?"

We come to a fork in the path, where we can follow the tunnel down to the Archives or climb into the fortress of the war college.

"There's no turning back from here," I say to the group, looking up the spiral staircase I've climbed so many times that I know each step by heart.

"Lead on!" Quinn orders, and we all jump about a foot in the air.

"Shhh!" Imogen hisses. "Some of us can get caught, you know."

"Right. Sorry." Quinn cringes.

"Everyone, remember the plan," I whisper. "No one deviates. *No one*."

They all nod, and we begin our silent climb up the dark stairs, then cling to the shadows as we cross the stone courtyard of Basgiath.

"Sure could use Xaden right about now."

"You're doing great," Andarna assures me in the happiest of tones. I swear, nothing bothers her. She's the most fearless kid I've ever met, and I grew up with Mira.

"It's six flights straight up," I whisper when we reach the next set of stairs, and we continue to climb as fast as we can without making any noise. Anxiety spikes, and my power rises in response, the relic in my back heating to an uncomfortable burn. It's always there lately, simmering beneath my skin, reminding me that performing lesser magics isn't going to be enough to vent it if I don't manifest a signet soon.

Eventually, we reach the top of the steps, and Liam leans out just far enough to see down the length of what's always felt like the world's longest hallway. "There are mage lights in sconces," he whispers. "And you were right." He withdraws into the safety of the stairwell. "There's only one guard stationed at the door."

"Was there any light under the door?" I ask quietly. My heart sounds like it's loud enough for the whole college to hear, even the infantry cadets sleeping hundreds of feet below us.

"No." He turns to Quinn. "The guard looks about six feet tall, but he seems pretty athletic. The other stairwell is down the hallway to the left, which means you'll have to get his attention and then book it."

Quinn nods. "No problem."

"Everyone else know what they're doing?" I ask.

There are eight nods.

"Then let's do this. Quinn, you're up. Everyone else, circle back down so he can't see us if he looks this way." I can't believe we're actually about to do this. If she catches us, there won't be any mercy. It's not in her nature.

We retreat, and Quinn charges up the stairs. Her voice is muffled by the stone walls, but we hear the guard's pounding footsteps clear as day as he charges past the stairway.

"Get back here! You can't be here!"

"Now!" Imogen orders.

We launch, leaving Rhiannon and Emery in the stairwell as we fly into the hallway. Sawyer rushes toward the opposite staircase, throwing the door shut and twisting the metal joints with his powers as we bolt down the hall.

I've never run this fast in my life, and Nadine is already at the door, trying to unweave whatever wards my mother has used.

Liam steps into the spot where the guard stood and lifts his chin in the air, taking the same posture. "Are you all right?"

"Yep," I answer, my chest heaving as Imogen steps in to help Nadine. Nadine's signet is the ability to unweave wards, which I never thought would come in this handy. Riders are always out there building the wards, keeping the shields up around Navarre. Then again, not many riders try to break into the commanding general's office. "And I'll be fine in there," I assure him, a smile tugging at my lips. "Which is funny, since I didn't think the same way the last time I was standing here."

"Got it!" Nadine whispers, nudging the door open.

"If you hear me whistle—" Liam starts, worry lining his forehead.

"We'll go out the window or something," I assure him as Ridoc and Sawyer rush past. "Relax." Leaving Liam to stand watch, I join the others in Mom's office.

"Don't touch the mage lights or she'll know," I warn them. "You have to make your own." I flick my wrist, twisting my power into a bright blue flame and letting it drift over me. It's one of the things I'm actually good at.

"How nice is this?" Ridoc flops down onto the red couch.

"We don't have time for you to be…you," Sawyer lectures, heading for the bookcase. "Help me search for something useful."

"We'll take the table." Imogen and Nadine start sorting through papers on the six-seater conference table.

"Which leaves me and the desk," I mutter, walking around the intimidating piece of furniture and praying I don't trigger any wards she's set. There are three folded missives in the middle, and I pick up the first, revealing a sharp dagger with an alloy-infused hilt and what looks to be a Tyrrish rune in the handle that she must be using as a letter opener or something. I unfold the letter with as much care as I can.

General Sorrengail,

The raids around Athebyne have spread the wing too thin. Being posted beyond the safety of the wards comes with considerable hazards, and though I am loath to request reinforcements, I must. If we do not reinforce the post, we may be forced to abandon it. We are protecting Navarrian citizens with life, limb, and wing, but I cannot adequately relay how dire the situation is here. I know you receive the dailies from our scribe attachment, but I would be remiss in my duties as executive officer of the Southern Wing if I did not write to you personally. Please find us reinforcements.

Sincerely,
Major Kallista Neema

I breathe past the ache that erupts in my chest at the plea in her letter. We've discussed nearly daily attacks in Battle Brief, but nothing on that scale.

Maybe they don't want to scare us.

But if it's that terrifying out there, we have every right to know—we'll likely be called into service before we graduate. Maybe even this year.

"These are all…numbers," Imogen says, rifling through the conference table papers.

"It's April," I say, reaching for the next missive. "She's working on next year's budget."

Everyone stops and turns to look at me, all wearing expressions of varying degrees of disbelief.

"What?" I shrug. "Did you think this place ran itself?"

"Keep looking," Imogen orders.

I unfold the next missive.

General Sorrengail,

Protests regarding conscription laws are growing within the province of Tyrrendor. Knowing that due to Tyrrendor's size, it provides the majority of our conscripts to replenish our front lines, we cannot afford to lose the support of the people again. Perhaps an influx of defensive spending on outposts here would not only bolster the province's economy and remind the Tyrrish how needed they are to the defense of our kingdom, but also ease the unrest. Please consider this solution as an alternative to suppressing the unrest with force.

Sincerely,

Lieutenant Colonel Alyssa Travonte

What the hell? I close the letter and put it back on Mom's desk, then turn to the giant map hanging on the wall directly above me.

Unrest isn't new to Tyrrendor, nor is the sentiment against conscription, but we certainly haven't heard any political rumblings in Battle Brief. Other than to quell discontent, it would make no sense to increase defensive spending there, especially since it holds our fewest number of outposts due to the natural barrier provided by the Cliffs of Dralor, which are unscalable by gryphons. Tyrrendor should already be one of the safest provinces on the Continent. Well, except Aretia. Where that capital should be, there is only a scorch mark, as though the burning of the city has singed the map as well.

I study the map for precious seconds, noting the battlement markers dotted along the countryside. Logically, there are more outposts along our more active border zones and, according to this map, more troops in those locations.

It shows all of Navarre, Krovla to the south, Braevick and Cygnisen to the east, and even the barriers of the Barrens, the ruined deserted lands at the southeastern tip of the Continent. It also shows each of our outposts and supply routes within Navarre.

A slow grin spreads across my face.

"Hey, Second Squad. I know what we need to steal."

It takes a matter of minutes for us to haul the map down and cut it away from its frame, then another to roll it, securing it with leather ties Imogen pulls out of her satchel.

Liam whistles, and my heart nearly leaps out of my chest.

"Shit!" Ridoc races to the door and cracks it open as we all prepare to flee. "What's going on out there?"

"He's pounding at the hall door! It's going to give any second. We have to go *now*," Liam whisper-shouts, holding the door open as we all race into the hallway. The map is too big for one person to carry, and Sawyer and Imogen struggle through the doorway as the guard kicks in the door farther down the hall.

My stomach hits the floor, and panic threatens to overwhelm logical thought.

"And we're fucked," Nadine announces.

"What the hell do you think you're doing?" the guard shouts, charging toward us.

"We're dead if he catches us with the map." Ridoc bounces on his toes like he's preparing to fight. On any given day, I'd argue that riders are the superior fighters—we have to be—but that Basgiath guard might just give us a run for our money.

"We can't hurt him," I protest.

The guard barrels past the first stairwell and Rhiannon steps into the middle of the hallway, her arms outstretched.

"Please work. Please work. Please work," Imogen chants.

The map disappears out of her hands and reappears down the hallway in Rhiannon's.

I barely have time to register that it worked as the guard stumbles, but he keeps running. Any closer and he'll see my face.

"This was not part of the plan." Liam moves to my side.

"Adapt! Emery!" Imogen hisses, and the third-year steps to the front of our little raiding party.

"I'm so sorry, man." He holds out his hands and pushes. A torrent of air rushes down the hallway, ripping tapestries from the walls and knocking into the guard, sending him flying against the stone wall. "Run!"

We sprint down the hall toward where the guard lies limp. "Put him in here," I hiss, forcing open the next door, the one that belongs to one of my mother's undersecretaries.

Liam and Ridoc haul the guard in, and I put my fingers to his neck. "Good strong pulse. He just knocked him out. Open his mouth." I snag the vial hidden in the pocket of my leathers, uncork it, and then let the tonic flow into the guard's mouth. "He'll sleep the rest of the night."

Liam's wide eyes meet mine. "You're kind of terrifying."

"Thank you." I grin, and we get out of there, running as fast as we can.

Fifteen minutes later, our chests are still heaving as we skid into the Battle Brief room, just under the clock.

We're the last to arrive, and the tick of Dain's jaw from where he sits in the top row with the other leadership tells me we're going to get an earful about it.

I drag my gaze away, and we find our seats as presentations begin in order of squad, giving us enough time to recover from our sprinting session before we have to take the stage.

A squad in First Wing stole Kaori's handwritten manual on the personal habits and flaws of all active dragons. Impressive.

A squad in Second Wing elicits an appreciative murmur when they reveal the uniform of one of the Infantry professors, fully intact with something riders never bear—a name tag. That would grant any enemy access to our outposts, given the rank on the shoulder.

Third Wing's best offering is a stunned, wide-eyed scribe, stolen straight from his bed, and given the way his mouth isn't moving… Yep, someone's signet power takes away speech. The poor thing is going to be traumatized when they finally let him go.

When it's our turn to take the stage, Sawyer and Liam, the two tallest in our squad, hold the top corners of our map so it's visible to all as it unrolls.

I stand back next to Imogen and search the leadership for a certain pair of onyx eyes. *There he is*.

Xaden is leaning against the wall near the other wingleaders, watching me with a pulse-quickening mix of curiosity and expectation.

"It was your idea," Imogen whispers, nudging me forward. "Present."

Markham's eyes flare wide as saucers as he forces himself to stand, followed quickly by Devera, whose mouth hangs so wide, it's almost comical.

I clear my throat and gesture to the map. "We have brought the ultimate weapon for our enemies. An up-to-date map of all current outposts of Navarrian wings, to include troop strength of infantry battlements." I point to the forts along the Cygnisen border. "As well as the locations of all current skirmishes in the last thirty days. Including last night."

A murmur rips through the quadrant.

"And how do we know this map is, in fact, current?" Kaori asks, holding his reclaimed journal under one arm.

There's no stopping the smile that spreads across my face. "Because we stole it from General Sorrengail's office."

Absolute mayhem breaks out, some of the riders rushing the stage as professors battle their way toward us, but I ignore it all as Xaden tilts one corner of that beautiful mouth and tips an imaginary hat to me, bowing his head for a heartbeat before bringing his gaze back to hold mine. Satisfaction fills every ounce of my being as I smile up at him.

It doesn't matter how the vote comes down.

I've already won.

There is no stronger bond than that between two mated dragons. It goes beyond the depth of human love or adoration to a primal, undeniable requirement for proximity. One cannot survive without the other.

—Colonel Kaori's Field Guide to Dragonkind

CHAPTER TWENTY-SIX

Flying for short distances is something I manage.

Flight maneuvers—the dips and dives that come with combat formations—send me spinning through the sky unless Tairn holds me on with bands of his own power.

But flying for six hours straight for our prize, a weeklong tour of a forward outpost, might just be the death of me.

"I'm pretty sure I'm dying." Nadine bends over, bracing her hands on her knees.

"I feel that." Every vertebra in my spine screams as I stretch, and the hands that were freezing only a few minutes ago start to sweat inside my leather gloves.

Naturally, Dain is minimally affected, his posture only slightly stiff as he and Professor Devera greet a tall man in rider black, who I assume is the outpost commander.

"Welcome, cadets," the commander says with a professional smile, folding his arms across the chest of his lightweight leathers. His salt-and-pepper hair makes it hard to determine his age, and he has that gaunt, weathered look all riders get when they've been stationed on the border for too long. "I'm sure you'd all like to get settled and into something a little more appropriate to the climate. Then we'll show you around Montserrat."

Rhiannon inhales sharply, her gaze sweeping over the mountains.

"You all right?"

She nods. "Later."

Later arrives in exactly twelve sweat-soaked minutes as we're shown to our double-occupancy barracks rooms. They're sparse, only furnished with two beds, two wardrobes, and a single desk under a wide window.

She's quiet the entire time we make our way through the bathing chamber to wash off the ride and alarmingly silent while we dress in our summer leathers. It may only be April here at Montserrat, but it feels like Basgiath in June.

"You going to tell me what's up?" I ask, stowing my pack beneath the bed before making sure all my daggers are where they're supposed to be. The hilts are barely visible in the sheaths I wear at my thighs, but I doubt many people this far east would recognize the Tyrrish symbols.

Rhiannon's hands tremble with what looks like nervous energy as she straps her sword to her back. "Do you know where we are?"

I mentally bring up a map. "We're about two hundred miles from the coast—"

"My village is less than an hour away on foot." Her eyes meet mine in an unspoken plea, so much emotion swirling in their dark-brown depths that my throat clogs, choking my words.

Taking her hands in mine, I squeeze, nodding. I know exactly what she's asking and exactly what it will cost if we're caught.

"Don't tell anyone," I whisper, even though it's just us in the tiny room. "We have six days to figure it out and we will." It's a promise and we both know it.

Someone pounds on our door. "Let's go, Second Squad!"

Dain. Nine months ago, I would have relished this time away with him. Now I find myself avoiding his constant expectations of me—or just avoiding him in general. Funny how much can change in such a short time.

We join the others, and Major Quade gives us the grand tour of the outpost. My stomach growls, but I ignore it, taking in the hectic energy of the base.

The fortress is basically four massive walls, filled with barracks and various chambers with turrets on each corner and a large, arched entrance that boasts a spiked portcullis that looks ready to drop at any second. On one end of the courtyard, there's a stable with a blacksmith and armory for the company of infantry stationed here, and on the other is the dining hall.

"As you can see," Major Quade tells us as we stand in the middle of the muddy courtyard, "we're built for siege. In the event of attack, we can feed and house everyone within for an adequate amount of time."

Adequate? Ridoc mouths, lifting his brows.

I press my lips together to keep from laughing, and Dain gives him a look that promises retribution from where he stands beside me. My smile falls away.

"As one of the eastern outposts, we have a full twelve riders stationed here. Three are out on patrol now, three wait, standing by in case they're needed, and the other six are in various stages of rest," Quade continues.

"What is that look for?" Dain whispers.

"What look?" I ask as the distinct roar of a dragon echoes off the stone walls.

"That should be one of our patrols returning now," Quade says, smiling like he wants to mean it but can't quite find the energy.

"The one where someone just sucked the joy out of your world," Dain responds, bending his head slightly and keeping his voice low enough that only I can hear him.

I could lie to him, but that would make our semi-truce even more awkward. "I was just remembering the guy I used to climb trees with, that's all."

He startles like I've slapped him.

"So we'll get you riders fed and put to bed, and then we'll work on who you'll be shadowing while you're here," Quade continues.

"Will we get to participate in any active scenarios?" Heaton asks, practically vibrating with excitement.

"Absolutely not!" Devera snaps.

"If you see combat, then I've failed as this being the safest place on the border to send you," Quade answers. "But you get bonus points for enthusiasm. Let me guess. Third-year?"

Heaton nods.

Quade turns slightly and smiles at three indistinct figures in rider black as they walk under the portcullis. "There they are now. Why don't you three come and meet—"

"Violet?"

My head whips toward the gate, and my heart combusts in a series of erratic beats that leaves me clutching my chest with the best kind of shock. *No way.* There's no way. I stumble for the gate, forgetting to be stoic, to be emotionally untouchable, as she breaks into a run, her arms opening just before we collide.

She sweeps me up, yanking me against her chest and squeezing tight. She smells like dirt and dragon and the coppery tang of blood, but I don't care. I hug her back just as hard.

"Mira." I bury my face against her shoulder, and my eyes burn as she rests her hand on top of the very braid she taught me how to do. It's as if the weight of everything that's happened over the last nine months comes crashing down, slamming into me with the force of a cross-bolt.

The wind of the parapet.

The look in Xaden's eyes when he realized I was a Sorrengail.

The sound of Jack swearing he'd kill me.

The smell of burning flesh that first day.

The look on Aurelie's face when she fell from the Gauntlet.

Pryor and Luca and Trina and…Tynan. Oren and Amber Mavis.

Tairn and Andarna choosing me.

Xaden kissing me.

Our mother ignoring me.

Mira pulls me back just long enough to look me over, as if she's checking for damage. "You're all right." She nods, her teeth digging into her bottom lip. "You're all right, aren't you?"

I nod, but she blurs in my vision because I might be alive, thriving even, but I'm not the same person she left at the base of that turret, and from the heaviness in her eyes, she knows it, too.

"Yeah," she whispers, tucking me in tight again. "You're all right, Violet. You're all right."

If she says it enough times, I might start to believe her.

"Are *you*?" I jerk back to study her. There's a new scar that stretches from her earlobe to her collarbone. "Gods, Mira."

"I'm fine," she promises, then grins. "And look at you! You didn't die!"

Irrational, giddy laughter bubbles up. "I didn't die! You're not an only child!"

We both burst into laughter, and tears track down my cheeks.

"Sorrengails are weird," I hear Imogen state.

"You have no idea," Dain answers, but when I turn to look, his lips are curved into the first genuine smile I've seen from him in months.

"Shut up, Aetos," Mira barks, throwing her arm over my shoulder. "Catch me up on everything, Violet."

We might be hundreds of miles from Basgiath, but I've never felt more at home.

It's early evening two days later, just after dinner, when Rhiannon and I climb out our first-story window and drop to the ground. Mira's out on patrol, and as wonderful as it's been to have her close, this is our only chance.

"We're on our way."

"Don't get caught," Tairn warns.

"Trying not to." Rhiannon and I sneak along the battlement wall, turning the corner toward the field—

I run into Mira so hard that I bounce backward.

"Shit!" Rhiannon exclaims as she catches me.

"Don't you at least check the corners?" Mira lectures, folding her arms over her chest and staring me down in a way I might deserve. Fine, I definitely deserve.

"In my defense, I didn't think you'd be there," I say slowly. "Because you're supposed to be on patrol."

"You were acting super weird at dinner." She tilts her head to the side and studies me just like we're kids again, seeing way too much. "So I switched shifts. Do you want to tell me what you're doing outside the walls?"

I glance at Rhiannon, and she looks away.

"Neither of you? Really?" She sighs and rubs the bridge of her nose. "You two need to sneak out of a heavily fortified defensive position because…?"

I look up at Rhiannon. "She's going to figure it out anyway. She's like a bloodhound with stuff like this. Trust me." My stomach clenches.

Rhiannon tilts her chin. "We're flying to my family's house."

Mira blanches. "You think you're *what*?"

"We're flying to her village. It's like a five-minute flight, according to Tairn, and—" I start.

"Absolutely not." Mira shakes her head. "Nope. You cannot fly off like you're on vacation. What if something happens to you?"

"At her parents' house?" I ask slowly. "Because there's some major ambush planned on the off chance that we might just be dropping in?"

Mira's eyes narrow.

Shit. This is not going well and, given the death grip Rhiannon has on my arm now, she doesn't think so, either.

"We'd be in less danger visiting her parents than we are at Basgiath," I argue.

Mira's lips purse. "Fair point."

"Come with us," I blurt. "Seriously. Come with us, Mira. She just wants to see her sister."

Mira's shoulders dip. She's softening, and I mercilessly go in for the kill. "Raegan was pregnant when Rhiannon left. Can you imagine not being there with me if I had a kid? Wouldn't you do anything, including escape a heavily fortified defensive position, if that meant holding your niece or nephew?" My nose scrunches as I brace for her answer. "Besides, with the hero of Strythmore at our side, what could possibly go wrong?"

"Don't even start with that." She looks at me, then Rhiannon, then back at me again before groaning. "Oh, fucking *fine*." Her finger comes out swinging when we both grin. "But if you even think about telling anyone, I'll make you regret it for the rest of your natural life."

"She means it," I whisper.

"I believe it," Rhiannon answers.

"You're here two days and already breaking the rules," Mira mutters. "Come on, it's quicker to cut down this path."

An hour later, Mira and I are stretched out on the cushioned benches that flank both sides of the dining table at Raegan's house, watching Rhiannon rock her nephew by the fireplace, lost in conversation with her sister as her parents and brother-in-law look on from the nearby couch.

Watching them reunite is worth everything.

"Thank you for helping us." I glance over the table at Mira.

"You would have done it with or without me." Her smile is soft as she watches the family, curling her hand around the pewter mug of wine Rhiannon's mom was kind enough to bring earlier. "Figured at least this way I'd know you're safe. What other rules have you broken, sis?" She sips her wine and cuts a look my way.

A smirk tugs at my mouth as I lift one shoulder. "Maybe a few here and there. I've gotten very good at poisoning my opponents before challenges."

Mira nearly spits out her wine, slamming her hand over her mouth.

I laugh, crossing one booted ankle over the other. "Not what you were expecting?"

Respect shines in her eyes. "I honestly don't know what I expected. I was just desperate for you to live. And then you went and not only bonded one of the most powerful dragons alive but a feathertail, too." She shakes her head. "My baby sister is a badass."

"Not sure Mom would agree with that." I rub my thumb over the handle of my mug. "I'm not exactly manifesting a signet yet. I'm solid at grounding and can hold a pretty strong shield, but..." I can't tell her the rest, the gift Andarna has given, at least for now, to me. "If I don't manifest my signet soon..."

We both know what will happen.

She quietly studies me in that way she has, then says, "Here's the thing. If you want your signet to manifest, then stop blocking it by thinking it has anything to do with Mom. Your power is yours and yours alone, Vi."

I squirm under her scrutiny and change the subject, my gaze dropping to her neck. "How did that happen?"

"Gryphon," she answers, nodding. "Near the village of Cranston about seven months ago. Thing came out of nowhere in the middle of a village raid. The wards went down, and usually my signet gives me a little immunity from the enemy wielders, but not their fucking birds. Took the healers hours to stitch me up. But it gave me a pretty cool scar." She tilts her chin to show it off.

"Cranston?" I think back over the Battle Briefs. "We never learned about that one. I..." Common sense tells me to shut my mouth.

"You what?" She takes another drink.

"I think there's way more going on along the borders than what we're told," I admit quietly.

Mira lifts her brows. "Well, of course there is. You don't expect Battle Brief to relay classified information, do you? You know better than that. And honestly, at the rate our borders are being attacked, they'd have to devote all day to Battle Brief in order to dissect each assault."

"That makes sense. Do you guys get all the information?"

"Only what we need. Like, I could have sworn I saw a riot of dragons across the border during this attack." She shrugs. "But questions about secret operations are above my pay grade. Think of it this way—if you were a healer, would you need to know the details about everyone else's patients?"

I shake my head. "No."

"Exactly. Now tell me, what the fuck is going on between you and Dain? I've seen less tension on a crossbow, and I don't mean the good kind." She gives me a look that leaves no room for excuses.

"I needed to change in order to survive. He wouldn't let me." It was the simplest explanation for the last nine months. "I got his friend Amber killed. She was a wingleader. And honestly, everything with Xaden just pushed us so far apart that I don't know how to repair our friendship. Not to what it was, at least."

"The execution of that wingleader is common knowledge. You didn't get her killed. She got herself killed by breaking the Codex." Mira studies me for a quiet moment. "Is it true Riorson saved you that night?"

I nod. "Xaden is a complicated subject." So complicated that I can't identify my own feelings. Thinking of him only jumbles me in a way that leaves me tangled in knots. I want him, but I can't trust him, not in the ways I want to. And yet in other ways, he's the person I trust most.

"I hope you know what you're doing there." Her grip tightens on her mug. "Because I distinctly remember warning you to steer clear of that traitor's son."

My stomach turns at Mira's description of Xaden. "Tairn clearly didn't heed the warning."

She snorts.

"But really, if Xaden hadn't shown up that night, or if I hadn't been sleeping in the armor…" I pause and lean forward to touch her hand. "I can't even begin to tell you how many times you've saved my life without even being there."

Mira smiles. "Glad it worked. I swear it took an entire molting season to collect all those scales."

"Have you thought of telling Mom about it? Getting them made for all riders?"

"I told my leadership." She leans back and takes another drink. "They said they're looking into it."

We watch Rhiannon kiss her nephew's perfect chubby cheeks. "I've never seen a family this happy," I admit. "Even when Brennan and Dad were alive, we weren't like…that."

"No, we weren't." A sad smile curves her mouth as she looks at me. "But I can remember plenty of nights we spent curled around the fire with Dad and that book you love."

"Ah yes, the book you made me leave in my old bedroom." I arch a brow.

"You mean the book I snagged just in case Mom got a wild hair and decided to clean out your things while you were in the quadrant?" Her smile morphs into a grin. "I have it at Montserrat. Figured you'd be pissed if you graduated and it was gone. I mean, whatever would you do if you forgot a minute detail of how the gallant riders took out the army of wyvern and the venin who sucked the land dry of magic?"

I blink. "Shit. I can't remember. But I guess I'll be able to read it again soon!" A bubble of joy rises in my chest. "You are the best."

"I'll give it to you at the outpost." She leans back and gives me a thoughtful look. "I know they're just stories, but I never used to get why the villains would choose to corrupt their souls and become venin, and now..." Her brow furrows.

"Now you empathize with the villain?" I tease.

"No." She shakes her head. "But we have the kind of power people would kill for, Violet. Dragons and gryphons are the gatekeepers, and I'm sure that to someone jealous enough, ambitious enough, risking a soul would be a fair price for the ability to wield." Her shoulders rise as she shrugs. "Just makes me glad our dragons are so discerning and our wards keep the gryphon riders at bay. Who the hell knows what kind of people those furry creatures choose?"

We stay another hour, until we know we're risking exposure if we stay a minute longer. Then Mira and I give Rhiannon some privacy to say goodbye to her family and head out of the house into the humid night. Tairn has been uncharacteristically quiet the last couple of hours.

"Have you been stationed with any riders of mated pairs?" I ask Mira as I close the door behind us.

"One," she answers, her eyes narrowing on the darkened path in front of the house. "Why?"

"I'm just wondering how long they can be separated."

"Turns out, about three days is their max." Xaden steps out of the shadows.

For valor above and beyond the call of duty in the battle of Strythmore, where her bravery resulted not only in the destruction of a battery behind enemy lines but also saved the lives of an entire company of infantry, I recommend Mira Sorrengail receive the Star of Navarre. But if the criterion is not met, which I assure you it has been, downgrading to the Order of the Talon would be a shame, but sufficient.

—Recommendation for Award from Major Potsdam to General Sorrengail

CHAPTER TWENTY-SEVEN

"So all we do is wait for something to happen?" Ridoc asks the next afternoon, leaning back in his chair and putting his boots on the end of the wooden table that runs the length of the briefing room.

"Yes," Mira says from the head of the table, then flicks her wrist and sends Ridoc flying backward. "And keep your feet off the table."

One of the Montserrat riders laughs, changing the markers on the large map that consumes the only stone wall in the curved, windowed room. This is the highest turret in the outpost, offering unmatched views of the Esben mountain range around us.

We've been split into two groups for the day. Rhiannon, Sawyer, Cianna, Nadine, and Heaton spent the morning with Devera in this room, studying previous battles at the outpost, and are now out on patrol.

Dain, Ridoc, Liam, Emery, Quinn, and I spent the morning on a two-hour flight around the surrounding area, with one extra tagalong—Xaden. He's been the worst kind of distraction since arriving last night.

Dain won't stop glaring at him and making snide remarks.

Mira keeps one eye on him at all times as well, suspiciously quiet since last night.

And me? I can't seem to keep my eyes to myself. There's a palpable energy in every room he enters, and it brushes over my skin like a caress each time our eyes meet. Even now, I'm aware of every breath he takes as he sits next to me midway down the table.

"Consider this your Battle Brief," Mira continues, side-eyeing Ridoc as he scrambles back into his chair. "This morning was about a quarter of the patrol we'd regularly fly, so normally we'd just be getting back about now and reporting our findings to the commander. But for the sake of killing time, since we're in this room as the reaction flight for this afternoon, let's pretend we'd come across a newly fortified enemy outpost crossing our border"—she turns to the map and sticks a pin with a small crimson flag near one of the peaks about two miles from the Cygnisen borderline—"here."

"We're supposed to pretend it just popped up overnight?" Emery asks, openly skeptical.

"For the sake of argument, third-year." Mira narrows her eyes on him, and he sits up a little straighter.

"I like this game," another one of the Montserrat riders says from the end of the table, lacing his fingers behind his neck.

"What would our objective be?" Mira glances around the table, noticeably skipping Xaden. Last night, she'd taken one look at the rebellion relic on his neck and walked by without saying a word. "Aetos?"

Dain startles from where he was glowering across the table at Xaden and turns to face the map. "What type of fortifications are there? Are we talking a haphazard wooden structure? Or something more substantial?"

"Like they had time to build a fortress overnight," Ridoc mutters. "It has to be wooden, right?"

"You are all so fucking literal." Mira sighs and rubs her thumb over her forehead. "Fine, let's say they occupied a keep that's already established. Stone and all."

"But the civilians didn't call for help?" Quinn asks, scratching her pointed chin. "Protocol calls for a distress signal this far into the mountains. They should have lit their distress beacon, alerting patrolling riders, at which time the dragons on patrol would have told all available dragons in the area. The very riders in this room would have mounted first as the reaction force and the others would have been woken from their rests, allowing the riders to prevent the loss of the keep in the first place."

Mira scoffs and braces her hands on the end of the table, staring us all down. "Everything you're taught at Basgiath is theory. You analyze past attacks and learn those very…theoretical combat maneuvers. But things out here don't always go according to plan. So why don't we talk about all the ways things can go sideways, so you'll know what to do when they do, as opposed to arguing that the keep shouldn't have fallen?"

Quinn shifts her weight uncomfortably.

"How many of you have been called out as third-years?" Mira stands straight, folding her arms over her black leathers and the strap that holds her sword to her back.

Emery and Xaden raise their hands, though Xaden's is barely a gesture.

Dain looks like his head is about to explode. "That's not correct. We're never called into service until graduation."

Xaden presses his lips in a tight line and nods, giving him a sarcastic thumbs-up.

"Yeah, all right." Emery laughs. "Just wait until next year. I can't count how many times we're the ones sitting in these very rooms in the midland forts because their riders have been called to the front for an emergency."

The color drains from Dain's face.

"Now that's settled." Mira reaches under the table and pulls out a set of models, putting a six-inch stone keep in the center of the table. "Catch." One by one, she tosses painted wooden models of dragons at us, keeping one for herself. "Pretend Messina and Exal don't exist back there, and we're the only squad available to take back that keep. Think of the power in this room. Think of what each individual rider brings to the table and how you'd use those powers in unison to conquer your objective."

"But they don't teach that to first-years," Liam says slowly from the other side of me.

Mira glances at the whirls of magic on his wrist, but to Liam's credit, he doesn't tug his sleeve down. It's hard to remember sometimes that the third-years are the first riders who will serve with the children of the leaders of the Tyrrish uprising—an uprising that could have left our borders eventually defenseless and the innocent people of Navarre war casualties.

Everyone in this room has become accustomed to Liam, Imogen...even Xaden. But those in active service have never flown with anyone marked by a rebellion relic.

The Tyrrish riders who remained loyal to Navarre during the uprising were promoted, not punished, and the riders who turned against king and country were killed or executed. And just like my grief at Brennan's loss was directed at Xaden that first day at the parapet, there will be more than one rider who misdirects their own anger at marked riders.

I clear my throat.

Mira's gaze meets mine, and I lift an eyebrow at her in clear warning. *Don't fuck with my friends.*

Her eyes widen ever so slightly, and she directs her attention back to Liam. "They might not teach you this battle strategy as first-years because you're all busy trying to stay on your dragons. You had your first taste of strategy during the Squad Battle, and it's almost May, which means final War Games should be beginning, right?"

"Two weeks," Dain answers.

"Good timing, then. Not all of you will survive the games if you're not prepared." She holds my gaze for a beat. "This kind of thinking will give your squad—your entire wing—an advantage, since I guarantee your wingleader is already assessing every rider for their own abilities."

Xaden flips his dragon model over his knuckles but doesn't reply. He hasn't spoken a word to Mira since arriving.

"So let's do this." Mira stands back. "Who is in command?" She glances toward Quinn. "And let's pretend that I don't have three years of seniority on even the highest-ranked of you."

"Then I'm in command." Dain sits up straight, his chin rising a good inch.

"Our *wingleader* is here," Liam argues, pointing at Xaden. "I would say that puts him in command."

"We can pretend I'm not here, just for the sake of the exercise." Xaden sets his dragon on the table and leans back in his chair, draping his arm across the back of mine, a move that makes Dain grit his teeth. "Give Aetos here the position we all know he craves."

"Don't be a dick," I whisper.

"You haven't even seen me start to be a dick."

My head turns so fast that it swims, and my mouth drops open as I stare at the side of Xaden's face. That was his voice...in my fucking *head*.

He turns, the golden flecks in his eyes catching the light, and I swear I hear him laughing in my mind, though his lips are closed, tilted in that pulse-quickening smirk of his.

"You're staring. It's going to get awkward in about thirty seconds if you don't stop."

"How?" I hiss.

"The same way you talk to Sgaeyl. We're all gloriously, annoyingly linked. This is just one of the perks. Though I'm starting to wish I'd tried it sooner. The look on your face is priceless." He winks and turns back to the table.

He. Fucking. *Winked.* And is that a hint of a smile?

"You're. The. Wingleader." Every word Dain speaks comes out through clenched teeth.

"I'm not even supposed to be here." Xaden shrugs. "But if it makes you feel better, for the purpose of War Games, you'd be getting your orders from your section leader, Garrick Tavis, which he'd get from me. You'll be carrying out your maneuvers as a squad for the good of the wing. Just pretend I'm another member of your squad and use me as you wish, Aetos." Xaden folds his arms across his chest.

I glance at Mira, who's watching the play-by-play with raised brows.

"Why are you even here?" Dain challenges. "No offense, *sir*, but we weren't exactly expecting senior leadership on this trip."

"You're more than aware that Sgaeyl and Tairn are mated."

"Three days?" Dain fires back, leaning in. "You couldn't make it three days?"

"It has nothing to do with him," I interrupt, setting my dragon down with a little more force than necessary. "That's up to Tairn and Sgaeyl."

"You never considered that it was you I couldn't stay away from?"

I crook my right arm and jab it into Xaden's biceps. He doesn't mean that. Not when he's still adamant that kissing me was a mistake. And if he does… I'm not going there.

"Now, now, you'll give our little communication secret away if you can't keep from being so…violent." He barely restrains a smile, obviously loving that he gets the last word.

I need to figure out how the hell he's doing it so I can mentally argue back.

"Of course you rush to defend him." Dain hurls a hurt glare at me. "Though how you can forget that this guy wanted to kill you six months ago is beyond me."

I blink up at him. "I cannot believe you went there."

"Good job remaining professional, Aetos." Xaden scratches the relic on his neck I'm all but certain doesn't actually itch. "Really shows those leadership qualities to their best advantage."

One of the riders down the table whistles low. "Do you boys just want to whip it out and measure? It would be faster."

Liam smothers a laugh, but his shoulders shake.

"Enough!" Mira slams her hands on the table.

"Oh, come on, Sorrengail," the rider down the table whines with a wide smile.

Both Mira and I look his way.

"I mean…the older Sorrengail. This is the best entertainment we've had in ages."

I shake my head and look around the table. "Mira has the ability to extend the shield if the wards are down, so the first thing I would do is send her to scout the area with Teine. We need to know if we're dealing with infantry or gryphon riders."

"Good." Mira moves her dragon closer to the castle. "Now let's assume there are gryphons."

"You want to do your job?" I ask Dain, smiling sweetly. "I mean, how you can forget you're the squad leader is beyond me."

His hand clenches around his own dragon as he rips his gaze from mine. "Quinn, can you astral project from the back of your dragon?"

"Yes," she answers.

"Then I would have you project into the fortress to check for signs of weakness," Dain orders. "And have you report back. Same with Liam. We'd use your farsight to see if you can locate where the gryphon riders are and if there are any traps."

"Good. The weaknesses are the wooden gate," Mira notes as Quinn and Liam move their dragons into position, "and the Navarrian citizens they have captive in the dungeons."

"So much for blasting the whole place," Ridoc says.

"You're an air wielder, right?" Dain asks Emery. "So you can shape your dragon's flames, lead them through the occupied parts of the keep without killing civilians."

"Yes," Emery answers. "But I'd have to be in the keep."

"Then you'll have to get into the keep," Mira says with a shrug.

Emery's eyes widen. "You want me to leave my dragon and go on foot?"

"Why do you think we get all that hand-to-hand training? Or are you going to leave all those innocent people to die?" Mira flicks her wrist and Emery's dragon goes flying out of his hand and into hers. She puts it in the center of the keep. "The real question is, how do we get you close enough without getting you killed?" She glances around the table. "Since I'm guessing the others will be busy fighting off the gryphons that launch once the fireworks start."

"What's your signet, Aetos?" Quinn asks.

"Above your pay grade," Dain answers, glancing around the table and skipping over Xaden, then making the rounds again, finally sighing. "Any ideas?"

Is the quadrant really making Dain keep the memory reading secret? Had him reaching for my head the day Amber burned been a loss of control? How has he gotten this far without telling *anyone* what his signet is? I shake my head.

"Sure." I pick up Xaden's dragon and shove it toward the keep, planting one mental foot in the Archives where I keep my power and using it to lift the dragon figurine into a hover above the structure. "You stop ignoring that you have an incredibly powerful shadow wielder at your disposal and ask him to black out the area so no one sees you land."

"She's not wrong," Mira agrees, but her words are clipped.

"You can do that?" Dain begrudgingly looks at Xaden.

"Are you seriously asking?" Xaden retorts.

"Just wasn't sure you could cover an area that—"

Xaden lifts a hand a few inches above the table, and shadows pour from underneath our seats, filling the room and turning it dark as midnight in a blink. My heart jumps as my sight goes black.

"Relax. It's just me." A ghost of a touch skims my cheek.

Just him is slightly…terrifying. I shove that thought at him, but there's no response. Maybe we have a one-way-communication thing going on over here, because I don't think I can talk to him the way he does me.

What had Sgaeyl said about signets? *It reflects who you are at the core of your being.* It makes sense. Mira is protective. Dain has to know everything. And Xaden…has secrets.

"Fuck me," someone says.

"I can surround this entire outpost, but I think that might freak some people out," Xaden says, and the shadows disappear, racing back under the table.

I draw in a full breath, noting that everyone at the table besides Emery—who has no doubt seen Xaden pull this kind of trick before—looks slightly greenish.

Even Mira, who's staring at Xaden like he's a threat she needs to assess.

My stomach turns.

"I hope you didn't get any ideas while we were in the dark there," Xaden teases, and just like that, my sympathy for the ass evaporates. I don't bother to face him, just raise one finger.

He chuckles, and I grit my teeth.

"Get him out of my head," I toss in Tairn's direction.

"You'll get used to it," Tairn responds.

"Is this normal with all mated pairs and their riders?"

"For some. It's a great advantage in a battle."

"Well, it's a pain in my ass right now." I miss Andarna. We're so far apart that I can barely feel her.

"Then shield him out the same way you do me—or start talking back," Tairn grumbles. *"You have the power to be a pain in the ass, too. Trust me."*

"And how exactly am I supposed to talk back at him?" I give Xaden a heavy dose of side-eye, but he's engrossed in the ongoing battle we've waged against an imaginary keep.

"Figure out which pathway into your mind is his."

Oh joy. That should be easy.

We finish the hypothetical operation, each of us using our power to its best ability…everyone except me. But when it's time to take the gryphons out in the air, Tairn overpowers every other dragon in the room.

"Good job," Mira says, glancing at her pocket watch. "Aetos, Riorson, and Sorrengail, I want to see you in the hallway. The rest of you are dismissed."

It's not like any of us has an option, so we follow Mira out to the spiral staircase.

She shuts the door behind us and throws up a line of blue energy that covers the entrance.

"Sound shield," Dain says with a smile. "Nice."

"Shut up." Mira spins on the top step, putting her finger in Dain's face. "I don't know what bug has crawled up your ass, Dain Aetos, but have you forgotten that you're a squad leader? That you have a very real chance of becoming a wingleader next year?"

Oh shit, she's pissed, and that's not anything I want a part of. I retreat another step, but with Xaden beneath me on the stairs, there's nowhere left to go.

"Mira—" Dain starts.

"Lieutenant Sorrengail," Mira responds. "You're blowing it, Dain. I know how badly you want his job next year." She points a finger at Xaden. "Don't forget that we've grown up about ten feet apart. And you are *blowing* it, because what? You're pissed that Violet bonded his dragon's mate?"

Heat stings my cheeks. She's never been one to mince words, but just… damn.

"He is the worst possible thing for her!" Dain counters.

"Oh, I'm not arguing that." She leans into his space. "But there's nothing anyone can do about the choices of dragons. They don't bother with the opinions of mere humans, do they? But whatever is going on between the two of you"—that finger swings between Dain and me—"is fucking up your squad. If I can see it after four days with you, then they sure as hell can tell. And if I'd known that you were going to be such a hard-ass with zero flexibility for the things she can't control, I never would have told her to find you after crossing the parapet." She glances at me, then back at him. "You two have been best friends since you were five years old. Figure your shit out."

Dain is so tense, he looks like he might crack in half, but he glances at me and nods.

I do the same.

"Good, now get back in there." She motions toward the door with her head, and Dain leaves, walking through the shield. "And as for you." She walks down two steps and pins Xaden with a glare. "Is this what she can expect next year?"

"Aetos being an asshole?" Xaden asks, leaving his hands loose at his sides. "Probably."

Mira's eyes narrow. "Mated dragons typically bond riders in the same year for a reason. You cannot expect your assigned wing or her instructors to let you both fly off every three days."

"Wasn't my choice." He shrugs.

"What are we supposed to do? Tell the giant, flame-throwing dragons how it's going to be?" I ask my sister.

"Yes!" she exclaims, turning toward me. "Because you can't live this way, Violet. You'll be the one who ends up missing the training you need, because he's the more powerful of the two of you right now. But if you don't get to focus on your training, then that's how it will always be. You won't ever become who Tairn can push you to be. Is that what you're after, Riorson?"

"Mira," I whisper, shaking my head. "You're wrong about him."

"Listen to me." She grasps my shoulders. "He might wield shadows, Violet, but give him his way, and you'll become one."

"That won't happen," I promise her.

"It will if he has anything to say about it." Her gaze flickers behind me. "Killing someone isn't the only way to destroy them. Keeping you from reaching your potential seems like a great path to the retribution he swore against our mother. Think long and hard. How well do you even really know him?"

I suck in a breath. I trust Xaden. At least, I think I do. But Mira's right; there are infinite ways to demolish someone without ending their life.

"That's what I thought." The look in her eyes turns to something worse than anger. It's pity. "Do you even know why he hates our mother so much? Why the kids like him are put on the para—"

"I'm right here," Xaden interrupts, rising to the same step to stand at my side. "In case you didn't notice."

"You're kind of hard to miss," she retorts.

"You're not listening." His voice lowers. "I. Am. Here. Tairn didn't drag her back to Basgiath. He didn't break through her shields and pour his emotions into her. He didn't demand she fly across the fucking kingdom. Your sister is still right here. I'm the one who left *my* post, *my* position, and *my* executive officer in charge of *my* wing. She's not missing out on *shit.*"

"And next year? When you're a brand-new lieutenant? What *shit* is she going to miss out on then?" Mira asks.

"We'll figure it out." I reach for her hand and squeeze. "Mira, he's taken every spare minute he has to train me on the mat for challenges or take me flying in hopes I'll finally figure out how to keep my damned seat without Tairn holding me in place. He's—"

She flinches. "You can't keep your seat?"

"No." It's barely a whisper, and the heat of embarrassment scorches my skin.

"How the hell can you *not*?" Her mouth hangs open.

"Because I'm not you!" I shout.

She rears back like I've slapped her, our hands breaking apart. "But you…you look so much stronger now."

"My joints and muscles are stronger because Imogen makes me lift these horrible weights, but that doesn't…fix me."

Mira blanches. "No. I didn't mean it like that, Vi. You're not anything that needs to be fixed. I just didn't know you couldn't hold your seat. Why didn't you tell me?"

"Because there's nothing you can do about it." I force a wry smile. "There's nothing *anyone* can do about the way I'm made."

A long, uncomfortable silence stretches between us. For as close as we are, there's still so much we don't share.

"She's getting better," Xaden offers, his voice calm and even. "The first few weeks were…disastrous."

"Hey, he caught me before I hit the ground," I argue.

"Barely," Xaden grumbles before turning back to Mira. "You don't have to trust me—"

"Good, because I don't," she says. "All of that power in the hands of someone with your history is bad enough, but to know your dragons are so tangled up that you can't be more than three days from Violet is unacceptable in every possible way I can think—" She goes completely still, her eyes un-focusing.

"There's a drift of gryphons headed this way!" Tairn bellows.

"Fuck! The wards are down," Mira mutters, apparently receiving the same alarm from Teine. She clutches my shoulders and yanks me into a hug. "You have to go."

"We can help!" I argue, but she holds me so tightly that I can't move.

"You can't. And if Tairn is using his power to keep you seated, then he's diminished as well. You have to *go*. Get out of here. If you love me, Violet, you'll go so I don't have to worry about you, too." She releases me, looking to Xaden as our squad pours out of the door above, thundering by as they run down the steps. "Get her out of here."

"Let's go!" Dain shouts. "Now!"

"Even if you don't trust me, I'm the best weapon you have," Xaden snarls at Mira.

"If what you say is true, then you're the best weapon *she* has. The other half of the squad will be here in moments, and Teine thinks we have about twenty minutes until the gryphons arrive." Mira's eyes meet mine. "You have to get to safety, Violet. I love you. Don't die. I'd hate to be an only child." There's no cocky grin like when she left me at Basgiath on Conscription Day.

Xaden hauls me against his side as Mira runs up the remaining stairs toward the roof.

This can't be happening. There's no way I can flee to safety and leave my sister here, with absolutely zero way of knowing if she's alive or dead. This feels like the exact sort of thing we'd never hear about in Battle Brief.

No fucking way. Every cell in my body rebels at the thought.

"No!" I fight, but there's no point. He's too strong. "Mira! What if you get hurt? Tairn's speed could be the only thing that saves you. At least let us stay."

She looks over her shoulder at the doorway, but there's steel in her expression. "You want me to trust you, Riorson? Get her the fuck out of here and find a way for her to keep her seat. We both know she's dead if she doesn't."

"Mira!" I scream, clawing at Xaden's arms, but he's already half carrying me down the stairs with an arm clamped around my waist as if I weigh less than the sword on his back. "I love you!" I call up the turret, but there's no way of knowing if she heard me.

"Can I trust you to get your own pack?" Xaden asks as he marches down the hallway of the barracks. "Or am I going to have to carry you out of here without whatever you brought?"

"I'll get it myself." I shove at him, and he lets me go.

It takes mere minutes to grab my pack and Rhiannon's, since we've left them intact, even cramming in our cloaks. Then I'm back in the hallway where Xaden waits, his own pack slung over his shoulder. It looks considerably smaller than the one he arrived with, and I don't want to even think about what he's left behind in order to force me out faster.

I don't bother looking at him, marching for the door, but he grabs my elbow and spins me around. "Nope. It's too dangerous to leave the fortress walls. We're going up." He wraps his arm around my waist and all but hauls me to the nearest turret. "Climb."

"This is bullshit!" I yell at him, uncaring that every other member of our squad who's climbing the same turret can hear. "Tairn could help them!"

"Your sister is right. You have to make it out, so we're leaving. Now fucking *climb*."

"Dain," I argue, realizing he's right in front of us.

He turns around and takes Rhiannon's pack, slinging it over his own shoulder. "For once, Riorson and I agree. It's not just you we have to get out, Violet. Think of every other first-year." The plea in his eyes shuts my mouth. "Are you going to sentence an entire *untrained* squad to death? Because I'll make it. Cianna, Emery, and Heaton will, too. And we all fucking know Riorson will. But what about Rhiannon? Ridoc? Sawyer? You want their deaths on your hands?" he asks, his words choppy as we race upward toward the open door.

This isn't about me.

We burst onto the roof as Emery mounts his dragon, who is precariously perched on the thinner-than-quadrant wall.

Oh gods, I'm never going to be able to mount Tairn at this angle.

"Ridoc and Quinn are already in the air," Liam tells us as Emery launches skyward, where Cath and Deigh hover, their wings beating the air.

"You're next!" Xaden shouts at Liam, and Dain nods.

Deigh crumbles the masonry with the force of his landing, and Liam takes off down the narrow walkway toward the large Red Daggertail.

"You next, Aetos," Xaden barks.

"Vi—" Dain starts to argue.

"That's an order." There's no room for argument in that tone, and we all know it, especially when Cath takes Deigh's place on the wall. "I've got her. Go."

"Go," I urge. I'd never be able to live with myself if something happened to Dain on my account. He may have been an ass the last few months, but that doesn't negate the years he's been my best friend.

Dain looks like he's about to fight but finally nods, turning to Xaden. "I'm trusting you to get her out."

"There's a lot of that going around today," Xaden retorts. "Now get on your dragon so I can get her on hers."

Dain gives me a long, intense look, then turns and runs, racing up Cath's foreleg in a way that's so reminiscent of the Gauntlet that I get flashbacks.

"Where are you?" I ask Tairn, seeing empty skies above us.

"Almost there. I was doing what could be done."

"I can't do this," I say to Xaden, turning in his arms to face him. "The others are gone. Call it the favor you owe me, I don't care. We can stay. I can't just leave her here. It's wrong, and it's something she'd never do to me. I have to stay for her. I just have to."

There's so much compassion, so much understanding in his eyes, that when he lets go of my waist, I think he might just let me stay. Then his hands are on my cheeks, sliding back to cup the base of my neck as he brings his mouth to mine.

The kiss is reckless and consuming, and I give it my all, knowing it might be the last one. His tongue licks into my mouth with an urgency I return, angling to take him deeper.

Gods, it's not just as good as I'd been fantasizing about, remembering that night. It's so much better. He was careful with me against that wall, but there is nothing hesitant about the way he lays claim to my mouth, nothing cautious about the ache that pulses low in my stomach. He only breaks the kiss when we're both panting, then rests his forehead against mine. "Leave for *me*, Violet."

"Almost there," Tairn says.

Xaden's been stalling to give Tairn and Sgaeyl time to arrive. My heart sinks like a rock, pinning my feet in place. "I will hate you for this."

"Yeah." He nods, a flash of pure regret crossing his face as he draws away. "I can live with that." His hands fall away from my face and reach for my arms, lifting them so I'm shaped like a T. "Arms up. Hold tight."

"Fuck. You."

The enormous shape of Tairn appears behind him, and Xaden drops to the stone floor just as Tairn flies directly above, his shadow falling over me a second before his foreclaw scoops me up like he's done countless times when I've fallen midflight.

"You have to take us back!"

"I have done everything I can and will not risk your life." He climbs in altitude, then throws me up onto his back in a practiced maneuver. *"Now, hold on so we can outfly them."*

I look over my shoulder and see Xaden on Sgaeyl, approaching quickly, and farther behind them, hundreds of feet below, a dozen gryphons envelop the keep.

Winning the War Games isn't about strength. It's about cunning. To know how to strike, you have to understand where your enemies—your friends—are most vulnerable. No one stays friends forever, Mira. Eventually those closest to us become our enemies in some way, even if it's through well-intentioned love or apathy, or if we live long enough to become their villains.

—Page eighty, the Book of Brennan

CHAPTER TWENTY-EIGHT

The stone wall outside Professor Markham's office in the Riders Quadrant digs into my back, irritating my relic as I brace all my weight next to the closed door. I'm ready to crawl out of my own skin with worry and the insufferable buildup of power that's threatening to combust at any moment.

It's been two days since we left Montserrat. One day of flight back to Basgiath and one excruciatingly long day of silence.

The sun is barely up. I haven't done library duty since returning, and I've somehow managed to get out the door before Liam even knows I'm gone. Breakfast doesn't matter. I couldn't give a shit if I miss formation. This is the only place I can contemplate being.

Footsteps on the circular staircase to the left make my stomach tense, and my pulse jumps as my gaze flies to the doorway, looking for the first sign of a cream tunic.

Instead, Xaden walks into the hallway, holding two steaming pewter mugs as he heads straight for me. "Still hate me?"

"Absolutely." That's not entirely true, but it's easy to blame all the guilt I've been eating for two straight days on him.

"Figured you'd already be waiting." He holds out one of the mugs as an offering. "It's coffee. Sgaeyl says you haven't slept."

"It's none of Sgaeyl's business if I'm sleeping," I snip. "But thanks." I take the cup. He looks like he's had a full eight hours and a vacation since yesterday. "I bet you're sleeping like a baby."

"Quit telling Sgaeyl about my sleep habits," I grumble at Tairn.

"I'm not dignifying that demand with a response."

"Andarna is my favorite."

Tairn snorts.

Xaden leans back against the wall across from me and sips his coffee. "I haven't slept well since the night my father left Aretia to declare the secession."

My lips part. "That was more than six years ago."

He stares at his coffee.

"You were—" I pause. "I don't even know how old you are now." Mira was right. I know almost nothing about him. And yet…I feel like I know *who* he is in the very marrow of his bones. Could my emotions be any more scattered when it comes to him?

"Twenty-three," he answers. "My birthday was in March."

And I didn't even know. "Mine is in—"

"July," he answers with a ghost of a smile. "I know. I made it my business to know everything there was to know about you the second I saw you on the parapet."

"Because that's not creepy." I let the coffee warm my freezing hands.

"Can't know how to ruin someone without understanding them first," he says quietly.

I lift my gaze to find that his is already on me. "And is that still your plan?" Mira's words have haunted me for two days.

He flinches. "No."

"What changed?" Frustration tightens my grip on the mug. "When exactly did you decide *not* to ruin me?"

"Maybe it was when I saw Oren holding a knife to your throat," he says. "Or maybe it was when I realized the bruises on your neck were fingerprints and wanted to kill them all over again just so I could do it slowly. Maybe it was the first time I recklessly kissed you or when I realized I'm fucked because I can't stop thinking about doing *more* than just kissing you." My breath catches at his admission, but he just sighs, lets his head fall back against the wall. *"Does it even matter when, as long as it changed between us?"*

"Don't do that," I whisper, and he lifts his head again to hold my gaze.

"Don't do what? Tell you I can't get you out of my head? Or speak directly into yours?"

"Either."

"You could learn to do it, too." Why the hell is it so impossible to look away from him? To remember that kiss on that tower had been a game to him, that this *all* might be a game to him? To quell this impossible ache that swirls in my stomach every time I think about him? *"Come on, give it a try."*

As I stare into his gold-flecked eyes, I decide he's right. I could at least meet him halfway and try. I put one mental foot in my Archives and feel power ripple through my veins. Bright orange, crackling energy streams in from the door behind me, and there's a golden light that shines from the window I created just for Andarna. I take a deep breath and turn slowly.

And there, swirling along the edge of the roofline, is a shadow of sparkling night. *Xaden.*

Footsteps sound on the stairs, and we both look.

"Guess you two had the same idea," Dain says when he sees us, coming to stand along the wall beside me. "How long have you been waiting?"

"Not long," Xaden answers.

"Hours," I say simultaneously.

"Damn, Violet." Dain runs a hand through his damp hair. "Are you hungry? Do you want to get breakfast?"

"No, dumbass, she doesn't, obviously." Xaden's snide commentary fills my head.

"Knock that the fuck off," I toss back. "No thank you."

"Look who figured it out." Xaden's mouth quirks upward for a heartbeat.

Another set of footsteps echoes up the staircase and I hold my breath, my eyes locked on the doorway.

Professor Markham pauses when he sees the three of us outside his office, then continues toward us. "To what do I owe the pleasure?"

"Just tell me if she's dead." I move into the center of the hall.

Markham looks at me with more than his fair share of disapproval. "You know I can't give out classified information. If there's anything to be discussed, we'll do it in Battle Brief."

"We were there. If it's classified, then we already know about it," I counter, my hands starting to tremble as I squeeze the pewter harder and harder.

Xaden takes the mug from me.

"It's hardly appropriate for me to—"

"She's my sister," I plead. "I deserve to know if she's alive, and I deserve *not* to hear about it in a room full of riders."

His jaw tightens. "There was considerable damage to the outpost, but we lost no riders at Montserrat."

Thank gods. My knees give out and Dain catches me, pulling me into his familiar hug as relief floods my system.

"She's fine, Vi," Dain whispers into my hair. "Mira's fine."

I nod, fighting against a swell of emotions to keep my control. I will not break down. I will not cry. I will not show weakness. Not here.

There's only one place I can go, one person who won't chide me for crumbling.

The second I have myself in hand, I step out of Dain's arms.

Xaden is gone.

I skip breakfast and miss formation to head to the flight field, holding myself together long enough to get to the middle of the meadow, where I drop to my knees.

"She's all right," I cry, my head falling into my hands. "I didn't leave her to die. She's alive." There's a ruffle of air and then the hard feel of scales against the backs of my hands. I lean forward into Andarna's shoulder, sagging against her. "She's alive. She's alive. She's alive."

I repeat it until I believe it.

"Do you have any siblings?" I ask Xaden the next time we're on the mat. Maybe it's Mira's comment about me not knowing enough about him, or maybe it's my own conflicting emotions, but he knows way more about me than I do him, and I need to level this playing field.

"No." He pauses in surprise. "Why?"

"Just asking." I take a fighting stance. "Let's go."

The next day, I ask him what his favorite food is in the middle of Battle Brief, using our mental connection. Pretty sure I hear him drop something at the back of the room before he answers.

"Chocolate cake. Stop being weird."

I grin.

A day later, after Tairn puts me through an absolutely draining set of advanced flight maneuvers most third-years couldn't stay seated through, either, we're perched on a mountain peak with Tairn and Sgaeyl when I ask him how he knows Liam, just to see if he'll tell me the truth.

"We were fostered together. What is with all the questions lately?"

"I barely know you."

"You know me well enough." He shoots me a look that says he's over it.

"Hardly. Tell me something real."

"Like what?" He turns in his seat to face me.

"Something like what those silver scars on your back are from." I hold my breath, waiting for the answer, waiting for him to say anything that might let me in.

Even from twenty feet away, I can see him tense. *"Why do you want to know?"*

My grip tightens on the pommel scales. I instinctively knew the scars were private, but his reaction says there's more to them than just a painful memory. *"Why don't you want to tell me?"*

Sgaeyl startles, then launches into the air, leaving Tairn and me behind.

"Are you pushing for a reason?" Tairn asks.

"Can you give me one not to?"

"He cares for you. That's already hard enough for him."

I scoff. *"He cares about keeping me alive. There's a difference."*

"Not for him there isn't."

The afternoon skies above Basgiath are crystal clear in the middle of May for the first battle of the War Games that signify the approach of graduation. As much as I want to feel excitement that I'm so close to actually surviving my first year in the Riders Quadrant, my stomach is tight with anxiety.

Battle Briefs are getting more redacted. Professor Carr is getting more anxious that I haven't manifested a signet like almost the entire first-year cadets. Dain is acting weird as fuck—friendly one minute and indifferent the next. Xaden is getting more secretive—if that were even possible—canceling some of our training for unexplained reasons. Even Tairn feels like there's something he's not telling me.

"What do you think our assignment is going to be?" Liam asks from my right as we stand in formation in the center of the courtyard with the rest of Fourth Wing. "Deigh thinks we're on offense. He won't stop going on about getting to kick Gleann's ass—" He pauses, as if listening to his dragon. "Guess dragons hold grudges," he finally whispers.

Leadership is gathered ahead of us, getting their assignments from Xaden.

"We're definitely on offense," Rhiannon answers from my left. "Otherwise, we'd already be in the field. I haven't seen a single rider from First Wing since lunch."

My stomach bottoms out. First Wing. Go figure they'd be our first opponent. *Anything* goes out there during War Games, and Jack Barlowe hasn't forgotten that I put him in the infirmary for four days. He gave me a wider berth for weeks after Xaden executed Oren and the other kids who had attacked me—and of course everyone stopped fucking with me after Amber Mavis. But still, I'd catch a look from him as we passed in the halls or in the cafeteria, pure hatred burning in the glacial blue depths of his eyes.

"I think she's right," I tell Liam, struggling not to fidget as the sun bakes through my flight leathers. It's been a while since I've envied the scribes and their cream uniforms, but this weather has me feeling like we got the shorter end of the uniform stick. It also doesn't help that I must have slept wrong, because my knee is *killing* me, and the stabilizing wrap feels like it's a million degrees. "Why do you think riders wear black anyway?"

"Because it's badass," Ridoc answers from behind me.

"So it's harder to see when we bleed," Imogen chimes in.

"Forget I asked," I mumble, watching for any signs that the leadership meeting will be over soon. Bleeding is the last thing I want to do today. *"Are we on offense or defense?"* I ask Xaden.

"Little busy right now."

"Oh no, am I distracting you?" A smile curves my mouth.

Shit, am I flirting? Maybe.

Do I care? Oddly enough…no.

"Yes." His tone is so gruff that I have to press my lips in a tight line to keep from laughing.

"Come on. You're taking forever over there. Give a girl a hint."

"Both," he growls, but he doesn't shut me out with his shields—which I know he can do—so I have a little mercy on him and the meeting he's supposed to be leading and leave him be.

Offense *and* defense? This afternoon should be interesting.

"You hear from Mira?" Rhiannon whispers, shooting me a quick glance.

I shake my head.

"That's just…inhumane."

"Did you honestly think they'd break the no-correspondence rule? Even if they tried, Mom would have shut that down with a quickness."

Rhiannon sighs, and I don't blame her. There's not much more to say on the subject.

The leadership meeting breaks up, and Dain heads over with Cianna. He's practically beaming, his hands clenching and unclenching with nervous energy.

"Which is it?" Heaton asks. "Offense or defense?"

"Both," he says as the other squad leaders report back to their riders.

I fake surprise and glance past him, but Xaden and the section leaders are nowhere to be seen.

"First Wing has taken a defensive position in one of the practice forts in the mountains, and they're guarding a crystal egg," Dain tells us, and the older riders in our squad murmur with excitement.

Makes sense. It's probably a symbolic nod to the different breeds of dragons bringing their eggs to Basgiath when Navarre unified.

"What are we missing?" Ridoc asks. "Because you guys seemed thrilled about an egg."

"From past years, we know that eggs are worth more points," Cianna says, grinning enthusiastically. "Flags have statistically been the lowest, and captured professors rank somewhere in the middle."

"But they like to switch it up," Dain adds. "The same way we could be going for a real objective on the line only to discover it's not as valuable as we thought."

"So how is this both offense and defense?" Rhiannon asks. "If they have the egg, then clearly we should go get the egg."

"Because we've also been given a flag to defend and no outpost to do it in." He grins. "And our squad has been assigned to carry it."

"You gave Dain the mission to defend Fourth Wing's flag?"

"I'm hoping he learned something from your sister's lesson at Montserrat," Xaden replies, but his voice is quieter, which I'm starting to learn means he's farther away. I can't help but wonder if we'll have the ability to communicate this way in a few months when more distance separates us.

My chest aches at the thought that he won't be here. He'll be risking his life on the front lines.

"And who is going to carry this flag?" Imogen asks.

Dain somehow manages to smile even wider. "That's going to be the fun part."

Over the next twenty minutes, we're drilled in strategy during the walk over to the flight field, and from the sound of it, Dain was paying attention to Mira.

The plan is simple: play to our individual strengths and pass the flag often, never giving First Wing a chance to spot who is carrying it.

When we get to the flight field, there are dozens upon dozens of dragons filling the muddy field, all positioned as though they had formation in their squads, too. It's easy to spot Tairn, seeing as his head rises above all others.

There's a palpable air of anticipation as we walk by the other squads, all mounting as the squad and section leaders give out last-minute orders.

"We're going to win," Rhiannon says with confidence, linking her arm with mine as we approach our section of the field.

"What makes you so sure?"

"We have you, Tairn, Riorson, and Sgaeyl. And obviously—me." She grins. "There's no way we're losing this."

"You are certainly—" My words die as Tairn comes into full view.

He stands tall and proud at the front of our section, not bothering to give deference to Cath as Dain's dragon, but it's not his position that steals my breath. It's the saddle strapped across his back that has me gawking.

"I hear it's all the fashion," Tairn brags.

"That's..." I don't even have words. The black metal bands look to be intricately linked as they loop around each foreleg and come together at the front of his chest, forming a triangular plate before rising above his shoulders to a saddle with strapped, secure stirrups. "That's a saddle."

"That's cool, that's what that is." Rhiannon thumps my back. "And it looks way more comfortable than Feirge's bony spine, I'll tell you that. See you up there." She walks past Tairn toward her own mount.

"I can't use that." I shake my head. *"It's not allowed."*

"I decide what's allowed and what's not," Tairn growls, lowering his head to my level and blasting me with a chuff of steam. *"There is no rule that says a dragon cannot modify their seat to serve their rider. You have worked just as hard—if not harder—than every rider in this quadrant. Just because your body is built differently than the others doesn't mean you don't deserve to keep your seat. It takes more than a few strips of leather and a pommel to define a rider."*

"He's right, you know," Xaden agrees as he approaches, and I briefly wonder where he'd gone that he's back so quickly.

"No one asked you." My pulse jolts and my skin flushes at the sight of him. Our uniforms make every rider look good, but Xaden takes even that up a notch with the way it cuts across the muscled lines of his body.

"If you don't use it, I'll take personal offense." He folds his arms across his chest and studies the rigging. "Considering I had it made for you and just about got myself burned alive in the process of trying to get it on him." He lifts a brow at Tairn. "Even though he helped design it, I might add."

"The first models were unacceptable, and you had the gall to pinch my chest scales when clumsily assembling it this morning." Tairn's golden eyes narrow on Xaden.

"How was I to know the leather from the prototype would burn so easily? And it's not like there are a lot of manuals on fitting a saddle to a *dragon*," Xaden drawls.

"It doesn't matter because I can't use it." I turn to face Xaden. "It's beautiful, a marvel of engineering..."

"And?" His jaw locks.

"And everyone here will know I can't keep my seat without it." Heat stings my cheeks.

"Hate to break it to you, Violence, but everyone already knows that." He gestures to the saddle. "That right there is the most practical way for you to ride. It has straps across your thighs to buckle yourself in once you're up, and theoretically, you should be able to change positions on long flights without unbuckling, since we built in a lap belt, too."

"Theoretically?"

"He wasn't amenable to me giving it a test flight."

"You can ride me when the flesh rots off my bones, wingleader."

Well, that's descriptive.

"Look, there's no rule against it. I checked. And if anything, you'll be doing Tairn a favor by freeing all his power and taking the weight of worry off his mind. Mine too, if that helps matters."

My fingernails bite into my palms as I search for another reason, another excuse, but there isn't one. I might not want to appear different than every other rider on this field, but I already am.

"Fuck, that stubborn, feisty look always makes me want to kiss you." Xaden's expression remains bland, bored even, but his eyes heat as his

gaze drops to my mouth.

"And you say this now, where people will see if you actually do." My breath catches.

"When did I ever give you the impression that I give a fuck what people think about me?" A corner of his mouth rises, and now it's all I can concentrate on, damn him. *"I only care what they think about you."*

Because he's a wingleader.

Nothing is worse than cadets gossiping that you've slept your way to safety. That's what Mira warned at Parapet.

"Mount up, Sorrengail. We have a battle to win."

I rip my gaze from his and study the exquisite, intricate structure of the saddle. "It's beautiful. Thank you, Xaden."

"You're welcome." He turns but leans into my space, and a shiver dances down my spine when his lips brush my ear. "Consider my favor fulfilled."

"Is that a saddle?"

I jump back from Xaden, but he doesn't budge an inch as Dain interrupts, holding a giant yellow flag on a four-foot pole, his eyes wide as he stares at Tairn.

"No, it's a collar," Tairn snips, snapping his teeth together.

Dain backs up a few steps.

"Yes," Xaden answers. "Have a problem with it?"

"No." Dain looks at Xaden like he's being unreasonable. "Why would I have an issue with it? I'm fine with whatever keeps Violet safe, if you haven't noticed."

"Good." Xaden nods once and turns toward me. *"Bet it would be even more awkward if I kissed you now, huh?"*

Yes, please.

"The next time we kiss had better not be just to piss off Dain." The next time had better only be because we want it.

"Next time, huh?" His gaze lowers to my mouth again.

And of course, now that's all I'm thinking about, the feel of his lips on mine, the way his hands always cradle the nape of my neck, the slide of his tongue. I stop myself from leaning in. Barely. "Go lead your wing—or do whatever it is you do."

"I'll be stealing an egg." His smile flashes before he turns back to Dain. "Keep our flag out of First Wing's hands."

Dain nods and Xaden leaves, heading across the field to where Sgaeyl waits.

"It's a great saddle," Dain says.

"It is," I agree, and Dain offers me a smile before walking toward Cath.

Moving toward Tairn's foreleg, I have to laugh as he dips his shoulder for me. "What? No ladder?"

"We thought about it and decided it would make you too vulnerable."

"Of course you thought about—" I pause before climbing when a flash of gold gallops toward me. "Andarna?"

"I want to battle, too." She skids to a halt directly in front of me.

My mouth opens and shuts. Andarna has been flying with us, and for short times, she can keep up with Tairn, but the way those scales shine in the sun is a beacon for…everyone.

But if I can have a saddle, then—

"Got it." My eyes sweep the flight field, which is at the height of its muddiest since the runoff season from the snowy peaks above. "Go roll." I point to the mud. "Unless that's going to mess with your wings? It's the scales on your belly I'm most worried about being easily spotted."

"No problem!" She races off, and I mount Tairn, finding the actual saddle covering the seat at the base of his neck and the pommel scales.

"I thought you said leather was bad?" The saddle itself is sumptuous black leather, complete with two raised pommels for my hands, and when I settle in, it fits like a dream. I bend and adjust the stirrups with the buckle system on the straps.

"The leather is a hazard on my chest if we take a fire attack, since your saddle would slide right off. But if you take a direct blast up there, sitting on a piece of metal isn't going to save you."

I don't bother pointing out that the only fire we'd be taking is from other dragons, which is a problem that doesn't exist, since gryphons are all beak and claw. Instead, I find the straps for my thighs and buckle in.

"This is ingenious," I say to Xaden.

"Let me know if it needs modifications after we win today."

Arrogant ass.

We're airborne moments later, Andarna keeping up and staying tucked close to Tairn just like we've practiced.

Our mission is to keep the flag out of enemy hands, so we skirt the perimeter of the hundred-mile battlefield that encompasses most of the central range while the other squads handle reconnaissance and retrieval.

About an hour into the afternoon, I'm wondering if this assignment is actually meant as punishment for Dain and not an honor. The twelve of us are split into two tight formations of six, seven when taking Andarna into account. Dain has the flag in his group just ahead of us, and when we reach yet another peak in the range, he splits to the right.

Tairn banks to the left, and my stomach pitches as we sweep down the side of the mountain. The wide straps dig into my thighs, holding me firmly in place, and my heart thunders as pure exhilaration hits as hard as the rush of wind against my face and goggles as we dive, and dive, and dive.

And for the first time, there's no fear that I'll tumble off his back. Slowly, I unclench my hands from the pommels and a heartbeat later, my hands are above my head as we plummet toward the valley below.

I've lived twenty years and never felt as alive as I do in this moment. Without even grounding in my Archives, power surges in my veins, crackling with a life all its own, jolting every single one of my senses to a degree that nears pain.

Tairn flares his wings, catching air and pulling out of the dive.

"You're going to have to work on those shoulder muscles, Silver One. We'll practice this week."

Leaning as far as I can out of the saddle, I see Andarna clutched in Tairn's claw as we level out in a glide along the valley floor.

"Thanks! I've got it now," Andarna says, and Tairn lets her free.

Power rattles my bones, as if it's looking for a way out, and I force myself upright. It's different than usual…like instead of standing ready to be molded by my hands, it wants to mold *me*.

A moment of fear skitters along my spine. What if the backlash of power from not manifesting a signet has chosen *today* to finally release? I shake my head. I do not have time to worry about what *might* happen—not in the middle of the War Games. My power is just feeling free because I'm finally not so focused on falling out of my seat. That's all it is.

Sitting tall in the saddle, I sweep my unsteady gaze along the landscape as Tairn begins to climb again, and my heart stutters. Up high on the western ridgeline is a gray tower that almost blends in to the cliffside. I would have missed it if not for the—

"Is that what I think it is?" Fear only feeds the uncontrollable energy prickling my skin.

Tairn's head is already turned in that direction. *"Dragons."*

I glance over my shoulder toward Liam and Rhiannon and see that Tairn must have relayed the message, because we break formation, scattering as three dragons launch from the cliff above us, diving in different directions.

We've given them multiple targets, but now we'll face them one-on-one.

A hail of ice pellets strikes my skin, bouncing off Tairn's scales, but he's forced to tuck his wings in tight to avoid damage.

My stomach launches into my throat as we free-fall, the valley floor rising up at us at an alarming rate. Heat and energy threaten to devour every inch of my body, and even my eyes feel like they're on fire. Oh fuck, my signet *is* going to backlash against me during the games.

"Ground now!" Tairn roars.

I slam my eyes shut, throwing both mental feet onto the marble floor of the Archives and throwing up the walls around me, only leaving entrances for Tairn's torrent of power, Andarna, and access to Xaden, and I immediately feel more in control.

When I open my eyes, we're ascending, Tairn's wings beating with so much force that I slide back in the saddle with every push.

He's left the ice-wielding First Wing cadet in a dive behind us, and I cringe as the dragon barely controls the descent, banking in the opposite direction we're headed.

"That's where they're guarding the egg." It has to be, considering another three dragons have taken the place of the others at the edge of the cliff, ready to launch.

"Agreed. Hold tight." Tairn barely has a second to shout before a dragon flies out of the valley to the right and blasts a stream of fire at us.

"Tairn!" I scream, watching in horror as the flames barrel toward us.

Tairn banks, taking the blast straight to his belly, shielding me from all but the sizzling heat that blazes by.

What the actual fuck?

"Andarna?" If something happens to her because First Wing is out for blood…

"Fireproof, remember?"

I let out a shaky breath. One worry down, but the other dragon is on our heels, opening its mouth and curling its tongue.

Tairn jerks and his tail swings, catching the offending dragon in the side, just below its wing. The other dragon roars, falling sideways, losing altitude at an alarming rate.

But I don't focus on the descent. Instead, I use the time to scan the mountainside for the outpost I spied earlier. My heartbeat quickens as I spot it peeking out from a ridge, only one remaining dragon guarding it.

"Xaden! The egg is here!" I relay.

"Already on my way. We're twenty miles out." The edge of panic lacing his tone puts a knot of fear in my throat, which only grows when I see Deigh and Liam locked in battle above us with a familiar Orange Scorpiontail—Baide.

Jack.

"We have to help Liam."

"On it." Tairn accelerates and Andarna falls away. Once I see her tuck into the mountainside where she'll be safe, I hunker down on Tairn's neck, giving him less wind resistance to fight as we climb faster than ever before. Wind yanks at the halo braid of my hair, the loosened strands whipping at my face as I keep my eyes locked on Deigh and Liam.

Baide snaps her tail at Deigh, the venomous bulb perilously close to Deigh's throat.

"His scales are thicker than you think. It's Liam who's in danger," Tairn warns, climbing higher.

We're almost there when Jack unsheathes his sword and jumps from Baide's back to Deigh's, catching Liam by surprise as the dragons grapple close to the tower we're approaching at breakneck speed.

There's barely time for Liam to gain his feet before Jack thrusts the sword through his side.

"Liam!" The scream tears from my throat as Jack kicks his boot into Liam's stomach, forcing Liam's body off the blade…and Deigh.

No. No. No.

Liam falls, his arms flailing as he plummets ahead of us.

"Catch him!" I demand, afraid we won't make it.

Deigh and Baide collide with the tower, and I glimpse Jack rolling to safety on the highest turret, his sadistic grin wide enough to see from here as Tairn changes course with a dramatic right roll.

Only the leather straps across my thighs keep me seated as we chase Liam's tumbling body, Tairn's wings tucked in tight, but the outcroppings are too close, and we're too high.

No. My throat closes. I refuse to lose him. Not when he's dedicated so many months of his life to keeping me alive. Failing isn't an option. It's just…not.

"Andarna?" I cry, already throwing open the window in my mind to where her glittering gift lies in wait.

"Do it," she answers. *"Focus on everything except you and Tairn!"*

She's right. There's no point in me catching up to Liam if Tairn is frozen.

"Do it!"

I reach for the golden power and my back arches as it barrels down my spine, flooding through my fingers and toes, enveloping every cell in my body before blasting outward in a shock wave that passes over Tairn.

Suddenly, we're the only ones moving, plunging through a windless sky toward Liam's frozen body, mere feet from the rugged outcropping of rocks below.

Heartbeats, that's all we have. My entire body trembles with the effort to hold it, the power flowing from Andarna ebbing as Tairn extends his wings and claw, snatching Liam's body from midair and taking out the rocks with the force of his tail as we barely escape death ourselves.

"Got him."

Time snaps back, wind blasting me in the face as we climb, turning tightly to avoid colliding with the ridgeline.

"Andarna?"

"Safe." Her voice is barely a whisper in my head.

Wrath and fury boil my blood as my eyes lock onto the figure on top of that tower. This is the last time this asshole will come after my friends or me.

Feirge appears from below, Rhiannon's arms outstretched as they rise beneath us. Tairn slows just enough to transfer Liam to her. He's alive—he has to be. It's the only outcome I'll accept.

In my peripherals, I see Cath and other dragons arrive from the north just as another squad launches from the cliff above.

Baide is airborne behind us, racing toward her asshole of a rider, who is still gloating on the top of that fucking tower.

"Climb!" I order, unsheathing a blade at my ribs and leaving one hand free to unsnap the buckles when it's time.

"You will not unseat yourself!" Tairn bellows at me as we surge forward, leaving the smaller orange dragon behind us. He swivels his head left, blasting a stream of fire toward the line of First Wing dragons to warn them off and succeeding as we barrel past.

A growing power sizzles in my chest as I lock my gaze on Jack. I can see the sick pleasure on his face as we fly closer, the blood that drips from his sword. Liam's blood.

An enormous dragon appears on the horizon. I don't need to look or even open my feelings to know it's Xaden, but I can't spare a moment for him. Tairn is climbing faster than we've ever climbed, and power is racing along my skin, scorching my blood.

If this is it, if my power is backlashing, then I'll be damned if I don't take that asshole with me. Tairn is fireproof—but not Jack.

"Faster!" I shout, my voice desperate with worry we won't make it in time.

Tairn charges the tower, his wings beating faster and faster, and I instinctually throw my hands forward, as though I can project all this power lashing within me toward the enemy who just tried to kill my friend, who has done his best to kill me at every opportunity.

That sizzle of magic grows to a lethal, swirling vortex of energy, and though my feet are still firmly grounded, the power rises to a breaking point and the roof of my Archives disintegrates. Power crackles above me, swirls around me, wraps along my feet below me.

I am the sky and the power of every storm that has ever been.

I am infinite.

A scream rips from my throat just as lightning splits the sky with a terrifying crack of thunder.

The bluish streak of silver death slams into the tower, and sparks flare as it explodes in a blast of stone. Tairn banks to avoid the blast, and I pivot in the saddle.

Jack falls down the mountainside in an avalanche of rock that I know he can't survive.

From the way Baide cries beneath us, she knows it, too.

My hand trembles as I sheathe the clean dagger at my ribs. The only blood to be found is on the rocks below, though I look at my hands as though they should be covered in death.

Tairn roars with the unmistakable sound of pride.

"Lightning wielder."

The death of a cadet is an inevitable yet acceptable tragedy. This process thins the herd, leaving only the strongest riders, and as long as the cause of death does not break the Codex, any rider involved in extinguishing another's life shall not be punished.

—Major Afendra's Guide to the Riders Quadrant (Unauthorized Edition)

CHAPTER TWENTY-NINE

We land in the flight field what feels like minutes later. Or maybe it's been a lifetime. I'm not sure.

The ground shakes as dragons arrive to the left and right, the field quickly filling with celebrating riders from Fourth Wing and angry ones from First. The dragons take off as soon as their riders dismount, with the exception of Andarna, who waits between Tairn's forelegs as I fumble with the buckles.

Jack is dead.

I killed him.

I'm the reason his parents will get a letter, the reason his name will be etched into stone.

Across the field, Garrick lifts the crystal egg above his head as Dain waves the flag, and those in Fourth Wing cheer, rushing toward the pair like they're gods.

Tairn's weight shifts beneath me as the last buckle slips through my fingers, and I slide out of the saddle. My head swims, stress no doubt bringing on the dizzy spell that makes it hard to keep my balance as I make my way to his shoulder and dismount.

I stumble in the mud, hitting my knees when I reach where Andarna lies between Tairn's forelegs, clearly exhausted.

"Tell me Liam is alive. Tell me it was worth it."

"Deigh says that he lives. The sword went through his side," Tairn says.

"Good. Good. That's good. Thank you, Andarna. I know how much that cost you." I look up into her golden eyes, and she blinks slowly back.

"Worth it."

Nausea holds me in its grip, and my mouth waters. *Killed him. I killed him.*

"Damn, Sorrengail!" Sawyer calls out. "Lightning? You've been holding out on us!"

Lightning I used to take a life.

My stomach heaves and a dark shadow envelops me, but it's not Xaden. Tairn has folded his wings over us, closing out the world while I retch up everything I've eaten today.

"You did what was necessary," Tairn says, but it doesn't stop my stomach from clenching and tightening again, trying its best to force up what's not even there.

"You saved your friend," Andarna adds.

Finally, my stomach settles, and I force myself to my feet, dragging the back of my hand over my mouth. "You need to get some rest, don't you?"

"I'm proud you're mine." Andarna's voice wavers, the blinks of her eyes becoming slower. *"Even if I need a bath."*

Tairn draws back his wings, and Andarna walks forward, then launches into the sky with steady wingbeats toward the Vale.

I stare up at the saddle. I need to get him out of this so he can rest, too. But all I can think is that I finally have a signet, a real, true signet, and the first thing I did with it was kill a man.

"Violet?" Dain appears on my left. "That was *you* with the lightning strike? The one that took down the tower?"

The one that killed Jack.

I nod, thinking of all the times I aimed for the shoulder instead of the heart. The poisons I used to incapacitate, not murder. I left Oren unconscious on the ground at Threshing and didn't even go for the throat when he invaded my room.

All because I didn't want to be a killer.

"I've never seen anything like it. I don't think there's been a lightning wielder in more than a century—" He pauses. "Violet?"

"I killed him," I whisper, studying the central chest plate of the saddle. That has to be where everything connects, right? He has to get out of this thing somehow.

Mom will be so proud to know I'm just like the others now. Just like her. My empty belly turns over again, and I retch like my body is trying to expel the guilt.

"Shit." He rubs his hand over my back. "It's all right, Vi."

It stops sooner this time, and Dain pulls me against his chest, rocking gently as his hand makes soothing motions up and down my spine.

"I killed him." Why the hell is that all I can say? I'm a broken music box, repeating the same melody over and over, and *everyone* can see me. Everyone knows I can't handle the consequences of my own signet.

"I know. I know." He presses a kiss to the top of my head. "And if you don't want to use that kind of power again, you don't have to—"

"Get the fuck away from her with that nonsense." Xaden pushes Dain's chest and tugs me out of his arms, then grips my shoulders, turning me to face him. "You killed Barlowe."

I nod.

"Lightning. Your signet is lightning, isn't it?" He looks at me with such intensity, as though my answer is the key to whatever he needs.

"Yes."

His jaw flexes and his head bobs once. "I thought so, but I wasn't sure until I saw you take that tower down."

He thought so? What the hell does that even mean?

"Listen to me, Sorrengail." He lifts one hand to stroke loose tendrils of hair behind my ear, his touch surprisingly gentle. "The world is a better place without Barlowe in it. We both know that. Do I wish I'd been the one to end his miserable life? Absolutely. But what you did will save countless others. He was nothing more than a bully and was only going to get worse as he grew more powerful. His dragon will choose another rider when she's ready. I'm glad he's dead. I am glad you killed him."

"I didn't mean to." It's barely a whisper. "I was just so fucking mad, and we'd just caught Liam. I thought my relic was backlashing finally." My eyes widen. "It was close, Xaden. It was *too* close. I had to do something."

"Whatever you did is what kept him alive." His thumb strokes over my cheek, the motion completely at odds with his tone, and his eyes flare just enough that I know he's aware of what I did.

"I don't want this," I blurt. "Rhiannon can move objects through space, and Dain has retrocognition—"

"Hey," Dain snaps.

"You think I didn't know that already?" Xaden barks over his shoulder.

"Kaori can bring his imagination to life, and Sawyer can bend metal. Mira can extend the wards. Everyone has a signet that isn't just useful for battle. They're tools for good in the world. And what the hell am I, Xaden? I'm a fucking *weapon*."

"You don't have to use your power, Vi," Dain starts, his voice soft and comforting.

"Stop. Fucking. Coddling. Her." Xaden bites out every word at Dain. "She is not a child. She's a full-grown woman. A rider. Start treating her like one and at least have the decency to give her the truth. You think Melgren or any other general—to include her own mother—is going to let her sit on a power like this? It's not like she can hide it, not the way she just *demolished* one of the practice forts."

"You just want her to be like you," Dain argues. "A cold-blooded killer. Soon you'll be telling her that it's all right, you get used to the killing."

I inhale a sharp breath.

Xaden nails him with a glare. "The blood in my veins is as warm as yours, Aetos, and if it's my job you want next year, then you'd better start understanding that you *never* get used to killing, but you do understand that it's necessary." He turns back to me, his dark gaze boring into mine. "This isn't primary school. This is war—and you heard me say it once before, but the ugly truth those not on the front lines choose to forget is there are *always* body bags in war."

I start to shake my head, but his eyes narrow on mine. "You might not like it, might even loathe it, but it's power like yours that saves lives."

"By killing people?" I cry. If Sgaeyl is right, and signets reflect who we are at our core, then I'm exactly as Xaden nicknamed me…Violence.

"By defeating invading armies before they get the chance to hurt civilians. You want to keep Rhiannon's nephew alive in that little border village? This is how. You want to keep Mira alive when she's behind enemy lines? This. Is. How. You are not just *a* weapon, Sorrengail. You are *the* weapon. You train this ability, own it, and you'll have the power to defend an entire *kingdom*." He smooths back more wind-loosened tendrils of my hair behind my ears, clearing my vision so I have no excuse but to see the honesty in his eyes. When he's sure I'm not going to argue further, he looks to his side. "Rhiannon, can you get her back to the citadel?"

"Absolutely." Rhiannon hustles over.

Dain scoffs and walks toward the other squad leaders, leaving us.

"The saddle—" I start.

"Tairn can get it off himself. It was one of his many design stipulations." Xaden turns to leave but pauses. "Thank you for saving Liam. He's important to me."

"You don't have to thank…" I sigh at his back. "And he's already gone."

"You two have the weirdest relationship," Rhiannon says, linking her arm with mine.

"We're not in a relationship." I look up at Tairn, who's surprisingly held his tongue through whatever that was with Xaden and Dain.

"Go," Tairn urges. *"But do not wallow in guilt, Silver One. Whatever you feel is natural. Allow yourself to feel it but then let it go. The wingleader made a valid point. With a signet like that, you are the best hope the kingdom has against the hordes of evil that seek to harm it. Rest and I will see you tomorrow. I'll get my own saddle off."*

"You're most definitely in a relationship," Rhiannon continues, tugging me off the field. "I just can't figure out if it's the opposites-attract partnership that has you two baring claws or the slow, lethal burn of scalding sexual tension." She glances sideways at me. "Now tell me how the hell you two moved that fast out there."

"What do you mean?"

"When Liam was falling, Feirge and I flew as fast as we could, but I knew we'd be too slow given our angle and speed, and I thought you…" She shakes her head. "It just looked like you were high above him one second and had him in the next. I've never seen a dragon fly that fast. It's like I blinked and missed it."

Now guilt bites into me for a whole other reason. Rhiannon is my friend, my closest one here, if I'm being honest about what Dain and I have become. Of everyone, she should know—

"Do not feel guilt that you cannot tell her. This secret belongs to dragonkind, not you," Tairn warns. *"No one has the right to risk our hatchlings. Not even you, Silver One."*

"Tairn is really fast," I say in way of explanation. It's not a lie, but it isn't the full truth, either.

"And thank gods for it. Zihnal must really love Liam, cheating death twice today."

But it wasn't Liam who cheated death.

It was me.

And I can't help but wonder if somewhere, on some plane of existence,

Malek sits on his throne, angry that I stole a soul from his grasp.

But then again, I gave him Jack's.

Of course, it might have broken mine forever.

The wooden target in my room wobbles as one of my daggers sinks into the wood beside the last one I threw. I might be angry with the world, but at least my aim isn't off. If I miss, there's a good chance the blade is flying out the window, considering where I have the target propped up on the wall.

I throw three more, rapid-fire, and hit the throat of the person-shaped target every single time.

What's the point of going for shoulders anymore if I'm already taking people out with bolts of lightning? What was my restraint for? With a flick of my wrist, I send the next dagger soaring, putting it straight through the figure's forehead just as there's a knock at my door.

It's either Rhiannon asking for the tenth time if I want to talk about what happened today or it's Liam—

I pause. It can't be Liam, checking to see if I'm actually turned in for the night, because Liam is still in the infirmary, healing from the sword he took to the side.

"Come in." Who cares if I'm in nothing but my dressing gown? It's not like I can't strike an intruder dead with a knife. Or lightning.

The door opens beside me, but I don't bother looking as I throw another dagger. That height? That hint of dark hair I catch in my peripheral vision? That incredible scent? I don't even need to look fully—my body tells me it's Xaden.

Then my body reminds me exactly what it feels like to have his mouth on mine, and my stomach flutters. Shit, I'm too on edge to deal with him or the way he makes me feel tonight.

"Imagining that's me?" he asks, shutting my door and leaning back against it, folding his arms across his chest. Then he does a double-take, his heated gaze roaming over my body.

Suddenly, the spring breeze coming through the open window isn't enough to cool my skin, not when he's looking at me like that.

My long braid swings across my back as I take another dagger off my dresser. "No. But it was you about twenty minutes ago."

"Who is it now?" He raises a brow, crosses one ankle over the other.

"No one you know." With a flick of my wrist, the next blade goes through the sternum. "Why are you here?" I glance his way just long enough to note that he's bathed and wearing our standard uniform instead of flight leathers, and definitely not long enough to note how fucking good he looks. Just once, I'd love to see him disheveled or unnerved, anything outside that calm control he wears like armor. "Let me guess. Since Liam is out of commission, it's your duty to lecture me about sleeping in plain cotton."

"I didn't come to lecture you," he says softly, and I can feel the warmth of his gaze like a caress as it rakes over the thin black straps of my dressing gown. "But I can definitely see that you're not wearing your armor."

"No one is going to be ridiculous enough to attack me now." I take another dagger from the dresser, my pile dwindling. "Not when I can kill them from fifty yards away." Tapping the end of the razor-sharp weapon, I pivot slightly, just enough to face him. "Do you think it works inside? I mean, how does someone wield lightning if there's no sky?" Keeping my eyes locked on his, I fling the dagger at the target. The satisfying sound of split wood tells me I hit true.

"Fuck, that's hotter than it should be." He pulls in a deep breath. "I think that's something you'll have to figure out." His gaze drops to my mouth and his arms tense.

"You're not going to step in and say you can train me? You can save me?" I click my tongue and have the absolutely ridiculous urge to run it up the lines of the relic on his neck, tracing the intricate pattern. "How very un-Xaden of you."

"I have no clue how to train a lightning wielder, and from what I witnessed today, you don't need saving." There's pure longing in his eyes as he scans the length of my body from my bare toes to the hemline that skirts my thighs, over my breasts to my neck, finally reaching my eyes.

"Only from myself," I mutter. The things I think about doing to him when he looks at me like that would surely ruin me, and tonight I'm not sure I care. That's a dangerous combination. "So then why are you here, Xaden?"

"Because I can't seem to stay away." He sounds anything but pleased by the admission, but my breath catches anyway.

"Shouldn't you be out there celebrating?" Everyone else is.

"We won a battle, not a war." He pushes off the door and takes a single step, closing the distance between us, and lifts my braid from over my shoulder, slowly rubbing his thumb along the strands. "And I figured you might still be upset."

"You told me to get over myself, remember? So why the fuck would you care if I'm upset?" I fold my arms across my chest, choosing anger over lust.

"I told you that you'd have to develop a stomach for killing. I never said you'd get over it." He drops my braid.

"I should, though, right?" I shake my head and retreat into the center of the room. "We spend three years here learning how to become killers, promoting and praising those who do it best."

He doesn't even flinch, just watches me in that observant, infuriatingly calm way of his.

"I'm not mad that Jack is dead. We both know he's wanted to kill me since Parapet, and eventually he would have. I'm mad that him dying changes *me*." I tap my chest right above my heart. "Dain told me that this place strips away the niceties to reveal who someone really is."

"Not going to argue there." He watches me as I begin to pace.

"And I just keep thinking that when I was younger, I asked my dad what would happen if I wanted to be a rider like Mom or Brennan, and he told me that I wasn't like them. That my path was different, except this place has peeled away my civility, my niceties, and it turns out my power is more destructive than *any* of theirs." I stop right in front of him and hold up my hands. "And it's not like I can blame this power on Tairn, not that I would. Signets are based on the rider, just fueled by the dragon, which means this has always been there under the surface, just waiting to be unleashed. And to think—" A knot forms in my throat. "All this time, I had this tiny, driving hope that I would be like Brennan, and *that* would be the twist in my little fable. That my signet would be mending, and I could put all the broken things back together. But instead, I'm made to split them apart. How many people will I kill with this?"

His eyes soften. "As many as you choose. Just because you gained power today doesn't mean you lost agency."

"What is wrong with me?" I shake my head, my hands clenching into fists. "Any other rider would be thrilled." Even now, I feel the power simmering just beneath my skin.

"You've never been like any other rider." He moves closer but doesn't touch me. "Probably because you never wanted to be here."

Gods, I want him to touch me, to wipe away the ugliness of the day, to make me feel something, anything but this welling shame.

"None of *you* wanted to be here." I glance pointedly at the rebellion relic on his neck. "You're all doing just fine."

He looks at me, really *looks*, and it feels like he sees entirely too much. "Most of us would burn this place to the ground if we had the option, but every marked one *wants* to be here because it's our only path for survival. It's not the same for you. You wanted a quiet life full of books and facts. You wanted to record the battles, not be in them. There is nothing *wrong* with you. You get to be angry that you killed a man today. You get to be angry that man tried to kill your friend. You get to feel however you want within these walls."

He's close enough now that I can feel his body heat through the thin cotton of my dressing gown.

"But not outside them." It's not a question.

"We're riders," he says, as if that's explanation enough. He takes hold of my hands and brings them to his chest. "So do whatever you need to get it out. You want to yell? Yell at me. You want to hit something? Hit me. I can take it."

Hitting him is the last thing I want to do, and suddenly, I'm done fighting it.

"Come on," he whispers. "Show me what you've got."

I surge up on my toes and kiss him.

Though not forbidden, cadets are strongly encouraged not to develop strong romantic attachments while studying in the quadrant for the efficiency of the unit.

—Article Five, Section Seven
The Dragon Rider's Codex

CHAPTER THIRTY

His body goes rigid for one beat, two, and then he spins us impossibly fast, putting my back against the door, jostling the frame. *Whoa.* He captures my wrists in one hand and holds them prisoner above my head. "Violet," Xaden groans against my mouth. The plea in his tone floods my veins with a whole different form of power. Knowing he's just as affected by our attraction as I am is a rush. "This isn't what you want."

"It's exactly what I want," I counter. I want to replace the anger with lust, the death of the day with the pulse-pounding assurance of my own life, and I know he's capable of delivering all that and more. "You said to do whatever I need." I arch my back, pressing the tips of my breasts against his chest.

His breathing changes, and there's a war in his eyes that I'm determined to win.

It's time to stop dancing around this unbearable tension and break it.

He leans down, his mouth only inches from mine. "And I'm telling you that I'm the last thing you need." The barely leashed growl of his voice rumbles up through his chest, and every nerve ending in my body flares to life.

"Are you suggesting someone else?" My heart races as I chance calling his bluff.

"Fuck no." The unmistakable flare of jealousy narrows his eyes for a heartbeat before his hips pin mine to the door, and my instant relief at his answer is replaced by a jolt of pure lust. I can see that infamous control of his hovering on the edge, balancing precariously on the point of a knife. All he needs is one. Little. Push. And I'm about to shamelessly shove.

"Good." I tilt my head up to his and draw his bottom lip between mine, sucking before gently nipping him with my teeth. "Because I only want you, Xaden."

The words breach something within him, and he gives.

Finally.

Our mouths collide, and the kiss is hot and hard and completely out of our control. Need streaks down my spine as he takes my ass in his hands and hauls me against his hips, my back raking the ridges of the door behind me as I use it as leverage to push closer to his strength.

I wrap my legs around his waist and lock my ankles. My dressing gown rises with the motion, but I don't care, not with the all-consuming way he's kissing me. The caress of his mouth and the strokes of his wicked tongue steal every logical thought, and my world narrows to this kiss, this minute, this man. *Mine.* In this moment, Xaden Riorson is *mine.*

Or maybe I'm his. Who fucking cares as long as he keeps kissing me?

Heat floods my body in an addictive rush, setting every inch of my skin aflame as his mouth slides down my neck in a sensual assault that makes me moan.

"Gods," he says against my throat, and then we're moving.

Wood scrapes the floor and crashes before my ass hits the desk, and my ankles fall from the small of his back when he leans over me, spearing his fingers through my hair at the nape of my neck as he takes my mouth again. I kiss him back with a hunger I've only known with him.

My hands fly back to brace my weight, knocking anything and everything out of my way, sending whatever careening to the floor. The clock stops ticking.

"You'll hate me in the morning. You. Don't. Really. Want. This." He punctuates each word with a kiss along my jaw, making his way to my ear. He bites the lobe, and my core liquefies, going molten.

"Stop telling me what I want." I breathe raggedly and thread my fingers through the short strands of his hair, tilt my head, giving him better access. He takes it, working his way down my neck to where it curves into my shoulder.

Fuck, that feels good. Every touch of his mouth to my heated skin is flame to kindling, and I suck in a sharp breath when he lingers on a sensitive spot, taking his time. But then he stills again, his breath hot and wet against the side of my neck.

My brow furrows with an unwelcome thought. "Unless *you* don't want *me*."

"Does this feel like I don't want you?" He takes my hand and slides it between our bodies, and my fingers curl around his length through his leathers. I whimper with pure want at the feel of how hard he is for me.

"I always fucking want you." He groans as I squeeze. Then he lifts his head, seizes my gaze with his, and I recognize the wild need in those gold-flecked depths. It mirrors my own. "You walk into a room, and I can't look away. I get anywhere near you, and this is what happens. Instantly hard. Fucking hell, I can barely *think* when you're around." He rocks his hips into my hand, and my grip tightens along with my stomach. "Wanting you is not the problem here."

"Then what is?"

"I'm trying to do the honorable thing and not take advantage of you after you've had a shit day." His jaw flexes.

I smile and kiss the side of his mouth. "It's always a shit day around here. And it's not taking advantage when I'm asking"—my teeth nip at his lips—"correction, *begging* you to make my day better."

"Violet." He says my name like a warning, as if he's something I should be wary of. *Violet.* He only says my name when it's just the two of us, when all the walls and the pretenses fall away, and gods if I don't want to hear it again and again, just like that.

"I don't want to think, Xaden. I just want to feel." I release him. One tug of the ribbon is all it takes to unravel the long, loose braid of my hair, and I run my fingers through the mass.

His eyes darken, and I know I've won.

"Fuck me, this hair," he says, then hovers his mouth over mine. "And this *mouth*. All I ever want to do is kiss you, even when you piss me off."

"So kiss me." I arch into him and claim his lips, kissing him like this might be the only time I'll get the chance. This kind of desperation isn't natural; it's a wildfire that's likely to burn us both to the ground if we let it.

The kiss is blatantly, deliciously carnal, and I melt against him, matching every thrust of his tongue with mine. He tastes like mint, and Xaden, and I can't get enough.

He's the worst kind of addiction, dangerous and impossible to sate.

"Tell me to stop," he whispers, his thumb skimming the hypersensitive skin of my inner thigh.

"Don't stop." I'll die if he does.

"Fuck, Violet," he groans, slipping his hand between my thighs.

Never mind. *That* is how I want him to say my name from now on. Just like that.

He glides the fabric of my underwear across my clit, and my back arches at the burst of pleasure that radiates through my body, so sweet I can taste it.

He captures my mouth with his again in a hungry assault, his tongue sliding against mine as his fingers stroke me through the fabric, expertly using it for friction. I try to rock my hips against his hand for more, but my feet dangle off the desk, robbing me of leverage. I can only have what he decides to give.

"Touch me," I demand, my fingernails biting into the back of his strong neck, desire pounding through me like a drumbeat.

His voice is ragged against my mouth. "If I get my hands on you, really, honestly get my hands on you, I don't know if I'll be able to stop."

He would. I know it in my soul. That's why I trust him with my body.

My heart? It isn't playing into this decision.

"Stop being so fucking *honorable* and fuck me, Xaden."

His eyes flare, and then he kisses me like I'm the air he's been missing, like his life depends on it, and I think mine just might. His fingers slide under my underwear and stroke my slickened core, and a moan tumbles from my lips. His touch is electric.

"So damned soft." He kisses me deeply as his fingers touch and tease, making that sweet coil of pleasure tighten in my core. I dig my nails into his shoulder, my back arching as he makes tighter and tighter circles against my swollen clit. "I bet you taste just as good as you feel."

Pleasure shudders through me, a living, breathing fire beneath my skin.

"More." It's all I'm capable of saying, demanding, as my skin flushes and my pulse skyrockets. I'm going to combust, to burst into flames, and all I can do is whimper against his mouth as he slides one finger inside me. My muscles clench around him, and he works in a second.

"You're so fucking hot." His voice drops, sounding like it's been scraped over coals. "It might damn us both, but I can't wait to feel you come around my cock."

"Oh *gods.*" That *mouth*. I throw my hands back against the wall for leverage, knocking something loose as my hips roll. Something shatters on the floor to the left as I ride his thrusting fingers. He curls them against my inner walls and I gasp, my thighs locking around his leather-clad hips. And when he uses his thumb to stroke my clit, the friction and pressure push me to the edge of mindless bliss.

I cry out, and he covers the sound with his mouth, kissing with devious strokes of his tongue that match the movement of his fingers within me. Power surges, rippling through my bones, and I grab onto Xaden even harder, surprised at the unexpected rush of crackling energy.

"Look at you. You're fucking beautiful, Violet. Let go for me." His words curl around my mind, his mouth fused to mine, and the intimacy of it pushes me to the limit of pleasure and then right over it.

He swallows my cry as my back bows, the first wave of my orgasm washing over me, releasing that tight coil of tension in a burst of sparks at the edge of my vision, breaking me into a million scattered stars. Lightning strikes outside my window, flashing light through the room again and again as he strokes me with an expertise that kicks the first climax into a second.

"Xaden," I moan as the pleasure ebbs and flares again.

He grins and slides his fingers from my body, and I'm nothing but ragged breaths and raw hunger as I reach for his shirt. I want it off *now*. He accommodates my urgency, ripping off the fabric, and then we're kissing again, all swirling tongues and roaming hands. The feel of his skin under my fingertips is divine, impossibly soft over yards of hard muscle. I trace the lines of his back, memorizing the dips and hollows as sinew ripples with every move he makes.

"I need you *now*," I gasp and reach for the buttons of his leathers.

"You know what you're saying?" he asks as I shove the fabric—and any cloth beneath—past his hips, freeing the thick length of his cock. It's hot and hard in my hand, and the moan that rips from his lips makes me feel invincible.

"I'm asking you to fuck me." I arch up and kiss him.

He groans, dragging my hips to the edge of the desk, then working my underwear down my legs, leaving me bare.

My pulse skyrockets. "I take the fertility suppressant." Of course, we both do. The last thing anyone wants are little quadrant babies running around. But it's better said than sorry.

"Same." He grips my hips, lifting me for a better angle, and the head of his cock rubs against my clit. I gasp and his eyes lock with mine. The hunger I see etched in every tense line of his body is my undoing. I don't care if it damns us. I need him.

No more holding back. Not anymore.

I reach between us, guiding the head of his cock to my entrance, but this position is shit. He's considerably taller than the desk, and if I wasn't so desperate for him, I'd laugh, but I am. I arch, but it doesn't help. Every second we wait feels like it stretches on for a decade.

"Fucking desk," he swears.

My thoughts exactly.

His biceps flex as he lifts me by the backs of my thighs, and I wrap my arms around his neck and my legs around his waist, my dressing gown caught between us as he pivots. Our mouths meet in a ravenous kiss as my back hits the armoire, but I barely blink, too consumed with the stroke of his tongue, the feel of him between my thighs.

"Shit. Are you all right?" he asks.

"I'm fine. You won't break me."

He pushes inside that first, tight inch of me, and I gasp at the fit, the stretch.

"More." I'm too busy kissing him to speak. *"I need all of you."*

"You're going to be the death of me, Violet." Whatever's left of his control slips, and he takes me completely with one hard thrust.

I moan into the kiss. *Deep*. He's so fucking deep that I feel him *everywhere*.

"Tell me you're all right." He's already moving, thank gods.

"I'm perfect." Better than perfect. Power blazes beneath my skin again, buzzing in wordless, frenzied demand.

"You feel so fucking good." He slams back into me, again and again, as he sets a brutal, steady pace, his mouth sliding down my neck as his hand rises to cup my breast.

I can't even think around the maddening pleasure as my back pounds the armoire door with every thrust, filling the room with the sound of our straining bodies and creaking wood. Every stroke is better than the last. My breaths stutter.

"Fuck, I'm never going to get enough of you, am I?" he says, his face buried in my neck as I arch into him.

"Shut up and fuck me, Riorson." Tomorrow is soon enough for regrets.

Reaching up, I grasp the top edge of the armoire with one hand so I can rock back with more force, meeting the drive of his hips, taking him deeper, harder. He drags one of my nightgown's straps off my shoulder, and the cool night air kisses the hardened peak of my nipple a heartbeat before his hot mouth covers it. The sensations spiral, spinning and coiling, forming a tight knot of pleasure so deep within me, the tension is sublimely unbearable.

The armoire door groans, then splinters off the hinges, and Xaden's shadows whip out, protecting me as the frame snaps and wood crashes around us. My power flares, rising in answer to his, sizzling beneath my skin as I grab ahold of his shoulders, my mouth finding his.

There's no stopping. We *can't* stop.

"Fuck," he curses as he takes me over and over, never stopping, turning us again so there's cloth against my back. But it's not the bed. It's the curtains shoved to the side of the window.

Energy crackles again as our mouths meet, and still he drives on, winding that knot inside me painfully tighter with every movement.

And the power…it's too much. It's burning me, heating my blood with the need for release. "Xaden," I cry out, simultaneously writhing yet holding on to him like he's the only thing anchoring me to the earth.

"I've got you, Violet," he promises, his breath ragged pants against my lips. "Let it out."

Lightning whips through me, flashing so bright that my eyes slam shut. Heat flares above me as thunder cracks immediately.

And I smell smoke.

"Shit." Xaden's power fills the room, eclipsing what light we had, and the curtain falls, but we're moving before the charred fabric can so much as touch my skin.

That knot of pleasure builds to a breaking point as he takes me to the floor, and *finally*, I have all of his weight as he drives into me. Shadows fall away and the sight of him above me, his dark gaze locked on mine in intense concentration, is the most beautiful sight I've ever seen.

"So. Very. Beautiful." I punctate each word with a kiss.

He draws back, his eyes searching mine for a heartbeat or two before he devastates me with another kiss that has me straining for more, rocking my hips against his.

This man kisses with his whole body, rolling his hips in time with the thrust of his tongue, bracing just enough of his weight so I can breathe while stroking his chest over my hypersensitive nipples. He keeps me on the same edge he's riding, and I don't know how much longer I can take it before I set this entire room on fire.

"I need...I need..." My frantic eyes search his. Where are my words?

"I know." He claims my mouth again and reaches between us, using those talented fingers to stroke me into another orgasm, and light flashes again, followed by thunder and darkness as I come apart under him.

Pleasure takes me in waves, rolling through me again and again until all I can do is clutch Xaden's shoulders and ride it out in blissful surrender.

"Beautiful," he whispers.

The second I come down, his rhythm breaks, and he presses my knee up toward my chest and takes me even deeper. I rock my hips up to meet his, sweat beading on our skin as I watch him unravel with rapt fascination. I love his loss of control just as much as I fear my own, and when I swirl my hips, he groans, arching his neck as he thrusts once. Twice.

On the third, he shouts, then shudders within me, and his power lashes out in streaks of shadows, the force splitting the wooden target on the other side of the window.

Pieces fly and Xaden throws out another wave of darkness that lasts just long enough to shield us from the debris. Then the shadows retreat and daggers clatter to the ground behind me.

He looks as shocked, and as enthralled, as I feel as we lay there, staring at each other, our chests heaving in the aftermath of what can only be described as complete and utter madness.

"I've never lost control like that," he says, bracing his weight on one arm and brushing my hair back from my face with the other. The move is so gentle, so at odds with what we've just experienced, that I can't help but blink, then smile.

"Me neither." The smile morphs into a full-out grin. "Not that I've ever had power to lose control of before."

He laughs and rolls us to his side, keeping me close and cushioning my head with his biceps.

I sniff at the smoke in the air. "Did I..."

"Set the curtains on fire?" He lifts a brow. "Yes."

"Oh." I can't find it in me to be embarrassed, so I brush the backs of my fingers across the stubble along his jaw. "And you put it out."

"Yes. Right before I destroyed your throwing target." He grimaces. "I'll get you a new one."

I glance over at the armoire. "And we..."

"Yep." He lifts his brows. "And I'm pretty sure you need a new chair, too."

"That was..." I didn't even get the man's pants entirely off, and my dressing gown is haphazardly hanging from one shoulder.

"Frighteningly perfect." He cups the side of my face. "We should get you cleaned up and to sleep. We can worry about...your room tomorrow. Ironically, your bed is the only thing we didn't wreck."

I sit up to confirm that the bed made it, and Xaden does the same next to me, leaning forward. Immediately, I lose interest in everything but the muscled lines of his back and the navy-blue relic Sgaeyl transferred to him.

I reach out and trace the dragon relic on his back, my fingers lingering on the raised silver scars, and he stiffens. They're all short, thin lines, too precise to be a whip, no rhyme or reason to their pattern but never intersecting. "What happened?" I whisper, holding my breath.

"You really don't want to know." He's tense but doesn't move away from my touch.

"I do." They don't look accidental. Someone hurt him deliberately, maliciously, and it makes me want to hunt the person down and do the same to them.

His jaw flexes as he looks over his shoulder, and his eyes meet mine. I bite my lip, knowing this moment can go either way. He can shut me out like always or he can actually let me in.

"There's a lot of them," I murmur, dragging my fingers down his spine.

"A hundred and seven." He looks away.

That number makes my stomach lurch, and then my hand pauses. *A hundred and seven.* That's the number Liam mentioned. "That's how many kids under the age of majority carry the rebellion relic."

"Yeah."

I shift so I can see his face. "What happened, Xaden?"

He brushes my hair back, and the look that passes over his face is so close to tender that it makes my heart stutter. "I saw the opportunity to make a deal," he says softly. "And I took it."

"What kind of deal leaves you with scars like that?"

Conflict rages in his eyes, but then he sighs. "The kind where I take personal responsibility for the loyalty of the hundred and seven kids the rebellion's leaders left behind, and in return, we're allowed to fight for our lives in the Riders Quadrant instead of being put to death like our parents." He averts his gaze. "I chose the chance of death over the certainty."

The cruelty of the offer and the sacrifice he made to save the others hits like a physical blow. I cradle his cheek and guide his face back to mine. "So if any of them betray Navarre…" I lift my brows.

"Then my life is forfeit. The scars are a reminder."

It's why Liam says he owes him everything. "I'm so sorry that happened to you." Especially when he wasn't the one who led the rebellion.

He looks at me like he sees into the very depths of who I am. "You have nothing to apologize for."

I grab his hand as he moves to stand. "Stay."

"I shouldn't." Two lines appear between his brows as he searches my eyes. "People will talk."

"When did I ever give you the impression that I give a fuck what people think?" I use his earlier words against him and sit up, curling my hand around the section of his neck that bears his relic. "Stay with me, Xaden. Don't make me beg."

"We both know this is a bad idea."

"Then it's *our* bad idea."

His shoulders dip, and I know I've won. He's mine for the night. We take turns sneaking out long enough to clean up, and then he slides into bed behind me. "Only within these walls," he says quietly, and I understand what he means.

"Only within these walls," I agree. It's not like we're in a relationship or anything. That would be…disastrous given the chain of command. "We're riders, after all."

"I just don't trust my temper if anyone says—"

I brush a kiss over his mouth, silencing him. "I know what you're saying. It's…sweet."

He nips at my skin. "I'm not sweet. Please don't mistake any part of me for soft or kind. That will only get you hurt, and whatever you do…" He buries his face in my neck, inhaling deeply. "Don't fall for me."

I stroke my hand over his marked arm and pray that's not exactly what I'm doing. This overwhelming juxtaposition of longing and satisfaction in my chest has to be the aftereffects of coming not once but three times, right? It can't be more.

"Violence?"

I look out my window at the infinite black sky and change the topic, my eyelids growing heavier by the second. "Why did you guess I could wield lightning?"

He stretches just enough to tuck my head under his chin. "I thought you did it the first night Tairn channeled power to you, but I wasn't sure, so I didn't say anything."

"Really?" I blink, thinking back, but my brain is full of a pleasant, dull hum as sleep fights to pull me under. "When?" My eyes drift shut.

His arms tighten around me as he tucks me closer, the backs of my thighs pressed tight against his pants as I start to drift off.

"The first time you kissed me."

When I wake, Xaden is gone, but that's not exactly a surprise. Him staying the night to begin with? Now that was the shocker.

Finding a jar on my nightstand with a handful of spring violets? My heart swells. I'm in so much fucking trouble.

He even moved all the debris to a pile in the corner, which means he must have used his shadows while I was sleeping because I didn't hear a thing.

I'm still exhausted, but I dress and pin my hair up quickly, noting the sun has already risen. With Liam in the infirmary, I'll be solo for my Archives trip today, but I might be able to sneak in to see him on the way back.

I'm lacing my boots when there's a knock at my door.

"You have to be kidding," I say loudly enough for the knocker to hear. "Just because Liam is healing doesn't mean I need another"—I wrench the door open and stumble over the last word—"bodyguard."

Professor Carr stands in my hallway, his hair standing on end as he looks at me with scientific appraisal, then lifts his eyebrows as he stares past me into the wreckage of my room. "We have work to do."

"I have Archives duty," I argue.

He snorts. "You're off Archives duty until we can be sure you're not going to burn the place down. Lightning and paper don't mix well. Trust me, Sorrengail, the scribes aren't going to want you anywhere near their precious books, and from the looks of it, you can't even control your powers in your sleep."

I try to ignore the sting of his words, since he's far off, but end up following him down the hall when he leaves. "Where are we going?"

"Somewhere you won't start a forest fire," he says without looking back.

Twenty minutes later, we're in the flight field, and to my surprise, Tairn is saddled.

"How the hell did you do that?"

He chuffs in indignation. *"As if I'd let them design something I couldn't figure out how to get on myself. Remember where you get your power from, Silver One."*

"How's Andarna?" I ask as Professor Carr thrusts a satchel into my hands. "What is this for?"

"Sleeping, but she's fine," Tairn promises.

"Breakfast," Carr answers. "With all the wielding you're about to do, you're going to need it." He climbs onto his Orange Daggertail and, after I mount Tairn and strap in, we're airborne.

The bite of spring wind stings my cheeks as we fly deep into the mountain range, and I'm thankful I dressed in flight leathers this morning, thinking I'd have a session before lunch.

We land almost a half hour later, high above the tree line.

I shiver and rub my arms to fight off the low temperatures that come with high altitude.

"Don't worry. You won't be cold for long," Carr assures, dismounting and pulling a small tome from his pocket. "According to what I read last night, this particular ability has the power to overheat your system, hence—" He gestures around us.

"Plus, there's not much to burn up here, is there?" And no witnesses if he decides to break my neck, either. I glance at him quickly before looking away, undoing the buckles of my saddle, then sliding down Tairn's foreleg. *"Don't leave me."*

"Never. I'll burn him alive before he takes a single step toward you."

"Exactly." He studies me carefully, and I avoid meeting his eyes as I check the wrap on my knee to make sure it hasn't slipped under my leathers. "It's always intriguing to me how nature finds the balance."

"I'm not sure I know what you mean, Professor."

"This kind of power found in one so…" He sighs. "Would you not call yourself fragile?"

"I am who I am." I bristle. I've never given this particular professor any reason to think of me as different.

"It's not an insult, cadet." He shrugs, looking at the saddle. "It's a balance. In the course of my duties, I've found a correlation of sorts that keeps a system of checks on power. Yours seems to be your body."

A growl rumbles in Tairn's chest as he edges Carr's smaller dragon out of his space.

"Your dragon doesn't trust me," Carr states, like it's an academic problem to be solved. "And considering he's the most powerful of them in the quadrant at the moment—"

"But not the Continent," Tairn admits.

"—that means you don't trust me, either, Cadet Sorrengail." He holds my gaze, and the mountaintop wind makes his white hair dance like feathers. "Why is that?"

"No point lying."

"Other than you calling me frail?" I stay at the base of Tairn's foreleg, ready to mount if necessary. "I was there the day you killed Jeremiah. His signet manifested, and you snapped his neck like a twig in front of all of us."

Carr tilts his head in thought. "Yes, well, he was in a considerable amount of panic, and it's widely known that inntinnsics aren't allowed to live. I ended his suffering before he could see the end coming."

"I'll never understand why mind-reading is a death sentence." I place my hand on Tairn's leg like I can absorb his strength, even though I already feel it flowing through me.

"Because knowledge is power. As a general's daughter, you should know that. We can't have someone walking around with unfettered access to classified material. They're a security risk to the entire kingdom."

And yet Dain is living.

"Because Aetos will be useful to them as long as they can keep him under their control." Tairn blasts a puff of steam over my head, and the Orange Daggertail backs up even more. *"His power is also limited to touch, so more controllable."*

"Now, you don't have to trust me, and you can even wield from your seat on your dragon if you like, but I hope you believe me when I tell you that I have no plans on killing you, Cadet Sorrengail. Losing an asset like you would be a tragedy for the war effort."

An asset.

"And the fact that you bonded Tairn makes you and Riorson the most coveted pair of riders this kingdom has seen in far too long. If I could offer a piece of advice?" His eyes narrow.

"Please do." At least he's brutally honest, so I know where I stand with him.

"Keep your loyalties clear. You and Riorson both have exceptional, lethal power that any rider would be envious of. But together?" His bushy brows furrow. "You would be a formidable enemy who command could simply not afford to let exist. Do you understand what I'm saying?" His voice softens.

"Navarre is my home, Professor. I will give my life to defend it just like every Sorrengail who has ridden before me."

"Excellent." He nods. "Now let's get to work. The sooner you can contain the lightning, the sooner we can both stop freezing our asses off."

"Good point." I look out over the range. "You just want me to…" I gesture to the mountains around us.

"Preferably anywhere but right here, yes."

I stare out at the mountains in the distance. "I'm not really sure what I did to call it before. It was an…emotional reaction." And what happened last night definitely isn't up for discussion.

"Interesting." He jots something down in his notebook with a piece of charcoal. "You've wielded lightning besides yesterday's display during the War Games?"

I debate keeping my answer to myself, but my silence isn't going to help. "A few times."

"And both times were the result of emotional reactions?"

Tairn snorts, and I smack his foreleg with the back of my hand. "Yes."

"Well, then start there. Ground in your power and try to feel whatever it was you were feeling." He goes back to his notebook.

"Should I get the wingleader?" Tairn flat-out laughs in my head.

"Shut up." I ground both feet in my Archives and power flows around me, through me. Andarna's golden light is there, too, but it's softened from having been drained yesterday, and high above me swirl the inky-black shadows I know represent the connection to Xaden.

"Problems?" Xaden asks, as if he feels my inquiry. *"And what are you doing so far away?"*

"Training with Carr." My cheeks heat at the sound of his low voice. *"And how do you know how far away I am anyway?"*

"Get stronger in wielding, and you'll be able to do it, too. There's nowhere

in existence you could go that I wouldn't find you, Violence." The promise should be a threat, but it's not. It's too damned comforting for that.

"Right now, I'd settle for wielding some lightning. Carr is staring at me, and it's about to get really fucking awkward if I can't figure out how—"

Images of…*me* flood my mind. It's last night, except I'm somehow seeing it through Xaden's eyes, feeling the unmistakable burn of insatiable desire. My control slips—no, it's Xaden's control slipping as I moan beneath him, my hips riding his hand, my nails biting into his skin with a pain that borders on pleasure as I writhe. Gods, I need—*no*—he needs me. His hunger walks the line of starvation to know my touch, my taste, the feel of—

Power floods my entire system, crackling along my skin, and light flashes behind my closed eyes.

The images stop, and my feelings are once again my own.

And fuck if I'm not so turned on that I have to shift my weight to ease the ache between my thighs.

"Good job!" Professor Carr nods, jotting something down.

"I can't believe you just did that."

"You're welcome."

My cheeks are flaming hot as I lift the backs of my hands to my skin.

"See, I told you." Carr lifts the notebook. "The last lightning wielder said it made them overheat. Now do it again."

Tairn chortles.

"Not a single fucking word out of you," I warn.

This time, I focus on the feeling of the power rush and not what got it there, opening every sense and letting white-hot energy course through me, gathering to a breaking point. Then I release it, and lightning strikes more than a mile away. Well, look at that. I am a certified badass.

"Maybe you could work at aiming it this time?" Professor Carr peers over his notebook. "Just remember not to exhaust the physical strength with which you control the power. No one wants to see you burn out. A power like Tairn's will eat you alive if you can't contain it."

Lightning strikes five more times before I'm exhausted, and none of it hits where I was aiming.

This is going to be harder than I thought.

July first, the anniversary of the Battle of Aretia, is hereby proclaimed Reunification Day and will be celebrated throughout Navarre on this date every year to honor the lives lost during the war to save our kingdom from separatists and those saved by the Treaty of Aretia.

—Royal Proclamation of King Tauri the Wise

CHAPTER THIRTY-ONE

There's a knock at my door as I take an armful of clothes from the skeletal remains of what used to be my armoire.

"Come in," I call out, dumping them on the bed.

The door opens and Xaden walks in, his hair windblown like he's just come from the flight field, and my pulse jumps.

"I just wanted—" he starts, then pauses, surveying the wreckage of my room from last night. "Somehow I'd convinced myself today that we hadn't done that much damage, but..."

"Yeah, it's..."

He looks at me, and we both crack a smile.

"Look, this doesn't have to be awkward or anything." I shrug, trying to ease the tension. "We're both adults."

His scarred brow rises. "Good, because I wasn't going to make it that way. But the least I can do is help you clean up." His attention shifts to the armoire, and he winces. "I swear it didn't look quite that ruined in the darkness when I left this morning. Turns out you set more than a few trees on fire last night, too. Took two water wielders to get them out."

My cheeks heat. "You took off early." I try to make my tone as nonchalant as possible as I walk toward my desk—which miraculously survived—and bend down to gather a few of my books we'd knocked to the floor.

"I had a leadership meeting and needed to get an early start." His arm brushes against mine as he leans down and picks up my favorite book of fables, the one Mira slipped into my rucksack once we'd gotten back to Montserrat that night.

"Oh." My chest lightens. "That makes perfect sense." I stand, putting my texts on the desk. "So it wasn't because I snore or anything."

"No." A corner of his mouth rises. "How did training with Carr go?"

Nice subject change.

"I can wield, but I can't aim, and it's completely exhausting." My mouth purses, thinking back to the first strike I wielded. "You know, you were kind of an asshole on the flight field yesterday."

His grip tightens on the book. "Yes. I told you what I thought you needed to hear to get through the moment. I know you don't like other people to see you vulnerable, and you..."

"Were vulnerable," I finish.

He nods. "If it makes you feel better, I couldn't keep anything down after the first time I killed anyone, either. I don't think less of you for having a reaction like that. Just means you still have your humanity."

"So do you," I say, gently taking the book from him.

"That's debatable."

Says the man who has one hundred and seven scars on his back. "It's not. Not to me."

He looks away, and I know he's going to have his defenses up any second now.

"Tell me something real," I say, desperate to keep him with me.

"Like what?" he asks, just like he did before when we were flying, when he left me sitting on that mountain when I had the nerve to ask about his scars.

"Like..." My mind races, looking for something to ask. "Like where you went the night I found you in the courtyard."

His brow furrows. "You're going to have to be more specific than that. Third-years get sent away all the time."

"You had Bodhi with you. It was right before the Gauntlet." I nervously run my tongue over my lower lip.

"Oh." He picks up another book and sets it on the desk, clearly stalling while he decides whether or not he'll open up to me.

“I would never tell anyone anything you tell me,” I promise. “I hope you know that.”

“I know. You never told a soul about what you saw under the tree last fall.” He rubs the back of his neck. “Athebyne. You can’t know why or ask anything else, but that’s where we were.”

“Oh.” That definitely wasn’t what I expected, but not out of the ordinary for cadets to run something to an outpost. “Thank you for telling me.” I move to put the book back and see that the binding is definitely worse for wear after we knocked the antique tome off the desk last night. “Damn.” I open the back cover and see that it’s split at the binding.

Something is peeking out.

“What is that?” Xaden asks, looking over my shoulder.

“Not sure.” Balancing the heavy book with one hand, I tug what looks to be a stiff piece of parchment free from where it’s been tucked behind the binding. Gravity shifts as I recognize my father’s handwriting, and it’s dated just a few months before his death.

My Violet,

By the time you find this, you’ll most likely be in the Scribe Quadrant. Remember that folklore is passed from one generation to the next to teach us about our past. If we lose it, we lose the links to our past. It only takes one desperate generation to change history—even erase it.

I know you’ll make the right choice when the time comes. You have always been the best of both your mother and me.

Love,

Dad

My brow furrows, and I pass the letter to Xaden, flipping through the book. The tales are all familiar, and I can still hear my father’s voice reading every word, as if I were still a child curled on his lap after a long day.

“That’s cryptic,” Xaden remarks.

“He got a little…cryptic in the years after Brennan died,” I admit softly. “Losing my brother made my father even more reclusive. I only really got to spend time with him because I was always in the Archives, studying to be a scribe.”

The pages flutter as I flip through stories of an ancient kingdom that spanned from ocean to ocean and a Great War among three brothers who fought to control the magic in this mystical land. Some of the fables tell stories of the first riders who learned to bond with dragons and how those bonds could turn on the rider if they tried to consume too much power. Others talk of a great evil that spread across the land as man became corrupted by dark magic and turned into creatures known as venin who created flocks of winged creatures called wyvern and scourged the land of all magic in the thirst for more power. Another talks about the dangers of wielding power from the ground instead of the skies, as one could easily start drawing magic from the earth and eventually be driven mad.

One of the purposes of the fables is to teach children about the dangers of too much power. No one wants to become a venin; they're the monsters that hide beneath our beds when we have nightmares. And we certainly never want to try to control magic without a dragon to ground us. But that's all they are, children's bedtime stories. So why did my dad leave me this cryptic note—and hide it inside the book?

"What do you think he was trying to tell you?" Xaden asks.

"I don't know. Every fable in this book is about how too much power corrupts, so maybe he felt someone in leadership was corrupt." I glance up at Xaden and joke, "I certainly wouldn't be surprised if General Melgren ripped a mask off one day and revealed he was a terrifying venin. That man has always given me the creeps."

Xaden chuckles. "Well, let's hope not that. My dad used to say venin were biding their time in the Barrens and one day were coming to get us—if we didn't eat our vegetables." He glances out the window to his left, and I know he's remembering his father. "He said one day there would be no magic left in the kingdom if we weren't careful."

"I'm sorry—" I start, but when he tenses, I decide a subject change is what he really needs. "So, which mess should we tackle first?"

"I have a better idea of how to spend our night," he says as he puts another pile of clothes on my bed.

"Oh?" I glance over and catch his eyes darkening as he stares at my mouth. My pulse immediately quickens, the thought of touching him sending a burst of energy through me.

Don't fall for me...

His words from last night cut a sharp contrast to the way he's looking at me now.

I take a step backward. "You said not to fall for you. Did you change your mind?"

"Absolutely not." His jaw tenses.

"Right." I don't expect that to hurt as much as it does, which is part of the problem. I'm already too emotionally involved to separate out the sex, no matter how phenomenal it is. "Here's the thing. I don't think I can separate sex from emotion when it comes to you." Well, shit, now I've said it. "We're already too close for that, and if we hook up again, I'm going to eventually fall for you." My heart pounds at the rushed confession, waiting for his response.

"You won't." Something akin to panic flares in his eyes, and he crosses his arms. I swear I can actually *see* the man building his defenses against his own feelings. "You don't really know me. Not at my core."

And whose fault is that?

"I know enough," I argue softly. "And we'd have all the time in the world to figure it out if you'd stop acting like such an emotional chickenshit and just admit that you're going to fall for me, too, if we keep this up." There's no way he would have designed that saddle, spent all that time training me to fight and fly, if he didn't feel *something*. He's going to have to fight for this, too, or it will never work.

"I have absolutely *no* intention of falling for you, Sorrengail." His eyes narrow and he enunciates every word, like I could possibly take that any other way.

Fuck. That. He let me in. He told me about his scars. He had an arsenal crafted for me. He cares. He's just as wrapped up in this as I am, even if he's shitty at showing it.

"Ouch." I wince. "Well, it's apparent that you're not ready to admit where this is going. So yeah, I think it's best we agree that this was just a onetime thing." I force my shoulders to shrug. "We both needed to blow off some steam, and we did, right?"

"Right," he agrees, apprehension lining his forehead.

"So the next time I see you, I'll just act as cool as you are right now and pretend that I'm not remembering what it feels like to have you sliding inside me." Warm and hard. He really does have an incredible body, but he doesn't get to dictate what I do with my heart.

He stalks forward with a smirk, his gaze warming every inch of my body. "And I'll just pretend that I'm not remembering the feel of your soft thighs around my hips or those breathy little sounds you make right before you come." His teeth rake over his lower lip, and it takes all my willpower not to suck that lip into my mouth.

"And I'll ignore the memory of your hands biting into my hips, pinning me to the armoire so you could take me deeper, and your mouth on my throat. Easy." My lips part as I retreat, my heart jumping in the best way when he follows, backing me against the wall.

His hand rests next to my head as he leans into my space, his lips curving into a half smile. "Then I guess I'll ignore the memory of how hot and slick you feel around my cock, and how you cry out for more until all I can think about is how to push every physical limit to be exactly what you need."

Shit. He's better at this game than I am. Heat flushes my skin. I want him closer. I want exactly what I had last night. But I want *more.* His breath hits my lips in ragged pants, and I'm in no better condition.

Fuck it. I can have him, right? I can take exactly what he's offering and enjoy every single minute. We can shred every piece of furniture in this room and then move to his. But where will that leave us in the morning?

Right here, both wanting and only one of us brave enough to take, and I deserve more than a relationship that's only on his terms.

"You want me." I put my hand on his chest and feel his heart pounding. "And I know that scares you even though I want you just as badly."

He stiffens.

"But here's the thing." I hold his gaze, knowing he could bolt at any second. "You don't get to dictate how I feel. You might give the orders out there, but not in here. You don't get to tell me we can fuck but I can't fall for you. That's not fair. You can only respect what I choose to do. So we're not doing this again until I *want* to risk my heart. And if I fall, then that's my problem, not yours. You're not responsible for my choices."

His jaw clenches once. Twice. And then he pushes off the wall, giving me space. "I think that's for the best. I'm graduating soon, and who knows where I'll end up. Besides, you and I are chained together because of Sgaeyl and Tairn, which complicates…everything." He retreats one step at a time, the distance more than just physical. "Besides, with all that *pretending*, I'm sure we'll eventually forget last night ever happened."

The way we're looking at each other tells me neither of us is *ever* going to forget. And he can avoid it all he wants, but we're going to end up right here time and again until he's willing to recognize what this is. Because if there's one thing I know for certain, it's that I'm going to fall for this man—if I haven't already—and he's halfway there, too, whether he realizes it or not.

Turning my back on him, I walk to the shattered halves of my throwing target and pick them up before heading back across my room. "I never figured you for a liar, Xaden." I shove the halves at his chest. "You can get me a new one when you're ready to come to your senses. Then we'll blow off some steam." I throw the aggravating man out.

"Did you hear that King Tauri is celebrating Reunification Day here?" Sawyer asks as he swings his leg over the bench beside me at lunch.

"Really?" I attack my roasted chicken with zeal. Since I've been training every day with Carr, my appetite somewhat resembles a bottomless pit. At least he only drags me to that mountaintop for an hour a day, but still, by the time breakfast comes, I'm ravenous.

After a month, I still can't aim lightning for shit. But I'm up to about twenty strikes an hour, so that's an improvement. Glancing down the tables, I catch Xaden's eye as he eats with the leadership on the dais.

He looks scrumptious this morning. Even the broody little cloud that follows him everywhere has a certain appeal as he rolls his eyes at something Garrick says.

"Don't look at me like that."

"Like what?" I arch an eyebrow.

His gaze flashes to mine. *"Like you're thinking about the sparring gym last night."*

"Well, duh," Rhiannon says across from me. "That's why Devera has about five hundred black dress uniforms in commons right now. Where the king travels, so does the party."

"Well, now that you mention it." My tongue flicks over my lower lip, remembering how his hips pinned mine to the mat after everyone had left for the night. How close we both came to giving in to the pulsing need between us.

His jaw flexes, and his grip tightens on his fork. *"Seriously. I can't think when you look at me like that."*

"Really? I figured those were for graduation?" Ridoc questions.

Imogen scoffs. "Like anyone dresses up for graduation. It's basically a giant formation where Panchek says, *Look, you lived. Good job. Come get your assignments and then pack your shit and leave.*"

Everyone laughs at her spot-on imitation.

"You're the one with the ridiculous rule about not falling for each other," I remind him.

"You're still looking." He forces his attention back to his plate.

"You make it hard to look away." I miss his mouth on my skin, the feel of his body pressed against mine. I miss the look on his face when he watched me come undone. But I miss the feeling of him curled around me in sleep more.

"I'm over here keeping my hands and memories to myself because you asked me to, and you're fucking me with your eyes. That's not playing fair."

I drop my fork and everyone at the table turns to stare.

"You all right over there?" Rhiannon asks, her eyebrows rising.

"Yep." I nod, ignoring the flush of heat creeping up my neck. "I'm great."

Liam sets his glass down and glances between Xaden and me, shaking his head as he fights a smile. Of course he knows what's going on. He'd have to be completely oblivious not to, considering he helped Xaden and Garrick move in the new armoire.

"Told you to stop staring." There's laughter in his voice, but his face is as expressionless as ever.

I tap my fork on my plate in pure frustration. You know what? Fuck this. Two can play at this game. *"If you'd just man up and admit there's something between us, I would strip down to my skin so you could see every single inch of me. And once I had you begging, I'd drop down to my knees, undo those flight leathers you're wearing, and wrap my lips around—"*

Xaden chokes.

Every head in the dining hall turns his way, and Garrick pounds on his back until Xaden waves him off, taking a drink of his water.

I grin, which earns me about six looks of confusion from our table and one set of rolled eyes from Liam.

"You're going to be the death of me."

• • •

We're only ten days away from graduation, and I'm counting every single one of them. That's when we'll find out how far Xaden is being sent from Basgiath. Most brand-new lieutenants are given midland posts, manning the forts along the roads that lead to the border outposts, but someone with Xaden's power? I don't even want to think about how far he'll be.

Or why he still hasn't admitted there's something between us. Or even hinted that at least he didn't regret that one night. I'd take that.

Don't fall for me…

I feel a familiar prickle along my scalp, and I know Xaden has filed into the Battle Brief room with the rest of the remaining cadets and leadership.

Professor Devera jumps right into today's brief, but I find it difficult to pay attention.

Today marks six years since Brennan was killed. He'd be a captain by now, or maybe even a major, given the way his career had taken off. Maybe he'd be married. Maybe I'd be an aunt. Maybe our father's heart wouldn't have given out that first time from the strain of losing him or that final time that spring two years ago.

"Take me to bed," I mentally blurt out, then sink down in my seat a little. I don't regret it, though. Today of all days, I need a distraction.

"It might be awkward in front of all these people."

I can't see him from where I know he's sitting at the top of the Battle Brief room, but his words feel like a caress on the back of my neck. *"Might be worth it."*

"And what would you have done differently?" Devera asks, scanning the crowd.

"I would have asked for reinforcements if I'd known the wards were weakening in the area," Rhiannon answers.

"I haven't changed my mind, Violence. There's no future for us."

"And when no reinforcements are available?" Devera asks, arching a brow. "You have noticed that the graduating classes from the Riders Quadrant are diminishing every year, while the uptick in attacks has cost us another seven riders *and* their dragons this year, haven't you? It takes at least a full company of infantry to make up for the loss of one rider."

"Graduation is ten days away." The approaching deadline has me on edge.

"I would have temporarily pulled riders from the midland posts to help rebuild the wards," Rhiannon answers.

"Don't remind me."

"Excellent." Devera nods.

"Are you seriously going to leave Basgiath without– " Without what? Declaring his undying...lust?

"Yes."

Of course he would. Xaden is a master of containing his emotions, which is probably why he's so fixed on containing mine, too. Or is there some other reason he's holding himself back that I'm not considering? The sex was great. Our chemistry? Explosive. We're even...friends, though the constant ache in my chest tells me it's gone far beyond that. If he could just be an asshole, then I'd write that night off as just sex—ridiculously *mind-blowing* sex—and move on. But he's not being an ass...not usually at least, and now I understand why he takes his job so seriously. He shoulders the responsibility for every marked one in here.

"Whatever you're thinking can wait until there's not a room of people between us," he says.

"What else do you have for me?" Devera continues, calling on a second-year.

It's been a month and a half since we destroyed my room—and we've managed to keep our hands off each other, even though one night wasn't enough to satisfy either of us, if the tension-filled evenings on the sparring mats are any indication. Of course, we both know anything more would only further complicate an already overly complicated situation.

But surely he's not relieving this sexual tension that stretches taut between us—with someone else. Surely. The insidious thought spreads with a sickening quickness.

I stop listening as my stomach twists at an all-too-real possibility. *"Is there someone else?"*

"I'm not having this discussion with you right now. Pay attention."

It takes everything I have not to turn around and yell at him. If I've spent every night tossing and turning in my sheets alone while he—

"That's a good idea, too, Aetos." Devera smiles. "A very wingleader answer, if I might say so."

Oh gods, Dain's ego is going to be unbearable today during sparring if Devera keeps complimenting him.

Sparring... I clasp my pen a little too hard as I remember the way

Imogen looked at Xaden that night. Shit. That would make sense. She carries a rebellion relic, and definitely isn't the daughter of the woman who killed his father, so she has that going for her, too. *"Is it Imogen?"*

I'm going to be sick.

"For fuck's sake, Violence."

"Is it? I know we said we weren't going there again, but—" I'm kicking myself for telling him I wanted more now, and for the fact that I should be paying attention instead of fighting with Xaden. *"At least tell me."*

"Sorrengail," Xaden snaps.

I freeze, feeling the weight of every gaze on me.

"Yes, Riorson?" Devera prompts.

He clears his throat. "If reinforcements were unavailable, I would have asked for Mira Sorrengail to temporarily transfer. The wards are strong at Montserrat, and with her signet, she could reinforce the weaknesses until other riders could arrive to strengthen those wards."

"Good idea." Devera nods. "And what riders are the most logical choice to help rebuild the wards in this particular mountain pass?"

"Third-years," I answer.

"Go on." Devera tilts her head at me.

"Third-years are taught to build wards, and at this point in the year, they're leaving anyway." I shrug. "May as well send them early so they can be of use."

"Point fucking made."

I slam my shield down and block him out.

"That's a logical choice," Devera says. "And that's all we have for today. Don't forget that you should be preparing for the last exercise of War Games before graduation. Also we expect each and every one of you in the courtyard in front of Basgiath tonight at nine for fireworks to celebrate Reunification Day. Dress uniforms only." She lifts her brows at Ridoc.

He shrugs. "What else would I be wearing?"

"One never knows what you'll come up with," Devera says, dismissing us.

"Anything I need to know about what's going on between you and..." Liam raises his eyebrows at me as we gather our things.

"Absolutely nothing is going on between us. Not one damn thing," I insist. If Xaden doesn't want to see if there might be more between us, message received. I turn to Rhiannon. "So are you excited to finally be able to write to your sister in ten days?"

She grins. "I've been writing her once a month since we got here. Now I'll finally get to post them."

At least one good thing is coming with graduation. We'll all be able to talk to our loved ones again.

Later that night, I adjust the sash across the bodice of my black dress uniform and tuck a loose strand of my hair back into the pretty arrangement Quinn helped me with earlier before meeting Rhiannon in the hallway.

She's unbound her hair from its usual braided, protective style, and the tight coils form a beautiful halo around her face, which she's dusted with gold-tinted blush. Her chosen option of sleek, tailored dress pants and a cross-body doublet that cuts across her torso on the diagonal looks phenomenal on her taller frame. "Hot," I say with a nod as she tugs on her sash.

I went with the high neck, sleeveless option to hide my armor and the flowing, floor-length skirt with the slit up the thigh, which Devera told me was for mobility in case of attack. Personally, I'm not against the flash of thigh it gives when I move, especially with all the work I've put in to strengthen my legs with Imogen. My sash is simple, the same black satin as everyone else's, with my name embroidered just beneath my shoulder and the star of a first-year.

"I heard there's going to be a mob of infantry guys there," Nadine says as she joins us.

"Don't you prefer a little brain with your brawn?" Ridoc slides right in, Sawyer at his side.

"You did *not* try to leave without me!" Liam shouts as he runs forward, darting through the crowd as we move toward the staircase that leads to Basgiath's main campus.

"I was hoping you'd been given the night off," I answer truthfully as he reaches my side. "Don't you look handsome."

"I know." He preens sarcastically, straightening his sash over a midnight-black doublet. "I've heard healer cadets have a thing for riders."

"Hardly." Rhiannon laughs. "As often as they have to put us back together? I bet they're more into scribes."

"What are scribes into?" Liam asks me as we descend the stairs in a sea of black, taking the path we tread every morning toward the Archives. "Seeing as you were almost one of them?"

"Usually other scribes," I answer. "But I guess riders, in my father's case."

"I'm just excited to see some people who aren't riders," Ridoc says, holding open the door so we can pass through the tunnel. "It's getting kind of incestuous around here."

"Agreed." Rhiannon nods.

"Oh, whatever. You and Tara have been on again, off again all year," Nadine says, then blanches. "Shit. Are you off again?"

"We're taking a breather until Parapet," she says, and we enter the Healer Quadrant.

"Hard to believe we'll be second-years in a little more than two weeks," Sawyer says.

"Hard to believe we've survived," I add. There was only one name on the death roll this week, a third-year who didn't come back from an overnight mission.

By the time we make it to the courtyard, the party is in full swing. There's a blend of pale blue for the healers, cream for the scribes, and the navy-blue uniforms of the infantry more than overwhelming the scattered black uniforms. There must be a thousand people or more in here.

Mage lights hang above us in the form of a dozen chandeliers, and drapes of rich velvets cover the stone walls of Basgiath, transforming the functional outdoor space into a ballroom of sorts. There's even a string quartet playing in the corner.

"Where are you?" I ask Xaden, but there's no answer.

We all seem to scatter as we enter, but Liam stays at my side, as tense as the string on my crossbow. "Tell me you're wearing your armor under all that."

"You think someone is going to knife me in front of my mother?" I gesture to the exposed balcony where Mom appears to be holding court, surveying her domain. Our gazes collide and she whispers something to the man next to her, disappearing from view.

Nice to see you, too.

"I think if anyone was going to knife you, now would be the time, especially knowing that killing you has a good chance of ending Fen Riorson's son." His voice tightens.

That's when I notice the stares of the officers and cadets around us. They're not gawking at my hair or the name on my sash. No, their gazes widen at Liam's wrist and the visible swirls of his rebellion relic.

I hook my arm through his and lift my chin. "I'm so sorry."

"There is absolutely nothing for you to be sorry about." He gives my hand a reassuring pat.

"Of course there is," I whisper. Oh gods, everyone is here to gather in celebration of the end of what he and the others call the apostasy. They're celebrating his mother's death. "You can go. You should go. This is…" I shake my head.

"I go where you go." His hand tightens over mine.

A boulder lodges in my throat, and I scan the crowd, instinctively knowing that he's not here. There's no Garrick, no Bodhi, no Imogen, and definitely no Xaden. No wonder he was in such a shit mood today.

"This isn't fair to you." I glare at the infantry officer who has the nerve to look appalled at the sight of Liam's wrist.

"I highly doubt you enjoy celebrating the anniversary of your brother's death, either." Liam holds himself with a dignity I could never imagine.

"Brennan would hate all of this." I gesture to the crowd. "He was more about getting the work done than celebrating its completion."

"Yeah, sounds like—" His words die, and I squeeze his arm tighter as I note the separating crowd before us.

King Tauri walks at my mother's side, and from the direction of his wide, toothy smile, he's headed this way. A purple sash crosses his doublet, pinned to his chest by a dozen medals he's never won from a hundred battlefields he's never stepped foot on.

Mom's medals are all earned, and they adorn her black sash like jewelry as it drapes across her high-necked, long-sleeve dress uniform.

"Go," I hiss at Liam in a whisper, forcing a smile for my mother's sake as General Melgren joins them. Melgren may be brilliant, but he's also unnerving as fuck to be around.

"When your greatest danger approaches? I think not." His spine straightens.

I'm going to rip Xaden's gorgeous head off for forcing Liam through this.

"Your Majesty," I murmur, dropping a foot behind me like Mira taught and bending as I bow my head, noting that Liam has bowed at the waist.

"Your mother tells me you've bonded with not one but *two* exceptional dragons," King Tauri says, smiling under his mustache.

"Yes, she is quite confident in your power," Melgren adds, his smile icy as he stares at me in blatant appraisal.

"I would not say the same at this time," I answer with a polite smile. I've spent enough time around egotistical generals, politicians, and royalty to know when to be humble. "I'm still learning how to wield."

"Don't be so modest, daughter," Mom chides. "From what her professors say, they've only seen a gift this powerful a few times in the last decade, in Brennan and the Riorson boy."

That *boy* is a twenty-three-year-old man, but I know better than to correct her and put an even bigger target on Xaden's back.

"And your gift?" King Tauri asks Liam.

"Farsight, Your Majesty," Liam responds.

Melgren's eyes narrow on Liam's exposed rebellion relic, then rise to his sash. "Mairi, as in Colonel Mairi's son?"

I squeeze his arm tighter against mine in silent support, and Mom notices.

"Yes, General. Though I was mostly brought up by Duke Lindell at Tirvainne." His jaw flexes, but that's the only physical sign of his discomfort.

"Ahh." King Tauri nods. "Yes, Duke Lindell is a good man, a loyal man." The superiority in his air makes me want to snatch the medals off his chest.

"I have him to thank for my fortitude, Majesty." Liam plays the game well.

"Yes, you do." Melgren nods again, his gaze scanning the crowd. "Now tell me, where is the Riorson boy? I always like to lay eyes on him once a year and make sure he's not causing trouble."

"No trouble," I answer, earning a swift glare from Mom. "He's our wingleader, actually. He saved my life when we were on the front lines at Montserrat." By making me leave instead of staying to help, but still, he deserves the credit for me not distracting Mira and getting her, myself, *and* Tairn killed. Xaden's done more than save me. He believed me when I told him Amber led the unbondeds to my room. He had an entire arsenal of daggers crafted just for me. He designed a saddle for Tairn so I can ride into battle with my peers. He'd protected me when I needed and taught me to defend myself so I wouldn't require protection forever.

And when others are quick to stand in front of me, Xaden always stands at my side, trusting me to hold my own.

But I don't say any of that. What's the point? Xaden wouldn't give a fuck what these people think of him—so I won't, either. Instead, I just continue to offer a simpering smile, seemingly in awe of the powerful men before me.

"Their dragons are mated," Mom offers, her smile chilling. "So she's grown quite close to him out of necessity."

Out of lust and need and the ache in my chest I'm terrified to define, but sure, *necessity* works.

"That's excellent." King Tauri beams. "It's good to have a Sorrengail on lookout for us. You'll let us know if he decides to, oh, I don't know." He laughs. "Start another war?"

Melgren is fully capable of seeing the outcome of any such absurdity, and yet he stares at Liam and me with unnerving focus.

My entire body tenses. "I can assure you, he's loyal."

"So where is he?" King Tauri scans the courtyard. "I asked that they all be here, all marked ones."

"I just saw him a little earlier." I smile through the not-quite lie. Battle Brief *was* earlier. "I'd check thc edges? He's not much for parties."

"Oh, look! There's Dain Aetos!" Mom says, nodding somewhere behind my shoulder. "He'd be so humbled if you said hello," she prompts the king.

"Of course." The three of them walk off, leaving Liam and me standing in complete silence as we pivot to watch them so we don't accidentally turn our backs on the king. I feel like I've just survived certain death, or at least some kind of natural disaster.

"I'm going to kill him for making you come to this," I mutter under my breath as Dain greets the king with perfect manners.

"Xaden didn't make me come."

"What?" My gaze jumps to his.

"He'd never ask this of me. Never ask it of anyone. But I told him I would keep you safe, and that's what I'm doing, keeping you safe." He flashes a crooked smile.

"You are a good friend, Liam Mairi." I rest my head on his arm.

"You saved my life, Violet. The least I can do is grin and bear it through a fucking party."

"I'm not sure I can grin and bear it." Not with the way people constantly glance at his wrist, like he's the one who personally led the army to the border.

Dain smiles as the king takes his leave, then glances over his shoulder, meeting my gaze and heading our way.

He grins, and it's all too easy to remember how many events just like this we've attended together over the years. His touch is gentle when he cups my cheek. "You look beautiful tonight, Vi."

"Thank you." I smile. "You look fabulous yourself."

His hand falls away as he turns to Liam. "Has this one tried to escape yet? She's always hated these things."

"Not yet, but the evening is young," Liam replies.

Dain must read the tense lines of Liam's face, because his smile slips when he looks back at me. "The staircase is about five feet to our right. I'll distract while you slip away."

"Thank you." I nod in thanks, offering him a soft smile. "Let's get out of here," I say to Liam.

Once we're out of the party and back in the Riders Quadrant, I walk straight into the courtyard and ground, letting power swirl around and through me. I sense the golden energy from Andarna, the blazing power from Tairn that connects me to Sgaeyl, and finally, the shimmering shadows of Xaden.

I open my eyes, tracing the ebb and flow of that shimmering shadow, and I know he's somewhere in front of me.

"Liam, you know I adore you, right?"

"Well, that's nice—"

"Go away." I walk straight ahead through the courtyard.

"What?" Liam catches up to me. "I can't just leave you out here by yourself."

"No offense, but I can fry this entire place with a lightning bolt if I want to, and I need to see Xaden, so go." I pat his arm and keep striding toward the feeling, using it to guide me.

"I mean, your aim is shit according to you, but I get the rest!" he calls out, falling behind.

I don't bother with a mage light as I pass the area where we usually stand in formation and keep walking toward the figures lounging against the only opening in this godsforsaken wall. There's only one place Xaden can be.

"Tell me he's not out there," I say to Garrick and Bodhi, whose features I can barely see in the moonlight.

"I could tell you that, but I'd be lying," Bodhi remarks, rubbing the back of his neck.

"You're not going to want to see him. Not tonight, Sorrengail," Garrick warns with a grimace. "Self-preservation is a thing. Notice we're not with him, and we're his best friends."

"Yeah, well, I'm his..." I open my mouth and shut it a few times because...fuck if I know what I am to him. But the longing that holds my heart hostage, this driving need to be at his side because I know he's suffering, no matter if it means throwing myself headfirst into uncertainty...I can't deny what he is to me. I kick off the leather slippers of my dress uniform—they're more of a hazard than anything, and in this wind? Well, we'll see how it goes. "I'm just...his."

For the first time since last year, I step up onto the parapet.

As for the 107 innocents, the children of the executed officers, they now carry what shall be known as the rebellion relic, transferred by the dragon who carried out the king's justice. And to show the mercy of our great king, they will all be conscripted into the prestigious Riders Quadrant at Basgiath, so they may prove their loyalty to our kingdom with their service or with their death.

—Addendum 4.2, the Treaty of Aretia

CHAPTER THIRTY-TWO

Walking the parapet on Conscription Day is a certifiable risk. Walking the parapet in a dress uniform, barefoot, in the dark? Now this is madness.

The first ten feet, while I'm still inside the walls, are the easiest, and as I reach the edge, where the wind ruffles my skirt like a sail, I start to doubt my plan. It's going to be hard to get to Xaden if I fall to my death.

But I see him sitting about a third of the way across the narrow stone bridge, staring up at the moon like it somehow adds to the burden he carries, and my heart fucking hurts. He had the lives of all one hundred and seven marked ones carved into his back, taking responsibility for them. But who takes responsibility—takes *care*—of him?

Everyone across the ravine is celebrating his father's death, and he's out here mourning it alone. When Brennan died, I had Mira and Dad, but Xaden's had no one.

You don't really know me. Not at my core. Isn't that how he replied when I told him that I'd end up falling for him? As if knowing him would somehow make me want him less, but everything I learn about him only makes me tumble harder and faster.

Oh gods. I know this feeling. Denying it doesn't make it any less true. My feelings are what they are. I haven't run from a challenge since I crossed this parapet a year ago, and I'm not about to start now.

The last time I stood here, I was terrified, but the distance to the ground isn't what has my pulse pounding now. There's more than one way to fall. *Shit.* That ache in my chest burns brighter than the power coursing through my veins.

I'm in love with Xaden.

It doesn't matter that he's leaving soon or that he probably doesn't feel the same for me. It doesn't even matter that he warned me not to fall for him. It's not an infatuation, our physical chemistry, or even the bond between our dragons that keeps me reaching in every way possible for this man. It's my reckless heart.

I've kept out of his bed—out of his arms—because he's adamant I can't fall for him, but that ship has long sailed, so what's the point in holding back? Shouldn't I grab hold of every moment we can have while he's still here?

I take the first step onto the narrow stone bridge and put my arms out for balance. It's just like walking along Tairn's spine, which I've done hundreds of times.

Except I'm in a dress.

And Tairn isn't going to catch me if I fall.

He's going to be so pissed when he hears that I did this—

"Already am."

Xaden's head snaps in my direction. "Violence?"

I take a step and then another, holding my frame upright with muscle memory I didn't have last year, and begin to cross.

Xaden swings his legs up and then fucking *jumps* to his feet. "Turn around right now!" he shouts.

"Come with me," I call over the wind, bracing myself as a gust whips my skirt against my legs. "Should have gone with the pants," I mutter and keep walking.

He's already coming my way, his strides just as long and confident as if he was on solid ground, eating up the distance between us as I move forward slowly until we meet.

"What the fuck are you doing out here?" he asks, locking his hands on my waist. He's in riding leathers, not a dress uniform, and he's never looked better.

What am I doing out here? I'm risking everything to reach him. And if he rejects me… No. There's no room for fear on the parapet.

"I could ask you the same thing."

His eyes widen. "You could have fallen and died!"

"I could say the same thing." I smile, but it's shaky. The look in his eyes is wild, like he's been driven past the point where he can contain himself in the neat, apathetic facade he usually wears in public.

It doesn't scare me. I like him better when he's real with me anyway.

"And did you stop to think that if you fall and die, then I can die?" He leans in and my pulse jumps.

"Again," I say softly, resting my hands on his firm chest, right above his heartbeat. "I could say the same thing." Even if Xaden's death wouldn't kill Sgaeyl, I'm not sure *I* could survive it.

Shadows rise, darker than the night that surrounds us. "You're forgetting that I wield shadows, Violence. I'm just as safe out here as I am in the courtyard. Are you going to wield lightning to break your fall?"

Fine. That's a good point.

"I…perhaps did not think that part through as thoroughly as you," I admit. I wanted to be close to him, so I got close, parapet be damned.

"You're seriously going to be the death of me." His fingers flex at my waist. "Go back."

It's not a rejection, not with the way he's looking at me. We've been sparring emotionally for the past month, hell, even longer than that, and one of us has to expose our jugular. I finally trust him enough to know he won't go for the kill.

"Only if you do. I want to be wherever you are." And I mean it. Everyone else—everything else in the world can fall away and I won't care as long as I'm with him.

"Violence…"

"I know why you said you don't see a future for us." My heart races like it's trying to take flight as I blurt out the words.

"Do you?" Of course he isn't going to make this easy. I'm not sure the man even knows what *easy* is.

"You want me," I say, looking him in the eyes. "And no, I'm not just talking about in bed. You. Want. Me, Xaden Riorson. You might not say it, but you do one better and *show* it. You show it every time you choose to trust me, every time your eyes linger on mine. You show it with every sparring lesson you don't have time for and every flight lesson that pulls you away from your own studies. You show it when you refuse to touch me because you're worried I don't really want you, then show it again when you take the time to hunt down violets before a leadership meeting so I don't wake up feeling alone. You show it in a million different ways. Please don't deny it."

His jaw flexes, but he doesn't deny it.

"You think we don't have a future because you're scared that I won't like who you really are behind all those walls you keep. And I'm scared, too. I can admit it. You're graduating. I'm not. You'll be gone in a matter of weeks, and we're probably setting ourselves up for heartbreak. But if we let fear kill whatever this is between us, then we don't deserve it." I lift one hand to the back of his neck. "I told you that I was the one who would decide when I'm ready to risk my heart, and I'm saying it."

The way he looks at me, with the same mix of hope and apprehension currently flooding my system, gives me absolute life.

"You don't mean that," he says, shaking his head.

And there he goes, sucking the life right out again.

"I mean it."

"If this is about the Imogen thing—"

"It's not." I shake my head, the wind catching the curls Quinn spent so much time on. "I know there's no one else. I wouldn't be walking the parapet in the middle of the night if I thought you were playing me."

His brow furrows, and he pulls me in closer against the warmth of his body. "Then what made you even think that? Have to admit, it pissed me off. I've given you exactly zero reasons to think I'm in anyone else's bed."

Which means he's only in mine.

"My own insecurities and the way she looked at you and Garrick sparring. You might not have a thing for her, but she definitely has one for you. I know that look. It's the same look I have when I'm watching you." Embarrassment heats my cheeks. I could change the subject or deflect, but it's not going to do our relationship—if that's even what this is—any favors if I hide my feelings, no matter how weak the irrational ones might make me seem.

"You're jealous." He bites back a smile.

"Maybe," I admit, then decide that answer is half-assed. "Fine. Yes. She's strong and fierce and has that same ruthless streak you do. I've always thought she was a better match for you."

"I know the feeling well." He shakes his head. "And you are strong and fierce and have a ruthless streak, too. Not to mention you're the smartest person I've ever met. That mind of yours is sexy as hell. Imogen and I are just friends. Trust me, she wasn't looking at me, and even if she were…" He pauses, his hand slipping to cradle the back of my head as he holds us steady despite the gusting wind. "Gods help me, I'm only looking at you."

Hope is a stronger buzz than anything they were serving at the party.

"She wasn't looking at you?"

"No. Rethink what you just said but take me out of the equation." He lifts his brows, waiting for me to come to the right conclusion.

"But on the sparring mat…" My eyes widen. "She has a thing for Garrick."

"Catching on fast, aren't you?"

"I am. Are you done pushing me away?"

He draws back, searching my eyes in the moonlight before glancing over my shoulder. "You done putting yourself in harm's way to get your point across?"

"Probably not."

He sighs. "There's only you, Violence. Is that what you needed to hear?"

I nod.

"Even when I'm not with you, there's only you. Next time, just ask. You've never had a problem being bluntly honest with me." Wind blows around us, but he's as immovable as the parapet itself. "As I remember, you've even thrown daggers at my head, which I greatly prefer over watching you get tangled up in your thoughts. If we're going to do this, then we have to trust each other."

"And you want to do this?" I hold my breath.

He sighs, long and hard, then admits, "Yes." His hand slides up, and he caresses my cheek with his thumb. "I can't make you any promises, Violence. But I'm tired of fighting it."

"Yes." One word has never meant so much to me. Then I blink, remembering his previous comment about jealousy. "What do you mean you know the feeling of jealousy well?"

His hands tighten on my waist, and he looks away.

"Oh no, if I have to trust you and tell you what I'm thinking, then I expect the same from you." I'm not going to be the only vulnerable one out on this ledge.

He grumbles, dragging his gaze back to mine. "I saw Aetos kiss you after Threshing and nearly lost my shit."

If I didn't already love him, that might have pushed me over the edge. "You wanted me then?"

"I've wanted you from the first second I saw you, Violence," he admits. "And if I was short with you today…well, it's just a shit day."

"I understand. And you know Dain and I are just friends, right?"

"I know that's how you feel, though I wasn't sure back then." He runs his thumb over the swell of my lips. "Now get your ass back on solid ground."

He wants to stay out here and wallow.

"Come with me." My fingers grasp the material of his flight leathers, ready to tug him along if I have to.

He shakes his head and looks away. "I'm not in a place to take care of anyone tonight. And yes, I know that's a shitty thing to say, since it's the anniversary of losing Brennan—"

"I know." I slide my hands down his arms. "Come with me, Xaden."

"Vi…" His shoulders dip, and the sadness that permeates the air between us puts a lump in my throat.

"Trust me." I step back out of his arms and take his hands. "Come on."

A moment of tense silence passes before he nods once, moving forward and holding me steady while I turn around. "I'm much better at this than I was last July."

"So I see." He stays close, one hand on my waist as I walk the last part of the parapet. "In a fucking dress."

"It's a skirt, actually," I say over my shoulder, only feet away from the wall.

"Eyes forward!" he grumbles, and it's only the fear in his tone that keeps me from doing something arrogant like skipping the last few feet.

The second we're within the confines of the wall, he hauls me against him, my back to his front. "Don't ever put your life at risk over something as trivial as talking to me again." It's as low as a growl against my ear, sending a shiver down my spine.

"Next year is going to be so much fun," I tease, walking forward and lacing my fingers with his so he follows.

"Liam will be here next year to make sure you're not doing asinine things," he mutters.

"You're going to *love* getting his letters," I promise, jumping the final foot off the parapet to the courtyard below. "Huh." I glance around the empty courtyard while putting my slippers back on. "Garrick and Bodhi were just here."

"They probably know I'm going to kill them for letting you out there. A dress, Sorrengail? Really?"

I take his hand in mine and head across the courtyard.

"Where are we going?" He sounds just as much the asshole as the day I met him.

"You're taking me to your room," I say over my shoulder as we approach the dormitory.

"I'm what?"

I throw open the door, grateful for the mage lights that make it easy to see him now, sneer and all. "You're taking me to your room." Turning left, I lead us past the hallway to my room and then start up the wide spiral staircase.

"Someone will see," he argues. "It's not my reputation I'm worried about, Sorrengail. You're a first-year and I'm your wingleader—"

"Pretty sure everyone already knows—we set half the forest on fire that night," I remind him as we climb past the door to the second-year hallway. "Did you know that the first time I climbed these steps with Dain, I was horrified that there wasn't a handrail?"

"Did you know I can't stand to hear his name on your lips while you're leading the way to *my* room?" He trudges up the steps behind me, shadows curling from the wall as if they sense his mood and want nothing to do with it. But his shadows don't scare me. There's nothing about this man that scares me anymore, except the magnitude of my feelings for him.

"Point is, and now look at me." I grin as we reach the third-year floor, and I push open the arched door. "All but dancing on the parapet in a dress."

"Probably not a good time to remind me." He follows me into the hallway. It looks like the second-year floor, except there are fewer doors and a high, vaulted roof.

"Which one is yours?"

"I should make you guess," he mutters but keeps my fingers laced with his as we walk to the end of the massively long hall. Of course it's the last one.

"Fourth Wing," I scoff. "Always has to go the farthest."

He unweaves his own wards and opens his door, standing back so I can walk in first. "I'm going to have to either ward your new door before I go or teach you how in the next ten days."

I'm not thinking about the looming deadline of his departure as I step into his room for the first time. It's twice as big as mine—and so is the bed. Surviving to third year has some serious perks. Or maybe the size reflects his rank, who knows.

It's immaculately clean, with a large armchair by the bed, dark-gray rug, wide wooden armoire, tidy desk, and a bookshelf that gives me instant envy. A sword rack consumes the area beside the door, complete with so many daggers that I can't possibly count them all, and across the space, next to the desk, stands a throwing target just like I have in my room. There's a table and chairs in the corner, and his window faces Basgiath but is framed by thick black curtains with Fourth Wing's emblem on the bottom.

"We do leadership meetings for the sections in here sometimes," he says from the doorway.

I pivot to find him watching me with curious eyes, like he's waiting for me to pass judgment on his space. Walking past the sword rack, I let my fingers graze across the handles of the different daggers. "How many challenges have you won anyway?"

"The better question is how many have I lost," he says, coming in and closing the door behind him.

"There's the ego I know and love so much," I mutter, making my way to the bed, which, just like mine, is outfitted in black.

"Have I told you how beautiful you look tonight?" His voice lowers. "If not, I'm a fool, because you are magnificently beautiful."

Heat rises in my cheeks, and my mouth curves into a smile. "Thank you. Now sit." I pat the edge of his bed.

"What?" His eyebrows rise.

"Sit," I order, staring him down.

"I don't want to talk about it."

"I never said you had to." There's no need to ask what *it* is, nor am I going to let what happened nearly six years ago drive a wedge between us, not even for one night.

To my absolute surprise, he does as I ask, sitting on the side of his bed. His long legs stretch out in front of him, and he leans back slightly on the heels of his hands. "Now what?"

I move between his thighs and run my fingers through his hair. He closes his eyes and leans into my touch, and I swear, I feel my heart crack wide open. "Now I take care of you."

His eyes fly open and gods, are they beautiful. I've memorized every gold fleck in those onyx depths, and it's a good thing, since I don't know where he'll be sent after graduation. Seeing him once every few days isn't the same as being able to touch him anytime I like.

Leaving his hair, I sink to my knees before him.

"Violet—"

"I'm just taking off your boots." A smirk plays at my lips as I unlace one, then the other, taking them off. I rise and carry his boots toward the armoire.

"You can just leave them there," he blurts.

I put them on the floor next to the armoire and walk back. "I wasn't going to go snooping through your clothes, and it's not like I haven't seen them all anyway."

His gaze locks on my skirt, heating every time the slit reveals a section of my thigh. "You've been wearing that all night?"

"That's what you get for walking behind me," I tease, coming to stand between his thighs again.

"I can't really argue about the view from the back, either." He tilts his chin to look up at me.

"Be quiet and let me get this off you." I undo the line of diagonal buttons across his chest, and he shrugs out of the leathers. "Were you flying tonight?"

"It usually helps." He nods as I lean over to set them on the armchair. "This day is always…"

"I'm sorry." I look him in the eyes as I say it, hoping he knows how very much I mean it as I return, reaching for his shirt.

"I'm sorry, too." He lifts his arms, and I tug the shirt off before putting it with the flight jacket.

"You have nothing to be sorry about." I keep my eyes on his as I cup the unrelenting angles of his face, then trace the scar that bisects a brow. "Challenge?"

"Sgaeyl." He shrugs. "Threshing."

"Most dragons scar their riders, but Tairn and Andarna have never hurt me," I say absent-mindedly, my hand slipping down his neck.

"Or maybe they knew you already carried a scar." He trails his fingers down the long silver scar on my arm from Tynan's blade. "I wanted to fucking kill them. And instead, I had to stand there and watch them go at you three-on-one. I was at the edge of my control and ready to step in when Tairn landed."

"It was only two-on-one once Jack ran," I reminded him. "And you couldn't have interfered. It's against the rules, remember?" But he took that step. That single step that told me he would have.

A corner of his mouth quirks into one of the sexiest smirks I've ever seen. "At the end of the day, you walked away with two dragons." His expression falls. "Two weeks from now, I won't even be here to watch when you're challenged, let alone do anything about it."

"I'll be fine," I promise. "Whomever I can't beat in a challenge, I'll just poison."

He doesn't laugh.

"Come on, let's get you to bed." I lean in and kiss the scar on his eyebrow. "It will be tomorrow when you wake up."

"I don't deserve you." His arm curls around my hips and he tugs me closer. "But I'm going to keep you all the same."

"Good." I lean in and brush my lips over his. "Because I think I'm in love with you." My heart beats erratically, and panic claws up my rib cage. I shouldn't have said it.

His eyes flare wide and his arms tighten around me. "You think? Or you know?"

Be brave.

Even if he doesn't feel the same, at least I will have spoken my truth. "I know. I'm so wildly in love with you that I can't imagine what my life would even look like without you in it. And I probably shouldn't have said that, but if we're doing this, then we're starting from a place of complete honesty."

He crushes his mouth to mine and pulls me fully into his lap so I'm straddling him. He kisses me so deep that I lose myself in it, in him. There are no words as he takes off my sash, my top, and unbuttons my skirt, all without breaking the kiss. "Stand," he says against my lips.

"Xaden." My heart thunders.

"I fucking *need* you, Violet. Right now. And I don't need *anyone*, so I'm not quite sure how to handle this feeling, but I'm giving it my best. And if you don't want this tonight, that's fine, but I'm going to need you to walk out that door right now, because if you don't, I'm going to have you naked on your back in the next two minutes."

The intensity in his eyes and the vehemence of his words should frighten me, but they don't. Even if this man loses every ounce of his self-control, I know he'll never hurt me.

Not with his body, at least.

"Walk away or stay, but either way, I need you to stand up," he begs.

"I think two minutes might be overestimating your skills with a corset." I glance down at my armor.

He grins and lifts me from his lap.

My feet hit the floor. "I'm timing you."

"Is that—"

"One. Two." I hold up my fingers. "Three."

He's on his feet in a heartbeat, and then his mouth is on mine, and I stop counting. I'm too busy chasing the strokes of his tongue, feeling the ripple of his muscles beneath my fingertips, to give a shit where my clothes are going.

I feel air rush against my legs as my skirt hits the floor, and I help him out by kicking off my slippers while I suck on his tongue.

He groans, his hands flying over my back. Laces loosen in record time, and the corset falls to the floor, leaving me in my underwear, since there wasn't much else fitting underneath that dress uniform.

Daggers, both his and mine, hit the ground as he unstraps the sheaths at my thighs and undoes his own. It's a glorious cacophony of metal until we're both naked and he's kissing me breathless.

Then his hands are in my hair, and pins fly until the mass falls down my back, unbound. He pulls back only long enough to rake his ravenous gaze down my body. "So fucking beautiful."

"I think that might have been a little longer than two—" I start, but he grabs the back of my thighs and lifts, sweeping my feet out from underneath me. My back hits the bed with a slight bounce, and honestly, I should have seen that move coming given that he's been putting me on my back for the better part of a year now.

"Still counting?" he asks, dropping to his knees beside the bed and dragging me across the soft coverlet to the edge.

"Do you need me to keep score?" I tease as my ass hits the end of the bed.

"Feel free." He grins, and before I can get another word in, his mouth is between my thighs.

I suck in a sharp breath and throw my head back at the sheer pleasure of his tongue, licking and swirling around my clit. "Oh *gods*."

"Which one are you calling out for?" he asks against my flesh. "Because it's just you and me in this room, Vi, and I don't share."

"You." My fingers tangle in his hair. "I'm calling out for you."

"I appreciate the elevation to deity, but my name will do." He licks me from entrance to clit, finally flicking his tongue over that sensitive bud, and I moan. "Fuck, you taste good." He lifts my thighs up onto his shoulders and settles in like he has nowhere else to be tonight.

Then he absolutely devours me with tongue and teeth.

Pleasure, hot and insistent, spirals in my stomach and I'm lost in sensation, my hips rising and falling as I chase the high he drives me toward with every expert stab of his tongue.

My thighs tremble when he takes up a rhythm against my clit and drives two fingers inside me. They lock when he strokes his fingers in time with his tongue. Mindless, I'm simply *mindless.*

Power rushes through me in a deluge, mingling with the pleasure until they're one and the same, and when he tips me over the edge of oblivion, it's his name I scream as that power whips outward with every wave of my climax.

Thunder booms, shaking the paneled glass in Xaden's windows.

"That's one," he says, kissing his way up my limp body. "Though I do think we're going to have to work on the fireworks show or people are always going to know what we're doing."

"Your mouth is…" I shake my head as his hands slide under me, moving us to the center of his bed. "There are no words for that."

"Delicious," he whispers, his lips skimming the plane of my stomach. "You are absolutely delicious. I never should have waited this long to get my mouth on you."

I gasp when he sucks the peak of my breast into his mouth, his tongue lashing and stroking my nipple as he works the other between thumb and forefinger, setting a whole new fire within me built on the embers of the first.

By the time he gets to my neck, I'm a writhing flame beneath him, touching every part of him I can reach, stroking my hands down his arms, his back, his chest. Gods, this man is incredible, every line of him carved for battle and built by sparring and swordplay.

Our mouths meet in a deep kiss, and I can taste us both in it as I draw my knees upward, settling his hips right where they're meant to be—between my thighs.

"Violet," he groans, and I can feel the head of him at my entrance.

"I don't get equal time to play?" I tease, arching my hips so he slides against me and making my own breath catch with the motion.

He nips my lower lip. "You can play all you want later if I can have you right now."

Yeah, that's a plan I can get with. "You already have me."

His gaze collides with mine as he hovers above me, bracing his weight to keep from crushing me. "You have everything I have to give."

That's enough…for now. I nod, arching my hips again.

Eyes locked with mine, he pushes into me with one long roll of his hips, consuming every inch and then taking another until he's seated to the hilt.

The pressure, the stretch, the fit of him is beyond words.

"You feel so damn good." I roll my hips because I can't help myself.

"I could say the same thing about you." He smiles, using my own words from earlier against me. Hard, deep, and slow, he sets a rhythm that has me arching for every thrust as we come together again and again and again.

He drives us up the bed, and I throw my arms back, bracing against the headboard for leverage as I meet every plunge of his hips. Gods, each is better than the last. When I urge him to move faster, he gives me a wicked grin and takes me at the same mind-blowing, heart-jolting pace. "I want this to last. I *need* this to last."

"But I'm…" That fire in my core is coiled tight and so ready to burst free that I can almost taste how sweet it will be.

"I know." He drives forward again, and I whimper at how fucking good it feels. "Just stay with me." He adjusts the angle so he hits my clit with every thrust and presses my knee forward, taking me even deeper.

I'm not going to survive this. I'm going to die right here in this bed.

"Then I'm going to die with you," he promises, kissing me.

I'm so far gone, I didn't even realize I said the words out loud, and then I remember that I don't have to. *"More. I need more."* Power simmers beneath my skin and my legs lock.

"You're almost there. Fuck, you feel so damn good around me. I'm never going to get enough of this, enough of you."

"I love you." The words are so incredibly freeing, even if he doesn't say them back.

His eyes flare and his control snaps as he pounds into me, and that coiled pleasure explodes as my powers whip out again, cracking through the room, shattering like glass as he throws his weight to the side, bringing me with him as he drives toward his own release, groaning into the side of my neck as the last waves of my orgasm leave me shuddering against him.

Long minutes pass before our breathing steadies, and a light breeze kisses my thigh that's thrown over his. "You're all right?" he asks, brushing my hair back from my face.

"I'm great. You're great. That was..."

"Great?" he supplies.

"Exactly."

"I was going to use the word 'explosive,' but I think 'great' covers it." His fingers tangle in my hair. "I fucking love your hair. If you ever want to bring me to my knees or win an argument, just let it down. I'll get the point."

I grin as the breeze rustles through the brown-to-silver strands.

Wait. There shouldn't be a breeze.

My stomach drops as I push myself up on an elbow to look over Xaden's shoulder. "Oh no, no, no." My hand covers my mouth as I glimpse the destruction. "I'm pretty sure I blew your window out."

"Unless there's someone else throwing lightning around, then yeah, that was you. See what I mean? Explosive." He laughs.

I gasp. That's why he threw himself sideways, to shield me from my own wreckage. "I'm so sorry." I scan over the damage, but there's only sand on the bed. "I'm going to have to get that under control."

"I threw up a shield. Don't worry about it." He pulls me back in for a kiss.

"What are we going to do?" Repairing a window is on a whole different level from replacing an armoire.

"Right now?" He strokes my hair back from my face again. "That was two, if we're still counting, and I say we clean up, get the sand out of the bed, and get you to three, maybe four if you're still awake."

My jaw drops. "After I just shattered your window?"

He smiles and *shrugs*. "I've got us covered just in case you decide to take out the dresser next."

I gaze down at his body, and the craving for him ignites again. How could it not when he looks like the gods blessed him and feels like the gods blessed *me*? "Yeah, let's go for three."

We're going for five, my hips in Xaden's hands while I slowly ride him, when I trail my fingers down the black swirls of the relic on his neck. I'm not sure how either of us is still moving, and yet we can't seem to stop tonight, can't get enough. "It really is beautiful," I tell him, rising up only to sink back down again, taking him deep within me.

His dark eyes flare as his hands flex. "I used to think of it as a curse, but now I realize it's a gift." He arches his hips, hitting me at a sublime angle.

"A gift?" Gods, he's robbing me of every thought.

Someone pounds on the door.

"Go the fuck away!" Xaden snarls, reaching up my back and hooking onto my shoulder to pull me down into his next thrust.

I fall forward, muffling my moan in his neck.

"I really wish I could." There's enough regret in the voice that I believe it.

"Someone better be dead if I get out of this bed, Garrick," Xaden retorts.

"I think there're *a lot* of people dead, which is why they're calling the full quadrant to formation, jackass!" Garrick growls.

Both Xaden and I startle, our gazes colliding in shock. I slide off him, and Xaden covers me with his blanket before shoving his legs into his leathers and striding for the door.

"What the fuck are you talking about?" he asks through a tiny opening in the door.

"Grab your flight leathers, and you'd better bring Sorrengail with you, too," Garrick says. "We're under attack."

The inability to control a powerful signet is just as dangerous to a rider—and everyone in their vicinity— as never manifesting one.

—Major Afendra's Guide to the Riders Quadrant (Unauthorized Edition)

CHAPTER THIRTY-THREE

I've never gotten dressed so fast in my entire *life*, and I'm not even bothering with the thigh sheaths. "What time is it?" I ask Xaden, pulling on my formal dress and slippers and blowing my hair out of my face.

Mandatory, urgent formation for the entire quadrant means *now*.

The wards are falling. How many Navarrians are we going to lose?

"Four fifteen." He finishes lacing his boots, already armed to the teeth as I'm picking up my sheaths, pretty sure I'm missing one of them. "You're going to freeze out there."

"I'll be fine." I drop to my knees and locate the missing dagger, hauling it out by the strap of the sheath before standing again.

"Here." Xaden throws one of his flight jackets over me, trapping my hair. "If Garrick's right and we're under attack, then my guess is they'll order the older years to staff the mid-guard posts, so you shouldn't be out in formation too long. I can't stand the thought of you being cold."

Which means *he'll* be leaving.

My heart somersaults as I clumsily shove my arms through the sleeves of his jacket. He'll be safe, right? It will just be a midland assignment, and he's the most powerful rider in the quadrant.

With my hands full of weapons, I don't argue about him buttoning the flight jacket over my chest.

"We have to get to formation." His hands cradle my face. "And if I have to go, then don't worry. I'm sure Sgaeyl will drag me back in a few days." He leans in and kisses me hard and quick. "Wanting you will be the death of me. Let's go."

The best thing about a war college in complete and utter chaos? No one notices when I slip out of my wingleader's room and into the sea of riders, all tugging on their own clothes to get to formation. Everyone is running on adrenaline, too busy getting their shit together to notice what I'm doing or the brief touch of Xaden's hand against mine before he heads toward leadership gathered near the dais in the courtyard.

I'm not the only one still in my dress uniform, either.

The wind has a bite to it as I make it into formation, but at least Xaden's flight jacket keeps my hair tucked away.

"This had better be good, because I was finally taking my shot with that gorgeous brunette healer," Ridoc whines as he steps into formation behind me.

Liam stands to my right, still buttoning the top on his uniform.

"Good night?" I ask Liam.

"Fine," he mutters, his cheeks turning pink in the moonlight.

"Anyone seen Dain?" I ask Nadine as she steps into formation ahead of me.

"All the squad leaders are with leadership," she answers over her shoulder as Rhiannon jogs up.

Rhi cracks a huge yawn, then glances my way and does a double-take. "Violet Sorrengail," she whispers, moving closer. "Are you wearing Riorson's flight jacket?"

Liam's head snaps in my direction, curse his stupidly good hearing.

"Why would you say that?" I do a shitty job of feigning shock and shove the sheaths into every available pocket in this thing. All three of them, which are considerably deeper than the ones in my own jacket.

"Oh, I don't know. Because it's huge on you and there are three stars right here?" She taps where there's only one star on her uniform.

Well, shit. Just goes to show that neither of us was thinking clearly.

"It could be any third-year's." I shrug.

"With a Fourth Wing shield on the shoulder?" She cocks an eyebrow.

"That does limit it a bit," I agree.

"And a *wingleader* emblem beneath those stars?" she teases.

"Fine, it's his," I whisper quickly as Commandant Panchek takes the dais, followed by Dain's father and the wingleaders. Xaden's damn good at keeping his eyes off me, but I can't say the same, especially when there's little doubt he's about to be sent away and I can still feel his mouth on my skin.

"I knew it!" Rhi grins. "Tell me it's good."

"I broke his window." I wince and my cheeks heat.

"Like...you threw something at it?" Her brow knits.

"No. As in, lightning struck...a lot, and I shattered his window." I glance toward the dais. "And look, there he is now, all calm, cool, and collected." My chest tightens as I wonder which is the *real* version of him? The one standing up there, in complete control, ready to command his wing? Or the one I had inside me less than a half hour ago? The one who declared that he doesn't deserve me but is going to keep me?

Xaden looks anything but pleased, and his gaze locks with mine for a millisecond. *"Fucking War Games."*

Relief and disbelief hit me in equal measure.

"You're kidding me." We got hauled out of bed for War Games?

"Nope."

"Damn." Rhiannon grins. "I wish someone made me shatter windows."

I turn toward her, rolling my eyes. "Oh please, you've had way more—"

"Hey, Aetos," Rhiannon says, leaning on my shoulder and quickly draping her hand over my collarbone to hide Xaden's insignia and rank. "Good morning, huh?"

Dain looks at Rhiannon like she's drunk too much mead as he approaches the squad. "Not really, no." He glances over the rest of us. "I know it's early...or late, depending on your night, but we've spent all year training for this, so wake the hell up." He turns to face the dais as Panchek takes the podium.

"Thanks," I whisper to Rhiannon as she stands back at my side. I'm not up for listening to Dain lecture me about my choices. Not tonight.

"Riders Quadrant!" Panchek shouts, his voice carrying across the courtyard. "Welcome to the last event of this year's War Games."

A murmur rips through the formation.

"The alert that was sounded is similar to what it would have been if this were a real-life attack—to see how fast you would muster—and we will continue this exercise as if it is. Were the borders to be simultaneously attacked, and the wards faltering, you would all be called into service to reinforce the wings. Colonel Aetos, would you do us the honor of reading the scenario?"

Dain's dad steps forward, scroll in hand, and begins to read. "The moment we've dreaded has arrived. The wards we've dedicated our lives to upholding are falling, and there has been an unprecedented, multilevel attack along our borders, putting villages under siege from drifts of gryphon riders. Mass casualties among civilians and infantry are already being reported, as are the deaths of multiple riders."

He's laying on the melodrama pretty thick.

"As we would if you were a battle-ready force, we are sending your wings in every direction," he continues, focusing on each wing until coming to ours. "Fourth Wing to the southeast. Each squad will pick which outpost they will reinforce within that region." He holds up a finger. "Choices are first come, first served. Wingleaders, however, will be assigned to theirs for the purposes of determining a headquarters for this exercise."

He turns to each wingleader, giving out orders, but glances in our direction—no doubt looking for Dain—before he turns toward Xaden. Something about the way his smile slips for a heartbeat makes the hair rise on the back of my neck.

"Riorson, you'll establish your headquarters for Fourth Wing at Athebyne. Wingleaders, assemble your headquarters squads at your own discretion, pulling from any and all riders within your wings. Consider this a test of leadership, as there are no limitations in a real-world scenario. You will receive the updated orders once you reach your selected outposts for this five-day exercise." He steps back.

Athebyne? That's beyond the wards…that's where Xaden flew his secretive mission. My gaze seeks out his, but he's focused on the colonel.

"Five whole days? This is going to be so much fun," Heaton exclaims with terrifying glee, running their hand over the purple flames dyed into their hair. "We're going to pretend war."

"Yeah," Imogen adds quietly. "I think we are."

"Just like real life, you squad leaders need to make your choices quickly, then report to the flight field within thirty minutes," Panchek decrees. "You're dismissed."

"Tairn."

"Already moving."

"We're going to claim the outpost at Eltuval, the northernmost one in our assigned region," Dain says, turning around to face us as Rhiannon leans over my shoulder again, blocking Xaden's insignia. "I'm not getting stuck at some coastal outpost when we know that's not how Poromiel would choose to attack. Anyone have a problem with that?"

We all shake our heads.

"Good, then you heard the commandant. You have thirty minutes to change, pack what you can carry for five days, and get your asses to the flight field."

Formation breaks and we all scurry to our dormitory rooms.

"What do you think our orders will be when we get there?" Rhiannon asks as we force our way through the bottleneck of cadets all trying to get into the barracks. "More eggs to hunt?"

"Guess we're about to find out."

It takes ten minutes to wrap my knees and support my shoulders for a long flight, then dress in my own flight leathers. It takes another five minutes to detangle my hair from Xaden's handling and braid it, which leaves me exactly five to pack. I throw Xaden's jacket in my rucksack just in case anyone snoops through my room while I'm gone.

"Wear every single dagger you own," Xaden demands, startling me.

"I'm already wearing twelve." I continue throwing items into my overnight pack.

"Good."

"I'll see you on the flight field, right?" If he leaves without saying goodbye, I'm going to track him down and kill him myself.

"Yes." His reply is curt, but I finish packing and head out, meeting Rhiannon and Liam in the hallway.

A buzz of excitement accompanies the crowd as we make our way to the flight field, taking rations the kitchen staff hands out near commons on our way. No doubt we'll be eating breakfast midflight.

When we arrive, it takes me a second to absorb the sight. Every dragon from the quadrant fills the field, standing in the same formation we keep in the courtyard, and hundreds of mage lights float overhead like hovering stars, giving the space an otherworldly feel, as though we're in a great hall instead of on the flight field. It's beautiful and menacing at the same time.

There's a nervous mix of energy and anticipation and more than one person hurling up whatever they've had to drink as the field floods with riders.

"We're going to win," Rhiannon states as we make our way through the wings amid way too many snarling dragons and snapping teeth. We're not the only ones anxious tonight. "We're the best. We'll win." Her face is set in lines of determination. "I can almost taste that squad leader designation for next year."

"You'll get it," I tell her, then turn toward Liam as we approach our section. "What about you? Want to distinguish yourself with glory so you can rise to squad leader?" He's a shoo-in with his hand-to-hand skills and stellar marks in classes.

"We'll see." He's unusually tense as we keep walking.

We make it to our dragons, and I can't help but notice that Tairn is standing in what should be Cath's spot, forcing Dain's dragon to the side as Dain does a head count. My egotistical dragon is already saddled with Andarna under his wing.

Shit. They're going to force Andarna to keep up with us.

"And if we take enemy fire, then you find the first available cover and hide just like last scenario. You're too shiny for your own good," Tairn tells her.

"All right."

"What are you wearing?" I ask Andarna, who struts out from under Tairn's wing with her head held high, boasting a contraption that reminds me of a saddle but isn't.

"The wingleader had it made for me. See? It hooks to Tairn's."

I can't help but smile as I see the shape of the triangle on Andarna's back that I'm sure fits the one on Tairn's chest. "It's amazing."

"It's just in case I can't keep up. Now I can come along!"

Just another reason to adore Xaden.

"Well, I love it." I turn to Tairn, who's busy snapping at Cath to give him more room. "Need me to attach anything?"

"I have it handled."

"I'm sure you do." Then it hits me. Five days. *Damn.* "Are you going to be all right if you're separ—"

"Second Squad!" Dain calls out. "Prepare for a four-hour first leg of our flight. We'll need to keep a tight formation for the first fifteen minutes as the squads disperse." He glances my way, then over my shoulder. "Wingleader?"

I pivot and see Xaden striding our way, the hilts of two swords strapped to his back rising above his shoulders, and my throat closes. How am I supposed to say goodbye to him in front of all these people? And worse, how are our dragons going to cope?

"Don't worry, Silver One," Tairn interjects, his tone resolved. *"Everything*

is as it should be."

"How can I help you?" Dain bites out, his shoulders straightening.

"I need you," Xaden says to me.

"I'm sorry?" Dain retorts before I can even nod.

"Relax, he just wants to say goodbye," I explain.

"If you're saying goodbye, it's to him," Xaden corrects, nodding at Dain. "I'm constructing my headquarters squad and you're coming with me. So are Liam and Imogen."

My jaw unhinges. I'm *what*?

"The fuck you are," Dain barks, stepping forward. "She's a first-year, and Athebyne is beyond the wards."

Xaden blinks. "I don't hear you giving me the same argument about Mairi."

I look over my shoulder, and sure enough, Liam stands with his chin raised in front of Deigh. It's almost as if he expected this.

"What is going on?" I ask Xaden.

"Liam is the best cadet among the first-years, even with you assigning him guard duty over Violet," Dain argues, folding his arms across his chest.

"And Sorrengail wields lightning," Xaden counters, taking a step closer so his arm brushes my shoulder. "And not that I owe you an explanation, *second-year*, because I don't, but Sgaeyl and Tairn can't be separated for longer than a few days—"

Of course. Now it makes sense.

"That you know of!" Dain exclaims. "Or can you honestly tell me Sgaeyl was at her wit's end when you showed up at Montserrat? You've never fully tested how long they can be apart."

"Feel like asking her yourself?" Xaden quips, arching a brow.

A low growl rumbles as Sgaeyl stalks forward, menace gleaming in her eyes. My heart launches into my throat on Dain's behalf. It doesn't matter how often I'm around her—there's always a part of me that sees her as the death sentence she is.

"Don't do this. Riders are known to die during War Games, and she's safer with me," Dain argues. "Anything could happen once we're away from Basgiath, let alone you taking her beyond the wards."

"I'm not dignifying that with a response. This is an order."

Dain's eyes narrow. "Or has this been your plan all along? To separate her from her squad so you can use her to get your need for revenge on her mother?"

"Dain!" I shake my head at him. "You know that's not going to happen."

"Do I?" he fires back. "He's made a big deal out of the whole if-she-dies-I-die thing, but do you know it for a fact? Do you know Tairn won't survive your death? Or has it all been a ploy to earn your trust, Violet?"

I suck in a sharp breath. "You need to stop right now."

"Please, do quit while you're behind, Aetos," Xaden seethes. "You want the truth? She's a fuck of a lot safer with me beyond the wards than she is with you within them. We both know it." The look in his eyes is similar to the one in Sgaeyl's, and it dawns on me why she chose him. They're both ruthless, both willing to annihilate whatever stands between them and what they want.

And Dain is in Xaden's path.

"Stop." I put my hand on Xaden's arm. "Xaden, stop. If you want me to go with you, I'll go. It's that simple."

His gaze shifts to meet mine and immediately softens.

"No fucking way," Dain whispers, but it reverberates in my bones like a lightning strike.

I pivot, dropping my hand from Xaden's arm, but it's obvious by Dain's expression that he now knows there's something between Xaden and me—and he's hurt. My stomach hits the ground. "Dain..."

"Him?" Dain's eyes widen and his face flushes. "You and...*him*?" He shakes his head. "People talk, and I thought that's all it was, but you..." Disappointment drops his shoulders. "Don't go, Violet. Please. He's going to get you killed."

"I know you think Xaden has ulterior motives, but I trust him. He's had every opportunity and has *never* hurt me." I move toward Dain. "At some point, you have to let this go."

Dain looks horrified for a second but quickly masks it. "If he's what you choose..." He sighs. "Then I guess that has to be enough for me, doesn't it?"

"Yes." I nod. Thank gods all this nonsense is about to be past us.

He swallows hard and leans in to whisper, "I'll miss you, Violet." Then he pivots on his heel and heads for Cath.

"Thank you for trusting me," Xaden says as I reach Tairn's foreleg.

"Always."

"We have to ride."

He pauses, like he's going to say more, but turns away instead. As he heads back to Sgaeyl, I can't help but note both of the important men are walking away from me right now, in opposite directions, and given the one I've chosen to follow, my life is about to change forever.

The first known gryphon attack occurred in 1 AU (After Unification) near what is now the trading post of Resson. At the edge of the dragon-protected border, the post has always been vulnerable to attack and, over the course of the past six centuries, has changed hands no less than eleven times in what has become a never-ending war to secure our borders from our power-hungry enemies.

—Navarre, an Unedited History by Colonel Lewis Markham

CHAPTER THIRTY-FOUR

We fly into the morning and then the afternoon, and when Andarna can't keep up, she hooks on to Tairn's harness midflight. She's asleep by the time Xaden chooses to skirt the thousands-foot-high Cliffs of Dralor that give Tyrrendor a geological advantage over every province in the kingdom—over every province on the Continent, really, and go around instead, heading into the mountains north of Athebyne.

There's a pulling sensation in my chest, then a *snap* as we cross the barrier of the wards.

"It feels different," I tell Tairn.

"Without the wards, magic is wilder here. It's easier for dragons to communicate within the wards. The wingleader will have to take that into account when commanding his wing from this outpost."

"I'm sure he's already thought of that."

It's nearly one o'clock in the afternoon when we approach Athebyne, stopping, at the orders of the dragons, at a lake closest to the outpost so they can drink. The surface of the lake is smooth as glass, reflecting the jagged peaks in front of us with breathtaking accuracy before the riot lands on the shoreline and sends ripples over the water in tiny shock waves. A thick forest of trees and heavy boulders surround one edge of the water, and nearby grass is trampled, which means we're not the first riot to rest here.

There are ten dragons in all with us, and though I might not recognize each one of them, I know that Liam and I are the only first-years in the group. Deigh lands beside Tairn, and Liam jumps from his seat like we haven't just spent seven hours in the sky.

"You both need to drink and probably eat something," I tell them as I unbuckle from the saddle. My thighs are sore and cramping, but it's not quite as bad as it was at Montserrat. The extra hours in the saddle this last month have helped.

Tairn pops a talon onto a latch, and Andarna plops to the ground, shaking her head, body, then tail.

"And you need to sleep," Tairn replies. *"You've been up all night."*

"I'll sleep when you do." Navigating his spikes carefully, I slide down his foreleg to the mossy edge of the shore.

"I can go for days without sleep. I'd rather you not fire off lightning bolts out of sleep deprivation."

It's on the tip of my tongue to retort that it takes effort to wield lightning, but after I shattered Xaden's window last night, I'm not sure I have any expertise on the subject. Or maybe it's just Xaden who makes me lose control. Either way, I'm dangerous to be around. I'm surprised Carr hasn't given up on me.

"It's strange to be beyond the wards," I say, changing the subject.

Tairn's talons dig into the soil as Liam approaches, stretching his neck high above his shoulders. From the general agitation of the riot, I wonder if it's something they all feel, this *wrongness* in the air that has the hairs on the back of my neck standing on end.

"We're twenty minutes out from Athebyne, so hydrate! We have no idea what kind of scenario is waiting for us," Xaden calls out, his voice carrying over the squad.

"You doing all right?" Liam asks, coming my way as Tairn and Andarna both take the few steps they need to access the water.

"Stay with Tairn," I tell Andarna. She's a shiny target this far from the protection of the Vale.

"I will."

Gods, I should have left her at Basgiath. What the hell was I thinking, bringing her out here? She's just a kid, and this flight has been grueling.

"It was never your choice," Tairn lectures. *"Humans, even bonded ones, do not decide where dragons fly. Even one as young as Andarna knows her own mind."* His words bring little comfort. When push comes to shove, I'm responsible for her safety.

"Violet?" Concern furrows Liam's brow.

"If I say I'm not sure, will you think less of me?" There are so many ways to answer that question. Physically, I'm sore but fine, but mentally… Well, I'm a mess of anxiety and anticipation for what the War Games will bring. We were warned the quadrant always loses ten percent of the graduating class in the final test, but it's more than that. I just can't put my finger on it.

"I'd think you're being honest."

I glance to the left and see Xaden deep in conversation with Garrick. Naturally, the section leader made the cut for Xaden's personal squad.

Xaden looks my way, our eyes locking for a second, and that's all it takes to remind my body that I had him naked a few hours ago, the lines of his carved muscles straining against my skin. I'm so damned in love with that man. How am I supposed to keep it off my face?

Just be professional. That's all I have to do. Though the way I'm hyperaware of each and every thing he's said and done since leaving his bedroom pretty much makes me a walking example of why first-years shouldn't sleep with their wingleaders, let alone fall in love with them. Good thing he's only my wingleader for another week or so.

"Keep looking at me like that and we'll be stopped longer than a half hour," he warns without looking at me.

"Promise?"

His gaze whips my way, and I swear I see him actually *smile* before turning back toward Garrick.

"You doing all right with whatever is going on there?" Liam asks, startling me.

"And if I tell you I'm not sure?" I give him the same answer, my lips curving.

"I'd think you got yourself in over your head." The look on his face is anything but teasing now.

"For someone who said he owes Xaden everything, that's not a glowing recommendation." I drop my pack to the ground and roll the tense muscles of my shoulders. "Don't turn into Dain on me."

"You feeling all right?" Xaden asks.

"Fine. Just a little sore." The last thing I want to be is a burden for him.

"It's not that." Liam grimaces. "It's just that I know his priorities."

"I'm really sorry you got dragged along on my account," I say quietly so the others won't hear. "You should be at one of the midland posts with Dain, not being hauled past the wards. Colonel Aetos is a fair man, but I have no doubt this assignment is meant to 'give the marked wingleader his due.'" I finish the last in a fair imitation of Dain's dad, and Liam rolls his eyes.

"I'm not scared, no one is *hauling* me, and believe it or not, Violet, sometimes my orders actually don't revolve solely around you. I do have other skills, you know," he teases with a grin, flashing a dimple as he hip-checks me.

"I've never once forgotten how amazing you are, Liam." And I mean it. He coughs, and I gesture him off. "Now, I need a moment of privacy."

He bows with a wave of a hand, as though introducing me to the forest behind us, and I head off into their shadowy depths.

When I return to the shore of the lake, Xaden walks away from Garrick and holds out his hand as he approaches.

My eyebrows rise. Is he… No. He wouldn't. Not in front of the eight other cadets.

He laces his fingers with mine. *Guess he would.* It's more than the touch of his skin that has my pulse leaping. He's breaking his own rule.

I glance pointedly toward where the others are gathered, all in various states of relaxation by the shore, but my hand tightens around his.

"None of them is going to say a single word about you—or us. I trust every single person here with my life," he says, leading me toward a cluster of boulders almost twice his height on the far side of the lake.

"People talk. Let them." I'm not ashamed of loving him, and I can handle any mean-spirited gossip that comes my way.

"You say that now." His jaw flexes. "Did you get enough to drink? Or eat?"

"I brought everything I needed in my pack. You don't have to worry about me."

"Worrying about you is ninety-nine percent of what I do." His thumb strokes the back of my hand. "When we make it to the outpost, I want you to rest after we get our scenario objective. Liam will stay while I most likely take the third-years out to patrol."

"I want to help," I immediately protest. Wasn't that why he brought me? For my lightning? Not that I'm exactly winning any accuracy awards, but still.

"You can, after you rest up. You have to be at full strength to wield that signet of yours, or you'll risk burning out. Tairn is too powerful."

He makes a decent point, but it doesn't mean I have to like it.

Once we're out of sight of the others, he backs me against the largest boulder and then lowers into a crouch before me.

"What are you doing?" I run my fingers through his hair just because I can. The fact that I get to touch this man is absolutely mind-blowing, and I plan on taking every advantage of the privilege while I can.

"Your legs are stiff." He starts at my calves, working the knots loose with his strong hands.

"I guess we can't really leave until the dragons are ready anyway, right?" His touch feels downright decadent.

"Right. We have another ten minutes or so." He flashes a wicked grin at me.

Ten minutes. Considering we really have no idea what the rest of the day will bring, I'm more than happy to grab ahold of what time we have.

I groan as my muscles melt and my head falls back to rest on the boulder. "That hurts so wonderfully. Thank you."

He laughs, making his way up to the tense muscles of my thighs. "Trust me, my motives aren't altruistic, Violence. I'll take any excuse I can get to put my hands on you."

The scruff on his cheeks scrapes my palms as I slide my hands down the sides of his face to cup the back of his neck. "The feeling is more than mutual."

His breathing changes when he reaches the top of my thighs, his fingers kneading my muscles into outright submission. "I'm sorry about this morning."

"What?"

He looks up at me, the sunlight catching the gold specks in his eyes, and arches his scarred brow. "We were in the middle of something, if you don't remember."

A slow smile spreads across my face. "Oh, I remember." The top button of his flight jacket is undone, and I grip the fabric and tug him toward me. At what point is this constant craving for him going to be assuaged? I've had him multiple times in the past twenty-four hours and could still go another round…or three. "Is it wrong to wish we'd had time to finish?"

"Not sure I'll ever be *finished*." He rises, every plane of his body caressing mine on the way up. "I'm way too fucking greedy when it comes to you."

He slants his head over mine and blurs out the rest of the world with a slow, luxurious kiss. His tongue slides between my parted lips to glide against mine like he has absolutely no other plans for the day but to memorize every corner of my mouth.

My entire body flares to life, then starts to simmer when he kisses a path down my throat. He palms my waist, pulling my curves flush with his hard angles, and I'm nothing but heat and need. My heart pounds so hard, it sounds like wingbeats in my ears. Gods, I'll never get enough of this.

He groans, one hand sliding to my ass. "Tell me what you're thinking."

I wind my arms around his neck. "I was thinking you are exactly as I predicted the first time you took me in my room."

"Oh yeah?" He draws back, curiosity sparking in his eyes. "And what exactly was that?"

"A very dangerous addiction." My gaze skims over the silver line of his scar, the thick lashes so many women would kill for, and over the bump in his nose to that perfectly sculpted mouth. I've already told him that I love him, so it's not like I'm keeping secrets over here. Hell, compared to him, I'm an open book. "Impossible to sate."

His eyes darken. "I'm going to keep you," he promises, just like he did last night. Or was it this morning? "You're mine, Violet."

I lift my chin. "Only if you're mine."

"I've been yours for longer than you could ever imagine." As if the words untether him, he clutches the nape of my neck and kisses me long and hard, stealing every breath, every thought beyond the sweep of his tongue and the rising tide of need that heats my skin.

Xaden yanks his mouth away with a gasp, breaking the kiss and cocking his head to the side as if listening for something.

"What's wrong?" I ask. He's gone rigid beneath my arms.

"Shit." His eyes widen as he drags his gaze back to mine. "Violet, I'm so sorry—"

"Is this seriously how you dragon riders spend your time?" a woman asks from behind Xaden, her voice like velvet dragged over a gravel road.

He spins around so quickly, he's a blur. Shadows envelop me, thick as a thundercloud.

I can't see shit.

"Xaden!" someone yells and multiple pairs of feet come crashing through the brush. Bodhi, maybe?

"Silly to hide what's already been seen," the woman says, her tone curt. "And if rumors are true, there's only one silver-haired rider in your death factory of a college, which means that's General Sorrengail's youngest."

"Fuck," Xaden swears. *"I need you to stay calm, Violence."*

Calm? Shadows fall away, and I leave my hands loose at my sides in case I need to grab a dagger or wield, sidestepping Xaden so I can see.

A pair of gryphon riders stands in the meadow about thirty feet away, their beasts eerily silent behind them. They're a third of the size of our dragons, but those beaks and claws look capable of shredding skin and scale just the same.

"Tairn!"

"Coming."

"Stay with Sgaeyl," I order Andarna.

"The gryphons look tasty from here," she responds.

"They're the same size you are. No."

"A fucking Sorrengail." The woman looks only a few years older than me, but she has the look of a veteran rider. She arches a dark brow, looking at me like I'm something that needs to be shoveled out of the horse stalls. The sound of beating wings fills the air as a handful of dragon riders barrel into the space around us. Imogen. Bodhi. A third-year with a scarred lip I recognize. Liam. But no one is reaching for a weapon.

At least the odds are in our favor now. Power unfurls under my skin, and I throw open that Archives door, letting energy rush over me in a torrent of scalding heat. The sky crackles.

"No!" Xaden turns and hauls me against his chest, wrapping his arms around me and pinning my arms to my sides.

"What are you doing?" I throw my weight against Xaden, but it's no use. He has me locked down tight.

A gust of wind hits my right side as Tairn lands.

"Holy shit, that one is *huge*," the woman says. Around Xaden's immovable arm, I see the gryphon riders retreat with quick steps, their eyes flying wide as they look up.

Xaden lifts one hand to cup the nape of my neck as I look up at him. What the actual fuck is he doing? Kissing me before we die? "If you have ever trusted me, Violet, I need you to do it now." The plea in his eyes leaves me stunned. Our enemies are feet away and he wants to… have a *moment*?

"Just stay here. Stay calm." His eyes search mine for an answer to a question I haven't been asked. Then he passes me to Liam.

Passes me. Like I'm a damned rucksack.

Liam pins my arms to my sides with careful but unyielding strength. "I'm sorry about this, Violet."

Why the hell is everyone apologizing?

"Let. Me. Go," I demand as Xaden strides toward the pair of gryphon riders, Garrick at his side. Fear squeezes my heart like a vise that he thinks he can take on the gryphons and their riders himself.

"I can't do that," Liam apologizes, his voice lowering. "I really wish I could."

Tairn roars from my right so hard that spit flies, smacking Liam in the face and making my ears ring. Liam drops his hands and backs away slowly, putting his palms up. "Got it. Point made. No touching."

Free from his grip, I spin toward the field as Xaden reaches the riders.

"You're fucking *early*," he says.

And my heart stops.

In his last days of interrogation, Fen Riorson lost touch with reality, railing against the kingdom of Navarre. He accused King Tauri, and all who came before him, of a conspiracy so vast, so unspeakable, that it does not bear repeating by this historian. The execution was swift and merciful for a madman who cost untold lives.

—Navarre, an Unedited History by Colonel Lewis Markham

CHAPTER THIRTY-FIVE

Somehow, I manage to keep breathing, which is impressive given my heart feels like it might shatter in a million pieces, and narrow my gaze on the enemy.

I've never seen a gryphon rider before. The dragons usually burn them to ash, along with their half-eagle, half-lion mounts.

"What happened to meeting tomorrow? We don't have a full shipment," Xaden says to the gryphon rider, his voice calm and even.

"The shipment isn't the issue," the woman says, shaking her head. Unlike our black, the riders' leathers are brown, matching the darker feathers of their beasts…who are currently staring at me like I'm dinner.

"If they try anything, they'll be a snack," Tairn says.

Shipment. I barely process what Tairn says through the shock of the rider's words. And Xaden knows them. He's *working* with them, aiding our enemy. Betrayal cuts my throat like glass as I try to swallow. This is why he's been sneaking off from the quadrant.

"So you were waiting nearby to chat on the off chance that we'd fly by a full day early?" Xaden asks.

"We were patrolling from Draithus yesterday—it's about an hour southeast from here—"

"I know where Draithus is," Xaden retorts.

"Never know, you Navarrians act like nothing exists beyond your borders," the male gryphon rider snarks. "I don't know why we're bothering to warn them."

"Warn us?" Xaden's head cocks to the side.

"We lost a village in the vicinity to a horde of venin two days ago. They decimated everything."

I startle, my eyes flying wide. She just said *what*?

"Venin never come this far west," Imogen says from my left.

Venin. Yep, that's what they both said. What the actual hell? I'd think someone was fucking with me if not for the two enormous gryphons looming behind the pair of riders. But no one is laughing.

"Until now," the woman replies, turning her gaze back to Xaden. "They were unmistakably venin and had one of their—"

"Don't say anything else," Xaden interrupts. "You know that none of us can know the details or we put everything at risk. All it takes is *one* of us being interrogated."

"Are you getting this?" I ask Tairn, glancing left and right to see if anyone else noticed the pure ridiculousness spewing from the woman's mouth, but everyone else looks…horrified, like they actually believe a village was destroyed by mythical creatures.

"Unfortunately, yes."

"Details or not, it looks like the horde is heading north," the male says. "Straight toward our trading post on the border across from your garrison at Athebyne. Are you armed?"

"We're armed," Xaden admits.

"Then our job here is done. You've been warned," the male says. "Now we have to go defend our people. As it is, this side trip only gives us about an hour to reach them in time."

Instantly, the atmosphere changes, intensifies, and the riders around me seem to brace for something.

Xaden looks over his shoulder at me, and instead of laughing at the utter absurdity of what they're discussing, his face is set in grim lines.

"If you think you'll ever convince a Sorrengail to risk their neck for anyone outside their own borders, then you're a fool," the man says with a sneer in my direction.

Power sizzles painfully beneath my skin, demanding an outlet.

The man leans slightly to the side and looks me up and down in obvious judgment. "I wonder what your king would be willing to pay in order to get back the daughter of his most illustrious general. I'm willing to bet your ransom would be worth enough weaponry to defend all of Draithus for a decade."

Ransom? Oh, I think not.

Tairn snarls.

"Fuck," Bodhi mutters, moving closer to me.

"Try. I dare you." I crook my fingers at them, releasing just enough power that light flashes within the clouds above us.

Shadows race menacingly from the pine trees on the edge of the meadow as Xaden raises his hands at his sides, and both gryphon riders tense when the darkness pauses only inches from their feet. "You take a step toward *that* Sorrengail and you'll be dead before you can even shift your weight," Xaden says, his voice dropping lethally. "She's not up for discussion."

The woman glances at the shadows, then sighs. "We'll be there with the rest of our drift. Just signal if you can get away from the disbelievers." She walks away, leading the man back toward their gryphons.

They mount within seconds and launch skyward.

Every head turns toward me with looks that vary from expectation to something akin to fear, and my stomach sinks. No one was surprised at the gryphon riders' familiarity or throwing words like "venin" around. And they all knew Xaden was aiding the enemy.

I'm the outsider here.

"Good luck, Riorson." Imogen tucks a piece of her pink hair behind her ear, her rebellion relic peeking out above the sleeve of her flight leathers as she turns to give us space.

My stomach drops and my mind races, grasping for anything but the obvious, devastating truth as they all slowly follow Imogen back toward the lake.

There's a rebellion relic winding up a third-year's forearm as he passes in front of me.

Garrick's here. He's a section leader, but he's...here, not with any of the Flame Section squads. So are Bodhi and Imogen. That brunette rider with the nose ring is Soleil, I think, and that's definitely a relic on her left forearm. The second-year from Claw Section? He has one, too.

And Liam...Liam is at my side.

"Tairn." I keep my breathing as even as possible as Xaden stares at me,

his face masked like an emotionless wingleader.

"Silver One?" Tairn's giant head swings in my direction.

"They all carry rebellion relics," I tell him. *"Everyone in this squad besides me is the child of a separatist."* In the chaos of the flight field, Xaden constructed an all-marked squad.

And they're all. Fucking. Traitors.

And I fell for it.

I fell for *him*.

"Yes. They are," he agrees, resignation in his tone.

My chest threatens to cave in as it truly hits me. This is so much worse than just Xaden betraying me, betraying our entire kingdom. There's only one explanation as to why my own dragons have been so damned docile in the presence of the enemy.

"You and Andarna lied to me, too." The treachery of it is too much, and my shoulders dip from the weight of it. *"You knew what he was doing."*

"We both chose you," Andarna says, like that makes it any better.

"But you knew." I look past where Liam dares to stare at me with sorrow, to Tairn, whose lethal focus lies straight ahead like he hasn't quite decided if he's going to burn Xaden alive or not.

"Dragons are bound by bonds," he explains as Xaden approaches. *"There is only one other bond more sacred than that of a dragon and its rider."*

A dragon and its mate.

Everyone knew but me. Even my own dragons. Oh gods, is Dain right? Has everything Xaden's done been a ploy to earn my trust?

The sweet glow of happiness, of love, trust, and affection that burned so brightly in my chest just a few minutes ago sputters painfully, gasping for oxygen like a campfire put out by a bucket of water once it outlives its usefulness. All I can do is watch as the embers drown and die.

Xaden watches me with increasing apprehension the closer he comes, like I'm some kind of cornered animal about to fight her way out with teeth and claws.

How was I ever foolish enough to trust him? How did I ever *fall* for him? My lungs ache and my heart screams. This can't be happening. I can't be this naive. But I guess I am, because here we are. His entire body is a fucking warning, especially the dark relic that's so glaringly visible on his neck right now. His father may have been the Great Betrayer, may have cost my brother his life, but Xaden's treachery cuts just as deep.

He flinches as my eyes narrow into a glare.

"Were we ever really friends?" I whisper at Liam, searching for the strength to yell.

"We are friends, Violet, but I owe him everything," Liam answers, and when I glance up, he's watching me with so much misery that I almost feel sorry for him. Almost. "We all do. And once you give him a chance to explain—"

There it is. Anger rushes to my aid, overpowering the hurt.

"You watched me train with him!" I shove at Liam's chest, and he stumbles backward through the grass. "You stood by and watched me fall for him!"

"Oh shit." Bodhi laces his hands behind his thick neck.

"Violence, let me explain," Xaden says. He's always known my true nature, and honestly, the shadows should have clued me in to his. He's a master of secrets.

Unspent power ripples in my very bones as I turn my back on Liam to face Xaden. "If you even think about touching me, I swear I'll fucking kill you." My power flares with my rage and lightning cracks across the sky, jumping from cloud to cloud.

"I think she means it," Liam warns.

"I know she does." Xaden's jaw ticks as our gazes collide and hold. "Everybody, go back to the shore. Now."

He watches me with apprehension as he draws closer.

"I know what you're thinking," Xaden says in that deceptively soft voice of his, and there's a flicker of fear in those onyx depths.

"You have no idea what I'm thinking." Fucking. Traitor.

"You're thinking I've betrayed our kingdom."

"Logical guess. Good for you." Another bolt of lightning whips free, streaking cloud to cloud. "You're working with gryphon riders?" I leave my arms loose at my sides just in case I need my hands free to wield, though I know I'm no match for him. Not yet. "Gods, you are such a cliché, Xaden. You're a villain hiding in plain fucking sight."

He winces. "Actually, they're called fliers," Xaden says softly, holding my gaze. "And I might be the villain to some, but not you."

"I'm sorry? Are we seriously arguing the semantics of your treason?"

"Dragons have riders, and gryphons have *fliers*."

"Which you know because you're in league with them." I retreat a few steps so I don't act on the overwhelming urge to punch him in the face. "You're working with our enemy."

"Did you ever once stop to think that sometimes you can start out on the right side of a war and end up on the wrong one?"

"In this particular case? No." I point toward the shore. "I was trained as a scribe, remember? All we've done is defend our borders for six hundred years. They're the ones who won't accept peace as a solution. What shipments have you been giving them?"

"Weapons."

My stomach hits the ground. "That they use to kill dragon riders?"

"No." He shakes his head emphatically. "These weapons are only to fight venin."

My jaw unhinges. "Venin are the stuff of fables. Like the book my father—" I blink. *The letter.* What had he written? *Folklore is passed from one generation to the next to teach us about our past.*

Was he trying to say… No. That's impossible.

"They're real," Xaden says softly, like he's trying to lessen a blow.

"You're saying people who can somehow tap into the source of magic without a dragon or gryphon to channel, corrupting their power beyond all salvation, actually exist." I say the words slowly just so we're crystal clear. "They're not just part of the creation fable."

"Yes." His forehead creases. "They drained all the magic out of the Barrens and then spread like an infestation."

"Well, at least that's in keeping with folklore." I fold my arms across my chest. "What was the fable again? One brother bonded to gryphon, one to dragon, and when the third grew jealous, he drew directly from the source, losing his soul and waging war on the other two."

"Yes." He sighs. "This was not how I wanted to tell you."

"Assuming you were *ever* going to tell me!" I glance to where Tairn watches, his head low as though he might have to incinerate Xaden at any moment. "Care to add to the discussion?"

"Not yet. I'd prefer you come to your own conclusion. I chose you for your intelligence and courage, Silver One. Don't let me down."

I barely restrain myself from flipping the middle finger at my own dragon.

"Fine. Were I to believe venin exist and roam the Continent wielding dark magic, then I'd also have to believe they never attack Navarre because…" My eyes widen at the possibility's logical conclusion. "Because our wards make all non-dragon magic impossible."

"Yes." He shifts his weight. "They'd be powerless the second they cross into Navarre."

Fuck, that makes sense, and I desperately don't want it to. "Which means I would have to believe that we have no clue that Poromiel is being relentlessly, viciously attacked by dark wielders just beyond our borders." My brow furrows.

He glances away and takes a deep breath before looking me in the eye. "Or you have to believe that we know and choose to do nothing about it."

Indignation lifts my chin. "Why the hell would we choose to do *nothing* about people being slaughtered? It goes against everything we stand for."

"Because the only thing that kills venin is the very thing powering our wards."

He doesn't say anything else as we stand there, the only sound the water lapping against the shore in time with the echo of his words beating against the edges of my heart.

"Is this why there have been raids along our borders? They're looking for the material we use to power our wards?" I ask. Not because I believe him, not yet, but because he's not trying to convince me. *The truth rarely needs effort*, my dad used to say.

He nods. "The material is forged into weapons to fight the venin. Here, take this."

Raising his right arm, he takes a black-handled dagger from the sheath at his side. I'm brutally aware of every move, horrifyingly aware that he's been able to kill me whenever he wants, and this moment is no different. Though it would have been a swifter death if he'd simply used one of the swords strapped across his back. He moves slowly, extending the dagger as an offering.

I take it, noting the sharpened blade, but it's the alloy embedded into the rune-marked hilt that makes me gasp. "You took this from my mother's desk?" My gaze jumps to his.

"No. Your mother probably has one for the same reason you should. To defend against venin." There's so much pity in his eyes that my chest tightens.

The dagger. The raids. It's all right there.

"But you told me there was no chance we could be fighting something like this," I whisper, clinging to the last of my hope that this is all a horrible joke.

"No." He moves closer, reaching for me and then dropping his hand as if he's thought better of it. "I told you I would hope that if this threat was out there, our leadership would tell us."

"You twisted the truth to suit your needs." My hand curls around the dagger's hilt, and I feel it hum with power. Venin are real. Venin. Are. Real.

"Yes. And I could lie to you, Violence, but I'm not. No matter what you think right now, I have *never* lied to you."

Sure. Right. "And how do I know this is the truth?"

"Because it hurts to think we're the kind of kingdom that would do this. It hurts to rearrange everything you think you know. Lies are comforting. Truth is painful."

I feel the hum of power within the blade and glare at Xaden. "You could have told me at any time, but instead you hid *everything* from me."

He flinches. "Yes. I should have told you months ago, but I couldn't. I'm risking *everything* by telling you now—"

"Because you have to, not because you want—"

"Because if your *best friend* sees this memory, everything is lost," he interrupts, and I gasp.

"You don't know that—"

"Dain wouldn't break a rule to *save your life*, Violet. What do you think he'd do if he had this knowledge?"

What *would* Dain do? "I have to believe he would not put the Codex above people suffering beyond our borders. Or maybe I could have built shields that would have kept Dain from prying. Or maybe he would continue to respect my boundaries and never look in the first place." I narrow my eyes. "But we'll never know, will we? Because you didn't trust me to know the right thing to do, Xaden, did you?"

He throws his hands wide. "This is bigger than you and me, Violence. And leadership will stop at nothing to sit behind their wards and keep the venin secret." His voice is raw as he pleads, "I watched my own father executed trying to help these people. I couldn't risk you, too." He leans into my space a little more with every word, launching my pulse, but I'm done letting my heart make my head's choices. "You love me, and—"

"Loved," I correct him, sidestepping so I can get some fucking *space* and then taking it.

"Love!" he shouts, stopping me in my tracks and earning us a glance from every rider within hearing distance. "You *love* me."

One of those little embers in my chest tries to come back to life, and I squash it before it has the chance to burn.

Slowly, I turn to face him. "Everything I feel—" I swallow, fighting to hold on to the anger so I don't fall apart. "*Felt* for you was based on secrets and deception." Shame burns in my cheeks that I was naive enough to fall for him in the first place.

"Everything between us is real, Violence." The intensity with which he says it hurts my heart even more. "The rest, I can explain with enough time. But before we get to our assigned outpost, I need to know if you believe me."

I glance at the dagger and hear the words in my father's letter as surely as if he'd spoken them. *I know you'll make the right choice when the time comes.* He warned me the only way he could have: through books.

"Yes," I say, handing the dagger back to Xaden. "I believe you. That doesn't mean I trust you anymore."

"Keep it." His posture softens in relief.

I sheathe it at my thigh. "You're giving me a weapon after just telling me that you've been deceiving me for months, Riorson?"

"Absolutely. I have another, and if what the fliers say is true, and venin are headed north, then you might need it. I never lied when I said I can't live without you, Violence." He backs away slowly, his lips curving in a sad smile. "And defenseless women have never been my type, remember?"

I'm not remotely ready to joke around with him. "Let's just get to Athebyne."

He nods, and a few minutes later, we're midflight.

"We know we didn't lie. We just didn't tell you everything," Andarna says, flying in the pocket of air behind Tairn with the least wind resistance as we make our way to the outpost.

"That's lying by omission," I argue. There's a lot of that going around today.

"She's right, Golden One." Tension radiates through every line of Tairn's body and the very beats of his wings. *"You have every right to be angry."* He banks, following the mountain range along the border. The straps on my saddle bite into my thighs. *"We made a choice to protect you—without your consent. It was an error, and one that I won't make again."* The guilt he feels overwhelms my own emotions, melting the hottest of my anger, and I begin to think.

Really, truly think.

If venin exist, we'd have record. And yet there weren't any copies of *The Fables of the Barren* in the Archives—the one location Navarre should have a copy of every book written or transcribed in the last four hundred years, which means Dad didn't just give me a rare book...but a forbidden one.

Four hundred years of tomes and not a single one—

Four hundred years. But our history spans over six. Everything is a copy of an earlier work. The only original text in the Archives older than four hundred years—around the time we fell into war with Poromiel—are the original scrolls from the Unification over six hundred years ago.

It only takes one desperate generation to change history—even erase it.

Gods, Dad spelled it all out for me. He'd always told me scribes hold all the power.

"Yes," Tairn says as we curve around the last peak, its jagged top bare of snow from the summer heat, and the mountainside outpost of Athebyne comes into view at the same time as the Cliffs of Dralor. *"One generation to change the text. One generation chooses to teach that text. The next grows, and the lie becomes history."*

He banks left, following the curve of the mountain, then slows as we approach the outpost's flight field.

My hands grip the pommels when we land in front of the looming structure perched on the side of the last peak in this range. Its design is identical to Montserrat, a simple square fortress with four towers and walls barely thick enough to launch a dragon. The military is nothing if not uniform.

I unbuckle from my saddle and slide down his foreleg. "And somehow we're supposed to be able to concentrate on the War Games," I mutter, adjusting my pack on my shoulders, thinking about a trading post that may or may not be under attack from mythical creatures soon.

The others dismount, and I look back to see Andarna already curled up between Tairn's feet.

Xaden walks with Garrick, looking my way with what feels like longing. I gave him everything, and he never truly let me in. Pain rips through my chest with the kind of cut that only heartbreak can give, sharp and jagged. I imagine this is what it feels like to be cleaved apart with a dull, rust-covered blade. It's not honed enough to slice quickly, and there's a one hundred percent chance the wound is going to fester. If I can't trust him, there's no future for us.

It's more than tense as the ten of us walk beneath the open portcullis and into the outpost. The very *empty* outpost.

"What the hell?" Garrick strides across the courtyard in the center of the structure, looking along the gathering spaces that should line the interior just like Montserrat.

"Stop," Xaden orders, surveying the walls that rise on every side above us. "There's no one here. Divide and search." He glances at me. "You don't leave my side. I don't think this is a War Game."

I start to argue that he couldn't possibly know that, but the whip of wind through the open gate makes me pause. The only sounds in a fortress that should house more than two hundred people are our footsteps on the rocky ground—and he's right. Everything feels *off*.

"Awesome," I reply with more than a small dose of sarcasm, and everyone but Liam—who's my shadow once again—scatters in groups of two or three, climbing various staircases.

"This way," Xaden says, beelining for the southwest tower. We climb and climb, finally reaching the top of the fourth floor, where the door leads us to an open-air observation point that overlooks the valley below, including the Poromish trading post.

"This is one of the most strategic garrisons we man," I say, looking for any sight of the infantry and riders who should be here. "There's no way they'd abandon it for War Games."

"That's exactly what I'm afraid of." Xaden looks out over the valley, then narrows his eyes on the trading post a thousand feet below. "Liam."

"On it." Liam moves forward, leaning on the stone battlement as he focuses on the structures in the distance beneath us. The trading post is maybe a twenty-minute walk along the wide gravelly path winding down the mountainside our outpost is perched on. The roofs of several buildings just poke out above the circular stone wall of its defenses, a drift of gryphons and their fliers approaching from the south.

Xaden turns on me, and the look in his eyes is anything but welcoming. "What did Dain say to you before we left? He leaned in and whispered something."

I blink, trying to remember. "He said something like…" I search my memory. "I'll miss you, Violet."

His body goes tense. "And he said I was going to get you killed."

"Yes, but he always says that." I shrug. "What would Dain have to do with emptying an entire outpost?"

"I have something!" Garrick calls from the southeast tower, holding what looks to be an envelope as he and Imogen cross the thick rampart, coming in our direction.

"Did you tell him about my trips here?" Xaden questions, his eyes hardening.

"No!" I shake my head. "Unlike some people, I never hid *anything* from you."

He draws back, his gaze shifting left and right as he thinks before settling on me again and widening. "Violence," he says softly, "did Aetos touch you after I told you about Athebyne?"

"What?" My brow furrows, and I shove an errant strand of hair out of my face as the wind swirls around us.

"Like this." He lifts his hand to my cheek. "His power requires touching someone's face. Did he touch you like this?"

My lips part. "Yes, but that's how he always touches me. He would n-never..." I sputter. "I would know if he read my memories."

Xaden's face falls, and his hand slips downward, cradling the back of my neck. "No, Violence. Trust me, you wouldn't." There's no accusation in his tone, just a resignation that hurts what's left of my heart.

"He wouldn't." I shake my head. Dain is a lot of things, but he would never violate me like that, never take something I hadn't offered. *Except he tried once.*

"It's addressed to you," Garrick says, handing the envelope to Xaden.

Xaden drops his hand from my face and breaks the seal. I can read the lettering as he opens the missive.

War Games for Xaden Riorson, Wingleader of Fourth Wing.

I recognize the handwriting—how could I not when I've seen it all my life? "That's from Colonel Aetos."

"What does it say?" Garrick asks, folding his arms over his chest. "What's our assignment?"

"Guys, I see something just past the trading post," Liam says from the battlement. "Oh shit."

Xaden's face drains of all color, and he crumples the missive in his fist before looking at me. "It says our mission is to survive if we can."

Oh *gods*. Dain read my memories without my permission. He must have told his father to where they've been sneaking off. I've unknowingly betrayed Xaden...betrayed them all.

"That's not…" Garrick shakes his head.

"Guys, this is bad," Liam shouts, and Imogen races to his side.

"This isn't your fault," Xaden says to me, then rips his gaze from mine and turns to his friends, who are running down the ramparts to join us. "We've been sent here to die."

For there, in the land beyond the shadows, were monsters that dwelled in the night and dined on the souls of children who wandered too close to the woods.

—"The Wyvern's Cry," The Fables of the Barren

CHAPTER THIRTY-SIX

Xaden hands Garrick the missive, and the rest of us rush to the battlements to see what we're up against, but I can't spot any threat in the valley below or the plains that stretch beyond for miles before the Cliffs of Dralor.

"Something is off," Tairn says. *"I felt it at the lake, but it's stronger here."*

"Can you pinpoint what it is?" I reply as panic creeps up my throat. If Dain's dad knows Xaden and the others have been supplying weapons to the gryphon fliers, there's every chance this is an execution.

"It's coming from the valley below."

"I can't see shit down there," Bodhi says, leaning over the edge of the masonry.

"Well, I can," Liam replies, "and if those are what I think they are, we're fucked."

"Don't tell me what you think they are—tell me what you're sure of," Xaden orders.

"The letter says this is a test of your command," the section leader reads behind us. "You have the choice of abandoning the village of our enemy or abandoning command of your wing."

"What the hell does that mean?" Bodhi reaches back and takes the letter.

"They're testing our loyalty without actually saying it." Xaden folds his arms over his chest, standing at my side. "According to the missive, if we leave now, we'll make it to the new location of headquarters for Fourth Wing at Eltuval in time to carry out our orders for War Games, but if we leave, the trading post of Resson and its occupants will be destroyed."

"By what?" Imogen asks.

"Venin," Liam responds.

My stomach drops.

"You're positive?" Xaden asks.

Liam nods. "As sure as I can be without having actually seen them before. Four of them. Purple robes. Distended red veins spidering all around bright red eyes. Creepy as shit."

"Sounds about right." Xaden's weight shifts.

"I liked it better when we just delivered the weapons," Bodhi mutters.

"Oh, and one guy with a giant-ass staff," Liam continues. "And I swear to Dunne, one second the plain was clear and the next they were just…there, walking toward the gates." His eyes are wide, his pupils blown as he uses his signet to see to the bottom of the valley.

"Red veins?" Imogen asks.

"Because magic corrupts their blood as they lose their souls," I murmur, looking up at Xaden, wondering if he remembers what Andarna said the night we took the tunnel to the flight field. "Nature likes everything in balance."

Every head but Liam's swings my way.

"If the fables are true, at least." A part of me hopes they are, or I know next to nothing about the enemy below. Of course, if they're true…

"Seven gryphons have landed next to us," Tairn tells me.

Everyone else stiffens, no doubt receiving the same message from their dragons.

"Andarna, stay with Tairn," I say. Xaden might trust the fliers, but Andarna is damn near defenseless.

"All right," she answers.

"The guy with the staff just—" Liam starts.

An explosion sounds, echoing up the sparsely treed valley, followed by a plume of blue smoke. My heart jolts at the sight.

"Those were the gates," he finishes.

"How many people live in Resson?" Bodhi asks.

"More than three hundred," Imogen answers as another boom cracks through the valley. "That's the post they do the yearly trades at."

"Then let's get down there." Bodhi turns and Xaden steps back, blocking his path with an outstretched hand. "You're kidding me, right?"

"We have no idea what we're walking into." Xaden's tone reminds me of that first day after Parapet. He's in full command mode.

"So we should just stand here while civilians die?" Bodhi questions, and I tense. We all do, watching Xaden.

"That's not what I'm saying." Xaden shakes his head. He has to choose. That's what the War Games missive said. He can abandon that village or his command, who's now waiting for him at Eltuval. "This isn't a fucking training exercise, Bodhi. Some—if not all—of us are going to die if we go down there. If we'd been assigned to an active wing, there would be far older, more experienced leadership making this decision, but there aren't. If we weren't marked with rebellion relics, if we hadn't been aiding the enemy"—his gaze darts to mine briefly—"we wouldn't even be here with this choice. So, all command structure aside, what are your thoughts?"

"We have the numbers," Soleil says, narrowing her brown eyes on the field and tapping her bright green fingernails rhythmically on the stone crenelations of the battlement. "And air superiority."

"At least there aren't any wyvern." I scan the skies just to be sure.

"Uh. What?" Bodhi's eyebrows rise.

"Wyvern. Fables say venin created them to compete with dragons and, instead of channeling *from* them, channel power *into* them." Let's hope there's something in that book that isn't true.

"Yeah, let's not borrow trouble." Xaden shoots a look sideways at me, then studies the sky.

"There are four venin and ten of us," Garrick says, walking away from the edge of the battlement.

"We have the weapons to kill them," Liam says, turning his back on the valley. "And Deigh told me seven gryphon fliers—"

"We're here," the older brunette from the lake says, striding down the battlement from the southeast corner of the outpost. "I left the rest of the drift outside once we noticed that your outpost seems to be...abandoned." She glances over the rampart at the clouds of smoke rising from the valley beneath with a look of resignation, her shoulders dipping. "I'm not going to ask you to fight with us."

"You're not?" Garrick's eyebrows rise.

"No." She gives him a sad smile. "Four of them is tantamount to a death sentence. The rest of my drift are making peace with our gods." She turns toward Xaden. "I came to tell you to leave. You have no clue what they're capable of wielding. It only took two of them to bring down an *entire* city last month. *Two. Of. Them.* We lost two drifts trying to stop them. If there're four down there..." She shakes her head. "They're after something, and they're going to kill every single person in Resson to get it. Take your riot and go home while you can."

Fear squeezes my chest, but my heart aches at the thought of leaving them to die. It goes against everything we stand for, even if they aren't Navarrian civilians.

"We have dragons," Imogen says, her pitch rising. "Surely that has to count for something. We're not afraid to fight."

"Are you afraid to die? Have any of you seen combat?" The brunette's gaze sweeps over us, and suddenly I feel...young as we reply with our silence. "Thought not. Your dragons do count for something. They can fly you far and fast. Dragon fire won't kill them. Only the daggers you've been bringing, and we have those." She looks at Xaden. "Thank you for everything you've done. You've kept us alive these last couple of years and given us a fighting chance."

"You're going down there to die," Xaden says matter-of-factly.

"Yes." She nods as another explosion sounds. "Get your riot out of here. Fast." Pivoting on her heel, she strides back down the rampart, her head held high before she disappears into the tower on the opposite end.

Xaden's jaw clenches, and I can see the battle raging in his eyes.

An unbearable heaviness settles in my stomach.

If we leave, they'll all die. Every civilian. Every flier. We won't have killed them, but we'll be complicit in their deaths all the same.

If we fight, we'll likely die with them.

We can live as cowards or die as riders.

Xaden's shoulders straighten, and the rock in my stomach turns to nausea. He's made a decision. I can see it in the lines of his face, the resolve in his posture. "Sgaeyl says she has never run from a fight, and today will not be the first. And I'm not going to stand by while innocent people are dying, either." He shakes his head. "But I'm not going to order any of you to join me. I'm responsible for *all* of you. None of you crossed that parapet because you *wanted* to. None of you. You crossed it because I made a deal. I'm the one who forced you into the quadrant, so I won't think less of anyone who wants to fly for Eltuval instead. Make your choice." He tears his hand through his hair. *"I don't want you in harm's way."*

In a perfect world, that would be all I need to hear. *"If the others get to make a choice, then so do I."*

His jaw flexes.

"We're riders," Imogen says as another explosion sounds. "We defend the defenseless. That's what we do."

"You saved every single one of us here, cousin," Bodhi says. "And we're thankful. Now, I'd like to do what we've trained for, and if it means I don't go home, then I guess my soul will be commended to Malek. I wouldn't mind seeing my mother anyway."

"I'll tell you the same thing I did after Threshing our first year when we decided to start smuggling weaponry out," Garrick says. "You kept us alive all these years; we get to decide how we die. I'm with you."

"Exactly!" Soleil says, drumming her fingertips just above the dagger sheathed at her thigh. "I'm in."

Liam steps forward so he stands at my side. "We watched as our parents were executed because they had the courage to do the right thing. I'd like to think my death would be just as honorable."

My chest tightens. Their parents died to expose the truth while mine sacrificed my brother to keep this heinous secret.

"Agreed." Imogen nods.

They all do.

One by one, everyone agrees, until there's only me.

Xaden captures my gaze.

If you think you'll ever convince a Sorrengail to risk their neck for anyone outside their own borders, then you're a fool. Isn't that what the flier said at the lake?

Fuck that.

"Tairn?" It's not just me going to war.

"We will feast on their bones, Silver One."

Graphic, but point made.

I will not leave innocent people to die, no matter what side of the border they live on. I will not let my squadmates risk their lives while I run, despite the plea I see in Xaden's eyes.

At least Rhiannon, Sawyer, and Ridoc aren't here. They'll live to be second-years.

Mira will understand. I have no doubt that she would do the same.

And as for Mom… The dagger on her desk means she knows and has done nothing to stop it. Guess I'll be the second child she sacrifices to keep the existence of venin a secret.

"I've been defenseless," I tell Xaden, lifting my chin. "And now I'm a rider. Riders fight."

The others shout in agreement.

A thousand emotions cross his face, but Xaden only nods as he walks toward the battlements. "Liam. Give me a report."

His foster brother moves to his side and focuses. "The fliers are engaged, all seven—six of them. Looks like they're trying to draw fire away from the civilians, but damn, the venin are wielding a kind of fire I've never seen among riders. Three surround the city, and one is making his way toward a structure in the middle. A clock tower."

Xaden nods, then divides us according to objectives. Garrick and Soleil will do a perimeter sweep for reconnaissance while the rest of us target the venin on various sides of Resson, keeping an eye on the advance on the clock tower as we near it on each pass through town. "The only way to take them out is by dagger."

"That means we'll have to dismount and fight once we get the townspeople to whatever safety we can find," Garrick adds, his face set in grim lines. "Don't throw your only weapons unless you're certain of your aim."

Xaden nods. "Save as many people as you can. Let's go."

We make our way down the steps and through the silent courtyard, Xaden leading the way. When we emerge from the outpost, our dragons wait, all perched on the edge of the ridgeline, shifting their weight in agitation as they survey the trading post below.

I walk directly between Tairn and Sgaeyl.

"I knew you'd make the right choice," Sgaeyl says, glancing toward where Xaden approaches with Liam, their footsteps dangerously close to the cliffside at my left. *"He did, too. Even if he doesn't like you putting yourself in danger, he knew you would."*

"Well, he knows me a great deal better than I know him." I lift a brow at her.

She blinks. *"You're a far cry from the trembling girl who stood in the courtyard and tried to mask her fear after Parapet. I approve."*

"I wasn't asking for your approval." If I'm going to die, I might as well be honest in my last moments.

She chuffs and nudges Tairn's head with hers, but he's solely focused on the trading post.

The rocky terrain crunches under my boots as I walk beneath Tairn to where Andarna stands between his forelegs, watching the attack unfold beneath us. I put myself right in front of her, blocking her view of what has to be carnage. "*Stay here and hide.*" I'm not taking a kid into battle, period.

"'*Stay here,*'" she grumbles sarcastically in response.

I bite back a sad smile. It's really too bad I won't get to see her go through her rebellious adolescent years.

"Agreed." Tairn dips a shoulder for me. *"You're a target, little one."*

"*I mean it,*" I order Andarna, stroking my hand over her scaly nose. "*If we're not back by morning, or if you think venin are approaching, you fly home to the Vale. Get behind the wards no matter what.*"

Her nostrils flare. *"I'm not leaving you."*

My chest hurts so badly, I fight the urge to rub the area above my heart, but I square my shoulders instead. It has to be said. "You'll feel the moment when you'll know that there's nothing to leave. And it might break your heart, but when you feel it, you fly. Promise me you'll fly."

Heartbeats pass before Andarna finally nods.

"Go," I whisper, stroking her beautiful jaw one last time. She'll be fine. She'll make it back to the Vale. I can't let myself believe any differently.

She turns around and heads for the outpost, and I pull my shit together and walk between Tairn's forelegs, taking one last, quick look at the valley. Xaden and Liam stand to my right, doing the same.

A screech rends the air, and an enormous gray dragon emerges from a valley two ridgelines to the south…across the Poromish border. It tucks its two legs up under its massive body as it flies away from us, heading straight for Resson.

"Do we have a riot nearby?" Liam asks.

"No," Xaden answers.

It's as though the ground beneath my feet shifts.

I could have sworn I saw a riot of dragons across the border. Isn't that what Mira said at Montserrat?

The dragon shrieks again, spewing a streak of blue fire down the mountainside, setting some of the smaller trees on fire before it reaches the plains where Resson stands. Blue. Fire.

No. No. *No.* "Wyvern." My heart launches into my throat. "Xaden, it has two legs, not four. It's not a dragon. It's a wyvern." Maybe if I say it a few more times, I'll believe what I'm seeing.

Holy. Shit. Is this what leadership has been *redacting*?

They're supposed to be myth, not flesh-and-blood beings. But then again, so are venin.

"Well, there went our air superiority," Imogen says across from us, then shrugs. "Fuck 'em. They can die, too."

"They have created abominations," Tairn says, a low growl rumbling in his chest.

"Did you know?"

"I suspected. Why do you think I've been so hard on you during flight maneuvers?"

"You and I are going to have to work on our communication skills."

"Guess we know all the details now," Liam says.

"Anyone want to change their minds?" Xaden asks down the line. None of us answer.

"No? Then mount up."

I walk toward Tairn's shoulder as Xaden strides over to me.

"Turn around, Violence," he orders, and I pivot, looking up at him. He unsheathes one of his daggers and slides it in the empty spot I have at my ribs. "Now you have two."

"You're not going to lecture me about staying safe in the outpost?" I ask, my emotions rioting at his nearness. He hid all of this from me, and yet my chest aches just looking at him.

"If I asked you to stay behind, would you?" His eyes bore into mine.

"No."

"Exactly. I try not to pick fights I know I can't win."

My eyes flare. "Speaking of knowing you'll win fights, General Melgren will know what's happened here. He'll be able to see the outcome of the battle even now."

He shakes his head slowly and points to his neck, to the rebellion relic snaking around his throat. "Do you remember how I told you I realized it was a gift, not a curse?"

"Yes." Back when I was in his bed.

"Just trust me—because of this, Melgren can't see a fucking thing."

My lips part, remembering Melgren saying he liked to lay eyes on Xaden once a year. "Any other secrets you're keeping from me?"

"Yes." He cups my neck and leans into my space. "Stay alive, and I promise I'll tell you whatever you want to know."

The simple confession makes my heart clench. As angry as I am, I can't imagine a world without him in it. "I need you to survive this, even if I hate that I still love you."

"I can live with that." A corner of his mouth lifts as he drops his hand and turns away from me, heading toward Sgaeyl.

Tairn dips his shoulder again and I mount, settling into the saddle and strapping my thighs in after I secure my pack behind the seat. It's time. *"Find a good hiding place, Andarna. I can't stand the thought of you being hurt."*

"Go for the throat," she says, walking into the abandoned outpost.

Sgaeyl launches to my right, and I hold the pommels tight when Tairn springs skyward with great, heavy beats of his wings.

"There's something in that trading post. We all feel it," Tairn says as he banks with Sgaeyl, plummeting from the ridgeline into a steep dive that leaves my stomach behind. The saddle straps dig into my thighs, but they do their job and keep me seated as I lower my riding goggles to shield my eyes from the wind. We fly into the shade, the sun sinking behind the Cliffs of Dralor and throwing the afternoon into shadow.

Another explosion hits, this time taking out a chunk of the post's high stone walls as Tairn pulls up, narrowly missing a gryphon rider and bringing us level across the post, flying too fast to hear anything more than the screams of townspeople as they run through the streets, fleeing for the exodus at the post gates.

"Where did the wyvern go?" I ask Tairn.

"Retreated into the valley. Don't worry—it will come back."

Oh. Joy.

My gaze sweeps the rooftops of the little post until I see it—him—whatever. There's a figure standing at the top of a wooden clock tower, wearing purple floor-length robes that billow in the wind while he hurls blue flames like daggers at the civilians below.

He's more terrifying than any illustrator could have depicted, rivers of red veins fanning in every direction around soulless eyes consumed by magic. His face is gaunt, with sharp cheekbones and thin lips, a gnarled hand gripping a long red cane made of some misshapen wood.

"Tairn!"

"Yes, let's." Tairn banks away from Sgaeyl, pulling us in a hard turn and taking us into the village. A few beats of his wings later, fire streams from his mouth, and he incinerates the clock tower on a flyby.

"Got him!" I turn in the saddle, watching as the wooden structure collapses in the blast. It's only a matter of seconds before the venin walks out of the flames, though, and there isn't a scratch on him. *"Oh, fuck. He's still there,"* I call out as we cut back across the post to get to our assigned area, mentally kicking myself for thinking it could have been that simple. There's a reason these creatures are what make up most Navarrians' nightmare stories—and it isn't because they're easy to kill. We have to get close enough to get a dagger in him.

I turn forward just in time to see a giant mass of wings and teeth cut across our path with an earsplitting screech, and Tairn's tail smashes into the stone walls behind me, knocking the masonry loose as he dodges the wyvern. We just barely evade the hissing curl of blue fire that streams from its mouth, catching a nearby tree on fire.

"The wyvern is back!"

"That's a different one," Tairn barks. *"I'm relaying orders to the others."*

Of course he is. Xaden might command the riders on this field, but Tairn is clearly leading the dragons.

The wyvern swings around and heads toward the town's center, tucking up two legs and beating spiderwebbed wings. It bears a female rider in maroon flight gear that resembles our own, and her eyes are the same eerie red color as the venin on the clock tower.

"Xaden, there's more than one wyvern."

There's a moment of silence, but I can feel Xaden's palpable shock, then rage. *"If you get separated from Tairn, call out, then fight until I get there."*

"No chance of that happening. I'm not letting her off my back, wingleader," Tairn growls as I get my first good look at the airspace above the city, flooded with dragons, gryphons, and wyvern, just like in the creation fable.

"Soleil found a sealed entrance to what looks to be a mine," Xaden says. *"I need—"*

Tairn turns abruptly, veering toward the mountains.

"—you to see if you can put down some cover so Garrick and Bodhi can get the townspeople evacuated," he finishes. *"Liam is on his way."*

"On it." My pulse leaps. *"Tairn, I can't aim."*

"You will," he says like it's a foregone conclusion. *"Orders are being dispersed amid the gryphons."*

"Dragons can speak to gryphons?" My eyebrows shoot up.

"Naturally. How do you think we communicated before humans got involved?"

I hunker down across his neck as we dart above the city, passing over a clinic, what looks to be a school, and rows and rows of an open-air market that's currently on fire. There's no sign of the purple-robed venin we first saw as we sail over the shriveled body of a gryphon and its rider near the center of town. My stomach turns, especially when I see a wyvern circling back toward them—and Sgaeyl is on an intercept course.

"She can hold her own," Tairn reminds me. *"And so can he. We have orders. Focus."*

Focus. Right.

We pass families scurrying from their ruined homes, then over the city walls, heading toward the opening in the side of the mountain where Soleil's Brown Clubtail swings its tail into the wood planks covering the abandoned tunnel. There are a few outbuildings lining the road but not much else.

Tairn pulls hard to the left as we approach, the strap digging into my legs as my weight shifts in the saddle with the abrupt motion. Then he flares his wings to hover in front of Soleil, facing Resson and the screaming crowd that runs the hundred yards between the city walls and us, led by a pair of gryphons and their fliers who continuously look behind them, scanning the skies.

But what they don't see is the venin striding our way from north of the gate, watching the crowd's movement with a narrowed red gaze. The veins on both sides of her eyes are more pronounced than the earlier rider's, and her long blue robe reminds me of the staff bearer who survived the clock-tower blast.

"I've already told Fuil. She'll protect Soleil," Tairn says, angling toward the threat.

"Get us away from the crowd." Power already sizzles beneath my skin.

A child stumbles on the dirt road, and my heart lurches as her father scoops her into his arms and continues to sprint.

Deigh passes, and I see him land out of the corner of my eye as I lift my arms and let my power rip free, focusing on the venin.

Lightning cracks. A section of the city wall crumbles.

Fuck.

"Keep going. Deigh says they need more time!" Tairn urges.

I make the mistake of turning in the saddle, noting that both Liam and Soleil are unseated, ushering the townspeople into the mine, while Deigh and Fuil guard separate sides of the evacuation path. If anything happens—if one of those wyvern circling the town decides to take notice—they're vulnerable. But so are the people they're protecting.

A trio of gryphons flies in, all three dangling townspeople from their talons, dropping them off at the entrance to the mine and looping back for another run.

Energy rips through me as I aim a bolt for the venin, this one shattering an outbuilding along the hillside to our right. Boards split and wood flies as it collapses.

The venin's attention whips upward, and my stomach twists when she spots me. There's pure malice in her red eyes as she reaches forward with her left hand, then flips it, fisting air.

Rocks tumble down the mountainside.

Soleil throws up her hands, stopping the slide before it can crush the people running into the mine below. Her arms shake, but the boulders fall on either side of the evacuation path, leaving the escape clear.

I whip back toward the venin and gasp.

Raw power is palpable in the air, lifting the hairs on my arms as the venin stands with her palms lowered to the ground. The grass around her turns brown, then the flowers of the wild clover bushes wilt and the leaves curl, losing all their color.

"Tairn, is she…"

"Channeling," he growls.

I fling another flare of energy as the blight spreads outward from the venin, as though she's draining the very essence of the land, but it hits too close to the road, and the straggler racing toward safety, for my comfort.

"Watch out. Deigh says that building on the other side of the road has a crate of something marked with Liam's family crest," Tairn tells me as I fire off another blast that lands nowhere near the venin. *"He says it's highly… unstable,"* he finishes, pausing as he relays the information.

"Not worried about the building,*"* I reply as the circle of death expands under Tairn's beating wings, and I draw more power from Tairn, poising to strike again.

Soleil charges toward the venin with Fuil on her heels, her dagger palmed and ready as the rest of the group of townspeople make it into the tunnel.

This is all worth it as long as they survive.

The wave of death pushes forward from the venin, flowing outward and catching up with the fleeing civilian in the middle of the road. He falls, then screams soundlessly, curling in on himself as his body becomes nothing but a husk of a shell.

Air freezes in my lungs and my heart stutters. The venin just…

"Soleil!" I yell, but it's already too late. The third-year stumbles a few steps into the dead zone, her dragon reaching for her as they both buckle and fall, Fuil throwing up a cloud of dirt with her heavy impact.

They desiccate in a matter of seconds, their bodies shriveling. A vise clamps around my chest, and for a second, I can't breathe. The venin has even more power now.

"Tell Deigh!" I look back over my shoulder to see Liam sprinting for

Deigh. He needs time.

"Already done." Tairn rolls left as a fireball churns up at us, the first of a volley that causes us to retreat across the road.

"We lost Soleil," I tell Xaden.

The only acknowledgment is a wave of sorrow, and I know it's his.

The gryphons take flight, their riders wielding what looks to be lesser magic at the venin as two wyvern approach, both riderless.

"Tell them to change tactics. They don't stand a chance if they can't get close to that venin," I tell Tairn.

The gryphons change course, and I loose my power again, hitting closer to the venin. She glares up at me, then turns at the sound of flapping wings.

Garrick and the other marked third-years are coming. She's outnumbered, and damn, I hope she knows it.

The gryphons team up, tearing into one of the approaching wyvern as Liam mounts and Deigh launches, escaping the spreading ring of death, but the other wyvern dips low, heading for the venin.

Right on course to pass by the outbuilding.

"You said that building has unstable material in it, right?" I ask.

"Yes."

I can't be sure I'll hit it, but—

"Excellent idea."

Tairn puts us into position, hovering about twenty feet aboveground as Liam flies for the gryphons above us, wielding spears of ice into the injured wyvern's throat. Blood streams as the wyvern falls from the sky with an ear-piercing cry.

One down.

The venin reaches the road, and the wyvern skids to a landing on the dirt path so she can mount.

"Now!" I shout.

Tairn breathes in deep and exhales pure fire as the wyvern takes off, sending the outbuilding up in a blaze that ignites whatever is within. Heat rushes my face, singeing my cheek as the building explodes, engulfing everything around it.

The firestorm nearly catches us, but Tairn banks left, narrowly missing the blast.

I shout, throwing up my fist as we circle back, the wind easing the sting in my cheek. We have one wyvern down, a good share of the townspeople evacuated, and there's no way anything survived that blast.

Tairn dips his right wing low and we turn sharply, getting set up to make another run through town. I glance to the right and gasp. Not only did that blast *not* kill the wyvern, but its rider is alive and well, too, flying toward—

Shit. Shit. *Shit.*

There are more wyvern than dragons exiting the valley to the south, and I'm trying hard not to panic when blazing-hot blue fire streams past us. I pivot in the saddle and see a wyvern on our tail, approaching frighteningly fast as we circle the post walls.

"Any idea how to kill that many wyvern?" I ask Tairn, panic sitting on my chest like an anchor that threatens to pull me under into the chaos of my thoughts.

There are at least six wyvern, from what I can see, all with terrifying wingspans and sharp teeth, and they're heading straight for us.

"The same methods that can kill us," Tairn says, leading the wyvern away from the post's center, where Garrick and Bodhi are both on foot, chasing down the venin from the clock tower, daggers in hand.

"I don't exactly have a cross-bolt handy!"

"No, but you do have lightning, and a bolt of that will stop any dragon's heart."

"Tell me you warned the others how Soleil and Fuil died." Everyone touching the ground is vulnerable.

"They all know what they risk."

Gods, there are still kids down there, some screaming, others heartbreakingly silent as their mothers drag their dead bodies from the streets.

There are no words.

"We need to draw them away from the city," I tell Xaden, turning back in the saddle as far as the bands across my thighs will let me to get a better vantage point of the airspace and the wyvern, some of which seemed to have slowed in order to circle the remains of the clock tower.

"Whatever they want must be there," Tairn says.

"Agreed on both counts. Do what you can to give the rest time to evacuate," Xaden responds. *"We're clearing the edge of town now."* He pauses, and a ripple of worry pushes through our emotional barrier. *"Try not to die."*

"Working on it."

A wyvern dives only to climb again with a human leg hanging from between its teeth.

We circle back, then head south through the trading post, away from the city's center and whatever Bodhi and Garrick are doing. *"They're not following,"* Tairn grunts. *"We'll need to draw them out."*

"That venin didn't seem to like when I wielded lightning."

"You're a threat."

"So let's get their attention and threaten."

He growls in approval.

I open the floodgates of Tairn's power, letting it roil and billow beneath my skin.

As soon as we're outside the walls, I throw my hands up and let it burst free.

Lightning streaks the sky, earning us the notice of the horde of wyvern, one of which peels off its flight pattern and soars in our direction, its poison-barbed tails flicking behind it.

Maybe this wasn't the best idea.

"We're committed now," Tairn reminds me.

Right.

They're finally outside the city walls.

I summon more power and wield, my arms trembling with the effort to control the deluge of raw energy. Lightning strikes once, missing the wyvern by more than I'd like to admit. Dread fills my mouth with the taste of ash. I'm not ready for this.

"Try again."

"I don't have enough control—"

"Try again!" Tairn demands.

I wield again, ripping down the walls between Tairn and me, and more of the energy he channels rips through me. Lightning splits the dusk-hued sky in a blast so bright, I blink.

"Again!"

I let the power overcome me again and again, concentrating on the location of the wyvern as Tairn dodges blasts of blue fire. Finally, a strike hits the one behind us, dropping him from the sky. It hits the hillside with a satisfying crash.

"What about the venin it's bonded to?" I tremble with the effort of controlling the power, fighting to keep it from overtaking me. Sweat drips down my face.

"Hopefully they're like us. Kill the wyvern and the rider dies, but it's hard to tell with so many riderless ones."

"'Hopefully' isn't the best word right now…" I turn in the saddle and watch in horror as two more riderless wyvern fly out of the valley. *"The*

civilians need more time to reach the mine. Let's give it to them."

Tairn growls in agreement, and we speed back over the post.

Xaden has one wyvern by the throat, strangling it with shadows as a third-year hurls ice at its rider, and the other four are doing everything they can to drive the newcomers back with a combination of dragon fire and magic.

Power jolts through me in wave after burning wave as I wield more lightning than I ever have in practice. I swing my arm around and aim another bolt at a wyvern flying near the front gate—or what used to be the front gate. I miss the wyvern but hit an empty tower, sending stone flying in all directions, a large chunk hitting a wyvern in the tail and causing it to spin in midair.

Tairn banks another hard turn and we come back around. I take a deep breath, then call a lightning bolt—this one striking a wyvern directly in its upper back with a satisfying sizzle. The giant beast shrieks, then smashes into a nearby hillside with a thunderous boom.

Coming back around again for another pass, and heady from my recent kill, I throw out three more bolts of lightning in quick succession. Unfortunately, more speed doesn't translate to more accuracy, and the adrenaline rush isn't helping my aim, either. I manage to cause three more alarming explosions, though—one of which distracts a rather large wyvern that had been on Bodhi's tail, giving him a moment's advantage, which his dragon seizes by banking hard left and coming up behind the wyvern and sinking its teeth into its leathery gray neck. There's an ominous crack, and then Bodhi's dragon releases the wyvern's lifeless body, letting it fall to the ground fifty feet below.

"*On the left*!" I shout as two more wyvern come into view on our rear flank.

I leave the evasive maneuvers up to Tairn and concentrate on bringing down as many strikes as possible as the wyvern gain speed on us. My arms tremble, growing weaker and weaker with each bolt I try to control to keep from hitting our own riders.

Sgaeyl is on the west side of the outpost, and my heart crawls into my throat when she flies low and Xaden does an impressive running jump off her back, landing with a roll onto the street below. Almost immediately, shadows pull in every direction and cover the people screaming as they try to run for cover from the snarling jaws of a hungry wyvern.

One of the wyvern on my tail must notice Xaden out of the saddle, because it tucks its wings for a moment, diving for the ground, only to widen them and pull out at the last minute, gliding mere feet above the silky shadows. Shit. It's heading straight for Xaden, its jaws opening wide as though it plans to just snatch Xaden up like a quick bite to eat.

"Xaden!" I scream out loud, but he's already noticed the wyvern, throwing a rope of shadows high above the buildings in a perfect lasso around Sgaeyl's head, and she yanks him up off the ground and out of the path of the oncoming wyvern. One minute Xaden is dangling from the shadow rope and the next he's back in his saddle as Sgaeyl banks for another low pass through town.

But I was so focused on Xaden, I completely forgot about the wyvern on my own tail. Tairn hasn't, though, and starts to climb higher and higher, leading the wyvern from the post as he gains altitude nauseatingly fast.

"Violence!" Xaden screams. *"Beneath you!"*

I look down and gasp. A stream of blue fire billows up toward us. *"Bank!"*

Tairn rolls left, and my ass leaves the saddle, held in only by the straps as he rolls us upside down to narrowly avoid the blast. But when he straightens, the wyvern is still on us. My heart lurches into my throat as its mouth gapes open, its sharp, bloodied teeth snapping as it lunges for Tairn's side.

"No!" I lift my arms to throw a bolt in its direction and prepare for impact.

A blur of blue shoots between us, and the wyvern is knocked away by the body of a navy dragon—Sgaeyl. Her jaws tear through the side of the wyvern in several rapid, brutal bites, flesh ripping and blood spraying in the most vicious midair meal I have ever seen. Then she flips and catches the devoured wyvern by the head with her daggertail, sending its dead body sailing several hundred feet before crashing to the ground.

Sgaeyl picks up speed, banks, and flies right by us, her wing gliding under Tairn's almost affectionately—which is in complete contrast to the menacing glare that seems directed at me, wyvern blood still dripping from her jaws. Message received. It's her job to keep an eye on Xaden's back, and mine is to watch Tairn's.

I do a quick turn in my saddle, checking all our sides for more wyvern, then tell Tairn, *"Let's climb so we can get a better count of what we're facing."*

We've barely made it a hundred feet above the town when I spy Liam and Deigh flying hard and fast in the opposite direction, with a venin riding a wyvern on his tail.

"Liam needs help!" I rush to explain.

"On it," Tairn says, flipping us in midair. We hang in the sky for a second before his massive wings catch the air and turn us so that we're heading straight for Liam.

The venin raises a staff of some sort, sending balls of blue flame at

Deigh, but he manages to avoid them all as Liam stands up and runs along Deigh's spine toward his daggertail. At the last second, Deigh uses his tail to whip Liam up into the air toward the wyvern. I don't even have time to scream before he lands in a crouch on the wyvern's rear and pulls out one of the runed daggers like the two Xaden gave me.

The venin whips around, raising his staff, but Liam is brutally fast and slits the venin's throat with sickening precision. The wyvern stops beating its wings within seconds, its heavy body free-falling to the ground, and Liam leaps from his back just as Deigh flies beneath, easily catching him.

A wyvern flies at us from the left, approaching with great beats of its wings.

"Tairn!" Power fills my veins and I lift my hands, but Tairn rolls, flipping my world upside down as he rakes his claws and morningstartail along the wyvern, from throat to tail, splitting it open in midair, then leveling out as the wyvern streaks a bloody path to the ground.

The rush in my head is a result of more than Tairn's acrobatics.

For the first time since we agreed to try to defend the civilians in this trading post, since we were told there were four venin and no way we could win, a little bit of the panic sitting on my chest starts to ease. We might actually be able to survive today. Maybe.

Just then, another wyvern drops out of a cloud above us, diving at Tairn, gaining speed as it tucks in its wings, becoming a teeth-tipped spear.

There's no time for evasive maneuvers. It's seconds away—but red fills my vision and Deigh is there, driving into the side of the massive gray beast.

There's no breath of relief as the collision sends Liam hurtling off Deigh's back and across the base of Tairn's neck at breakneck velocity.

"Violet!"

"Liam!" I catch his scrambling hands as he slides by and hold on, a cry escaping as my shoulders pop and subluxate from the strain of catching his weight, and Tairn pitches in a sharp turn to follow Deigh. "Hold on!"

Grimacing, Liam crawls forward on his elbows despite the impossible angle, then grasps the pommels of the saddle. I throw myself over him, sheltering his head and holding on with everything I have as Tairn rolls and banks to keep close but clear of Deigh and the massive gray wyvern.

Locked in battle only a few feet away, their talons shred through the scales of the other amid snapping teeth—and Deigh's catastrophic roars of pain. They're too close for me to act, and there's no guarantee I'll hit the wyvern and not Deigh with my lightning.

There's nothing I can do but secure Liam.

Grabbing the lap belt I never use, I wind it around Liam's torso and buckle it. "That should hold you until we can get you back to Deigh, but I can't wield without hitting him!" I yell as wind whips around us.

The agony in his eyes steals my breath.

"Why did you do that?" I cry, my fingers searching for purchase on his leathers to pull him closer. I settle for the back of his collar and yank. "Why would you risk it?" Gods, if anything happens to them…

His gaze collides with mine. "That thing was going to take a chunk out of Tairn. You've saved my life and now it's my turn. No matter what you think of me for keeping secrets, we're friends, Violet."

Response is impossible as Tairn rolls again, lifting Liam's entire body, and the leather belt slips to just under his arms. I fist my hands in the back of his flight leathers, but there's not much to grab on to. Heartbeats pass and I can't breathe, can't think past the desperation to keep Liam safe, until Tairn levels out again, trying to stay as close as he can to Deigh without risking any of us in the process.

But then Deigh's scream slices me to the bone as the two lock into a dive.

"Can't you do something?" I beg Tairn.

"Working on it!" He pitches right and plummets, positioning himself around the downward-spiraling duel to strike. It should be us fighting for our lives, not Liam and Deigh.

And gods, Deigh is losing, which means Liam—

My throat constricts. *No.* Not going to happen.

"Get over here!" I shout at Xaden. Energy crackles through my hands, but there's no clear target. They're moving too fast.

"I'm hunting the venin at the walls!" he answers.

"Deigh is fighting for his life!"

The heartbeat of terror squeezing my chest like a vise isn't mine. It's Xaden's. *"If I leave, these civilians are all dead!"*

We're on our own. A quick glance at the field tells me every other dragon is locked in its own battle.

Tairn's tail swings out, slamming into the wyvern's hindquarters, and comes away bloody, but the fucking thing doesn't release Deigh. Its claws flex, burrowing deeper beneath the red's scales.

"Deigh!" Liam's scream is raw, his voice breaking at the end.

Tairn lunges, snapping at the wyvern's shoulder and drawing blood, but it's not enough. He swings around to get a better angle on the wyvern, and the force nearly costs Liam his grip, but the buckle holds.

Another riderless wyvern flies at us from the right. *"On the right!"*

Tairn whips his body faster than I've ever felt and rips out the throat of the new threat, shaking the wyvern like a doll, then releases his jaws and lets the thing fall hundreds of feet to the mountainside below.

Then Tairn dives to catch up with Deigh and the wyvern as they race toward the ground.

Dread settles in my chest, ominous and heavy.

"We're on our way!" Xaden says.

But he'll be too late.

"Violet!" Liam shouts over the wind, and I rip my attention from the gruesome battle alongside us as we spiral downward. "We have to take out the riders."

"I know!" I reply. "We will!" He just needs to hang on. They both do.

"No, I mean that's the—"

Tairn lunges again, and we're thrown sideways as he rips another hole in the wyvern's wings with his teeth, raking down its tail with his talons, but the creature has Deigh in a death lock. Its wings are shredded now, but it doesn't seem to care as its claws dig into Deigh's underbelly, like it's willing to mindlessly die to make the kill.

"It's going to be all right," I promise Liam, wind stinging my cheeks. It has to be all right; even though the ground rushes at us, closer and closer each second, it just…has to be.

Deigh screams again, the sound weaker and higher-pitched than the last. It's a cry.

"We have to pull up!" Tairn warns.

"He's dying!" Liam lunges across Tairn's back, reaching for his dragon as if so he can touch the Red Daggertail one last time.

"Just hold—" I start, but Deigh's shriek of pain closes my throat, strangling the words. He's being eviscerated, and there's nothing we can do.

The wyvern roars in victory a heartbeat before they crash into the hillside with a sickening thud. The wyvern limps away on its hind legs and the talons that tip its wings.

Deigh doesn't move.

Liam's raw scream shatters my heart, and Tairn flares his wings, banking hard to keep us from the same gruesome fate.

"DEIGH." Tairn's grief blasts through my body as he streams fire at the wyvern's retreating back, and Andarna's cry fills my head.

No. If Deigh…

"Is he—" I can't bring myself to finish.

"He's gone." Tairn reverses course, barreling for the hillside outside the city walls where Deigh has fallen.

No. No. *No.* That means...

"Liam!" I grab for my friend as we land at speed, Tairn's claws digging into the ground to stop us close to Deigh's body.

"You only have minutes," Tairn warns.

"Deigh," Liam whispers, falling limp against Tairn's back.

"I'll get you to him," I promise, already fumbling with the strap's buckle.

"Deigh's gone," I cry to Xaden, my voice a trembling mess. *"Liam is dying."*

"No." I feel his terror, his sorrow, and his overpowering anger wrap around my mind, mixing with my own until it hurts to breathe.

Minutes. We have minutes.

"Just hold on," I whisper to Liam, fighting not to cry as he looks up at me with those sky-blue eyes, wide with shock and pain. After everything Liam has given up for me, this is the least I can do for him. I can get him to Deigh the same way I know he would carry me to Tairn or Andarna. Tairn lies down completely, flattening his massive frame as much as possible as I unstrap my thighs. Then I wrap my arms around Liam's bulky frame and we slide down Tairn's side, hitting our feet on the rocky hillside far from the trading post.

Deigh lies a couple of dozen feet away, his body folded at an unnatural angle.

This isn't fair. This isn't right. Not Deigh. Not...Liam. They're the strongest of our year. They're the best of us.

"Can't make it," Liam says, stumbling forward and tripping.

I rush to catch him as he goes down, but his substantial weight is too much for me, and we both fall to our knees. "We can make it," I force out through my tightening throat, trying to hook his arm over my shoulders. We're so close.

If a venin comes along, then I'll deal with it.

"We can't." He crumples against me, sliding down my side. I fall back on my heels and his head lands in my lap as his body goes limp. "It's all right, Violet," he says, looking up at me, and I shove my goggles on top of my head so I can see him clearer.

He's struggling to breathe.

"It's not all right." I want to scream with the injustice of it, but that won't help. My hand trembles as I slide his riding goggles up to his forehead, then brush his blond hair back off his forehead. "None of this is all right.

Please stay," I beg, tears I can't fight rolling unchecked down my cheeks. "Fight to stay. Please, Liam. Fight to stay."

"At Parapet—" His face twists in pain. "You have to take care of my sister."

"Liam, no." I choke on the words as tears clog my throat. "You'll be there." I stroke his hair. He's fine. He's physically, perfectly fine, and yet I'm watching him slip away. "You have to be there." He has to smile at the sister he's missed for years and flash that dimple of his. He has to give her the stack of letters he's written. He *deserves* it after all he's been through.

He can't die for me.

"Tairn," I cry. *"Tell me what to do."*

"There's nothing you can do, Silver One."

"We both know I won't. Just promise you'll take care of Sloane," he begs, his eyes searching mine as his breaths grow ragged. "Promise."

"I promise," I whisper, taking his hand and squeezing, not bothering to wipe my tears. "I'll take care of Sloane." He's dying and there's nothing I can do. Nothing *anyone* can do. How can all this power be so fucking *useless*?

The pulse under my thumb slows.

"Good. That's good." He forces a weak smile, and that dimple makes a faint appearance before his expression falters. "And I know you feel betrayed, but Xaden needs you. And I don't just mean alive, Violet. He needs *you*. Please hear him out."

"All right." I nod, fighting to force a watery smile. He could ask for anything right now, and I'd give it to him. "Thank you, Liam. Thank you for being my shadow. Thank you for being my friend." He blurs in my vision as the tears come faster.

"It's been. My honor." Liam's chest rattles as his lungs struggle.

A gust of wind blows the loosened strands of my braid back from my face. Seconds later, I feel Xaden racing toward us, a torrent of his emotions overwhelming my own.

"No, Liam," Xaden chokes out as he crouches in front of us, the muscles in his face working to control his expression, but there's no hiding the despair that pushes at our mental connection.

"Deigh," Liam pleads in a strangled whisper, turning his head toward Xaden.

"I know, brother." Xaden's jaw flexes and our gazes lock above Liam as tears overflow my eyes. "I know." He leans forward and lifts Liam into his arms, then stands, carrying him. "I'll take you."

He walks slowly across the gravelly terrain to Deigh's body, saying things I can't hear from where I kneel, the rocks digging into my knees through the fabric of the leather as I watch Xaden say goodbye.

Xaden lowers Liam, sitting him against Deigh's unblemished shoulder, then kneels beside him, nodding slowly at whatever Liam has said.

The cry of a wyvern splits the air above us, and I look up instinctively.

A cloud of flapping gray wings moves toward us from higher up the valley. Wyvern. Dozens and *dozens* of wyvern.

"Look up at the valley!"

Liam's head rolls slowly as they both look.

Xaden's head bows, and my breath freezes in my lungs as shadows momentarily whip out around him, like a blast of menace and sorrow.

Seconds later, his soundless, soul-rending scream fills my head with such force that my heart shatters like glass against a stone floor.

I don't need to ask. Liam is gone.

Liam, who never complained about being my shadow, never hesitated to help, never bragged about being the best of our year. He died protecting me. Oh gods, and I just asked him if we'd ever really been friends an hour ago.

Just one of those beasts managed to kill my friend; what the hell can *that* many accomplish?

A bloodied wyvern dives for us, and Tairn throws his wing over me. I hear the sound of his teeth snapping and a sharp cry above me before his wing retracts.

"We're targets on the ground," Tairn says as the wyvern flies away.

"Then let's be the ones who hunt." I stumble to my feet in time to see Xaden running my way.

"Violence!" Xaden grasps my shoulders, determination lining his features. "Liam told me to tell you that there are two riders with that horde."

"Why would he tell me and not—" An anvil sits on my chest.

"Because he knew I'd have to be the one who holds off the wyvern as long as possible." He studies my face like he'll never see it again.

"And I'm the one who can kill them all." It will kill me to wield that many times, but I'm the best shot we have. The best shot *he* has to survive.

"You can kill them." He yanks me close and kisses my forehead. "There is no me without you," he says against my skin.

Before I can react, he turns toward the valley and lifts his arms—throwing up a wall of shadow that consumes the space between the ridgelines. *"Go! I'll give you as much time as I can!"*

Every second matters, and these are bound to be my last—*our* last.

In the span of one heartbeat, I look over my shoulder, past Tairn, and see the flaming ruins of the trading post. Townspeople run from the city walls, fleeing the wyvern that circle above. My stomach drops at our failure—we haven't managed to evacuate all the civilians.

At the second beat, I draw a stuttered breath of smoke-laden air as a lone gryphon flies through the haze, followed by Garrick and Imogen on their dragons, and I can only hope the others are still alive.

In the third heartbeat, I turn back toward Liam's and Deigh's lifeless bodies, and rage floods my veins faster than any lightning strike I've ever wielded. The horde of wyvern behind Xaden's wall will tear into Tairn and Sgaeyl just like Deigh.

And *Xaden*... No matter how strong he is, Xaden won't be able to hold them forever. His arms already shake with the effort of controlling so much power. He'll be the first to die if I'm not exactly what he called me under that tree all those months ago. *Violence*.

There are dozens of wyvern and one of me.

I have to be as strategic as Brennan and as confident as Mira.

I've spent the last year trying to prove to myself I'm nothing like my mother. I'm not cold. I'm not callous. But maybe there *is* a part of me that's more like her than I care to admit.

Because right now, standing near the dead body of my friend and his dragon—all I want is to show these assholes exactly how violent I can be.

I pull my goggles down as I turn to Tairn's shoulder, mounting quickly. There's no need to ask him to launch, not when our emotions are aligned like this. We want the same exact thing. Revenge.

I buckle the straps across my thighs as Tairn springs upward, taking off with heavy beats of his massive wings. The bloodied wyvern has doubled back, and Tairn flies straight at it. I don't even care if it's the same one that just killed our friends. They're all going to die.

As soon as we get close enough, I throw my hands out, letting all my power loose with a guttural scream. Lightning hits the wyvern on the first shot, sending the monster plummeting to the ground near the city walls.

But I never see the one coming at us from the left.

Not until I feel Tairn's roar of pain.

But it was the third brother, who commanded the sky to surrender its greatest power, who finally vanquished his jealous sibling at a great and terrible price.

—"The Origin," The Fables of the Barren

CHAPTER THIRTY-SEVEN

I whip around in the saddle and see a venin—the one who killed Soleil, distended, branchlike veins spreading from her red eyes—grasping the sword she's stabbed in between Tairn's scales in the area behind his wings.

"There's a venin on your back!" I shout at Tairn as the venin whips a ball of fire toward my head. It comes so close that I feel the singe of heat along my cheek.

Tairn rolls, executing a dizzying climb that throws my weight back into the saddle, and yet the venin holds fast, grabbing on to the embedded sword as her feet fly out from under her. The second Tairn levels off, the venin stares at me like I'm her next meal, striding for me with nothing but resolve in her eyes and fisting serrated green-tipped daggers.

"Three more riderless ones on my tail!" Tairn shouts.

Fuck. There's something I'm missing. It's taunting me from the edge of my mind like the answer to a test I know I've studied for.

"Aren't you a little small for a dragon rider?" the venin hisses.

"Big enough to kill *you.*" Tairn and I are dead if I don't do something.

"I need you to stay level," I tell Tairn, unbuckling my thigh straps.

"You will not *unseat!"* Tairn growls.

"I won't let her kill you!" I climb to my feet and unsheathe the two daggers Xaden gave me today. Every challenge, every obstacle, every hour Imogen spent in the weight room, every single time Xaden has taken me to the mat has to be worth something, right?

This is just a challenge...with a not-so-fictitious dark wielder...on the parapet.

A moving, flying parapet.

"Get back in your seat!" Tairn orders.

"You can't shake her. She'll cut into you again. I have to kill her." I shove the fear aside. There's no room for it here.

By the dying sunlight and the eerie glow of the burning city below us, I dodge the first swipe of her knife, then the second, ducking low and throwing up my forearm to block a downward thrust, halting the plunge of metal jabbing toward my face. The force of impact results in a snap I know is one of my bones.

Excruciating pain momentarily freezes me as the dagger flies out of my hand. I'm down to only one. My heart pounds as my feet catch on one of Tairn's spikes, and I stumble.

I can't even cradle my ruined, throbbing arm as she advances, gaining on me with every lunge and swipe of her green-tipped daggers. It's as if she knows exactly what I'm going to do before I do it. She counters every one of my attacks with a quicker one of her own, as if she's adapting to my fighting style from mere moments of combat. She's unnaturally quick. I've never seen Xaden or Imogen move this fast.

I manage to parry each of her attacks, but there's no question that I'm on the defense. She's not even in leathers, just a fluttering sail of a robe, and still—

Pain flares in my side, hot and sharp, and I fall back in disbelief when I find one of her daggers protruding low in my side, just beneath the edge of the dragon-scale armor.

Tairn roars and Andarna shrieks.

"Violet!" Xaden screams.

"She's too fast!" I doubt the dagger has struck anything vital from its position, and I fight through mouthwatering nausea to balance the only venin blade I have left and yank hers out. But something isn't right. The wound begins to *burn*, and I immediately battle to keep my balance as acid races through my veins. The tip on the knife is no longer green as it falls from my fingers.

"Such untapped power. No wonder we were called here. You could command the sky to surrender all its power, and I bet you don't know what to do with it, do you? Riders never do. I'm going to split you open and see where all that astonishing lightning comes from." She waves the other dagger at me, and I realize she's *playing* with me. "Or maybe I'll let *him* do it. You'll wish for death if I hand you over to my Sage."

She has a *teacher*?

She's a damn student, just like me, and I'm lethally outmatched. I can barely keep track of which hand her blade is in. My arm has its own heartbeat, and my side screams.

"Level the playing field," Xaden orders. He's split his power and shadows rush in from the cliffs at my left, throwing the world around me—and the venin—into a cloud of complete darkness.

And I have the power of light.

I'm the one in control now, and I know the terrain of Tairn's back like my own hand. Moving to the right, where I can feel the slope of his shoulder, I take up a fighting stance, grip my dagger in my good hand, and let my power explode through the dark, illuminating the sky for one crackling, priceless second.

The venin is disoriented, her back turned toward me. I plunge the runed dagger between her ribs—right where Xaden showed me all those months ago—and yank it out so I don't lose it. She staggers backward, her face turning an ashen gray before she falls from Tairn's back.

I falter, swaying as the acid in my veins burns brighter, harsher, incinerating me from the inside out.

"She's dead," I manage to tell them, throwing the word out toward Tairn, Xaden, Andarna, Sgaeyl…whoever might be listening.

The shadows fall away, letting in the fading light of dusk as I stumble toward the saddle, holding my side to stanch the flow of blood from the stab wound.

"You're hurt," Tairn accuses.

"I'm fine," I lie, staring with wide eyes as dark-black blood sludges through my fingers. Not good. So not good.

I won't be able to fight another in hand-to-hand, not with the wound in my side, and soon I'll be too weak to wield. The strength is flowing out of me with my blood. I sheathe the dagger. My best weapon now is my mind.

Taking a deep breath, I fight to steady my heartbeat and *think.*

"They're falling," Tairn says, and I jerk my gaze from my side to see three wyvern tumble from the sky and crash to the earth.

Riderless wyvern.

Created by venin.

And they all died because I killed one venin.

That's what Liam was trying to tell me. When a dragon dies, so does its rider. But apparently when a venin dies, so do the wyvern they created. All of them. That's how we can save everyone on this battlefield.

There are two riders among the horde Xaden is holding back.

"We have to take out the riders," I whisper.

"Yes," Tairn agrees, following my thoughts. *"Excellent idea."*

"You're willing to gamble your life on it?" If I'm wrong, we're both dead, and so are Xaden and Sgaeyl.

"I will bet my life on you as I have from the first day," he says, banking to fly back to the valley as the other dragons rush with their riders to follow us, no doubt following Tairn's command. Only Garrick and his Brown Scorpiontail are ahead of us, flying low and fast toward Xaden. *"Three of the venin are dead, but one is—"*

I watch in horror as a venin with a staff as tall as he is strides out of the darkness, his menacing gaze locked on Xaden.

"To the left!" I scream at Xaden.

Sgaeyl spins and blasts fire at the venin, but he doesn't so much as pause.

Garrick leans from his seat and flings a dagger, but before it can reach the venin, the robed figure slams his staff into the ground and disappears like he was never there in the first place.

He moved. But to where?

"The hell?" I shout into the wind.

"A general can recognize another general, and that's their leader," Tairn says.

The Sage?

"I can't hold them back much longer!" Xaden yells, his arms shaking so hard, it looks like his body is tearing itself apart at the very seams as we rush toward the mouth of the valley.

"New plan," I tell Xaden as Tairn pushes himself to the max. *"I need you to let the shadows fall."*

"WHAT?" He's already wavering; I can see it by the straining shapes against his shadows, wyvern desperate to push their way through.

"So much suffering." The hurt in Andarna's voice jars me.

I whip my head back toward the trading post and catch the glint of gold. My heart seizes. *"No! It's not safe for you here!"*

"You need me!" she yells.

"Please hide. One of us has to survive this," I tell her as Tairn flies past

Xaden and Sgaeyl.

"Xaden, you have to drop the shadows. It's the only way."

"Tairn!" Sgaeyl shouts, fear edging her tone in a way I've never heard.

"Don't ask that of me." Even Xaden's *voice* shakes. Those shadows are coming down whether or not he wants them to. He's approaching burnout.

"If you've ever trusted me, Xaden, I need you to do it now," I use his earlier words, barely breathing through the searing pain in my side. He'll lose himself to burnout if he doesn't trust me.

"Fuck!" In a blink, the wall of shadow falls, and the wyvern fly toward us with terrifying speed. If I can't do this, no one will survive. There are too many of them.

"Spot the more powerful rider, Tairn." It's the best bet. The only bet.

We're a minute away from a collision.

"Once I've taken the rider out, that only leaves one, Xaden. Just kill that one and the rest of the wyvern will fall."

"I'm coming."

But I'll get there first. Tairn is faster than Sgaeyl. *"You saved us by holding them back this long."*

When he starts to respond, I slam my shield down, blocking him out to concentrate.

Tairn's head swivels left and right, searching, and I break apart the last of my Archives walls, keeping one foot firmly on that marble floor.

"There," Tairn says, his head turned to the right. *"That one."*

At the corner of the flying horde is a seated venin, crimson veins streaking his temples and traveling down his cheeks.

"You're sure?" I ask.

"Positive."

Blue fire erupts from the horde, and I barely draw breath before a torrent of shadows rises from the edges of the valley, snuffing out the flame.

Power ripples in my bones, vibrating my very being with the amount of energy I'm forcing my body to contain.

"Tell me your plan isn't to try and jump on the wyvern's back?" Tairn asks as my breath hitches. Just a few more seconds and we'll be close enough.

"I don't have to," I tell him. *"Didn't you hear what the venin said? I can command the sky to surrender all its power, but I'm going to need every ounce of yours to do it."* I unleash my signet and strike once, missing the wyvern, then again, missing once more.

They're almost on us as I strike again and again, pushing myself to the limit as Xaden smothers the blue flames before they have a chance to burn me alive.

I can't aim. I'm not ready. Maybe if I had another year or two to practice, but not now. *"I need more, Tairn!"*

"You will burn out, Silver One!" he growls, dodging a flame Xaden misses. *"You already walk the edge."*

My arms shake as I lift them again. *"This is the only way I can save them. I can save Sgaeyl. You just have to decide to live, Tairn. Even if I don't."*

"I will not watch another rider die because they do not know their own limitations. One more strike could be your last. I feel your waning strength."

"I know exactly what I'm capable of," I promise as energy fills my body once again, and my heart jolts, struggling to find the right rhythm. Hot. I'm so damned hot, I feel like I could burst into flame myself. I've taken too much power. *"I'm not Naolin."*

Fear threatens to consume me as the venin rides at us, close enough that I can see his snarling mouth, but it's not my terror. It's Tairn's.

"Let me help!" Andarna shouts, and my heart swells even as it stutters from the energy flowing through my veins. I don't have time to look to see where she is—I only hope she's still in the outpost.

"*Only what I need,*" I say to her.

I swallow hard, my good hand clutching the blood-tipped dagger as we fly toward the wall of wyvern. I reach for her golden power, and it spreads down my spine and explodes through me, time pausing around us.

Tairn flares his wing, bringing us to a hover as the wyvern move toward us inch by precious inch, fighting against Andarna's magic with their own.

I have to *want* to kill that venin, and gods help me, I do.

"Now!" I push my arms toward the venin and command lightning to split the sky, and it does, branching out in every direction, but I only need to control one of its silver-blue veins. I focus on the one closest to the venin, bringing it down in slow bursts that defy time. My arms vibrate, and I feel Tairn's power push the boundaries of my body as I yank the branch sideways in its descent, inch by inch with the last of my strength, positioning it over the venin. *"More, Tairn!"*

He roars and lightning itself rips through me, sizzling my lungs and charring my very breath as Andarna's gift ebbs. I don't have to be near her to feel her fatigue, her strength ebbing. But I only take what I need. Andarna will live today, even if she is the only one.

I have only a few heartbeats or this much power will burn through me and take me under.

Xaden screams through the barrier in my mind, and the sounds of his anguish and fear are nearly more than I can bear. But there's no time to focus on him, to wonder what will happen if I don't succeed. Because right now, I am focused on vengeance with a coldness that would make even my mother proud.

Finally dragging the lightning down into place as my skin sizzles and burns, I release time and hold myself upright long enough to see it strike true, killing the venin at the first touch of its energy. As if time were still frozen, his body slowly topples from the top of his wyvern.

In the next breath, more than half the monsters fall from the sky, as if they were struck themselves, and, as if it had been waiting for me to accomplish my goal, the wound in my side threatens to burn me alive.

"On the left!" Tairn roars, swinging toward the wyvern and its rider as they barrel toward us with murder in their eyes.

A rope of shadow flies up, wrapping around the venin's neck as Tairn banks left to avoid the hit, and I barely manage to keep my seat.

Xaden pulls the venin from the wyvern's back and yanks him downward, right into the dagger he holds in his outstretched hand.

Damn, sometimes I forget just how beautifully lethal he is.

Knowing they'll all live, I let gravity claim my body and slide from Tairn's back.

"VIOLET!" I hear Xaden's scream as I fall.

In the event that you come across a poison you do not recognize, it is best to treat with any and every antidote. Either way, the patient will die, but at least this way you would have learned something.

—Major Frederick's Modern Guide for Healers

CHAPTER THIRTY-EIGHT

I think I might die today.

Air rushes by and my stomach feels like it's somewhere above me.

Because I'm falling.

Endlessly falling.

Tairn roars, and it's the panic, the pitch of that bellow that forces my eyes open just long enough to see him diving for me, but I can't feel him in my head, can't feel my feet on the Archives floor, can't access my power. I'm cut off, no longer grounded.

My back slams into something, knocking the breath from my lungs, slowing my descent but not stopping it, and shimmering gold rises and ebbs around me. Wind stills, the cries of mayhem and destruction pause, but the burn inside rages on, consuming me with fiery teeth. *Time.*

Andarna has stopped time with what strength she has left.

I'm on her back, falling...because she isn't strong enough to carry me, but she's brave enough to fly into this battle. Now my eyes are burning, too. She shouldn't be here. She should be tucked away in the outpost, safe from the wyvern three times her size.

Are there any wyvern left? Did we get them all?

When time starts again, wind whipping at my exposed skin, I slip from her back and am gathered close by strong human arms.

"Violet." I know that deep, panicked voice. *Xaden*. But I can't move, can't even force my lips apart to scream with the pain of it all when he puts pressure on the wound. "Fuck, it must be poison. You have to fight it."

Poison. The green-tipped dagger.

But what poison could paralyze me not only physically but magically?

"I'll take care of you. Just...just live. Please live."

Of course he wants me to live. I'm integral to his survival.

It takes all my strength, but I manage to lift my eyelids for a second, and the blatant fear in his eyes jolts my heart before I lose consciousness.

"Maybe it isn't poison," someone says in a deep voice as I wake but can't pry my eyes open. Garrick, maybe? Gods, everything *hurts.* "Maybe it's magic."

"Did you see the way she whipped that lightning straight at that venin's head?" someone asks.

"Not now," Bodhi practically growls. "She saved your fucking life. She saved *all* our lives."

But I didn't. Soleil and...Liam are dead.

"Her blood is fucking *black*," Xaden snaps and his arms tighten, holding me to his chest.

"It has to be poison," Imogen cries—a sound I've never heard from her. "Look at it! We have to get her back to Basgiath. Nolon *might* be able to help."

Yes. Nolon. They need to take me to Nolon. But I can't say it, can't make my lips move, can't even reach out along the mental pathways that have become as familiar to me as breathing. Being cut off from Tairn, from Andarna...from Xaden is a torture all on its own.

"That's a twelve-hour flight." Xaden's voice rises. "And I'm pretty sure her arm is broken."

I'll be dead in twelve hours. The promise of sweet oblivion already hovers at the edge of my consciousness, a promise of peace if I agree to just let go.

"There's somewhere closer," Xaden says quietly, and I feel his fingers skim over my cheek. The motion is unnervingly tender.

Another wave of fire consumes me, singeing every nerve, but all I can do is lie there and take it.

Make it stop. Gods, make it stop.

"You can't be serious." Someone's voice lowers to a hiss.

"You'll put everything at risk," Garrick warns as sleep tugs at me, the only escape from the searing pain.

Tairn bellows so loudly, my rib cage vibrates. At least he's close.

"I wouldn't say that again," Imogen mutters, "or he'll probably eat you. And don't forget, if she dies, there's a damn good chance Xaden does, too."

"I'm not saying he shouldn't, just reminding him what the stakes are," Garrick replies.

Can Tairn feel the disconnect between us? Is he suffering the same way I am? Was the sword poisoned, too? Can Andarna fly? Or does she need to sleep?

Sleep. That's what I want. Cool, blissful, empty sleep.

"I don't give a fuck what happens to me!" Xaden yells at someone. "We are going and that's an order."

"No need for orders, man. We'll save her." That's Bodhi. I think.

"Live up to your nickname and fight this, Violence," Xaden whispers against my ear. Then he says louder, to someone farther away, "We have to get her to him. We ride." I feel the shift as he begins to walk, but the agony of movement against the wound is too much, and I fade into blackness.

Hours pass before I wake again. Maybe seconds. Maybe days. Maybe it's forever and I've been sentenced to an eternity of torture by Malek for my sheer recklessness, but I can't bring myself to regret saving them.

Maybe it's better if I die. But then Xaden might die.

Whatever is wedged between us right now, I don't want him dead. I'll never want that.

A steady rush of wind at my face and the rhythmic beat of wings tells me we're flying, and it takes all the energy I have to lift a single eyelid as we pass over the Cliffs of Dralor. The thousand-foot drop is unmistakable. It's what made the Tyrrish rebellion not only possible but nearly successful.

The poison scorches every vein, every nerve ending in my body as it runs through me unchecked, slowing my heartbeat. Even the irony that I'm going to die by poison, something I have unparalleled knowledge of, can't make me muster the energy to speak, to offer any thoughts on an antidote. How can I when I don't even know what's been used on me? Until a few hours ago, I didn't even know venin existed outside fables, and now there's nothing but pain and death.

It's only a matter of time, and mine is short.

Death would be preferable to existing for another second in this pyre of a body, but it's apparently a mercy I'm not allowed as I'm jostled awake.

Air. There's not enough air. My lungs struggle to inhale.

"You're sure about this?" Imogen asks.

Each step Xaden takes brings a new wave of agony that starts in my side and ripples through my whole body.

"Stop fucking asking him that," Garrick snaps. "He made his decision. Support him or get the fuck out, Imogen."

"And it's a bad one," another man retorts.

"When *you* have a hundred and seven scars on your back, then you get to make the fucking decisions, Ciaran," Bodhi snarls.

Tairn's roar startles me, and I twitch, which only intensifies the already indescribable torture racking my body now.

"What was that?" Garrick asks from somewhere to the left.

"He basically said that he'll cook me alive if I fail," Xaden replies, holding me closer. I guess that part of the bond is still in place. My cheek falls against his shoulder, and I swear I feel him brush a kiss over my forehead, but that can't be right.

You don't keep secrets from someone you care about, let alone secrets that are going to cost me my life any second if the stuttering beat of my heart is any indication.

It's struggling to pump the liquid fire that's cauterizing my veins.

Gods, I wish he'd just let me die.

I deserve it. I'm the reason Liam is dead. I'm so weak-minded that I didn't even realize Dain took my memories and used them against me—against Liam.

"You have to fight, Vi," Xaden whispers against my forehead as we move. "You can hate me all you want when you wake up. You can scream, hit, throw your fucking daggers at me for all I care, but you have to live.

You can't make me fall for you and then die. None of this is worth it without you." He sounds so sincere that I almost believe him.

Which is exactly what got me into this situation in the first place.

"Xaden?" a familiar voice calls out, but I can't place it. Bodhi, maybe? One of the second years? So many strangers. And no friends.

Liam is dead.

"You have to save her."

You're all cowards.

—The last words of Fen Riorson (redacted)

CHAPTER THIRTY-NINE

-XADEN-

"*She'll be all right.*" Sgaeyl's voice is gentler than she's ever deigned to use with me. Then again, she didn't choose me because I needed coddling. She chose me for the scars on my back and the simple fact that I am the grandson of her second rider—the one who didn't make it through the quadrant.

"*You don't know that she'll be all right. No one does.*" It's been three fucking days, and Violet hasn't woken up. Three never-ending days I've spent in this armchair, walking a knife's edge between sanity and madness, studying every rise and fall of her chest just to be sure she's still breathing.

My lungs only fill when hers do, and the time between my heartbeats is filled with sharp, all-consuming fear.

She's never looked fragile to me, but she does now, lying in the middle of my bed, her lips pale and chapped, the ends of her hair duller than their usual bladelike hue. For three days, everything about her has felt as though the life was leached from her body, only a shadow of her soul left beneath her skin.

But today, at least, the morning light shows her cheeks have a little more color along the darker line of her flight goggles than yesterday.

I'm a fucking fool. I should have left her at Basgiath. Or sent her with Aetos, even if it strained Sgaeyl and Tairn. She never should have suffered the punishment Colonel Aetos delivered. For a crime she didn't even know

I was committing. Didn't even suspect.

I run a hand through my hair. She wasn't the only one who suffered.

Liam would be alive.

Liam. Guilt pairs with soul-sucking grief, and I can barely inhale around the pain in my chest. I'd ordered my foster brother to keep her safe, and that order got him killed. His death is on me.

I should have known what was waiting for us at Athebyne—

"You should have told her about the venin. I waited for you to impart the information, and now she's suffering," Tairn growls. The dragon is the living, fire-breathing embodiment of my shame. But at least the bond that links the four of us is still in place, even if he can't communicate with her—which means Violet's alive.

He can yell at me all he wants as long as her heart's beating.

"I should have done a lot of things differently." What I shouldn't have done was fought my feelings for her. I should have grabbed on to her after that first kiss the way I wanted and kept her at my side, should have let her all the way in.

My eyelids scratch like sandpaper each time I blink, but I'm fighting sleep with every bone in my body. Sleep is where I hear her heartbreaking scream, hear her cry that Liam died, hear her call me a fucking traitor over and over.

She can't die, and not just because there's a chance I won't survive. She can't die because I *know* I can't live without her even if I do. Somewhere between the shock of our attraction at the top of that turret to realizing she risked her own life by giving up a boot for someone else on the parapet that first day to her throwing those daggers at my head under the oak tree, I wavered. I should have realized the danger of getting too close the first time I put her on her back and showed her how easily she could kill me on the mat—a vulnerability I've allowed no one else—but I brushed it off as an undeniable attraction to a uniquely beautiful woman. When I watched her conquer the Gauntlet, then defend Andarna at Threshing, I stumbled, stunned by both her cunning and her sense of honor. When I burst into her room and found Oren's treacherous hand at her throat, the rage that made it so easy to kill all six of them without batting an eye should have told me I was headed for a cliff. And when she smiled at me after mastering her shield in mere minutes, her face lighting up as the snow fell around us, I fucking fell.

We hadn't even kissed, and I fell.

Or maybe it was when she threw her knives at Barlowe or when jealousy ate me alive seeing Aetos kiss the mouth I'd dreamed about countless times. Looking back, there were a thousand tiny moments that pulled me over the edge for the woman asleep in the bed I always pictured her in.

And I never told her. Not until she was delirious with poison. Why? Because I was scared to give her power over me when she already held it all? Because she's Lilith Sorrengail's daughter? Because she kept giving Aetos second and third chances?

No. Because I couldn't give her those words without being totally, completely honest with her, and after the way she looked at me at the lake, the utter betrayal—

The rustle of sheets makes my gaze whip to her face, and I take my first full breath since she fell from Tairn's back. Her eyes are open.

"You're awake." My voice sounds like it's been dragged across gravel when I thought it'd only been my heart.

I stagger to my feet and take the two steps that separate me from her bedside. She's awake. She's alive. She's…smiling? That must be a trick of the light. This woman likely wants to set me on fire.

"Can I check your side?" The mattress depresses slightly as I sit near her hip.

She nods and stretches her arms up like a cat who's been napping in the sun before reaching for the blankets.

Drawing back the covers, I untie the robe covering the short nightdress I changed her into that first evening and slowly lift the hem above the silken skin of her hip, preparing myself for the black tendrils that discolored her veins during the flight but receded slowly since we arrived. There's nothing. Just a thin silver line an inch above her hipbone. Air gushes from my lungs in relief. "Miraculous."

"What's miraculous?" she croaks, looking down at her new scar.

Shit. I would be a horrible healer. "Water." My hand shakes with exhaustion, or relief, I don't even care which, as I pour a glass from the pitcher on my bedside table. "You must be parched."

She pushes herself to sit, then takes the glass, drinking the entire thing down. "Thanks."

"*You* are." I set the empty glass on the nightstand and then turn back to her, gazing into the hazel eyes that have haunted me since Parapet. "You are miraculous," I finish in a whisper. "I was fucking terrified, Violet. There aren't adequate words."

"I'm fine, Xaden," she says softly, her hand rising to rest above my pounding heart.

"I thought I was going to lose you." The confession comes out strangled, and maybe it's pushing my luck after all I've put her through, but I can't keep from leaning forward and brushing my lips over her forehead, then her temple. Gods, I'd kiss her forever if I thought it would keep the coming argument at bay, keep us in this one pristine moment where I can actually believe that everything might be all right between us, that I haven't irrevocably fucked up the best thing that's ever happened to me.

"You aren't going to lose me." She gives me a puzzled look, smiling like I've said something peculiar. Then she leans in and kisses me.

She still wants me. The revelation makes my heart fucking *soar*. I take the kiss deeper, swiping my tongue over her soft lower lip and gently sucking on the tender curve. That's all it takes for need to flood my system, hot and demanding. It's always like this between us—the slightest spark sets off a wildfire that consumes every thought that isn't related to how many ways I can make her moan. We'll have a lifetime of these moments ahead of us, when I can strip her down to her skin and worship every curve and hollow of her body, but this isn't one of them, not when she's barely been awake for five minutes. I draw back, slowly releasing her mouth. "I'll make it up to you," I promise, holding her delicate hands between my rough ones. "I'm not saying we won't fight or you won't want to throw those daggers at me when I'm inevitably an ass, but I swear I will always strive to do better."

"Make what up to me?" She pulls away with an inquisitive smile.

I blink as my brow furrows. Has she lost her memories? "How much do you remember? By the time we got you here, the poison spread to your brain and—"

Her eyes flare, and something shifts, something that sinks my stomach like a rock as she tugs her hands from mine.

She glances away, and her eyes glaze in that way that tells me she's checking in with her dragons.

"Don't panic. Everything is fine. Andarna isn't quite the same, but she's… her." She's fucking huge now, but I'm not about to say that to Violet. Her gift is also gone, according to Tairn, but there's plenty of time to share that news. Instead, I say, "The healer told me he isn't sure what lasting effects the poison might have, because it was something he's never seen, and no one really knows how long it will take to get your memories back if there's any lasting damage, but I'll tell you—"

She throws up her hand and looks around the room, as if noticing where we are for the first time, then scrambles backward out of bed, pulling her robe closed. The look in her eyes puts a vise around my chest as she stumbles to the large windows that line my bedchamber.

The windows that look out over the mountain this fortress is built upon down to the valley below and its line of charred trees marking where the earth was scorched all the way to stone and the quiet town—which used to be a city—of Aretia beneath us.

The town we've worked our asses off to rebuild from a pile of cinder and ruins.

"Violet?" I keep my shields up, trying to respect her privacy as I walk to her side, but gods, I need to know what she's thinking.

Her eyes widen as her gaze sweeps over the town, each structure with its identical green roofs, then pauses on the Temple of Amari, which was the most noted landmark besides our library.

"Where are we? And don't you dare lie to me," she says. "Not again."

Not again. "You remember."

"I remember."

"Thank gods," I murmur, shoving my hand into my hair. It's a good thing, proving that she's truly healed, but…fuck.

"Where. Are. We?" She bites out every word, her eyes narrowing on me. "Say it."

"The way you're looking at me says you already know." There's no way this brilliant woman doesn't recognize that temple.

"This looks like Aretia." She gestures to the window. "There's only one temple with those particular columns. I've seen the drawings."

"Yes." Brilliant. Fucking. Woman.

"Aretia was burned to the ground. I've seen *those* drawings, too, the ones the scribes brought back for the public notices. My mother told me she saw the embers with her own eyes, so where are we?" Her voice rises.

"Aretia." It feels incredibly freeing to tell her the truth.

"Rebuilt or never burned?" She turns her back on me.

"In the process of rebuilding."

"Why haven't I read about this?"

I start to tell her, but she holds up a hand and I wait. It only takes her a minute to work it out, too.

She points to my rebellion relic and says, "Melgren can't see the outcome when more than three of you are together. That's why you're not allowed to assemble."

I can't help it. I smile. This brilliant fucking woman is mine. Or was mine. Will be mine again if I have anything to say about it. Which I probably don't. I sigh, losing the smile immediately. Fuck.

No, I'm not giving up until she tells me to.

Things might be complicated, but so are both of us.

"That and we're not big enough to warrant the attention of the scribes anymore. We're not hidden. We're just not…advertising our existence." Which is also the reason this place is still technically…mine. Nobles weren't exactly eager to throw their money at a scorched city or be taxed on unusable land. Eventually they'll notice. Eventually I'll lose it. Then I'll lose my head. "You can know whatever you want. Just ask."

She stiffens. "Tell me one thing right now."

"Anything."

"Is…" Her shoulders stutter as she inhales. "Is Liam really dead?"

Liam. A fresh stab of sorrow pierces my ribs. Heartbeats pass in silence as I try to find the right words, but there aren't any, so I take from my pocket the palm-size, freshly finished carving of Andarna Liam had been working on.

She turns in my direction, her gaze immediately locking on the figurine, and her eyes water. "It's my fault."

"No, it's mine. If I had just told you everything sooner, you would have been prepared. You probably would have schooled us all on how to kill them." My soul breaks all over again when she swipes at twin tears with the backs of her hands. I set the carving in her hand. "I know I should have, but I couldn't bear to burn it. We laid him to rest yesterday. Well, the others did. I haven't left this room since we got here." Our gazes collide, and it's all I can do not to reach for her, but I know I'm the last place she'll seek comfort. "I haven't left you."

"Well, you do have a vested interest in my survival," she quips with a watery, sarcastic smile. "Give me a second to get dressed, and then we'll talk."

"Kicking me out of my own room." I reach for that sarcastic, teasing tone that used to be so easy when it came to her and back away. "New one."

"Now, Riorson."

I can't keep from wincing. She never uses my last name. Maybe it's because she doesn't like to remember that I'm Fen Riorson's son, and all my father cost her, but I've always been Xaden to her. The loss feels like a bottomless abyss, like a death blow. "Bathing chamber is through there." I point to the far wall and stride for the exit, swinging my sword over my back on the way out.

My cousin is leaned up against the wall, talking to Garrick, who's boasting a new six-inch scar from temple to jaw, but they both fall silent as I shut my door behind me. They tense and Garrick stands to his full height. "She's awake."

"Thank Amari," Bodhi says, his shoulders sagging. His arm is still in a sling, recovering from the four places a venin fractured it.

"She's going to have to choose." I look at Garrick, noting the worry in his eyes. He's already told me he thinks she'll keep our secret. That worry is for my mental state if she doesn't forgive me for not telling her sooner. "She'll either keep our secret or she won't."

"That's something you'll have to figure out," he replies. "And then teach her how to hide it from Aetos if she chooses."

"Any word from the fliers?"

"Syrena is alive, if that's what you're asking," Bodhi answers. "So is her sister. But the rest…" He shakes his head.

At least they made it out, and now that Violet is awake, I can finally breathe. "You figure out what that box was that Chradh was drawn to back at Resson?" I ask. Garrick's dragon is remarkably sensitive to runes, which allowed them to locate and retrieve the small iron box beneath the rubble of the clock tower.

"They're working on it right now. Hopefully we'll have an answer in the next couple of hours. I'm glad she's all right, Xaden. I'll tell the others." He nods once and heads down the hall, almost as familiar with the castle's layout as I am, considering he spent every summer here before the apostasy, or *secession*, as the Navarrians call Dad's rebellion.

Funny how people rename everything that makes them feel uncomfortable. We lost faith that our king would ever do the right thing. And they call *us* traitors.

Bodhi wrinkles his nose.

"What?"

"You smell like dragon ass."

"Fuck off." I chance a whiff and can't argue. "I'm using your room."

"I would consider it a personal favor."

I extend my middle finger and head toward his room.

An hour later, I'm bathed and impatient as I wait outside my room in a fresh set of leathers with Bodhi, who's doing his best to lighten my mood just like he always does, when the door opens and Violet stands there.

I nearly swallow my tongue at the sight of her unbound, damp hair curling just under her breasts. I can't even articulate what it is about the strands that pushes me straight into need-to-fuck-her-now territory, and I'm too busy fighting to keep my hands at my sides to question the why of it.

She exists, and I get turned on. I've come to accept that particular truth over the last year.

Bodhi grins, flashing a smile that looks exactly like my aunt's used to. "Good to see you up and about, Sorrengail." Then he smacks me on the shoulder as he walks off, looking back over his shoulder. "I'll fetch the backup plan. Good luck."

Gods, I want to haul her into my arms and love her until she forgets everything except how good we are together, but I'm sure that's the last thing she'll ever want again.

"Come back in," she says softly, and my heart lurches.

"As long as you've invited me." I walk in, loathing the distrust in her eyes.

Whether or not Violet will believe me, I've never lied to her. Not once.

I've just never been entirely truthful, either.

"Is all this original?" she asks, her gaze sweeping over my bedroom.

"The majority of the fortress is stone," I say as she studies the detailed arches at the ceiling, the natural lighting from the windows that consume the western wall. "Stone doesn't burn."

"Right."

I swallow. Hard. "I think after all you've seen, the question I have to ask before I tell you everything is pretty simple. Are you in? Are you willing to fight with us?" She could just as easily decide to turn us all in. She didn't know enough to condemn us, but she does now.

"I'm in." She nods.

Relief surges through me in a rush more powerful than anything I could channel from Sgaeyl, and I reach for her. "I'm so sorry I had to keep…" My words die on my tongue as she steps back, avoiding me.

"Not happening." A world of hurt flashes in those hazel eyes, and I fucking *wither*. "Just because I believe you and am willing to fight with you doesn't mean I'll trust you with my heart again. And I can't be with someone I don't trust."

Something in my chest crumples. "I've never lied to you, Violet. Not once. I never will."

She walks over to the window and looks down, then slowly turns back to me. "It's not even that you kept this from me. I get it. It's the ease with which you did it. The ease with which I let you into my heart and didn't get the same in return." She shakes her head, and I see it there, the love, but it's masked behind defenses I foolishly forced her to build.

I love her. Of *course* I love her. But if I tell her now, she'll think I'm saying it for all the wrong reasons, and honestly, she'd be right.

I'm not going to lose the only woman I've ever fallen for without a fight. "You're right. I kept secrets," I admit, pressing forward again, taking step after step until I'm less than a foot from her. I palm the glass on both sides of her head, loosely caging her in, but we both know she could walk away if she wanted. But she doesn't move. "It took me a long time to trust you, a long time to realize I fell for you."

Someone knocks. I ignore it.

"Don't say that." She lifts her chin, but I don't miss the way she glances at my mouth.

"I fell for you." I lower my head and look straight into her gorgeous eyes. She might be rightfully pissed, but she sure as Malek isn't fickle. "And you know what? You might not trust me anymore, but you still love me."

Her lips part, but she doesn't deny it. "I gave you my trust for free once, and once is all you get." She masks the hurt with a quick blink.

Never again. Those eyes will never reflect hurt I've inflicted ever again.

"I fucked up by not telling you sooner, and I won't even try to justify my reasons. But now I'm trusting you with my life—with *everyone's* lives." I've risked it all by just bringing her here instead of taking her body back to Basgiath. "I'll tell you anything you want to know and everything you don't. I'll spend every single day of my life earning back your trust."

I'd forgotten what it felt like to be loved, really, truly loved—it'd been so many years since Dad died. And Mom… *Not going there.* But then Violet gave me those words, gave me her trust, her heart, and I remembered. I'll be damned if I don't fight to keep them.

"And if it's not possible?"

"You still love me. It's possible." Gods, do I ache to kiss her, to remind her exactly what we are together, but I won't, not until she asks. "I'm not afraid of hard work, especially not when I know just how sweet the rewards are. I would rather lose this entire war than live without you, and if that means I have to prove myself over and over, then I'll do it. You gave me your heart, and I'm keeping it." She already owns mine, even if she doesn't realize it.

Her eyes widen, as if she's finally seeing the resolve in mine.

It's time she knew everything. Knowing Violet, she won't stay tucked away, safe behind Basgiath's walls, especially not now that she knows just how corrupt those walls are.

She'll fight this war at my side.

There's another insistent knock at the door.

"Fuck is he impatient," I mutter. "You have about twenty seconds to ask a question, if I know him."

She blinks. "I'm still hoping that missive at Athebyne was really about the War Games. Do you think there's any chance we just happened to end up in the middle of a wyvern attack at that outpost?"

"That definitely wasn't an accident, little sister," he says from the doorway.

I sigh and move to the side, watching Violet's eyes widen as she sees him standing in the doorway. "Told you I knew better poison masters," I tell her softly. "You weren't healed. You were mended."

"Brennan?" She stares at her brother in open-mouthed shock.

Brennan just grins and opens his arms. "Welcome to the revolution, Violet."

Acknowledgments

First and foremost, thank you to my Heavenly Father for blessing me beyond my wildest dreams.

Thank you to my husband, Jason, for being the best inspiration an author could ever have for the perfect book boyfriend and for your endless support of my dream-chasing ways. Thank you for holding my hand when the world went wonky, getting me to every doctor's appointment, and managing the overwhelming the calendar that comes with having four sons and a wife with a connective tissue disorder. Through the surgeries and specialists, you've been our rock. Thank you to my six children, who teach me more than I will ever teach them. You guys are my reason. Never doubt that you are essential to my existence. To my sister, Kate, love you, mean it. To my parents, who are always there when I need them. To my best friend, Emily Byer, for always hunting me down when I disappear into the writing cave for months.

Thank you to my team at Red Tower. There isn't enough gratitude in the world for my editor Liz Pelletier, for giving me the chance to spread my wings and write fantasy and keeping me fed and laughing during our twenty-one-day stint of finishing edits. No laptops were harmed in the making of this book. But seriously, this book is my dream. Thank you for making it come true with your advice, input, patience, and endless support—it wouldn't have been possible without you. To Stacy for copy editing during sleepless nights. Heather, Curtis, Molly, Jessica, Riki, Meredith, and everyone at Entangled and Macmillan for answering endless streams of emails and for bringing this book to the marketplace. To Madison and

Nicole for all the incredible notes and staying up all night during the read-through. Elizabeth, thank you for this beautiful cover, and to Bree and Amy for the exquisite art. Thank you to my phenomenal agent, Louise Fury, who didn't bat an eye when I said I wanted to write a fantasy and who makes my life easier simply by standing at my back.

Thank you to my wifeys, our unholy trinity, Gina Maxwell and Cindi Madsen—I'd be lost without you. To Kyla, who made this book possible. To Shelby and Cassie for keeping my ducks in a row and always being my number one hype girls. To Candi for handling everything that comes our way with grace and laughter. To Stephanie Carder for taking the time to read. To every blogger and reader who has taken a chance on me over the years, I can't thank you enough. To my reader group, The Flygirls, for bringing me joy every day.

Lastly, because you're my beginning and end, thank you again to my Jason. There's a little bit of you in every hero I write.

Ready for even more from
Basgiath War College?

Read on for bonus content—
an exclusive new chapter
from Xaden's point of view,
in print for the first time ever!

CHAPTER TWENTY-SEVEN

-XADEN-

Dain Aetos is dancing on my last fucking nerve. Between the petty comments he's been making all afternoon and what I'm sure he thinks are menacing glares, I'm ready to lean over and introduce his face to the Montserrat briefing table.

But Violence wouldn't like that, and as satisfying as it would be to hear his nose crunch against the polished wood, I'm not about to do anything that could end this little training session early and jeopardize Imogen's mission, should her squad realize she isn't actually vomiting in the infirmary.

Not that the healer will remember her ever being there, thanks to Imogen's handy little signet. If she's on schedule, she'll be on her way back from delivering the drop I brought with me. The thought makes me reinforce my shields just in case Dain acts on the threat in his eyes. I'm not letting that fucker's hands anywhere near me.

"So all we do is wait for something to happen?" Ridoc Gamlyn asks—by Dunne, did he just put his dirty-ass boots on the briefing table?

"Yes," the older Sorrengail sister answers from the head of the table to my left, then gestures with her right hand, knocking Gamlyn on his ass with lesser magic. "And keep your feet off the table."

The taller of the riders stationed here chuckles and updates the battle map behind Violet's sister, but his face falls quickly, his eyes narrowing with suspicion when he catches me watching him. I scratch my neck at the top of my collar, right over my relic, and hold his gaze until he drops it.

Shit like that is why I keep my inconvenient feelings about Violet to my damned self, no matter how good she looks today or how delectable she smells sitting next to me, like some kind of citrus that makes me want to bury my face in the side of her neck and see just how pink I can get her cheeks to flush. No, if I did that, every rider in this room would look at her differently, and not in a good way. Leave it to me to fall for the one woman on the Continent I can never fucking have.

Still, I'd put myself right between her and Liam, ignoring his knowing little smirk, when I took the chair closest to Violet. There's nothing going on there, but he can back the fuck up when I'm around.

"Consider this your Battle Brief," Mira Sorrengail lectures as Gamlyn scurries back into his chair at the foot of the table. "This morning was about a quarter of the patrol we'd regularly fly, so normally we'd just be getting back about now and reporting our findings to the commander. But for the sake of killing time, since we're in this room as the reaction flight for this afternoon, let's pretend we'd come across a newly fortified enemy outpost crossing our border"—she pivots to the map and marks a nearby location with a red flag—"here."

Aetos is too busy glaring at me to look, so I settle back into my seat and do what I do best—stare right back.

"We're supposed to pretend it just popped up overnight?" There's a little snark in Emery Barnes's tone, but I keep my attention on making Dain as uncomfortable as possible just for fun.

"For the sake of argument, third-year," Mira retorts.

Dain's hands curl into fists on the tabletop, and a corner of my mouth rises. He's pathetically easy to rile.

"I like this game," the shorter of the lieutenants stationed here comments from Mira's side.

"What would our objective be?" Mira asks. "Aetos?"

Dain startles and jerks his focus to the map. *I win*. "What type of fortifications are there? Are we talking a haphazard wooden structure? Or something more substantial?"

At least he asks good questions.

"Like they had time to build a fortress overnight," Ridoc quips. "It has to be wooden, right?"

"You are all so fucking literal." Mira rubs at her forehead like we're a headache she can't kick. "Fine, let's say they occupied a keep that's already established. Stone and all."

Which means there would be civilians or possibly prisoners inside. Wide-scale dragon fire is out. Fine. Liam scouts out their defenses, then I drench the place in shadow for our assault. Half of us dismount while the other half take out the gryphons in the air, and I move in darkness below to free the prisoners while Emery directs controlled blasts of fire by air-wielding, using Quinn as a scout.

My mind runs through three other battle strategies, then stutters on a fourth as I glance in Violet's direction and catch her lips pursing in concentration. Gods, that *mouth*. I dream about that mouth. Fantasize about that mouth. That kiss is burned into my memory like a relic, taunting me with what will never happen again, with what I never should have tasted in the first place.

Mira and Quinn start arguing about the scenario's parameters, and I force my attention back to the briefing.

"How many of you have been called out as third-years?" Mira folds her arms.

Emery raises his hand, and I lift a couple of fingers.

Violet's eyebrows rise, but she stays quiet, just like she has been all afternoon. I crack open my shields just enough to sense that wispy silver bond that's been steadily growing between the two of us—the one she hasn't noticed yet.

"I told you, it's been known to happen between the riders of bonded pairs," Sgaeyl reminds me, annoyance sharpening her tone.

"And has Tairn told her?*"* I ask, to which she doesn't bother replying.

Dain turns a shade that reminds me of a tomato. "That's not correct. We're never called into service until graduation."

I bite back a laugh and offer him a sarcastic thumbs-up.

"Yeah, all right." Emery huffs a laugh. "Just wait until next year. I can't count how many times we're the ones sitting in these very rooms in the midland forts because their riders have been called to the front for an emergency."

Aetos pales.

If he knew half of what's actually happening beyond the borders, he'd probably pass out.

"Now that's settled..." Mira sets a six-inch model of a stone keep in the center of the table. "Catch," she warns before throwing each of us a wooden replica of a dragon.

"Yours are better," I whisper under my breath to Liam.

"I know." He grins, running his thumb over the chunky wings of the figure.

"Pretend Messina and Exal don't exist back there, and we're the only squad available to take back that keep," Mira orders. "Think of the power in this room. Think of what each individual rider brings to the table and how you'd use those powers in unison to conquer your objective."

"But they don't teach that to first-years," Liam says like he hasn't been taught battle strategy since we were kids. Lewellen made sure of it once he took guardianship of us after the execution.

Mira's gaze drops to the rebellion relic on Liam's wrist, and I lift my chin. They'd better get used to us being in rooms like this, because we're here to stay. At least until we get Aretia's forge up and running.

Violet clears her throat, and Mira's gaze shifts to her little sister, her eyes flaring before focusing back on Liam.

My chest tightens annoyingly. Whatever look Violet shot her sister, it was obviously in our defense, and damn if that doesn't hit me straight between the ribs.

"They might not teach you this battle strategy as first-years because you're all busy trying to stay on your dragons. You had your first taste of strategy during the Squad Battle, and it's almost May, which means final War Games should be beginning, right?"

"Two weeks," Dain informs her like he needs to remind everyone he's still at the table.

"Good timing, then. Not all of you will survive the games if you're not prepared." Mira's gaze lingers on Violet long enough to prick my temper. Of all the people in this room, Mira should know how capable Violet is. "This kind of thinking will give your squad—your entire wing—an advantage, since I guarantee your wingleader is already assessing every rider for their own abilities."

I roll the dragon figurine over my knuckles and keep my mouth shut, since I'm not supposed to be here.

"So let's do this." Mira backs up, and I glance around the table, curiosity settling my attention on Aetos. "Who is in command? And let's pretend that I don't have three years of seniority on even the highest-ranked of you."

"Then I'm in command." Aetos sits up stiffly, like someone's called formation.

To my credit, I don't laugh.

"Our *wingleader* is here." Liam points in my direction. "I would say that puts him in command."

The wispy silver bond solidifies, an emotion—pride—dancing down the pathway even though Violet doesn't move a muscle. Holy shit, we really are connected. This could be—

"Dangerous? Reckless? An unaffordable distraction?" Sgaeyl snaps, and I swear I hear her teeth clash.

"Fun." There's no denying the bond between us when it's shining at me like a fucking mage light. "We can pretend I'm not here, just for the sake of the exercise." I put my figurine on the table and settle in my chair, then wrap my arm around the back of Violet's seat and enjoy the sight of Dain grinding his teeth. "Give Aetos here the position we all know he craves."

His jaw flexes, and I leave my arm planted like a battle marker. The command, he can have. I'm mildly curious to see what he does with it. But that's the *only* position I'm ceding to the spoiled whiner.

"Don't be a dick," Violet whispers.

"You haven't even seen me start to be a dick." I send the words down the bond.

Her head whips toward mine, her lips parting as she openly gawks at me.

It *worked*. My heart stumbles, and I bite back a laugh. I was wrong. This isn't just *fun*, it's instantly vital to my existence. I turn toward her, letting a corner of my mouth rise, and look straight into those hypnotic hazel eyes. *"You're staring. It's going to get awkward in about thirty seconds if you don't stop."*

"How?" She spits out the whisper like an accusation.

"The same way you talk to Sgaeyl. We're all gloriously, annoyingly linked. This is just one of the perks. Though I'm starting to wish I'd tried it sooner. The look on your face is priceless." I wink and turn my attention back to the seething pot of jealousy boiling over across the table.

"You're. The. Wingleader." Dain chokes out the words, and I can't help but wonder if he's submitting to my rank or accusing me of inappropriate behavior with a subordinate.

Not that I give a fuck either way. If it were safe for Violet, I'd be ecstatically guilty of inappropriate behavior. Wickedly inappropriate. In my bed. In hers. On a table in the Archives. In the bathing chamber and every room with a door to lock so no one else can see what's mine. I'd be so decadently inappropriate that her voice would turn hoarse from screaming my name every single day.

But though she'd be the best thing that ever happened to me, I'd be the worst thing that ever happened to her. The truth of it sinks like a stone in my stomach.

"I'm not even supposed to be here." I shrug. "But if it makes you feel better, for the purpose of War Games, you'd be getting your orders from your section leader, Garrick Tavis, which he'd get from me. You'll be carrying out your maneuvers as a squad for the good of the wing. Just pretend I'm another member of your squad and use me as you wish, Aetos." I withdraw my hold on Violet's chair and cross my arms.

"Why are you even here?" Dain whines. "No offense, *sir*, but we weren't exactly expecting senior leadership on this trip."

"Yes, why are *you here?"* Sgaeyl doesn't disguise the mockery in her tone.

"You're more than aware that Sgaeyl and Tairn are mated." My voice stays respectfully level. *"It was your idea to bring the daggers."* I'm careful to only speak down Sgaeyl's bond.

"It seemed a prudent course of action, considering your insufferable intolerance to being separated from the general's daughter." She huffs.

"Three days?" Dain fires back, leaning in. "You couldn't make it three days?"

"Insufferable? That's a bit far."

"'Where's Violet now?'" she mocks. *"'What is she doing? Is she thinking of me? Is she missing me? Is she getting closer to Aetos? Does she dream about that kiss? How many days until Violet's—'"*

"Point fucking taken." She's going to be unbearable on the flight home.

"It has nothing to do with him." Violet slams her dragon figurine on the table. "That's up to Tairn and Sgaeyl."

And there she goes again, defending me. Fuck, I love this woman.

"You never considered that it was you I couldn't stay away from?" I ask her. She jabs the point of her elbow into my biceps, and I fight the upward curve of my mouth. I love that she isn't scared of me, that she'll call me out in a way no one else besides Sgaeyl does. Everything she does—even blatantly elbowing me in front of her squad—turns me on. I'm fucked on every level known to man when it comes to Violet Sorrengail. *"Now, now,*

you'll give our little communication secret away if you can't keep from being so…violent."

"Of course you rush to defend him," Dain whines yet again. "Though how you can forget that this guy wanted to kill you six months ago is beyond me."

He's not lying, but that was when I hated the idea of her, before I knew her—loved her.

Violet stiffens. "I cannot believe you went there."

The hurt in her tone sets my teeth on edge. "Good job remaining professional, Aetos." I scratch the relic on my neck to remind him exactly who the fuck I am. "Really shows those leadership qualities to their best advantage."

A rider stationed here whistles. "Do you boys just want to whip it out and measure? It would be faster."

Liam stifles what's obviously a laugh, and I shoot him a sideways look.

"Enough!" The table vibrates as Mira slams her hands onto the surface.

"Oh, come on, Sorrengail," the shorter rider on her left whines jokingly, and both Sorrengails glance his way.

"I mean…the older Sorrengail. This is the best entertainment we've had in ages."

Violet shakes her head, clearly having had enough. "Mira has the ability to extend the shield if the wards are down, so the first thing I would do is send her to scout the area with Teine. We need to know if we're dealing with infantry or gryphon riders."

Excellent point. I hadn't considered Mira in my own calculations.

"Good." Mira sets her dragon close to the castle. "Now let's assume there are gryphons."

"Speaking of gryphons," I say to Sgaeyl. *"Any news from Glane?"*

"Still out of range," she replies.

Sending Imogen an hour south, toward the Braevick border, was a calculated risk given that I hadn't had much time to get a message to Syrena and her drift, but rendezvousing there was a far better choice than risking her being caught by Cygnis fliers. Cygnis fliers would take the daggers and then kill Imogen to make a point. Stubborn assholes.

"You want to do your job?" Violet's smile practically drips venomous sugar as she turns it on Dain. "I mean, how you can forget you're the squad leader is beyond me."

Fucking *love* her.

His knuckles whiten around his figurine. "Quinn, can you astral project from the back of your dragon?"

"Yes," she answers.

"Then I would have you project into the fortress to check for signs of weakness," Dain says. "And have you report back. Same with Liam. We'd use your farsight to see if you can locate where the gryphon riders are and if there are any traps."

"Good. The weaknesses are the wooden gate," Mira adds as the two cadets move their figurines, "and the Navarrian citizens they have captive in the dungeons."

"So much for blasting the whole place," Ridoc mutters.

"You're an air wielder, right?" Dain asks Emery. "So you can shape your dragon's flames, lead them through the occupied parts of the keep without killing civilians."

"Yes," Emery answers with a nod. "But I'd have to be in the keep."

"Then you'll have to get into the keep." Mira's shoulders rise and fall in a shrug.

Emery's eyes flare. "You want me to leave my dragon and go on foot?"

"Why do you think we get all that hand-to-hand training? Or are you going to leave all those innocent people to die?" Mira flicks her wrist and Emery's dragon goes flying up into the air. Mira catches it, then sets it in the center of the model. "The real question is, how do we get you close enough without getting you killed? Since I'm guessing the others will be busy fighting off the gryphons that launch once the fireworks start."

"What's your signet, Aetos?" Quinn asks.

"Above your pay grade," Dain answers.

Does he actually think that? Or is he so brainwashed by Daddy that he doesn't see they're going to use him as a weapon against other riders?

He looks at every cadet except me, then sighs. "Any ideas?"

Violet shakes her head, then says, "Sure." She snatches my dragon and pushes it at the keep, flaring her hand so the figurine levitates above the model. I shouldn't be impressed—it's just lesser magic—but damn she's sexy when she takes charge. "You stop ignoring that you have an incredibly powerful shadow wielder at your disposal and ask him to black out the area so no one sees you land."

Spot-on.

"She's not wrong." Mira bites the words out.

"You can do that?" Aetos slowly looks in my direction.

"Are you seriously asking?" I reach for Sgaeyl's power, and it pours into my veins.

"Just wasn't sure you could cover an area that—"

I lift my palms just enough to clear the table and summon the cooling darkness of the shadows. They stream out from under the table and blanket the room in less than a heartbeat, devouring all traces of light.

Panic skitters down the silver bond.

"Relax. It's just me." I crook a finger, and a strand of shadow solidifies to skim along Violet's cheek.

"Fuck me," a rider to the left says.

"I can surround this entire outpost, but I think that might freak some people out." I close my hands, and the shadows jolt back to their natural state, letting light pour in through the windows. Damn, that was fun. It was even worth the threat assessment I'm getting from Mira. Violet tenses like she spotted it, too. *"I hope you didn't get any ideas while we were in the dark there."*

She lifts her middle finger without even looking my way, and a laugh sneaks past my lips as Mira leads us through the rest of the exercise.

"Good job," Mira finally says, checking the time. "Aetos, Riorson, and Sorrengail, I want to see you in the hallway. The rest of you are dismissed."

This should be fun.

She leads the way, then shuts the door behind us once we're in the staircase and throws a blue wave of energy over the doorway. It's an interesting use of power, when I'm more than capable of constructing a colorless one for the sake of privacy.

"Sound shield." Dain smiles. "Nice."

What a suck-up.

"Shut up." Mira pivots a few steps above me, one above Violet, and shoves a finger in Aetos's face. "I don't know what bug has crawled up your ass, Dain Aetos, but have you forgotten that you're a squad leader? That you have a very real chance of becoming a wingleader next year?"

Gods help every cadet if *that* happens.

Violet retreats a step in my direction, and my brow furrows. Sibling dynamics are something I'll never understand.

"Mira—" Aetos begins.

"Lieutenant Sorrengail," Mira interrupts. "You're blowing it, Dain. I know how badly you want his job next year." She swings that finger toward me. "Don't forget that we've grown up about ten feet apart. And you are *blowing* it, because what? You're pissed that Violet bonded his dragon's mate?"

Harsh, but I respect her candor.

"He is the worst possible thing for her!" Dain raises his voice.

Huh. Guess we actually agree on something.

"Oh, I'm not arguing that." Mira invades his space. "But there's nothing anyone can do about the choices of dragons. They don't bother with the opinions of mere humans, do they? But whatever is going on between the two of you"—her finger flies between Violet and Aetos—"is fucking up your squad. If I can see it after four days with you, then they sure as hell can tell. And if I'd known that you were going to be such a hard-ass with zero flexibility for the things she can't control, I never would have told her to find you after crossing the parapet. You two have been best friends since you were five years old. Figure your shit out." That last part is directed at them both.

Dain stiffens, then looks Violet's way and nods, which she returns.

An irrational, ugly feeling sours my stomach. They have the kind of history that lingers, the kind that has me really contemplating the word "jealousy."

"Glane approaches from the south," Sgaeyl tells me. *"They were successful."*

"Thank you." Now to get Imogen to the infirmary, and no one will realize she'd even been missing.

"Good, now get back in there." Mira nods toward the door, and Dain departs, heading through the shield. "And as for you." She descends two stairs and narrows her eyes on me. "Is this what she can expect next year?"

"Aetos being an asshole?" I keep my hands off my weapons. Killing Mira might appease the burning need for revenge I've learned to live with, but it's not worth upsetting Violet or dealing with the oldest Sorrengail sibling, either. "Probably."

Mira glares at me, and the resemblance to her mother is uncanny. "Mated dragons typically bond riders in the same year for a reason. You cannot expect your assigned wing or her instructors to let you both fly off every three days."

"Wasn't my choice." I shrug. Lying is easy, except when it comes to Violet. I haven't quite figured that one out yet.

"What are we supposed to do? Tell the giant, flame-throwing dragons how it's going to be?" Violet questions.

"Yes!" Mira shouts, facing her sister. "Because you can't live this way, Violet. You'll be the one who ends up missing the training you need, because he's the more powerful of the two of you right now. But if you don't get to focus on your training, then that's how it will always be. You won't ever become who Tairn can push you to be. Is that what you're after, Riorson?"

My gut twists with anger, and power rushes through me. Fuck it, Violet would get over her sister's death eventually.

"Mira," Violet whispers and shakes her head. "You're wrong about him."

Only in some ways. The beating organ behind my ribs soothes the anger, and my power recedes.

"Listen to me." Mira grabs Violet's shoulders. "He might wield shadows, Violet, but give him his way, and you'll become one."

And the power races back in, shadows pulsing at the edges of the stairwell. I'm the one pushing Violet instead of babying her. If Aetos had his way, she'd be smothered in cream robes.

"That won't happen," Violet vows.

"It will if he has anything to say about it." Mira pins a look on me that I don't appreciate. "Killing someone isn't the only way to destroy them. Keeping you from reaching your potential seems like a great path to the retribution he swore against our mother. Think long and hard. How well do you even really know him?"

Violet's swift intake of breath slices like a knife to my side.

"That's what I thought." Mira's expression softens, and I wait to see if she's going to take the Dain route. "Do you even know why he hates our mother so much? Why the kids like him are put on the para—"

Oh, fuck no, she isn't ready to hear *half* of what their mother did to me.

"I'm right here." I step up to Violet's side. "In case you didn't notice."

"You're kind of hard to miss," Mira counters.

"You're not listening." I hold her accusing stare and lower my voice. "I. Am. Here. Tairn didn't drag her back to Basgiath. He didn't break through her shields and pour his emotions into her. He didn't demand she fly across the fucking kingdom. Your sister is still right here. I'm the one who left *my* post, *my* position, and *my* executive officer in charge of *my* wing. She's not missing out on *shit.*" The truth of the words stings. I might be accomplishing a very risky run, but Sgaeyl is right. We're here because I couldn't concentrate for shit knowing that Violet was this close to the border. I chose Violet over my wing.

"And next year? When you're a brand-new lieutenant? What *shit* is she going to miss out on then?" Mira asks.

Yeah, fuck if I know. At this rate, they'll have to station me at Basgiath if I can't get my shit under control and get over—

"Love isn't something you get over," Sgaeyl reminds me. *"Why do you think I flew you all the way out here?"*

"To mock me while cavorting with your mate."

"I didn't say it was without its perks."

"We'll figure it out." Violet grabs Mira's hand. "Mira, he's taken every spare minute he has to train me on the mat for challenges or take me flying in hopes I'll finally figure out how to keep my damned seat without Tairn holding me in place. He's—"

Mira flinches. "You can't keep your seat?"

Oh shit.

"No." Violet's voice drops to a whisper.

"How the hell can you *not*?" Mira's jaw drops.

Fuck. What are the rules when it comes to interfering with sisters? Am I supposed to step in? Let Violet handle it? Lewellen let Liam and me beat the shit out of each other when we fought, but I'm not sure that's the right approach here. I'm also not about to infantilize Violet when her sister is doing a damned good job of it herself.

"Because I'm not you!" Violet shouts.

Mira jolts backward. "But you…you look so much stronger now."

"My joints and muscles are stronger because Imogen makes me lift these horrible weights, but that doesn't…fix me." Violet's shoulders drop, and shadows pulse at the edges of the steps.

The color fades from Mira's face. "No. I didn't mean it like that, Vi. You're not anything that needs to be fixed. I just didn't know you couldn't hold your seat. Why didn't you tell me?"

"Because there's nothing you can do about it." Violet's smile is anything but happy. "There's nothing *anyone* can do about the way I'm made."

The way she's made? She's fucking *perfect*. Everything about her is what makes her…Violet.

When the silence grows awkward, my power ebbs. "She's getting better," I tell Mira, just to get her off Violet's back. "The first few weeks were…disastrous."

"Hey, he caught me before I hit the ground." Violet shoots me a *not helpful* look.

"Barely," I admit, then rip my gaze from Violet to face down her sister. "You don't have to trust me—"

"Good, because I don't," she says. "All of that power in the hands of someone with your history is bad enough, but to know your dragons are so tangled up that you can't be more than three days from Violet is unacceptable in every possible way I can think—" She freezes, her eyes going unfocused.

Unnatural quiet falls, and unease ripples down my spine at the lack of the steady, quiet hum of background noise that always accompanies proximity to stored power. My stomach clenches. The wards are down.

"Drift incoming from the east!" Sgaeyl snarls.

"Let me guess. They're not friendly?" My gaze shoots to the top of the steps. I can have Violet on the ramparts in thirty seconds or less.

"Definitely not."

"Fuck! The wards are down." Mira grabs Violet into a hug. "You have to go."

"We can help!" Violet's voice pitches toward panic.

"Is this us?" Wards will only fall this quickly if the power supply is compromised...or stolen.

"No."

Which means we have enemies within the keep already.

"You can't." Mira's voice cuts like steel. "And if Tairn is using his power to keep you seated, then he's diminished as well. You have to *go*. Get out of here. If you love me, Violet, you'll go so I don't have to worry about you, too."

"Western rampart." Violet needs to be airborne *now*.

"Where do you think we're already headed?" Sgaeyl snaps. *"And you'd better be there with her."*

The squad races out of the briefing room and hurries down the steps as Mira releases Violet and pins me with a look that's equal parts order and desperation. "Get her out of here."

My head rears back. Did she just tell me to go *with* her? Fuck that.

"Let's go!" Aetos yells. "Now!"

"Even if you don't trust me, I'm the best weapon you have," I remind Mira in a less-than-amiable tone.

"If what you say is true, then you're the best weapon *she* has. The other half of the squad will be here in moments, and Teine thinks we have about twenty minutes until the gryphons arrive." Her expression shifts to a quick but blatant plea before turning to her sister. "You have to get to safety, Violet. I love you. Don't die. I'd hate to be an only child."

"I can get Violet out and track down whoever brought down the wards—"

"If you stay, so will she," Sgaeyl growls. *"And need I remind you what happens to us all if she's killed while you're off proving your acumen?"*

Fuck. Every instinct but one demands I fight, but it's that lone, sharply insistent slice of intuition screaming to keep Violet safe above all else that quickly conquers every other impulse. I breathe in sharply, then exhale pure frustration, mentally shifting to a new plan as I whip my arm around Violet's waist and pull her against my side.

She flat-out *fights* me as Mira sprints up the stairs to the roof.

"No!" Violet throws her body weight against my grip, but I hold fast. "Mira! What if you get hurt? Tairn's speed could be the only thing that saves you. At least let us stay."

Mira pivots at the doorway to face us. "You want me to trust you, Riorson? Get her the fuck out of here and find a way for her to keep her seat. We both know she's dead if she doesn't."

I nod, then shift my grip on Violet's waist, locking my elbow around the delicate curve, and haul her ass down the stairs.

"Mira!" Violet rakes her nails along my forearm. "I love you!" she screams over her shoulder.

Her cry rips into my very soul, but I'm not risking her life, even for her sister. Shadows race ahead of us, pouring over the steps. If anyone is coming up this direction, I'll know before they so much as see us.

"Close yet?" I ask Sgaeyl as we turn the curve into the barracks' hall.

"Not quite. Glane has rerouted as well."

Good. Gives us enough time for me to get my pack. If anyone finds the alloy-hilted dagger I keep stored there, I'm fucked.

"Can I trust you to get your own pack?" I ask Violet, setting her on her feet. "Or am I going to have to carry you out of here without whatever you brought?"

"I'll get it myself." She pushes at me, and I release my grip.

Two seconds later, she slams the door to the room she shares with Matthias in my face, and I head into mine just down the hall, finding Liam standing with his arms folded in the center of my room, his pack strapped to his back.

"Was it us?" he says. It's more accusation than question.

"No." I shove what few belongings I brought into my pack.

"Was it us?" He shouts this time, standing in my way when I turn for the door, like he could actually stop me from leaving if he wanted to.

"No," I repeat, looking him straight in the eye. "I already asked Sgaeyl; we have no operations in the area— "

"Except what Imogen pulled off today," he retorts, his hands clenching.

My jaw flexes. "This wasn't us, Liam. You know I'd never risk civilian casualties by taking down an entire *outpost*. Imogen carried *two dozen* daggers across the border, but even that amount of power wouldn't be enough to affect an outage like this." I sheathe my swords in the scabbards sewn into my pack, then swing it onto my back.

Liam's shoulders dip. "This isn't on us."

"No." I shake my head, then clasp his shoulder. "Get to the roof. We need to mount."

He nods. "I'll get Vi— "

"I've got her." I drop my hand and walk past him, swinging open the door to the hallway. "She's not exactly in favor of leaving. Now, go."

We split at the hallway, and Violet keeps me waiting less than a minute before barreling through her door carrying two packs and avoiding my gaze as she marches toward the door that leads to the courtyard.

I catch her elbow and spin her to face the correct direction. "Nope. It's too dangerous to leave the fortress walls. We're going up." I hook my arm around her waist before she can even think about fighting me, then carry her to the crowded stairwell before setting her down. "Climb."

"This is bullshit!" Her cheeks flush as she narrows her eyes on me, members of her squad pushing past. "Tairn could help them!"

And she could die in the process. My resolve hardens to stone. "Your sister is right. You have to make it out, so we're leaving. Now fucking *climb*." Or so help me, Dunne, I will throw her over my damned shoulder right in front of everyone.

"Dain." Her gaze swings to the squad leader just ahead of us like he's any fucking use right now.

He takes Matthias's pack from Violet. "For once, Riorson and I agree. It's not just you we have to get out, Violet. Think of every other first-year. Are you going to sentence an entire *untrained* squad to death?" He starts climbing and, lucky for me, Violet follows. "Because I'll make it. Cianna, Emery, and Heaton will, too. And we all fucking know Riorson will. But what about Rhiannon? Ridoc? Sawyer? You want their deaths on your hands?"

Is it just me or is he already out of breath as we climb through the third floor and out onto the roof?

Emery mounts ahead of us on the annoyingly narrow rampart. The design is great for preventing fliers from doing the same, but it's not doing us any favors at the moment.

"Ridoc and Quinn are already in the air," Liam announces, watching Emery launch on his Brown Clubtail.

I spot Deigh next to Cath, hovering with shallow beats of their wings.

"You're next!" I order Liam, and thankfully for our time's sake, Dain agrees, which means I don't have to kill him.

Chunks of masonry tumble to the bailey below as Deigh lands, and Liam wastes no time, taking the rampart at a run just like we'd practiced hundreds of times in Lewellen.

"You next, Aetos." My gaze rakes the sky for any sign of Tairn.

"Coming behind you," the surly behemoth deigns to speak to me. *"She's not going to like the method."*

"Vi—" Aetos has the nerve to object.

"That's an order." Just because I loathe the simpering daddy's boy doesn't mean I *want* to be responsible for the death of a younger cadet. Plus, I can't afford Aetos Senior making my life hell. "I've got her. Go."

"Go," Violet pleads.

Aetos turns my way and offers me his best impression of a threatening glare. "I'm trusting you to get her out."

I don't have time for this bullshit. "There's a lot of that going around today," I snap. "Now get on your dragon so I can get her on hers."

He heads down the rampart toward Cath, but he's nowhere as fast as Liam.

"What method isn't she going to like?" I ask Tairn, choosing the pathway that excludes Violet the same way he had.

"I'm going to have to..." He pauses, and I note Violet scanning the sky above us. *"Scoop her up. It won't be her most dignified moment."*

Oh, she's going to *love* that.

"I can't do this." Violet twists in my grip, turning those hazel eyes on me. "The others are gone. Call it the favor you owe me, I don't care. We can stay. I can't just leave her here. It's wrong, and it's something she'd never do to me. I have to stay for her. I just have to."

Fuck. I get it. I really do. Liam and Bodhi are the closest things I have to siblings, and I wouldn't leave with their lives on the line, either. But this isn't Liam. Or Bodhi. It's *her*. And we aren't at Basgiath. That approaching drift—and whoever is responsible for compromising the power supply for the wards—will kill her if given the chance, and that's not something I'll ever let happen.

But damn, her courage has me tripping over my feelings for her.

"Approaching," Sgaeyl informs me.

"Not fast enough."

Violet isn't going to leave of her own accord; I can see it in her eyes, feel it in the tense lines of her back. I drop my shields, and her emotions hurtle down the bond. Determination. Fear—

She's going to bolt.

And there's only one way to stop her. I lift my hands from her waist to the velvet-soft skin of her cheeks, memorizing every color in her eyes as I cup the back of her neck, preparing to commit what she'll think is an unforgivable sin.

I kiss her. It's hard and raw, wild and desperate, and the way she opens for me, kissing me back with abandon, nearly takes me out at the knees. Gods, I'll never get enough of this woman. Her mind. Her tenacity. Her *mouth*.

I kiss her like this might be the last time she'll let me, like this is an alternate reality and there's a chance she could love me back.

I kiss her like she's *mine*.

It's a stolen moment—it can never be anything more—but it's ours.

Wingbeats approach, and I ignore them, stroking my tongue against hers again and again, keeping my hands at the nape of her neck by sheer force of will, denying the urge to explore every curve, every hollow of her tight body. I've never wanted anyone the way I want her, never craved a woman's laugh as much as her touch or needed her trust more than my next breath. Only Violet.

I tear my mouth away, the steady pulses of wings undeniable as Tairn and Sgaeyl approach. Wind gusts, catching the loosened strands of her hair as I lean my forehead against hers. "Leave for *me*, Violet."

She stiffens, accusation filling her eyes so quickly that I know she's figured out that I just used our attraction to distract her. "I will hate you for this."

Ouch.

"Yeah." I nod, accepting the consequences of my actions. "I can live with that." I can live with *anything* as long as she's still breathing, so I drop my hands to her arms and force them out at her sides. "Arms up. Hold tight."

"Fuck. You." She hisses out the words as a shadow falls over us, and I hit the floor, catching myself with my hands as a black claw fills the space I just occupied, hooking Violet's arms and snatching her into the sky.

"She'll never forgive me," I tell Sgaeyl as she lands on the narrow perch ahead of me. *"Especially if something happens to her sister."*

She tilts her head, staring at me with typical impatience as I launch to my feet and sprint down the rampart toward her. We're airborne in seconds, her wings pummeling the air before I even reach the seat. *"If she can't forgive you for the least of your transgressions, then she doesn't deserve you."*

"I don't think she'll see it that way." I get a good grip on her scales and settle in for the flight.

"Then you'd better start praying to your gods that her sister survives."

Can't get enough of *Fourth Wing*?

Turn the page for two more bonus chapters from Xaden's point of view—previously published in the *Fourth Wing* Special Edition hardcover.

Chapter Nine

-XADEN-

"You don't think you'll need those?" Sorrengail asks, gripping two of her daggers and facing me on the mat with an impressive lack of trembling. Hell, she looks more pissed than she does terrified that I'm about to end her, even though I've handed my weapons to Imogen.

"This is reckless," Sgaeyl lectures.

"Nope. Not when you brought enough for the both of us." My mouth quirks into a smile as I crook my fingers at her, then lock my shields firmly in place, since Aetos hovers close by. The second-year is good on the mat, even if he's a little too straight-laced to really be the best in this place. "Let's go."

She takes a fighting stance, and I forget the members of Second Squad surrounding the mat, forget the mission I'm due to fly this weekend, focusing solely on her. Violet Sorrengail. The five-foot-nothing daughter of the general who executed my father. I have every right to ruin her, according to the Codex. She might fall under my chain of command, but she's not in my squad.

I could snap her neck and no one in this room would interfere. But the hundred and seven souls I'm responsible for would pay the price. So what the fuck am I doing on this mat?

Her posture changes subtly, her wrist flicking a second before she flings a dagger at my damned chest.

I catch it by pure reflex, then cluck my tongue at her. "Already seen that move."

That is what I'm doing out here. Took me all of two weeks to realize she's somehow figured out who she'll be facing and has been poisoning her opponents. That brilliant, devious mind might regrettably be a complete turn-on, but she's going to get herself killed if she depends solely on that method—and flinging daggers like a carnival act. To my surprise, the thought doesn't sit right with me. Nothing about her does.

She attacks in a typical first-year swipe-and-kick combo, which is as easy to predict as it is to block. I pluck the badly balanced dagger from her grip and catch her by the thigh, using her own momentum and slight bodyweight against her to drop her to the mat.

Her hazel eyes flare wide as she stares up at me, fighting to draw breath, and I drop the dagger at her side and kick it out of her reach, toward the squad leader who should have taught her better.

Were she any other opponent, I'd put the blade against her throat, proving my point and ending the match, but fuck me if I don't feel like I somehow owe the first-year for keeping her mouth shut about the meeting she saw under the oak tree. My form of gratitude just happens to be not killing her as she lies at my feet, battling her own lungs.

Her ribs finally rise, and she heaves herself upward to a sitting position, then tries to plunge a knife in my thigh.

Oh, for fuck's sake.

I block the strike with my right forearm, then take hold of her wrist with my left hand and disarm her as I lean down into her space, mere inches from her face. "Going for blood today, are we, Violence?" I whisper.

Rage shines in those mesmerizing eyes as I drop her blade to the mat and kick it out of reach also. She's too easy to disarm, and her false confidence that she's not will get her killed. And why the fuck isn't she using weapons suited for her body type and fighting style? Not that she actually *has* a fighting style yet.

"My name is *Violet*," she retorts, and I half expect her to hiss at me like a cat. That's exactly what she reminds me of, all sleek lines and bared claws. Only the pulse fluttering beneath my fingertips gives away her fear.

Violet is too soft of a name for her. Too breakable. I'm well aware of the shit people talk about her bones and joints, but from what I've seen, the woman has a core of steel.

"I think my version fits you better." I release her wrist and stand to my full height, offering her a hand up and hoping she's too smart to take it. "We're not done yet."

But she does.

Fuck me, she's naive. I pull her to her feet, then whip her around before she can get her bearings, twisting her arm behind her back and trapping our hands between us as I tug her hard against my chest. Too naive for this place.

"Damn it!" she snaps.

I slip one of her obnoxiously big daggers from her thigh sheath and lift it to the soft skin of her throat, pinning her in place with my forearm. Her head falls back against my chest, the silver ends of her hair braided up like a crown. She barely reaches my collarbone, so I dip my head so the others won't hear, and gods she smells really *fucking* good like—

No thinking about how she smells, jackass.

"Don't trust a single person who faces you on this mat," I lecture quietly near the shell of her ear, careful to keep my mouth off her. Since when do I think about putting my *mouth* on an opponent?

"Even someone who owes me a favor?" she retorts, keeping her voice equally low.

Warmth flares in my chest in appreciation of her discretion, her quick observation that this lesson isn't for public dissemination, and I drop the knife, kicking it to her squad leader just like the other two and ignoring the bluster of threat in his stern expression.

"I'm the one who decides when to grant that favor. Not you." I release her so I don't dislocate her shoulder and step back.

She acts immediately, spinning with a raised fist, and I bat it away from my throat.

"Good." I can't help but smile as I block her next attempt just as easily. "Going for the throat is your best option, as long as it's exposed."

Her cheeks flush, anger narrowing her eyes as she kicks in the same fucking combination she's already tried, and I grab hold of her thigh again, unsheathing the last dagger there and letting it fall before I release her. I lift my scarred eyebrow in sheer disappointment. She's smarter than that. "I expect you to learn from your mistakes." I kick it to Aetos.

She retrieves her next weapon from her rib sheath and takes a defensive stance as she circles me. It's all I can do not to sigh in complete, utter annoyance. I don't need to see her to hear every step on the mat behind me as she hesitates.

"You going to prance or are you going to strike?" That should get her moving.

The shadows on the mat give her away, and I twist and duck as she jabs forward, the knife slicing through the air where I'd been standing. At least she really went for it, but the move leaves her exposed, so I use her arm to flip her around the side of my torso, sending her face-first into the mat and following her down.

She gasps when I wrench her arm into a submission hold, forcing her to drop the dagger. Careful to balance most of my weight on my right, I set my left knee onto her back just enough to stress her. She has to learn how to move under pressure, how to think on the edge of death. I strip away another of her daggers and fling it at the squad leader's feet, then pull another from her ribs and set it to the exposed skin beneath her jaw.

Then I invade what little space she has. "Taking out your enemy before the battle is really smart; I'll give that to you," I whisper into her ear, and she tenses beneath me. *Yeah, Violence, I know what you've been up to.* "Problem is, if you aren't testing yourself in here"—I drag the blade down her neck, careful not to draw blood—"then you're not going to get any better."

"You'd rather I die, no doubt," she spits back, the side of her face squished against the mat.

"And be denied the pleasure of your company?" Sarcasm drips from my retort.

"I fucking hate you."

A corner of my mouth lifts. Gods, she's just as merciless as Sgaeyl when it comes to her tongue. "That doesn't make you special."

I gain my feet and kick the knives to Aetos, leaving Sorrengail with two more to fight with as I offer my hand again.

She scowls, but doesn't take the help this time, standing on her own, and another smile curves my mouth. I can't remember the last time I had so much fun. Every single one of her expressions is beautifully raw. There's no guile. No artifice. But there's also no control. "She can be taught."

"She's a quick learner," she fires back.

"That remains to be seen." I take two steps backward and beckon her forward by crooking my fingers again.

"You've made your damn point." Her voice rises to a public level, and Imogen gasps behind me, no doubt worried that I'll lose my temper and kill the first-year.

But killing her is the last thing on my mind.

"Trust me, I've barely gotten started." I cross my arms and shift my weight back, curious to see what she does next and even more perplexed as to why I care so damned much.

Sure, she's beautiful, but I've never let the symmetry of someone's facial features sway me. And it's not the palpable hatred in her ever-changing eyes, either. I'm used to being loathed. But the combination of her hatred and her silence about seeing us meet is too intriguing to ignore—

She moves, and I'm too fucking distracted to react like usual, and when she kicks for the backs of my knees, I fall. Hard.

Holy shit.

"What did I say about being reckless?" Sgaeyl pushes through my shields. *"The silver-haired girl is a distraction you can't aff—"*

I plant my feet on that mental hillside in Tyrrendor and reinforce my shields, blocking her out. She's *never* going to let me live this down.

Sorrengail lands on my back and attempts a headlock. Good for her. It's a solid choice, but she isn't physically strong enough to cut off my air supply. She's fighting like she's six inches taller and has another forty pounds on her instead of leaning into her actual strengths.

I don't bother with her arms. Twisting quickly, I break her grip and grasp the backs of her thighs in one motion, throwing us into a roll that ends with me pinning her back to the mat. Before she can take another breath, I put my forearm against the delicate line of her throat but don't press.

There are over a dozen different ways to end her in this position, and I have all the leverage. But though my hips anchor hers to the mat, I have most of my weight braced on my left arm so I don't crush her.

She's well and fucking caught, and the flash of fear that's quickly masked by fury in her eyes tells me she knows it, too.

Damn it. I don't *want* to crush her.

What the fuck is happening to me?

She grabs for a dagger and makes the monumental mistake of going for my shoulder.

I abandon her throat and capture her wrist, pinning it above her head. Then I watch her face with rapt fascination as her expression shifts from wide-eyed shock, to tensing fear, to pursed-lipped anger all in a matter of seconds. The speed with which she processes information and compartmentalizes her feelings is such an advantage, and I doubt she even knows it.

Pink flushes up her neck and into her cheeks, and suddenly I find myself studying her for an entirely different reason. The blush, the skittered pulse, the way her gaze flicks toward my mouth for less than a second… I'm not the only one attracted here.

Fuck. This is dangerous. *She* is dangerous.

The world outside the mat ceases to exist as my focus narrows to just Violence. She really is stunning, especially when pissed. Tension surges between us, and my heartbeat jumps despite my best effort to lock that shit down. But damn if I'm not critically aware of the feel of her body beneath mine, the warmth of her skin under my fingertips, the way her breath catches as I lower my face to hers slowly.

Sliding my fingers up the heel of her hand, I force her fist open, then toss the blade across the mat before freeing her wrist.

"Get your dagger," I demand.

"What?" Her eyes fly wide.

"Get. Your. Dagger," I repeat, moving her hand with mine and dragging it to her ribs, to the last of her daggers. I curl my fingers around hers, grabbing the hilt.

Even her hands are soft. Fragile. Breakable. And if I don't teach her how to use her petite size to her advantage, the next opponent will use it to shatter her. And for some fucking reason I can't identify or deny…I care.

Gods damn it.

"You're tiny." Anger simmers in my stomach.

"Well aware." She glares.

"So stop going for bigger moves that expose you." I bring our laced hands to my side and drag the tip down my ribs. "A rib shot would have worked just fine." Then I lead our hands around to my back, leaving myself vulnerable for the first time since I walked into this prison of a war college. "Kidneys are a good fit from this angle, too."

She swallows, and I fight the urge to watch the motion of her throat, holding her gaze instead. I swear, her eyes seem different every time I look into them. No wonder I can't look away.

I bring our hands to my waist, keeping my eyes locked on hers. "Chances are, if your opponent is in armor, it's weak here. Those are three easy places you could have struck before your opponent would have had time to stop you."

Her lips part, and she draws a shaky breath.

"Do you hear me?" I'm sure as hell not repeating this lesson.

She nods.

"Good. Because you can't poison every enemy you come across," I whisper, watching the blood drain from her face as I level the accusation. "You're not going to have time to offer tea to some Braevi gryphon rider when they come at you."

"How did you know?" She tenses under me, and *fuck*, her thighs clench around my hips.

I have to get the fuck off her before she realizes she has another weapon at her disposal when it comes to me. "Oh, Violence, you're good, but I've known better poison masters. The trick is to not make it quite so obvious."

Brennan would give one of his frustrated sighs if he knew just how obvious his little sister was. Then again, he'd also try to kick my ass for the position I have Violence in.

A bitter taste floods my mouth. She has no clue he's alive.

She opens her mouth like she's about to speak.

"I think she's been taught enough for the day," Aetos barks.

It takes every ounce of control I possess not to startle at the sudden reminder that we're not alone. "He always that overprotective?" I mutter, putting a couple of inches between us.

"He cares about me." She narrows her eyes at me, which I'm starting to think is her default expression.

"He's holding you back. Don't worry. Your little poisoning secret is safe with me." I arch my scarred brow and hope she gets the hint to keep my secret safe, too. Then I slide our joined hands along her side and sheathe the jewel-hilted blade she has no business carrying. It's too fucking big for her. Too easy to knock loose.

"You're not going to disarm me?" she questions as I slip my fingers from hers and lift my weight off her.

Thank *gods* she has the common sense to release my hips from the grip of her thighs, because mine has fled, replaced by the urge to leave them right where they were and carry her to the nearest empty room to see just how *attracted* we both are.

But that way lies absolute disaster.

"Nope. Defenseless women have never been my type. We're done for today." I stand immediately, leaving her there, and walk to the edge of the mat to get my weapons from Imogen.

"What the hell was that?" she whispers, handing back the last of my knives.

"Aetos." I ignore her question and turn toward the squad leader across the mat, who's busy coddling Violence as usual.

His head snaps toward mine, and the anger there almost makes me smile.

"She could use a little less protection and a little more instruction." I level an accusatory look on him until he nods, then turn and walk away.

"You in the mood to spar with first-years?" Garrick asks, keeping pace with me once I'm a few steps from Second Squad, a smile tugging at his mouth. "Or just *that* particular first-year?"

"Sometimes I hate how fucking observant you are."

"It's hard to miss the way you look at her," he says, lowering his voice.

"Like I want to kill her?" I retort, spotting an interesting match in Claw Section.

"Or fu—"

"Don't finish that sentence when I'm in the mood to hit people." We're mutually assured destruction against each other, which makes us the perfect sparring partners, but I'm just aggravated enough to do some real damage to my best friend, despite the size he has on me.

"Oh, would you, please?" He puts his hand to his heart and grins. "I need you to use those big, strong hands to show me—"

I shove his shoulder hard enough to send him staggering sideways and keep walking out of his section and into Claw. The farther the better when it comes to Sorrengail.

Chapter Sixteen

-XADEN-

"Don't you see what happened? What Xaden's done?" Aetos asks Sorrengail, panicking like the infantry soldier he should have been and insinuating that I changed the outcome of Threshing.

If I act every time someone drags my name through a pile of bullshit, I'll never get anything done. For the most part, I take note of the offense, file it away for future consideration, and move on. As Sgaeyl loves to remind me, dragons are not concerned with the opinions of the sheep… or most humans.

But Aetos's fingers dent in on the shoulders of Sorrengail's uniform, right above the bandage from where she took the blade from that limp-dick first-year Tairn incinerated, and unexplainable rage pumps into my veins like little shards of ice, cutting everything in its path. I slam my mental shields down just like I do every time I'm near *anyone*, let alone a memory-reader.

"Please, do tell me what it is you think I've done." I step into the moonlight that illuminates most of the flight field and sever the flow of power from Sgaeyl, letting the night's shadows fall back into their natural state so this asshole can see me clearly.

"You manipulated Threshing." Aetos takes his hands off Sorrengail's shoulders, and I decide to let him keep them. For now.

Seriously. Of all the laws I break around here, *that's* the one he goes with?

I almost laugh, but then the asshole puts himself in front of Sorrengail, like Violence actually needs his protection. He didn't see her out there on the field today like I did, or he wouldn't be hovering like a nanny.

"Dain, that's..." Sorrengail steps out from behind him.

"Is that an official accusation?" Gods, please give me a reason to beat the pompous, Codex-loving shit out of him. Just once.

"He's nothing but an irritant. Have some self-control," Sgaeyl lectures, like her affection for the little gold dragon isn't what put us in this fucking situation.

I keep my gaze locked on Aetos and off Sorrengail's wide, hazel eyes and the scrapes that mar her skin. I definitely don't let my attention wander down those tight curves—

Fuck, she's a distraction. One I can't afford, and yet one I've just been saddled with for the rest of my godsforsaken life. And instead of glaring up at me with that fire I can't seem to stay the fuck away from, it's fear making her eyes appear more amber than blue in the moonlight.

Fear for...Aetos? Something unpleasant twists in my gut.

"Did you step in?" Aetos questions, his voice pitching toward whiny.

"Did I what?" I lift my brow, letting all my loathing for his spoiled ass shine through. The pint-size morsel of straight-up arsenic nearly got herself *killed* on that field, and his concern is for protocol? "Did I see her outnumbered and already wounded? Did I think her bravery was as admirable as it was fucking *reckless*?" I make the monumental mistake of looking at her, and the rigid hold I keep on my temper slips. She could have died out there. She almost did. Right in front of me.

"And I would do it again." She tilts her stubborn chin at me.

"Well-the-fuck-aware!" *Shit.* So much for only *slipping*—my control just evaporated. "Did I see her fight off *three* bigger cadets?" I narrow my eyes at Aetos. "Because the answer to all of those is yes. But you're asking the wrong question, Aetos. What you should be asking is if *Sgaeyl* saw it, too."

"You did not just bring me into this nonsense."

"You sure as hell dragged me *into it. Since when do you get all mushy over smaller dragons?"* Not that the golden one isn't cute. But going soft

on *cute* gets you killed out here, which is exactly what makes Sorrengail so dangerous for me.

Aetos looks away nervously, as he should.

"His mate told him," Sorrengail whispers. Guess someone filled her in on Tairn and Sgaeyl's mating bond.

"Since when do you get emotional over human women?" Sgaeyl challenges.

"I'm pissed, not emotional," I correct her. "She's never been a fan of bullies," I confirm. "But don't mistake it as an act of kindness toward you. She's fond of the little dragon. Unfortunately, Tairn chose you all on his own."

"Fuck," Aetos murmurs, finally putting it together.

"My thought exactly." I shake my head at the squad leader. "Sorrengail is the last person on the Continent I'd ever want to be chained to me. I didn't do this." In one second on that field, my attitude toward Violence changed from maybe-I'll-kill-her-or-maybe-I-won't to protect-her-at-all-costs.

And not because she's brilliant, or beautiful, or infuriatingly capable of shredding my carefully crafted control, even though she's absolutely all of those things. No. I had *no* choice in this. Tairn made my decision for me.

"And even if I had." I step into Aetos's space, and to his credit, he doesn't retreat as I hover over him. "Would you really level that accusation knowing it would have been what saved the woman you call your best friend?" At some point, Sorrengail is going to have to recognize that the last year in the quadrant has changed her little friend into someone she doesn't actually know.

His silence is fucking delicious, saying more to incriminate him than I ever could.

"There are…rules," he stammers, trying his best to stare me down even though I have inches on him. Odd time to grow a spine, but good for him.

"And out of curiosity, would you have, let's say, *bent* those rules to save your precious little Violet in that field?" Her name tastes odd on my tongue, softer than the nickname I prefer.

"This is cruel, even for you," Sgaeyl notes with a hint of amusement.

"It's unfortunate that it hurts her, but she's going to have to toughen up to survive our partnership, and Aetos can't be anywhere around us."

"Oh, so we're not discussing that you were already moving when Tairn landed?" she fires back. *"That had he not arrived, you'd be guilty of the very thing the colonel's offspring accuses you of doing?"*

"I moved on instinct to protect—"

"Let's not embarrass each other by letting you finish that sentence."

I fucking hate when she does that. She's the only being on the Continent with a sharper tongue than mine. Well. Violence might give her a run for her money.

Damn, Aetos *still* hasn't answered.

"That's unfair to ask him." Sorrengail walks straight up to me, putting herself beside Aetos as the rhythmic beat of dragon wings fills the air. Guess the Empyrean has made its choice as to if they'll let her bond both dragons.

"I'm ordering you to answer, *squad leader.*" I lock my gaze on his. *Come on. Show her who you really are.*

Aetos swallows so obnoxiously loud that I can hear it, then squeezes his eyes shut. "No. I wouldn't have."

I scoff. Fucking rule-loving coward. He doesn't deserve to breathe the same air as Violence. She's half his size and a thousand times braver. Talk about a disproportionate relationship. There's no rule in this godsforsaken college that would keep me from saving Bodhi's, Garrick's, or Liam's life… and now *hers*.

Aetos swings his face toward Sorrengail, but even I can see the damage is done. She looks like someone just shredded her favorite book.

Shit. What is that uncomfortable weight sitting in my lungs? Is that… No. It can't be guilt. I can't remember the last time I felt guilty about… well…anything that didn't involve a marked one.

"It would have killed me to watch something happen to you, Vi, but the rules—" Aetos whines.

"It's all right," she interrupts, lifting her hand to his shoulder.

And it's enough to turn the guilt to nausea, which I'm oddly thankful for.

"The dragons are returning." I note the obvious as they start to land, causing cadets to scramble out of the way. "Get back to formation, squad leader."

Aetos scurries away like the little rat he is.

"Why would you do that to him?" Sorrengail damn near shouts at me, then shakes her head. "Forget it." She dismisses me, walking away without another word.

I blink. Swear to Amari, the five-foot-nothing pain in my ass is the only person who *ever* has the nerve to *dismiss* me. I'm moving before my common sense can tell me to leave well enough alone.

"Because you put too much faith in him." I catch up to her in a matter of steps. "And knowing who to trust is the only thing that will keep you alive—keep *us* alive—not only in the quadrant but after graduation."

"There is no *us*," she retorts, barely avoiding a collision with another rider running by, causing my heart to jolt. Yesterday, I might not have cared.

Today, her blood is my blood.

"Oh, I think you'll find that's no longer the case." I grab hold of her elbow and pull her out of the path of another imminent collision. Is *this* what it's going to be like, trying to keep this woman alive? She'll stand up to three armed bullies to defend the smallest dragon, but she won't watch where the fuck she's *walking*? "Tairn's bonds are so powerful, both to mate and rider, because *he's* so powerful. Losing his last rider nearly killed him, which, in turn, nearly killed Sgaeyl. Mated pairs' lives are—"

"Interdependent, I know that," she snaps back, anger highlighting the blue in her eyes as she rips her gaze from mine, focusing on the movement of the riot as they land.

What in Dunne's name is wrong with me that I'm noticing shit like that?

"Now who's getting mushy?" Sgaeyl asks.

"Attracted and mushy aren't the same thing." And I'm already pissed at myself for the first. I'm sure as hell not slipping into the second. "Each time a dragon chooses a rider, that bond is stronger than the last, which means that if you die, Violence, it sets off a chain of events that potentially ends with *me* dying, too. So yeah, unfortunately for everyone involved, there's now an *us* if the Empyrean lets Tairn's choice stand."

Her eyes flare and her lips part.

And I'm *definitely* not thinking about her mouth, not when I have bigger concerns like how to keep her alive. Not thinking about the best angle to kiss her, either. Or what her *perfect* ass would feel like in my hands.

"And now that Tairn is in play, that other cadets know he's willing to bond…" Gods, they're going to come after her. On the mat. In the halls. In the damned bathing chamber that I can't exactly patrol. I force my gaze away and exhale with enough force to actually call it a sigh.

"That's why Tairn told me to stay with you," she whispers, like she's finally grasping the severity of our situation. "Because of the unbonded."

"The unbonded are going to try to kill you in hopes they'll get Tairn to bond *them*."

Garrick heads my way, and I shake my head. Any news he has from last night's mission has to wait. *"Of all the people in the quadrant, Tairn had to bond Sorrengail?"* Life is about to get infinitely more complicated.

"Feel free to question his motives," Sgaeyl suggests.

"Hell no. I prefer my head attached." He's one surly motherfucker. "Tairn is one of the strongest dragons on the Continent, and the vast power he channels is about to be yours. The next few months, the unbonded will try to kill a newly paired rider while the bond is weak, while they still have a chance of that dragon changing its mind and picking them so they're not set back a full year. And for Tairn? They'll do just about anything." I can't help but sigh for real this time. "There are forty-one unbonded riders for which you are now target number one." I hold up my pointer finger.

"And Tairn thinks you'll play bodyguard." She snorts. "Little does he know just how much you dislike me."

"He knows exactly how much you dislike *her and how often you stare—"*

"I will volunteer for every cold-weather mission in existence if you—"

"Rude. As if your inability to control your own hormones should result in my discomfort." She mentally shudders. Ruthless and vicious as my girl might be, she draws the line at the cold unless we're flying for Aretia.

"He knows exactly how much I value my *own* life," I counter, my gaze roaming down Sorrengail's body. There's absolutely *nothing* to dislike about what I see. In fact, if Amari herself ever designed a woman with my downfall in mind... Well, fuck. Maybe that's exactly what Violence is—my downfall. Soft skin. Sharp mind. Fierce temper. Deadly with a dagger. Brave to a fault. And utterly unruffled. "You're freakishly calm for someone who just heard she's about to be hunted." What makes her lose complete control? What kind of man would she let unravel her?

"She's two years your junior and in your chain of command." Sgaeyl feigns outrage.

"And you're fifty years younger than Tairn. Your point?"

"It's a typical Wednesday for me." Sorrengail shrugs, and my gaze locks onto the flush in her cheeks, that delicate bloom of pink that tells me she's not as unaffected by me as she likes to pretend. "And honestly, being hunted by forty-one people is a lot less intimidating than constantly watching dark corners for *you*."

Fair point.

The gold dragon lands behind us, followed by the monstrosity Sgaeyl calls a mate, and I walk the hell away as quickly as possible now that Sorrengail's protected, heading across the field to where Sgaeyl waits at the end of the row with the other wingleaders' dragons.

Garrick stands just off to the side of Chradh—his Brown Scorpiontail—and lifts his eyebrows as I approach. "So, you and the general's daughter..."

"Not funny." I shake my head and ignore Sgaeyl's chuff beside me as General Melgren takes the front of the dais. My skin crawls, just like it always does when he's near. Fucking murderer. It's not hard to tune him out; I've practiced ignoring him for years. Besides, I don't need to listen in order to know what he's going to say.

Tairn will get his way. She'll bond both dragons. Even the Empyrean isn't going to tell the second-largest dragon on the Continent no when he finally wants to bond. They want him back on the battlefield.

"Is this going to be a problem?" Garrick asks as Melgren prattles on.

"No."

"Right." The word drips with sarcasm.

"I'm fine." I scan the first-years who survived Threshing.

"I've seen corpses more *fine* than you," my best friend mutters.

"Of course corpses are fine. They have *nothing* to worry about." And I've just been handed Violet-fucking-Sorrengail to protect if I want to live. Which I do. Or rather, I have to. Especially since Melgren just announced that she gets to bond her dragons.

I lower my shields just enough to feel for the bond. The hard sapphire one I share with Sgaeyl is locked into place as always, but now there are two more. The onyx I recognize as Tairn, and the other, a glimmering strand of...silver, like the ends of her hair. *Fuck*. He really did bond her. Only a mating bond like Sgaeyl and Tairn's could link me to another rider whether or not I want it.

Sorrengail looks across the field at me, and I slam my shields back into place and hold up my pointer finger. She's now target number one around here, and my biggest liability.

"Guess we'll need to keep her alive," Garrick mutters as General Sorrengail steps forward to give her yearly speech about family even though she threw hers to the dragons.

"Yes." How the hell am I going to keep her alive through all the first-year shit I'm nowhere near? I look across the field and spot Liam, my foster brother, standing in front of his new Red Daggertail as the dragons gift their riders with relics to channel magic. "Maybe I should move Liam into her squad."

"Liam?" Garrick questions.

"He's the best in his year." I nod as the first-years break out in celebration. "I trained him to fight, so I know he's capable of protecting her." Plus, he's as loyal to me as I am to him.

"Or you could give her a chance to make it on her own first." Garrick folds his arms across his chest and glances sideways at me.

There are a multitude of reasons he might be right.

"But if that's the route you choose, everyone likes Liam, so hopefully she will, too. It will make it easier for him to guard her."

"She'll like him." That unpleasant feeling flares in my gut again, twisting into a knot.

Garrick grins. "Don't worry. He won't fuck her."

My eyes narrow at Garrick. "Why would I care if he..." The words die on my tongue as Aetos walks behind Sorrengail and reaches for her back. That asshole is unlacing her armor. He's got his hands on her skin. I breathe in through my nose and out through my mouth to quell the quickly rising nausea.

"Relax, he's lacing her back up," Garrick says, and I know without looking the asshole is still smiling. "See? She's already turning around."

Sorrengail turns in Aetos's arms, and he lifts his hands to her face. No doubt he's pilfering through her memories to see if I actually interfered.

"Nothing to... Oh shit." Garrick's voice fades to a whisper as Aetos lowers his head and kisses Sorrengail.

Fire rushes through my veins and shadows spasm around me, distorting my vision for a second. Dain-fucking-Aetos has his mouth on *my* Violence.

Not mine. But that doesn't stop the knot in my stomach from unfurling, spreading like acid into my system, burning through my chest and making it hard to draw breath until that snot-nosed asswipe lifts his head.

"Damn. You all right over there?" Garrick asks, laughter lacing his tone.

"I'm..." I pin my feet to the field with shadows to keep from marching over there and feeding Aetos my fist. How fucking dare he kiss the mouth he wouldn't bend a rule to protect, when I would—

"Yes, what would *you do?"* Sgaeyl asks.

Fuck me. What *wouldn't* I do?

"You're looking a little green." Garrick flat-out laughs, and I force air in and out of my lungs as Sorrengail steps back from Aetos.

He grins down at her, but...wait. She isn't returning the sentiment. No, Sorrengail looks like she just accidentally kissed her cousin and can't retreat fast enough. Talk about awkward.

"In twenty years, I don't think I've ever seen you jealous before. This is amazing." Garrick claps his hand on my shoulder.

Jealous. That's exactly what this hot, corrosive feeling is—jealousy. And now I'm linked to this woman for the rest of our lives.

I need to stay as far away from her as possible.

"But you won't," Sgaeyl predicts, and I'd be tempted to raise my middle finger if I didn't think she'd bite the damned thing off as a reminder that she can.

CONNECT WITH US ONLINE

@redtowerbooks

@RedTowerBooks

@redtowerbooks

RED TOWER
BOOKS™